DIRECTORY

OF

BOOK
PRINTERS

1991 EDITION

An international directory of book printers
capable of printing from 50 to 1,000,000 copies of a book,
catalog, magazine, journal, genealogy, software manual,
directory, yearbook, or other bound publication

COMPILED AND EDITED BY
JOHN KREMER

Published by:
Ad-Lib Publications
51 N. Fifth Street
P. O. Box 1102
Fairfield, Iowa 52556-1102
(515) 472-6617; (800) 669-0773
Fax: (515) 472-3186

Printed and bound by Walsworth Publishing of Marceline, Missouri.

Cover photo provided by Publishers Press of Salt Lake City, Utah.

ISSN: 0895-139X

Foreword

This sixth edition of the *Directory of Book Printers* features 784 printers of books, catalogs, magazines, and other bound publications. Of that number, at least 50 are new listings which have not appeared in previous editions. In addition, about 100 printers have changed addresses, names, owners, or other important details. Finally, we have deleted about 300 printers from the last edition, either because they have gone out of business or because they are general commercial printers who do not print that many bound publications.

Besides listing the company name, person to contact, address, phone numbers, and fax number, this *Directory* also provides many additional details about each printer. Among other items, this *Directory* lists the printers' optimum print runs, standard book sizes, binding capabilities, and types of printed items besides books. This edition also lists the various services each printer offers, including whether or not the printer can do color separations, maintain lists, handle fulfillment, do typesetting, or provide design and layout. Also, in keeping with the times, this edition notes which printers stock acid-free or recycled papers.

For those of you who wanted more information about each printer, this edition now also lists the equipment used by the printer, its annual sales and number of employees, when it was founded, and whether it is a union shop or not. It also indicates the turnaround times for books, magazines, and catalogs. Finally, for those of you who would like to work with a printer accustomered to working with your kind of organization (whether book publisher, business, non-profit organization, school, or whatever), we have indicated the percentage of their business which comes from various segments of the market.

We hope you like these new additions to the book. The information contained in the listings of this *Directory* are based on what the printers wrote on the survey forms we sent to them in September of 1991. Where the printer did not return the survey form to us, we have had to rely on information available from other published sources, the printer's advertisements, and/or reports received from people who have used their services. Because some printers are not above exaggerating their capabilities, services, or turnaround times, you should read each listing with a skeptic's mind.

I hope this *Directory* will help you locate the most appropriate printers for your various publication needs. We have worked hard to make this *Directory* the most comprehensive of its kind. Nonetheless, we know there is still vast room for improvement. Although we have listed all the major book printers as well as the top commercial printers according to the GAM 100 and Printing Impressions 500, we know that we've still over-looked a good number of reliable printers capable of printing books, catalogs, magazines, and other bound publications.

To make this *Directory* even more comprehensive and complete, we need your help. Please send us any further information you discover about the printers we now list. Also send us the names and addresses of any printers we have overlooked. Write direct to me. I'll be sure to follow up on your letter and immediately update our PrintBase data files to reflect any changes you send to me. Thanks for your help.

John Kremer
November 15, 1990

Note: To cut our costs in typesetting this *Directory* (so we could keep the retail price low), we have designed the book using Ventura Publisher and then outputted the camera-ready copy at 100% on plain paper using an HP LaserJet II. As a result, some of the smallest print (especially the boxed info at the bottom of the listings) might lack the detail and clarity you would normally expect to see in a book like this. We mention this little detail because we don't want you to think that the printers of this book are at fault. On the contrary, they have done a superb job.

Table of Contents

Chapter 1

Introduction: How to Use This Directory

This *Directory* is designed to save you time and money in finding the best printer for your next book, catalog, journal, magazine, manual, annual report, directory, or other bound publication. It could save you hundreds, even thousands of dollars in printing and binding costs alone. Plus, of course, it can save you time as well as production hassles.

As one user of this *Directory* wrote, "Without your *Directory* I ended up paying $12,500 for the first printing of one book—and I got plenty of production hassles. With the *Directory*, I paid $4,500 for the identical job —and not one problem."

Two Steps to Savings

How can you get these savings? You need to do two things:
1) Contact the appropriate printers, and
2) Query them in a professional manner.

This *Directory* will help you with both steps.

First, its listings of 780 printers will enable you to select the appropriate one for your job. If you have a particular project in mind, you can use the 79 pages of indexes to help you target those printers who have the right combination of capabilities and services to meet your needs. Or, if you'd rather, you can browse through the book simply reading the listings until you locate several printers capable of meeting your needs.

Read each listing carefully. Check to see which printers can offer the services you require. Can they print the quantity you want? Do they offer the type of binding you need? What about their other services, their credit terms, their normal turnaround times?

Once you have located five or ten printers who you think could do the job you require, query them. Always query at least five printers. Don't get hooked on using one printer all the time (except, of course, for a continuing publication such as a magazine where you might contract with a printer for an entire year). As your needs change, you will find that you may also have to change printers to find one who can handle the different quantities, sizes, or bindings that you require ... with the quality you want ... at a price you can afford ... and with great service and dependability.

To query a printer, develop a standard Request for Quotation (RFQ) form that you can send to all printers. For examples, see the sample book RFQs on pages 21 and 28 to 29. For more details about querying printers, read Chapter 3.

Printer Listings — The Details

This 1991 edition of the *Directory* has been updated to list over 700 printers capable of printing books, catalogs, magazines, and other bound publications. Where known, the following information is listed about each printer:

- **Main Focus**—This code indicates whether they are primarily a book, catalog, or magazine printer, or a general commercial printer, or a printing broker.

- **Company Address**—The name of the company, the main person to contact for queries, the address, phone number, and fax number.

- **Print Runs**—Their minimum press run, their normal maximum print run, and their optimum print run for bound publications. Not only will this give you a good idea of the range of their capabilities, but the optimum print run should indicate at what quantity they can offer you their best price.

- **Sizes**—We list whether they are capable of printing the six most common sizes for books as well as whether or not they can handle other odd sizes. The six most common sizes are as follows:
    4¼ x 7 inches — massmarket paperback
    5½ x 8½ inches — common trade paperback
    6 x 9 inches — common hardcover book
    7 x 10 inches — less common size
    8½ x 11 inches — workbook or magazine
    9 x 12 inches — large art or coffee-table book

- **Bindings**—We indicate whether they offer the following bindings inhouse or can subcontract them from outside suppliers:
    Casebound — hardcover, edition binding
    Comb-bound — plastic binding (e.g., cookbooks)
    Glue Bound — used in some low-priced catalogs
    Looseleaf Binders — for software manuals, etc.

Perfectbound — common paperback
Saddlestitched — stapled in center (magazines)
Sidestitched — like *National Geographic*
Spiral Bound — like a notebook
Wire-O Bound — similar to spiral binding

- **Items** — The types of items they regularly print, including annual reports, books, catalogs, cookbooks, directories, journals, magazines, mass-market paperbacks, newsletters, textbooks, software manuals, yearbooks, brochures, calendars, greeting cards, maps, posters, and so forth.

- **Services** — We indicate which of the following services they are capable of providing in-house:

  4-color printing on text pages
  Color separations in-house
  Design and artwork
  Fulfillment and mailing services
  List maintenance
  Opti-Copy prepress system
  Rachwal prepress system
  Acid-free paper stocked
  Recycled paper stocked
  Typesetting
  Typesetting from disks or via modem
  Warehousing

- **Equipment** — We list the kinds of printing presses they use and, when known, the number and sizes of each kind. The five most common kinds are:

  Cameron Belt Press — cost-effective for quantities between 5000 and 30,000 of trade paperback books. For more information about the Cameron belt press, write to **Cameron Graphic Arts, Somerset Technologies, P. O. Box 791, New Brunswick NJ 08903; (201) 356-6000.** They will send you a booklet describing how a Cameron belt press works and why it is cost-effective for certain publications.

  Letterpress — While offset presses have replaced letterpresses as the standard printing technology, letterpresses are still commonly used for printing die-cut, embossed, and perforated items. They are also used by printers of limited edition books and other "fine" printing.

  Sheetfed Offset Press — Commonly used for press runs under 10,000 copies. Web presses tend to be more cost-effective for print runs over that quantity (at least for books and other publications).

  Web Offset Press — Cost-effective for print runs over 10,000. Used for print runs as high as 7,000,000.

  Gravure (Rotogravure) — Because of its high makeready costs, this press is most cost-effective for print runs over half a million.

- **Annual Sales** — This information is listed for those of you who want to know more about the printer you will be working with. Annual sales will indicate whether or not the printer has the cash flow and resources to serve your needs over an extended period of time (especially crucial for magazine and catalog publishers).

- **Number of Employees** — Again, this figure indicates whether the printer has the resources (in this case, the personnel) to handle big jobs or heavy demand.

- **Turnaround Times** — We asked the printers to indicate their typical turnaround time for printing and binding (1) books, (2) catalogs, and (3) magazines. The turnaround time is the number of working days it takes them to complete the job, from camera-ready copy to shipment. The listed turnaround times are taken from the printer's reports. We cannot guarantee that the printer will live up to these "typical" turnaround times on every job.

- **Customers** — We also asked the printers to indicate what percentage of their business comes from the following customers:
  - Book publishers
  - Businesses
  - Colleges and universities
  - Magazine publishers
  - Non-profit groups
  - Other organizations
  - Schools (elementary and secondary)
  - Self-publishers (including authors, genealogists, etc.)
  - Others

  This information will be most useful to those of you who would like to work with a printer accustomed to working with similar organizations. While this information may be especially useful for self-publishers, schools, and non-profit groups, it may also be useful to magazine publishers who want to work with a printer accustomed to servicing the special needs of magazine publishers.

- **Union** — We have noted which printers use union workers because we have received a number of requests from unions and non-profit groups who must use union suppliers.

- **Year Established** — In general, the longer a printer has been in business, the more reliable they ought to be. They should have gotten the kinks out of their business long ago. Of course, some businesses become more inept as they age, so use this information only as a guide. Always check a printer's references.

- **Terms** — These are the standard terms offered by the printer. Most printers will offer net 30 terms with approved credit, but some require a deposit when working with a new customer. Note that terms are always negotiable, especially if you have a good credit rating *and* the printer is hungry for business.

- **Statement**—The statements are written by the printers to describe, in their own words, their goals and services. In some cases, these statements have been taken from the printers' advertisements or printed brochures rather than from their statements on our survey form. But in every case, these statements are in their own words.

- **Comments**—These comments are written by the editor of this *Directory*. In some cases, they may reflect the opinion of the editor or the general consensus of those who have used the printer before (and reported their experiences to the editor). In most cases, however, the comments amplify the details listed in that printer's entry, thereby highlighting information that the standard listing failed to bring out.

Other Features

Besides the information contained in the alphabetical listings of the printers, this *Directory* also includes the following information:

- **Short-Run 4-Color Printers**—Chapter 6 features a listing of more than 30 printers who specialize in printing 4-color catalog sheets, postcards, and other items in short runs (from 500 to 25,000 copies).

- **Foreign Printers**—Chapter 7 features a listing of more than 120 overseas printers and printing brokers. While we do encourage you to use printers in the U.S. and Canada, it is possible to save considerable amounts of money by getting certain items printed overseas (especially 4-color books in short runs).
  The introduction to Chapter 7 describes how to best work with overseas printers. It also describes the advantages and disadvantages to working with such printers.

- **Other Publishing Services**—Chapter 8 features a listing of about 20 related publishing services.

- **Glossary**—The glossary provides definitions for about 300 terms commonly used in the printing trade (and in this book). If you find a word somewhere in this introduction or in one of the listings that you do not understand, refer to the glossary.

- **Bibliography**—This section provides a list of books we recommend for further reading. Of all these books, the most important is *Getting It Printed* by Mark Beach, Steve Shepro, and Ken Russon. This book should be required reading for all printers and all printing buyers. A second bibliography lists books published by Ad-Lib Publications.

- **Indexes**—To make this book as useful as possible, we have provided 79 pages of indexes indicating which printers specialize in the capabilities and services you need. Among these indexes is a special listing of all printers by city and state (or province), so you can locate those printers who are nearest you.

- **Choosing a Printer**—In the following chapter, we've listed 20 points to consider when selecting a printer. Read these points over carefully. While many smaller publishers tend to select printers solely on price, that can often be a mistake. These points will describe what you should look for in a printer.

  There is an old saying in the printing industry: "Price, speed, and quality—you can have any two." If you want to have top quality, you have to pay the price. If you want speed, you also may have to pay more. No printer can offer you the best of all three (lowest price, fastest turnaround, best quality). Almost all print buying decisions are, therefore, compromises. Know what to look for so you can make the most informed decision.

- **Requests for Quotations**—Chapter 3 describes how to query printers to obtain a reliable pricing quotation for your printing jobs. A well-prepared Request for Quotation (RFQ) will ensure that you get the best price and service from your printer. It also provides the basis for any contract you sign with a printer.

- **Tips on Saving Money**—In Chapter 4, we list some 40 tips that could help you save money on the typesetting and printing of your books and other publications. You should find several points that will help you to streamline your production or save you money, time, or hassles dealing with printers.

- **Printer Database**—The information contained in this *Directory* is also available as data files for use with your favorite database program. These data files allow quick and easy selection of all those printers who can match your needs. For example, using these data files and your favorite database program, you could print out labels for all printers capable of producing short-run books in a matter of minutes. These data files can save you time when sending out RFQ's or other requests for information.

  Currently, these data files are available as comma-delimited or tab-delimited ASCII (mail-merge) files for IBM or Macintosh compatible computers. They are also available ready to use for those of you who have an IBM compatible computer and the PC-File database program. Call **800-669-0773** for details.

Chapter 2

20 Points to Consider When Selecting a Printer

Too many publishers evaluate printers only on the basis of price. That is a mistake. The cheapest printer is not always the best printer. To help you in your evaluation of prospective printers, here are 20 points you should consider.

- **Experience** — How long have they been printing books? How long have they been in business? What kind of books and other printed items are they accustomed to producing?

- **Reputation** — Do they have a reputation for doing quality work and delivering on schedule? Do you know anyone who has used them before? Can they provide references?

- **Quality of Work** — Do they produce good-looking, well-made books? Do their books hold together? Is the printing clear — neither overinked nor underinked? Have you seen samples of their work? Be sure to get a sample of their work before you commit to them — preferably a sample similar in size and binding to the book or other publication you want produced.

- **Price** — How do their prices compare to other printers? If their prices are higher than other printers, what added benefits do they offer? Faster delivery? Better quality? Greater reliability? More services?

- **Service** — Are they willing to work with you to produce the best book for the price you are able to pay? Do they answer your phone calls, letters, and other queries quickly and courteously? Do they put forth that extra bit of effort that makes working with them a pleasure?

- **Dependability** — Do they deliver books, catalogs, or other publications when promised? Do they live up to their promises, both verbal and written? Again, check their references to verify their dependability.

- **Timing** – Do they offer faster delivery than other printers? Most book printers offer a 4 to 6 week lead time for books printed from camera-ready copy. Can this printer offer a faster delivery time and yet produce a quality publication?

- **Terms** – What kind of terms can they offer you? Do they require a large downpayment? Do they offer any discounts for prepayment or quicker payment?

- **Other Services** – Can they provide warehousing and fulfillment services for you? Can they do typesetting and pasteup in house? Do they have teletypesetting capabilities? Can they maintain your lists?

- **Quantities** – What quantities are they capable of producing? Will they be able to follow up an initial short run with a much larger second run, or will you have to go to another printer to do a higher quantity when your book begins to sell or when you want to roll out a catalog after a test run?

- **Capabilities** – What kind of books or other publications are they accustomed to doing? What sizes and types of bindings? Is your book a special size or binding? Will it economically fit their presses and binding capabilities.

- **Specialization** – Whenever possible, use a printer who specializes in the type of publication you want to publish. Find out which sizes, quantities, bindings, etcetera, they are accustomed to doing. Can they do odd sizes? And, if so, are they set up for easy handling of such odd sizes or bindings?

- **Choices** – Does the printer offer a choice of paper and cover stocks? Do they keep them in stock, or will they have to special order them? Special orders will usually require more time.

- **Location** – Where are they located? Location may be important for several reasons: 1) You may be able to get speedier delivery – both in getting copy to them and in getting books from them; 2) It will be easier to make changes in the galleys if necessary; and 3) If you live nearby, you may have a chance to visit their plant and see more samples of their work and meet the people you will be working with.

- **Equipment** – Is the printer's equipment up to date? Can it handle the type of book or publication you want to publish? Is the equipment messy and dirty, or well maintained? (If they do not care how their plant or equipment looks, do you think they will care what your book looks like?)

- **Working Conditions** – If you get a chance to visit the printing plant, check out the following points. Is the plant well lighted and ventilated? Does it appear to be a pleasant place to work? Are the floors clean? Is there enough space for the equipment and storage? Enough room for the workers to get around efficiently? Does the flow of work seem well thought out?

- **Personnel**—Do the workers seem happy? Are they interested in their work? Do you like the customer service rep you will be working with? Do all the personnel seem responsive to your needs? Do they have the knowledge and experience to do the job?

- **Packing and Shipping**—Will the printer pack the books properly so that they are not damaged in shipment? Can they provide shrinkwrapping of books? Can they ship to more than one destination? Can they ship by both UPS and truck? Do they have the capability to handle your list maintenance and fulfillment (for catalogs, magazines, and other periodicals)?

- **Fitness**—Be sure to select a printer who is right for the job you want done. Don't go to a quick printer for a casebound book, or to a web printer for 100 copies of a short brochure. Use this Directory to help you select those printers who can best serve your needs.

- **Long-Term Relationship**—Never work with a printer you would not be happy to work with again. Aim to develop long-standing relationships with your printers so you can come back to them again and again with confidence.

Chapter 3

How to Request a Printing Quotation

To obtain a reliable quote for the printing of your book or other publication, you should supply all the information the printer will need to make a valid estimate. To ensure that you have included all the necessary information—and to ensure that the same basic data is used by all printers you query—use a Request for Quotation (RFQ) form on your letterhead. See the next page for a copy of the RFQ we sent out when requesting quotations for this *Directory*.

You do not need to copy the form we used; you may adapt it to your own requirements. Regardless of what kind of format you decide to use, you should provide the printer with the following basic information, all of which they need in order to make an accurate estimate:

- **Title of the publication**—If you do not have a title yet, give some reference title or number.

- **Quantity**—State the number of copies you want printed. You may list several options if you are not sure how many copies you want printed, but don't ask for more than two or three (just as a common courtesy). You may also ask for a quote for a preliminary test run and a follow-up roll-out quantity.

  For magazines, you will need to indicate the number of issues per year, plus the projected print runs for each issue through the coming year.

- **Number of Pages**—Include all pages: title page, copyright page, index, blank pages, and so on. Note that most printers can give you a better price if the total number of pages in your book is a multiple of 32 pages (96, 128, 160, 192, 224, ...). If the publication uses a self-cover, the cover should also be included in the page count; otherwise, the cover should be quoted separately.

Ad-Lib Publications, Box 1102, Fairfield, IA 52556
(515) 472-6617 / Fax: (515) 472-3186

Request for Quotation

Contact: John Kremer

Please quote by October 15, 1990

Quote your best price and turnaround time for the following job:

Specifications:

Book Title:	Directory of Book Printers, 1991 Edition
Total Pages:	288 pages
Trim Size:	6 x 9 inches
Text Paper:	55 lb. or 60 lb. offset — Please quote on your best house stock. If possible, quote on a recycled paper grade as well.
Text Ink:	Black
Cover Stock:	10 pt C1S plus film lamination
Cover Ink:	4-color, sides 1 and 4, separations will be provided by customer
Binding:	Perfectbind and shrinkwrap individually
Material Provided:	Camera-ready copy plus some negatives (for about 20 pages of ads). Blue lines required.
Packing:	Pack in tightly sealed cartons (275 lb test) not to exceed 40 lb. total weight.

Quote:

Quantity:	12,000 copies — $_____
Delivery:	Working days from receipt of camera-ready copy to shipment — _____
Terms:	Net 30 (credit references available upon request).
Remarks:	

Printer:
Address:

Phone:

Thank you. We look forward to working with you on this book.

Illustration 3.1 — Sample RFQ

- **Trim Size** — State the dimensions of the publication, whether 8½ x 11 or 8⅜ x 10⅞ or whatever. If the dimensions must be exact, note the specification in your RFQ. Otherwise, the printer could well substitute a near fit (for example 5⅜ x 8⅜ for 5½ x 8½ because that size better suits their presses).

  Standard trim sizes (such 5½ x 8½, 6 x 9, or 8½ x 11 for books) will enable you to get a better price from many printers *and* will fit the standard shelving units of libraries and booksellers, but don't rule out an odd size if it is appropriate for the contents of your book. If you want an odd size, be sure to describe its dimensions clearly.

- **Text Paper** — Most books are printed on 50 lb. or 60 lb. white offset or book paper, but if you are publishing a children's or photo book, you will probably want to use a different paper stock. If you want the book to last a hundred years or more, be sure to specify acid-free paper (which is, however, often more expensive). If you intend to supply your own paper, be sure to let the printer know.

- **Text Ink** — If you do not specify a color of ink, it will be black. If you want a four-color book or another accent color, be sure to specify it. In some RFQs, this may also be referred to as Press Work.

- **Binding** — Do you want your book to be a perfectbound softcover (like this book), or a saddlestitched book (stapled like a magazine), or a smyth-sewn casebound (hardcover), or comb or spiral bound (like many cookbooks)? You must specify exactly what kind of binding you want for the book.

  If you are publishing a casebound book, you need to specify the grade of binders board and cloth you want to use, plus other specifics. Discuss your options with several printers to get an idea of the specifications you want to use.

- **Cover Stock** — Most trade paperbacks use a 10 pt. C1S (coated one side) cover, though other cover stocks are available. Magazines and catalogs usually use a lighter stock. Again, if you don't know how to specify the cover stock, send the printers samples of the sort of cover stock you want to use. They can take it from there.

  For softcover books, we recommend that you ask for a varnish or, better yet, a film lamination or UV coating for the cover (to better protect its surface during shipping and handling; also, it looks better). This additional coating will cost you between 4¢ and 10¢ per copy.

- **Cover Ink** — Will the cover be printed with one or more colors? Any dropouts or screens? Also specify whether you want the cover printed sides 1 and 4 only (the outside) or all sides (including the inside).

- **Copy** — Will you provide camera-ready copy, negatives, press-ready plates, or will you require typesetting and pasteup services? If you require typesetting, you need to provide them with an accurate estimate of the number of words in the book, type size, fonts, and so on.

Will the copy have any photos? Bleeds? Extensive solid areas? If the book is to be printed in full color, will you be providing the color separations or transparencies?

Packing—Do you want your books shrinkwrapped singly or in convenient multiples (5 to 10 books) to protect them during shipment? Do you have any other special packing or shipping requirements?

In general, it is best if you can specify exactly how they should pack your books or other publications and how they should ship them.

For magazines and catalogs, will you provide the packing envelope, labels (in 4-up cheshire format?), and so on, or will the printer be asked to provide many of these fulfillment services as well? In such a case, how often will you be publishing? What kind of mailing schedule will they have to maintain? How many pieces?

Resources for Preparing an RFQ

An RFQ form lays out all the necessary information in a clear, understandable format so that any printer should know exactly what you want. If you do not know how to specify all the details regarding paper stocks, bindings, typesetting, and so on, then do one or more of the following:

- **Read some books on graphics arts and printing.** We highly recommend the following book: *Getting It Printed* by Mark Beach, Steve Shepro, and Ken Russon. If every printer and publisher had a copy of this book (and used it), 90% of all printing problems would disappear. It has an excellent glossary, detailed discussion of printing contracts, many superb tips, and much more.

- **Find a local graphic designer** who can help you

- **Ask questions of the printers** you are considering using. Most will be more than willing to answer your questions if you are seriously considering using them to print your job.

- **Several printers issue publications** to help you understand all the terminology and will send these to you free if you write on your letterhead requesting copies. Here are several of the best:

    Braun-Brumfield's *Book Manufacturing Glossary, Book Paper Samples*, and *Type Sample Book*
    Delta Lithograph's *Planning Guide*
    Dinner & Klein's *Catalogs, Brochures, and Flyers*
    R R Donnelley's *Guide to Book Planning*
    Friesen Printers' *Book Publishers' Guide*
    Griffin Printing's *Signature* newsletter
    Marrakech Express's *Shortruns* newsletter
    McNaughton & Gunn's *Book Manufacturing Intro Kit*
    Thomson-Shore's superb *Printer's Ink* newsletter

More Notes on RFQs

- On your RFQ form, besides providing the specifications for your book, you should also require a few other details from the printer. For instance, always ask for their credit terms, normal delivery times, and the approximate delivery charges to your firm (if any).

- Normal terms of credit are net 30 with approved credit. In other words, if your credit is good, you will be expected to pay for the books 30 days after the books are shipped. If your credit is shaky or your business is new, then most printers will require at least ⅓ down, another ⅓ with returned proofs, and the balance on delivery.

- Delivery times can vary from as short as 10 working days (2 weeks) to as long as 8 to 12 weeks for camera-ready copy. If your book requires typesetting or case binding, the time can vary from as short as 4 weeks to as long as 20 or more weeks. If you need fast turnaround, let them know that when you query them.

  If you require delivery by a specific date, be sure to state that on your RFQ when first querying the printer.

- Printing times for magazines and catalogs are usually shorter than books. Weekly magazines, such as *Time* and *Newsweek*, for example, are produced by printers who specialize in large runs at fast speeds and turnarounds. Note also that such magazines are often produced by more than one plant (with regional editions being printed by printers in various parts of the country).

- When choosing a printer, be sure to consider more than just price. How about their turnaround time, their quality, their service, their terms? Read Chapter 2 to make sure you've considered all the facts before committing yourself to a printer.

- Always ask the printer to quote by a specific date (allow 2 - 3 weeks minimum). Printers say they can produce a quote in 1 - 7 days and they should be able to, but our experience is that most printers take much longer. By setting a cutoff date, you ensure that all serious bids will be sent to you in time for you to make a decision.

- Also ask them to state how long the quoted prices are good for. This is vital if you won't be publishing right away (or if there is any chance of a delay).

- Stand by your dates. Make sure you send in your camera-ready copy, negatives, or other artwork when you say you will. You can't expect printers to live up to their commitments unless you live up to yours. If you are going to be delayed in getting materials to them, be sure to let them know.

  If you stand by your dates and get material to them on time and if you return your bluelines in a timely manner, then the printer can offer you the kind of service you'd like.

- When you've narrowed your choice to two or three printers, ask them to send you samples of their work. Be sure to inspect these samples carefully.

- Also ask them to give you the names and phone numbers of some of their recent customers. Call these customers and ask them for feedback regarding the printer's service and quality of work. Do this before you send your money or camera-ready copy to a printer. You do not want to spend thousands of dollars for books you would not be proud to sell.

- Be prepared for a significant difference in the response to your queries from different printers. Some printers are very aggressive in marketing their services while others are incredibly blasè. Here, for example, are the responses of a variety of printers to a neophyte book publisher's query:

  1) *Their rep was a sweetheart. Spent lots of time talking with me. Sent me books and information up the yingyang. They don't miss a beat ... very professional. Their rep said they were going after the small publishers with fervor. He came down from his original quote twice.*

  2) *Never responded.*

  3) *Sent paper samples. No letter, no brochure, no hello, never heard from them again.*

  4) *They really seemed to want the job. Very personable. Kept in touch by phone every few days. Changed their bid twice.*

  5) *Sent a bit of information; nothing to snow you. Never called, just sent a bid.*

  6) *Was always consistent on their prices. They never had to budge because they were always the lowest in everything but shipping. They were very professional and helpful. I talked to them quite a bit ... asked every basic question possible.*

  7) *Good price, personable people. Didn't kill themselves trying, though. Do send out packets of beautiful and expensive brochures. They spend a lot of money on you.*

  8) *My runnerup. Very friendly. Answered all my questions. Took a lot of time with me. Very professional.*

  9) *Sent paper samples and a book, but they never followed up. Their bid was good, but I was so busy making friends with other printers that kept calling me that I didn't pursue them.*

  10) *They were very helpful and gave me a couple sample books. Promised to send me paper samples, etc. A month passed and nothing sent. I called, and two weeks latter they got around to sending me books, samples of paper, brochures, and an estimate. But too late by then.*

  11) *Very nice rep, kept in touch, sent me books. Too bad her estimate was high.*

12) *Visited their plant. Very nice people, knocked themselves out for me. But their price was too high.*

13) *Visited them, too. Very nice, but not professional. And their bid was astronomical.*

- Note that printers do vary in their response to your query. If you are seriously interested in working with a printer, call them if they don't call you first.

- If your favorite printers come out significantly higher on a job quote than several other printers, you might want to ask them why. They might offer to come down a bit to match the others or at least come close enough to make the difference negligible when taking into consideration other factors such as their service and quality. If they do lower their price, be sure to get a written verification of the change.

- When you are ready to send in your manuscript or camera-ready copy, phone the printer beforehand to confirm prices and the printing schedule. Quoted prices may change due to changes in paper prices, and delivery schedules vary with the printer's workload. Be sure to confirm both.

- When you do send in your copy, enclose a written letter of confirmation (or contract) that describes the agreed-upon price and delivery schedule. This will save you from problems if some question should come up later regarding prices, services, or delivery.

- Always keep a copy of any manuscripts or camera-ready copy you send them. The postal service and printers have both been known to lose or spoil even the best prepared and packaged copy.

Note: Be sure to let printers know you read about them in the *Directory of Book Printers*. It will show them that you are serious about getting good quality work for a reasonable price.

Sample RFQs

In this book, we have included several sample Requests For Quotations which you may use as a pattern to develop your own RFQ for various publications.

The RFQ on page 19 is the one we used to request price quotations for the printing of this **Directory**. It is a simple and straightforward RFQ. Use one like it when the job isn't too complicated. As the job becomes more detailed or complicated, you might want to use an RFQ like the one on pages 26 to 27.

The sample RFQ on pages 26 to 27 is taken from *Getting It Printed* (reprinted by permission of the publisher, Coast to Coast Books, Portland Oregon). This sample RFQ is written on a universal RFQ form which can be used to request prices for almost any printing job. A copy-ready version of this form can be found on pages 225 and 226 of *Getting It Printed*. Because the form is so comprehensive and detailed, it should not be used by someone who does not know anything about printing terminology. If you want to use this form, be sure to read the book first.

Getting It Printed accurately defines all the terms and standards you would use to describe any job. It defines, for instance, the differences between basic, good, premium, and showcase quality printing. It also defines all the various grades of paper. If you do not know the differences, you need to read the book. Check your local library, or order the book by calling toll-free **800-669-0773**.

Request for Quotation

Job name __SUMMER CATALOG__   Date __3/2/87__

Contact person __JOHN BRIGHTON__   Date quote needed __3/9/87__

Business name __WILLIAMS MARKETING__   Date job to printer __3/19/87__

Address __919 SECOND AVENUE, ANTELOPE USA 10123__   Date job needed __4/15/87__

Phone __800-282-5800__ **Please give** ☑ firm quote ☐ rough estimate ☐ verbally ☑ in writing

This is a ☑ new job ☐ exact reprint ☐ reprint with changes _____

Quantity 1) __25,000__   2) __50,000__   3) __40,000__   ☑ additional __1,000__ s

Quality ☐ basic ☐ good ☑ premium ☐ showcase   comments __CRITICAL FABRIC MATCH__

Format product description __CATALOG WITH ORDER FORM INSERT__

   flat trim size ____ x ____   folded/bound size __8½__ x __11__

   # of pages __16__ ☐ self cover ☑ plus cover

Design features ☑ bleeds ☑ screen tints # __60__ ☑ reverses # __20__ ☑ comp enclosed

Art ☑ camera-ready ☐ printer to typeset and paste up (manuscript and rough layout attached)

   ☐ plate-ready negatives with proofs to printer's specifications

   trade shop name and contact person _____

Mechanicals color breaks ☐ on acetate overlays ☑ shown on tissues   # pieces separate line art __4__

Halftones ☐ halftones # ____ ☐ duotones # ____

Separations ☑ from transparencies # __30__ ☑ from reflective copy # __1__ ☐ provided # ____

   finished sizes of separations __5 @ 3×5; 8 @ 8½×11; 10 @ 4×4; 8 @ 5×8__

Proofs ☐ galley ☐ page ☑ blueline ☑ loose color ☑ composite color ☐ progressive

Paper	weight	name	color	finish	grade
cover	80#	SUPERCOTE	WHITE	GLOSS	COVER
inside	70#	SNOWLIGHT	WHITE	GLOSS	COATED BOOK
INSERT	70#	RYAN OPAQUE	CREAM	VELLUM	UNCOATED BOOK

☐ send samples of paper ☐ make dummy   buy paper from __RIVER PAPER__

Illustration 3.2 — Sample RFQ, Page 1

Request for Quotation (continued)

Printing   ink color(s)/varnish   ink color(s)/varnish

cover   side 1 4-COLOR + SILVER + VARNISH   side 2 4-COLOR + VARNISH

inside   side 1 4-COLOR + VARNISH   side 2 4-COLOR + VARNISH

INSERT side 1 BLACK + ONE COLOR   side 2 BLACK + ONE COLOR

_____ side 1 _____   side 2 _____

Ink ☐ special color match ☑ special ink METALLIC SILVER ON COVER ☐ need draw down

coverage is ☐ light ☑ moderate ☐ heavy ☑ see comp attached ☑ need press check

Other printing (die cut, emboss, foil stamp, engrave, thermograph, number, etc.) _____

_____

Bindery

☐ deliver flat press sheets	☐ round corner	☐ pad	☐ Wire-O
☑ trim	☐ punch	☐ paste bind	☐ spiral bind
☐ collate or gather	☐ drill	☑ saddle stitch	☐ perfect bind
☐ plastic coat with _____	☑ score/perforate	☐ side stitch	☐ case bind
☑ fold _____		☐ plastic comb	☐ tip in _____

comments SCORE COVER; PERFORATE INSERT _____

Packing ☐ rubber band in # ___ s ☐ paper band in # ___ s ☐ shrink/paper wrap in # ___ s

☐ bulk in cartons/maximum weight ___ lbs ☑ skid pack ☐ other _____

Shipping ☐ customer pick up ☑ deliver to QUICK-OUT MAILING SERVICES

_____

☐ quote shipping costs separately ☐ send cheapest way ☐ other _____

Miscellaneous instructions PRINT 500 EXTRA COVERS; SHRINK WRAP

100 CATALOGS IN 10'S; DELIVER EXTRA COVERS AND CATALOGS

TO SUSAN PRESTON WHEN RETURNING MECHANICALS

AND PHOTOS

Illustration 3.2 — Sample RFQ, Page 2

Chapter 4

How to Save Money on Your Book Printing Bill

Here are a few ways you can save money on the design, typesetting, printing, and binding of your books:

- **No rush jobs.** Don't wait until the last minute. Rush jobs only cause headaches, result in errors of omission, and can cost more money in overtime pay and shipping.

- **Present clean typewritten copy** to the typesetter with as few editorial changes as possible. Clean copy allows the typesetter to operate faster, resulting in a lower charge for the typesetter's time.

- **Typeset from disk.** According to the National Composition Association, keyboarding the original input and proofreading make up 53% of the typical costs of regular typesetting. Corrections account for another 13% of typical costs. By providing your own proofread and corrected input, you can save up to 66% of total typesetting costs. Check with your printer or typesetter to see how much you can save by doing your own keyboarding. For instance, one printer will typeset text from disk for $7.00/page versus $12.00/page from manuscript. See the Services Index for printers capable of typesetting from your computer disks or via modem.

- **Use desktop publishing.** If you have a computer and want to have a book that appears professionally typeset, consider using a desktop publishing program. And then output via a laser printer (as this book was done) or to a typesetting machine capable of taking input from a desktop publishing program.

- **Seek the help of your printers in cutting costs.** Talk to them early in the planning of the layout and design of your books and other publications. They may be able to suggest minor changes in your specs that will save you money without affecting the quality of your publications.

- **Standardize your format.** Prepare your camera-ready copy so all the pages can be shot using the same camera setting (requiring no special reductions or enlargements.

- **Make all your editorial changes before you send your copy to the typesetter.** Making changes after the copy has been typeset will cost you at least two to three times as much.

- **Use special effects.** You can obtain a two-color effect with only one color by using screens, dropouts, and reverses.

- **Skip the press checks or blue lines.** If you provide complete camera-ready copy to your printer, you may not need to see press proofs. Most quality printers will reproduce your camera-ready copy exactly as you provided it. Hence, you can save the proof charges (which cost anywhere from $50 to $250) and save the time that would otherwise be taken up in sending the proofs back and forth for approval. However, when working with a printer for the first time, it is always safer to require press proofs — and check your press proofs thoroughly.

  This tip, of course, only applies to straight text copy. If your copy involves many halftones, colors, or special effects, you will certainly want to review the proofs before okaying the print run.

- **Avoid close registrations** when doing two or three-color printing. They require extra prep time and can result in a higher reject rate as well.

- **Check with your printer to see how they define camera-ready copy.** With some printers you will be able to save money by providing your camera-ready copy on single sheets that are the same size as the finished book page. Others require you to use their special layout pages. Check first to find out what they want from you.

- **Avoid special requests** (odd sizes, unusual papers, special effects) unless they contribute to the content of the publication. Extras cost time and money.

- **Design your books to fit the press** (in signatures of 4, 8, 16, or 32 pages). A book of 158 pages will usually cost as much or more than a book of 160 pages because of additional labor charges in handling the incomplete signature. Add several empty pages or, better yet, use those extra pages to advertise some of the other books you publish. Or just add a coupon so people can order additional copies of the book itself (for themselves or for friends).

- **Build up your credit rating by paying your bills on time.** Also, take advantage of any discounts for paying early (you can save from 1% to as much as 5%).

- **A lighter weight paper can save you money,** both on the cost of the paper itself and in postage for mailing the book. Many 50 lb. or 55 lb. book papers are now as opaque and as durable as any 60 lb. papers.

- **You can save money by gang-running your books** (that is, by printing several books at the same time). If you can arrange to publish several books in the same size and quantity, you can save on prep costs while getting better quantity discounts on paper costs. You will also save time and money in preparing manuscripts for typesetting and in designing your books if you have a standard format for all your books.

Some printers offer lower prices if you allow your 4-color catalog or brochures to be grouped with others. However, there are some problems to gang-running your 4-color work with others: You have less control over the resulting color match. You must run with certain quantities. You may have to wait longer. Nonetheless, if you want only 25,000 or less copies of a 4-color job, gang-running offers a cost-effective alternative to custom work.

In this directory, we provide a list of short-run color printers, who offer great prices on full-color catalog sheets.

- **Check your quotes.** It is important to check specifications as well as quoted prices when you receive quotes back from printers, since many printers may change one or two specifications to save costs or to fit your book to their capabilities. The most common changes are paper stock and trim size (for example, 5 3/8 x 8 3/8 trim size rather than 5 1/2 x 8 1/2). Be sure that any such changes are acceptable to you.

- **Be sure to get an updated quote** whenever you change any specifications, including the time of printing. Otherwise, you could get a big surprise when the printing bill comes.

- **Book papers are different from offset grades** — they are more opaque, made to a consistent bulk (which is important for accurately fitting covers), and usually have less filler and stronger fiber (making them more flexible so they tend to lie flatter). But they also tend to be more expensive. You must make the choice.

- **Paper grades vary for coated stock as well.** If the look or feel of your catalog or other publication is important, be sure to see samples of the paper options offered by the printer or by your paper supplier.

- **Query at lease five to ten printers on every book**, especially when the format differs from your standard format or when you're varying the quantity.

- **Print during the off-season.** Some book printers will lower their quotes when work is slow. For instance, we know of one publisher who had three printers call him back to revise their quotes because work was slow in the summer.

- **Plan your printing and publishing schedules.** At the very least, you should have a schedule of what books you will be publishing in the coming year. Planning will save you from the unnatural disasters of rush jobs.

- **You can save money by buying your own paper for your books** (if you know what you are doing). To learn more about how to judge, specify, and buy paper, read *Getting It Printed*.

- **Get everything in writing.** Any modifications in your specifications that you agree to over the phone or in a conversation should be put into writing (either included in the contract or attached thereto). If you don't require a signed contract when you work with a printer, you should at least send a letter of confirmation with your manuscript or camera-ready copy. This letter should reconfirm the specifications in the written quote you received from the printer (including final price and delivery date). Attach a copy of your original RFQ as well.

- **Never ask for delivery ASAP** (as soon as possible); always specify the exact date when you expect delivery of the completed job. In turn, always stand by your own commitments to get camera-ready materials to the printer on time. If something holds you up, be sure to let the printer know in plenty of time. Otherwise, you might be charged for the printer's downtime.

- **Use a self-cover.** For some of your booklets, manuals, and catalogs, you may be able to use a self-cover (where the cover stock is the same as the text stock). By using a self-cover, you will save the cost of a separate press run.

- **Note shipping costs.** When comparing price quotes, don't forget to include the cost of shipping the books to your warehouse. Shipping costs can make a significant difference. In fact, some West Coast book printers refuse to provide quotes for people on the East Coast because by the time shipping costs are added, they can't be competitive with the Ann Arbor printers.

- **Send everything at the same time.** Provide your printer with all the camera-ready copy, photographs, and instructions at the same time. There is far less room for mistakes to creep into the job if the printer gets everything at once.

- **Try to figure out your true costs for producing books** — including the cost of your time. Value your time. It may be your major expense in producing books and other publications.

- **Match your printing jobs to the printer's capabilities.** You'll save money by using a printer set up to do the kind of job you want. Use this directory to select the most appropriate printers for the kind of books you publish.

- **Look around for inexpensive photo and art sources.** Use stock photo and clip art services rather than hiring freelancers. Or use art students from your local college. You can also get excellent free photos from your local historical society and from many corporate or government PR offices.

- **Edit more carefully.** You can save money on your printing bills by editing your books more thoroughly. Does the book really have to be as long as it is? Can some chapters be trimmed or even deleted without hurting the content, design, and message of the book?

- **Set a firm publishing schedule** and, in turn, a firm production schedule — with plenty of leeway to allow you time to make changes if they are needed. Set a realistic schedule, put it in writing, and stick to it. Don't rush yourself. Rush jobs are sloppy jobs. And sloppy jobs cost you money. Either you must pay to correct the mistakes or, if you don't correct them, you can lose sales because the book is not suitable.

- **Use photographs only when necessary** since each halftone can add from $5 to $25 in prep costs.

- **You can have a number of your photos shot as half-tones at one time.** The photos must have uniform contrasts and be the same size (or be reduced by the same percentage). Then the halftones can be stripped into the production negatives as usual.

- **Always ask for samples of the printer's work.** And be sure to check these samples. Open the book flat, test the binding, check the coating, and so on.

- **In some cases it is possible to save money by using more than one supplier.** For instance, some book binders offer lower prices than are available in-house from a printer.

- **You might try to arrange a long-term contract** with one of your printers to produce a series of books for you. Ask them to quote on the entire job at once. They should be able to give you a lower price because such a long-term contract will allow them to make fuller use of their facilities, save on quantity purchases, and secure a more reliable cash flow.

- **Remember:** The lowest price is not necessarily the best bargain. Don't sacrifice quality, service, or delivery just to save a few dollars.

Chapter 5

How to Read the Printer Listings

The following pages (pages 38 through 157) provide an alphabetical listing of over 650 printers of books, catalogs, magazines, and other bound publications. The details in most of these listings were derived from surveys we sent out in September and October of 1990. Where a printer did not return the survey form, we listed whatever public information we were able to obtain (from advertisements, other listings, and articles). A complete listing includes the following details.

Company Name and Address

Company Name — the name of the printing company.
Contact Person — the name and title of the person to contact for printing quotations.
Address — the complete address, including city, state, and zip code.
Phone Numbers — the phone and fax numbers for the company.

Main Focus

At the top right of each listing, we have indicated the main business focus of that printer whether, for example, they are primarily book printers, catalog printers, magazine printers, or general commercial printers. Where their main focus isn't known, they have been listed as general commercial printers.

BK — Book printers
BR — Printing brokers
CA — Catalog printers
GC — General commercial printers
MG — Magazine printers
MS — Short-run magazine printers

Print Runs

After the name and address of the company, we list their minimum, maximum, and optimum print runs for publications (where known).

Min: — Minimum print run.

Max: — Maximum print run.

Opt: — Optimum print run (usually the quantity that best fits their equipment and, hence, the quantity for which they can generally offer the best price).

Sizes

Each listing indicates which of six standard sizes of publications the printers are capable of printing and whether they are also capable of printing other sizes. The six standard sizes are coded by numbers 1 through 6.

1 — 4 1/4 x 7 inches (or similar sizes)
2 — 5 1/2 x 8 1/2 inches
3 — 6 x 9 inches
4 — 7 x 10 inches
5 — 8 1/2 x 11 inches
6 — 9 x 12 inches
X — other sizes, including odd sizes

Bindings

Each listing indicates which bindings the printer is capable of providing in-house and which they can arrange to have done by a regular outside supplier. An "**I**" after the code (e.g., **HCI**) indicates that they can provide the binding service in-house; an "**O**" (e.g., **PBO**) indicates they use an outside bindery; an "**X**" (e.g., **LBX**) means that they did not specify whether they could do the binding in-house or that they use an outside bindery.

HC — Casebinding (hardcovers)
CB — Plastic comb binding
GB — Glue or paste binding (used in some inexpensive catalogs)
LB — Looseleaf binders
PB — Perfect binding (softcovers)
SS — Saddle stitching (stapled in the center)
SD — Side stitching (like *National Geographic*)
SB — Spiral binding (like notebooks)
WB — Wire-O binding

Printed Items

This line in the listing indicates the kinds of publications and other printed items the printer regularly produces. The items are indicated by letter codes as follows:

A — Annual Reports
B — Books
C — Booklets
D — Catalogs
E — Cookbooks
F — Directories
G — Galley Copies
H — Journals
I — Magazines
J — Massmarket Paperbacks
K — Newsletters
L — Software Manuals
M — Textbooks
N — Workbooks

O — Yearbooks
P — Brochures
Q — Calendars
R — Comic Books
S — Direct Mail Letters
T — Envelopes
U — Greeting Cards
V — Labels / Stickers
W — Maps
X — Newspapers / Tabloids
Y — Postcards
Z — Posters
1 — Stationery

Services

These codes indicate whether the printers offer any of twelve addition-al services to their customers, everything from color separations through warehousing.

4C   — 4-color (full-color process) printing
CS   — Color separations
DA   — Design, layout, and artwork
FF   — Fulfillment and mailing services
LM   — List maintenance
OC   — Uses the OptiCopy prepress system
RA   — Uses the Rachwal prepress system
AF   — Stocks acid-free paper
RP   — Stocks recycled paper
TY   — Typesetting and composition
TD   — Typesetting via disk, modem, etc.
WA   — Warehouse or store books

Equipment

This line indicates the kind, number, and sizes of printing equipment the printer uses. These details, which can help you decide whether or not the printer has the capabilities to fill your needs, are listed in abbreviated form. For example, 2CB indicates they have two Cameron belt presses; 4SO(to 24x38) indicates they have four sheetfed presses, the largest capable of printing 24 by 38 inch sheets.

CB   — Cameron belt press
LP   — Letterpress
SO   — Sheetfed offset press
WO   — Web offset press
gravure — Rotogravure press

Annual Sales

Where known, we have listed the printer's most recent annual sales. In many cases, these annual sales figures are reported by the printers themselves. Some sales figures, however, are excerpted from the *GAM* 100 (*Graphics Arts Monthly* report on printers) or the *Printing Impressions* 500 listing of the top printers in North America.

Number of Employees

Again, these figures are either taken from the printer's self report or from the *GAM* 100 or *Printing Impressions* 500. The annual sales figures and number of employees should provide a good indication of the printer's ability to meet your needs, especially if those needs are long term.

Turnaround Times

These codes indicate the normal turnaround times for the printer to produce a job from camera-ready copy to shipment. These times are expressed as a range of working days; e.g., "**B4**" indicates that the printer can produce a book within 21 to 30 working days after receipt of camera-ready copy while "**M2**" indicates that they can produce a magazine within 6 to 10 working days from receipt of camera-ready copy (or negatives).

Note that these turnaround times are those reported by the printer; we have no way to verify their normal turnaround times.

B1 — 1 to 5 working days.
B2 — 6 to 10 working days.
B3 — 11 to 20 working days.
B4 — 21 to 30 working days.
B5 — 30 to 45 working days.
B6 — over 45 days.

If the code starts with a "**C**", it indicates the turnaround time for a catalog while an "**M**" indicates the turnaround time for a magazine. Hence, **C3** indicates that the printer can deliver a finished catalog in 11 to 20 working days. Similarly, an **M2** indicates that they can deliver a finished magazine in 6 to 10 working days.

Customers

These figures indicate what percentage of their printing business is done for various types of customers. For example, **BP25** indicates that 25% of their business is for book publishers, while **NP50** indicates that 50% of their business is with non-profit groups. In other words, the number after the code letters indicates the percentage.

This information is most useful to those of you who want to work with a printer who is accustomed to serving the needs of clients similar to you.

It's useful, for example, if you are a magazine publisher to work with a printer whose major source of business is other magazine publishers because that printer will be more aware of the potential problems that can arise in producing a magazine on a regular basis.

BP — Book publishers
BU — Businesses, both large and small
CU — Colleges and universities
MP — Magazine publishers
NP — Non-profit groups and organizations
OR — Other organizations and clubs
SC — Schools, elementary and secondary
SP — Self-publishers, authors, genealogists
OT — Other

Union Shop

A **Y** indicates that they are a union shop while an **N** indicates that they employ non-union workers.

Year Established

Where known, we have listed the year in which the printer began business. In a few cases, this date might indicate the year they started printing bound publications rather than the year they began business.

Terms

This line lists the printer's standard terms of payment. Most indicate that they offer net 30 with approved credit. That means that if you have good credit, then you may pay your printing bill 30 days after the job is finished. On the other hand, some require that you pay ⅓ of the bill at the time you give them your camera-ready copy, ⅓ when you approve the proofs or blues, and the final ⅓ before they ship the finished job or upon delivery.

Statement and Comments

The **statement** consists of the printer's own words describing their goals and services.

The **comments**, on the other hand, are written by the editor either to expand upon the details in the listing or to clarify those details.

Alphabetical Printer Listings

A

Academy Books **BK**
Robert A Sharp, General Manager
10 Cleveland Avenue
P O Box 757
Rutland, VT 05701
802-773-9194

Min: 100 **Max:** 5,000 **Opt:** 5,000
Sizes: 2356X
Bindings: HCI-CBO-PBI-SSI-SBO
Items: ABCDEHINP
Services: AF
Union shop: N
Year established: 1946
Terms: 1/3 down, 1/3 proofs, 1/3 done

Comments: A division of Sharp Offset
Printing, Academy has been printing books
since 1946.

Accurate Web **BK**
2 Allwood Avenue
Central Islip, NY 11722
516-234-3590

Min: 7,000 **Max:** 200,000 **Opt:** 25,000
Sizes: 25
Bindings: PBI
Items: BDF
Equipment: WO

Ad Infinitum Press **BK**
7 N MacQuesten Parkway
P O Box 2212
Mount Vernon, NY 10551
914-664-5930

Min: 100 **Max:** 50,000 **Opt:**
Bindings: PBI-SSI
Items: BCFGHMN
Services: 4C-CS-DA-TY-WA
Equipment: LP-SO

Statement: We accept print runs of any
quantity that are suitable for sheetfed presses. We offer editorial services, typesetting,
design and pasteup, and galley copies.

Adams & Abbott **BK**
46 Summer Street
Boston, MA 02110
617-542-1621

Min: 100 **Max:** 10,000 **Opt:**
Sizes: 25X
Bindings: CBX-PBX-SSX-SBX
Services: DA-TY

Comments: Their specialty has been
typesetting and printing foreign language
texts and mathematics books.

The Adams Group **GC**
225 Varick Street
New York, NY 10014
212-255-4900

Min: 5,000 **Max:** 2,000,000 **Opt:**
Sizes: 123456X
Bindings: PBI-SSI
Items: ABCDFIKNPZ
Services: 4C-CS-DA-TY
Equipment: 6SO-2WO
Annual sales: $12,500,000
Number of employees: 125

Adams Press **BR**
Beverly Freid, Sales Manager
25 E Washington Street
Chicago, IL 60602
708-676-3426

Min: 250 **Max:** 5,000 **Opt:** 2,000
Sizes: 123456
Bindings: HCO-CBO-LBO-PBI-
          SSI-SDI-SBI-WBI
Items: ABCDEHIMN
Services: 4C-AF-TY-TD

PRINTED ITEMS			
A Annual Reports	**G** Galley Copies	**N** Workbooks	**U** Greeting Cards
B Books	**H** Journals	**O** Yearbooks	**V** Labels / Stickers
C Booklets	**I** Magazines	**P** Brochures	**W** Maps
D Catalogs	**J** Mass-Market Books	**Q** Calendars	**X** Newspapers
E Cookbooks	**K** Newsletters	**R** Comic Books	**Y** Postcards
F Directories	**L** Software Manuals	**S** Direct Mail Letters	**Z** Posters
	M Textbooks	**T** Envelopes	**1** Stationery

Equipment: 4SO(17X22)
Annual sales: $1,000,000
Number of employees: 20
Turnaround times: B5C5M5
Customers: BP5-CU5-SP90
Union shop: N
Year established: 1942
Terms: 50% deposit, balance with proof

Statement: Our primary objective is to help self-publishers get their books in print. We supply a professionally printed book at a reasonable cost. We also secure copyrights and Library of Congress catalog card numbers. We pay shipping charges to any address in the USA. Write for our catalog and price list.

Comments: Having advertised in *Writer's Digest* for years, Adams Press is accustomed to working with writers.

BK
Advanced Duplicating & Printing
Sandy Wagner
7419 Washington Avenue South
Edina, MN 55439
612-944-6050; Fax: 612-944-9683

Min: 25 **Max:** 5,000 **Opt:** 1,000
Sizes: 12345
Bindings: CBI-LBI-PBI-SSI-SBI-SBI-WBI
Items: BCFLMN
Equipment: SO-WO
Annual sales: $2,500,000
Number of employees: 35
Turnaround times: B2
Customers: BP15-BU85
Union shop: N
Year established: 1977
Terms: Net 30

Statement: We print one-color books. We have a complete bindery for perfect binding, spiral binding, and wire-o binding.

BK
Adviser Graphics
4757 - 60th Street, Bag 5012
Red Deer, Alberta T4N 6R4 Canada
403-347-8866

Min: Max: 100,000 **Opt:** 10,000
Sizes: 123456
Bindings: HCO-PBO-SSI-SDI-SBI-WBO

Items: ABCDEFHKPQSTXYZ1
Services: 4C-LM-AF-TY-TD
Equipment: 2LP(17")-4SO(to 25")-
1WO(35")
Annual sales: $5,000,000
Number of employees: 30
Turnaround times: B6C3
Customers: BP12-BU60-CU15-NP5-OR8
Union shop: N
Year established: 1979
Terms: COD

CA
Alden Press
2000 Arthur Avenue
Elk Grove Village, IL 60007-6071
312-640-6000

Min: 50,000 **Max:** 5,000,000 **Opt:**
Sizes: 35X
Bindings: SSI
Items: D
Services: 4C-FF
Equipment: 12WO
Annual sales: $163,000,000
Number of employees: 700
Year established: 1948

GC
Algen Press Corporation
18-06 130th Street
College Point, NY 11356
718-463-4605; Fax: 718-359-0384

Min: 1,000 **Max:** 35,000 **Opt:** 15,000
Sizes: 123456X
Bindings: SSX
Items: CDPUYZ
Services: 4C-CS

Comments: They specialize in printing 4-color case covers and dust jackets, but they also print some catalogs, pamphlets, and brochures.

BK
Alger Press Ltd
P O Box 100, 61 Charles Street
Oshawa, Ontario L1H 7K8 Canada
416-725-3501

Min: 2,000 **Max:** 250,000 **Opt:**
Sizes: 2345
Bindings: CBI-PBI-SSI-SBI-WBI

SERVICES				BINDINGS			
4C	4-Color Printing	RA	Rachwal System	HC	Hardcover	SD	Side Stitching
CS	Color Separations	AF	Acid-Free Paper	CB	Comb Binding	SB	Spiral Binding
DA	Design / Artwork	RP	Recycled Paper	GB	Glue Binding	WB	Wire-O Binding
FF	Fulfillment/Mailing	TY	Typesetting	LB	Loose-Leaf Binding	I	In-House
LM	List Maintenance	TD	Typeset w/ Disk	PB	Perfect Binding	O	Out of House
OC	OptiCopy System	WA	Warehousing	SS	Saddle Stitching	X	Unknown

Items: BCEFLMN
Services: 4C-FF-WA
Equipment: SO-WO
Statement: We offer complete book manufacturing service from manuscript to distribution.

Allen Press   **MS**
1041 New Hampshire Street
P O Box 368
Lawrence, KS 66044
913-843-1234

Min: 200 Max: 20,000 Opt: 7,000
Sizes: 23456
Bindings: GBI-PBI-SSI
Items: H
Services: 4C-FF-LM-AF-TY-TD-WA
Equipment: 7SO(19X25-28X41)
Customers: CU30-NP70
Union shop: N
Year established: 1952
Terms: Cash, Net 30

Comments: They specialize in printing scholarly and scientific journals. They offer advice on all aspects of journal publishing, including editing and marketing.

Allied Graphics Arts   **CA**
1515 Broadway, 42nd Floor
New York, NY 10036
212-730-1414

Min: 25,000 Max: 2,000,000 Opt:
Sizes: 2345X
Bindings: SSI
Items: D
Services: 4C-CS-DA
Annual sales: $60,000,000
Customers: BU100

Allied Printing   **GC**
Bill Fongheiser, President
1414 Kenmore Boulevard
P O Box 3737
Akron, OH 44314
216-753-8436; Fax: 216-753-0870
Toll-free: 800-824-8719

Min: 20,000 Max: 500,000 Opt: 100,000
Sizes: 1245X
Bindings: PBI-SSI
Items: ABCDIKNPQ
Services: 4C-FF
Equipment: 6SO(19X25-25X38)-2WO(to 23X38)
Annual sales: $7,000,000
Number of employees: 75
Turnaround times: B3C3M3
Customers: BP5-BU80-CU5-MP10
Union shop: Y
Year established: 1962
Terms: 1% 10, net 30

Statement: We have full-color web and sheetfed capabilities. We specialize in square book formats (8 3/8" x 8 3/8" or 11" x 11"). We offer full mailing and lettershop capabilities.

Alonzo Printing   **GC**
1094 San Mateo Avenue
S San Francisco, CA 94080
415-873-0522

Sizes: 25
Bindings: SSI
Items: BCDIKNX
Services: 4C-FF
Equipment: WO

Alpine Press   **BK**
100 Alpine Circle
Stoughton, MA 02072
617-341-1800; Fax: 617-341-3973
Toll-free: 800-343-5901

Min: 500 Max: 100,000 Opt: 15,000
Sizes: 123456X
Bindings: HCI-CBI-PBI-SBI-WBI
Items: BFM
Services: RA
Equipment: 6SO-WO(19x22)
Annual sales: $15,000,000
Number of employees: 250
Customers: BU-CU-OR-SC
Year established: 1917

Comments: This division of Courier Graphics specializes in producing books for colleges, businesses, and professionals.

PRINTED ITEMS					
A Annual Reports	G Galley Copies	N Workbooks	U Greeting Cards
B Books	H Journals	O Yearbooks	V Labels / Stickers
C Booklets	I Magazines	P Brochures	W Maps
D Catalogs	J Mass-Market Books	Q Calendars	X Newspapers
E Cookbooks	K Newsletters	R Comic Books	Y Postcards
F Directories	L Software Manuals	S Direct Mail Letters	Z Posters
	M Textbooks	T Envelopes	1 Stationery

American Offset Printers **BK**

Bill Rakow, Sales Manager
Group Printing California
3600 S Hill Street
Los Angeles, CA 90007
213-231-4133

Min: 3,000 **Max:** 100,000 **Opt:** 20,000
Sizes: 12345
Bindings: HCX-CBX-PBX-
    SSX-SBX-WBX
Items: BCDFHJLMN
Services: 4C-CS-FF-AF-WA
Equipment: 3SO(40")-1WO(38")
Number of employees: 35
Turnaround times: B3C3M3
Customers: BP20-BU45-
    CU5-NP5-SC5-SP20
Union shop: Y
Year established: 1938
Terms: 2% 10, Net 30

Statement: Our company has specialized for 50 years in the production of books, catalogs, manuals, and directories for commercial and trade customers.

Comments: A division of Merrill Corporation of Saint Paul, Minnesota ($69 million in annual sales from 3 plants with 584 employees).

American Press Inc **MS**

2911 Hunter Mill Road #202
Oakton, VA 22124
703-255-4666; Fax: 703-255-9857
Toll-free: 800-283-4666

Min: 10,000 **Max:** 800,000 **Opt:** 50,000
Items: DI
Services: 4C-CS-DA-FF

American Printers & Litho **GC**

Richard D Krebs, Sales Manager
6701 W Oakton Street
Chicago, IL 60648-0271
708-966-6500; Fax: 312-267-6553

Sizes: 23456
Bindings: HCO-CBO-LBO-PBO-
    SSI-SDO-SBO-WBO
Items: ABCDEPWZ

Services: 4C
Equipment: 5LP-19SO(11x17-54x77)
Annual sales: $35,000,000
Number of employees: 260
Turnaround times: B3C2
Customers: BP8-BU90-MP2
Union shop: Y
Year established: 1965
Terms: Net 30

Comments: They specialize in printed premiums, including finger puppets, puzzles, cutouts, punchouts, stickers, mobiles, masks, caps, hats, die-cut menus, and scratch-off promotions.

American Signature Graphics **CA**

Storm Printing
6320 Denton Drive
Dallas, TX 75235
214-358-1371

Min: 20,000 **Max:** 3,000,000 **Opt:**
Bindings: PBI-SSI
Items: ADIPZ
Services: 4C-CS-FF
Annual sales: $351,000,000
Number of employees: 2,480

American Signature Graphics **CA**

Frye & Smith
150 E Baker Street
Costa Mesa, CA 92626
714-540-7005

Min: 20,000 **Max:** 3,000,000 **Opt:**
Bindings: PBI-SSI
Items: ADIPZ
Services: 4C-CS-FF

American Signature Graphics **CA**

Executive Offices
40 West 40th Street
New York, NY 10018-3988
212-703-5101

Min: 20,000 **Max:** 3,000,000 **Opt:**
Bindings: PBI-SSI
Items: ADIPZ
Services: 4C-CS-FF

SERVICES				BINDINGS			
4C	4-Color Printing	**RA**	Rachwal System	**HC**	Hardcover	**SD**	Side Stitching
CS	Color Separations	**AF**	Acid-Free Paper	**CB**	Comb Binding	**SB**	Spiral Binding
DA	Design / Artwork	**RP**	Recycled Paper	**GB**	Glue Binding	**WB**	Wire-O Binding
FF	Fulfillment/Mailing	**TY**	Typesetting	**LB**	Loose-Leaf Binding	**I**	In-House
LM	List Maintenance	**TD**	Typeset w/ Disk	**PB**	Perfect Binding	**O**	Out of House
OC	OptiCopy System	**WA**	Warehousing	**SS**	Saddle Stitching	**X**	Unknown

CA
American Signature Graphics
Storm Publications Printers
P O Box 30208
Memphis, TN 38130
601-895-4242

Min: 20,000 **Max:** 3,000,000 **Opt:**
Bindings: PBI-SSI
Items: ADIPZ
Services: 4C-CS-FF

MS
American Web Offset
4900 East 41st Avenue
Denver, CO 80216
303-321-2422

Min: 10,000 **Max:** 200,000 **Opt:** 45,000
Sizes: 245X
Bindings: PBI-SSI
Items: HIK
Services: 4C-CS
Equipment: 2WO(22X36)
Annual sales: $15,000,000
Number of employees: 100
Turnaround times: M2
Customers: BU5-MP95
Union shop: N
Year established: 1981
Terms: 1% 10, Net 30

Statement: We are dedicated to serving
the needs of short-run, specialty interest
magazine publishers.

BK
Americomp
Henry Burr
American-Stratford Graphic Services
Putney Road, Box 8128
Brattleboro, VT 05304
802-254-6073; Fax: 802-254-5240
Toll-free: 800-451-4328

Min: 100 **Max:** 10,000 **Opt:** 1,000
Sizes: 23
Bindings: PBI
Items: BGHILN
Services: TY-TD
Equipment: SO
Turnaround times: B2
Year established: 1990

GC
Amherst Printing Corporation
245 Seventh Avenue
New York, NY 10001-7302
212-924-0205

Min: 2,000 **Max:** 50,000 **Opt:**
Sizes: 25
Bindings: SSI

GC
Amidon Graphics
1966 Benson Avenue
Saint Paul, MN 55116-3299
612-690-2401; Toll-free: 800-328-6502

Min: 5,000 **Max:** 5,000,000 **Opt:** 50,000
Sizes: 25
Bindings: SSX
Items: CDKNPRSTY1
Services: 4C-CS
Equipment: 4WO(20x22)
Annual sales: $5,000,000
Number of employees: 25
Turnaround times: B3C3
Customers: BU70-MP10-NP10-OR5-SC5
Union shop: N
Year established: 1951
Terms: Net 30

Statement: We specialize in medium and
long-run web printing of direct mail pieces,
postcards, self-mailers, restaurant place-
mats, and guest checks — all from one color
to full color.

MS
Amos Press
911 Vandemark Road, P O Box 4129
Sidney, OH 45365
513-498-2111; Toll-free: 800-848-4406

Min: 5,000 **Max:** 250,000 **Opt:** 50,000
Items: IKS
Services: DA-FF-TY
Annual sales: $30,000,000
Number of employees: 250

Statement: We provide newsletter publishers with full in-house services from creative
design to printing and mailing. In as short
as 36 hours, we have typeset, keylined,
printed, and mailed 110,000 newsletter
packages.

PRINTED ITEMS					
A Annual Reports	G	Galley Copies	N Workbooks	U	Greeting Cards
B Books	H	Journals	O Yearbooks	V	Labels / Stickers
C Booklets	I	Magazines	P Brochures	W	Maps
D Catalogs	J	Mass-Market Books	Q Calendars	X	Newspapers
E Cookbooks	K	Newsletters	R Comic Books	Y	Postcards
F Directories	L	Software Manuals	S Direct Mail Letters	Z	Posters
	M	Textbooks	T Envelopes	1	Stationery

Anderson Lithograph   GC
1101 East 18th Street
Los Angeles, CA 90021
213-749-4383

Equipment: SO-LP
Annual sales: $10,000,000
Number of employees: 430
Year established: 1962

Anderson, Barton & Dalby   BR
3715 Northside Parkway
200 Northcreek #600
Atlanta, GA 30327
404-231-9357; Fax: 404-231-9427

Items: B
Services: DA

Andover Press   BR
516 West 34th Street
New York, NY 10001
212-594-3556

Min: 500 Max: 10,000 Opt: 5,000
Sizes: 23
Bindings: HCX-CBX-PBX-SSX-SBX
Items: BE
Services: DA-TY

Comments: Andover is the printing arm of
Vantage Press, a vanity press.

Anundsen Publishing Company   GC
Erik Anundsen
108 Washington Street
P O Box 230
Decorah, IA 52101
319-382-4295; Fax: 319-382-5150

Min: 35 Max: 5,000 Opt: 500
Sizes: 2345
Bindings: HCO-CBO-LBO-
    PBI-SSI-SDI-SBO-WBO
Items: BPT1
Services: 4C-AF-TY
Equipment: 3LP-7SO(10x15-20x29)
Annual sales: $1,000,000
Number of employees: 25

Turnaround times: B4C3
Customers: BU25-CU25-SP33-
    genealogies-17%
Union shop: N
Year established: 1871
Terms: Net 30; genealogies cash only

Statement: We specialize in short-run (35
to 300 copies) genealogical books for individuals nationwide.

Arandell-Schmidt   CA
N82 W13118 Leon Road
P O Box 405
Menomonee Falls, WI 53051
414-255-4400; Toll-free: 800-558-8724

Min: 50,000 Max: 3,000,000 Opt:
Sizes: 23456X
Bindings: SSI
Items: D
Services: 4C
Annual sales: $80,000,000
Number of employees: 450
Year established: 1980

Arcata Graphics / Baird Ward   MG
Thompson Lane & Powell Avenue
P O Box 305127
Nashville, TN 37230
615-385-0460; Fax: 615-297-8539

Min: 50,000 Max: 20,000,000 Opt:
Bindings: PBI-SSI
Items: DI
Services: 4C-FF
Annual sales: $550,000,000
Number of employees: 7,400
Turnaround times: M1
Customers: BU10-MP90
Terms: Net 30

Arcata Graphics / Buffalo   MG
Tom Carroll, Marketing Director
TC Industrial Park
Depew, NY 14043
716-686-2756; Fax: 716-684-5191

Min: 20,000 Max: 20,000,000 Opt:
Sizes: 125X

SERVICES				BINDINGS			
4C	4-Color Printing	RA	Rachwal System	HC	Hardcover	SD	Side Stitching
CS	Color Separations	AF	Acid-Free Paper	CB	Comb Binding	SB	Spiral Binding
DA	Design / Artwork	RP	Recycled Paper	GB	Glue Binding	WB	Wire-O Binding
FF	Fulfillment/Mailing	TY	Typesetting	LB	Loose-Leaf Binding	I	In-House
LM	List Maintenance	TD	Typeset w/ Disk	PB	Perfect Binding	O	Out of House
OC	OptiCopy System	WA	Warehousing	SS	Saddle Stitching	X	Unknown

Bindings: PBI-SSI
Items: DIJX
Services: 4C-CS-FF-OC-WA
Equipment: 4WO-12OT(gravure)
Annual sales: $60,000,000
Number of employees: 1,000
Turnaround times: B2M1
Customers: BU40-MP60
Union shop: Y
Year established: 1925
Terms: Net 30

Statement: Arcata Graphics/Buffalo is one
of eleven operating facilities of Arcata
Graphics. Headquartered in Baltimore,
Maryland, Arcata Graphics has annual
sales in excess of $550 million and is
among this country's largest publication
and book printers. The Buffalo division
specializes in printing magazines and mass-
market paperbacks.

Arcata Graphics / Fairfield   BK
Dan Hill, Marketing Director
100 N Miller Street
P O Drawer AN
Fairfield, PA 17320
717-642-5871; Fax: 717-642-8485
Toll-free: 800-356-0603

Min: 1,500 Max: 1,500,000 Opt: 20,000
Sizes: 23X
Bindings: HCI-PBI
Items: BDEFLM
Services: AF-RP
Equipment: 1CB-10SO
Turnaround times: B4
Customers: BP80-CU20
Union shop: N
Year established: 1976
Terms: Net 30

Comments: This division specializes in
producing one and two-color trade books
and college textbooks.

Arcata Graphics / Halliday   BK
Christine Ladd, Sales Manager
Circuit Street
West Hanover, MA 02339
617-826-8385; Fax: 617-826-6653
Toll-free: 800-356-0603

Min: 500 Max: 500,000 Opt: 6,000
Sizes: 235X
Bindings: HCI-CBI-PBI-SSI-SBI
Items: BM
Number of employees: 750
Turnaround times: B5
Union shop: N
Year established: 1948
Terms: Net 30

Comments: Halliday specializes in printing
and binding high quality trade books and
professional textbooks.

Arcata Graphics / Kingsport   BK
Roger Marshall
P O Box 1977
201 W Market Street
Kingsport, TN 37662
615-378-1000; Fax: 615-378-1109
Toll-free: 800-356-0603

Min: 2,000 Max: 1,500,000 Opt:
Sizes: 123456X
Bindings: HCI-CBI-GBI-LBI-
     PBI-SSI-SDI-SBI-WBI
Items: ABCDEFGHLMNO
Services: 4C-CS-OC-RA-AF-TY-TD-WA
Equipment: 3CB-23SO-26WO
Number of employees: 2,000
Turnaround times: B4C5
Customers: BP85-BU5-CU5-OT5
Union shop: Y
Year established: 1923
Terms: Net 30

Statement: Arcata is dedicated to being a
one-stop shopping source for publishers.

Arcata Graphics / Martinsburg   BK
1989 Arcata Boulevard, P O Box 11
Martinsburg, WV 25401
304-267-3600; Fax: 304-267-0989
Toll-free: 800-356-0603

Min: 1,000 Max: 2,000,000 Opt: 50,000
Sizes: 123456X
Bindings: HCI-CBI-GBI-LBI-
     PBI-SSI-SDI-SBI-WBI
Items: BDEFHJLMNOQW
Services: 4C-CS-FF-AF-TY-TD-WA

PRINTED ITEMS			
A Annual Reports	G Galley Copies	N Workbooks	U Greeting Cards
B Books	H Journals	O Yearbooks	V Labels / Stickers
C Booklets	I Magazines	P Brochures	W Maps
D Catalogs	J Mass-Market Books	Q Calendars	X Newspapers
E Cookbooks	K Newsletters	R Comic Books	Y Postcards
F Directories	L Software Manuals	S Direct Mail Letters	Z Posters
	M Textbooks	T Envelopes	1 Stationery

Equipment: 3CB-23SO-26WO
Turnaround times: B5
Customers: BP80-BU10-CU5-OT5
Union shop: N
Year established: 1989
Terms: Net 30

MG

Arcata Graphics / San Jose
696 E Trimble Road, P O Box 6363
San Jose, CA 95150
408-435-2300; Fax: 408-435-2383

Min: 50,000 Max: 20,000,000 Opt:
Bindings: PBI-SSI
Items: DI
Services: 4C-FF
Turnaround times: M1
Customers: BU10-MP90
Terms: Net 30

CA

Argus Press
7440 Natchez Avenue
Niles, IL 60648
312-647-7800

Min: 200 Max: 50,000 Opt: 30,000
Sizes: 123456
Bindings: HCO-CBO-GBO-LBI-
    PBI-SSI-SDI-SBI-WBO
Items: ACDKPQSUVYZ1
Services: 4C-CS-FF-TY-WA
Equipment: 2LP(14x20-23x35)-
    10SO(28x41)
Annual sales: $15,000,000
Number of employees: 100
Turnaround times: C2M2
Customers: BP5-BU65-CU5-MP10-OR15
Union shop: N
Year established: 1968
Terms: Net 30

GC

Arizona Lithographers
351 N Commerce Park Loop
Tucson, AZ 85745
602-622-7667

Min: 5,000 Max: 50,000 Opt: 20,000
Bindings: HCO-PBI-SSI
Items: ADKY art prints
Services: 4C

Comments: Arizona Litho is a sheetfed commercial and art print lithographer.

GC

Artcraft Press
P O Box 7
Waterloo, WI 53594
414-478-2176

Min: 5,000 Max: 2,000,000 Opt:
Sizes: 2345X
Bindings: PBI-SSI
Items: ACDFINPXYZ
Services: 4C-FF

BR

Artex Publishing
Les Zielinski, President
P O Box 202
Stevens Point, WI 54481
715-341-6959

Min: 500 Max: 5,000 Opt:
Sizes: 235
Bindings: PBI-SSI
Items: BCHIK
Services: TY
Turnaround times: B5
Customers: MP40-SP60
Union shop: N
Year established: 1985
Terms: 50% down, balance before print

Statement: Our goal is to provide economically priced products with good quality with a fast turnaround.

GC

Associated Printers
401 Hill Avenue
Grafton, ND 58237
701-352-0640

Sizes: 256X
Bindings: PBX-SSI
Items: CDIPSX
Services: 4C-FF-TY

GC

Atelier
147 West 25th Street #1001
New York, NY 10001-7205
212-620-9079

SERVICES				BINDINGS			
4C 4-Color Printing	**RA** Rachwal System			**HC** Hardcover	**SD** Side Stitching		
CS Color Separations	**AF** Acid-Free Paper			**CB** Comb Binding	**SB** Spiral Binding		
DA Design / Artwork	**RP** Recycled Paper			**GB** Glue Binding	**WB** Wire-O Binding		
FF Fulfillment/Mailing	**TY** Typesetting			**LB** Loose-Leaf Binding	**I** In-House		
LM List Maintenance	**TD** Typeset w/ Disk			**PB** Perfect Binding	**O** Out of House		
OC OptiCopy System	**WA** Warehousing			**SS** Saddle Stitching	**X** Unknown		

Opt: 20,000
Sizes: 235
Bindings: SBI
Items: BE

Automated Graphic Systems   BK
P O Box 188
188 DeMarr Road
White Plains, MD 20695
301-843-1800; Fax: 301-843-6339
Toll-free: 800-678-8760

Min: 500 Max: 50,000 Opt: 20,000
Sizes: 2345X
Bindings: HCO-CBI-PBI-SSI-SBI
Items: BCDEFHP
Services: DA-FF-TY-TD-WA
Terms: Net 30

Comments: Besides printing and binding, they provide the following services: art, composition, storage, mailing, and database management.

Autumn House Graphics Group   MG
Steve Hall, Marketing Director
55 W Oak Ridge Drive
Hagerstown, MD 21740
Toll-free: 800-444-7532

Bindings: SSI
Items: I
Services: 4C-CS-DA-FF-TY
Equipment: SO-1WO

Comments: They are specialists in the design of magazines.

B

B & R Printing   GC
420 5th Avenue
Post Falls, ID 83854
208-773-1103

Min: 100 Max: 10,000 Opt: 2,000
Sizes: 123456
Bindings: HCO-CBI-GBI-LBI-
PBI-SSI-SDI-SBO-WBO

Items: ACDEFKLMNOPSTY1
Services: DA-AF-TY-TD
Equipment: 2SO
Annual sales: $150,000
Number of employees: 7
Turnaround times: B2
Customers: BP3-BU70-NP5-
OR5-SC2-SP10-OT5
Union shop: N
Year established: 1981
Terms: COD or net 30 with approval

Statement: We are a small printer catering to short-run, fast-turnaround customers.

Baker Johnson   BK
Wayne A Johnson
2810 Baker Road
P O Box 280
Dexter, MI 48130
313-426-0200; Fax: 313-426-0301

Min: 100 Max: 25,000 Opt: 4,000
Sizes: 123456
Bindings: LBI-PBI-SSO
Items: BDEFHLMN
Services: 4C-CS-AF-WA
Equipment: 3SO(19x26-41x54)
Annual sales: $1,000,000
Number of employees: 16
Turnaround times: B3C3M3
Customers: BP60-BU8-
CU20-NP5-OR2-SP5
Union shop: N
Year established: 1989
Terms: Net 30 on approved credit

Statement: Since we feature a limited number of bindings, we are able to offer high quality at competitive prices. Our turnaround time is typically the best in the area.

Balan Printing   CA
5377 Kings Highway
Brooklyn, NY 11203
718-629-2900

Min: 5,000 Max: 1,000,000 Opt: 100,000
Sizes: 1245X
Bindings: GBI-PBI-SSI-SBI
Items: BCDEFGHIJKMNOPRSXZ

PRINTED ITEMS					
A Annual Reports	G Galley Copies	N Workbooks	U Greeting Cards
B Books	H Journals	O Yearbooks	V Labels / Stickers
C Booklets	I Magazines	P Brochures	W Maps
D Catalogs	J Mass-Market Books	Q Calendars	X Newspapers
E Cookbooks	K Newsletters	R Comic Books	Y Postcards
F Directories	L Software Manuals	S Direct Mail Letters	Z Posters
	M Textbooks	T Envelopes	1 Stationery

Services: 4C-FF-LM-TY-TD-WA
Equipment: 2SO(25x38)-4WO(22x36)
Annual sales: $5,000,000
Number of employees: 75
Turnaround times: B1C1M1
Customers: BP20-BU35-MP25-SP20
Union shop: Y
Year established: 1963
Terms: Net 30

Bang Printing   **BK**
Junction Highways 18 & 25
Brainerd, MN 56401
218-829-2877

Banta Commercial Group   **CA**
641 Fairview Avenue N
Saint Paul, MN 55104-1792
612-645-4422

Min: 5,000 Max: 3,000,000 Opt:
Sizes: 23456X
Bindings: SSI
Items: ACDFIKNPSWXZ
Services: 4C-CS-DA-FF-TY
Equipment: LP-5SO-8WO
Annual sales: $568,000,000
Number of employees: 3,800

Banta Corporation   **BK**
Pat Coenraad, Marketing Admininstrator
Curtis Reed Plaza, P O Box 60
Menasha, WI 54952
414-722-7771; Fax: 414-722-8541
Toll-free: 800-722-3324

Min: 2,500 Max: 1,000,000 Opt: 25,000
Sizes: 123456X
Bindings: HCI-CBI-LBO-
    PBI-SSI-SDO-SBI-WBI
Items: BCDEFJLMN
Services: 4C-CS-FF-OC-AF-RP-WA
Equipment: 3CB-5SO(25x38-28x40)-14WO
Annual sales: $568,000,000
Number of employees: 3,800
Turnaround times: B3C3
Customers: BP80-BU17-OT3
Union shop: Y
Year established: 1901
Terms: Net 30

Comments: Besides books, Banta also
prints game boards, game cards, educational workbooks, software and video packages, and magazines.

Banta-Harrisonburg   **BK**
3330 Willow Spring Road
Harrisonburg, VA 22801
703-433-2517

Min: 2,500 Max: 1,000,000 Opt: 25,000
Sizes: 123456X
Bindings: PBI-SSI
Items: BCDFILN
Services: 4C-CS-FF-OC-AF-RP-WA
Terms: Net 30

Bawden Printing   **BK**
Lisa Christison, Marketing Coordinator
400 South 14th Avenue
Eldridge, IA 52748
319-285-4800; Fax: 319-285-4828

Min: 3,000 Max: 200,000 Opt: 50,000
Sizes: 1235
Bindings: HCO-CBI-LBO-
    PBI-SSI-SDO-SBI-WBI
Items: BDFLN
Services: FF-OC-AF-RP-TY-WA
Equipment: 2LP-2SO(19x25)-3WO
Annual sales: $35,000,000
Number of employees: 270
Turnaround times: B3C3
Customers: BP40-BU35-CU15-NP5-OT5
Union shop: Y
Year established: 1921
Terms: Net 30 with approved credit

Statement: We are a one and two-color
medium to high volume web printer. We
also have five-color sheetfed cover press
capability, plus full in-house saddlestiching,
perfect binding, labeling, mailing, promotion fulfillment, and distribution.

Bay Port Press   **BK**
Bruce Collin
100 West 35th Street #P
National City, CA 92050
619-420-6296; Fax: 619-420-2217

SERVICES				BINDINGS			
4C	4-Color Printing	RA	Rachwal System	HC	Hardcover	SD	Side Stitching
CS	Color Separations	AF	Acid-Free Paper	CB	Comb Binding	SB	Spiral Binding
DA	Design / Artwork	RP	Recycled Paper	GB	Glue Binding	WB	Wire-O Binding
FF	Fulfillment/Mailing	TY	Typesetting	LB	Loose-Leaf Binding	I	In-House
LM	List Maintenance	TD	Typeset w/ Disk	PB	Perfect Binding	O	Out of House
OC	OptiCopy System	WA	Warehousing	SS	Saddle Stitching	X	Unknown

Min: 500 **Max:** 100,000 **Opt:** 10,000
Sizes: 1245
Bindings: HCO-CBO-LBI-
   PBI-SSI-SDI-SBO-WBO
Items: BCDEFKLMNPSY
Services: DA-AF-TY-TD
Equipment: SO-WO
Annual sales: $2,500,000
Number of employees: 21
Turnaround times: B3
Customers: BP5-BU40-
   CU10-NP10-SC5-SP15
Union shop: N
Year established: 1978
Terms: Net 30 upon credit approval

Statement: We are a commercial non-heat-set web printer specializing in perfectbound, saddlestitched, and loose leaf publications in one and two colors on high grade stock.

GC
Beacon Press
4731 Eubank Road
Richmond, VA 23231
804-226-2120

Min: 50,000 **Max:** 2,000,000 **Opt:**
Sizes: 2345X
Bindings: GBI-PBI-SSI-SDI
Items: BCDHIKSX
Services: 4C
Equipment: 1SO-3WO

GC
Beacon Wholesale Printing
Chad Ernst, General Manager
101 4th Avenue S
P O Box 1750
Seattle, WA 98111-1750
206-624-9699; Fax: 206-726-8394
Toll-free: 800-426-0244

Min: 100 **Max:** 1,000,000 **Opt:** 5,000
Sizes: 123456
Bindings: HCO-CBI-LBI-
   PBO-SSI-SDI-SBI-WBO
Items: ABCDEKLNPSTVY1
Services: 4C-FF-LM-AF-RP-TY-WA
Equipment: 3LP-4SO(to 15x20)-1WO
Annual sales: $7,500,000
Number of employees: 25
Turnaround times: B4C3

Customers: BP30-BU40-CU5-
   NP5-OR5-SP5-OT10
Union shop: N
Year established: 1916
Terms: 1% 10, net 30 with approved credit

GC
Bell Publications
P O Box 2491
Iowa City, IA 52244
319-354-3600

Min: 1,000 **Max:** 100,000 **Opt:**
Sizes: 25
Bindings: GBI-LBI-PBI-SSI
Items: ABCDKNPSXZ1
Services: TY

BK
Harold Berliner Printer
224 Main Street
Nevada City, CA 95959
916-273-2278

Min: 100 **Max:** 2,000 **Opt:** 1,000
Sizes: 123456
Bindings: HCX-SSX
Items: BWZ1
Equipment: 2LP(22x28)-1SO(23x29)
Turnaround times: B5
Customers: BP10-SP90
Union shop: N
Terms: 10 days after deposit

BK
Berryville Graphics
Jerry Allee, VP Sales
Springsbury Road
P O Box 272
Berryville, VA 22611
703-955-2750; Fax: 703-955-4268

Min: 2,500 **Max:** 2,000,000 **Opt:** 20,000
Sizes: 123456
Bindings: HCI-CBO-PBI-
   SSI-SDI-SBO-WBO
Items: BCE
Services: 4C-OC-RA-AF-TY-TD-WA
Equipment: 2LP-5SO-3WO
Annual sales: $114,000,000
Number of employees: 430
Turnaround times: B5
Customers: BP97-BU1-CU1-NP1

PRINTED ITEMS							
A	Annual Reports	G	Galley Copies	N	Workbooks	U	Greeting Cards
B	Books	H	Journals	O	Yearbooks	V	Labels / Stickers
C	Booklets	I	Magazines	P	Brochures	W	Maps
D	Catalogs	J	Mass-Market Books	Q	Calendars	X	Newspapers
E	Cookbooks	K	Newsletters	R	Comic Books	Y	Postcards
F	Directories	L	Software Manuals	S	Direct Mail Letters	Z	Posters
		M	Textbooks	T	Envelopes	1	Stationery

Union shop: N
Year established: 1957
Terms: Various, net 30
Statement: A division of Bertelsmann.

BK
Bertelsmann Printing
Gregg Aponte
245 Park Avenue, 42nd Floor
New York, NY 10167
212-984-7676; Fax: 212-984-7600

Min: 1,500 **Max:** 1,000,000 **Opt:** 20,000
Sizes: 123456X
Bindings: HCI-CBO-LBO-
PBI-SSI-SDI-SBO-WBO
Items: BCEFGJLMNPQZ
Services: 4C-CS-OC-RA-AF-RP-TD-WA
Equipment: 57SO-33WO
Annual sales: $95,000,000
Number of employees: 1,211
Turnaround times: B3
Customers: BP70-BU10-CU2-NP15-OT3
Union shop: Y
Year established: 1960
Terms: Net 30 from invoice date

Statement: BPMC is a full integrated book manufacturing company consisting of plants in Pennsylvania, Virginia, and California. This is the main corporate offices for Berryville Graphics, Delta Lithograph, and Offset Paperback.

Comments: BMPC is a division of Bertelsmann, a large German publisher which also owns Bantam/Doubleday/Dell.

MG
Beslow Associates
2537 W Montrose
Chicago, IL 60618
312-539-6486

Min: 10,000 **Max:** 3,000,000 **Opt:**
Sizes: 23456X
Bindings: PBI-SSI
Items: BDFHI
Services: 4C-CS-FF-TY-TD
Annual sales: $9,000,000
Number of employees: 30

Statement: We offer complete processing of directories, catalogs, business magazines, and newsstand publications.

BK
T H Best Printing Company
J Kirby Best, President
33 Kern Road
Don Mills, Ontario M3B 1S9 Canada
416-447-7295; Fax: 416-447-7444

Min: 250 **Max:** 1,100,000 **Opt:** 7,000
Sizes: 123456X
Bindings: HCI-CBO-GBI-
LBO-PBI-SSO-SBO-WBI
Items: ABEFLMNOR
Services: OC-RP-WA
Equipment: 4SO
Annual sales: $15,000,000
Number of employees: 100
Turnaround times: B2
Customers: BP70-BU30
Union shop: N
Year established: 1893
Terms: Net 30

Statement: We are committed to achieving the highest standards of quality and service thru hiring and developing the best people.

BK
Blake Printery
2222 Beebee Street
San Luis Obispo, CA 93401
805-543-6843; Toll-free: 800-792-6946

Min: 1,000 **Max:** 300,000 **Opt:** 5,000
Sizes: 123456X
Bindings: HCO-CBI-PBO-SSI
Items: BCDEHIPQUYZ
Services: 4C-DA-TY

CA
Blazing Graphics
1120 Wellington Avenue
Cranston, RI 02910
401-941-8090

Min: 2,000 **Max:** 50,000 **Opt:**
Sizes: 25X
Bindings: PBI-SSI
Items: DP
Services: 4C-CS-DA-TY-TD
Equipment: 1SO

Comments: Primarily a design and color separation house, they also print short to medium runs of catalogs, trade ads, and catalog sheets.

SERVICES				BINDINGS			
4C	4-Color Printing	**RA**	Rachwal System	**HC**	Hardcover	**SD**	Side Stitching
CS	Color Separations	**AF**	Acid-Free Paper	**CB**	Comb Binding	**SB**	Spiral Binding
DA	Design / Artwork	**RP**	Recycled Paper	**GB**	Glue Binding	**WB**	Wire-O Binding
FF	Fulfillment/Mailing	**TY**	Typesetting	**LB**	Loose-Leaf Binding	**I**	In-House
LM	List Maintenance	**TD**	Typeset w/ Disk	**PB**	Perfect Binding	**O**	Out of House
OC	OptiCopy System	**WA**	Warehousing	**SS**	Saddle Stitching	**X**	Unknown

BK

Blue Dolphin Press
Paul M Clemens, President
12380 Nevada City Highway
Grass Valley, CA 95945
916-265-6923

Min: 500 **Max:** 3,000 **Opt:** 2,000
Sizes: 123
Bindings: HCO-CBI-PBI-SSI-SBI-WBO
Items: ABCDEFKPSTYZ1
Services: 4C-DA-AF-TY-TD
Equipment: 1LP(10x15)-5SO(up to 24")
Annual sales: $1,000,000
Number of employees: 16
Turnaround times: B5
Customers: BP10-BU70-NP10-SP10
Union shop: N
Year established: 1978
Terms: 1/3 down, 1/3 blues, 1/3 delive

Comments: Affiliated with Blue Dolphin Publishing, this company provides typesetting, design, and printing services.

MS

Bolger Publications
Mary Kronholm
3301 Como Avenue SE
Minneapolis, MN 55414
612-645-6311; Fax: 612-645-1750
Toll-free: 800-999-6311

Min: 1,000 **Max:** 50,000 **Opt:** 20,000
Sizes: 123456X
Bindings: HCO-CBO-LBI-PBI-SSI-SDO-SBO-WBO
Items: ABCDEFHIKLMNPQYZ
Services: 4C-CS-DA-OC-RP-TY-TD
Equipment: 4SO(25"-40")
Annual sales: $15,000,000
Number of employees: 105
Turnaround times: B4C3M3
Union shop: N
Year established: 1954
Terms: Net 30

Statement: We are a high quality, extremely customer oriented, full-service color printer solving customer communication needs with specialty services and products. Specialty products include short to medium run company and association publications, product literature, auction brochures, directories, and catalogs.

BK

Book Makers Inc
6227 14th Avenue
Kenosha, WI 53140
414-658-2952

Min: 25 **Max:** 2,000 **Opt:** 300
Sizes: 123456X
Bindings: HCO-CBI-GBI-LBO-PBO-SSO-SDI-SBO-WBO
Items: BCDEFGKLNO
Services: DA-TY-TD-WA
Equipment: 4LP(12x24)-2SO(up to 24")
Annual sales: $200,000
Number of employees: 7
Turnaround times: B2C3
Customers: BP5-BU50-CU10-NP5-SC25-SP5
Union shop: N
Year established: 1980
Terms: Net 30

BK

The Book Press
Daniel Byrne, Marketing Director
Putney Road
Brattleboro, VT 05301
802-257-7701; Fax: 802-257-9439
Toll-free: 800-732-7310

Min: 1,000 **Max:** 2,000,000 **Opt:**
Sizes: 23456X
Bindings: HCI-CBO-LBO-PBI-SSO-SDI-SBO-WBO
Items: BCDEFLMN
Services: OC
Equipment: 1CB-4SO(23x29-54x77)-5WO
Annual sales: $22,000,000
Number of employees: 350
Turnaround times: B4M4
Customers: BP90-OT10
Union shop: Y
Year established: 1949

Comments: The Book Press is now owned by Quebecor Printing.

BK

The Book Printer
117 S Third Street
Laurens, IA 50554

Items: B
Services: TY

PRINTED ITEMS							
A	Annual Reports	G	Galley Copies	N	Workbooks	U	Greeting Cards
B	Books	H	Journals	O	Yearbooks	V	Labels / Stickers
C	Booklets	I	Magazines	P	Brochures	W	Maps
D	Catalogs	J	Mass-Market Books	Q	Calendars	X	Newspapers
E	Cookbooks	K	Newsletters	R	Comic Books	Y	Postcards
F	Directories	L	Software Manuals	S	Direct Mail Letters	Z	Posters
		M	Textbooks	T	Envelopes	1	Stationery

BK
BookCrafters
Customer Service
140 Buchanan Street, P O Box 370
Chelsea, MI 48118
313-475-9145; Fax: 313-475-7337

Min: 250 Max: 2,000,000 Opt: 6,000
Sizes: 123456X
Bindings: HCI-CBI-GBI-
LBI-PBI-SSI-SBI-WBI
Items: BCDEFHLMN
Services: 4C-FF-AF-RP-TY-WA
Equipment: 1CB(38")-16SO(20x29-38x50)
Annual sales: $35,000,000
Number of employees: 630
Turnaround times: B4C3
Customers: BP30-BU5-CU30-OR15-SP20
Union shop: N
Year established: 1965
Terms: Net 30; terms to be arranged

Statement: A division of American Business Products of Atlanta, BookCrafters provides complete printing & binding services, specializing in short to medium runs. We have a fully automated distribution center as well as two manufacturing plants.

BK
BookCrafters / Fredericksburg
Lee Hill Industrial Park, P O Box 892
Fredericksburg, VA 22401
703-371-3800; Fax: 703-475-8591

Min: 300 Max: 1,000,000 Opt: 6,000
Sizes: 123456
Items: BCDEFHLMN
Services: 4C-FF
Equipment: 1CB(38")-12SO(29-38-40-50")
Turnaround times: B4
Customers: BP60-BU3-CU7-
NP5-SP15-OT10
Union shop: N
Year established: 1965
Terms: Net 30; terms to be arranged

GC
Booklet Publishing Company
Joe Olcott, President
1902 Elmhurst Road
Elk Grove Village, IL 60007
312-364-1544; Fax: 312-364-0284

Min: 500 Max: 50,000 Opt: 2,500
Sizes: 25
Bindings: PBI-SSI
Items: BCDFKLNP
Turnaround times: B2C2

BK
Book-Mart Press
Michelle Gluckow, VP Marketing
2001 42nd Street
North Bergen, NJ 07047
201-864-1887; Fax: 201-864-7559

Min: 300 Max: 30,000 Opt: 2,500
Sizes: 123456X
Bindings: HCI-CBI-GBI-LBI-PBI-SSI-
SPO-WBO
Items: ABCDEFHLMN
Services: FF-AF-WA
Equipment: 8SO(23x23-41x56)
Annual sales: $8,000,000
Turnaround times: B3C3
Union shop: N
Year established: 1976
Terms: To be arranged

Statement: We specialize in manufacturing short to medium runs of both soft and hardcover books and scholarly journals. Our service is impeccable.

 BookMasters
638 Jefferson St., P. O. Box 159
Ashland, Ohio 44805
800/537-6727
In Ohio call 419/289-6051

BK
BookMasters
Ray Sevin, General Manager
638 Jefferson Street
P O Box 159
Ashland, OH 44805
419-289-6051
Toll-free: 800-537-6727
Min: 300 Max: 100,000 Opt: 1,000
Sizes: 123456
Bindings: HCO-CBO-PBO-
SSO-SBO-WBO
Items: BCDEFHJMN
Services: DA-FF-TY-TD-WA

SERVICES				BINDINGS			
4C	4-Color Printing	**RA**	Rachwal System	**HC**	Hardcover	**SD**	Side Stitching
CS	Color Separations	**AF**	Acid-Free Paper	**CB**	Comb Binding	**SB**	Spiral Binding
DA	Design / Artwork	**RP**	Recycled Paper	**GB**	Glue Binding	**WB**	Wire-O Binding
FF	Fulfillment/Mailing	**TY**	Typesetting	**LB**	Loose-Leaf Binding	**I**	In-House
LM	List Maintenance	**TD**	Typeset w/ Disk	**PB**	Perfect Binding	**O**	Out of House
OC	OptiCopy System	**WA**	Warehousing	**SS**	Saddle Stitching	**X**	Unknown

Turnaround times: B3
Customers: PB75-CU15-SP10
Union shop: N
Year established: 1972
Terms: Subject to review

BK

William Boyd Printing Company
49 Sheridan Avenue
Albany, NY 12210
518-436-9686; Fax: 518-436-7433

Min: 1,000 **Max:** 250,000 **Opt:**
Sizes: 2345
Bindings: HCO-CBO-LBI-PBI-SSI-SBO
Items: BEFHILO
Services: 4C-DA-FF-LM-TY-WA
Equipment: SO-WO
Annual sales: $8,000,000
Number of employees: 130
Turnaround times: B3
Year established: 1889
Terms: Net 30 with approved credit

Comments: They print United Nations publications, law books, journals, and commercial work as well as trade paperbacks.

MS

Braceland Brothers
7625 Suffolk Avenue
Philadelphia, PA 19153
215-492-0200; Fax: 215-492-8538
Toll-free: 800-338-1280

Min: 2,000 **Max:** 100,000 **Opt:** 50,000
Sizes: 25
Bindings: CBO-CBI-GBI-LBO-
PBI-SSI-SDI-SBO-WBO
Items: BCDFHIMN
Services: DA-FF-TY-TD
Equipment: 4SO(34"-58")-4WO
Annual sales: $28,000,000
Number of employees: 400
Turnaround times: B4C3M3
Customers: BP10-BU50-CU5-OR20-SC15
Union shop: N
Year established: 1899
Terms: Net 30

Comments: Braceland has plants in Pennsylvania, Ohio, and Georgia.

CA

Bradley Printing Company
2170 S Mannheim Road
Des Plaines, IL 60018
708-635-8000

Min: 100 **Max:** 2,000,000 **Opt:**
Sizes: 25
Bindings: HCO-CBO-GBO-LBO-
PBI-SSI-SDI-SBO-WBO
Items: ACDFKLPQSTUWYZ1
Services: 4C-CS-DA-FF
Equipment: LP-18SO(13x20-28x40)-
4WO(22x38)
Annual sales: $107,000,000
Number of employees: 725
Turnaround times: C2
Customers: BU80-CU5-MP5-NP5-OR5
Union shop: Y
Year established: 1964
Terms: Net 30

Statement: Bradley is a division of Graphisphere Corporation.

BK

Braun-Brumfield
Janice E Cooch, Marketing Director
100 N Staebler Road
P O Box 1203
Ann Arbor, MI 48106
313-662-3291; Fax: 313-662-1667

Min: 100 **Max:** 5,000 **Opt:** 2,000
Sizes: 23456
Bindings: HCI-CBO-LBO-PBI-
SSI-SDO-SBO-WBO
Items: BDEFHMN
Services: FF-OC-RA-AF-RP-TY-TD-WA
Equipment: 10SO(up to 38x50)
Annual sales: $28,000,000
Number of employees: 400
Turnaround times: B4C4
Customers: BP75-CU20-SP5
Union shop: N
Year established: 1950
Terms: Net 30

Statement: We are a complete in-house book manufacturer committed to quality and customer satisfaction. To honor this commitment, we utilize the best materials, the most efficient technology available, and that most vital element—dedicated people.

PRINTED ITEMS	G	Galley Copies	N	Workbooks	U	Greeting Cards
A Annual Reports	H	Journals	O	Yearbooks	V	Labels / Stickers
B Books	I	Magazines	P	Brochures	W	Maps
C Booklets	J	Mass-Market Books	Q	Calendars	X	Newspapers
D Catalogs	K	Newsletters	R	Comic Books	Y	Postcards
E Cookbooks	L	Software Manuals	S	Direct Mail Letters	Z	Posters
F Directories	M	Textbooks	T	Envelopes	1	Stationery

Comments: Braun-Brumfield is now owned by the Sheridan Group, which also includes The Sheridan Press. Write for their excellent resource booklets, *Book Manufacturing Glossary, Book Paper Samples,* and *Type Sample Book.*

Brennan Printing   BK
Robert Brennan, Owner
100 Main Street
Deep River, IA 52222
515-595-2000

Min: 500 **Max:** 10,000 **Opt:** 2,000
Sizes: 235
Bindings: HCO-CBI-GBI-LBI-
      PBI-SSI-SDI-SBO-WBO
Items: EKV
Services: TY
Equipment: 2SO(16x23)
Turnaround times: B6
Customers: NP70-SP1-OT29
Union shop: N
Year established: 1978
Terms: Net 30

Statement: Cookbooks are our specialty.

Brookshore Lithographers   GC
2075 Busse Road
Elk Grove Village, IL 60007
312-593-1200; Toll-free: 800-323-6112

Min: 50,000 **Max:** 2,000,000 **Opt:**
Sizes: 123456X
Bindings: SSI
Items: CDPSVYZ
Services: 4C

Comments: Now owned by Banta, Brookshore prints direct mail formats, including catalogs, mini-catalogs, brochures, gatefolds, inserts, poster pull-outs, and other direct mail packages.

Brown Printing   MS
U S Highway 14 West
Waseca, MN 56093
507-835-2410
Min: 20,000 **Max:** 3,000,000 **Opt:**

Sizes: 25X
Bindings: PBI-SSI
Items: ACDFHIKPUWZ
Services: 4C-CS-FF-TY
Equipment: 10WO
Annual sales: $410,000,000
Number of employees: 3,300
Year established: 1957

Comments: A subsidiary of Gruner-Jahr AG, a German company, Brown has branches in Kentucky and Pennsylvania. The three branches specialize in printing magazines and catalogs.

Brown Printing / East Greenville   CA
Route 29
East Greenville, PA 18041

Min: 20,000 **Max:** 3,000,000 **Opt:**
Bindings: PBI-SSI
Items: DHIP
Services: 4C-CS-FF-TY
Equipment: 4WO

Brown Printing / Franklin   MG
Broderson Road
Franklin, KY 42134
507-835-2410

Min: 500,000 **Max:** 10,000,000 **Opt:**
Sizes: 5X
Bindings: PBI-SSI
Items: DIX
Services: 4C-CS-FF
Equipment: 3OT(gravure)

William C Brown Printing   BK
Edmund O'Neill, Vice President
Manufacturing Division
2460 Kerper Boulevard
Dubuque, IA 52001
319-588-1451

Bindings: PBI
Items: B

Comments: Brown is a book publisher with its own printing plant. They do some outside book printing for other companies.

SERVICES				BINDINGS			
4C	4-Color Printing	RA	Rachwal System	HC	Hardcover	SD	Side Stitching
CS	Color Separations	AF	Acid-Free Paper	CB	Comb Binding	SB	Spiral Binding
DA	Design / Artwork	RP	Recycled Paper	GB	Glue Binding	WB	Wire-O Binding
FF	Fulfillment/Mailing	TY	Typesetting	LB	Loose-Leaf Binding	I	In-House
LM	List Maintenance	TD	Typeset w/ Disk	PB	Perfect Binding	O	Out of House
OC	OptiCopy System	WA	Warehousing	SS	Saddle Stitching	X	Unknown

BK

Brunswick Publishing Company
Walter J Raymond, President
P O Box 555
Lawrenceville, VA 23868
804-848-3865; Fax: 804-848-0607

Min: Max: 5,000 Opt: 1,500
Sizes: 123456X
Bindings: HCO-CBI-LBI-PBI-SSI-SDI
Items: ABCDEFKLNOPST1
Services: AF-TY-TD
Equipment: 3SO(11x17-18x24)
Annual sales: $400,000
Number of employees: 7
Turnaround times: B3C2
Customers: BU15-CU5-NP10-OR10-SP50
Union shop: N
Year established: 1978
Terms: 50% advance, balance on delivery

Comments: Brunswick is a publishing
company which also does some outside
book printing, including subsidy publishing
for authors.

GC

R L Bryan Company
301 Greystone Boulevard
P O Drawer 368
Columbia, SC 29202
803-779-3560

Min: 1,000 Max: 100,000 Opt: 40,000
Sizes: 123456X
Bindings: HCO-CBO-GBI-LBO-
PBI-SSI-SDI-SPO-WBO
Items: ABCDEFHIKPQSTVWZ1
Services: 4C-CS-DA-FF-TY-TD-WA
Equipment: 3LP(to 41")-10SO(to 40")
Annual sales: $7,000,000
Number of employees: 100
Turnaround times: B6C4M2
Customers: BU65-CU6-NP1-SP22-OT6
Union shop: N
Year established: 1915
Terms: Net 30 with approved credit

GC

BSC Litho
3000 Canby Street
Harrisburg, PA 17105
717-238-9469

Min: 1,000 Max: 2,000,000 Opt:
Sizes: 123456
Bindings: HCO-CBO-GBO-LBO-
PBO-SSI-SDI-SBO-WBO
Items: ABCDEFIKPQSY
Services: 4C-DA-TY-WA
Equipment: 2LP(14x16)-6SO(20x28)-
2WO(18x23)
Annual sales: $7,000,000
Number of employees: 100
Turnaround times: B5C4M5
Customers: CU20-MP20-OR60
Union shop: N
Year established: 1921
Terms: Net 30

MS

William Byrd Press
2901 Byrdhill Road
P O Box 27481
Richmond, VA 23261
804-264-2711

Sizes: 5X
Bindings: PBX-SSX
Items: HI
Services: TY-TD

Statement: A division of Cadmus Communications ($160 million in annual sales
from 10 plants with 1,950 employees).

C

BK

C & M Press
850 East 73rd Avenue #12
Thornton, CO 80229
303-289-4757

Min: 100 Max: 5,000 Opt: 1,000
Sizes: 123456X
Bindings: HCI-CBI-LBI-PBI-SSI-SBI-WBI
Items: ABCDEFJKLMN
Equipment: 8SO(13x17)
Annual sales: $5,000,000
Number of employees: 30
Turnaround times: B3
Customers: BP20-BU60-CU10-SC5-SP5
Union shop: N
Year established: 1983
Terms: Net 30

PRINTED ITEMS					
A	Annual Reports	G	Galley Copies	N	Workbooks
B	Books	H	Journals	O	Yearbooks
C	Booklets	I	Magazines	P	Brochures
D	Catalogs	J	Mass-Market Books	Q	Calendars
E	Cookbooks	K	Newsletters	R	Comic Books
F	Directories	L	Software Manuals	S	Direct Mail Letters
		M	Textbooks	T	Envelopes

U	Greeting Cards
V	Labels / Stickers
W	Maps
X	Newspapers
Y	Postcards
Z	Posters
1	Stationery

Statement: We are highly specialized and provide no printing services other than the production of books, manuals, and computer documentation.

GC

Cal Central Press
P O Box 551
2629 Fifth Street
Sacramento, CA 95608
916-441-5392

Min: 5,000 **Max:** 2,000,000 **Opt:**
Sizes: 2345X
Bindings: SSI-SDI
Items: ABCFINSZ
Services: 4C-CS-TY
Equipment: LP-SO-WO
Annual sales: $23,000,000
Number of employees: 250

BK

Caldwell Printers
Bob E Caldwell, Owner
29 S First Avenue
Arcadia, CA 91006
818-447-4601

Min: 50 **Max:** 5,000 **Opt:** 2,000
Sizes: 2356
Bindings: HCO-PBO-SSI
Items: BCD
Services: DA-TY
Terms: 50% deposit, balance on delivery

Statement: We are a family-owned business of conscientious craftsmen who print short runs of manuals, poetry, and autobiographies.

MS

California Offset Printers
620 W Elk Avenue
Glendale, CA 91204
213-245-6446

Min: 10,000 **Max:** 20,000,000 **Opt:** 35,000
Sizes: 25X
Bindings: PBO-SSI
Items: DFIKLNPX
Services: 4C-FF
Equipment: 5WO
Annual sales: $25,000,000

Number of employees: 170
Turnaround times: C2M2
Customers: BU25-CU5-MP40-OT30
Union shop: Y
Year established: 1963
Terms: Net 30 on approved credit

Statement: We print four basic formats: standard newspapers, tabloids, magazines, and digest. 70% of our business is printing publications.

BK

Camelot Book Factory
Donald Spencer, President
39-B Coolidge Avenue
Ormond Beach, FL 32174
904-672-5672

Min: 50 **Max:** 300 **Opt:** 200
Sizes: 25
Bindings: CBI-PBI-SSI
Items: BCDEFGLMNPSZ
Services: DA-TY
Equipment: Xerox copiers
Annual sales: $250,000
Number of employees: 5
Turnaround times: B2C2
Customers: BP50-BU30-CU10-SP10
Union shop: N
Year established: 1972
Terms: Payment in full with order

Statement: We specialize in ultra short-run books and booklets. If you give us camera-ready copy, we give back a finished product fast and at low cost. We issue free descriptive brochures and prices. We can deliver books in as short as five days.

GC

Camelot Fine Printing
3600 Central SE
Albuquerque, NM 87108
505-266-3600

Min: 100 **Max:** 100,000 **Opt:** 30,000
Sizes: 123456
Bindings: CBI-GBO-LBI-
    PBO-SSI-SDI-SBI-WBO
Items: ABCDEFHIKLMNPQSTUWYZ1
Services: 4C-CS-DA-TY-TD
Equipment: 3SO(11x17-12x18-18x25)
Annual sales: $500,000

Number of employees: 10
Turnaround times: B3C2
Customers: BU75-NP20-OT5
Union shop: N
Terms: 1/2 on order, balance delivery

Canterbury Press   MS
Walter Ranger
301 Mill Street, P O Box 4299
Rome, NY 13440
315-337-5900; Fax: 315-337-4070

Min: 500 Max: 2,500 Opt: 1,000
Sizes: 23456X
Bindings: HCO-CBI-PBI-SSI-SBO-WBO
Items: ABCDFHIKNPT
Services: 4C-AF-RP-TY-TD-WA
Equipment: 6SO(19x25-36x49)
Annual sales: $7,000,000
Number of employees: 82
Turnaround times: C4M3
Customers: BU10-CU10-OR5
Union shop: Y
Year established: 1952
Terms: Net 30

Statement: We primarily produce short-run paperback books as how-to or field guides. Additionally, we provide competitive quality printing with a special expertise in the medical/pharmaceutical and scientific fields (short to medium runs).

Capital City Press   BK
Airport Drive, P O Box 546
Montpelier, VT 05602
802-223-5207

Min: 300 Max: 30,000 Opt: 5,000
Sizes: 23456X
Bindings: HCX-PBI-SSI
Items: BFHI
Services: FF-TY-TD
Equipment: SO
Annual sales: $11,000,000
Number of employees: 150
Year established: 1908
Terms: 2% 10, Net 30

Comments: They print over 140 medical and technical journals as well as trade paperbacks and hardcovers.

Capital Printing Company   GC
Barkley Edwards, President
4001 Caven Road (78744)
P O Box 17548
Austin, TX 78760-7548
512-442-1415; Fax: 512-441-1448

Min: 1,000 Max: 25,000 Opt: 10,000
Sizes: 123456X
Bindings: HCO-CBO-LBO-PBI-SSI-SDO-SBO-WBO
Items: ABCDEFHIKLNPSXYZ
Services: 4C-DA-FF-LI-OC-AF-RP
Equipment: 2SO(40")
Annual sales: $2,000,000
Number of employees: 50
Turnaround times: B3C3M2
Customers: BP10-BU10-CU10-MP60-OR5-SC5
Union shop: N
Year established: 1960
Terms: 1% 10, net 30 with approval

Statement: Our goals are to provide only the highest quality product, give total customer satisfaction, listen to our customers so we can give them what they want, constantly innovate to improve our product and service, honor commitments whatever the cost or effort, and take pride in our craftsmanship. Each of us is the company.

Carlson Color Graphics   MS
3310 SW 7th Street
Ocala, FL 32674
904-732-7787; Fax: 904-351-5199

Min: 10 Max: 200,000 Opt: 50,000
Bindings: SSI
Items: DI
Services: 4C-DA-FF-TY

Carter Rice   BK
Donald Page, Vice President
273 Summer Street
Boston, MA 02101
617-542-6400
Toll-free: 800-225-6673

Items: B

PRINTED ITEMS			
A Annual Reports	G Galley Copies	N Workbooks	U Greeting Cards
B Books	H Journals	O Yearbooks	V Labels / Stickers
C Booklets	I Magazines	P Brochures	W Maps
D Catalogs	J Mass-Market Books	Q Calendars	X Newspapers
E Cookbooks	K Newsletters	R Comic Books	Y Postcards
F Directories	L Software Manuals	S Direct Mail Letters	Z Posters
	M Textbooks	T Envelopes	1 Stationery

Cascio-Wolf   **CA**
Bobbie Cascio, Sales
6621 Iron Place
Springfield, VA 22151
703-750-0001

Min: 5,000 Max: 2,000,000 Opt:
Sizes: 25X
Bindings: SSI
Items: ADKOST
Services: 4C-CS-FF
Equipment: 8SO(to 50")-1WO(17x26)

Case-Hoyt Corporation   **CA**
Donald McCloskey, VP Sales
100 Beaver Road, P O Box 259
Rochester, NY 14601
716-889-5670; Fax: 716-889-3418

Min: 10,000 Max: 5,000,000 Opt:
Sizes: 23456X
Bindings: CBI-PBI-SSI-SBI
Items: DP
Services: 4C-FF-TY
Equipment: SO-6WO-OT(screen)
Annual sales: $85,000,000
Number of employees: 700
Turnaround times: C4
Year established: 1917

Statement: Case-Hoyt was recently bought
by Continental Graphics of Los Angeles.

Catalogue Publishing Company   **CA**
Earl D Unger, President
809 Virginia Avenue
Martinsburg, WV 25401
304-267-2673

Min: 2,000 Max: 200,000 Opt:
Sizes: 12356
Bindings: GBI-SSI
Items: ACDFKPSTVY1
Services: 4C-DA-FF-LM-TY-WA
Equipment: 2SO(10X15-11X17)-
    1WO(17X22)
Annual sales: $500,000
Number of employees: 8
Turnaround times: C3
Customers: BU10-SP90
Union shop: N

Year established: 1975
Terms: Cash & carry; net 30 D&B rated

Statement: We are designers, producers,
and printers of upscale catalogs.

Celo Press   **BK**
1901 Hannah Branch Road
Burnsville, NC 28714
704-675-4925

Centax of Canada   **BK**
1048 Fleury Street
Regina, Saskatchewan S4N 4W8 Canada
306-359-3737

Min: 1,000 Max: 100,000 Opt: 20,000
Sizes: 235
Bindings: HCO-CBI-PBO-SBI
Items: BEM
Services: 4C
Equipment: 1SO-1WO

Central Publishing Company   **GC**
401 N College Avenue
P O Box 1657
Indianapolis, IN 46202
317-636-4504

Min: 300 Max: 30,000 Opt: 15,000
Sizes: 123456
Bindings: HCO-CBO-GBI-LBI-
    PBO-SSI-SDI-SBO-WBO
Items: ABCDEFGHIKLPT
Services: 4C-CS-TY-TD
Equipment: 7SO(11x17-28x41)
Annual sales: $5,000,000
Number of employees: 25
Turnaround times: B4C3M2
Customers: BU50-NP40-OR10
Union shop: Y
Year established: 1920
Terms: Net 30 with approved credit

Champion Printing   **GC**
3250 Spring Grove Street
Cincinnati, OH 45225
513-541-1100; Fax: 513-541-9398
Toll-free: 800-543-1957

SERVICES				BINDINGS			
4C	4-Color Printing	**RA**	Rachwal System	**HC**	Hardcover	**SD**	Side Stitching
CS	Color Separations	**AF**	Acid-Free Paper	**CB**	Comb Binding	**SB**	Spiral Binding
DA	Design / Artwork	**RP**	Recycled Paper	**GB**	Glue Binding	**WB**	Wire-O Binding
FF	Fulfillment/Mailing	**TY**	Typesetting	**LB**	Loose-Leaf Binding	**I**	In-House
LM	List Maintenance	**TD**	Typeset w/ Disk	**PB**	Perfect Binding	**O**	Out of House
OC	OptiCopy System	**WA**	Warehousing	**SS**	Saddle Stitching	**X**	Unknown

Min: 10,000 Max: 250,000 Opt:
Sizes: 5X
Bindings: SSI
Items: CDKNPST
Services: FF

Comments: Champion is a specialist in printing direct mail formats, including self-mailers, catalogs, and catalog inserts.

Charles Communications   MG
621 Avenue of the Americas
New York, NY 10011
212-924-7551

Min: 20,000 Max: 2,000,000 Opt:
Bindings: SSI
Items: DIX
Services: 4C
Equipment: 4SO-6WO
Annual sales: $190,000,000
Number of employees: 350
Year established: 1948

Comments: They print publications and newspaper inserts.

Citizen Prep & Printing   MS
805 Park Avenue
P O Box 558
Beaver Dam, WI 53916

Min: 20,000 Max: 500,000 Opt: 100,000
Sizes: X
Bindings: SSI
Items: IX
Services: 4C-DA-TY
Equipment: WO

Statement: Citizen specializes in printing 20,000 to 500,000 copies of uncoated tabloid publications.

City Printing Company   GC
291 State Street
North Haven, CT 06473
203-281-4254

Min: 3,000 Max: 1,000,000 Opt: 500,000
Sizes: 25
Bindings: HCO-GBO-PBO-
    SSI-SDO-SBO-WBO

Items: ACDIKPQST
Services: 4C
Equipment: 1LP-7SO(25x38-54x77)-
    4WO(23x38)
Annual sales: $29,000,000
Number of employees: 300
Turnaround times: C4
Customers: BP10-BU90
Union shop: N
Year established: 1936
Terms: Net 30

Clark Printing Company   MS
Marketing Director
Banta Publications Group
1534 Burlington Street
Kansas City, MO 64116
816-842-8282

Min: 10,000 Max: 500,000 Opt: 250,000
Sizes: 245X
Bindings: PBI-SSI
Items: DIX
Services: 4C-CS-FF-LM-TD
Equipment: 3S0(25x38)-8WO(23")
Customers: CU10-MP70-NP20
Union shop: Y
Year established: 1927
Terms: Net 30

Statement: Clark is a division of Banta Corporation, which has $568 million in annual sales, 21 plants and 3,800 employees in all its divisions.

Clarkwood Corporation   BK
Marketing Director
690 Union Boulevard
Totowa, NJ 75120
201-256-2456

Min: 2,000 Max: 2,000,000 Opt:
Sizes: 5
Bindings: LBI
Items: BL
Services: FF-LM
Equipment: SO-WO

Comments: Clarkwood specializes in printing and distributing looseleaf books and subscription services.

PRINTED ITEMS						
A	Annual Reports	G	Galley Copies	N	Workbooks	U	Greeting Cards
B	Books	H	Journals	O	Yearbooks	V	Labels / Stickers
C	Booklets	I	Magazines	P	Brochures	W	Maps
D	Catalogs	J	Mass-Market Books	Q	Calendars	X	Newspapers
E	Cookbooks	K	Newsletters	R	Comic Books	Y	Postcards
F	Directories	L	Software Manuals	S	Direct Mail Letters	Z	Posters
		M	Textbooks	T	Envelopes	1	Stationery

Coach House Press   **BK**
Stan Bevington, President
401 Huron Street (Rear)
Toronto, Ontario M5S 2G5 Canada
416-919-2217

Min: 500 Max: 5,000 Opt: 1,000
Sizes: 2
Bindings: HCX-PBX
Items: BHKPYZ
Services: 4C-TY
Equipment: LP
Year established: 1965

Comments: This small Canadian publisher
also does typesetting and printing for other
small Canadian publishers.

Cody Publications   **MS**
P O Box 2028, 410 W Verona Street
Kissimmee, FL 32741
305-846-2800; Toll-free: 800-432-9192

Min: 1,000 Max: 25,000 Opt: 9,000
Sizes: 123456
Bindings: CBO-LBO-PBO-SSI-SBO-WBO
Items: ABCDEFHIKNP
Services: 4C-CS-DA-FF-LM-AF-TY-TD
Equipment: 3SO(19x25-28x41)
Annual sales: $5,000,000
Number of employees: 30
Turnaround times: B5C4M3
Customers: MP90-OT10
Union shop: N
Year established: 1946
Terms: Net 30 with approved credit

A Colish Inc   **BK**
40 Hartford Avenue
Mount Vernon, NY 10550
914-667-1000

Services: DA-TY

The College Press   **GC**
Dale Collins
4981 Industrial Drive, P O Box 400
Collegedale, TN 37315-0400
615-396-2164; Fax: 615-238-3546
Toll-free: 800-277-7377

Min: 1,000 Max: 50,000 Opt: 20,000
Sizes: 235
Bindings: HCO-CBI-LBO-PBI-
   SSI-SDI-SBO-WBO
Items: ABCDEFIKLMNPT1
Services: 4C-CS-DA-TY-TD
Equipment: 9SO(25"-26"-38")
Annual sales: $2,500,000
Number of employees: 30
Turnaround times: B3C3M3
Customers: BP15-BU20-CU20-MP25-NP20
Union shop: N
Year established: 1917
Terms: Net 30

Colonial Graphics   **GC**
John V Turi, President
P O Box 1013, 92 Maryland Avenue
Paterson, NJ 07533-2113
201-345-0600; Fax: 201-345-0083

Min: 1,500 Max: 50,000 Opt: 25,000
Sizes: 25
Bindings: CBX-SSX-SDX-SBX-WBX
Items: ABCDEFHKLPQSWZ
Services: FF-OC-TY-WA
Equipment: 3SO(to 28x40)-1WO(22x35)
Annual sales: $2,500,000
Number of employees: 16
Turnaround times: B3C3
Union shop: N
Year established: 1984
Terms: per client

Statement: We have provided in-house
prep to fulfillment for 33 years. We have
furnished our plant with perfecting presses,
both sheet and web offset, allowing more
product for your dollar.

Color Graphics   **GC**
1819 Underwood Boulevard
P O Box 1025
Delran, NJ 08075
609-461-7001; Toll-free: 800-257-9569

Items: PST
Services: 4C
Equipment: SO-WO

Comments: They specialize in direct
response formats.

SERVICES			
4C 4-Color Printing	**RA**	Rachwal System	
CS Color Separations	**AF**	Acid-Free Paper	
DA Design / Artwork	**RP**	Recycled Paper	
FF Fulfillment/Mailing	**TY**	Typesetting	
LM List Maintenance	**TD**	Typeset w/ Disk	
OC OptiCopy System	**WA**	Warehousing	

BINDINGS			
HC Hardcover		**SD**	Side Stitching
CB Comb Binding		**SB**	Spiral Binding
GB Glue Binding		**WB**	Wire-O Binding
LB Loose-Leaf Binding		**I**	In-House
PB Perfect Binding		**O**	Out of House
SS Saddle Stitching		**X**	Unknown

Color House Graphics BK
Van Moore, Marketing Director
3505 Eastern Avenue SE
Grand Rapids, MI 49508-2408
616-241-1916; Fax: 616-245-5494

Min: 500 Max: 25,000 Opt: 7,000
Sizes: 23456X
Bindings: HCO-CBI-PBI-SSI-SBI-WBI
Items: ABCDEFKMNOP
Services: 4C
Equipment: 2SO(28x40)
Annual sales: $2,500,000
Number of employees: 22
Turnaround times: B4C4
Customers: BP70-BU22-CU3-NP2-OT3
Union shop: N
Year established: 1987
Terms: Net 30 with approved credit

Statement: Our specialty is printing and binding perfectbound books. Our goal is to develop long term collaborative relationships with our customers by providing quality products, reasonable prices, and excellent service on a timely basis.

Color World Printers GC
Leslie Schultz, Sales Rep
201 E Mendenhall (59715)
P O Box 1088
Bozeman, MT 59771-1088
406-587-4508; Toll-free: 800-332-3303

Min: 100 Max: 300,000 Opt: 20,000
Sizes: 123456X
Bindings: HCO-CBI-LBI-PBI-SSI
Items: ABCDEFHIKLMNPQSUYZ
Services: 4C-DA-FF-AF-TY-TD
Equipment: 4SO(19x25 to 23x29)
Annual sales: $2,300,000
Number of employees: 35
Turnaround times: B4C5M4
Customers: BP-BU-CU-MP-SP
Union shop: N
Year established: 1967
Terms: New customers: 1/3, 1/3, 1/3

Statement: We can produce your book from manuscript, disc, or camera-ready copy. We are a family-owned business and are committed to quality. Our Montana location keeps our prices very competitive.

ColorGraphics GC
4500 S Garnett #600
Tulsa, OK 74146
918-664-6002

Bindings: PBI-SSI
Items: ACDPSZ
Services: 4C-DA-FF-TY
Equipment: 3SO-2WO

Colorlith Corporation CS
777 Hartford Avenue
Johnston, RI 02919
401-521-6000; Toll-free: 800-556-7171

Min: 2,500 Max: 50,000 Opt: 5,000
Items: DP
Services: 4C-CS
Equipment: SO

Colortone Press BK
2400 17th Street NW
Washington, DC 20009
202-387-6800

Sizes: 235X
Bindings: HCX-CBX-PBX-SSX-SBX
Items: ABCDEINPQZ
Services: 4C-DA-TY-TD

Comments: Colortone is the printing arm of Acropolis Press. They specialize in printing books that require high quality color work.

Columbus Book Binders & Printers BK
Tom Goodlett
1326 Tenth Avenue
P O Box 8193
Columbus, GA 31908
404-323-9313; Fax: 800-553-2987
Toll-free: 800-553-7314

Bindings: CBI-PBI-SSI
Items: BCDFHILMN
Services: TY-TD
Customers: SP100

PRINTED ITEMS					
A Annual Reports	G Galley Copies	N Workbooks	U Greeting Cards
B Books	H Journals	O Yearbooks	V Labels / Stickers
C Booklets	I Magazines	P Brochures	W Maps
D Catalogs	J Mass-Market Books	Q Calendars	X Newspapers
E Cookbooks	K Newsletters	R Comic Books	Y Postcards
F Directories	L Software Manuals	S Direct Mail Letters	Z Posters
	M Textbooks	T Envelopes	1 Stationery

Combined Communication Services

MS

American Press
4601 Paris Road
Columbia, MO 65201
314-474-6126

Min: 5,000 **Max:** 500,000 **Opt:** 100,000
Sizes: 2345
Bindings: PBI-SSI
Items: DHI
Services: 4C-CS-FF-TY
Equipment: 3SO-2WO
Annual sales: $58,243,000
Number of employees: 750

Comments: CCS specializes in producing special interest magazines.

Combined Communication Services

MS

1501 W Washington Road
Mendota, IL 61342
815-539-7402

Min: 5,000 **Max:** 500,000 **Opt:** 100,000
Sizes: 2345
Bindings: PBI-SSI
Items: DHI
Services: 4C-CS-FF-TY
Equipment: 3SO-2WO

Commercial Printing Company

BK

Cleve Tooker, VP Operations
2661 S Pacific Highway
P O Box 1165
Medford, OR 97501
503-773-7575; Fax: 503-773-1832

Min: 1,000 **Max:** 100,000 **Opt:** 50,000
Sizes: 14X
Bindings: PBI-SSI-SBI-WBI
Items: ABCL
Services: 4C-CS-FF-TY-TD-WA
Equipment: 3LP-7SO(28x41)-
    2WO(23x38-19x32)
Annual sales: $17,000,000
Number of employees: 67
Turnaround times: B3C3
Customers: BP15-BU85

Union shop: N
Year established: 1906
Terms: Net 30

Statement: CPC is one of the West Coast's largest manufacturers of software manuals. Our laser scanning and electronic color page makeup system make us an excellent choice for color brochures, short-run journals, collateral color advertising, as well as coffee-table books.

Community Press

BK

5600 N University Avenue
Provo, UT 84504
801-225-2299

Min: 500 **Max:** 50,000 **Opt:** 10,000
Sizes: 123456X
Bindings: HCI-CBI-PBO-SSI-SBI
Items: ABCDEFHIKMNOPQZ
Services: 4C-DA-TY-WA
Equipment: SO
Terms: Net 30 with approved credit

Comput-A-Print

GC

1040 Matley Lane #3
Reno, NV 89502
702-786-2300

Min: 100 **Max:** 10,000 **Opt:** 2,000
Sizes: 123456
Bindings: HCO-CBI-GBI-LBI-
    PBI-SSI-SDI-SBI-WBO
Items: ABCDEFGKLMNOPQSTVYZ1
Services: TY-WA
Equipment: 5SO(to 15x18)
Annual sales: $500,000
Number of employees: 7
Turnaround times: B3
Customers: BU80-NP5-OT5-SC5-SP5
Union shop: N
Year established: 1976
Terms: 50% deposit, balance on delivery

Concord Litho Company

GC

92 Old Turnpike Road
P O Box 464
Concord, NH 03301
603-225-3328; Toll-free: 800-258-3662

Min: 10,000 Max: 2,000,000 Opt:
Sizes: 2345X
Bindings: SSI
Items: DPSTU
Services: 4C-CS
Equipment: 8SO(28x40-54x77)-
    5WO(17x26)
Annual sales: $24,000,000
Number of employees: 200

Comments: They specialize in direct
response formats, including ruboffs, die-
cuts, inserts, and brochures.

Coneco Laser Graphics   BK
Dennis Brower, Vice President
58 Dix Avenue
P O Box 3255
Glen Falls, NY 12801-3255
518-793-3823

Min: Max: 20,000 Opt: 5,000
Sizes: 12345
Bindings: HCO-CBI-GBI-LBI-
    PBI-SSI-SDI-SBO-WBO
Items: ABCFHIKLPQZ
Services: AF-TY-TD
Equipment: 5SO
Annual sales: $5,000,000
Number of employees: 30
Turnaround times: B5C6M5
Customers: BP10-BU38-CU15-
    MP2-SP10-OT25
Union shop: N
Year established: 1984
Terms: 1/3, 1/3, 1/3

Connecticut Printers   MG
55 Granby Street
Bloomfield, CT 06002
203-242-0711

Min: 50,000 Max: 1,000,000 Opt: 500,000
Sizes: 123456
Bindings: PBI-SSI
Items: DINW
Services: 4C-FF-TY-TD-WA
Equipment: 2SO(43x60)-5WO(36-38)
Annual sales: $27,000,000
Number of employees: 350
Turnaround times: B3C2M3
Customers: BU30-MP60-SC10

Union shop: N
Year established: 1832
Terms: Net 30; 1 1/2% on balances

Statement: We are a publication printer
serving the high quality, 4-color requirements of magazine and catalog customers
in the Northeast.

Consolidated Printers   GC
2630 Eighth Street
Berkeley, CA 94710
415-843-8524

Min: 2,000 Opt: 50,000
Sizes: 123456X
Bindings: PBI-SSI-SBI
Items: ABCDEFLNP
Equipment: SO-WO

Continental Web   GC
1430 Industrial Drive
Itasca, IL 60143
312-773-1903; Fax: 312-773-1909

Min: 25,000 Max: 2,000,000 Opt:
Sizes: 245
Bindings: SSI
Items: ADIKPSUWXYZ
Services: 4C-CS-AF-WA
Equipment: 9WO(23x38)
Annual sales: $66,100,000
Number of employees: 450
Turnaround times: C3M2
Customers: MP25
Union shop: N
Terms: Net 30

Martin Cook Associates   BR
Martin Cook, President
1141 Broadway
New York, NY 10001
212-686-3533

Min: 1,500 Max: 1,000,000 Opt: 20,000
Sizes: 123456
Bindings: HCO-CBO-GBO-LBO-
    PBO-SSO-SBO-WBO
Items: ABCDEFJLMNOQUYZ
Services: 4C-CS-DA-TY
Equipment: none

PRINTED ITEMS						
A	Annual Reports	G	Galley Copies	N	Workbooks	U	Greeting Cards
B	Books	H	Journals	O	Yearbooks	V	Labels / Stickers
C	Booklets	I	Magazines	P	Brochures	W	Maps
D	Catalogs	J	Mass-Market Books	Q	Calendars	X	Newspapers
E	Cookbooks	K	Newsletters	R	Comic Books	Y	Postcards
F	Directories	L	Software Manuals	S	Direct Mail Letters	Z	Posters
		M	Textbooks	T	Envelopes	1	Stationery

Annual sales: $500,000
Number of employees: 2
Turnaround times: B5C5
Customers: BP50-OR20-OT30
Union shop: N
Year established: 1976
Terms: Net 30 with approved credit

Cookbook Publishers   **BK**

2101 Kansas City Road
P O Box 1260
Olathe, KS 66061
913-764-5900; Toll-free: 800-821-5745

Min: 200 **Max:** 50,000 **Opt:** 5,000
Sizes: 23
Bindings: CBI-PBO
Items: E
Services: 4C

Comments: They specialize in printing comb-bound cookbooks for organizational fundraisers. They also have a separate division, the Cookbook Collection, which distributes such cookbooks.

Copen Press   **CA**

Bob Brower, Marketing Director
100 Berriman Street
Brooklyn, NY 11208
718-235-4270

Min: 5,000 **Max:** 100,000 **Opt:** 20,000
Sizes: 25
Bindings: GBI-PBI-SSI
Items: ABCDEFKPQST
Equipment: 2SO(17x22)-1WO(23x35)
Annual sales: $5,000,000
Number of employees: 30
Turnaround times: B3C2
Customers: BU70-CU5-SP10-OT15
Union shop: Y
Year established: 1950
Terms: Net 30

Comments: They specialize in printing one and two-color booklets and newsprint catalogs. They can also print tabloids. They publish a standard price list which they will send to you upon request.

Copple House / Macon Graphics   **BK**

Road's End
P O Box 285
Lakemont, GA 30552
404-782-2134

Min: 300 **Max:** 10,000 **Opt:**
Sizes: 12345X
Bindings: HCX-CBX-PBX-SSX
Items: BCEFHNPYZ1
Services: 4C-CS-DA-TY
Equipment: SO
Year established: 1960

Statement: We are not a get-it-today and out-tomorrow company. We are a small company and prefer customers who want to get the best they can for the money they have to spend.

Coral Graphic Services   **GC**

11 Commercial Street
Plainview, NY 11803
516-935-5900; Fax: 516-935-5902

Services: 4C-CS

Corley Printing Company   **GC**

David C Deibel, Vice President
3777 Rider Trail South
Earth City, MO 63045
314-739-3777; Fax: 314-739-1436

Min: 500 **Max:** 250,000 **Opt:** 10,000
Sizes: 45
Bindings: PBI-SSI-SSI
Items: BCDFKLN
Services: 4C
Equipment: 2SO(23x35,19x25)-
   1WO(22x36)
Annual sales: $7,500,000
Number of employees: 49
Turnaround times: B3C3
Customers: BP15-BU80-SC5
Union shop: N
Year established: 1929
Terms: 1% 10; net 30 (best terms)

Statement: Our corporate motto, "Better People ... Better Products" says it all.

Cornay Web Graphics **BR**
623 Dublin Street
New Orleans, LA 70118
504-865-9426; Toll-free: 800-888-9426

Min: 5,000 **Max:** 3,000,000 **Opt:**
Sizes: 123456X
Bindings: HCO-CBO-GBO-LBO-
    PBO-SSO-SDO-SBO-WBO
Items: ABCDEFHIPQSTVWXY1
Services: 4C-CS-DA-FF-TY
Equipment: none
Turnaround times: B4C3
Union shop: N
Year established: 1947
Terms: Net 30

Statement: We are a full service graphics house specializing in printing production.

Country Press **BK**
Fuller Street
P O Box 489
Middleborough, MA 02346
617-947-4485

Min: 100 **Max:** 10,000 **Opt:** 500
Sizes: 23
Bindings: PBI
Items: G
Equipment: SO
Turnaround times: B2

Comments: They specialize in producing bound galley proofs with a fast turnaround.

Country Press **GC**
Carol Ann Vercz, Owner
RD #1, Box 71
Ward Road
Mohawk, NY 13407
315-866-7445

Min: 100 **Max:** 2,000,000 **Opt:**
Sizes: 123456X
Bindings: HCO-CBI-GBI-LBI-
    PBI-SSI-SDI-SBI-WBO
Items: ABCDEFGHIJKLMNPQSTUYZ1
Services: 4C-DA-OC-RP-TY-TD
Equipment: 1SO(11x17)
Annual sales: $300,000
Number of employees: 6

Turnaround times: B1C1M1
Customers: BP10-BU40-
    CU10-NP20-OR30-SP35
Union shop: N
Year established: 1985
Terms: Payment on delivery

Courier Corporation **BK**
165 Jackson Street
Lowell, MA 01852
508-458-6351; Fax: 508-453-0344

Min: 5,000 **Max:** 2,000,000 **Opt:**
Sizes: 5
Bindings: PBI
Items: F
Annual sales: $95,950,000
Number of employees: 1,385
Customers: OT(phone directories)

Comments: Courier prints telephone directories in its Lowell plant. It also owns Alpine Press, Murray Printing, National Publishing Company, and the English book printer, Anchor Brendon.

Courier Graphics **GC**
P O Box 18640
4325 Old Shepherdsville Road
Louisville, KY 40218
502-947-5303

Items: PV
Equipment: SO

Comments: They print book covers and labels as well as other commercial printing.

Craftsman Press **CA**
1155 Valley Street
Seattle, WA 98109
206-682-8800

Min: 5,000 **Max:** 2,000,000 **Opt:**
Sizes: 25X
Bindings: PBI-SSI-SDI
Items: DI
Services: 4C-CS-FF-TY
Equipment: SO-5WO(to 22x38)
Annual sales: $16,000,000
Customers: BU60-MP40

PRINTED ITEMS		G	Galley Copies	N	Workbooks	U	Greeting Cards
A	Annual Reports	H	Journals	O	Yearbooks	V	Labels / Stickers
B	Books	I	Magazines	P	Brochures	W	Maps
C	Booklets	J	Mass-Market Books	Q	Calendars	X	Newspapers
D	Catalogs	K	Newsletters	R	Comic Books	Y	Postcards
E	Cookbooks	L	Software Manuals	S	Direct Mail Letters	Z	Posters
F	Directories	M	Textbooks	T	Envelopes	1	Stationery

Comments: They print about 30 different magazines plus many catalogs, including the Leanin' Tree catalog.

Crane Duplicating Service   BK
Kenyon Gregoire, Marketing Director
1611 Main Street
Barnstable, MA 02668
508-362-3441; Fax: 508-362-5445

Min: 10 Max: 5,000 Opt: 500
Sizes: 12345
Bindings: CBI-PBI-SSI-SBI
Items: ABCDEFGHJKLMNOP
Services: 4C-CS-DA-AF-RP-TY-TD
Equipment: 7SO(to 13x18)
Annual sales: $5,000,000
Number of employees: 25
Turnaround times: B1
Customers: BP60-CU10-SP30
Union shop: N
Year established: 1955
Terms: 50% deposit, rest 2% 10, net 30

Statement: Crane provides bound galleys to the publishing industry. Our goal is to provide the best short-run bound galley and book manufacturing services in the country for runs of 1000 or less.

Creative Web Systems   GC
371 N Oak Street
Inglewood, CA 90049
213-216-7887

Min: 3,000 Max: 2,000,000 Opt:
Sizes: 2345X
Bindings: GBI-SSI
Items: CIKPSZ
Services: 4C
Equipment: 2WO

Statement: We are direct response specialists.

Crest Litho   BK
2550 Ninth Avenue
P O Box 428
Watervliet, NY 12189
518-272-0292

Min: 100 Max: 500,000 Opt: 75,000
Sizes: 123456X
Bindings: CBI-PBI-SSI-SBI
Items: ABCDEFHIMNP
Services: 4C-WA
Annual sales: $11,000,000
Number of employees: 150
Terms: Net 30

Statement: We can do it all, from textbooks and instruction manuals to commercial printing. Our reputation has been built on quality, service, and dependability.

Crusader Printing & Typesetting   GC
Joe W Lewis Jr., Sales Manager
10th & State Street
East Saint Louis, IL 62201
618-271-2000; Fax: 618-271-2045

Min: 500 Max: 500,000 Opt:
Sizes: 123556
Bindings: HCO-CBI-LBO-
   PBO-SSI-SDI-SBO-WBO
Items: ABCDEFHIJKLMNOPQSTUXZ1
Services: 4C-DA-FF-LM-RP-TY-TD
Equipment: 3LP-12SO(up to 23x35)-1WO
Number of Employees: 21
Turnaround times: B2C2M2
Year established: 1941
Terms: Flexible, net 60

Comments: This Black-owned printing company prints books, catalogs, newspapers, and many other items. They are especially supportive of African-American publishers.

Cummings Printing Company   MS
Edward Bellemare, Sales Manager
P O Box 4687, 215 Canal Street
Manchester, NH 03108
603-625-6901

Min: 1,000 Max: 35,000 Opt: 20,000
Sizes: 25
Bindings: PBI-SSI
Items: HI
Services: FF-TY
Equipment: SO
Number of employees: 77
Year established: 1917

SERVICES					BINDINGS			
4C	4-Color Printing	RA	Rachwal System		HC	Hardcover	SD	Side Stitching
CS	Color Separations	AF	Acid-Free Paper		CB	Comb Binding	SB	Spiral Binding
DA	Design / Artwork	RP	Recycled Paper		GB	Glue Binding	WB	Wire-O Binding
FF	Fulfillment/Mailing	TY	Typesetting		LB	Loose-Leaf Binding	I	In-House
LM	List Maintenance	TD	Typeset w/ Disk		PB	Perfect Binding	O	Out of House
OC	OptiCopy System	WA	Warehousing		SS	Saddle Stitching	X	Unknown

BK
Cushing-Malloy
Thomas F Weber, Sales Manager
1350 N Main Street, P O Box 8632
Ann Arbor, MI 48107
313-663-8554; Fax: 313-663-5731

Min: 150 Max: 8,000 Opt: 2,500
Sizes: 123456X
Bindings: HCO-CBO-PBI-SSI-SBO-WBO
Items: BCDEFHJM
Services: AF
Equipment: 6SO
Annual sales: $9,000,000
Number of employees: 100
Turnaround times: B4C4
Customers: BP50-CU35-SP10-OT5
Union shop: N
Year established: 1948
Terms: Net 30

Statement: Cushing-Malloy's philosophy is simple: To deal honestly, consistently and professionally with our customers and to produce a product with excellent value and quality, on schedule, time after time.

D

GC
D D Associates
Steve Bearden
570 Martin Avenue
Santa Clara, CA 95050
408-988-5150

Min: 100 Max: 25,000 Opt: 10,000
Sizes: 123456X
Bindings: CBX-LBX-PBX-SSX-WBX
Items: ABCDEFHIKLMNPS
Services: 4C-CS-FF-LM-TY-TD-WA
Equipment: 4SO(19x25)
Annual sales: $7,500,000
Number of employees: 54
Turnaround times: B2C1M1
Customers: BP5-BU80-CU5-OR5-SP5
Union shop: N
Year established: 1964
Terms: 2% 10, net 30

Statement: We produce quality controlled manuals, books, and brochures.

Daamen Printing Company **BK**
Debi Saldi
Industrial Park
P O Box 97
West Rutland, VT 05777
802-438-5472; Fax: 802-438-5477

Min: 50 **Max:** 10,000 **Opt:** 1,500
Sizes: 2345
Bindings: HCO-CBO-LBI-PBI-
   SSI-SDI-SBO-WBO
Items: ABCEHMNO
Services: TY
Equipment: 4SO(29"-36"-38")
Annual sales: $2,000,000
Turnaround times: B3
Customers: BP75-CU5-SP5-OT15
Union shop: N
Year established: 1978
Terms: 2% 10, 1% 20, net 30

Danbury Printing & Litho **CA**
Prindle Lane
P O Box 2479
Danbury, CT 06813-2479
203-792-5500; Toll-free: 800-231-8712

Min: 5,000 **Max:** 2,000,000 **Opt:**
Sizes: 25X
Bindings: SSI
Items: ADPPS
Services: 4C-CS-DA-TY
Equipment: 6SO(to 28x42)-6WO(to 22x36)
Annual sales: $48,000,000
Number of employees: 339

Statement: A printer of upscale catalogs.

Danner Press **BK**
Tim Angbrandt, Marketing Manager
1250 Camden Avenue SW (44706)
P O Box 8349
Canton, OH 44711-8349
216-454-5692; Fax: 216-454-4727

Min: 25,000 **Max:** 2,000,000 **Opt:** 100,000
Sizes: 25
Bindings: PBI-SSI-SBO-WBO
Items: BDIMN
Services: 4C-CS-OC-FF
Equipment: 3SO-5WO

Annual sales: $64,000,000
Number of employees: 350
Customers: BP43-BU30-MP27
Union shop: Y
Year established: 1938

Statement: Our major products are color educational workbooks, magazines, and catalogs. Specialized services include ink jet printing and polybagging.

Comments: See its related company, The Press of Ohio.

Dartmouth Printing **MS**
69 Lyme Road
Hanover, NH 03755
603-643-2220

Min: 5,000 **Max:** 2,000,000 **Opt:**
Sizes: 25X
Bindings: PBI-SSI
Items: DIP
Services: 4C-CS-FF-TY-TD
Equipment: 4SO(25"-41")-
   3WO(23x17-22x34)
Annual sales: $21,000,000
Number of employees: 250
Year established: 1843

Comments: Among other magazines, Dartmouth prints *Catalog Age, Folio, Cape Cod Life,* and *U.S. Banker.*

Dataco **GC**
1712 Lomas Boulevard NE
Albuquerque, NM 87106
505-243-2841

Min: Max: 20,000 **Opt:** 5,000
Sizes: 123456
Bindings: HCO-CBI-GBO-LBI-
   PBO-SSI-SDI-SBO-WBO
Items: ABCDFHIKLPQSTUYZ1
Services: 4C-DA-FF-LM-TY
Equipment: 2SO(19x25)-1WO(14x17)
Annual sales: $5,000,000
Number of employees: 30
Turnaround times: B3C3
Customers: BP5-BU60-CU5-
   MP2-NP3-OR10-OT15
Union shop: N
Terms: Net 30

SERVICES				BINDINGS			
4C	4-Color Printing	RA	Rachwal System	HC	Hardcover	SD	Side Stitching
CS	Color Separations	AF	Acid-Free Paper	CB	Comb Binding	SB	Spiral Binding
DA	Design / Artwork	RP	Recycled Paper	GB	Glue Binding	WB	Wire-O Binding
FF	Fulfillment/Mailing	TY	Typesetting	LB	Loose-Leaf Binding	I	In-House
LM	List Maintenance	TD	Typeset w/ Disk	PB	Perfect Binding	O	Out of House
OC	OptiCopy System	WA	Warehousing	SS	Saddle Stitching	X	Unknown

Dellas Graphics **GC**

835 Canal Street
Syracuse, NY 13210
315-474-4641

Min: 100 Max: 500,000 Opt: 25,000
Sizes: 123456
Bindings: CBI-GBO-PBO-SSI-SDI
Items: ABCDKLPSTYZ
Services: 4C-DA-FF-LM-TY-TD-WA
Equipment: 10SO(10x15-25x38)
Annual sales: $5,000,000
Number of employees: 30
Turnaround times: B3C3M3
Customers: BU60-CU10-NP20-OR10
Union shop: N
Year established: 1982
Terms: Net 30

Delmar Printing Company **BK**

Curt Cox, National Sales Manager
9601 Monroe Road (28226)
P O Box 1013
Charlotte, NC 28201-1013
704-847-9801; Fax: 704-845-1218
Toll-free: 800-438-1504

Min: 100 Max: 100,000 Opt: 7,000
Sizes: 23456X
Bindings: HCI-CBI-GBO-LBO-
    PBO-SSI-SDO-SBO-WBI
Items: ABCDEFMNOPQ
Services: 4C-CS-DA-FF-AF-TY-TD
Equipment: 8SO(25x38-28x40)
Annual sales: $30,000,000
Number of employees: 250
Turnaround times: B5C5M5
Customers: BP35-SC65
Union shop: N
Year established: 1944
Terms: 1/3 order, 1/3 proofs, net 10

Statement: We are a medium-sized company which offers personal attention to our client's needs. We strive to provide a quality product for a fair price with an acceptable turnaround time.

Comments: Delmar is a division of Continental Graphics Corporation of Los Angeles ($292 million in annual sales from 17 plants with 3400 employees.

Delta Lithograph **BK**
Ute Schroff, Marketing Director
28210 N Avenue Stanford
Valencia, CA 91355-1111
805-257-0584; Fax: 805-257-3867
Toll-free: 800-323-3582

Min: 1,000 Max: 750,000 Opt: 10,000
Sizes: 123456X
Bindings: PBI-SSI-WBI
Items: ABCDEFHKLMNPRWZ
Services: 4C-DA-FF-LM-
    OC-AF-RP-TY-WA
Equipment: 6SO(38"-40")-3WO(30"-35")
Annual sales: $30,000,000
Number of employees: 200
Turnaround times: B3C3
Customers: BP40-BU20-CU15-
    NP5-OR5-SC5-SP10
Union shop: N
Year established: 1954
Terms: Net 30 on approved credit

Statement: Delta is a full service media production specialist: Delta Lithograph for softcover book manufacturing and binding; Corporate Publishing Services for data collection, updating, retrieval, and printing of directories, guides, and manuals; Printing on Demand for fast turnaround of publications; and Delta Mailing and Fulfillment for packaging, mailing, and list maintenance. Delta is a division of Bertelsmann Printing Corporation.

Democrat Printing & Litho **MS**

P O Box 191
Little Rock, AR 72203
501-374-0271

Min: 5,000 Max: 100,000 Opt:
Sizes: 5
Bindings: SSI
Items: DI
Annual sales: $16,000,000
Number of employees: 150

PRINTED ITEMS					
A	Annual Reports	G	Galley Copies	N	Workbooks
B	Books	H	Journals	O	Yearbooks
C	Booklets	I	Magazines	P	Brochures
D	Catalogs	J	Mass-Market Books	Q	Calendars
E	Cookbooks	K	Newsletters	R	Comic Books
F	Directories	L	Software Manuals	S	Direct Mail Letters
		M	Textbooks	T	Envelopes

U	Greeting Cards
V	Labels / Stickers
W	Maps
X	Newspapers
Y	Postcards
Z	Posters
1	Stationery

Comments: They specialize in short-run to medium-run business and technical magazines as well as catalogs.

GC

Des Plaines Publishing
Jim Forbing, Sales Manager
1000 Executive Way
Des Plaines, IL 60018
708-824-1111; Fax: 708-824-1112
Toll-free: 800-283-1776

Sizes: 5X
Items: CDFIPSX
Services: 4C-FF-TY-TD
Equipment: WO

GC

Desaulniers Printing Company
4905 77th Avenue
Milan, IL 61264
309-799-7331

Min: 500 Max: 2,000,000 Opt:
Sizes: 25X
Bindings: CBI-PBI-SSI

Items: ABCDFHIKNPQSXZ
Services: 4C-CS-FF-LM-TY-WA
Equipment: 4SO(to 28x40)-3WO(to 22x36)
Annual sales: $25,000,000
Number of employees: 280
Customers: BP-BU-CU-OR
Year established: 1895
Terms: Net 30

GC

Deven Lithographers
15 Huron Street
Brooklyn, NY 11222
718-392-6740

Bindings: PBI-SSI
Services: 4C
Equipment: WO

BK

John Deyell Company
Cairn Capital
2235 Sheppard Avenue E #903
Willowdale, Ontario M2J 5B5 Canada
416-491-8811; Fax: 416-491-3893

Min: 500 Max: 50,000 Opt: 15,000
Sizes: 23456X
Bindings: HCI-CBX-PBI-SSX
Items: BCEFHMN
Services: TY
Equipment: 5SO
Annual sales: $61,000,000
Number of employees: 200
Turnaround times: B3
Year established: 1912

Comments: John Deyell is a division of
Cairn Inc. ($61 million in annual sales
from 8 plants).

GC

Dharma Press
Terry Ryder, Marketing Director
1241 21st Street
Oakland, CA 94607
415-839-3931; Fax: 415-839-0954

Min: 500 Max: 60,000 Opt: 20,000
Sizes: 23456
Bindings: LBX-PBX-SSX-SBX-WBX
Items: ABCDFHIKLNPQSUWYZ
Services: 4C-FF-AF-RP-TY-TD
Equipment: 5SO(29/36/36/40/65)
Annual sales: $7,500,000
Number of employees: 70
Turnaround times: B2
Union shop: N
Year established: 1970
Terms: Net 30

Statement: We offer fast turnaround, 2 to
4-color, medium to high quality, medium
to long run printing. We have a service in-
tensive, very experienced, stable work
force.

GC

Diamond Graphics
Patrick Canter, Marketing Manager
6324 W Fond du Lac Avenue
Milwaukee, WI 53218
414-462-2205
Min: 1,000 Max: 10,000 Opt: 3,000
Sizes: 123456X
Bindings: HCO-CBI-LBI-
   PBI-SSI-SBO-WBO
Items: ABCDEFIKLMNOPQSTVYZ
Services: 4C-DA-FF-LM-TY-TD-WA

Equipment: 7SO(19x26)
Annual sales: $500,000
Number of employees: 20
Turnaround times: B2C2M2
Customers: BP10-BU60-CU5-
   MP3-NP10-SC5-SP7
Union shop: N
Year established: 1976
Terms: 50% down, 50% on delivery

Statement: Our motto: Quality, service,
and integrity.

BK

Dickinson Press
Bob Worcester, Sales Manager
5100 33rd Street SE
Grand Rapids, MI 49512
616-957-5100; Fax: 616-957-1261

Min: 3,000 Max: 200,000 Opt: 7,500
Sizes: 12356X
Bindings: HCO-CBO-PBI-
   SSI-SDO-SBO-WBO
Items: BCDFIJMN
Services: 4C-RA-AF
Equipment: 2SO(28x40-37x49)-3WO
Annual sales: $15,000,000
Number of employees: 116
Turnaround times: B4C4
Customers: BP75-BU15-CU5-MP5
Union shop: Y
Year established: 1884
Terms: 2% 10, Net 30

Statement: We are a full service book,
catalog, and Bible manufacturer serving
religious, institutional, educational and
general trade publishers as well as industrial catalog companies. Our purpose is
to competitively develop, produce, and
deliver quality printed material in a service
oriented environment.

CA

The Dingley Press
119 Lisbon Road
Lisbon, ME 04250
207-353-4151

Min: 150,000 Max: 2,000,000 Opt: 500,000
Sizes: 34X
Bindings: SSI
Items: DIP

PRINTED ITEMS						
A	Annual Reports	G	Galley Copies	N	Workbooks	U	Greeting Cards
B	Books	H	Journals	O	Yearbooks	V	Labels / Stickers
C	Booklets	I	Magazines	P	Brochures	W	Maps
D	Catalogs	J	Mass-Market Books	Q	Calendars	X	Newspapers
E	Cookbooks	K	Newsletters	R	Comic Books	Y	Postcards
F	Directories	L	Software Manuals	S	Direct Mail Letters	Z	Posters
		M	Textbooks	T	Envelopes	1	Stationery

Services: 4C-CS-FF
Equipment: 2WO
Year established: 193?

Comments: Dingley specializes in printing catalogs that are 7 1/2" x 9" in size.

Dinner & Klein   CA
600 S Spokane Street, P O Box 3814
Seattle, WA 98124
206-682-2494

Min: 1,000 **Max:** 150,000 **Opt:** 50,000
Sizes: 25
Bindings: GBI-PBI-SSI
Items: ABCDFKNPS
Equipment: SO-WO
Year established: 1948
Terms: Payment in full with order

Comments: Write for their standard price list for self-cover catalogs and booklets on a variety of paper stocks.

Dittler Brothers   GC
1375 Seaboard Industrial Blvd NW
Atlanta, GA 30318
404-355-3423; Toll-free: 800-927-0777

Min: 200,000 **Max:** 5,000,000 **Opt:**
Sizes: 25X
Bindings: PBI-SSI-SDI
Items: PST
Equipment: SO-WO-OT(gravure)
Annual sales: $85,000,000
Number of employees: 1,000
Year established: 1903

Comments: Dittler is a division of Southam Printing of Toronto, Ontario ($586 million in annual sales from 21 plants with 4,200 employees). They print many direct mail formats, including personalized pieces, pop-ups, scratch-offs, holograms, and database printing.

Diversified Printing   CA
Frank Kubat Jr, General Manager
2632 Saturn Street
Brea, CA 92621
714-993-4541

Min: 2,000 **Max:** 500,000 **Opt:** 50,000
Sizes: 235
Bindings: CBI-GBI-PBI-SSI-SDI-SBI-WBI
Items: ABCDFLMNR
Services: FF
Equipment: 1SO-3WO
Turnaround times: B3C4
Customers: BP50-BU25-CU15-SC10
Union shop: N
Year established: 1965
Terms: 2% 10, Net 11

Comments: A division of Quebecor Printing, Diversified prints books, manuals, directories, and catalogs.

Dollco Printing   GC
Peter Vineberg, Sales Director
P O Box 8620
2340 St Laurent Boulevard
Ottawa, Ontario K1G 3M5 Canada
613-738-9181; Fax: 613-738-4655

Min: 5,000 **Max:** 1,000,000 **Opt:** 100,000
Sizes: 2345X
Bindings: HCO-CBO-LBO-
    PBI-SSI-SDO-SBO-WBO
Items: ABCDFHIKMOPSTUVWXYZ1
Services: 4C-CS-AF-RP-TY-TD-WA
Equipment: 3LP-12SO(10x14-28x40)-
    2WO(26/36)
Annual sales: $15,000,000
Number of employees: 140
Turnaround times: B3M2
Customers: BU30-MP30-NP20-OR20
Union shop: N
Year established: 1958
Terms: Net 30

Statement: Also owns Gladstone Press.

Donihe Graphics   CA
Route 1, Brookside Road
P O Box 1788
Kingsport, TN 37662
615-246-2800; Toll-free: 800-251-0337

Min: 10,000 **Max:** 500,000 **Opt:**
Sizes: 123456X
Bindings: SSI
Items: ABCDEFIKLNPQSWXYZ
Services: 4C-CS-DA-FF-TY-WA

SERVICES				BINDINGS			
4C	4-Color Printing	RA	Rachwal System	HC	Hardcover	SD	Side Stitching
CS	Color Separations	AF	Acid-Free Paper	CB	Comb Binding	SB	Spiral Binding
DA	Design / Artwork	RP	Recycled Paper	GB	Glue Binding	WB	Wire-O Binding
FF	Fulfillment/Mailing	TY	Typesetting	LB	Loose-Leaf Binding	I	In-House
LM	List Maintenance	TD	Typeset w/ Disk	PB	Perfect Binding	O	Out of House
OC	OptiCopy System	WA	Warehousing	SS	Saddle Stitching	X	Unknown

Equipment: 1SO-1WO(17x26)
Annual sales: $9,000,000
Number of employees: 75
Turnaround times: B5C5M4
Customers: BU70-CU10-MP5-OT15
Union shop: N
Year established: 1977
Terms: 50% down, balance on delivery

R R Donnelley & Sons **BK**
Chuck Harpel
Crawfordsville Division
Route 32 West
Crawfordsville, IN 47933
317-362-1659; Fax: 317-364-3921
Toll-free: 800-428-0832

Min: 1,000 Max: 2,000,000 Opt: 25,000
Sizes: 235X
Bindings: HCI-CBI-PBI-SSI-SDI-SBI-WBI
Items: ABCDEFGHIJLMNPQWX
Services: 4C-FF-OC-AF-RP
Equipment: SO-WO
Turnaround times: B3C3M3
Union shop: N
Terms: Net 30

Statement: We are a major book manufacturer of all types of books and other full
service capabilities from prepress through
printing and binding to distribution.

R R Donnelley & Sons **BK**
Donnelley Book Group
2223 S Martin Luther King Drive
Chicago, IL 60616
312-326-7721; Fax: 312-326-7307
Toll-free: 800-428-0832

Min: 1 Max: 10,000,000 Opt: 100,000
Sizes: 235X
Bindings: HCI-CBI-PBI-SSI-SDI-SBI-WBI
Items: ABCDEFGHIJLMNPQWX
Services: 4C-FF-OC-AF-RP
Equipment: SO-WO-OT(gravure)
Annual sales: 3,122,000,000
Number of employees: 26,100
Turnaround times: B3C3M3
Customers: BP95-NP5
Union shop: N
Year established: 1864
Terms: Net 30

R R Donnelley, Harrisonburg **BK**
1400 Kratzer Road
Harrisonburg, VA 22801
703-434-8833; Fax: ext. 256
Toll-free: 800-428-0832

Min: 1,000 Max: 2,000,000 Opt: 25,000
Sizes: 12345X
Bindings: HCI-PBI
Items: BCEFLMN
Services: 4C-CS-DA-FF-LM
Equipment: CB-SO-WO
Turnaround times: B3
Union shop: N
Terms: Net 30

R R Donnelley, Willard **BK**
Gilbert McLondon, Manager
1145 Conwell Avenue
Willard, OH 44809
419-935-1230; Fax: 419-933-5360
Toll-free: 800-428-0832

Min: 1,000 Max: 2,000,000 Opt: 25,000
Sizes: 12345X
Bindings: HCI-PBI
Items: BCEFLMN
Services: 4C-CS-DA-FF-LM
Equipment: SO-WO
Turnaround times: B3
Union shop: N
Terms: Net 30

Dragon Press **BK**
P O Box 298
Delta Junction, AK 99737
907-895-4231

Min: 500 Max: 10,000 Opt: 2,000
Sizes: 2345
Bindings: HCX-PBI-SSI
Items: BCDFHMNP

Dynagraphics **MS**
6200 Yarrow Drive
Carlsbad, CA 92009
619-438-3456

PRINTED ITEMS							
A	Annual Reports	G	Galley Copies	N	Workbooks	U	Greeting Cards
B	Books	H	Journals	O	Yearbooks	V	Labels / Stickers
C	Booklets	I	Magazines	P	Brochures	W	Maps
D	Catalogs	J	Mass-Market Books	Q	Calendars	X	Newspapers
E	Cookbooks	K	Newsletters	R	Comic Books	Y	Postcards
F	Directories	L	Software Manuals	S	Direct Mail Letters	Z	Posters
		M	Textbooks	T	Envelopes	1	Stationery

Min: 10,000 **Max:** 500,000 **Opt:** 60,000
Sizes: 2345
Bindings: PBI-SSI
Items: CDFIPQ
Services: 4C-CS
Equipment: 1WO(17x26)-1OT
Annual sales: $5,000,000
Number of employees: 30
Turnaround times: C2M2
Customers: BU20-CU10-MP70
Union shop: N
Year established: 1977
Terms: Cash

E

E & D Web   CA

Edwards & Deutsch
4633 West 16th Street
Cicero, IL 60650
312-656-6600; Toll-free: 800-323-5733

Min: 25,000 **Max:** 2,000,000 **Opt:**
Sizes: 235X
Bindings: SSI
Items: CDKPSTXYZ
Services: 4C
Equipment: 5WO
Annual sales: $23,000,000
Number of employees: 130
Year established: 1896

Comments: E & D specializes in producing color direct mail promotions, including catalogs, magazine bind-ins, package inserts, newspaper inserts, newsletters, lift letters, and tip ons.

Eagle Web Press   GC

P O Box 12008
Salem, OR 97309
503-393-7980

Sizes: 235
Bindings: SSI
Items: CDKPSYZ1
Equipment: WO

East Village Enterprises   GC

37 West 20th Street #206
New York, NY 10001
212-463-7800

Min: 100 **Max:** 500,000 **Opt:** 15,000
Sizes: 123456X
Bindings: CBI-GBO-LBO-
PBO-SSI-SDO-SBO-WBO
Items: ABCDFGHKLPSTUVYZ1
Services: 4C-DA-LM-TY-TD
Equipment: 4SO(20")-2WO(17")
Annual sales: $500,000
Number of employees: 9
Turnaround times: B4C3M3
Customers: BU40-MP5-NP10-
SC5-SP10-OT30
Union shop: N
Year established: 1979
Terms: 50% down, balance on delivery

Eastern Press   BK

654 Orchard Street
P O Box 1650
New Haven, CT 06507
203-777-2353

Bindings: CBX-PBI-SBX
Items: BP
Services: 4C-CS-TY
Annual sales: $12,000,000
Number of employees: 150

Comments: One of their specialties is 4-color art books.

Eastwood Printing & Publishing   GC

2901 Blake Street
Denver, CO 80205
303-296-1905

Min: 1,000 **Max:** 1,000,000 **Opt:** 10,000
Sizes: 23456
Bindings: HCO-LBI-PBI-SSI-SDI-WBI
Items: ABCDFIKLMNPUWZ
Services: 4C-CS-TY-TD
Equipment: 2SO(26x38)-
2WO(23x36-39x40)
Annual sales: $5,000,000
Number of employees: 100

SERVICES				BINDINGS			
4C	4-Color Printing	**RA**	Rachwal System	**HC**	Hardcover	**SD**	Side Stitching
CS	Color Separations	**AF**	Acid-Free Paper	**CB**	Comb Binding	**SB**	Spiral Binding
DA	Design / Artwork	**RP**	Recycled Paper	**GB**	Glue Binding	**WB**	Wire-O Binding
FF	Fulfillment/Mailing	**TY**	Typesetting	**LB**	Loose-Leaf Binding	**I**	In-House
LM	List Maintenance	**TD**	Typeset w/ Disk	**PB**	Perfect Binding	**O**	Out of House
OC	OptiCopy System	**WA**	Warehousing	**SS**	Saddle Stitching	**X**	Unknown

Turnaround times: B4C4M2
Customers: BP15-BU15-CU10-
    MP5-NP5-OR20-OT3
Union shop: Y
Year established: 1905
Terms: Net 30

Statement: We are printers of book format products and maps.

Ebsco Media   **MS**
801 Fifth Avenue S
Birmingham, AL 35233
205-323-1508; Toll-free: 800-624-9454

Min: 5,000 Max: 50,000 Opt: 40,000
Sizes: 5
Bindings: SSI
Items: H
Services: 4C-FF
Equipment: SO
Annual sales: $20,000,000
Number of employees: 100

Statement: Ebsco is a state-of-the-art printing and mailing plant geared to serve the smaller publisher.

Economy Bookcraft   **BR**
3001 Pacific Avenue
San Francisco, CA 94115
415-777-9509

Economy Printing Concern   **MG**
169 S Jefferson Street
Berne, IN 46711
219-589-2145

Min: 10,000 Max: 2,000,000 Opt: 250,000
Sizes: 123456
Bindings: PBI-SSI-SDI
Items: DEFILNX
Services: 4C-CS-DA-TY-WA
Equipment: 3SO(25x38)-7WO(various)
Annual sales: $14,000,000
Number of employees: 150
Turnaround times: B3C3M2
Customers: BP19-MP78-OT3
Union shop: N
Year established: 1925
Terms: Net 30

Edison Lithographing   **BK**
3725 Tonnelle Avenue
North Bergen, NJ 07047-2421

Min: 5,000 Max: 2,000,000 Opt:
Sizes: 25X
Bindings: PBX-SSX
Items: BCDIPZ
Services: TY
Equipment: SO

Edison Press   **GC**
547 Broad Street
Glen Rock, NJ 07452

Min: 300 Max: 10,000 Opt: 1,000
Sizes: 5
Bindings: HCO-CBI
Items: BCDFKLP
Terms: Net 30 with approved credit

Editors Press   **MS**
6200 Editors Park Drive
Hyattsville, MD 20782
301-853-4900

Min: 50,000 Max: 1,000,000 Opt: 250,000
Sizes: 25X
Bindings: PBI-SSI
Items: ADISX
Services: 4C-FF-LM-WA
Equipment: 1SO(26x40)-3WO(23x38)
Annual sales: $26,000,000
Number of employees: 250
Turnaround times: C2M2
Customers: MP78-OR22
Union shop: Y
Year established: 1958
Terms: Net 30

Comments: A subsidiary of Kiplinger Washington Editors, they print magazines, catalogs, direct mail promotions, and tabloids.

Edwards & Broughton   **GC**
1821 North Boulevard
Raleigh, NC 27611
919-833-6601

PRINTED ITEMS						
A	Annual Reports	G	Galley Copies	N	Workbooks	U	Greeting Cards
B	Books	H	Journals	O	Yearbooks	V	Labels / Stickers
C	Booklets	I	Magazines	P	Brochures	W	Maps
D	Catalogs	J	Mass-Market Books	Q	Calendars	X	Newspapers
E	Cookbooks	K	Newsletters	R	Comic Books	Y	Postcards
F	Directories	L	Software Manuals	S	Direct Mail Letters	Z	Posters
		M	Textbooks	T	Envelopes	1	Stationery

Min: 3,000 Max: 250,000 Opt: 60,000
Sizes: 2345X
Bindings: HCO-CBI-PBI-SSI-SBI
Items: ABCDEFHIKNPQSUYZ1
Services: 4C-DA-TY-TD
Equipment: SO-WO
Terms: Net 30 with approved credit

Comments: A division of Graphics Industries of Atlanta ($310 million in annual sales from 38 plants with 3,070 employees), they can print brochures, folders, large 4-color posters, and point of purchase displays.

BK
Edwards Brothers
Thomas R Prince
2500 S State Street
P O Box 1007
Ann Arbor, MI 48106-1007
313-769-1000; Fax: 313-769-4756

Min: 500 Max: 100,000 Opt: 1,500
Sizes: 23456
Bindings: HCI-CBI-PBI-SSI-SBI-WBI
Items: BDFHLMN
Services: 4C-CS-FF-OC-
  AR-RP-TY-TD-WA
Equipment: 12SO(20x29-43x60)-
  1WO(18x26)
Annual sales: $51,000,000
Number of employees: 700
Turnaround times: B3C3
Customers: BP20-BU20-CU20-NP20-
  OR10-OT10
Union shop: N
Year established: 1893
Terms: Net 30

Statement: Our mission is to compete as a world class manufacturer in the information transfer business, primarily in the North American markets, focusing on the printing of books and journals in the short to medium-run market (1 and 2-color).

BK
Edwards Brothers / Raleigh
800 Edwards Drive
P O Box 1027
Lillington, NC 27546
919-893-2717

Min: 1,000 Max: 20,000 Opt: 5,000
Sizes: 23456
Bindings: HCX-GBX-LBX-
  PBX-SSX-SBX-WBX
Items: BCDEFHLMN
Services: 4C-FF-AF-TY-TD-WA
Turnaround times: B3C3
Union shop: N
Terms: Net 30

BK
Eerdmans Printing Company
Don Miller
231 Jefferson Avenue SE
Grand Rapids, MI 49503
616-451-0763; Fax: 616-459-4356

Min: 1,000 Max: 200,000 Opt: 50,000
Sizes: 12345
Bindings: HCI-CBO-LBO-
  PBI-SSI-SBO-WBO
Items: ABCDEFJLMNQ
Services: 4C-AF
Equipment: 2SO(25x38-26x40)-
  1WO(23x35)
Annual sales: $5,500,000
Number of employees: 60
Turnaround times: B5C4
Customers: BP80-BU10-SP10
Union shop: N
Year established: 1950
Terms: Net 30 with good credit

Statement: We work with customers in getting books ready and doing a quality job in a reasonable time and at a reasonable price.

GC
Einson Freeman Graphics
20-10 Maple Avenue
Fairlawn, NJ 07410
201-423-4200

Min: 5,000 Max: 2,000,000 Opt:
Sizes: 2345X
Bindings: HCX-PBI-SSI-SDI
Items: ABCDIKNPUWZ
Services: 4C
Equipment: LP-SO-WO
Annual sales: $16,000,000
Number of employees: 100

SERVICES				BINDINGS			
4C	4-Color Printing	RA	Rachwal System	HC	Hardcover	SD	Side Stitching
CS	Color Separations	AF	Acid-Free Paper	CB	Comb Binding	SB	Spiral Binding
DA	Design / Artwork	RP	Recycled Paper	GB	Glue Binding	WB	Wire-O Binding
FF	Fulfillment/Mailing	TY	Typesetting	LB	Loose-Leaf Binding	I	In-House
LM	List Maintenance	TD	Typeset w/ Disk	PB	Perfect Binding	O	Out of House
OC	OptiCopy System	WA	Warehousing	SS	Saddle Stitching	X	Unknown

Eureka Printing Company   **GC**
106 T Street
Eureka, CA 95501
707-442-5703

Items: BD

Eusey Press   **BK**
27 Nashua Street
Leominster, MA 01453
617-534-8351; Toll-free: 800-678-6299

Items: BLN
Services: 4C
Equipment: CB
Annual sales: $25,000,000
Number of employees: 335

Comments: Eusey is a subsidiary of Quebecor Printing ($1.7 billion in annual sales from 60 plants with 10,000 employees).

Eva-Tone   **GC**
4801 Ulmerton Road
P O Box 7020
Clearwater, FL 33518-7020
813-577-7000; Toll-free: 800-382-8663

Min: 5,000 **Max:** 2,000,000 **Opt:**
Sizes: 2345X
Bindings: SSI
Items: CPST
Services: 4C-FF
Equipment: SO
Year established: 196?

Comments: Eva-Tone's primary business is as a producer of sound sheets (flexible phonograph discs) and audio cassettes.

Evangel Press   **BK**
Jon Stepp, Manager
2000 Evangel Way
P O Box 189
Nappanee, IN 46550-0189
219-773-3164; Toll-free: 800-822-5919

Min: 500 **Max:** 10,000 **Opt:** 3,000
Sizes: 123456

Bindings: HCO-PBI-SSI-SBO
Items: BEHI
Services: TY
Equipment: 2SO(20"-41")
Annual sales: $3,000,000
Number of employees: 22
Turnaround times: B4
Customers: BP50-CU10-MP20-NP10-SP10
Union shop: N
Year established: 1920
Terms: Net 30

Statement: Our current primary interest is with short and medium-run book work and one or two-color magazines.

Everton Publishers   **BK**
P O Box 368
Logan, UT 84321

Min: 100 **Max:** 5,000 **Opt:** 500
Items: BCF
Customers: OR20-SP80(genealogists)

Statement: We specialize in short runs of family histories and genealogies.

William Exline Inc   **GC**
12301 Bennington Avenue
Cleveland, OH 44135
216-941-0800; Toll-free: 800-321-3062

Min: 300 **Max:** 50,000 **Opt:** 10,000
Sizes: X
Items: CT1

Comments: Among other items, Exline prints bank books and purse books with sewn bindings.

Exposition Press of Florida   **BR**
Edward Uhlan, President
1701 Blount Road #C
Pompano Beach, FL 33069
305-979-3200

Min: 100 **Max:** 100,000 **Opt:** 3,000
Sizes: 123446X
Bindings: HCX-PBX
Items: BEF

Comments: A vanity or subsidy press.

PRINTED ITEMS						
A	Annual Reports	G	Galley Copies	N	Workbooks	U	Greeting Cards
B	Books	H	Journals	O	Yearbooks	V	Labels / Stickers
C	Booklets	I	Magazines	P	Brochures	W	Maps
D	Catalogs	J	Mass-Market Books	Q	Calendars	X	Newspapers
E	Cookbooks	K	Newsletters	R	Comic Books	Y	Postcards
F	Directories	L	Software Manuals	S	Direct Mail Letters	Z	Posters
		M	Textbooks	T	Envelopes	1	Stationery

F

Faculty Press
BK

Walter Heitner, VP Sales
1449 - 37th Street
Brooklyn, NY 11218
718-851-6666

Min: 500 **Max:** 35,000 **Opt:** 6,000
Sizes: 123456X
Bindings: HCO-CBO-PBI-SSI-SBO-WBO
Items: ABCDEFHIKLNOPQSUWZ
Services: 4C-CS-DA-AF-RP
Equipment: 8SO(11x17-41x54)
Annual sales: $2,500,000
Number of employees: 45
Turnaround times: B3C2
Customers: BP20-BU20-CU15-
   MP10-NP20-SC10
Union shop: Y
Year established: 1950
Terms: Net 30 with approved credit

Statement: We offer high quality production of single and multi-colored materials for publishers and other clients in the New York metro area. We specialize in the printing of promotional items such as mailers, posters, and catalogs.

Fast Print
GC

2841 E State Boulevard
Fort Wayne, IN 46815
219-484-5487

Min: 100 **Max:** 5,000 **Opt:** 1,000
Sizes: 123456
Bindings: PBO-SSI-SDI-SBI-WBO
Items: ABCDEFKNPQSTVYZ1
Services: DA-TY-TD
Equipment: 1LP(10x15)-3SO(10x15-13x18)
Annual sales: $500,000
Number of employees: 8
Turnaround times: B2C2
Customers: BU50-CU5-NP20-
   OR15-SC5-SP5
Year established: 1976
Terms: Net 30

Statement: We are a quick printing company that offers printing and typesetting at a reasonable price.

William Feathers Printer
GC

235 Artino Street
Oberlin, OH 44074
216-774-1500

Min: 10,000 **Max:** 2,000,000 **Opt:**
Sizes: 5
Bindings: SSI
Items: CD
Services: 4C
Equipment: WO
Annual sales: $20,000,000
Number of employees: 80

Federated Lithographers
BK

Daniel Byrne, Marketing Director
369 Prairie Avenue
P O Box 158
Providence, RI 02901
401-781-8100; Fax: 401-467-8120

Min: 500 **Max:** 2,000,000 **Opt:**
Sizes: 123456X
Bindings: HCO-CBO-LBO-
   PBO-SSI-SDO-SBI-WBI
Items: BCDEFLMNPQTUVWZ
Services: 4C
Equipment: 9SO(up to 55x78)
Annual sales: $22,000,000
Number of employees: 200
Turnaround times: B4
Customers: BP50-OT50
Union shop: Y
Year established: 1868

Comments: Owned by Quebecor America Book Group.

Fetter Printing
GC

P O Box 33128
Louisville, KY 40232-3128
502-634-4771

Min: 5,000 **Max:** 2,000,000 **Opt:**
Sizes: 2345X
Bindings: SSI-SDI
Items: CDIKPS
Services: 4C-CS-DA-FF-TY-WA
Equipment: 3SO(28x41-43x60)-
   1WO(18x23)
Year established: 1890

SERVICES				BINDINGS			
4C	4-Color Printing	RA	Rachwal System	HC	Hardcover	SD	Side Stitching
CS	Color Separations	AF	Acid-Free Paper	CB	Comb Binding	SB	Spiral Binding
DA	Design / Artwork	RP	Recycled Paper	GB	Glue Binding	WB	Wire-O Binding
FF	Fulfillment/Mailing	TY	Typesetting	LB	Loose-Leaf Binding	I	In-House
LM	List Maintenance	TD	Typeset w/ Disk	PB	Perfect Binding	O	Out of House
OC	OptiCopy System	WA	Warehousing	SS	Saddle Stitching	X	Unknown

Fisher Printing `GC`
405 Grant Street, P O Box 56
Galion, OH 44833
419-468-2190

Min: 10,000 Max: 2,000,000 Opt:
Sizes: 2345X
Bindings: SSI
Items: PST
Services: 4C
Equipment: SO(28x41)-WO

Comments: Fisher prints direct mail components and, through Fisher Envelope Corporation, also prints envelopes.

Fisher Web Printers `MG`
2121 N Towne Lane NE
P O Box 1366
Cedar Rapids, IA 52406
319-393-5405

Min: 50,000 Max: 2,000,000 Opt:
Sizes: 25X
Bindings: SSI
Items: CDFHIKNPSVWXZ
Services: 4C-CS-FF
Equipment: 2WO

Comments: Besides direct mail letters, brochures, inserts, and other promotional materials, they can also print magazines in quantities from 50,000 to 1,000,000 and digests from 100,000 to 2,000,000.

Fleetwood Litho & Letter `GC`
304 Hudson Street
New York, NY 10013
212-924-4422

Bindings: SSI
Items: CDPSZ
Services: 4C-CS-FF-TY

Comments: Promotional printers and mailers for publishers and ad agencies.

Foote & Davies `CA`
3101 McCall Drive
Atlanta, GA 30340
404-451-4511

Min: 200,000 Max: 2,000,000 Opt:
Sizes: 23456X
Bindings: PBI-SSI
Items: ADIP
Services: 4C-CS-FF-TY
Equipment: SO-21WO
Annual sales: $351,000,000
Number of employees: 2,480
Year established: 1887

Comments: Foote & Davies became a division of American Signature in early 1990.

Foote & Davies / Lincoln `MG`
P O Box 81608
3700 NW 12th Street
Lincoln, NE 68501
402-474-5825

Min: 50,000 Max: 2,000,000 Opt:
Sizes: 2345X
Bindings: PBI-SSI
Items: CDFINPX
Services: 4C-FF
Equipment: 10WO

Fort Orange Press `BK`
31 Sand Creek Road
P O Box 828
Albany, NY 12201
518-489-3233; Toll-free: 800-448-4468

Min: 500 Max: 50,000 Opt: 15,000
Sizes: 23456X
Bindings: HCI-CBI-LBI-PBI-SSI-SBI
Items: ABCDEFGHJMNPZ
Services: 4C-DA-TY-TD-WA
Equipment: LP-SO
Terms: Net 30 with credit approval

Foster Printing Service `GC`
4295 S Ohio Street
P O Box 2089
Michigan City, IN 46360
219-879-8366; Toll-free: 800-382-0808

Min: 100 Max: 25,000 Opt:
Sizes: 123456
Bindings: PBI-SSI

PRINTED ITEMS						
A	Annual Reports	G	Galley Copies	N	Workbooks	U	Greeting Cards
B	Books	H	Journals	O	Yearbooks	V	Labels / Stickers
C	Booklets	I	Magazines	P	Brochures	W	Maps
D	Catalogs	J	Mass-Market Books	Q	Calendars	X	Newspapers
E	Cookbooks	K	Newsletters	R	Comic Books	Y	Postcards
F	Directories	L	Software Manuals	S	Direct Mail Letters	Z	Posters
		M	Textbooks	T	Envelopes	1	Stationery

Items: ACGKPZ
Services: 4C-TY
Equipment: LP-10SO(10x15-25x35)
Annual sales: $5,000,000
Number of employees: 30
Customers: MP70-OT30
Union shop: Y
Terms: Net 30

Comments: They specialize in promotional printing, including ad reprints, brochures, spec sheets, statement stuffers, and catalog sheets.

The Four Corners Press   BR
Charlotte Ellison, President
2056 College SE
Grand Rapids, MI 49507
616-243-2015

Min: 500 **Max:** 10,000 **Opt:** 2,000
Sizes: 235
Bindings: HCO-PBO
Items: BFHMN
Services: DA-TY
Year established: 1977

Statement: Four Corners is a full service brokerage with design, typographical, and production management for foundations, corporations, learned societies, and small publishers.

Friesen Printers   BK
Tim Fast
P O Box 720
Altona, Manitoba R0G 0B0 Canada
204-324-6401; Fax: 204-324-1333

Min: 3,000 **Max:** 50,000 **Opt:** 10,000
Sizes: 3456
Bindings: HCI-CBI-PBI-SSI-SBI-WBI
Items: BEHMNOPQ
Services: 4C-CS-FF-CO-AF-RP-WA
Equipment: 10SO(up to 38 x 50)
Annual sales: $32,000,000
Number of employees: 350
Turnaround times: B4
Customers: BP75-SC25
Union shop: N
Year established: 1907
Terms: Net 30

Statement: We are a sheet-fed printer specializing in 4-color work. We believe that we are the lowest-cost producer of color books this side of Hong Kong.

Comments: They have a U.S. address:
    Friesen Printers
    P O Drawer B
    Neche ND 58265.

Fundcraft   BK
410 Highway 72 West
P O Box 340
Collierville, TN 38017
800-325-1994; Toll-free: 800-351-7822

Min: 500 **Max:** 25,000 **Opt:** 2,000
Sizes: 23
Bindings: CBI
Items: E
Services: 4C-DA-TY
Customers: OR100
Terms: No downpayment

Comments: Fundcraft specializes in printing cookbooks for fundraising organizations.

Futura Printing   GC
Bob Steinmetz, President
517 E Ocean Avenue
P O Drawer 99
Boynton Beach, FL 33425-0099
305-734-0825; Fax: 305-734-0862

Min: 50 **Max:** 5,000 **Opt:**
Sizes: 123456
Bindings: CBX-LBX-PBX-SSX
Items: ABCDEFIKLTX1
Services: 4C-TY
Equipment: 2SO(11x17-18x24)
Annual sales: $400,000
Number of employees: 6
Turnaround times: B5C3
Customers: SC30-SP30-OT40
Union shop: N
Year established: 1977
Terms: 1/2 down, balance on delivery

Statement: We publish books for those who cannot get published otherwise.

SERVICES			BINDINGS			
4C	4-Color Printing	**RA** Rachwal System	**HC**	Hardcover	**SD**	Side Stitching
CS	Color Separations	**AF** Acid-Free Paper	**CB**	Comb Binding	**SB**	Spiral Binding
DA	Design / Artwork	**RP** Recycled Paper	**GB**	Glue Binding	**WB**	Wire-O Binding
FF	Fulfillment/Mailing	**TY** Typesetting	**LB**	Loose-Leaf Binding	**I**	In-House
LM	List Maintenance	**TD** Typeset w/ Disk	**PB**	Perfect Binding	**O**	Out of House
OC	OptiCopy System	**WA** Warehousing	**SS**	Saddle Stitching	**X**	Unknown

G

Gagne Printing Ltd   BK
Guy Lefebvre, VP Marketing
Imprimerie Gagne Ltee
80 Avenue Saint Martin
Louiseville, Quebec J5V 1B4 Canada
819-228-2768; Toll-free: 800-567-2154

Min: 800 **Max:** 600,000 **Opt:** 10,000
Sizes: 123456X
Bindings: HCO-CBO-GBI-LBI-
    PBI-SSO-SDO-SBI-WBO
Items: BCDEFIJMNOP
Services: 4C-AF-TY-TD-WA
Equipment: 4SO(28x41)-3WO(38"-78")
Annual sales: $20,000,000
Number of employees: 125
Turnaround times: B3C3
Customers: BP75-CU10-SC10-OT5
Union shop: Y
Year established: 1890
Terms: Net 30

Ganis & Harris   BK
39 West 14th Street #205
New York, NY 10011-7432
212-685-5444

Min: 3,000 **Max:** 100,000 **Opt:** 10,000
Sizes: 123456X
Bindings: HCI-CBI-PBI-SSI-SBI
Items: BCFHMN
Services: 4C-DA-TY
Year established: 194?
Terms: Net 30 with approved credit

Comments: They specialize in heavily illustrated and detailed technical books.

Gateway Press   GC
4500 Robards Lane
P O Box 32548
Louisville, KY 40232
502-454-0431

Min: 25,000 **Max:** 2,000,000 **Opt:** 300,000
Sizes: 1245
Bindings: HCO-CBI-GBI-LBI-
    PBI-SSI-SDI-SBI-WBO

Items: ABCDEFIMNPQWZ
Services: 4C-FF-TY
Equipment: 6SO(17x23-26x49)-
    4WO(23x36)
Annual sales: $17,000,000
Number of employees: 250
Customers: BP8-BU50-CU12-MP20-OT10
Union shop: N
Year established: 1950
Terms: Net 30

Gateway Press   BR
1001 N Calvert Street
Baltimore, MD 21202
301-837-8271

Customers: SP(genealogists)

Comments: They broker printing services for genealogists.

Gaylord Ltd   BK
633 N LaPeer Drive
West Hollywood, CA 90069
213-274-5407

Min: 500 **Max:** 10,000 **Opt:** 4,000
Sizes: 123456
Bindings: HCX-PBX-SSX-SBX-WBX
Items: BCDEFHIKLMNOP
Services: 4C-CS-FF-AF-TY
Equipment: 4SO(25x38)
Annual sales: $750,000
Number of employees: 30
Turnaround times: B4C4M4
Customers: BP40-BU5-MP10-NP5-SP40
Union shop: N
Year established: 1982
Terms: Net 30

Gaylord Printing   GC
15555 Woodrow Wilson Boulevard
Detroit, MI 48238
313-883-7800

Min: 5,000 **Max:** 2,000,000 **Opt:**
Sizes: 2345X
Bindings: SSI
Items: ACDKNPSWXZ
Services: 4C-CS
Equipment: SO-WO

PRINTED ITEMS						
A	Annual Reports	G	Galley Copies	N	Workbooks	U	Greeting Cards
B	Books	H	Journals	O	Yearbooks	V	Labels / Stickers
C	Booklets	I	Magazines	P	Brochures	W	Maps
D	Catalogs	J	Mass-Market Books	Q	Calendars	X	Newspapers
E	Cookbooks	K	Newsletters	R	Comic Books	Y	Postcards
F	Directories	L	Software Manuals	S	Direct Mail Letters	Z	Posters
		M	Textbooks	T	Envelopes	1	Stationery

Annual sales: $19,000,000
Number of employees: 190

BK

Geiger Brothers
Eugene Geiger, President
P O Box 1609
Mount Hope Avenue
Lewiston, ME 04240
207-783-2001

Sizes: 25X
Bindings: LBI-SSI-SBI
Items: B
Equipment: LP-SO

Comments: They specialize in printing looseleaf time management systems and address books.

GC

General Offset Company
Murray H Berger, President
234 16th Street
Jersey City, NJ 07302
201-420-0500; Fax: 201-420-9086

Min: Max: Opt: 15,000
Sizes: 123456
Bindings: HCO-SBO-GBO-LBO-
PBO-SSO-SDO-SB0-WBO
Items: ABCDEKLNOPQUWZ
Services: 4C-CS-AF
Equipment: 5SO(23x29-43x60)
Annual sales: $7,000,000
Number of employees: 43
Turnaround times: B5C3
Customers: BP65-OT35
Union shop: Y
Year established: 1940
Terms: Net 30

Comments: They specialize in color printing and halftone inserts. They do many children's books.

GC

George Lithograph
650 Second Street
San Francisco, CA 94107
415-397-2400

Min: 500 **Max:** 25,000 **Opt:** 10,000
Sizes: 235

Bindings: HCO-CBI-PBI-SSI-SBI
Items: ABCDFHIKLNP
Services: DA-TY-TD-WA
Equipment: SO
Annual sales: $15,000,000
Number of employees: 225
Terms: Net 30 with approved credit

Comments: They specialize in printing manuals, directories, training manuals, and computer documentation.

GC

Germac Printing
207 Tigard Plaza
P O Box 23877
Tigard, OR 97223
503-639-0898

Min: 10 **Max:** 40,000 **Opt:** 6,000
Sizes: 235
Bindings: HCI-CBO-PBI-SSI-SBO
Items: ABCDFNP
Services: DA-TY
Equipment: SO(15x18)
Terms: Net 10 with approved credit

GC

Geryon Press
Stuart McCarty, Owner
P O Box 770
Tunnel, NY 13848
607-693-1572

Min: 10 **Max:** 1,000 **Opt:** 400
Sizes: 23
Bindings: HCO-PBI-SSI
Items: BCDEPYZ
Services: DA-TY
Equipment: LP
Union shop: N
Terms: To be arranged

Comments: Geryon is a small letterpress shop specializing in typesetting and printing poetry books, postcards, and broadsides.

BK

Giant Horse and Company
400 Talbert Street
Daly City, CA 94014
415-468-0573

SERVICES				BINDINGS			
4C	4-Color Printing	RA	Rachwal System	HC	Hardcover	SD	Side Stitching
CS	Color Separations	AF	Acid-Free Paper	CB	Comb Binding	SB	Spiral Binding
DA	Design / Artwork	RP	Recycled Paper	GB	Glue Binding	WB	Wire-O Binding
FF	Fulfillment/Mailing	TY	Typesetting	LB	Loose-Leaf Binding	I	In-House
LM	List Maintenance	TD	Typeset w/ Disk	PB	Perfect Binding	O	Out of House
OC	OptiCopy System	WA	Warehousing	SS	Saddle Stitching	X	Unknown

Min: 100 Max: 100,000 Opt: 6,000
Sizes: 123456X
Bindings: HCO-CBI-GBI-LBI-
   PBI-SSI-SDI-SBO-WBO
Items: ABCDEFHKLNOPSZ
Equipment: 3SO(10x15-19x26)
Annual sales: $500,000
Number of employees: 30
Turnaround times: B2C2
Customers: BU75-OT25
Union shop: N
Terms: Net 30 with credit approval

Statement: Our specialty is the production
of black and white, short-run books,
catalogs, manuals, and newsletters.

Gibbs-Inman Company   CA
P O Box 32030
Louisville, KY 40232
502-966-3151; Toll-free: 800-626-2365

Min: 25,000 Max: 250,000 Opt:
Sizes: 5X
Bindings: SSI
Items: DP
Equipment: WO

Gilliland Printing Company   BK
Patsy Sweeley, Sales Manager
215 N Summit Avenue
P O Box 1170
Arkansas City, KS 67005
316-442-0500
Toll-free: 800-332-8200

Min: 1,000 Max: 30,000 Opt: 8,000
Sizes: 12345
Bindings: PBI-SBI-SSI
Items: BDEFHJLR
Services: 4C-DA-TY-TD
Equipment: 4SO(25x38)
Annual sales: $7,500,000
Number of employees: 125
Customers: BU20-CU10
Union shop: N
Year established: 1969
Terms: Net 30

Statement: Gilliland specializes in printing
college catalogs.

Gladstone Press   GC
Peter Vineberg, Sales Director
430 Gladstone Avenue
Ottawa, Ontario K2P 0Z1 Canada
613-232-7450; Fax: 613-232-4943

Min: 5,000 Max: 1,000,000 Opt: 100,000
Sizes: 2345X
Bindings: HCO-CBO-LBO-
   PBI-SSI-SDO-SBO-WBO
Items: ABCDFHIKMOPSTUVWXYZ1
Services: 4C-CS-AF-RP-TY-TD-WA
Equipment: 3LP-12SO(10x14-28x40)-
   2WO(26/36)
Annual sales: $15,000,000
Number of employees: 140
Turnaround times: B3M2
Customers: BU30-MP30-NP20-OR20
Union shop: N
Year established: 1958
Terms: Net 30

Comments: A division of Dollco Printing.

Globe-Comm   GC
301 N Frio
P O Box 7789
San Antonio, TX 78207-0789
512-227-9185

Sizes: 123456X
Bindings: HCO-CBO-GBO-LBI-
   PBO-SSI-SDO-SBO-WBO
Items: ACDFKPQSTVYZ1
Services: 4C-CS-DA-FF-LM-TY-WA
Equipment: LP-SO-WO
Annual sales: $5,000,000
Number of employees: 30
Turnaround times: B1C2M3
Customers: BU50-NP30-OR15-OT5
Union shop: N
Year established: 1936
Terms: COD, credit with approval limit

Statement: We specialize in producing
direct marketing services and materials.

Glundal Color Service   CA
6700 Joy Road
East Syracuse, NY 13057
315-437-1391

PRINTED ITEMS					
A Annual Reports	G Galley Copies	N Workbooks	U Greeting Cards
B Books	H Journals	O Yearbooks	V Labels / Stickers
C Booklets	I Magazines	P Brochures	W Maps
D Catalogs	J Mass-Market Books	Q Calendars	X Newspapers
E Cookbooks	K Newsletters	R Comic Books	Y Postcards
F Directories	L Software Manuals	S Direct Mail Letters	Z Posters
	M Textbooks	T Envelopes	1 Stationery

Min: 15,000 Max: 3,000,000 Opt: 500,000
Sizes: 25
Bindings: CBO-LBO-PBO-SSI-SBO-WBO
Items: ACDFIKPQZ
Services: 4C-CS-DA
Equipment: 4SO(25x38)-1WO(17x23)
Annual sales: $7,000,000
Number of employees: 100
Turnaround times: C3M4
Customers: BP10-BU70-CU10-OR10
Union shop: N
Terms: Net 30

BK
Golden Horn Press
2506 Shattuck Avenue
Berkeley, CA 94704
415-845-4355

Min: 300 Max: 10,000 Opt:
Sizes: 12
Bindings: PBX-SSX
Items: BJ

Comments: They specialize in printing smaller books (4 x 7 and 5 1/2 x 8 1/2) in quantities from 300 to 10,000.

BK
Goodway Graphics of Virginia
Kathryn Sheller, Sales Rep
6628 Electronic Drive
Springfield, VA 22151
703-941-1160; Fax: 703-658-9511

Min: 500 Max: 25,000 Opt: 15,000
Sizes: 35
Bindings: PBI-CBI-SSI
Items: BCDEFHLN
Equipment: 4SO(35x45)-2WO(26x36)
Number of employees: 250
Year established: 196?

Statement: We are primarily a black and white book, catalog, and directory printer. Our pricing is best on 8 1/2 x 11 and 6 x 9 high volume work.

GC
Gorham Printing
334 Harris Road
Rochester, WA 98579
206-273-0970

Min: 250
Sizes: 25
Bindings: PBX-SSX
Items: BCDFKLNP
Services: DA-TY
Year established: 1974

GC
Gowe Printing Company
620 E Smith Road
P O Box 1048
Medina, OH 44258
216-725-4161

Min: 5,000 Max: 2,000,000 Opt:
Sizes: 2345X
Bindings: SSI
Items: DFINPX
Services: 4C
Equipment: SO-WO
Annual sales: $28,000,000
Number of employees: 350

Comments: A subsidiary of Sun Media, Gowe prints catalogs, magazines, newspapers, directories, and brochures.

MS
Graftek Press
11595 McConnell Road
P O Box 628
Woodstock, IL 60098
815-338-6750

Min: 50,000 Max: 350,000 Opt: 150,000
Sizes: 4X
Bindings: HCO-GBO-PBI-SSI-SBO
Items: CDFHIX
Services: 4C-CS
Equipment: 3SO(18x25-28x40)-
    9WO(23x36)
Annual sales: $43,247,000
Number of employees: 545
Turnaround times: M2
Customers: BU2-CU1-MP95-NP2
Union shop: N
Year established: 1970
Terms: Net 30

Comments: Printers of medium-run special interest and trade publications, they have two printing facilities: Graftek Press in Crystal Lake, Illinois, and Elkhorn Web Press in Elkhorn, Wisconsin.

SERVICES				BINDINGS			
4C	4-Color Printing	RA	Rachwal System	HC	Hardcover	SD	Side Stitching
CS	Color Separations	AF	Acid-Free Paper	CB	Comb Binding	SB	Spiral Binding
DA	Design / Artwork	RP	Recycled Paper	GB	Glue Binding	WB	Wire-O Binding
FF	Fulfillment/Mailing	TY	Typesetting	LB	Loose-Leaf Binding	I	In-House
LM	List Maintenance	TD	Typeset w/ Disk	PB	Perfect Binding	O	Out of House
OC	OptiCopy System	WA	Warehousing	SS	Saddle Stitching	X	Unknown

Graphic Arts Center `CA`
2000 NW Wilson Street
Portland, OR 97209
503-224-7777

Min: 2,000 **Max:** 2,000,000 **Opt:**
Sizes: 23456X
Bindings: HCI-PBI-SSI-SDI-SBI-WBI
Items: ADPS
Services: 4C-CS-FF-TY
Equipment: 5SO(to 26x40)-4WO(to 23x36)
Annual sales: $123,000,000
Number of employees: 650

Comments: GAC specializes in printing catalogs of all shapes and sizes. They also publish their own calendars and coffee-table books.

Graphic Arts Publishing `CA`
2285 Warm Springs Avenue
Boise, ID 83712
208-34203549; Toll-free: 800-523-9675

Min: 1,000 **Max:** 1,000,000 **Opt:**
Sizes: 235
Bindings: SSI
Items: D
Equipment: SO-WO

Comments: They will print as few as a 1000 catalogs or as many as 1,000,000.

Graphic Design & Printing `BK`
Richard Heppard, President
23844 Sherwood
Center Line, MI 48015-1091
313-758-0480; Fax: 313-748-0035
Toll-free: 800-343-5840

Bindings: CBI-PBI-SSI-WBI
Items: ABCDFPQ
Services: DA-TY-TD
Equipment: 2LP-12SO(10x15-38x50)-
1WO(36")

Graphic Litho Corporation `BK`
Jesse Kamien
130 Shepard Street, Industrial Park
Lawrence, MA 01843
508-683-2766

Min: 2,000 **Max:** 100,000 **Opt:** 25,000
Sizes: 123456
Bindings: CBI-PBI-SSI-SSI
Items: ABCDEFMNPQSUWYZ
Services: 4C
Equipment: 3SO(42x58 - 52x76 - 54x77)
Annual sales: $2,000,000
Number of employees: 16
Turnaround times: B3
Customers: BP45-BU25-OT30
Union shop: N
Year established: 1964
Terms: 1% 10, net 30

Statement: Quality color work is our specialty.

Graphic Printing Division `BK`
McGregor & Werner
310 N Clay Street
New Carlisle, OH 45344
513-845-3752

Min: 100 **Max:** 20,000 **Opt:** 5,000
Sizes: 123456X
Bindings: HCO-CBI-GBI-LBI-
PBI-SSI-SDI-SBI-WBI
Items: BCDFGHKLMNPS
Services: 4C
Equipment: 7SO(29"-55")
Annual sales: $12,000,000
Number of employees: 125
Turnaround times: B3
Customers: BP20-BU15-CU10-
NP40-SC10-SP5
Union shop: N
Year established: 1950
Terms: 1% 10, Net 30 w/approved credit

Comments: A division of McGregor & Werner.

Gray Printing `MS`
401 E North Street
P O Box 840
Fostoria, OH 44830
419-435-6638

Min: 8,000 **Max:** 200,000 **Opt:** 50,000
Sizes: 25X
Bindings: CBI-PBI-SSI-WBI

PRINTED ITEMS					
A Annual Reports	G Galley Copies	N Workbooks	U Greeting Cards
B Books	H Journals	O Yearbooks	V Labels / Stickers
C Booklets	I Magazines	P Brochures	W Maps
D Catalogs	J Mass-Market Books	Q Calendars	X Newspapers
E Cookbooks	K Newsletters	R Comic Books	Y Postcards
F Directories	L Software Manuals	S Direct Mail Letters	Z Posters
	M Textbooks	T Envelopes	1 Stationery

Items: ADFHIKLNPXZ
Services: 4C-DA-TY-TD
Equipment: 6SO(to 28x40)-3WO(23x38)
Annual sales: $14,000,000
Number of employees: 200
Turnaround times: B4C3M2
Customers: BU25-CU10-MP60-NP5
Union shop: Y
Year established: 1888
Terms: Net 30

Comments: If you are a magazine publisher, write for a copy of their quarterly *Gray Matter* newsletter.

Greater Buffalo Press   MG
302 Grote Street
Buffalo, NY 14207
716-876-6410

Min: 200,000 **Max:** 2,000,000 **Opt:**
Sizes: 25X
Bindings: GBI
Items: DIX
Services: 4C-CS-DA-FF-TY
Equipment: 24 + LP - 20 + WO
Annual sales: $360,000,000
Number of employees: 2,500
Year established: 1926

Comments: GBP prints magazines, tabloids, and catalogs in satellite plants in Dunkirk, New York; Marengo, Iowa; Lufkin, Texas; Pittsburgh, California; York, Pennsylvania; Stevensville, Ontario; and Sylacauga, Alabama.

Greenfield Printing & Publishing   MS
Wilson L Moon
1025 N Washington Street
Greenfield, OH 45123
513-981-2161
Toll-free: 800-543-3881

Min: 2,000 **Max:** 250,000 **Opt:**
Sizes: 2345X
Bindings: PBI-SSI
Items: I
Services: 4C-CS-FF
Equipment: 2SO-2WO

The Gregath Company   GC
Ann Gregath, Owner
P O Box 1045
Cullman, AL 35056-1045
205-739-0508

Sizes: 123456
Bindings: LBI-PBI-SDI-WBI
Items: ABCDEFGHIJKMNOPSTUVYZ1
Services: 4C-CS-DA-LM-AF-TY
Equipment: 1LP-6SO(14x20)
Annual sales: $500,000
Number of employees: 9
Turnaround times: B3C2M2
Customers: BP60-BU10-CU10-MP10-SC10
Union shop: N
Year established: 1977
Terms: 50% down, balance on delivery

Comments: They specialize in editing, designing, printing, and distributing genealogies and regional histories.

Griffin Printing & Lithograph   BK
Richard Ford, Marketing Director
544 W Colorado Street
Glendale, CA 91204
818-244-2128; Fax: 818-242-1172
Toll-free: 800-826-4049

Min: 500 **Max:** 50,000 **Opt:** 8,000
Sizes: 123456X
Bindings: HCO-CBO-GBI-LBI-
PBI-SSI-SDI-SBO-WBO
Items: ABCDEFHIJLMNP
Services: 4C-CS-DA-FF-
LM-AF-TY-TD-WA
Equipment: 4SO-4WO(22 3/4")
Annual sales: $10,000,000
Number of employees: 85
Turnaround times: B3C4
Customers: BP60-CU10-MP5-OR10-SP15
Union shop: N
Year established: 1924
Terms: 2% 14, Net 30

Statement: Griffin provides a monthly newsletter and regular seminars as educational services to the publishing industry. Write for a free subscription to our *Signature* newsletter.

SERVICES				BINDINGS			
4C	4-Color Printing	RA	Rachwal System	HC	Hardcover	SD	Side Stitching
CS	Color Separations	AF	Acid-Free Paper	CB	Comb Binding	SB	Spiral Binding
DA	Design / Artwork	RP	Recycled Paper	GB	Glue Binding	WB	Wire-O Binding
FF	Fulfillment/Mailing	TY	Typesetting	LB	Loose-Leaf Binding	I	In-House
LM	List Maintenance	TD	Typeset w/ Disk	PB	Perfect Binding	O	Out of House
OC	OptiCopy System	WA	Warehousing	SS	Saddle Stitching	X	Unknown

Griffin Printing Company   BK
Cecil Carson, General Manager
1801 Ninth Street
Sacramento, CA 95814
916-448-3511; Fax: 916-448-3597
Toll-free: 800-448-3511

Min: 1,000 Max: 25,000 Opt: 5,000
Sizes: 25
Bindings: HCO-CBO-LCO-
   PBI-SSI-SDO-SBO-WBO
Items: BCDEFKLMN
Services: OC
Equipment: 1SO-1WO
Annual sales: $3,000,000
Number of employees: 30
Turnaround times: B3
Customers: BP70-BU30
Union shop: N
Year established: 1924
Terms: Net 30 with approved credit

Statement: We offer personalized service and 3 to 4 week turnarounds.

Comments: Formerly Spilman Printing, this company has merged with Griffin.

GRIT PRINTING SERVICES

Grit Commercial Print   GC
Thomas Stein, Mktg Director
208 W Third Street
Williamsport, PA 17701-9988
717-326-1771; Fax: 717-326-6940
Toll-free: 800-223-8455

Min: 500 Max: 10,000,000 Opt: 25,000
Sizes: 2356
Bindings: HCO-CBO-LBO-
   PBO-SSI-SDI-SBO-WBO
Items: ACDEFIKPQSTWX1
Services: 4C-DA-FF-AF-RP-TY-TD-WA
Equipment: 6SO(11x14-25x38)-1WO(61")
Annual sales: $3,000,000
Number of employees: 100
Turnaround times: B4C2
Customers: BU40-CU10-MP10-
   NP6-OR9-SC5-SP20
Union shop: Y
Year established: 1884
Terms: Net 30

Statement: Our goal is to produce the highest quality product in accordance with providing the highest quality customer satisfaction. We also provide direct mailing services.

Comments: Grit Printing is a division of *Grit* magazine.

BK
GRT Book Printing
3960 East 14th Street
Oakland, CA 94601
415-534-5032

Min: 100 **Max:** 2,000 **Opt:** 1,000
Sizes: 123456
Bindings: CBI-LBI-PBO-SSI-SBO-WBO
Items: BCEFHLMN
Equipment: 6SO(to 11x17)
Annual sales: $500,000
Number of employees: 30
Turnaround times: B2C2M2
Customers: BP20-BU42-
      CU19-MP2-NP3-SP14
Union shop: N
Year established: 1973
Terms: 50 down, balance COD

Statement: GRT specializes in short-run book printing for customers located in California only.

BK
GTE Directories Printing Corp.
111 Rawls Road
Des Plaines, IL 60018
312-296-8850

Min: 5,000 **Max:** 2,000,000 **Opt:**
Sizes: 23
Bindings: PBI
Items: BF
Equipment: WO
Customers: BU-OT

Statement: GTE is a directory printer. We print millions of telephone books.

GC
Gulf Printing
2210 W Dallas Avenue
Houston, TX 77019
713-529-4201; Toll-free: 800-423-9537

Min: 2,000 **Max:** 2,000,000 **Opt:**
Sizes: 2345X
Bindings: PBI-SSI-SDI
Items: ABCDFIKPSZ
Services: 4C-CS-FF
Equipment: 5SO(20x28-43x60)-2WO
Annual sales: $105,000,000
Number of employees: 529

Comments: A subsidiary of Southwestern Bell Corporation.

OF NEW MEXICO

GC
Guynes Printing Company
Robert A Johnson, Vice President
2709 Girard Boulevard NE
Albuquerque, NM 87107
505-884-8882; Fax: 505-889-3148

Min: 500 **Max:** 20,000 **Opt:** 5,000
Sizes: 12345X
Bindings: HCO-CBI-LBI-
      PBI-SSI-SDI-SBI-WBI
Items: ABCDEFIJKLPQSUYZ
Services: 4C-CS-FF-AF-RP-TY-TD
Equipment: 4SO(19x25-26x40)
Annual sales: $6,000,000
Number of employees: 84
Turnaround times: B3C2
Customers: BP15-BU15-CU2-SP10
Union shop: N
Year established: 1932
Terms: 2% 10, net 30 days

H

BK
Haddon Craftsmen
Ash Street & Wyoming Avenue
Scranton, PA 18509
717-348-9211; Fax: 717-348-9266
Toll-free: 800-225-6538

Min: 1,000 **Max:** 500,000 **Opt:** 7,000
Sizes: 23456X
Bindings: HCI-PBI

SERVICES				BINDINGS			
4C	4-Color Printing	**RA**	Rachwal System	**HC**	Hardcover	**SD**	Side Stitching
CS	Color Separations	**AF**	Acid-Free Paper	**CB**	Comb Binding	**SB**	Spiral Binding
DA	Design / Artwork	**RP**	Recycled Paper	**GB**	Glue Binding	**WB**	Wire-O Binding
FF	Fulfillment/Mailing	**TY**	Typesetting	**LB**	Loose-Leaf Binding	**I**	In-House
LM	List Maintenance	**TD**	Typeset w/ Disk	**PB**	Perfect Binding	**O**	Out of House
OC	OptiCopy System	**WA**	Warehousing	**SS**	Saddle Stitching	**X**	Unknown

Items: BEFLM
Services: 4C-FF-TY-WA
Equipment: 5WO
Annual sales: $50,000,000
Number of employees: 1,000
Turnaround times: B2
Year established: 1890

BK

Hamilton Printing Company
P O Box 232
Rensselaer, NY 12144
518-477-9345

Min: Max: Opt:
Bindings: HCI-CBI-LBI-PBI-SSI-SBI-WBI
Items: BCDFHIMN
Services: 4C-FF
Equipment: SO
Annual sales: $10,000,000
Number of employees: 180

BK

Hamilton Reproductions
70 W Cedar Street
P O Box H
Poughkeepsie, NY 12602
914-471-3110

BR

Harlin Litho
24 Oakbrook Road
Ossining, NY 10562-2620
914-948-8630

Sizes: 123456X
Bindings: HCO-CBO-GBO-LBO-
   PBO-SSO-SDO-SBO-WBO
Items: ACDEFIKPSTUVWYZ1
Services: 4C-CS-TY
Turnaround times: C3M3
Customers: BU75-CU10-MP10-OT5
Union shop: N
Terms: Net 30

BK

Harlo Press
Kitty Russo
50 Victor Avenue
Detroit, MI 48203
313-883-3600; Fax: 313-883-0072

Min: 250 Max: 10,000 Opt: 3,000
Sizes: 123456
Bindings: HCO-CBI-LBO-
   PBI-SSI-SDI-SBI-WBI
Items: ABCDEFKLMNOPQSTYZ1
Services: 4C-DA-FF-AF-TY-TD-WA
Equipment: LB-SO-WO
Annual sales: $2,500,000
Number of employees: 25
Turnaround times: B3C3
Customers: NP20-OR10-SC10-SP60
Union shop: N
Year established: 1946
Terms: 2% 10, net 30

Comments: Harlo has advertised in *Writer's Digest* for years and, therefore, is quite accustomed to working with writers and self-publishers.

GC

Hart Graphics
8000 Shoal Creek Boulevard
P O Box 968
Austin, TX 78767-9979
512-454-4761; Toll-free: 800-531-5471

Min: 50,000 Max: 2,000,000 Opt:
Sizes: 25X
Bindings: GBI-PBI-SSI
Items: BDPS
Services: 4C-CS-FF-TY
Equipment: LP-SO-WO
Annual sales: $58,152,000
Number of employees: 750

Comments: Their speciality is full-color magazine inserts and envelopes. They can provide inserts with perforations, rub-offs, scratch-n-sniff, and other special effects. They are one of the few companies in the country which currently use the Otabind system.

MG

Hart Graphics
800 SE Main Street
Sampsonville, SC 20681
803-967-7821

Min: 100,000 Max: 2,000,000 Opt:
Sizes: X
Bindings: PBI
Items: CI

PRINTED ITEMS					
A	Annual Reports	G	Galley Copies	N	Workbooks	U	Greeting Cards
B	Books	H	Journals	O	Yearbooks	V	Labels / Stickers
C	Booklets	I	Magazines	P	Brochures	W	Maps
D	Catalogs	J	Mass-Market Books	Q	Calendars	X	Newspapers
E	Cookbooks	K	Newsletters	R	Comic Books	Y	Postcards
F	Directories	L	Software Manuals	S	Direct Mail Letters	Z	Posters
		M	Textbooks	T	Envelopes	1	Stationery

Services: 4C-FF
Equipment: WO
Number of employees: 100

Comments: This plant is designed to produce only perfectbound digests. They print *TV Guide* as well as other digest-size books and publications.

MS
Hart Press
333 Central Avenue
Long Prairie, MN 56347
612-732-2121

Min: 10,000 **Max:** 500,000 **Opt:** 250,000
Sizes: 245X
Bindings: PBI-SSI
Items: DIX
Services: 4C-CS-FF-LM-TD
Equipment: 3S0(25x38)-8WO(23")
Customers: CU10-MP70-NP20
Union shop: Y
Year established: 1927
Terms: Net 30

Statement: We provide efficient, quality service for 220 short to long-run publications.

Comments: Hart is a division of Banta Corporation ($568 million in annual sales from 21 plants with 3,800 employees).

BK
Hawkes Publishing
John D Hawkes, President
3775 South 5th West
P O Box 15711
Salt Lake City, UT 84115
801-262-5555

Bindings: HCX-PBX
Items: B
Services: TY

Comments: Their specialty is genealogies.

BK
Heart of the Lakes Publishing
Walter Steesy, Owner
2989 Lodi Road
Interlaken, NY 14847-9763
607-532-4997

Min: 200 **Max:** 10,000 **Opt:** 2,000
Sizes: 235
Bindings: HCO-CBO-PBI-SSO
Items: BFH
Services: DA-TY
Customers: OR50-SP50
Terms: 1/3, 1/3, 1/3

Comments: They specialize in historical and genealogical publications.

MS
Heartland Press
520 2nd Avenue East
Spencer, IA 51301
712-262-6353; Toll-free: 800-932-9675

Min: 10,000 **Max:** 200,000 **Opt:** 75,000
Sizes: 12345
Bindings: PBO-SSI
Items: DFHIPX
Equipment: 2WO(36")
Annual sales: $5,000,000
Number of employees: 125
Turnaround times: C2M2
Customers: BP10-BU25-MP65
Union shop: N
Year established: 1976
Terms: 2% 10, Net 30

BK
Heffernan Press
Hillary Heffernan
35 New Street
P O Box 15061
Worcester, MA 01615-0061
508-791-3661; Fax: 508-754-3936
Toll-free: 800-343-6016

Min: 500 **Max:** 20,000 **Opt:** 10,000
Sizes: 2345
Bindings: HCO-CBI-GBI-
LBI-PBI-SSI-SDI-WBI
Items: BCFHLMN
Services: FF-AF-RP-WA
Equipment: 8SO(18x25-44x65)
Annual sales: $7,500,000
Number of employees: 100
Turnaround times: B2M2
Customers: BP66-BU2-CU5-MG10-NP5-
OR10-SP2
Union shop: N
Year established: 1888
Terms: Net 30 with approved credit

SERVICES				BINDINGS			
4C	4-Color Printing	RA	Rachwal System	HC	Hardcover	SD	Side Stitching
CS	Color Separations	AF	Acid-Free Paper	CB	Comb Binding	SB	Spiral Binding
DA	Design / Artwork	RP	Recycled Paper	GB	Glue Binding	WB	Wire-O Binding
FF	Fulfillment/Mailing	TY	Typesetting	LB	Loose-Leaf Binding	I	In-House
LM	List Maintenance	TD	Typeset w/ Disk	PB	Perfect Binding	O	Out of House
OC	OptiCopy System	WA	Warehousing	SS	Saddle Stitching	X	Unknown

Statement: Hefferenan Press is geared up for quick turnaround. Our production schedule is as fast as two weeks. We have a variety of text and cover stocks for you to choose from for your next job whether it's one color or four, short or medium run, 10 pages or 1000.

Henington Publishing   BK
112 W Main, P O Drawer N
Wolfe City, TX 75496
214-496-2226

Min: 100 **Max:** 3,000 **Opt:** 1,000
Sizes: 23456X
Bindings: HCI-CBI-PBI-SSI-SDI-WBI
Items: BOP
Services: 4C
Equipment: 4SO(22"-38")
Annual sales: $5,000,000
Number of employees: 75
Turnaround times: B5
Customers: BP20-BU5-SC50-SP25
Union shop: N
Year established:
Terms: 1/3 down, 1/3 blues, 1/3 finish

Comments: This is a family-owned business that does contract printing for business and government as well as genealogies and histories for self-publishing clients.

Hennegan Company   CA
311 Genesee Street
Cincinnati, OH 45202
513-621-7300

Min: 5,000 **Max:** 2,000,000 **Opt:**
Sizes: 23456X
Bindings: PBI-SSI
Items: ACPZ
Services: 4C-CS-FF
Equipment: 5LP-8SO(to 44x60)-1WO(22x38)
Annual sales: $20,000,000
Number of employees: 200

Herbick & Held Printing   GC
1117 Wolfendale Street
Pittsburgh, PA 15233
412-321-7400

Min: 10,000 **Max:** 2,000,000 **Opt:** 250,000
Sizes: 25X
Bindings: HCO-CBO-GBO-LBO-PBO-SSI-SDO-SBO-WBO
Items: ACDKPQZ
Services: 4C-DA-TY-TD
Equipment: 4S0(25x38-43x60)-2WO(23")
Annual sales: $15,000,000
Number of employees: 300
Turnaround times: C3
Customers: BU95-NP5
Union shop: Y
Year established: 1903
Terms: Net 30

Statement: Our emphasis is on printing annual reports and catalogs.

Heritage Printers   BK
William E Loftin, President
510 W Fourth Street
Charlotte, NC 28202
704-372-5784

Min: 100 **Max:** 5,000 **Opt:** 2,000
Sizes: 123456
Bindings: HCO-PBO
Items: BEH
Services: AF-TY
Equipment: 2LP(28x41)
Annual sales: $750,000
Number of employees: 12
Turnaround times: B6
Customers: BP50-CU50
Union shop: N
Year established: 1956
Terms: Net 21 days

Statement: We are almost one-of-a-kind Linotype and Monotype (hot metal) composition and letterpress printers—not as a hobby or private press, but as a commercial operation. We are trying to keep alive the proud tradition.

D B Hess Company   BK
1150 McConnell Road
Woodstock, IL 60015
815-338-6900

Min: 3,000 **Max:** 250,000 **Opt:** 30,000
Sizes: 5
Bindings: PBI-SSI-SBI

PRINTED ITEMS						
A	Annual Reports	G	Galley Copies	N	Workbooks	U Greeting Cards
B	Books	H	Journals	O	Yearbooks	V Labels / Stickers
C	Booklets	I	Magazines	P	Brochures	W Maps
D	Catalogs	J	Mass-Market Books	Q	Calendars	X Newspapers
E	Cookbooks	K	Newsletters	R	Comic Books	Y Postcards
F	Directories	L	Software Manuals	S	Direct Mail Letters	Z Posters
		M	Textbooks	T	Envelopes	1 Stationery

Items: BDFMN
Services: 4C-FF
Equipment: 2SO(28x40)-4WO(22)
Annual sales: $15,000,000
Number of employees: 75
Turnaround times: B4C2M2
Customers: BP60-BU40
Union shop: N
Year established: 1978
Terms: Net 30

Comments: They have two divisions: educational (for workbooks, lab manuals, and test booklets) and commercial (for catalogs, annual reports, and training manuals). Both divisions specialize in one standard format, 8 1/2 x 11 inches, in one, two, or four colors.

Hignell Printing   BK
Kevin Polley, Marketing Director
245 Burnell Street
Winnepeg, Manitoba R3G 2B4 Canada
204-783-7237; Fax: 204-774-4053

Min: 500 Max: 10,000 Opt: 3,000
Sizes: 1235
Bindings: HCI-CBO-LBO-
 PBI-SSI-SDO-SBO-WBO
Items: BDFHKMNV
Services: 4C-AF-RP-TY-TD
Equipment: 3SO(29"-38"-40")
Annual sales: $7,500,000
Number of employees: 50
Turnaround times: B3C3
Customers: BP70-BU5-CU15-OT10
Union shop: N
Year established: 1940
Terms: New accounts: 1/3, 1/3, 1/3

Statement: We are short-run book specialists with excellent turnaround time and top quality.

Hinz Lithographing Company   GC
1750 W Central Road
Mt Prospect, IL 60067-9990
312-253-2020

Min: 5,000 Max: 25,000,000 Opt:
Sizes: 1235
Bindings: HCO-PBO-SSI-SBO

Items: ACDIKPQSWZ
Services: 4C-CS-TY
Equipment: 2SO(25x38)-2WO(18x26)
Annual sales: $5,000,000
Number of employees: 100
Turnaround times: B3C3M2
Customers: BU98-SC2
Union shop: N
Year established: 1947
Terms: Net 30

A B Hirschfeld Press   GC
Trent Cunningham, Marketing Director
5200 Smith Road
Denver, CO 80216
303-320-8500; Fax: 303-329-3111

Min: 10,000 Max: 1,500,000 Opt: 75,000
Sizes: 123456X
Bindings: HCI-CBI-LBI-
 PBI-SSI-SDI-SBI-WBI
Items: ABCDEHIKLPQSTUWYZ
Services: 4C-CS-DA-FF-RP-TY-TD-WA
Equipment: 11SO-4WO(22x36-31x46)
Annual sales: $30,000,000
Number of employees: 250
Turnaround times: B3C2M2
Customers: BP5-BU70-CU3-
 MP3-SC5-SP3-OT11
Union shop: Y
Year established: 1920
Terms: 50% down, balance prior to ship

Statement: We are proud to have the reputation of quality and on-time delivery in an industry full of empty promises. Please call for a competitive bid.

Hoechstetter Printing   GC
218 N Braddock Avenue
Pittsburgh, PA 15208
412-241-8200; Fax: 412-242-3835

Bindings: PBI-SSI
Items: BCDIN
Services: 4C
Equipment: SO

Comments: A division of Graphics Industries of Atlanta ($310 million in annual sales from 38 plants with 3,070 employees).

SERVICES			BINDINGS		
4C	4-Color Printing	RA Rachwal System	HC Hardcover	SD Side Stitching
CS	Color Separations	AF Acid-Free Paper	CB Comb Binding	SB Spiral Binding
DA	Design / Artwork	RP Recycled Paper	GB Glue Binding	WB Wire-O Binding
FF	Fulfillment/Mailing	TY Typesetting	LB Loose-Leaf Binding	I In-House
LM	List Maintenance	TD Typeset w/ Disk	PB Perfect Binding	O Out of House
OC	OptiCopy System	WA Warehousing	SS Saddle Stitching	X Unknown

MS
Holladay-Tyler Printing Corp.
Graden Laycook
7100 Holladay-Tyler Road
Glenn Dale, MD 20769
301-464-6066; Toll-free: 800-444-8953

Min: 20,000 **Max:** 2,000,000 **Opt:**
Bindings: HCX-PBX-SSX-SDX
Items: BCDFHIN
Services: 4C
Equipment: WO
Annual sales: $53,000,000
Number of employees: 530

Comments: Holladay-Tyler is a division of
Southam Printing of Toronto, Ontario
($586 million in annual sales from 21
plants with 4,200 employees).

BK
Holyoke Lithography
Daniel Byrne, Marketing Director
655 Page Boulevard
Springfield, MA 01104
413-732-7405; Fax: 413-731-8961

Min: 1,000 **Max:** 2,000,000 **Opt:**
Sizes: 123456
Bindings: HCO-CBO-LBO-PBO-
    SSO-SDO-SBO-WBO
Items: BCDEFLMNPQ
Services: 4C
Equipment: 5SO(to 54x77)
Annual sales: $2,500,000
Turnaround times: B4M4
Customers: BP75-OT25
Union shop: Y

Comments: Holyoke is owned by Quebecor Printing ($1.7 billion in annual sales
from 60 plants with 10,000 employees).

BK
Hooven-Dayton Corporation
430 Leo Street
Dayton, OH 45404
513-224-110

Min: 500 **Max:** 75,000 **Opt:** 25,000
Sizes: 25
Bindings: CBI-PBI-SSI
Items: ABCDEFHIKLMNP
Services: TY-WA

Year established: 195?
Terms: Net 30

Comments: They have been printing for
the U.S. Government Printing Office for
30 years but are now branching out to do
more private sector work.

BK
Horowitz/Rae Book Manufacturers
Alan Horowitz, VP Marketing
300 Fairfield Road
P O Box 1308
Fairfield, NJ 07006
201-575-7070; Fax: 201-575-4565

Min: 1,000 **Max:** 250,000 **Opt:** 15,000
Sizes: 123456X
Bindings: HCI-PBI-SSO-SDI-SBO-WBO
Items: BDEM
Services: 4C-CS-FF-AF-WA
Equipment: 8SO(20x28-54x77)-
    1WO(22x36)
Annual sales: $30,000,000
Number of employees: 400
Turnaround times: B5
Customers: BP90-CU2-OR8
Union shop: N
Year established: 1920
Terms: Net 30

Statement: We specialize in manufacturing
high quality 4-color juvenile and art books
(as well as duotone and B&W illustrated
books). We also print and finish book jackets and covers. We received the 1989 LMP
award in book manufacturing.

GC
Humboldt National Graphics
380 North Avenue
North Abington, MA 02351
617-878-6373; Toll-free: 800-344-1033

Min: 5,000 **Max:** 2,000,000 **Opt:**
Sizes: 2345X
Bindings: SSI
Items: DIPS
Services: 4C-TY-FF
Equipment: 6SO(to 40")-7WO(23x38)
Annual sales: $16,000,000
Number of employees: 210

PRINTED ITEMS							
A	Annual Reports	G	Galley Copies	N	Workbooks	U	Greeting Cards
B	Books	H	Journals	O	Yearbooks	V	Labels / Stickers
C	Booklets	I	Magazines	P	Brochures	W	Maps
D	Catalogs	J	Mass-Market Books	Q	Calendars	X	Newspapers
E	Cookbooks	K	Newsletters	R	Comic Books	Y	Postcards
F	Directories	L	Software Manuals	S	Direct Mail Letters	Z	Posters
		M	Textbooks	T	Envelopes	1	Stationery

Comments: They have 4 printing plants: Humboldt Press in N. Abington, Massachusetts; Humboldt Printing in Fortuna, California; Journal Press in Belfast, Maine; and Portland Litho in Portland, Maine.

GC

Hunter Publishing Company
2505 Empire Drive
Winston-Salem, NC 27113
919-765-0070

Min: 1,000 **Max:** 1,000,000 **Opt:** 30,000
Sizes: 123456
Bindings: HCI-CBO-GBI-LBO-
　　PBI-SSI-SDI-SBO-WBO
Items: ABCDEFGHIKLMNOPQXYZ
Services: 4C-CS-DA-TY-TD-WA
Equipment: 8SO(25x38-28x40)
Annual sales: $23,000,000
Number of employees: 375
Turnaround times: B5C3M3
Customers: BP5-BU40-CU50-MP5
Union shop: N
Terms: Net 30

I

BK

Independent Printing Company
5-15 49th Avenue
Long Island City, NY 11101
212-689-5100

Min: 25 **Max:** 2,000 **Opt:** 1,000
Sizes: 235
Bindings: CBI-LBI-PBI-SSI-WBI
Items: BGHP
Equipment: SO-miniWO
Terms: Net 30 with credit approval

Comments: They specialize in printing and ultra-short runs, from 25 to 2500 copies.

BR

Independent Publishing Company
Ned Burke, Marketing Director
P O Box 15126
Sarasota, FL 34277
813-366-9850

Min: none **Max:** 2,000 **Opt:** 500
Sizes: 25
Bindings: HCO-CBO-PBI-SSI-SDI
Items: BCDEFIKPST1
Services: DA-TY-TD
Equipment: 3SO
Annual sales: $250,000
Number of employees: 4
Turnaround times: B4C2
Customers: BU5-MP5-SP90
Union shop: N
Year established: 1986
Terms: Payable in advance

Statement: We try to provide a low-cost, high- quality option for self-publishers who want a personal working relationship with their printer. We especially enjoy helping writers with short-run books. Independent also publishes *New Writer's Magazette*.

BK

Infopress/Saratoga Printing Co.
Robert Beach, Estimator
120 Henry Street
Saratoga Springs, NY 12866
518-584-2054; Fax: 518-587-9077

Min: 500 **Max:** 50,000 **Opt:** 10,000
Sizes: 23456
Bindings: HCO-CBI-PBO-SSI-SBO-WBO
Items: ABCDEFHIKLMNPQSTWYZ1
Services: 4C-AF-RP-TY-TD
Equipment: 5SO(up to 41")
Annual sales: $1,000,000
Number of employees: 21
Turnaround times: B4C3
Customers: BP5-BU75-CU20
Union shop: N
Year established: 1947
Terms: 50% down, 50% on delivery

Statement: We produce books, signatures, covers, dustjackets, and more. We do high quality color work at a fairly reasonable price.

GC

Inland Lithograph Company
1201 Pratt Boulevard
Elk Grove Village, IL 60007-5780
312-965-0500

SERVICES				BINDINGS			
4C	4-Color Printing	RA	Rachwal System	HC	Hardcover	SD	Side Stitching
CS	Color Separations	AF	Acid-Free Paper	CB	Comb Binding	SB	Spiral Binding
DA	Design / Artwork	RP	Recycled Paper	GB	Glue Binding	WB	Wire-O Binding
FF	Fulfillment/Mailing	TY	Typesetting	LB	Loose-Leaf Binding	I	In-House
LM	List Maintenance	TD	Typeset w/ Disk	PB	Perfect Binding	O	Out of House
OC	OptiCopy System	WA	Warehousing	SS	Saddle Stitching	X	Unknown

Min: 1,000 Max: 1,000,000 Opt: 375,000
Sizes: 123456
Bindings: HCO-CBO-GBO-LBO-
PBO-SSO-SCO-SBO-WBO
Items: ABCDEFKLMNPQSTWZ
Services: 4C
Equipment: 3SO(55x78)-2WO(17x26)
Annual sales: $12,000,000
Number of employees: 115
Turnaround times: B2C1
Customers: 10BP-90BU
Union shop: Y
Year established: 1904
Terms: Net 30

Statement: Inland is a service-oriented lithographer of informational products and promotional components. We specialize in "Color Lithography At Its Best."

Insert Color Press   **MG**
90 Air Park Drive
Ronkonkoma, NY 11779
516-981-5300; Toll-free: 800-356-3943

Sizes: 5X
Bindings: SSI
Items: IX

Intelligencer Printing   **CA**
Stephen J Brody, Sales Manager
330 Eden Road, P O Box 1768
Lancaster, PA 17601
717-291-3100; Toll-free: 800-233-0107

Min: 25,000 Max: 2,000,000 Opt:
Sizes: 23456X
Bindings: PBI-SSI-SDI
Items: ADIPQUZ
Services: 4C-CS
Equipment: SO-WO
Annual sales: $23,000,000
Number of employees: 225
Year established: 1794

Statement: Write for a copy of their *Intellectual* newsletter.

Interstate Printers   **BK**
19 N Jackson Street, P O Box 594
Danville, IL 61832-0594
217-446-0500

Min: 300 Max: 100,000 Opt: 20,000
Sizes: 2345X
Bindings: HCI-CBI-PBI-SSI-SBI
Items: ABCDEFJILMNP
Services: 4C-DA-FF-TY-WA
Equipment: SO-WO
Year established: 1908
Terms: Net 30 with approved credit

Comments: Interstate is both a printer and a publisher. They print monthly and quarterly magazines as well as some general commercial printing. They also publish textbooks and related materials (with over 1200 active titles) in the fields of agriculture and special education.

Interstate Printing Company   **CA**
2002 N 16th Street
P O Box 3667
Omaha, NE 68103
402-341-8028

Min: 3,000 Max: 2,000,000 Opt:
Sizes: 25X
Bindings: GBI-SSX
Items: ABCDKNPQRSWXYZ
Services: 4C-FF-TY-TD-WA
Equipment: CB-LP-SO-WO
Annual sales: $5,000,000
Number of employees: 125
Turnaround times: B5C2M2
Customers: BU75-CU15-NP5-SC5
Union shop: Y
Year established: 1917
Terms: Net 10 following month

Comments: They specialize in gang printing and mailing of insurance company letters, magazines with print runs between 20,000 and 500,000, and direct mail catalogs and inserts with runs between 50,000 and 1,000,000.

J

Japs-Olson Company   **GC**
30 N 31st Avenue
Minneapolis, MN 55411
612-522-4461

PRINTED ITEMS						
A	Annual Reports	G	Galley Copies	N	Workbooks	U	Greeting Cards
B	Books	H	Journals	O	Yearbooks	V	Labels / Stickers
C	Booklets	I	Magazines	P	Brochures	W	Maps
D	Catalogs	J	Mass-Market Books	Q	Calendars	X	Newspapers
E	Cookbooks	K	Newsletters	R	Comic Books	Y	Postcards
F	Directories	L	Software Manuals	S	Direct Mail Letters	Z	Posters
		M	Textbooks	T	Envelopes	1	Stationery

Sizes: 23456
Bindings: SSI
Items: CDKPSTV
Services: 4C-FF-TY
Equipment: 8SO(to 26x40)-7WO(to 26x23)
Annual sales: $23,000,000
Number of employees: 225
Turnaround times: C2M2
Customers: BU65-MP20-NP10-SP5
Union shop: N
Terms: Net 30

Comments: We are complete printers for the direct marketing industry: order envelopes, web and sheetfed catalogs, service bureau, and mailing.

Jersey Printing Company　MS
Steven Schnoll, President
111 Linnet Street
P O Box 79
Bayonne, NJ 07002
201-436-4200; Fax: 201-436-0116

Min: 100 Max: 50,000 Opt: 10,000
Sizes: 123456
Bindings: PBI-SSI
Items: ABCDFHIKPQYZ
Services: 4C-CS-DA-FF-TY-TD-WA
Equipment: 9LP-5SO(20x28-25x38)
Annual sales: $20,000,000
Number of employees: 125
Turnaround times: B5C4M2
Customers: BP3-BU36-
　　CU5-MP38-NP5-OT13
Union shop: Y
Year established: 1910
Terms: Net 30

Statement: Jersey prints museum and gallery quality posters, catalogs of art reproductions, annual reports, house organs, publications, and advertising brochures.

The Job Shop　GC
P O Box 305
Woods Hole, MA 02543
617-548-9600

Min: 100 Max: Opt: 1,000
Sizes: 12345
Bindings: HCO-CBI-LBI-PBI-SSI-SDI

Items: BCDFKLNPSTVY1
Services: DA-TY-TD
Equipment: 2SO(11x17-14x18)
Annual sales: $200,000
Number of employees: 5
Turnaround times: B4C3
Customers: BP10-BU25-CU5-
　　NP15-OR20-SP5-OT2
Union shop: N
Year established: 1967
Terms: 30% down, 30% delivery, net 30

Statement: Our goal is to be as adaptable as possible to the needs of short-run publishers of books and newsletters.

JohnsBryne Microdot　MS
7350 Croname Road
Niles, IL 60648-3932
312-647-2211; Fax: 312-647-2238

Bindings: SSI
Items: DIKQZ
Services: 4C-CS
Equipment: SO

Johnson & Hardin Company　MS
Andrew M Jamison
3600 Red Bank Road
Cincinnati, OH 45227
513-271-8874; Fax: 513-271-3603

Min: 5,000 Max: 2,000,000 Opt: 100,000
Sizes: 2345X
Bindings: HCX-PBX-SBX
Items: ABCDEFHIKLMNP
Services: 4C-TY
Equipment: LP-SO-WO
Year established: 1902

Johnson Graphics　GC
120 Frentress Lake Road
East Dubuque, IL 61025
815-747-6511

Min: 2,000 Max: 50,000 Opt:
Sizes: 2345X
Bindings: SSI
Items: ACDFIKNP
Services: FF
Equipment: SO

SERVICES		BINDINGS		
4C 4-Color Printing	RA Rachwal System	HC Hardcover	SD Side Stitching	
CS Color Separations	AF Acid-Free Paper	CB Comb Binding	SB Spiral Binding	
DA Design / Artwork	RP Recycled Paper	GB Glue Binding	WB Wire-O Binding	
FF Fulfillment/Mailing	TY Typesetting	LB Loose-Leaf Binding	I In-House	
LM List Maintenance	TD Typeset w/ Disk	PB Perfect Binding	O Out of House	
OC OptiCopy System	WA Warehousing	SS Saddle Stitching	X Unknown	

Johnson Publishing Company **GC**
Dennis Collier
1880 South 57th Court, P O Box 990
Boulder, CO 80306
303-443-1576; Fax: 303-443-1679

Min: 500 Max: 50,000 Opt: 5,000
Sizes: 23456X
Bindings: HCO-CBI-LBI-PBI-
   SSI-SDO-SBI-WBI
Items: BCDEFHKLP
Services: 4C-DA-FF-AF-RP-TY-TD-WA
Equipment: 8SO(to 28x40)-1WO
Annual sales: $18,000,000
Number of employees: 150
Turnaround times: B3C3
Customers: BP25-BU65-CU3-NP5-SP2
Union shop: N
Year established: 1946
Terms: Net 30

Statement: We are a fully integrated manufacturer of print and related services. We provide commercial printing and many types of book production to business, publishers, and educational institutions.

Jostens / Clarksville **BK**
1312 Dickson Highway, P O Box 923
Clarksville, TN 37040
615-647-5211

Min: 100 Max: 100,000 Opt: 10,000
Sizes: 123456X
Bindings: HCI-CBI-PBI-SSI-SBI
Items: BCDEINOQZ
Services: 4C-CS-DA-TY-TD
Equipment: many SO(25x38)
Annual sales: $153,000,000
Number of employees: 8,000
Union shop: N
Year established: 1950
Terms: Net 30 with approved credit

Statement: A yearbook publisher with divisions in CA, KS, PA, and TN.

Jostens / State College **BK**
401 Science Park Road, P O Box 297
State College, PA 16801
814-237-5771

Min: 100 Max: 100,000 Opt: 10,000
Sizes: 123456X
Bindings: HCI-CBI-PBI-SSI-SBI
Items: BCDEINOQZ
Services: 4C-CS-DA-TY-TD
Equipment: many SO(25x38)
Union shop: N
Terms: Net 30 with approved credit

Jostens / Topeka **BK**
4000 S Adams Street, P O Box 1903
Topeka, KS 66609
913-266-3300

Min: 100 Max: 100,000 Opt: 10,000
Sizes: 123456X
Bindings: HCI-CBI-PBI-SSI-SBI
Items: BCDEINOQZ
Services: 4C-CS-DA-TY-TD
Equipment: many SO(25x38)
Union shop: N
Terms: Net 30 with approved credit

Jostens / Visalia **BK**
29625 Road 84, P O Box 991
Visalia, CA 93279
209-651-3300

Min: 100 Max: 100,000 Opt: 10,000
Sizes: 123456X
Bindings: HCI-CBO-GBO-LBO-
   PBI-SSI-SDI-SBO-WBO
Items: BCDEFHILNOPQSYZ
Services: 4C-CS-DA-TY
Equipment: 7SO(25x38)
Turnaround times: B4C4M4
Customers: BP5-BU30-MP35-
   OR8-SC10-SP8-OT4
Union shop: N
Terms: 35% down, 35% proofs, 30% net30

Judd's Incorporated **MS**
1500 Eckington Place NE
Washington, DC 20002
202-635-1200

Bindings: PBI-SSI
Items: I
Annual sales: $113,000,000
Number of employees: 1,200

GC

Julin Printing
Ruth Julin, President
225 S Locust Street
Monticello, IA 52310
319-365-2135

Min: 2,000 **Max:** 2,000,000 **Opt:** 10,000
Sizes: 123456
Bindings: HCO-CBI-GBI-LBI-
    PBI-SSI-SDI-SBI-WBI
Items: ABCDEFIKPQSTUWYZ1
Services: 4C-CS-DA-AF
Equipment: 6SO(17"-61")
Annual sales: $5,000,000
Number of employees: 20
Turnaround times: B3C3M3
Customers: BP10-BU60-CU20-MP10
Union shop: N
Year established: 1954
Terms: Net 30

K

GC

K & S Graphics
601 Hagan Street
Nashville, TN 37203
615-242-3474

Sizes: 2345X
Bindings: SSI
Items: ACDKPZ1
Services: 4C-DA-TY

Comments: A two-color specialist, they
can design, typeset, and print newsletters,
booklets, and catalogs.

CA

K-B Offset Printing
1006 W College Avenue
State College, PA 16801
814-238-8445

Sizes: 2345X
Bindings: SSI
Items: ACDIKP
Services: 4C

Statement: 4-color brochures at prices
you've been looking for. Also catalogs,
reports, and periodicals.

GC

K/P Graphics San Diego
420 Andreasen Drive
Escondido, CA 92026
619-745-3666

Min: 1,000 **Max:** 100,000 **Opt:** 10,000
Sizes: 123456
Bindings: HCO-CBO-GBO-LBI-
    PBO-SSI-SDI-SBO-WBO
Items: ABCDEFIKLMNPQSTVYZ1
Services: 4C-CS-DA-FF-TY-TD-WA
Equipment: 5SO(1lxl7-28x40)
Annual sales: $52,500,000
Number of employees: 625
Turnaround times: B4C3M3
Customers: BP10-BU60-CU5-
    MP2-OR1-SP2-OT20
Union shop: N
Year established: 1970
Terms: Net 30

Comments: Headquartered in Berkeley,
California.

CA

Kable Printing Company
404 N Wesley Avenue
Mount Morris, IL 61054
815-734-4121; Toll-free: 800-678-6299

Min: 250,000 **Max:** 2,000,000 **Opt:**
Sizes: 235X
Bindings: PBI-SSI
Items: DX
Services: 4C-CS-FF
Equipment: 8WO-13OT(gravure)

Comments: A division of Quebecor.

GC

Kaufman Press Printing
Gary J Dedell
P O Box 68
Syracuse, NY 13207
315-471-1817

Min: 1,000 **Max:** 20,000 **Opt:**
Sizes: 123456X
Bindings: HCO-DBI-GBI-LBI-
    PBO-SSI-SDI-SBO-WBO
Items: ACDHIKLPQSTVWXYZ1
Services: 4C-CS-DA-FF-TY-WA
Equipment: 14LP-11SO-5WO
Annual sales: $1,000,000

SERVICES				BINDINGS			
4C	4-Color Printing	RA	Rachwal System	HC	Hardcover	SD	Side Stitching
CS	Color Separations	AF	Acid-Free Paper	CB	Comb Binding	SB	Spiral Binding
DA	Design / Artwork	RP	Recycled Paper	GB	Glue Binding	WB	Wire-O Binding
FF	Fulfillment/Mailing	TY	Typesetting	LB	Loose-Leaf Binding	I	In-House
LM	List Maintenance	TD	Typeset w/ Disk	PB	Perfect Binding	O	Out of House
OC	OptiCopy System	WA	Warehousing	SS	Saddle Stitching	X	Unknown

Number of employees: 50
Turnaround times: B3C2M2
Customers: BP5-BU60-CU5-
MP5-NP20-OR8-SC5
Union shop: Y
Year established: 1910
Terms: 1% 10, net 20

Kaumagraph Corporation **GC**
14 & Poplar Streets
Wilmington, DE 19899
302-575-1500

Equipment: WO-OT(gravure/silk screen)

Kern International **GC**
Chris Korites
190 Duckhill Road
Duxbury, MA 02332
617-871-4982

Min: 120 Max: 100,000 Opt: 1,000
Sizes: 123456
Bindings: CBI-GBI-LBI-PBI-SSI-SBI-WBI
Items: ABCDEFGKLMNPQSW1
Services: DA-FF-LM-TY-TD-WA
Equipment: 1SO(12x18)
Annual sales: $400,000
Number of employees: 25
Turnaround times: B2C2
Union shop: N
Year established: 1985
Terms: C.O.D.

Kimberly Press **BK**
Bill McNally, President
P O Box 399, 5390 Overpass Road
Santa Barbara, CA 93111-2008
805-964-6469

Min: 500 Max: 5,000 Opt: 2,000
Sizes: 2345
Bindings: HCI-PBI-SSI
Items: BCGHI
Services: 4C-FF

Statement: We are serious local printers in
a high overhead resort area. Our prices
will never be as low as printers in
Michigan. We specialize in producing
scholarly books and journals.

KNI Book Manufacturing **BK**
1261 S State College Parkway
Anaheim, CA 92806
714-956-7300; Fax: 714-635-1744

Min: 200 Max: 25,000 Opt: 5,000
Sizes: 12345
Bindings: CBX-LBX-PBX-
SSX-SCX-SBX-WBX
Items: BCDEFHLMNRS
Equipment: 2SO(12x18-14x20)-
2WO(11x17-22x17)
Annual sales: $5,000,000
Number of employees: 125
Turnaround times: B3C3
Customers: BP50-BU30-CU5-SC5-SP10
Union shop: N
Year established: 1970
Terms: Various

The Kordet Group **CA**
15 Neil Court
Oceanside, NY 11572
516-766-4111

Sizes: 5
Bindings: SSI
Items: DP
Services: 4C-CS-DA-TY
Equipment: SO
Annual sales: $40,000,000
Number of employees: 375

C J Krehbiel Company **BK**
3962 Virginia Avenue
Cincinnati, OH 45227
513-271-6035

Min: 3,000 Max: 250,000 Opt:
Sizes: 23456X
Bindings: HCI-CBI-PBI-SSI-SBI
Items: BDN
Services: 4C
Equipment: SO-WO
Annual sales: $10,000,000
Number of employees: 150
Terms: Net 30

Comments: They specialize in printing
trade books and workbooks in one, two, or
four colors.

PRINTED ITEMS					
A	Annual Reports	G	Galley Copies	N	Workbooks	U	Greeting Cards
B	Books	H	Journals	O	Yearbooks	V	Labels / Stickers
C	Booklets	I	Magazines	P	Brochures	W	Maps
D	Catalogs	J	Mass-Market Books	Q	Calendars	X	Newspapers
E	Cookbooks	K	Newsletters	R	Comic Books	Y	Postcards
F	Directories	L	Software Manuals	S	Direct Mail Letters	Z	Posters
		M	Textbooks	T	Envelopes	1	Stationery

L

Lancaster Press
MS

Prince & Lemon Streets
Lancaster, PA 17603
717-394-7241

Min: 5,000 Max: 95,000 Opt:
Sizes: 235
Bindings: PBI-SSI
Items: BDHI
Services: 4C-CS-FF-TY-TD
Equipment: SO-WO
Annual sales: $17,000,000
Number of employees: 225

The Lane Press
MS

305 Saint Paul Street
Burlington, VT 05401
802-863-5555

Min: 2,000 Max: 2,000,000 Opt:
Sizes: 2345X
Bindings: PBI-SSI
Items: BCDHI
Services: 4C-FF-TY-TD
Equipment: SO-WO
Annual sales: $27,000,000
Number of employees: 300

Lasky Company
CA

67 E Willow Street
Milburn, NJ 07041
201-376-9200

Min: 5,000 Max: 2,000,000 Opt:
Sizes: 2345X
Bindings: PBO-SSO
Items: ACDIKPXZ
Services: 4C-CS-TY
Equipment: 4SO(25x39-28x40)-
    4WO(to 23x38)
Annual sales: $60,000,000
Number of employees: 430
Year established: 1917

Statement: We love to print jobs that
other printers say are too tough or impos-
sible to do. Because that's where we always
show our true colors.

Latham Process Corporation
GC

200 Hudson Street
New York, NY 10013
212-966-4500

Sizes: 2345
Bindings: GBI-LBI-PBI-SSI-SDI
Items: CDFHIKLMNPX
Services: 4C-TY-TD
Equipment: 8SO-7WO
Annual sales: $30,000,000
Number of employees: 400
Turnaround times: C1M1
Customers: BU95
Union shop: Y
Year established: 1940

Comments: A financial printer as well as a
general commercial printer.

Lawson Graphics
GC

3620 Lakeshore Boulevard W
Toronto, Ontario M8W 1N9 Canada
416-251-3171

Min: 25,000 Max: 5,000,000 Opt: 1,000,000
Sizes: 123456
Bindings: HCO-PBO-SSI-SDO-SBO-WBO
Items: ACDIPQ
Services: 4C
Equipment: 5WO(17x26-45x56)
Annual sales: $35,000,000
Number of employees: 125
Turnaround times: C1M1
Union shop: Y
Year established: 1972

Statement: We specialize in 4-color printing on coated stock.

Legacy Books
BK

2901 4th Street SE
Minneapolis, MN 55414
Toll-free: 800-367-BOOK

The Lehigh Press
GC

Cooper Parkway Building West
7001 N Park Drive
Pennsauken, NJ 08109
609-665-5200

SERVICES				BINDINGS			
4C	4-Color Printing	RA	Rachwal System	HC	Hardcover	SD	Side Stitching
CS	Color Separations	AF	Acid-Free Paper	CB	Comb Binding	SB	Spiral Binding
DA	Design / Artwork	RP	Recycled Paper	GB	Glue Binding	WB	Wire-O Binding
FF	Fulfillment/Mailing	TY	Typesetting	LB	Loose-Leaf Binding	I	In-House
LM	List Maintenance	TD	Typeset w/ Disk	PB	Perfect Binding	O	Out of House
OC	OptiCopy System	WA	Warehousing	SS	Saddle Stitching	X	Unknown

Min: 20,000 Max: 2,000,000 Opt:
Sizes: 23456X
Bindings: SSI
Items: ADIPSTWYZ
Services: 4C-CS-LM
Equipment: WO
Annual sales: $162,000,000
Number of employees: 1,060
Year established: 1924

Comments: Lehigh prints magazines,
catalogs, direct mail components, inserts,
book covers, and book jackets.

Lehigh Press / Cadillac   GC
25th & Lexington Street
Broadview, IL 60153
312-681-0333

Min: 20,000 Max: 2,000,000 Opt:
Sizes: 23456X
Bindings: SSI
Items: ADIPSTWYZ
Services: 4C-CS-LM
Equipment: WO

Comments: This division of Lehigh specializes in printing direct mail components,
magazine inserts, and point of purchase
selling aids.

Lehigh Press / Dallas   MG
1515 Round Table Drive
Dallas, TX 75247
214-631-3130

Min: 20,000 Max: 2,000,000 Opt:
Sizes: 23456X
Bindings: SSI
Items: ADIPSTYZ
Services: 4C-CS-LM
Equipment: WO

Statement: This plant prints digest-sized
publications, including the Southwest edition of *TV Guide*, as well as catalogs.

Les Editions Marquis   BK
305 E Tache Boulevard
Montmagny, Quebec G5V 1C7 Canada
418-248-0737

Min: 300 Max: 10,000 Opt: 2,000
Sizes: 24
Bindings: HCO-CBO-GBO-LBO-
    PBI-SSO-SDO-SBO-WBO
Items: ABCDEFLMNOPWZ
Services: 4C-CS-AF-TY-TD
Equipment: 6SO(19x25-28x40)
Annual sales: $4,000,000
Number of employees: 35
Turnaround times: B3C3
Customers: BP70-BU5-CU15-SP5-OT5
Union shop: Y
Year established: 1937
Terms: Net 30

Statement: We print top quality paperbacks and color publications and are competitive for low runs.

Liberty York Graphic Industries   GC
Marketing Director
171 Greenwich Street
Hempstead, NY 11550
516-481-8500

Min: 10 Max: 100,000 Opt: 15,000
Sizes: 2345X
Bindings: HCO-CBI-PBI-SSI-SBI
Items: ABCDFHKNP
Services: TY
Equipment: SO
Terms: Net 30 with approved credit

Comments: A full-service commercial
printer, they produce short-run, multi-page
newsletters, reports, financial statements,
and brochures.

Litho Prestige   BK
Marketing Director
1330 Michaud
Drummondville, Quebec, Canada
819-472-1171

Min: 10,000 Max: 2,000,000 Opt: 20,000
Sizes: 2345X
Bindings: PBI
Items: BCDFJMN
Services: 4C
Equipment: CB-WO

PRINTED ITEMS						
A	Annual Reports	G	Galley Copies	N	Workbooks	U	Greeting Cards
B	Books	H	Journals	O	Yearbooks	V	Labels / Stickers
C	Booklets	I	Magazines	P	Brochures	W	Maps
D	Catalogs	J	Mass-Market Books	Q	Calendars	X	Newspapers
E	Cookbooks	K	Newsletters	R	Comic Books	Y	Postcards
F	Directories	L	Software Manuals	S	Direct Mail Letters	Z	Posters
		M	Textbooks	T	Envelopes	1	Stationery

Litho Specialties
GC

Duane Pogue
1280 Energy Park Drive
Saint Paul, MN 55108
612-644-3000; Fax: 612-644-4839

Min: 3,000 **Max:** 1,000,000 **Opt:** 10,000
Sizes: 123456X
Bindings: HCO-CBO-
    SSI-SDO-SBO-WBO
Items: ABCDEPQSUZ
Services: 4C-CS-AF-RP
Equipment: 5SO(28x40)-1WO(17x26)
Annual sales: $15,000,000
Number of employees: 145
Turnaround times: B2
Customers: BP5-BU85-CU5-OR5
Union shop: N
Year established: 1975
Terms: Net 30

Statement: Litho Specialties produces four, five, and six-color fine photography and art books and catalogs. We also produce annual reports and commercial catalogs.

Lithocolor Press
BK

John Matheson, General Manager
9825 W Roosevelt Road
Westchester, IL 60153
708-345-5530; Fax: 708-345-1283

Min: 3,000 **Max:** 100,000 **Opt:** 15,000
Sizes: 123456X
Bindings: HCO-CBO-LBO-
    PBI-SSI-SDO-SBO-WBO
Items: BCDFIJLN
Services: 4C-AF
Equipment: 3SO(23x29-25x38)-
    2WO(22"-38")
Annual sales: $7,500,000
Number of employees: 66
Turnaround times: B4C3
Customers: BP45-CU5-MP5-NP45
Union shop: N
Year established:
Terms: Net 30

Statement: We are a service-oriented company with sufficient flexibility in our operations to enable us to cater to our customer's needs.

LithoCraft
GC

50 Broad Street
Carlstadt, NJ 07072
201-939-6440; Toll-free: 800-223-0574

Min: 500 **Max:** 1,500,000 **Opt:**
Sizes: 123456X
Bindings: CBO-GBI-LBO-PBO-
    SSI-SDI-SBO-WBO
Items: ABCDEIPQVZ
Services: 4C-CS-FF
Equipment: 3SO(25x38-38x50)-
    3WO(17x26-24x38)
Annual sales: $25,000,000
Number of employees: 150
Turnaround times: B4C3M3
Customers: BU70-CU5-MP5-NP10-OR10
Union shop: Y
Terms: Net 30

Statement: We specialize in all areas of commercial printing — catalogs, direct mail flyers, point of purchase display sheets, and posters in long and short runs.

Little River Press
BK

55 NE 73rd Street
Miami, FL 33138
305-757-7504

Min: 1,000 **Max:** 500,000 **Opt:** 15,000
Sizes: 125
Bindings: HCO-PBI-SSI
Items: ABCDFHIJKNP
Services: 4C
Terms: 1% 10, Net 30

Long Island Web Printing
CA

Janice Kerner, Sales Manager
26 Jericho Turnpike
Jericho, NY 11753
516-997-7000; Fax: 516-334-4055

Min: 5,000 **Max:** 500,000 **Opt:** 250,000
Sizes: 45X
Bindings: GBI-SSI
Items: CDFX
Services: 4C-DA-TY
Equipment: 2WO(22x35)
Annual sales: $2,500,000
Number of employees: 30

Turnaround times: C1
Customers: BU70-CU10-SP10-OT10
Union shop: N
Year established: 1967
Terms: Net 30

Statement: A division of Marks-Roiland Communications, we specialize in the printing and handling of lightweight paper stocks such as newsprint, groundwood, and directory stock. We also offer cheshire mailing services.

Longacrea Press   GC
85 Weyman Avenue
New Rochelle, NY 10805
914-235-9700

Min: 1,000 **Max:** 50,000 **Opt:**
Sizes: 23456X
Bindings:
Items: PSYZ
Services: 4C-CS
Equipment: SO

Comments: This general commercial printer specializes in fine art reproductions, book covers and jackets, and promotional pieces.

John D Lucas Printing Company   BK
1820 Portal Street
Baltimore, MD 21224
301-633-4200; Toll-free: 800-638-2850

Min: 1,000 **Max:** 500,000 **Opt:**
Sizes: 23456X
Bindings: HCI-PBI-SSI
Items: ABCDFHIKMNPQSUYZ
Services: 4C-CS-TY
Equipment: 6SO(to 58")-2WO(22x36)
Annual sales: $30,000,000
Number of employees: 320
Terms: 1/3 down, 1/3 proofs, 1/3 done

Comments: This commercial printer produces lottery tickets, game boards, cards, calendars, posters, catalogs, annual reports, books, directories, technical journals, and textbooks.

M

Mack Printing   MS
20th & Northampton Streets
Easton, PA 18042
215-258-9111

Min: 10,000 **Max:** 500,000 **Opt:** 80,000
Sizes: 56X
Bindings: PBI-SSI
Items: DFHILX
Services: 4C-DA-FF-LM-TY-TD-WA
Equipment: 7SO(18x25-25x38)-6WO(23x38)
Annual sales: $55,000,000
Number of employees: 621
Turnaround times: C3M3
Customers: MP40-OR60
Union shop: N
Year established: 1907
Terms: Net 30

Comments: Mack recently bought Monroe Printing (which includes Science Press and Hughes Printing).

Mackintosh Typography   BK
Lynne Stark, Estimator
319 Anacapa Street
Santa Barbara, CA 93101
805-962-9915

Min: 300 **Max:** 3,000 **Opt:** 2,000
Sizes: 123456
Bindings: HCO-PBI-SSI
Items: BCDHIKPVYZ
Services: 4C-CS-DA-TY-TD
Equipment: 1LP(10x15)-1SO(18x25)
Number of employees: 10
Customers: BP60-CU10-SP15-OT15
Union shop: N
Terms: 1/2 down, 1/2 on completion

Statement: We do fine book production for literary and academic publishers.

Maclean Hunter Printing   MG
4601 Yonge Street, City of North York
Willowdale, Ontario M2N 5L9 Canada
416-221-1131

PRINTED ITEMS						
A	Annual Reports	G	Galley Copies	N	Workbooks	U	Greeting Cards
B	Books	H	Journals	O	Yearbooks	V	Labels / Stickers
C	Booklets	I	Magazines	P	Brochures	W	Maps
D	Catalogs	J	Mass-Market Books	Q	Calendars	X	Newspapers
E	Cookbooks	K	Newsletters	R	Comic Books	Y	Postcards
F	Directories	M	Textbooks	S	Direct Mail Letters	Z	Posters
				T	Envelopes	1	Stationery

Min: 20,000 Max: 2,000,000 Opt:
Sizes: 25X
Bindings: PBI-SSI
Items: DHIP
Services: 4C-CS-TY
Equipment: 7SO-7WO
Annual sales: $75,000,000
Number of employees: 600

Comments: Maclean-Hunter is also a publisher of magazines in Canada and the US.

BK

The Mad Printers
800 Wickham Avenue
Mattituck, NY 11952
516-298-5100

Min: 300 Max: 10,000 Opt:
Sizes: 2345
Bindings: PBI
Items: BH
Services: TY-TD
Equipment: SO

CA

Mail-O-Graph
206 West 4th Street, P O Box 407
Kewanne, IL 61443
309-852-2602

Min: 10,000 Max: 2,000,000 Opt: 50,000
Sizes: 245
Bindings: GBI-SSI-SDI
Items: CDFHSTX
Services: 4C-TY-WA
Equipment: 6WO
Annual sales: $4,000,000
Number of employees: 30
Turnaround times: B3C3M3
Customers: BU90-CU2-MP2-NP2-OR4
Union shop: Y
Year established: 1933
Terms: Net 30

BK

Malloy Lithographing
Tim Scarbrough
5411 Jackson Road
P O Box 1124
Ann Arbor, MI 48106
313-665-6113; Fax: 313-665-2326
Toll-free: 800-722-3231

Min: 1,000 Max: 50,000 Opt: 5,000
Sizes: 123456X
Bindings: HCO-CBI-LBI-PBI-
    SSI-SDO-SBO-WBO
Items: BDEFHLMN
Services: OC-RA-AF-RP
Equipment: 5SO(20x29-41x54)-4WO(to 45)
Annual sales: $25,000,000
Number of employees: 330
Turnaround times: B4
Customers: BP80-BU5-CU5-NP5-SP5
Union shop: N
Year established: 1960
Terms: Net 30

Statement: Malloy exists to provide the best possible printing services to our customers. The mission of Malloy is to meet and exceed the book manufacturing needs of our customers.

CA

Maple Leaf Press
58 Elliot Street
Brattleboro, VT 05301
802-257-5121

Items: DP
Services: TY

BK

Maple-Vail Book Manufacturing
Willow Springs Lane, P O Box 2695
York, PA 17405
717-764-5911

Min: 500 Max: 250,000 Opt:
Sizes: 235
Bindings: HCI-CBI-PBI-SBI
Items: BCDE
Services: FF-TY-TD
Equipment: SO-WO
Annual sales: $65,000,000
Number of employees: 1,200
Year established: 1903
Terms: To be established

GC

Maquoketa Web Printing
Route 4, Box 8
Industrial Park
Maquoketa, IA 52060
319-652-4971; Fax: 319-652-4666

SERVICES			
4C 4-Color Printing	**RA** Rachwal System	**SD** Side Stitching	
CS Color Separations	**AF** Acid-Free Paper	**SB** Spiral Binding	
DA Design / Artwork	**RP** Recycled Paper	**WB** Wire-O Binding	
FF Fulfillment/Mailing	**TY** Typesetting	**I** In-House	
LM List Maintenance	**TD** Typeset w/ Disk	**O** Out of House	
OC OptiCopy System	**WA** Warehousing	**X** Unknown	

BINDINGS		
HC Hardcover	**SD** Side Stitching
CB Comb Binding	**SB** Spiral Binding
GB Glue Binding	**WB** Wire-O Binding
LB Loose-Leaf Binding	**I** In-House
PB Perfect Binding	**O** Out of House
SS Saddle Stitching	**X** Unknown

Min: 2,000 Max: 2,000,000 Opt:
Sizes: 25X
Bindings: SSI
Items: DX
Services: 4C
Equipment: WO
Year established: 1946

Mariposa Press   GC
447 E Channel Road
Benicia, CA 94510
707-746-0800

Bindings: PBI
Items: BDHIP
Services: 4C-FF
Equipment: WO
Annual sales: $14,000,000
Number of employees: 75

Mark IV Press   BK
325 Rabro Drive
Hauppauge, NY 11785
516-348-5252

Min: 500 Max: 20,000 Opt:
Sizes: 2345
Bindings: CBI-LBI-PBI-SBI
Items: BCDEFGJL
Services: 4C-CS-DA-FF-TY-TD
Equipment: SO

Marrakech Express   BK
Shirley Copperman
500 Anclote Road
Tarpon Springs, FL 34689-6701
813-942-2218; Fax: 813-937-4758
Toll-free: 800-940-6566

Min: 250 Max: 10,000 Opt: 2,500
Sizes: 123456
Bindings: LBI-PBI-SSI-SDI-SBO
Items: ABCDEFHIKLMOPSTV1
Services: 4C-CS-FF-AF-RP-TY-TD-WA
Equipment: 6SO
Annual sales: $2,500,000
Number of employees: 17
Turnaround times: B3C2
Customers: BP30-BU26-CU4-
    MP27-NP4-SP8-OR11

Union shop: N
Year established: 1976
Terms: To be arranged

Statement: We give personal attention to
the needs of small book and magazine
publishers with quality workmanship and
the lowest possible pricing. For us, the
challenge is always to finish up with a publication you can proudly sell. Write for a
copy of our *Shortruns* newsletter.

Mars Graphic Services   GC
1 Deadline Drive
Westville, NJ 08093
609-456-8666

Bindings: SSI
Items: CIPST
Services: 4C
Equipment: 5WO
Annual sales: $14,000,000
Number of employees: 140

Maverick Publications   BR
Ken Asher, Producer
P O Drawer 5007
Bend, OR 97708
503-382-6978; Fax: 503-382-4831
Toll-free: 800-627-7932

Min: 200 Max: 50,000 Opt: 2,000
Sizes: 2356
Bindings: CBX-PBX
Items: BCEFLMN
Services: 4C-CS-DA-TY-TD
Equipment: 4SO(19x25)
Turnaround times: B4C4
Customers: BP20-BU3-CU3-
    NP2-OR2-SC2-SP68
Union shop: N
Year established: 1968
Terms: 1/2 down, 1/2 with proofs

The Mazer Corporation   GC
Jim Mosher, Customer Service Manager
2501 Neff Road
Dayton, OH 45414
513-276-6181; Fax: 513-278-9506

PRINTED ITEMS							
A	Annual Reports	G	Galley Copies	N	Workbooks	U	Greeting Cards
B	Books	H	Journals	O	Yearbooks	V	Labels / Stickers
C	Booklets	I	Magazines	P	Brochures	W	Maps
D	Catalogs	J	Mass-Market Books	Q	Calendars	X	Newspapers
E	Cookbooks	K	Newsletters	R	Comic Books	Y	Postcards
F	Directories	L	Software Manuals	S	Direct Mail Letters	Z	Posters
		M	Textbooks	T	Envelopes	1	Stationery

Min: 500 Max: 25,000 Opt: 7,500
Sizes: 123456X
Bindings: HCO-CBI-LBI-
    PBI-SSI-SDI-SBI-WBI
Items: BCDEFGHKLMNTZ
Services: 4C-DA-FF-RA-AF-
    RP-TY-TD-WA
Equipment: 1LP(18x22)-
    6SO(28-40)-2WO(22")
Annual sales: $35,000,000
Number of employees: 300
Turnaround times: B3C3
Customers: BP75-BU10-CU10-NP5
Union shop: N
Year established: 1964

Statement: We are a full service supplier
of books and ancillary materials for publishers and corporate clients. We specialize
in runs under 25,000 units and offer the
finest quality.

McClain Printing Company   GC
George A Smith Jr, President
212 Main Street
Parson, WV 26287
304-478-2881; Fax: 304-478-4658

Min: 250 Max: 10,000 Opt: 2,000
Sizes: 2356
Bindings: HCO-CBI-LBI-
    PBI-SSI-SDI-SBO-WBO
Items: ABCDEFHIKLMNOPQSZ
Services: 4C-CS-FF-AF-TY-TD-WA
Equipment: 5SO(19x25-20x29)
Annual sales: $2,500,000
Number of employees: 20
Turnaround times: B5C4M4
Customers: BU60-CU5-NP5-SP30
Union shop: N
Year established: 1958
Terms: Net 30

Statement: We are the right choice for
profitable results.

McDowell Publications   BK
1129 Pleasant Ridge Road
Utica, KY 42376
502-275-4075

Min: 100 Max: 5,000 Opt: 500
Bindings: HCX-PBX-SSX

Items: BCF
Customers: OR20-SP80(genealogists)

Comments: They specialize in printing
genealogies and local histories.

The McFarland Company   MS
Crescent and Mulberry Streets
P O Box 3645
Harrisburg, PA 17105
717-234-6235

Min: 3,000 Max: 20,000 Opt: 10,000
Sizes: 25
Bindings: CBO-PBI-SSI-SPO-WBO
Items: ACDFHIKLMPQUVWZ
Services: 4C
Equipment: 5SO(25x38-70")
Annual sales: $5,000,000
Number of employees: 125
Turnaround times: B4C3M2
Customers: BP10-BU30-MP30-NP30
Union shop: Y
Year established: 1886
Terms: Net 30

McGregor & Werner   BK
6411 Chillum Place NW
Washington, DC 20012
202-722-2200

Min: 100 Max: 20,000 Opt: 5,000
Sizes: 123456X
Bindings: HCO-CBI-GBI-LBI-
    PBI-SSI-SDI-SBI-WBI
Items: BCDFGHKLMNPS
Services: 4C
Equipment: 7SO(29"-55")
Annual sales: $5,000,000
Number of employees: 100
Turnaround times: B3
Customers: BP20-BU15-
    CU10-NP40-SC10-SP5
Union shop: N
Year established: 1950
Terms: 1% 10, Net 30 w/approved credit

Comments: They specialize in conference
publications and reprints, but also print
newsletters, posters, books, and journals.
They have two printing divisions: Graphic
Printing in New Carlisle, Ohio, and Saint
Mary's Press in Hollywood, Maryland.

SERVICES			BINDINGS			
4C	4-Color Printing	RA Rachwal System	HC	Hardcover	SD	Side Stitching
CS	Color Separations	AF Acid-Free Paper	CB	Comb Binding	SB	Spiral Binding
DA	Design / Artwork	RP Recycled Paper	GB	Glue Binding	WB	Wire-O Binding
FF	Fulfillment/Mailing	TY Typesetting	LB	Loose-Leaf Binding	I	In-House
LM	List Maintenance	TD Typeset w/ Disk	PB	Perfect Binding	O	Out of House
OC	OptiCopy System	WA Warehousing	SS	Saddle Stitching	X	Unknown

McKay Printing Services   GC
14851 Greenwood Road
Dolton, IL 60419
312-841-7300; Toll-free: 800-227-1432

Items: CDIKNP
Services: FF

Comments: McKay is a graphic arts company specializing in quality printing and mailing/fulfillment, with special emphasis on direct mail advertising.

McNaughton & Gunn   BK
Ronald Mazzola, Sales Director
960 Woodland Drive
Saline, MI 48176
313-429-5411; Fax: 800-677-BOOK

(P O Box 2070, Ann Arbor MI 48106)

Min: 100 Max: 50,000 Opt: 4,500
Sizes: 123456
Bindings: HCO-CBI-LBO-
     PBI-SSI-SDI-SBO-WBO
Items: BCDEFHLMN
Services: 4C-CS-FF-RA-AF-RP
Equipment: 7SO(24x32-41x55)-1WO(35")
Annual sales: $19,000,000
Number of employees: 240
Turnaround times: B3C3
Customers: BP75-BU5-NP10-SP10
Union shop: N
Year established: 1975
Terms: Net 30 with approved credit

Statement: We are a book manufacturer which produces predominantly perfectbound books, one- and two-color, in the sheet-fed and web market. We are committed to our customers as demonstrated by providing superior service, dependable quality, reliable schedules, and competitive prices.

Meaker the Printer   GC
802 W Jefferson Street
Phoenix, AZ 85007
602-254-2171

Min: 300 Max: 2,000,000 Opt: 7,000
Sizes: 2345X
Bindings: HCO-CBI-PBO-SSI
Items: ABCDEFHIKNPSYZ1
Services: 4C-DA-TY-TD
Terms: Net 10 with approved credit

Media Printing   CA
8050 NW 74th Avenue
Miami, FL 33166
305-888-1300; Toll-free: 800-544-WEBS

Min: 50,000 Max: 2,000,000 Opt:
Sizes: 5X
Bindings: SSI
Items: DP
Services: 4C-FF
Equipment: 3WO(19x33-23x38)
Year established: 1971

Statement: We are your one source for fine quality catalogs, brochures, flyers, coupons, business reply cards, and more.

Meehan-Tooker & Company   GC
55 Madison Circle Drive
East Rutherford, NJ 07073
201-933-9600; Fax: 201-933-8322

Min: 5,000 Max: 2,000,000 Opt:
Sizes: 235X
Bindings: PBO-SSO
Items: ADPSWXZ
Services: 4C-CS
Equipment: 1SO(28x40)-7WO(22x38)
Annual sales: $89,080,000
Number of employees: 380

Comments: Meehan-Tooker is an employee-owned company specializing in printing inserts, catalogs, coupons, annual reports, and other direct response promotions. They can provide die-cutting, microfragrances, perfs, rub-offs, and other special effects.

Mercury Printing Company   GC
2929 Convair Road
Memphis, TN 38132
901-345-8480

PRINTED ITEMS			
A Annual Reports	G Galley Copies	N Workbooks	U Greeting Cards
B Books	H Journals	O Yearbooks	V Labels / Stickers
C Booklets	I Magazines	P Brochures	W Maps
D Catalogs	J Mass-Market Books	Q Calendars	X Newspapers
E Cookbooks	K Newsletters	R Comic Books	Y Postcards
F Directories	L Software Manuals	S Direct Mail Letters	Z Posters
	M Textbooks	T Envelopes	1 Stationery

Min: 500 Max: 200,000 Opt: 20,000
Sizes: 123456X
Bindings: HCO-CBI-GBO-LBO-
    PBI-SSI-SDI-SBO-WBO
Items: ABCDEFIKLMNOPQRTVWYZ1
Services: 4C-DA-FF-AF-TY-TD-WA
Equipment: LP-5SO(19x25-28x41)
Turnaround times: B2C3M2
Customers: BU90-CU3-MP6-OT1
Union shop: N
Year established: 1961
Terms: Net 30

Statement: A division of Graphics Industries of Atlanta ($310 million in annual
sales from 38 plants with 3,070 employees).

MG

Meredith/Burda
1716 Locust Street
Des Moines, IA 50336
515-284-2553

Min: 25,000 Max: 5,000,000 Opt:
Sizes: 2345X
Bindings: PBI-SSI

Items: CDIP
Services: 4C-CS-FF-LM
Equipment: 8WO-18OT(gravure)
Annual sales: $456,000,000
Number of employees: 3,100

Comments: Recently acquired by R R
Donnelley, this printer of long-run magazines has plants in Iowa, Arizona, Virginia,
and North Carolina.

BK

Messenger Graphics
Sam Freedman, Account Executive
110 S 41st Avenue (85009)
P O Box 29096
Phoenix, AZ 85038
602-233-3700; Fax: 602-352-2335
Toll-free: 800-847-2844

Min: 1,000 Max: 50,000 Opt: 10,000
Sizes: 123456
Bindings: HCO-CBO-GBI-LBO-
    PBI-SSI-SDI-SBO-WBO
Items: ABCDEFHIJKLMNPQSWYZ
Services: 4C-FF-OC-TY-TD

Equipment: 2LP(29")-
7SO(28x40)-3WO(to 40")
Annual sales: $15,000,000
Number of employees: 175
Turnaround times: B3C3M3
Customers: BP20-BU50-CU10-MP15-OT5
Union shop: Y
Year established: 1925
Terms: Net 30 with credit approval

Metromail Corporation   GC
901 W Bond Street
Lincoln, NE 68521
402-475-4591

Min: 200 Max: 7,000 Opt: 2,000
Sizes: 5
Bindings: GBI-PBI-SSI
Items: DFN
Services: TY
Equipment: 1SO(19x25)-2WO(24x36)
Turnaround times: C3
Union shop: N
Year established: 1978
Terms: Net 30 with approved credit

Comments: Metromail specializes in short-
run printing of large size directories and
other high page count books. They can
typeset from mag tape or floppy discs.

Metroweb   MS
Judy Leidy
P O Box 18760
1282 Cox Avenue
Erlanger, KY 41018
606-525-1168; Fax: 606-525-8219

Min: 15,000 Max: 500,000 Opt: 50,000
Sizes: 5X
Bindings: PBI-SSI
Items: DHIKPX
Services: 4C-FF-OC-AF-RP-TD-WA
Equipment: 2WO(17x26)-1WO(23x36)
Annual sales: $17,000,000
Number of employees: 165
Turnaround times: C2M1
Customers: BU5-CU15-MP30-NP40-OR10
Union shop: N
Year established: 1977
Terms: Net 30 upon credit approval

Statement: Metroweb is a full service
printer dedicated to producing high-quality
magazines and journals in standard and
tabloid sizes, saddle and perfect bound.
Specializing in magazine-format printing
has enabled Metroweb to provide extremely fast turnaround time. And our in-house
mailing program provides the most efficient way to maximize postal savings.

Mideastern Printing   GC
7 Delmar Drive
P O Box 205
Brookfield, CT 06804-0205
203-775-0451

Min: 1,000 Max: 100,000 Opt: 35,000
Sizes: 2356
Bindings: HCO-CBI-GBO-LBI-
PBO-SSI-SDI-SBO-WBO
Items: ADEIKLNPQSTUWZ
Services: 4C-CS-DA-FF-TY-TD
Equipment: 9SO(10x13-28x40)
Annual sales: $15,000,000
Turnaround times: B4C1M3
Customers: BU70-NP10-SC10-OT10
Union shop: N
Year established: 1967
Terms: Net 30

Mitchell Press   GC
P O Box 6000
1706 W First Avenue
Vancouver, British Columbia V6B 4B9
Canada
604-731-5211

Min: 2,000 Max: 2,000,000 Opt:
Sizes: 2345X
Bindings: PBI-SSI
Items: ABCDFHIKNP
Services: 4C-CS-DA-TY
Equipment: SO-WO

Mitchell-Shear   BK
713 W Ellsworth Road
Ann Arbor, MI 48108
313-995-2505

PRINTED ITEMS						
A	Annual Reports	G	Galley Copies	N	Workbooks	U	Greeting Cards
B	Books	H	Journals	O	Yearbooks	V	Labels / Stickers
C	Booklets	I	Magazines	P	Brochures	W	Maps
D	Catalogs	J	Mass-Market Books	Q	Calendars	X	Newspapers
E	Cookbooks	K	Newsletters	R	Comic Books	Y	Postcards
F	Directories	L	Software Manuals	S	Direct Mail Letters	Z	Posters
		M	Textbooks	T	Envelopes	1	Stationery

Min: 200 Max: 30,000 Opt: 3,000
Sizes: 23456
Bindings: HCO-CBI-GBO-LBO-
    PBI-SSI-SDI-SBO-WBO
Items: ABCDEFHKLMPQSTYZ1
Services: 4C-CS-AF-WA
Equipment: 4SO
Annual sales: $5,000,000
Number of employees: 35
Turnaround times: B3C3M3
Customers: BP55-BU15-CU15-NP5-SP10
Union shop: N
Year established: 1980
Terms: Net 30 on approved credit

Comments: Mitchell-Shear is a division of
Lithographics, a general commercial
printer.

BK

MMI Press
Mountain Missionary Institute
P O Box 279
Harrisville, NH 03450
603-827-3361; Toll-free: 800-367-1888

Min: 3,000 Max: 100,000 Opt:
Sizes: 2345X
Bindings: HCI-PBI-SSI
Items: BCDFJMN
Services: 4C
Equipment: CB

Comments: Besides printing their own
publications, they sometimes take on outside work.

CA

Moebius Printing
300 N Jefferson Street
P O Box 302
Milwaukee, WI 53202
414-276-5311

Min: 5,000 Max: 5,000,000 Opt:
Sizes: 23456X
Bindings: SSI
Items: ACDJIPQSUYZ
Services: 4C-CS-FF
Equipment: 3SO-5WO
Annual sales: $98,000,000
Number of employees: 380
Year established: 1911

Monument Printers & Lithographers, Inc.
6th St. & Madalyn Ave.,
Verplanck, N.Y. 10596
(914) 737-0992
800-227-2081

BK

Monument Printers & Lithographer
Norman McGowan
6th Street & Madalyn Avenue
P O Box 629
Verplanck, NY 10596
914-737-0992; Fax: 914-737-0783
Toll-free: 800-227-2081

Min: 100 Max: 20,000 Opt: 5,000
Sizes: 123456
Bindings: CBX-PBX-SSX-SDX-SBX
Items: BCDFG
Services: TY-TD
Equipment: 6SO(25"-38")
Annual sales: $3,000,000
Number of employees: 50
Turnaround times: B3C3
Customers: BP70-BU5-CU10-OT15
Union shop: N
Year established: 1950
Terms: Net 30; new accounts 50% down,
    50% on delivery

GC

Moore Response Graphics
1113 S Milwaukee Avenue
Libertyville, IL 60048
708-680-0111; Toll-free: 800-722-9001

Min: 100,000 Max: 2,000,000 Opt:
Bindings: SSI
Items: CDPS
Equipment: WO
Annual sales: 2,500,000,000

Comments: They print sweepstakes and
other game tickets as well as premium
books (with die cuts, decals, scratch-offs,
and other special effects) in quantities of
250,000 or more.

SERVICES				BINDINGS			
4C	4-Color Printing	**RA**	Rachwal System	**HC**	Hardcover	**SD**	Side Stitching
CS	Color Separations	**AF**	Acid-Free Paper	**CB**	Comb Binding	**SB**	Spiral Binding
DA	Design / Artwork	**RP**	Recycled Paper	**GB**	Glue Binding	**WB**	Wire-O Binding
FF	Fulfillment/Mailing	**TY**	Typesetting	**LB**	Loose-Leaf Binding	**I**	In-House
LM	List Maintenance	**TD**	Typeset w/ Disk	**PB**	Perfect Binding	**O**	Out of House
OC	OptiCopy System	**WA**	Warehousing	**SS**	Saddle Stitching	**X**	Unknown

Moran Colorgraphic GC
5425 Florida Boulevard
P O Box 66538
Baton Rouge, LA 70896
504-923-2550

Min: 2,000 **Max:** 200,000 **Opt:** 20,000
Sizes: 123456
Bindings: HCO-CBO-GBO-LPO-
  PBI-SSI-SDI-SBO-WBO
Items: ABCDEFGHIKLPQSZ
Services: 4C-DA-AF-TY-TD-WA
Equipment: 6LP(to 50")-6SO(to 40")
Annual sales: $3,000,000
Number of employees: 75
Turnaround times: B2C2M2
Customers: BP10-BU25-MP10-SP5-OT50
Union shop: Y
Year established: 1880
Terms: Net 30

Statement: Our goal is to become recognized as the best in our region.

Morgan Press GC
145 Palisade Street
Dobbs Ferry, NY 10522
914-693-0023

Min: 1,000 **Max:** 50,000 **Opt:**
Bindings: SSI
Items: ABCDHKPQTUYZ1
Services: 4C-DA-TY-WA
Equipment: 2LP(22x30)5SO(11x17-38x50)
Annual sales: $3,000,000
Number of employees: 30
Turnaround times: B6C4
Customers: BP25-BU65-NP10
Union shop: N
Year established: 1965
Terms: Net 30 with proper credit

Statement: We do short-run commercial printing. We are publishers of greeting cards and technical photographic books under the Morgan and Morgan name.

Morgan Printing BK
Michael Morgan, President
900 Old Koenig Lane #135
Austin, TX 78756
512-459-5194

Min: 50 **Max:** 3,000 **Opt:** 800
Sizes: 235X
Bindings: HCO-CBI-PBI-SSI
Items: BCDFIKNPZ
Services: 4C-AF-RP-TY-TD
Equipment: 4SO(14x20-20x26)
Annual sales: $650,000
Number of employees: 15
Turnaround times: B4C3
Customers: BP30-BU10-CU20-
  NP2-OR8-SP30
Union shop: N
Year established: 1980
Terms: 50% down, 50% COD

Comments: Send for their price list and newsletter.

Morningrise Printing GC
Jane McLaughlin, Trustee
1525 W MacArthur Boulevard #1
Costa Mesa, CA 92626
714-957-8494; Fax: 714-549-1241

Min: 200 **Max:** 5,000 **Opt:** 2,000
Sizes: 1245
Bindings: HCO-CBO-GBO-
  PBO-SSI-SDI-SBO-WBO
Items: BCDKLPT
Services: DA-TY
Equipment: 2SO(12x18)
Annual sales: $300,000
Number of employees: 5
Turnaround times: B4C2
Customers: BU80-SP15-OT5
Union shop: N
Year established: 1978
Terms: 50% deposit, 50% on delivery

Statement: We operate under the premise that every job is a portrait of the person who did it. If our customers aren't happy, we're not happy—and we want to be happy.

Cookbooks by Morris Press BK
P O Box 1681
Kearney, NE 68848
800-652-9314; Toll-free: 800-445-6621

Min: 200 **Max:** **Opt:** 500
Sizes: 25
Bindings: CBI-LBI-SBI

PRINTED ITEMS						
A Annual Reports	G	Galley Copies	N	Workbooks	U	Greeting Cards
B Books	H	Journals	O	Yearbooks	V	Labels / Stickers
C Booklets	I	Magazines	P	Brochures	W	Maps
D Catalogs	J	Mass-Market Books	Q	Calendars	X	Newspapers
E Cookbooks	K	Newsletters	R	Comic Books	Y	Postcards
F Directories	L	Software Manuals	S	Direct Mail Letters	Z	Posters
	M	Textbooks	T	Envelopes	1	Stationery

Items: E
Services: 4C-DA-TY
Equipment: 14SO
Annual sales: $3,000,000
Number of employees: 75
Turnaround times: B6
Customers: NP90-OT10
Union shop: N
Year established: 1937
Terms: 50% net 37 days, balance 90 day

Comments: They specialize in printing personalized cookbooks for fundraising groups. Write for their *Cookbook Planning Guide*.

Motheral Printing   CA
510 S Main Street
P O Box 629
Fort Worth, TX 76101
817-335-1481

Min: 5,000 Max: 2,000,000 Opt:
Sizes: 2345X
Bindings: SSI
Items: ACDHIPZ
Services: 4C
Equipment: SO-WO
Year established: 1934

Muller Printing   GC
3550 Thomas Road
P O Box 698
Santa Clara, CA 95070
408-988-8400

Min: 5,000 Max: 350,000 Opt: 175,000
Sizes: 25
Bindings: HCO-CBO-GBO-LBI-
    PBO-SSI-SDO-SBO-WBO
Items: ACDHILPQSZ
Services: 4C-CS
Equipment: 4SO19x25-28-40)-1WO
Annual sales: $18,000,000
Number of employees: 125
Turnaround times: B2C3M3
Customers: BU90-MP10
Union shop: N
Year established: 1956
Terms: Net 30

Multiprint Inc   BR
Martin Schwalbaum, Manager
80 Longhill Lane
Chatham, NY 07928
201-635-6400; Fax: 201-635-6402

Min: 100 Max: 3,000 Opt: 1,000
Sizes: 25
Bindings: CBI-LBI-PBI-
    SSI-SDI-SBO-WBO
Items: BCEFGHLMN
Services: RP
Equipment: 8SO(up to 35x45)
Annual sales: $1,500,000
Number of employees: 4
Turnaround times: B3
Customers: BP60-CU15-SP25
Union shop: N
Year established: 1958
Terms: 1/2 w/order, 1/2 on completion

Statement: We specialize in brokering book printing jobs of 100 to 2000 copies in paper covers. We offer three week turnaround. We are also very helpful with production details.

Murphy's Printing   GC
1731 Dell Avenue
Campbell, CA 95008

Min: 100 Max: Opt: 2,000
Sizes: 123456X
Bindings: PBO-SSI
Items: ABCDKPSTVYZ1
Services: 4C

Murray Printing Company   BK
Daniel N Bach, VP National Sales
2500 W Progress Drive
P O Box 395
Kendallville, IN 46755-0395
219-347-3044; Fax: 219-347-3507

Min: 1,000 Max: 200,000 Opt: 20,000
Sizes: 2345
Bindings: HCO-GBI-PBI-SSI
Items: BEFLMN
Services: AF

PRINTED ITEMS						
A	Annual Reports	G	Galley Copies	N	Workbooks	U	Greeting Cards
B	Books	H	Journals	O	Yearbooks	V	Labels / Stickers
C	Booklets	I	Magazines	P	Brochures	W	Maps
D	Catalogs	J	Mass-Market Books	Q	Calendars	X	Newspapers
E	Cookbooks	K	Software Manuals	R	Comic Books	Y	Postcards
F	Directories	L	Software Manuals	S	Direct Mail Letters	Z	Posters
		M	Textbooks	T	Envelopes	1	Stationery

Equipment: 6SO(60"-77")-llWO(19"-38")
Annual sales: $95,951,000
Number of employees: 400
Turnaround times: B5
Customers: BP90-BU5-CU5
Union shop: N
Year established: 1898
Terms: Net 30

Comment: A division of Courier Graphics.

BK

Murray Printing Company
Daniel N Bach, VP National Sales
Pleasant Street
Westford, MA 01886
508-692-6321; Fax: 508-692-7292

Min: 1,000 Max: 100,000 Opt: 15,000
Sizes: 2345
Bindings: HCI-GBI-PBI-SSI
Items: BEFLMN
Services: AF-OC
Equipment: 6SO(60"-77")-llWO(19"-38")
Turnaround times: B5
Customers: BP90-BU5-CU5
Union shop: N
Terms: Net 30

N

CA

National Bickford Foremost
10 Park Lane
Providence, RI 02907
401-944-2700

Min: 5,000 Max: 2,000,000 Opt:
Sizes: 2345X
Bindings: PBI-SSI
Items: ACDIPUXZ
Services: 4C-CS-FF
Equipment: 5SO(26x40)-2WO(23x38)
Annual sales: $20,000,000
Number of employees: 175

Statement: Capturing the art of color is the specialty of our house: from separations right through to final delivery.

GC

National Graphics Corporation
724 E Woodrow Avenue, P O Box 719
Columbus, OH 43216
614-445-3200

Min: 25,000 Max: 2,000,000 Opt:
Sizes: 235X
Bindings: PBI-SSI
Items: ABCDFINWXZ
Services: 4C-FF-TY
Equipment: SO-WO

BK

National Publishing Company
Clinton Matlack, Commercial Manager
24th & Locust, P O Box 8386
Philadelphia, PA 19101-8386
215-732-1863; Fax: 215-732-1314

Min: 10,000 Max: 1,000,000 Opt: 50,000
Sizes: 25
Bindings: HCI-PBI
Items: BDFM
Services: FF
Equipment: WO
Turnaround times:
Customers: BP80-BU20
Union shop: Y
Terms: Net 30

Comment: A division of Courier Graphics.

BK

National Reproductions Corp.
Cathy Franczck, General Manager
12749 Richfield Court
Livonia, MI 48150
313-591-4130; Fax: 313-591-0557

Min: 50 Max: 3,000 Opt: 1,000
Sizes: 2356
Bindings: CBI-PBI-SSI-SDI
Items: BCDEFGHLMNPS
Services: 4C-CS
Equipment: SO
Annual sales: $5,000,000
Number of employees: 30
Turnaround times: B3C3
Customers: NP-OR-SP
Union shop: N
Year established: 1953
Terms: Net 30 with approved credit

SERVICES				BINDINGS			
4C	4-Color Printing	RA	Rachwal System	HC	Hardcover	SD	Side Stitching
CS	Color Separations	AF	Acid-Free Paper	CB	Comb Binding	SB	Spiral Binding
DA	Design / Artwork	RP	Recycled Paper	GB	Glue Binding	WB	Wire-O Binding
FF	Fulfillment/Mailing	TD	Typeset w/ Disk	LB	Loose-Leaf Binding	I	In-House
LM	List Maintenance	TY	Typesetting	PB	Perfect Binding	O	Out of House
OC	OptiCopy System	WA	Warehousing	SS	Saddle Stitching	X	Unknown

Nationwide Printing   GC
5906 Jefferson Street
Burlington, KY 41005
606-586-9005

Min: 1,000 **Max:** 100,000 **Opt:** 25,000
Sizes: 123456
Bindings: SSI
Items: ACDHKLMNPQSTYZ1
Services: 4C
Equipment: 5SO(19x25)
Annual sales: $750,000
Number of employees: 10
Turnaround times: C2M2
Customers: BU65-NP15-SC20
Union shop: N
Year established: 1984
Terms: Net 30

Statement: Nationwide specializes in direct response envelopes as well as all types of direct mail printing.

Naturegraph Publishers   BK
Barbara Brown, Manager
3543 Indian Creek Road, P O Box 1075
Happy Camp, CA 96039
916-493-5353

Min: 500 **Max:** 15,000 **Opt:** 5,000
Sizes: 12346
Bindings: HCO-CBI-LBO-
    PBI-SSI-SDO-SBO-WBO
Items: ABCDEP
Services: 4C
Equipment: 2SO(18x24-19x26)
Annual sales: $400,000
Number of employees: 7
Turnaround times: B4C3
Customers: BP20-MP20-SP60
Union shop: N
Year established: 1963
Terms: 1/2 down, balance on completion

Statement: We publish our own publications (almost 100 in print), but we also do some commercial work for others.

Neibauer Press   GC
Nathan Neibauer, President
20 Industrial Drive
Warminster, PA 18974
215-322-6200

Min: 1,000 **Max:** 100,000 **Opt:** 5,000
Sizes: 123456
Bindings: HCO-LBI-PBO-
    SSI-SDI-SBO-WBO
Items: ABCDEFGHIKLMNOPQSZ
Services: 4C-CS-DA-FF-TY-TD-WA
Equipment: 2SO(23x29-28x41)
Annual sales: $3,000,000
Number of employees: 32
Turnaround times: B4C3M3
Customers: BP20-BU20-CU10-NP40
Union shop: N
Year established: 1967
Terms: Net 20 days

Statement: We offer high quality short-run printing on coated or uncoated paper.

Nevada Web Graphics   CA
451 E Glendale Avenue
Sparks, NV 89431
702-331-4497

Min: 20,000 **Max:** 2,000,000 **Opt:**
Sizes: 2345X
Bindings: SSI
Items: D
Services: 4C
Equipment: WO
Annual sales: $21,000,000
Number of employees: 150

Comments: A division of George Rice & Sons, they print catalogs.

Newsfoto Publishing Company   BK
P O Box 1392, 2027 Industrial Boulevard
San Angelo, TX 76902
915-949-3776

Bindings: HCI
Items: BFO
Services: 4C-CS-TY
Equipment: SO

Statement: A subsidiary of Taylors.

Neyenesch Printers   MS
2750 Kettner Boulevard
San Diego, CA 92101
619-297-2281; Fax: 619-299-7250

PRINTED ITEMS							
A	Annual Reports	G	Galley Copies	N	Workbooks	U	Greeting Cards
B	Books	H	Journals	O	Yearbooks	V	Labels / Stickers
C	Booklets	I	Magazines	P	Brochures	W	Maps
D	Catalogs	J	Mass-Market Books	Q	Calendars	X	Newspapers
E	Cookbooks	K	Newsletters	R	Comic Books	Y	Postcards
F	Directories	L	Software Manuals	S	Direct Mail Letters	Z	Posters
		M	Textbooks	T	Envelopes	1	Stationery

Min: 5,000 Max: 25,000 Opt: 15,000
Sizes: 2345X
Bindings: PBI-SSI-SDI
Items: ABCDFHIKNSWZ
Services: 4C-CS-TY
Equipment: LP-SO-WO

Nielsen Lithographing GC
3731 Eastern Hills Lane
Cincinnati, OH 45209
513-321-5200

Min: 1,000 Max: 1,000,000 Opt: 150,000
Sizes: 123456X
Bindings: PBI-SSI-SDO-SBO-WBO
Items: ACDIPQSVYZ
Services: 4C-CS
Equipment: SO-WO
Annual sales: $16,000,000
Number of employees: 165
Turnaround times: C4M4
Union shop: N
Terms: Net 30

Nimrod Press GC
170 Brookline Avenue
Boston, MA 02215
617-437-7900

Min: 300 Max: 50,000 Opt: 3,000
Sizes: 235X
Bindings: HCX-CBI-PBI-SSI-SBI
Items: ABCDEFHILMNP
Services: 4C-TY-TD
Equipment: S0
Annual sales: $17,000,000
Number of employees: 185
Terms: Net 30

Comments: A financial and general commercial printer, Nimrod also prints book jackets and some books.

Noble Book Press BR
Philip Weinreich, President
900 Broadway
New York, NY 10003-1210
212-777-1300; Fax: 212-473-7855

Min: 500 Max: 5,000 Opt:
Sizes: 23456

Bindings: no bindery
Items: BCDLO
Services: 4C-CS-DA-AF
Equipment: no presses
Annual sales: $1,000,000
Turnaround times: B4C4

Noll Printing Company CA
100 Noll Plaza
Huntington, IN 46750
219-356-2020; Fax: 219-356-4584
Toll-free: 800-348-2886

Min: 75,000 Max: 1,000,000 Opt: 250,000
Sizes: 1245X
Bindings: GBI-PBI-SSI
Items: CDFHIJXZ
Services: 4C-CS-FF-LM-AF-TY-TD
Equipment: 5WO(22x36-22x38)
Annual sales: $45,000,000
Number of employees: 391
Turnaround times: B3C3M3
Customers: BU60-MP15-NP10-OR5-SC10
Union shop: Y
Year established: 1930
Terms: Net 30 with approved credit

Statement: A subsidiary of Our Sunday Visitor Inc., we are experts in printing lightweight stocks to save postage.

North Plains Press MG
1216 S Main, P O Box 1830
Aberdeen, SD 57401-0501
605-225-5360

Sizes: 5X
Bindings: SSI
Items: BCDFHIKPX
Services: 4C-DA-FF-LM-TY
Equipment: SO-WO
Year established: 188?

Northeast Web Printing GC
425 Smith Street
Farmingdale, NY 11735
516-753-9035

Min: 5,000 Max: 300,000 Opt: 15,000
Sizes: 25
Items: BDX

SERVICES			
4C 4-Color Printing	RA Rachwal System		
CS Color Separations	AF Acid-Free Paper		
DA Design / Artwork	RP Recycled Paper		
FF Fulfillment/Mailing	TY Typesetting		
LM List Maintenance	TD Typeset w/ Disk		
OC OptiCopy System	WA Warehousing		

BINDINGS			
HC Hardcover	SD Side Stitching		
CB Comb Binding	SB Spiral Binding		
GB Glue Binding	WB Wire-O Binding		
LB Loose-Leaf Binding	I In-House		
PB Perfect Binding	O Out of House		
SS Saddle Stitching	X Unknown		

Services: DA
Equipment: 17WO(22x36)
Annual sales: $5,000,000
Number of employees: 125
Turnaround times: B1C4M1
Customers: BU5-OT95
Union shop: N
Year established: 1978
Terms: Net 30

Comments: Their primary business is as a printer of weekly newspapers.

GC

Northlight Studio Press
Lew Bell, Marketing Director
Route 14, P O Box 568
Barre, VT 05641-0568
802-479-0565; Fax: 802-479-5245

Min: 100 Max: 5,000 Opt: 1,500
Sizes: 2356
Bindings: HCO-CBI-GBI-LBO-PBI-SSI-
    SDO-SBO-WBO
Items: ABCDEFGKPT1
Services: 4C-RP-TY-TD
Equipment: 3SO(19x25)
Annual sales: $2,500,000
Number of employees: 16
Turnaround times: B3C3
Customers: BP20-BU45-CU30-OT5
Union shop: N
Year established: 1974
Terms: Net 30

Statement: We strive to provide the best possible product to our customers.

MS

Northprint
406 Pokegama Avenue N
Grand Rapids, MN 55744
800-662-5784; Toll-free: 800-346-5767

Min: 25,000 Max: 500,000 Opt:
Bindings: SSI
Items: DI
Equipment: WO

CA

Northwest Web
3592 West 5th Avenue
Eugene, OR 97402
503-345-0552

Min: 30,000 Max: 5,000,000 Opt: 500,000
Sizes: 25X
Bindings: SSI
Items: DIPX
Services: 4C-TY
Equipment: 2WO(22x36-22x39)
Annual sales: $18,000,000
Number of employees: 125
Turnaround times: C1M1
Customers: BU90-MP5-SC5
Union shop: N
Terms: Net 30

GC

Nystrom Publishing Company
Jerry Nystrom, President
9100 Cottonwood Lane
Maple Grove, MN 55369
612-425-7900; Fax: 612-425-0898

Min: 1,000 Max: 80,000 Opt: 5,000
Sizes: 23456
Bindings: HCO-PBO-SSI-SBO-WBO
Items: ABCDFHIKPW
Services: 4C-FF-RP-TY-TD-WA
Equipment: 3SO(18x24-25x38)
Annual sales: $2,500,000
Number of employees: 13
Turnaround times: B4C3M3
Customers: BP5-BU25-MP10-
    NP30-SC25-OT5
Union shop: N
Year established: 1978
Terms: Net 30

Statement: We offer quality printing at reasonable prices with a quick turnaround.

O

BK

O'Neil Data Systems
2034 Armacost Avenue
Los Angeles, CA 90025
213-820-8343

Min: 100 Max: 100,000 Opt: 25,000
Sizes: 25
Bindings: CBI-PBI-SSI
Items: BCDFN

PRINTED ITEMS						
A	Annual Reports	G	Galley Copies	N	Workbooks	U	Greeting Cards
B	Books	H	Journals	O	Yearbooks	V	Labels / Stickers
C	Booklets	I	Magazines	P	Brochures	W	Maps
D	Catalogs	J	Mass-Market Books	Q	Calendars	X	Newspapers
E	Cookbooks	K	Software Manuals	R	Comic Books	Y	Postcards
F	Directories	L	Software Manuals	S	Direct Mail Letters	Z	Posters
		M	Textbooks	T	Envelopes	1	Stationery

Services: FF-TY-TD
Equipment: SO-WO
Turnaround times: B1

Oaks Printing Company
GC

195 Nazareth Pike
Bethlehem, PA 18017
215-759-8511

Min: 10 **Max:** 2,000,000 **Opt:** 8,000
Sizes: 123456X
Bindings: HCO-CBO-GBO-
LBI-PBO-SSI-SDI-WBO
Items: ABCDEFGHIKMNPSTUVWYZ1
Services: 4C-TY-TD
Equipment: 7SO(10x15-25x36)
Annual sales: $5,000,000
Number of employees: 125
Turnaround times: B5C5M5
Customers: BU70-CU20-NP5-OR5
Union shop: Y
Year established: 1974
Terms: Net 30

Odyssey Press
BK

Douglas Stone
Forum Court #15
113 Crosby Road
Dover, NH 03820
603-749-4433; Fax: 603-749-1425

Min: 10 **Max:** 1,500 **Opt:** 500
Sizes: 12345
Bindings: PBI-SSI-SDI
Items: BCFGHLN
Services: FF-AF-TY-TD-WA
Equipment: 5SO(12x18)
Annual sales: $600,000
Number of employees: 14
Turnaround times: B3C3
Customers: BP45-BU5-
CU25-NP10-OR5-SP10
Union shop: N
Year established: 1989
Terms: Net 30

Statement: Our desire is to provide the
ultrashort run book market with an
economical source for quick turnaround
products.

Offset Paperback Manufacturers
BK

Robert O'Connor, VP of Sales
Route 309, P O Box N
Dallas, PA 18612
717-675-5261; Fax: 717-675-8714

Min: 5,000 **Max:** 2,000,000 **Opt:** 100,000
Sizes: 12X
Bindings: PBI
Items: BJ
Services: 4C-CS-FF-WA
Equipment: 2SO(25x38)-
9WO(22x36-29x60)
Annual sales: $40,000,000
Number of employees: 500
Turnaround times: B4
Customers: BP100
Union shop: Y
Year established: 1972
Terms: Net 30 but negotiable

Comments: A division of Bertelsmann
Printing.

Oklahoma Graphics
MG

P O Box 26488, 5400 NW 5th Street
Oklahoma City, OK 73127
405-947-0711

Min: 50,000 **Max:** 5,000,000 **Opt:**
Sizes: 5X
Bindings: SSI
Items: DIX
Services: 4C-FF
Equipment: 4WO
Annual sales: $38,000,000
Number of employees: 300

Comments: A division of Shea Communications ($107 million in annual sales from
3 plants with 700 employees).

Olympic Litho
GC

116 Nassau Street
Brooklyn, NY 11201
718-522-2400

Max: 75,000
Bindings: SSO
Items: CDKPQSUYZ
Services: 4C-CS-DA
Equipment: 3SO(23x36-28x41)

SERVICES				BINDINGS			
4C	4-Color Printing	RA	Rachwal System	HC	Hardcover	SD	Side Stitching
CS	Color Separations	AF	Acid-Free Paper	CB	Comb Binding	SB	Spiral Binding
DA	Design / Artwork	RP	Recycled Paper	GB	Glue Binding	WB	Wire-O Binding
FF	Fulfillment/Mailing	TY	Typesetting	LB	Loose-Leaf Binding	I	In-House
LM	List Maintenance	TD	Typeset w/ Disk	PB	Perfect Binding	O	Out of House
OC	OptiCopy System	WA	Warehousing	SS	Saddle Stitching	X	Unknown

Annual sales: $5,000,000
Number of employees: 30
Turnaround times: C3
Customers: BU80-CU5-NP5-OR5-OT5
Union shop: N
Year established: 195?
Terms: Net 30

Statement: Our professional staff has produced, and often designed, brochures, posters, catalogs, point-of-purchase displays, direct mail pieces, and a wealth of things in between.

GC

Omaha Printing
4700 F Street
Omaha, NE 68117
402-734-4400

Min: 1,000 **Max:** 2,000,000 **Opt:**
Sizes: 123456X
Bindings: LBO-PBO-SSI-SDI-SBO-WBO
Items: ACDEIKPQSTVYZ1
Services: 4C-CS-TY-TD-WA
Equipment: 4LP(13x19)-9SO(to 25x38)-3WO-1 Other
Annual sales: $13,000,000
Number of employees: 150
Turnaround times: B4C4M2
Customers: BU80
Union shop: N
Year established: 1858
Terms: Net 30

Statement: We specialize in direct mail and related pieces.

BK

Omnipress
Steve Harrell, Sales Manager
2600 Anderson Street, P O Box 7214
Madison, WI 53707-7214
608-246-2600; Fax: 608-246-4237
Toll-free: 800-828-0305

Min: 50 **Max:** 2,000 **Opt:** 500
Sizes: 5
Bindings: CBI-GBI-LBI-PBI-SDI-SBI
Items: BFGHLMN
Services: FF-RP
Turnaround times: B2
Union shop: N
Year established: 1977
Terms: No credit extended

Statement: OMNIPRESS specializes in quick and dependable service on the reproduction of high page count, standard size books and manuals from 100 to 2000 copies.

BK

Optic Graphics
101 Dover Road
Glen Burnie, MD 21061
301-768-3000; Toll-free: 800-638-7107

Min: 500 **Max:** 2,000,000 **Opt:** 8,000
Sizes: 123456X
Bindings: HCI-CBI-LBI-PBI
Items: ABFLNP
Equipment: 2SO(54")
Annual sales: $14,000,000
Number of employees: 250
Terms: 2% 10, Net 30

Comments: They can manufacture both vinyl and cloth looseleaf binders in-house. They assemble binders and/or slipcases as well as print manuals for the computer software industry.

GC

Original Copy Centers
Ten Leader Building
Cleveland, OH 44114
216-861-0620

Min: 100 **Max:** 2,000 **Opt:** 500
Sizes: 5
Bindings: LBX-SSX
Items: BCDFLN
Services: demand printing

GC

Ortlieb Press
3333 Drusilla, P O Box 172
Baton Rouge, LA 70809
504-923-0202

Min: **Max:** 2,000,000 **Opt:** 100,000
Sizes: 123456X
Bindings: HCO-CBI-GBI-LBO-PBI-SSI-SDI-SBO-WBO
Items: ABCDEFHIKLNOPQSTUVXYZ1
Services: 4C-CS-DA-FF-LM-TY-WA
Equipment: LP-SO-WO-OP(Sreen)
Annual sales: $5,000,000
Number of employees: 30

PRINTED ITEMS		G	Galley Copies	N	Workbooks	U	Greeting Cards
A	Annual Reports	H	Journals	O	Yearbooks	V	Labels / Stickers
B	Books	I	Magazines	P	Brochures	W	Maps
C	Booklets	J	Mass-Market Books	Q	Calendars	X	Newspapers
D	Catalogs	K	Newsletters	R	Comic Books	Y	Postcards
E	Cookbooks	L	Software Manuals	S	Direct Mail Letters	Z	Posters
F	Directories	M	Textbooks	T	Envelopes	1	Stationery

Turnaround times: varies
Year established: 1901
Terms: Negotiable

Outstanding Graphics **GC**
1417 50th Street
Kenosha, WI 53140
414-658-8990

Min: 1,000 Max: 250,000 Opt: 10,000
Sizes: 123456
Bindings: PBX-SSX-SDX
Items: CDKOPSTYZ1
Services: 4C-CS-DA-AF
Equipment: 3SO(10x15-23x29)
Annual sales: $500,000
Number of employees: 20
Turnaround times: B4C3M4
Customers: BU55-CU20-
    MP10-NP5-OR5-SC5
Union shop: N
Year established: 1977
Terms: Net 10

Statement: We are dependable printers who specialize in two-color top-quality printing.

Ovid Bell Press **MS**
1201-05 Bluff Street
P O Box 381
Fulton, MO 65251
314-642-4117; Toll-free: 800-835-8919

Min: 2,000 Max: 75,000 Opt: 16,000
Sizes: 2356
Bindings: PBI-SSI
Items: BCHIP
Services: 4C-AF-TY-TD
Equipment: 7SO(25x38)
Annual sales: $5,000,000
Number of employees: 125
Turnaround times: B4M2
Customers: BP5-CU5-MP85
Union shop: N
Year established: 1927
Terms: Net 30, interest thereafter

Statement: We provide full service to the small magazine publisher, with close attention to detail.

Oxford Group **BK**
P O Box 269
Norway, ME 04268
207-743-8958

Min: 1,000 Max: 2,000,000 Opt:
Sizes: 2345X
Bindings: PBX-SSI
Items: BCHI
Services: TY-TD
Equipment: SO-WO

Oxford Group, New Hampshire **BK**
351 Main Street
P O Box 38
Berlin, NH 03570
603-752-2339

Min: 1,000 Max: 2,000,000 Opt:
Sizes: 2345X
Bindings: PBX-SSI
Items: BCHI
Services: TY-TD
Equipment: SO-WO

Oxmoor Press **BK**
100 W Oxmoor Road
P O Box 980
Birmingham, AL 35201
205-942-0511

Bindings: HCX-PBX-SSX
Items: BCDFNR
Equipment: LP-SO

Comments: Oxmoor is a subsidiary of Stevens Graphics and associated with Oxmoor Publishing Company. They can print Bibles, catalogs, directories, and coloring books.

P

Pacific Lithograph **GC**
2555 Bayshore Boulevard
San Francisco, CA 94134
415-467-5200

SERVICES				BINDINGS			
4C	4-Color Printing	RA	Rachwal System	HC	Hardcover	SD	Side Stitching
CS	Color Separations	AF	Acid-Free Paper	CB	Comb Binding	SB	Spiral Binding
DA	Design / Artwork	RP	Recycled Paper	GB	Glue Binding	WB	Wire-O Binding
FF	Fulfillment/Mailing	TY	Typesetting	LB	Loose-Leaf Binding	I	In-House
LM	List Maintenance	TD	Typeset w/ Disk	PB	Perfect Binding	O	Out of House
OC	OptiCopy System	WA	Warehousing	SS	Saddle Stitching	X	Unknown

Min: 2,000 Max: 2,000,000 Opt:
Sizes: 2345X
Bindings: GBI-SSI-SDI
Items: ACDPSXZ
Services: 4C-CS
Equipment: SO-WO
Annual sales: $31,800,000
Number of employees: 165

PAK Discount Printing   GC
38771 N Lewis Avenue
Zion, IL 60099
312-249-1789

Min: 200 Max: 25,000 Opt: 3,000
Sizes: 25X
Bindings: SSI
Items: CDKNPSTVYZ1
Services: TY
Equipment: SO

Comments: PAK is a general commercial
printer who does much business by mail.
Write for their price list.

Pantagraph Printing   BK
P O Box 1406
217 W Jefferson Street
Bloomington, IL 61701
309-829-1071

Bindings: HCX-PBX
Items: BFHMN
Services: TY
Equipment: SO-WO

Paraclete Press   BK
Jacquelin Cleverly
P O Box 1568
Orleans, MA 02653
508-255-4685; Fax: 508-255-5705
Toll-free: 800-451-5006

Min: 500 Max: 25,000 Opt: 3,000
Sizes: 23456
Bindings: PBI-SSI
Items: ABCDEFIJKNPQWZ
Services: 4C-DA-AF-TY
Equipment: 2SO(12x18-20x28)
Annual sales: $750,000
Number of employees: 50

Turnaround times: B3
Customers: BU50-MP25-SP25
Union shop: N
Year established: 1981
Terms: 1/2 down, net 30, first time

Statement: We provide high quality printing, particularly 4 color, with a conscientious effort to make our commitments.

Park Press   GC
930 East 162nd Street
South Holland, IL 60473
708-331-6352

Min: 5,000 Max: 100,000 Opt: 15,000
Sizes: 5X
Bindings: GBI-SSX
Items: CD
Equipment: WO
Year established: 1954

Parker Graphics   GC
712 N Main Street
P O Box 159
Fuquay-Varina, NC 27526-0159
919-552-9033

Min: 500 Max: 50,000 Opt: 10,000
Sizes: 123456
Bindings: CBI-GBI-LBI-PBI-SSI-SDI
Items: CDEFKNPTV1
Services: 4C-TY
Equipment: 6SO(10x15-20x28)-IWO(23x38)
Annual sales: $200,000
Number of employees: 5
Turnaround times: C6M5
Customers: BU90-NP5-SP5
Union shop: N
Year established: 1969
Terms: Net on receipt

Patterson Printing Company   BK
1550 Territorial Road
P O Box 1244
Benton Harbor, MI 49022
616-925-2177; Fax: 616-925-6057

Min: 100 Max: 100,000 Opt: 10,000
Sizes: 235X

PRINTED ITEMS	G	Galley Copies	N	Workbooks	U	Greeting Cards
A Annual Reports	H	Journals	O	Yearbooks	V	Labels / Stickers
B Books	I	Magazines	P	Brochures	W	Maps
C Booklets	J	Mass-Market Books	Q	Calendars	X	Newspapers
D Catalogs	K	Newsletters	R	Comic Books	Y	Postcards
E Cookbooks	L	Software Manuals	S	Direct Mail Letters	Z	Posters
F Directories	M	Textbooks	T	Envelopes	1	Stationery

Bindings: HCO-CBI-LBI-PBI-SSI
Items: BCFHIMNP
Services: 4C-FF-RA
Equipment: SO-WO
Number of employees: 120
Customers: BP-CU-NP-SC
Year established: 1949
Terms: Net 30 with approved credit

Comments: Patterson specializes in printing information materials (educational textbooks, student workbooks, technical manuals, spirit masters, transparencies, and educational kits).

Paust Inc   GC
14 N 10th Street
P O Box 1326
Richmond, IN 47375
317-962-1507

Min: 10 Max: 2,000,000 Opt: 1,000
Sizes: 123456
Bindings: HCO-CBO-GB0-LBI-
    PBO-SSI-SDI-SBI-WBO
Items: ABCDFIKLNPQSTUVWYZ1
Services: 4C-CS-DA-LM-AF-TY
Equipment: 10SO(10x15-23x29)
Annual sales: $5,000,000
Number of employees: 35
Turnaround times: B3C2M2
Customers: BP10-BU70-CU10-NP10
Union shop: N
Year established: 1945
Terms: Payment in full with order

Pearl Pressman Liberty Printing   BK
Fifth and Poplar Streets
Philadelphia, PA 19123
215-925-4900

Bindings: HCX-PBX-SSX
Items: BCM
Services: 4C-TY-FF
Equipment: SO
Annual sales: $15,000,000
Number of employees: 140

Comments: They specialize in printing book covers and jackets as well as multicolor medical textbooks and juvenile picture books.

Pelican Pond Publishing   BK
13386 N Bloomfield Road
Nevada City, CA 95959

Comments: This publisher does some printing for outside companies.

Pendell Printing   MS
1700 James Savage Road
P O Box 2066
Midland, MI 48640-2066
517-496-3333; Toll-free: 800-448-4200

Min: 5,000 Max: 300,000 Opt: 80,000
Sizes: 25X
Bindings: PBI-SSI
Items: ACDIPZ
Services: 4C-CS-DA-TY-WA
Equipment: 2SO(25x38-28x40)-3WO
Annual sales: $16,000,000
Number of employees: 200
Turnaround times: C3M2
Customers: BU37-CU3-MP60
Union shop: N
Year established: 1972
Terms: Net 30

Comments: A division of Quebecor Printing, Pendell specializes in short to medium-run publications.

PennWell Printing   MS
1421 S Sheridan Road
P O Box 1260
Tulsa, OK 74112
918-832-9338

Min: 10,000 Max: 500,000 Opt:
Sizes: 5
Bindings: HCO-CBO-GBI-LBO-
    PBI-SSI-SDO-SBO-WBO
Items: DHIPX
Services: 4C-FF-LM-TY-TD-WA
Equipment: 3SO(to 38x40)-2WO(23x36)
Annual sales: $35,000,000
Number of employees: 150
Turnaround times: M2
Customers: BU10-MP90
Union shop: Y
Year established: 1910
Terms: Net 30

SERVICES				BINDINGS			
4C	4-Color Printing	RA	Rachwal System	HC	Hardcover	SD	Side Stitching
CS	Color Separations	AF	Acid-Free Paper	CB	Comb Binding	SB	Spiral Binding
DA	Design / Artwork	RP	Recycled Paper	GB	Glue Binding	WB	Wire-O Binding
FF	Fulfillment/Mailing	TY	Typesetting	LB	Loose-Leaf Binding	I	In-House
LM	List Maintenance	TD	Typeset w/ Disk	PB	Perfect Binding	O	Out of House
OC	OptiCopy System	WA	Warehousing	SS	Saddle Stitching	X	Unknown

Statement: PennWell is a full service commercial printing company which specializes in producing special interest publications.

BK

Pentagram
212 North Second Street
Minneapolis, MN 55401
612-340-9821

Min: 50 Max: 1,000 Opt: 300
Sizes: 123456X
Bindings: HCO-CBO-GBO-PBI-SSI
Items: BTU1
Services: DA-AF-TY
Equipment: 3LP(10x15-15x20)
Annual sales: $200,000
Number of employees: 3
Turnaround times: B5
Customers: BP50-SP50
Union shop: N
Year established: 1975

Statement: Pentagram is a small letterpress shop. We print and publish books on good mouldmade or handmade papers.

MG

Penton Press
680 N Rocky River Road
Berea, OH 44017
216-243-5700

Min: 1,000 Max: 500,000 Opt:
Sizes: 2345X
Bindings: PBI-SSI
Items: CDIPX
Services: 4C
Equipment: SO-WO

CA

Perlmuter Printing
5604 Valley Belt Road
Independence, OH 44131
216-398-1905; Toll-free: 800-321-6228

Min: 2,000 Max: 2,000,000 Opt:
Sizes: 25X
Bindings: SSI
Items: ACDIKNPQYZ
Services: 4C-CS-DA-FF-TY
Equipment: 3SO(28x40)-3WO(22x38)
Annual sales: $23,000,000
Number of employees: 210
Year established: 1917

Statement: Perlmuter is a full service commercial printer offering customers a single source from creative to distribution. We currently print more than 50 catalogs.

CA

Perry Printing
575 W Madison Street
P O Box 97
Waterloo, WI 53594
414-478-3551

Min: 100,000 Max: 5,000,000 Opt:
Sizes: 1245
Bindings: GBI-PBI-SSI
Items: ACDFHINPVXZ
Services: 4C-FF-TD-WA
Equipment: 14WO
Annual sales: $175,000,000
Number of employees: 1,600
Turnaround times: C1M1
Customers: MP40-OR60
Union shop: Y
Year established: 1956
Terms: Net 30

Comments: A subsidiary of Journal Communications, they print many catalogs.

GC

Perry/Baraboo
1300 Sauk Avenue
Baraboo, WI 53913
414-478-3551

Min: 100,000 Max: 5,000,000 Opt:
Sizes: 1245
Bindings: GBI-PBI-SSI
Items: ACDFHINPVXZ
Services: 4C-FF-TD-WA
Equipment: 14WO
Turnaround times: C1M1
Customers: MP40-OR60
Union shop: Y
Terms: Net 30

GC

Petty Printing Company
420 W Industrial Avenue
Effingham, IL 62414
217-347-7721

Min: 50,000 Max: 5,000,000 Opt:
Sizes: 25X

PRINTED ITEMS	G	Galley Copies	N	Workbooks	U	Greeting Cards
A	Annual Reports	H	Journals	O	Yearbooks	V	Labels / Stickers
B	Books	I	Magazines	P	Brochures	W	Maps
C	Booklets	J	Mass-Market Books	Q	Calendars	X	Newspapers
D	Catalogs	K	Newsletters	R	Comic Books	Y	Postcards
E	Cookbooks	L	Software Manuals	S	Direct Mail Letters	Z	Posters
F	Directories	M	Textbooks	T	Envelopes	1	Stationery

Bindings: SSI
Items: DPST
Services: FC-FF-TY
Equipment: 1SO(24x36)-7WO(to 22x38)
Annual sales: $71,000,000
Number of employees: 450

Comments: Petty specializes in producing various direct mail formats, including catalogs, self-mailers, inserts, game cards, coupons and bind-ins.

BK
PFP Printing Corporation
Frank Wood, Marketing Director
8041 Cessna Avenue #132
Gaithersburg, MD 20879-4118
301-258-8353; Fax: 301-670-4147

Min: 10 **Max:** 6,000 **Opt:** 750
Sizes: 123456X
Bindings: HCO-CBI-LBI-PBI-
    SSI-SDI-SBO-WBO
Items: BCDEFGHIKLMNOPSTY1
Services: FF-AF-RP-TY-TD
Equipment: 3SO(up to 14x20)-1 perfector
Annual sales: $1,000,000
Number of employees: 7
Turnaround times: B2
Customers: BP20-BU40-MP40-
    NP20-SC10-SP20
Union shop: N
Year established: 1986
Terms: Net on delivery

Statement: We strive to achieve customer satisfaction regarding quality, schedule, cost, and headache-free service in the manufacture of softbound books in short and medium run lengths, principally single-color text with single or multi- color covers.

BK
Phillips Brothers Printing
Lori Tucker, Marketing Director
1555 W Jefferson
P O Box 580
Springfield, IL 62705
217-787-3014

Min: 1,000 **Max:** 500,000 **Opt:** 50,000
Sizes: 136
Bindings: HCO-CBI-PBI-SSI-SBO

Items: BCDEFLMP
Equipment: 5SO(23x29-28x41)-
    2WO(11x17-19x33)
Annual sales: $6,000,000
Number of employees: 125
Turnaround times: B5C5M4
Customers: BP20-CU48-OT32
Union shop: Y
Year established: 1883
Terms: Net 30

Comments: Phillips is a family-owned printer specializing in web offset printing of catalogs and annual reports.

GC
Pine Hill Press
700 East 6th Street
Freeman, SD 57029

Min: 200 **Max:** 10,000 **Opt:** 1,000
Sizes: 25
Bindings: SSI
Items: CDNP
Terms: Net 30 with approved credit

GC
Pioneer Press
1232 Central Avenue
Wilmette, IL 60091
312-256-7625

Min: 5,000 **Max:** 1,000,000 **Opt:**
Sizes: 2345X
Bindings: SSI
Items: BCDFIKPS
Services: 4C-TY
Equipment: SO-WO

GC
Plain Talk Publishing Company
511 E Sixth Avenue
Des Moines, IA 50309
515-282-0483

Sizes: 123456
Bindings: none
Items: ACDEFHIKLPQSTVXYZ1
Services: 4C
Equipment: 3LP(to 21x26)-6SO(to 26x40)
Annual sales: $5,000,000
Number of employees: 125

SERVICES				BINDINGS			
4C	4-Color Printing	RA	Rachwal System	HC	Hardcover	SD	Side Stitching
CS	Color Separations	AF	Acid-Free Paper	CB	Comb Binding	SB	Spiral Binding
DA	Design / Artwork	RP	Recycled Paper	GB	Glue Binding	WB	Wire-O Binding
FF	Fulfillment/Mailing	TY	Typesetting	LB	Loose-Leaf Binding	I	In-House
LM	List Maintenance	TD	Typeset w/ Disk	PB	Perfect Binding	O	Out of House
OC	OptiCopy System	WA	Warehousing	SS	Saddle Stitching	X	Unknown

Turnaround times: B4C3M3
Customers: BP2-BU65-CU5-
MP2-NP5-OR16-SP5
Union shop: Y
Year established: 1869
Terms: Net 30

BK

Plus Communications
2828 Brannon Avenue
Saint Louis, MO 63137-1461
314-868-7587

Min: 1,000 Max: 100,000 Opt: 20,000
Sizes: 2356
Bindings: CBI-LBI-PBI-SSI-SDI
Items: BCDFHKLMNPQ
Services: 4C-DA-FF-TY-TD-WA
Equipment: 3SO(26"-40")-1WO(35")
Annual sales: $5,000,000
Number of employees: 30
Turnaround times: B4C4
Customers: BP40-BU15-CU25-NP10-SP10
Union shop: N
Year established: 1979
Terms: Net 30

Statement: We are short to medium-run
book printers. We provide high quality
covers with lamination and good one or
two-color text.

BK

Port City Press
1323 Greenwood Road
Pikesville, MD 21208
301-486-3000; Fax: Ext 323

Min: 300 Max: 50,000 Opt: 25,000
Sizes: 2345
Bindings: HCX-PBI-SSI-SDI
Items: ABCDHIPX
Services: 4C-DA-FF-TY-WA
Equipment: SO-WO
Annual sales: $32,000,000
Number of employees: 350
Turnaround times: B3
Year established: 1961
Terms: Net upon receipt of invoice

Comments: A subsidiary of Judd's Incorporated, Port City specializes in printing
and binding softcover books.

MS

Port Publications
William Schanen III
125 E Main Street
P O Box 349
Port Washington, WI 53074
414-284-3494; Fax: 414-284-0067

Min: 2,500 Max: 50,000 Opt: 15,000
Sizes: 245X
Bindings: HCO-CBO-PBO-
SSI-SDI-SBO-WBO
Items: ACDHIPRXZ
Services: 4C
Equipment: 3SO(18x25)-1WO(23x36)
Annual sales: $3,000,000
Number of employees: 50
Turnaround times: B3C3
Customers: MP70-OR30
Union shop: Y
Year established: 1940
Terms: Net 30

Statement: We have just moved into a new
building and installed more equipment.

GC

Practical Graphics
135 West 20th Street, 3rd Floor
New York, NY 10011
212-463-7800; Fax: 212-463-7803

Sizes: 123456
Bindings: HCO-CBI-LBO-
PBI-SSI-SDI-SBO-WBO
Items: ABCDFHIKPSTUVYZ1
Services: 4C-DA-LM-RP-TY-TD
Equipment: CB-SO-WO
Annual sales: $2,500,000
Customers: BU50-CU10-MP5-
NP15-OR5-SC5-SP10
Union shop: N
Year established: 1979
Terms: 50% deposit, balance on delivery

Statement: We strive to provide the best
quality products and service.

GC

Precision Offset Printing
8000 West Chester Pike
Upper Darby, PA 19082
215-789-8350

PRINTED ITEMS					
A	Annual Reports	G	Galley Copies	N	Workbooks
B	Books	H	Journals	O	Yearbooks
C	Booklets	I	Magazines	P	Brochures
D	Catalogs	J	Mass-Market Books	Q	Calendars
E	Cookbooks	K	Newsletters	R	Comic Books
F	Directories	L	Software Manuals	S	Direct Mail Letters
		M	Textbooks	T	Envelopes

U	Greeting Cards
V	Labels / Stickers
W	Maps
X	Newspapers
Y	Postcards
Z	Posters
1	Stationery

Min: 5,000 **Max:** 500,000 **Opt:**
Sizes: 2345X
Bindings: SSI
Items: ADPZ
Services: 4C
Equipment: 5SO
Year established: 195?

Comments: Precision specializes in printing plastic specialty items, such as overhead transparencies, overlays, and posters.

Preferred Graphics   BK
Tom Morgan
1151 E Broadway
Winona, MN 55987
507-452-8581; Fax: 507-452-1661
Toll-free: 800-247-7841

Min: 1,000 **Max:** 50,000 **Opt:** 10,000
Sizes: 123456
Bindings: HCI-CBO-GBI-LBO-
    PBI-SSI-SDI-SBO-WBO
Items: ABCDEFHIKPQSTWYZ1
Services: 4C-DA-AF-RP-TY-TD
Equipment: 4LP(25x38)-2SO(25x36)
Annual sales: $2,500,000
Number of employees: 56
Turnaround times: B4C3M4
Customers: BP10-BU53-CU20-MP2-NP15
Union shop: N
Year established: 1987
Terms: Net 30

Statement: We offer top quality with on time delivery.

Press America   GC
Attn: New Order Department
1001 Nicholas Boulevard
Chicago, IL 60641
312-228-0333

Min: 1,000 **Max:** 25,000 **Opt:**
Sizes: 25
Bindings: SSI
Items: CDKNPST1
Equipment: SO

Comments: A general commercial printer. Send for their price list.

The Press of Ohio   BK
3765 Sunnybrook Road
Brimfield, OH 44240
216-678-5868; Fax: 216-677-3346

Min: 25,000 **Max:** 2,000,000 **Opt:** 100,000
Sizes: 25
Bindings: PBI-SSI-SBO-WBO
Items: BDIMN
Services: 4C-CS-OC
Equipment: 2SO-4WO
Annual sales: $25,000,000
Number of employees: 250
Customers: BP39-BU39-MP22
Union shop: N
Year established: 1986

Statement: The Press of Ohio and Danner Press specialize in quality color printing of educational workbooks, magazines, and catalogs.

Princeton University Press   BK
Stan Cooper
3175 Princeton Pike
Lawrenceville, NJ 08648
609-896-2111

Min: 500 **Max:** 20,000 **Opt:** 2,000
Sizes: 235
Bindings: PBX-SSX
Items: BCDJM
Services: TY-TD
Year established: 1908

Comments: This university press also prints books for other university presses and trade publishers.

Prinit Press   BK
Bob Goodwin, Owner
2151 Franklin Street
P O Box 65
Dublin, IN 47335
317-478-4885

Min: 50 **Max:** 5,000 **Opt:** 2,000
Sizes: 1235
Bindings: HCO-CBO-GBI-
    PBI-SSI-SDI-SBO-WBO
Items: BCDEFKPQSTYZ1

SERVICES			BINDINGS		
4C	4-Color Printing	RA	Rachwal System	HC	Hardcover	SD	Side Stitching
CS	Color Separations	AF	Acid-Free Paper	CB	Comb Binding	SB	Spiral Binding
DA	Design / Artwork	RP	Recycled Paper	GB	Glue Binding	WB	Wire-O Binding
FF	Fulfillment/Mailing	TY	Typesetting	LB	Loose-Leaf Binding	I	In-House
LM	List Maintenance	TD	Typeset w/ Disk	PB	Perfect Binding	O	Out of House
OC	OptiCopy System	WA	Warehousing	SS	Saddle Stitching	X	Unknown

Services: 4C-DA-TY
Equipment: 3SO(11x17-17x22)
Annual sales: $500,000
Number of employees: 7
Turnaround times: B6C6M6
Customers: SP90-OT10
Union shop: N
Year established: 1969
Terms: 50% down, 50% on completion

Statement: We specialize in book printing for self-publishers and writers.

Print Northwest   GC
4918 20th Street E
P O Box 1418
Tacoma, WA 98401
206-922-9393

Min: 3,000 Max: 3,000,000 Opt: 80,000
Sizes: 1235
Bindings: CBI-PBI-SSI-SDI-WBI
Items: ACDEFIKLPQWYZ
Services: 4C
Equipment: 5LP-6SO(to 25x38)-
     1WO(17x26)
Annual sales: $15,000,000
Number of employees: 125
Turnaround times: C3M2
Customers: BU80-CU2-MP3-NP5
Union shop: Y
Year established: 1972
Terms: Net 30

The Printer Inc   CA
7401 Kilmer Lane
Maple Grove, MN 55369
612-424-7446

Min: 150,000 Max: 2,000,000 Opt:
Sizes: 5X
Bindings: PBI-SSI
Items: ADIX
Services: 4C-FF-TY
Equipment: 4WO
Annual sales: $30,000,000
Number of employees: 125
Turnaround times: C2M2
Customers: BU90-MP10
Union shop: N
Year established: 1985
Terms: Net 30

Printing Corporation of America   GC
620 SW 12th Avenue
Pompano Beach, FL 33060
305-781-8100

Min: 2,000 Max: 40,000 Opt: 15,000
Sizes: 2356X
Bindings: HCX-CBX-PBI-SSI-SBX
Items: ABCDFHIKNPQSTYZ
Services: 4C-CS-DA-TY
Terms: 50% down, balance COD

Printing Dimensions   GC
12104-J Indian Creek Court
Beltsville, MD 20705
301-953-2112

Sizes: 123456X
Bindings: CBI-LBI-PBI-SSI
Items: BCDFHIL[QSTYZ1
Services: DA-TY-TD-WA
Equipment: 9SO(10x15-28x40)
Annual sales: $5,000,000
Number of employees: 125
Turnaround times: B3C2M3
Union shop: N
Terms: 2% I0, Net 30

Progress Printing   GC
Daniel P Thornton, VP Sales
3523 Waterlick Road, P O Box 4575
Lynchburg, VA 24502
804-239-9213; Fax: 804-237-1618
Toll-free: 800-572-7804

Min: 1,000 Max: 5,000,000 Opt: 200,000
Sizes: 23456
Bindings: HCO-CBI-GBI-LBI-
     PBI-SSI-SDI-SBI-WBO
Items: ABCDEFHIKLNPQSTUVWYZ1
Services: 4C-CS-DA-OC-AF-RP-TY-TD
Equipment: 3LP(to 28x41)-15SO-
     2WO(17x23)
Annual sales: $30,000,000
Number of employees: 305
Turnaround times: B3-C3-M3
Customers: BP10-BU40-
     CU20-MP10-NP2-OT18
Union shop: N
Year established: 1962
Terms: Net 30

PRINTED ITEMS	G	Galley Copies	N	Workbooks	U	Greeting Cards
A Annual Reports	H	Journals	O	Yearbooks	V	Labels / Stickers
B Books	I	Magazines	P	Brochures	W	Maps
C Booklets	J	Mass-Market Books	Q	Calendars	X	Newspapers
D Catalogs	K	Newsletters	R	Comic Books	Y	Postcards
E Cookbooks	L	Software Manuals	S	Direct Mail Letters	Z	Posters
F Directories	M	Textbooks	T	Envelopes	1	Stationery

Progressive Typographers   **BK**
York County Industrial Park
P O Box 278
Emigsville, PA 17318
717-764-5908

Bindings: SSI
Items: BCDHI
Services: TY-TD
Equipment: SO

Comments: Primarily typesetters, they also print and bind saddlestiched publications in short runs.

ProLitho   **GC**
1775 South 350 East
Provo, UT 84601
801-373-7335

Items: ABCDFKLNPSTYZ1
Services: 4C
Equipment: 4SO-1WO
Number of employees: 100

Comments: A general commercial printer, ProLitho also produces computer software manuals and support materials.

Promotional Printing Corporation   **CA**
6902 Palestine Road
Houston, TX 77020
713-673-1005

Min: 50,000 Max: 2,000,000 Opt:
Sizes: 5X
Bindings: SSI
Items: DIPS
Services: 4C-CS-TY
Equipment: 2WO(21x36)

Comments: This subsidiary of the Houston Chronicle Company specializes in printing catalogs.

Providence Gravure   **CA**
10 Orms Street
Providence, RI 02904
401-331-1771; Toll-free: 800-678-6299

Min: 250,000 Max: 2,000,000 Opt:
Sizes: 235X
Bindings: PBI-SSI
Items: DX
Services: 4C-CS-FF
Equipment: 8WO-13OT(gravure)
Annual sales: $235,000,000
Number of employees: 1,650

Comments: A division of Quebecor.

Publishers Press   **BK**
Brent McPhie, Marketing Director
1900 West 2300 South
P O Box 27408
Salt Lake City, UT 84127-0408
801-972-6600; Fax: 801-972-6601
Toll-free: 800-456-6600

Min: 1,000 Max: 150,000 Opt: 10,000
Sizes: 123456X
Bindings: HCI-CBO-GBI-
    LBO-PBI-SSI-SBO-WBO
Items: BCDEFHJLMN
Services: 4C-FF-OC-AF
Equipment: 5SO(36"-41")-
    2WO(17x26-19x30)
Annual sales: $30,000,000
Number of employees: 115
Turnaround times: B4C4
Customers: BP50-BU20-CU5-SP25
Union shop: N
Year established: 1958
Terms: Net 30 upon credit approval

Statement: Our goal is to meet the needs of our clients, whatever those needs. We take great pride in the number of repeat customers we have.

Publishers Printing   **MS**
One Fourth Avenue
Shepherdsville, KY 40165
502-543-2251; Toll-free: 800-626-5801

Min: 10,000 Max: 2,000,000 Opt:
Bindings: PBI-SSI
Items: BCDHI
Services: 4C-FF
Equipment: SO-WO
Annual sales: $71,000,000
Number of employees: 1,000

SERVICES				BINDINGS			
4C	4-Color Printing	RA	Rachwal System	HC	Hardcover	SD	Side Stitching
CS	Color Separations	AF	Acid-Free Paper	CB	Comb Binding	SB	Spiral Binding
DA	Design / Artwork	RP	Recycled Paper	GB	Glue Binding	WB	Wire-O Binding
FF	Fulfillment/Mailing	TY	Typesetting	LB	Loose-Leaf Binding	I	In-House
LM	List Maintenance	TD	Typeset w/ Disk	PB	Perfect Binding	O	Out of House
OC	OptiCopy System	WA	Warehousing	SS	Saddle Stitching	X	Unknown

Q

MG
**Quad Graphics -
   Thomaston Press**
100 McIntosh Parkway
Thomaston, GA 30286
404-691-5020

Min: 50,000 Max: 2,000,000 Opt:
Sizes: 25X
Bindings: PBI-SSI
Items: JIX
Services: 4C-FF-TY
Equipment: 8WO
Turnaround times: M1
Comments: This division of W R Bean
was recently sold to Quad Graphics.

MG
Quad/Graphics, Lomira
952 Badger Road
Lomira, WI 53048
414-269-4700

Min: 100,000 Max: 7,000,000 Opt:
Sizes: 2345X
Bindings: PBI-SSI
Items: ACDIPW
Services: 4C-CS-FF-TY
Equipment: WO-3OT(gravure)
Turnaround times: M1
Customers: BU25-MP75

MG
Quad/Graphics, Pewaukee
W224 N3322 Duplainville Road
Pewaukee, WI 53072
414-691-9200

Min: 100,000 Max: 7,000,000 Opt:
Sizes: 2345X
Bindings: PBI-SSI
Items: ACDIPW
Services: 4C-CS-FF-TY
Equipment: 24WO
Annual sales: $376,000,000
Number of employees: 4,771
Turnaround times: M1
Customers: BU25-MP75
Year established: 1972

Comments: Quad Graphics prints many of
the largest circulation magazines and
catalogs in the United States.

MG
Quad/Graphics, Saratoga Springs
100 DuPlainville Road
Saratoga Springs, NY 12866
518-583-1920

Min: 100,000 Max: 7,000,000 Opt:
Sizes: 2345X
Bindings: PBI-SSI
Items: ACDIPW
Services: 4C-CS-FF-TY
Equipment: 24WO
Turnaround times: M1
Customers: BU25-MP75

CA
Quad/Graphics, Sussex
N63 W23075 Highway 74
Sussex, WI 53089
414-691-9200

Min: 100,000 Max: 7,000,000 Opt:
Sizes: 2345X
Bindings: PBI-SSI
Items: ACDIPW

BK
Quebecor America Book Group
Daniel Byrne, Marketing Director
9 East 38th Street
New York, NY 10016
212-779-2772; Fax: 212-779-2779

Min: 1,000 Max: 2,000,000 Opt: 30,000
Sizes: 23456X
Bindings: HCI-CBI-LBI-PBI-
       SSI-SDI-SBI-WBI
Items: BCDEFLMNPQTUVWZ
Services: 4C-OC
Equipment: 1CB-22SO(to 55x78)-
       10WO(various)
Annual sales: 1,700,000,000
Number of employees: 10,000
Turnaround times: B4
Customers: BP70-OT30
Union shop: Y
Terms: Net 30

PRINTED ITEMS			
A Annual Reports	G Galley Copies	N Workbooks	U Greeting Cards
B Books	H Journals	O Yearbooks	V Labels / Stickers
C Booklets	I Magazines	P Brochures	W Maps
D Catalogs	J Mass-Market Books	Q Calendars	X Newspapers
E Cookbooks	K Newsletters	R Comic Books	Y Postcards
F Directories	L Software Manuals	S Direct Mail Letters	Z Posters
	M Textbooks	T Envelopes	1 Stationery

Quinn-Woodbine   **BK**
Oceanview Road, P O Box 515
Woodbine, NJ 08270
609-861-5352; Fax: 609-861-5352

Min: 200 Max: 5,000 Opt: 1,000
Sizes: 2345
Bindings: HCI-CBO-PBI-SSI-SBO
Items: BFH
Equipment: SO
Number of employees: 72
Turnaround times: B4
Terms: Net 30 with approved credit

Quintessence Press   **BK**
Linomarl Beilke
356 Bunker Hill Mine Road
Amador City, CA 95601
209-267-5470

Min: 100 Max: 1,500 Opt: 1,000
Sizes: 235X
Bindings: HCI-CBI
Items: BCEKTUVYZ1
Services: DA-AF-RP-TY
Equipment: 11LP(14x20)
Annual sales: $250,000
Number of employees: 2
Turnaround times: B6
Customers: BP5-BU60-CU5-NP20-SP10
Union shop: N
Year established: 1976
Terms: 50% down, 50% on delivery

Statement: We print exclusively by letterpress, hence we accept no camera-ready
artwork. We have 2500 Ludlow, Linotype,
and handset typefaces. We are a working
pressroom printing museum.

Quixott Press   **BK**
Charles Ingerman, President
3291 Church School Road
Doylestown, PA 18901
215-794-7101
Min: 300 Max: 1,000 Opt: 500
Sizes: 12345
Bindings: HCO-PBI-SSI-SDI
Items: BETYZ1
Services: DA-TY

Equipment: 3LP(5x8/8x12/10x15)
Turnaround times: B5
Customers: NP5-SC10-SP40
Union shop: N
Year established: 1966

Comments: They specialize in all handset
letterpress publications.

R

Rand McNally   **BK**
Book Manufacturing Division
Box 84, US Bypass 60
Versailles, KY 40383-1496

Statement: This book and map publisher
also prints books for other companies.

Rapid Printing & Mailing   **GC**
9320 J Street
Omaha, NE 68127
402-331-0600

Min: 10,000 Max: 5,000,000 Opt: 1,000,000
Sizes: 12345
Bindings: GBI-LBO-PBO-
        SSI-SDI-SBO-WBO
Items: CDFKMNPSX
Services: 4C-DA-FF-LM-TY-WA
Equipment: 11SO(11x17-25x38)-6WO
Annual sales: $23,000,000
Number of employees: 230
Turnaround times: C3
Customers: BU93-CU2-SP5
Union shop: N
Year established: 1973
Terms: Net 10

Statement: A subsidiary of the *Omaha
World Herald*, we will provide full design,
production, and distribution of catalogs
and direct mail pieces on a regional basis.

RBW Graphics   **CA**
1749 - 20th Street E
P O Box 550
Owen Sound, Ontario N4K 5R2 Canada
519-376-8330

SERVICES			BINDINGS		
4C 4-Color Printing	**RA** Rachwal System		**HC** Hardcover	**SD** Side Stitching	
CS Color Separations	**AF** Acid-Free Paper		**CB** Comb Binding	**SB** Spiral Binding	
DA Design / Artwork	**RP** Recycled Paper		**GB** Glue Binding	**WB** Wire-O Binding	
FF Fulfillment/Mailing	**TY** Typesetting		**LB** Loose-Leaf Binding	**I** In-House	
LM List Maintenance	**TD** Typeset w/ Disk		**PB** Perfect Binding	**O** Out of House	
OC OptiCopy System	**WA** Warehousing		**SS** Saddle Stitching	**X** Unknown	

Min: 50,000 Max: 6,000,000 Opt: 250,000
Sizes: 25X
Bindings: HCI-PBI-SSI
Items: BDFINQ
Services: 4C-FF-TY-TD
Equipment: 1LP-4SO(to 28x41)-
    7WO(38x47)
Annual sales: $45,000,000
Number of employees: 600
Turnaround times: B5C5M3
Customers: BP17-BU43-CU5-MP30-NP5
Union shop: N
Year established: 1853
Terms: Net 30

Comments: A division of Southam, RBW
is a major catalog, magazine, and book
printer in Canada.

Realtron Multi-Lith   BK
165 S Union Boulevard
Denver, CO 80228
303-987-2338

Min: 10 Max: 1,000 Opt: 300
Sizes: 5
Bindings: PBI
Items: BCDFHLN
Services: TY-TD
Equipment: SO
Terms: Net 30

Comments: Realtron specializes in short
runs of high page count books, directories,
and manuals.

Recorder Sunset Press   MG
99 S Van Ness Avenue
San Francisco, CA 94103
415-621-5400

Min: 8,000 Max: 1,000,000 Opt: 100,000
Sizes: 25
Bindings: HCI-CBI-PBI-SSI-SBI
Items: BCDFILN
Services: 4C-TY-TD
Equipment: WO
Annual sales: $15,000,000
Terms: Net 30 with approved credit

Statement: We are the only printer in San
Francisco with a full heat-set web.

Regensteiner Press   MG
1833 Downs Drive
West Chicago, IL 60185
312-231-8600; Fax: 312-231-7273

Min: 50,000 Max: 2,000,000 Opt:
Sizes: 2345X
Bindings: PBI-SSI
Items: ABCDHIPSX
Services: 4C-CS-FF
Equipment: 6WO
Annual sales: $46,000,000
Number of employees: 300
Union shop: N
Year established: 1890

Repro-Tech   GC
250 Lackawanna Avenue
P O Box 600
West Patterson, NJ 07424
201-785-0011

Min: Max: 5,000 Opt: 3,000
Sizes: 235
Bindings: HCX-CBX-GBX-LBX-
    PBX-SSX-SDX-SBX-WBX
Items: ABCDEFGKLNPSTV1
Services: DA-LM-TY-TD-WA
Equipment: 5SO(11x17-14x18)
Annual sales: $4,000,000
Number of employees: 75
Turnaround times: B2C2
Union shop: N

Statement: We are a full-service commercial printing company offering typesetting,
electronic publishing, graphic design, offset
printing, and binding. We specialize in runs
between 500 and 5000.

Reproductions Inc   GC
12401 Washington Avenue
Rockville, MD 20852-1888
301-770-3333

Min: 500 Max: 500,000 Opt: 25,000
Sizes: 123456
Bindings: HCO-CBI-GBO-LBI-
    PBO-SSI-SDI-SBO-WBO
Items: ABCDEFHIKLMNPQRSTXYZ1
Services: 4C-DA-TY

PRINTED ITEMS				
A Annual Reports	G Galley Copies	N Workbooks	U Greeting Cards
B Books	H Journals	O Yearbooks	V Labels / Stickers
C Booklets	I Magazines	P Brochures	W Maps
D Catalogs	J Mass-Market Books	Q Calendars	X Newspapers
E Cookbooks	K Newsletters	R Comic Books	Y Postcards
F Directories	L Software Manuals	S Direct Mail Letters	Z Posters
	M Textbooks	T Envelopes	1 Stationery

Equipment: 7SO(11x17-28x40)-
2WO(36"-38")
Annual sales: $6,000,000
Number of employees: 125
Turnaround times: B2C2M2
Customers: BP5-BU20-CU15-
MP5-NP15-OR15-OT2
Union shop: N
Year established: 1967
Terms: 1% 10, Net 30

George Rice & Sons
GC

2001 N Solo Street
Los Angeles, CA 90032
213-223-2020

Bindings: SSI
Items: AI
Annual sales: $103,500,000
Number of employees: 540

Rich Printing Company
BK

P O Box 90472
7131 Centennial Boulevard
Nashville, TN 37209
615-385-3500

Min: 1,000 Max: 2,000,000 Opt:
Sizes: 2345X
Bindings: PBI-SSI
Items: BCDFHINP
Services: 4C-TY
Equipment: SO-WO
Year established: 1902

Rich Publishing Company
BR

H E Dobson, President
10611 Creektree
Houston, TX 77070
713-469-9165

Items: B
Services: DA
Annual sales: $300,000
Number of employees: 2
Customers: SP100
Union shop: N
Year established: 1982
Terms: 50% with order, 50% at printing

Statement: We specialize in working with self-publishers by providing manuscript evaluation, editing, jacket design, composition, proofreading, and subcontracting printing services.

Ringier America
GC

Ron Covelli, VP, Book Sales
One Pierce Place #800
Itasca, IL 60143-1272
708-285-6000; Fax: 708-285-6584

Min: 25,000 Max: 40,000,000 Opt: 200,000
Sizes: 123456X
Bindings: HCI-CBI-PBI-SSI-SDI
Items: BDEFHIJM
Services: 4C-CS-FF
Equipment: SO-WO-
OP(gravure & flexographic)
Annual sales: $665,000,000
Number of employees: 5,700
Turnaround times: B4C4M4
Customers: BP20-BU40-MP30-OR10
Union shop: N
Terms: Net 30

Statement: We are the nation's largest privately held printer. Nationwide, we bring the finest prepress, bindery, and distribution technology available today—and the first opportunity to use the technology of tomorrow.

Ringier America - Brookfield
MG

12821 W Blue Mound Road
Brookfield, WI 53005-8098
414-786-6000

Min: 10,000 Max: 2,000,000 Opt:
Sizes: 2345
Bindings: PBI-SSI
Items: ABDIMPQ
Services: 4C-CS-TY-WA
Equipment: 39WO

Ringier America - Corinth
MG

Corinth Division
1 Golden Drive
Corinth, MS 38834
601-287-3744

SERVICES				BINDINGS			
4C	4-Color Printing	RA	Rachwal System	HC	Hardcover	SD	Side Stitching
CS	Color Separations	AF	Acid-Free Paper	CB	Comb Binding	SB	Spiral Binding
DA	Design / Artwork	RP	Recycled Paper	GB	Glue Binding	WB	Wire-O Binding
FF	Fulfillment/Mailing	TY	Typesetting	LB	Loose-Leaf Binding	I	In-House
LM	List Maintenance	TD	Typeset w/ Disk	PB	Perfect Binding	O	Out of House
OC	OptiCopy System	WA	Warehousing	SS	Saddle Stitching	X	Unknown

Min: 200,000 Max: 2,000,000 Opt:
Sizes: 5X
Bindings: SSI-SDI
Items: DIWXZ
Services: 4C-FF
Equipment: WO-OT(gravure)

BK
Ringier America - Dresden
Mass Market Book Division
2073 Evergreen Street
Dresden, TN 38225
901-364-3171; Fax: ext. 315

Min: 30,000 Max: 2,000,000 Opt: 100,000
Sizes: 1
Bindings: PBI
Items: J

Comments: This division of Ringier specializes in printing mass-market books.

CA
Ringier America - Jonesboro
4708 Krueger Drive
Jonesboro, AR 72401-9198
501-935-7000

Min: 10,000 Max: 2,000,000 Opt:
Sizes: 2345
Bindings: SSI
Items: ADIMPQ

BK
Ringier America - New Berlin
16555 W Rogers Drive
New Berlin, WI 53151-2223
414-784-2000; Fax: 414-784-0968

Min: 1,500 Max: 2,000,000 Opt:
Sizes: 123456
Bindings: HCI-PBI
Items: ABDIMPQ
Services: 4C-CS-TY-WA
Equipment: 39WO
Turnaround times: B4

Comments: This division specializes in printing softcover and casebound books, especially elementary and high school textbooks, reference sets, and continuity series.

BK
Ringier America - Olathe
2115 E Kansas City Road
Olathe, KS 66201
913-764-5600; Fax: 913-764-3403
Toll-free: 800-678-0003

Min: 1,000 Max: 2,000,000 Opt: 5,000
Sizes: 123456X
Bindings: HCI-CBI-PBI-SSI-SBI
Items: BD
Services: 4C-TY-WA
Turnaround times: B3
Terms: Net 30 with approved credit

Comments: Formerly Interstate Book Manufacturers, this division specializes in one or two-color books of any trim size.

CA
Ringier America - Phoenix
2802 West Palm Lane
Phoenix, AZ 85009-2599
602-272-3221

Min: 10,000 Max: 2,000,000 Opt:
Sizes: 2345
Bindings: SSI
Items: ADIMPQ

CA
Ringier America - Pontiac
1600 N Main Street
P O Box 140
Pontiac, IL 61764-1060
815-844-5181

Min: 10,000 Max: 2,000,000 Opt:
Sizes: 2345
Bindings: SSI
Items: ADIMPQ

MS
Ringier America - Senatobia
121 Matthews Drive
P O Box 568
Senatobia, MS 38668-2304
601-562-5252

Min: 5,000 Max: 75,000 Opt:
Sizes: 2345
Bindings: PBI-SSI
Items: ABDIMPQ

PRINTED ITEMS							
A	Annual Reports	G	Galley Copies	N	Workbooks	U	Greeting Cards
B	Books	H	Journals	O	Yearbooks	V	Labels / Stickers
C	Booklets	I	Magazines	P	Brochures	W	Maps
D	Catalogs	J	Mass-Market Books	Q	Calendars	X	Newspapers
E	Cookbooks	K	Newsletters	R	Comic Books	Y	Postcards
F	Directories	L	Software Manuals	S	Direct Mail Letters	Z	Posters
		M	Textbooks	T	Envelopes	1	Stationery

Comments: This division specializes in printing quality magazines in economical standard formats in quantities from 5,000 to 75,000.

The Riverside Press GC
4901 Woodall Street
Dallas, TX 75247
214-631-1150

Min: 2,000 **Max:** 500,000 **Opt:**
Sizes: 25X
Bindings: SSI
Items: ACDKNPVZ
Services: 4C-CS
Equipment: SO-WO
Annual sales: $42,000,000
Number of employees: 400

John Roberts Company CA
9787 East River Road
Minneapolis, MN 55433
612-755-5500

Min: 10,000 **Max:** 750,000 **Opt:**
Sizes: 25X
Bindings: SSI
Items: ABCDNPZ
Services: 4C-CS
Equipment: 6LP(to 22x32)-
    14SO(to 28x40)-4WO
Annual sales: $19,000,000
Number of employees: 180
Year established: 1951

Rollins Press BK
1624 Forsyth Road
Orlando, FL 32807
305-667-5533

Bindings: PBI-SSI
Items: BCFHN
Services: TY
Equipment: LP-SO

Ronalds Printing CA
8000 Blaise Pascal
Montreal, Quebec H1E 2S7 Canada
514-648-1880

Min: 75,000 **Max:** 4,000,000 **Opt:**
Sizes: 5
Bindings: HCO-CBO-GBI-LBO-
    PBI-SSI-SDO-SBO-WBO
Items: ABCDEFHIJKLPRSXZ
Services: 4C-FF-WA
Equipment: 27SO-135WO
Turnaround times: C2M2
Customers: BU65-MP35
Union shop: Y
Year established: 1890
Terms: Credit to be arranged

Comments: Ronalds is a division of Quebecor Printing.

Ronalds Printing GC
1070 SE Marine Drive
Vancouver, British Columbia V5X 2V4
Canada
604-321-2231

Min: 10,000 **Max:** 275,000 **Opt:** 150,000
Sizes: 12345
Bindings: HCO-CBO-GBO-LBO-
    PBI-SSI-SDO-SBO-WBO
Items: BCDFHILMNPQSWZ
Services: 4C-FF-TY-TD
Equipment: 1LP-4SO(to 59")-5WO(23x38)
Turnaround times: B3C2M2
Customers: BP3-BU47-MP25-OT25
Union shop: Y
Year established: 1950
Terms: Net 30

Ronalds Printing CA
10481 Yonge Street
Richmond Hill, Ontario L4C 3C6 Canada
416-884-9121

Min: 75,000 **Max:** 4,000,000 **Opt:**
Sizes: 5
Bindings: HCO-CBO-GBI-LBO-
    PBI-SSI-SDO-SBO-WBO
Items: ABCDEFHIJKLPRSXZ
Services: 4C-FF-WA
Equipment: 27SO-135WO
Turnaround times: C2M2
Customers: BU65-MP35
Union shop: Y
Year established: 1890
Terms: Credit to be arranged

SERVICES			
4C 4-Color Printing	**RA** Rachwal System	**BINDINGS**	
CS Color Separations	**AF** Acid-Free Paper	**HC** Hardcover	**SD** Side Stitching
DA Design / Artwork	**RP** Recycled Paper	**CB** Comb Binding	**SB** Spiral Binding
FF Fulfillment/Mailing	**TY** Typesetting	**GB** Glue Binding	**WB** Wire-O Binding
LM List Maintenance	**TD** Typeset w/ Disk	**LB** Loose-Leaf Binding	**I** In-House
OC OptiCopy System	**WA** Warehousing	**PB** Perfect Binding	**O** Out of House
		SS Saddle Stitching	**X** Unknown

Rose Printing Company
BK

Charles Rosenberg, President
Rose Industrial Park
2503 Jackson Bluff Road
Tallahassee, FL 32304
904-576-4151; Fax: 904-576-4153
Toll-free: 800-227-3725

Min: 300 Max: 100,000 Opt: 3,500
Sizes: 123456X
Bindings: HCI-PBI-SSI
Items: BEFILMN
Services: OC-RP-TD
Equipment: 7SO(23x29-41x51)-
    3WO(21x39)
Annual sales: $18,000,000
Number of employees: 185
Turnaround times: B3C3
Customers: BP75-BU15-CU5-OR5
Union shop: N
Year established: 1932
Terms: Net 30 with approved credit

Statement: We commit to deliver a quality on-time product and service conforming to your expectations at a mutually beneficial value.

S Rosenthal & Company
MS

9933 Alliance Road
Cincinnati, OH 45242
513-984-0710; Fax: 516-984-5643
Toll-free: 800-325-7200

Min: 35,000 Max: 20,000,000 Opt:
Sizes: 23456
Bindings: PBI-SSI
Items: ACDFHIPQSXZ
Services: 4C-CS-DA-FF-TY-TD-WA
Equipment: 3SO(25x38)-
    4WO(22x38-31x46)
Annual sales: $26,000,000
Number of employees: 255
Turnaround times: B3C3M2
Customers: BU10-CU5-MP80-SC5
Union shop: Y
Year established: 1868
Terms: Net 30

Statement: Affiliated with the same company that publishes *Writer's Digest*, they print special interest magazines, catalogs, digests, and magazine inserts.

Roxbury Publishing Company
BK

Claude Teweles, Executive Editor
619 Baylor Street
P O Box 491044
Los Angeles, CA 90049
213-458-3493

Min: 100 Max: 2,000,000 Opt:
Sizes: 123456X
Bindings: HCO-CBI-GBO-LBO-
    PBI-SSI-SDI-SBO-WBO
Items: BEFJMN
Services: 4C-CS-DA-FF-AF-TY-TD-WA
Equipment: 5SO(to 41x54)-3WO(to 40x45)
Annual sales: $400,000
Number of employees: 75
Turnaround times: B5
Customers: BP50-SP50
Union shop: Y
Year established: 1979
Terms: 1/2 down, 1/2 with blues

Comments: Roxbury, a textbook and trade publishing company, does typesetting and printing of books for outside customers, including self-publishers.

Royle Printing
GC

The Royle Group
112 Market Street
Sun Prairie, WI 53590
608-837-5161

Min: 5,000 Max: 2,000,000 Opt:
Sizes: 2345X
Bindings: PBI-SSI
Items: ACDFINPXYZ
Services: 4C-FF
Equipment: SO-WO

Statement: See also the Artcraft Press.

RPP Enterprises
GC

1920 Enterprise Court
Libertyville, IL 60048
312-680-9700; Fax:
Toll-free: 800-

Min: 5,000 Max: 2,000,000 Opt:
Sizes: 256
Bindings: SSI-SDI

PRINTED ITEMS					
A Annual Reports	G Galley Copies	N Workbooks	U Greeting Cards
B Books	H Journals	O Yearbooks	V Labels / Stickers
C Booklets	I Magazines	P Brochures	W Maps
D Catalogs	J Mass-Market Books	Q Calendars	X Newspapers
E Cookbooks	K Newsletters	R Comic Books	Y Postcards
F Directories	L Software Manuals	S Direct Mail Letters	Z Posters
	M Textbooks	T Envelopes	1 Stationery

Items: ACDFKPQ
Services: 4C-DA-WA
Equipment: 3LP-5SO(to 25x38)-
   1WO(18x23)
Annual sales: $5,000,000
Number of employees: 125
Turnaround times: C3
Customers: BU90-OR10
Year established: 1927
Terms: Net 30

S

BK

Sabre Printers
Linda Lee
Sabre Group Inc
P O Box 518
Rogersville, TN 37857
615-272-3030; Fax: 615-272-7607

Min: 1,000 **Max:** 10,000 **Opt:** 2,500
Sizes: 1235
Bindings: PBI-SSI
Items: BCEFH
Equipment: SO
Year established: 1962

Comments: Write for a copy of their
Sabre's Edge Book Report newsletter.

MS

Saint Croix Press
1185 S Knowles Avenue
New Richmond, WI 54017
715-246-5811; Fax: 715-243-7555
Toll-free: 800-826-6622

Min: 1,000 **Max:** 150,000 **Opt:** 25,000
Sizes: 5
Bindings: PBI-SSI-SDI
Items: DEFHIPSZ
Services: 4C-FF-TY
Equipment: 5SO(25x38)-2WO
Annual sales: $15,000,000
Number of employees: 125
Turnaround times: C2M2
Customers: MP90-OR10
Union shop: Y
Year established: 1955
Terms: 2% 10, Net 30

GC

Saint Joseph Printing
3 Benton Road
Toronto, Ontario M6M 3G2 Canada
416-248-0721

Bindings: SSI
Items: DIQ

BK

Saint Mary's Press Division
Airport View Drive
Hollywood, MD 20636
301-373-5827

Min: 100 **Max:** 20,000 **Opt:** 5,000
Sizes: 123456X
Bindings: HCO-CBI-GBI-LBI-
   PBI-SSI-SDI-SBI-WBI
Items: BCDFGHKLMNPS
Services: 4C
Equipment: 7SO(29"-55")
Turnaround times: B3
Customers: BP20-BU15-CU10-
   NP40-SC10-SP5
Union shop: N
Year established: 1950
Terms: 1% 10, Net 30 w/approved credit

Comments: A division of McGregor &
Werner.

BK

Sanders Printing Company
P O Box 160
Garretson, SD 57030
Toll-free: 800-648-3738

Items: B
Services: TY-TD

BK

The Saybrook Press
146 Elm Street
P O Box 629
Old Saybrook, CT 06475
203-388-5737

Bindings: HCI-PBI
Items: BFH
Services: 4C-TY
Equipment: SO

Comments: They specialize in short run
journal typesetting and printing.

SERVICES				**BINDINGS**			
4C	4-Color Printing	RA	Rachwal System	HC	Hardcover	SD	Side Stitching
CS	Color Separations	AF	Acid-Free Paper	CB	Comb Binding	SB	Spiral Binding
DA	Design / Artwork	RP	Recycled Paper	GB	Glue Binding	WB	Wire-O Binding
FF	Fulfillment/Mailing	TY	Typesetting	LB	Loose-Leaf Binding	I	In-House
LM	List Maintenance	TD	Typeset w/ Disk	PB	Perfect Binding	O	Out of House
OC	OptiCopy System	WA	Warehousing	SS	Saddle Stitching	X	Unknown

Schiff Printers & Lithographers

GC

T Scott Barthelmes, Sales
1107 Washington Boulevard
P O Box 5131
Pittsburgh, PA 15206
412-441-5760; Fax: 412-441-0133

Min: 2,500 **Max:** 500,000 **Opt:** 50,000
Sizes: 123456
Bindings: PBI-SSI-SDI
Items: ABCDFKLNPS
Services: 4C-CS-AF-RP-TY-TD
Equipment: 5SO(17x22-28x41)
Annual sales: $3,000,000
Number of employees: 30
Turnaround times: B3C2
Customers: BP5-BU25-CU20-NP50
Union shop: N
Year established: 1954
Terms: Net 30

Statement: We are equipped and staffed to produce newsletters, bulletins, paperback books, industrial product literature, brochures, and folders—from typesetting to the finished product.

Schlasbach Printers

BK

RR 1, Box 301
Sugarcreek, OH 44681

Min: 100 **Max:** 200,000 **Opt:**
Annual sales: $200,000
Number of employees: 6
Year established: 1979

Schumann Printers

MS

701 S Main Street
P O Box 128
Fall River, WI 53932
414-484-3348; Fax: 414-484-3661

Min: 10,000 **Max:** 250,000 **Opt:** 50,000
Sizes: 5
Bindings: SSI-PBI
Items: HI
Services: 4C-CS-FF
Equipment: WO
Year established: 1963

Science Press

BK

Volker Kruhoeffer, Mktg Director
Monroe Printing
300 W Chestnut Street
Ephrata, PA 17522
717-738-9300; Fax: 717-738-9424

Min: 2,000 **Max:** 50,000 **Opt:** 10,000
Sizes: 123456
Bindings: PBI-SSI-SDI
Items: ABCDEFHLMNO
Services: 4C-FF-OC-RA-
    AF-RP-TY-TD-WA
Equipment: 6SO(25x38-41x50)-
    1WO(22x36)
Annual sales: $33,000,000
Number of employees: 405
Turnaround times: B3C3
Customers: BP20-BU10-
    CU10-MP30-NP20-OR10
Union shop: N
Year established: 1901
Terms: Net 30

Statement: We offer complete compositor/database services for journal, book, directory, and catalog publishers. We also print by sheetfed, low-run high-quality four-color catalogs and art books. Mack Printing recently bought Monroe Printing and Science Press.

Semline Inc

BK

Daniel Byrne, Marketing Director
180 Wood Road
Braintree, MA 02184
617-843-8100; Fax: 617-843-3643

Min: 1,000 **Max:** 2,000,000 **Opt:** 30,000
Sizes: 23456X
Bindings: HCO-CBI-LBI-
    PBI-SSI-SDI-SBI-WBI
Items: BCDEFLMNP
Services: 4C-OC
Equipment: 4SO(to 54x77)-5WO(23x38)
Annual sales: $33,000,000
Number of employees: 300
Turnaround times: B4M4
Customers: BP65-CU2-OT33
Union shop: Y
Year established: 1896
Terms: Net 30

PRINTED ITEMS						
A	Annual Reports	G	Galley Copies	N	Workbooks	U Greeting Cards
B	Books	H	Journals	O	Yearbooks	V Labels / Stickers
C	Booklets	I	Magazines	P	Brochures	W Maps
D	Catalogs	J	Mass-Market Books	Q	Calendars	X Newspapers
E	Cookbooks	K	Newsletters	R	Comic Books	Y Postcards
F	Directories	L	Software Manuals	S	Direct Mail Letters	Z Posters
		M	Textbooks	T	Envelopes	1 Stationery

Comments: Semline is now owned by Quebecor Printing ($1.7 billion in annual sales from 60 plants with 10,000 employees).

BK

Service Printing Company
2725 Miller Street
San Leandro, CA 94577
415-352-7890

Min: 1,000 **Max:** 25,000 **Opt:** 5,000
Sizes: 245X
Bindings: HCX-CBX-PBX-SSX-SBX
Items: BCDFLN
Equipment: SO
Turnaround times: B2
Year established: 1925
Terms: Net 30

Comments: They specialize in producing training and technical manuals for the computer/technical industry. Their routine delivery is 5 to 7 working days from receipt of camera-ready copy.

MS

Sexton Printing
Mike Poquette
250 E Lothenbach Avenue
West Saint Paul, MN 55118
612-457-9255; Fax: 612-457-7040

Min: 10 **Max:** 20,000 **Opt:** 5,000
Sizes: 123456X
Bindings: HCO-PBO-SSI
Items: ABCDFHIKNP
Services: 4C-DA-FF-LM-OC-TY-TD
Equipment: 1LP(10x15)-11SO(11x15-28x40)
Customers: BU-NP-OR
Year established: 1949

Comments: Sexton specializes in printing newsletters, house organs, and magazines for clubs, associations, and businesses.

MG

Shepard Poorman Communications
P O Box 68110
7301 N Woodland Drive
Indianapolis, IN 46268
317-293-1500

Bindings: SSI
Items: ACDFHIK
Services: OC-TY
Annual sales: $17,500,000
Number of employees: 220
Year established: 1977

MS

The Sheridan Press
Donald G Ford, VP Sales
Fame Avenue
Hanover, PA 17331
717-632-3535; Fax: 717-633-8900
Toll-free: 800-352-2210

Min: 500 **Max:** 50,000 **Opt:** 10,000
Sizes: 235X
Bindings: HCO-CBO-PBI-SSI-SDI-SBO
Items: DEFHIK
Services: 4C-DA-FF-LM-TY-TD
Equipment: 9SO
Annual sales: $51,000,000
Number of employees: 800
Turnaround times: B3M3
Customers: BU-CU-MP-NP-OR-SC
Year established: 1915
Terms: Net 30

Comments: Sheridan, which recently bought Braun-Brumfield, specializes in printing medical, technical, and scholarly journals in press runs from 500 to 50,000.

MS

Sheridan Printing Company
1425 Third Avenue
Alpha, NJ 08865
201-454-0700

Min: 1,000 **Max:** 50,000 **Opt:**
Sizes: 5
Bindings: PBI-SSI
Items: DI
Services: 4C-FF-TY

GC

Skillful Means Press
1241 - 21st Street
Oakland, CA 94607
415-839-3931

Min: 2,000 **Max:** 50,000 **Opt:** 20,000
Sizes: 235

SERVICES			BINDINGS		
4C 4-Color Printing	RA Rachwal System		HC Hardcover	SD Side Stitching	
CS Color Separations	AF Acid-Free Paper		CB Comb Binding	SB Spiral Binding	
DA Design / Artwork	RP Recycled Paper		GB Glue Binding	WB Wire-O Binding	
FF Fulfillment/Mailing	TY Typesetting		LB Loose-Leaf Binding	I In-House	
LM List Maintenance	TD Typeset w/ Disk		PB Perfect Binding	O Out of House	
OC OptiCopy System	WA Warehousing		SS Saddle Stitching	X Unknown	

Bindings: HCX-CBX-PBX-SSX-SBX
Items: BCDFHKNPSTYZ1
Services: 4C-TY
Equipment: SO
Union shop: N
Year established: 1959
Terms: 50% down, balance net 30

Comments: Formerly known as Dharma Press, Skillful Means is a general commercial printer.

Slater Lithographers   GC
645 West 44th Street
New York, NY 10036
212-757-8877

SLC Graphics   MG
50 Rock Street
Hughestown Borough
Pittston, PA 18640
717-655-9681

Min: 100,000 **Max:** 400,000 **Opt:** 100,000
Sizes: 23456X
Bindings: PBI-SSI
Items: I
Services: 4C-CS-FF-WA
Equipment: 3WO(22x36-38x54)
Annual sales: $16,000,000
Number of employees: 200
Turnaround times: M4
Customers: MP100
Union shop: Y
Year established: 1970
Terms: Net 30

R E Smith Printing   GC
900 Jefferson Street
P O Box 1800
Fall River, MA 02722
617-679-2131

Min: 1,000 **Max:** 100,000 **Opt:** 20,000
Sizes: 35
Bindings: CBO-LBO-PBO-SSI-SDI-SBO-WBO
Items: ADFIKLNPQYZ
Services: 4C-TY

Equipment: 11LP(to 27x41)-9SO(to 28x40)-2WO
Annual sales: $5,000,000
Number of employees: 125
Turnaround times: B3C3M3
Customers: BU75-CU5-MP5-NP3-SC3-SP2-OT5
Union shop: N
Year established: 1964
Terms: Net 30

Statement: R. E. Smith is a division of Close Manufacturing.

Smith-Edwards-Dunlap   GC
2867 E Allegheny Avenue
Phildelphia, PA 19134
215-425-8800

Bindings: SSI
Items: ACDHIKNPSZ
Services: 4C-FF-TY
Equipment: LP-SO-WO
Annual sales: $25,000,000
Number of employees: 410

Snohomish Publishing   BK
114 Avenue C
P O Box 1248
Snohomish, WA 98290
206-339-3301

Min: 500 **Max:** 50,000 **Opt:** 3,000
Sizes: 25
Bindings: HCO-PBI-SSI
Items: ABCDEFIKLNPQX
Services: 4C-TY-TD
Equipment: 2SO(18x23-23x29)-2WO(22x36)
Annual sales: $5,000,000
Number of employees: 30
Turnaround times: B4C3M3
Customers: BP5-SP35-OT60
Union shop: N
Year established: 1965
Terms: 1/2 down, 1/4 delivery, net 30

Statement: We provide the author with the guidance and facilities to produce their self-published book.

Southam Printing   **MG**
P O Box 510
2973 Weston Road
Weston, Ontario M9N 3R3 Canada
416-741-9700

Min: 50,000 **Max:** 10,000,000 **Opt:**
Sizes: 2345X
Bindings: SSI
Items: ABCDFHINX
Services: 4C-CS-TY
Equipment: LP-WO-OT(gravure)
Annual sales: $585,921,000
Number of employees: 4,200

Comments: Southam specializes in printing 4-color magazines, catalogs, books, and annual reports.

Southeastern Printing Company   **GC**
3601 SE Dixie Highway
P O Box 2476
Stuart, FL 33495
407-287-2141; Fax: 407-288-3988
Toll-free: 800-228-1583

Min: 5,000 **Max:** 100,000 **Opt:**
Sizes: 2356
Bindings: CBI-GBI-PBI-SSI-SDI-WBI
Items: ABCDEILMPQUWYZ
Services: 4C-FF-WA
Equipment: 4SO(28x40)
Annual sales: $12,500,000
Number of employees: 130
Turnaround times: B5C4
Customers: BU100
Union shop: N
Year established: 1924
Terms: Net 30

Statement: We are a sheetfed lithographer serving the corporate, professional, creative, financial, industrial, and publishing markets.

Southern California Graphics   **MS**
8432 Stellar Drive
Culver City, CA 90232
213-559-3600

Bindings: SSI
Items: AIP

Southern Tennessee Publishing   **BK**
P O Box 91
Waynesboro, TN 38485
615-722-5404

Min: 50 **Max:** 2,000 **Opt:** 500
Sizes: 125
Bindings: HCO-PBO-SSI
Items: BCHP
Services: 4C-DA-TY
Equipment: SO
Customers: SP100
Terms: Payment in full with order

Comments: They are a small printer serving self-publishers. Send for their standard price list.

Sowers Printing Company   **MG**
N 10th & Scull Street
P O Box 479
Lebanon, PA 17042-0479
717-272-6667; Toll-free: 800-233-7028

Min: 2,000 **Max:** 2,000,000 **Opt:**
Sizes: 2345X
Bindings: PBI-SSI
Items: BCDFHIKN
Services: 4C-FF-LM
Equipment: SO-WO

Speaker-Hines & Thomas   **GC**
P O Box 11120
Lansing, MI 48901
517-321-0740; Toll-free: 800-292-2630

Min: 25,000 **Max:** 2,000,000 **Opt:**
Sizes: 235X
Bindings: GBI-PBI-SSI-SDI
Items: CDHIKNPSX
Services: 4C-CS-FF
Equipment: LP-SO-WO
Annual sales: $17,000,000
Number of employees: 145

Spencer Press   **CA**
90 Industrial Park Road
Hingham, MA 02043
617-749-5000; Toll-free: 800-343-5690

SERVICES			**BINDINGS**		
4C 4-Color Printing	**RA** Rachwal System		**HC** Hardcover	**SD** Side Stitching
CS Color Separations	**AF** Acid-Free Paper		**CB** Comb Binding	**SB** Spiral Binding
DA Design / Artwork	**RP** Recycled Paper		**GB** Glue Binding	**WB** Wire-O Binding
FF Fulfillment/Mailing	**TY** Typesetting		**LB** Loose-Leaf Binding	**I** In-House
LM List Maintenance	**TD** Typeset w/ Disk		**PB** Perfect Binding	**O** Out of House
OC OptiCopy System	**WA** Warehousing		**SS** Saddle Stitching	**X** Unknown

Min: 50,000 Max: 5,000,000 Opt:
Sizes: 235X
Bindings: GBI-SSI
Items: ACDPSX
Services: 4C-CS-FF-TY
Equipment: 6WO
Annual sales: $55,000,000
Number of employees: 480
Year established: 1940

Spencer Press / Wells   CA
90 Spencer Drive
Wells, ME 04090
617-749-5000; Toll-free: 800-343-5690

Min: 50,000 Max: 5,000,000 Opt:
Sizes: 235X
Bindings: GBI-SSI
Items: ACDPSX
Services: 4C-CS-FF-TY
Equipment: 6WO
Annual sales: $55,000,000
Number of employees: 480
Year established: 1940

Staked Plains Press   GC
P O Box 816
Canyon, TX 79015
806-655-1061

Bindings: CBI-SBI
Items: BCELP
Services: 4C-CS-TY
Equipment: SO

Standard Printing Service   BK
162 N State Street
Chicago, IL 60601
413-686-0441

Bindings: HCI
Items: BFM
Services: TY
Equipment: SO-WO

Standard Publishing   CA
8121 Hamilton Avenue
Cincinnati, OH 45231
513-931-4050; Toll-free: 800-543-1301

Min: 50,000 Max: 4,000,000 Opt:
Sizes: 2345X
Bindings: GBI-PBI-SSI-SDI
Items: DFHNPXZ
Services: 4C-FF-TY
Equipment: 4SO-3WO
Annual sales: $450,000,000
Number of employees: 4,000
Year established: 1866

Comments: They are a full service commercial printer who prints many industrial catalogs as well as religious publications.

Stephenson Inc   CA
5731 General Washington Drive
Alexandria, VA 22312
703-642-9000; Toll-free: 800-336-4637

Min: 2,000 Max: 2,000,000 Opt:
Sizes: 2345X
Bindings: PBI-SSI
Items: ABCDFHIKNPSWXZ
Services: 4C-CS-FF
Equipment: 7SO(40")-2WO
Annual sales: $20,000,000
Number of employees: 180

Stewart Publishing & Printing   BK
Jonathan Stewart, Manager
646 Pomeroy Road
Marble Hill, MO 63764
314-238-4273

Min: 50 Max: 5,000 Opt: 2,500
Sizes: 123456
Bindings: PBI-SSI-SBI
Items: ABCDEFHJKNOPSTYZ1
Services: 4C-DA-TY-TD
Equipment: 3SO(19x15)
Annual sales: $200,000
Number of employees: 5
Turnaround times: B5C4
Customers: BP5-BU10-
    CU10-NP20-SC5-SP50
Union shop: N
Year established: 1977
Terms: 50% down, 50% net 30

Statement: Our goal is to help self-publishers obtain the highest quality books at the most reasonable costs. We also provide editorial and marketing assistance.

PRINTED ITEMS							
A	Annual Reports	G	Galley Copies	N	Workbooks	U	Greeting Cards
B	Books	H	Journals	O	Yearbooks	V	Labels / Stickers
C	Booklets	I	Magazines	P	Brochures	W	Maps
D	Catalogs	J	Mass-Market Books	Q	Calendars	X	Newspapers
E	Cookbooks	K	Newsletters	R	Comic Books	Y	Postcards
F	Directories	L	Software Manuals	S	Direct Mail Letters	Z	Posters
		M	Textbooks	T	Envelopes	1	Stationery

Stinehour Press **BK**
P O Box 159
Lunenburg, VT 05906-0159
802-328-2507; Fax: 802-328-3821

Min: 100 Max: 75,000 Opt:
Sizes: 123456X
Bindings: HCI-PBI-SSI
Items: ABHQUYZ
Services: 4C-CS-DA-FF-TY-TD-WA
Equipment: LP-SO
Annual sales: $5,000,000
Number of employees: 75
Turnaround times: B5
Union shop: N
Year established: 1887
Terms: varies

Straus Printing Company **GC**
1028 E Washington Avenue
P O Box 2118
Madison, WI 53701
608-251-3222

Min: 10,000 Max: 1,000,000 Opt:
Sizes: 25X
Bindings: PBI-SSI
Items: ACDEFIPQSVWYZ
Services: 4C-CS
Equipment: 2SO(38"-40")-1WO(17x26)
Annual sales: $5,000,000
Number of employees: 75
Turnaround times: C3M2
Customers: BU70-CU10-MP10-OR10
Union shop: N
Year established: 1920
Terms: Net 30

Comments: Their specialties are medium runs of high quality 4-color catalogs and annual reports as well as posters and other color brochures.

The Studley Press **BK**
P O Box 214
151 E Housatonic Street
Dalton, MA 01226
413-686-0441

Min: 1,000 Max: 20,000 Opt: 10,000
Sizes: 235

Bindings: HCI-CBX-PBI-SSX-SBX
Items: ABCHIP
Services: 4C-DA-TY-TD
Equipment: SO
Terms: Net 30

Suburban Publishers **CA**
Stevens Lane
Exeter, PA 18643
717-655-6881

Min: 100,000 Max: 10,000,000 Opt: 500,000
Sizes: 12456X
Bindings: HCO-CBO-GBI-LBO-
   PBI-SSI-SDI-SBO-WBO
Items: ACDFIPX
Services: 4C-CS-DA-LM-TY-WA
Equipment: 6WO(22x38)
Annual sales: $30,000,000
Number of employees: 250
Turnaround times: B4C2M2
Customers: BP3-BU80-CU1-MP6-OT10
Union shop: N
Year established: 1967
Terms: Net 30

Comments: A subsidiary of Jewelcor.

Sun Graphics **CA**
Larry Reed, Marketing VP
1818 Broadway
Parsons, KS 67357
316-421-6200; Fax: 316-421-2089
Toll-free: 800-835-0588

Bindings: SSI
Items: DP
Services: 4C-CS-TY

Statement: Primarily color separators.

Sundance Press **MS**
817 East 18th Street (85719)
P O Box 26605
Tucson, AZ 84726
602-622-5233; Toll-free: 800-528-4827

Min: 1,000 Max: 10,000 Opt: 10,000
Sizes: 5
Bindings: SSI
Items: I
Equipment: SO

SERVICES				BINDINGS			
4C	4-Color Printing	RA	Rachwal System	HC	Hardcover	SD	Side Stitching
CS	Color Separations	AF	Acid-Free Paper	CB	Comb Binding	SB	Spiral Binding
DA	Design / Artwork	RP	Recycled Paper	GB	Glue Binding	WB	Wire-O Binding
FF	Fulfillment/Mailing	TY	Typesetting	LB	Loose-Leaf Binding	I	In-House
LM	List Maintenance	TD	Typeset w/ Disk	PB	Perfect Binding	O	Out of House
OC	OptiCopy System	WA	Warehousing	SS	Saddle Stitching	X	Unknown

Sweet Printing CA
P O Box 49390 (Austin)
1000 S Interstate 35
Round Rock, TX 78681
512-255-1055

Min: 5,000 Max: 2,000,000 Opt:
Sizes: 2345X
Bindings: PBI-SSI
Items: ADHINPSWZ
Services: 4C-CS-DA-FF-TY
Equipment: 1SO-2WO

Statement: We print catalogs, flyers, magazines, and maps—anything that will take ink on paper.

John S Swift Company GC
1248 Research Boulevard
P O Box 28252
Saint Louis, MO 63132
314-991-4300

Min: 100 Max: 15,000 Opt: 5,000
Sizes: 23456X
Bindings: CBI-PBI-SSI-SBI
Items: ABCDKPQSTWYZ1
Services: 4C-TY
Equipment: SO-WO
Year established: 1912

John S Swift, Chicago GC
17 N Loomis Street
P O Box 7261
Chicago, IL 60607
312-666-7020

John S Swift, Cincinnati GC
2524 Spring Grove
Cincinnati, OH 45214
513-721-4147

John S Swift, Teterboro GC
U S Route 46
Teterboro, NJ 07608
201-288-2050

T

T A S Graphic Communications GC
11191 Lappin
Detroit, MI 48234
313-372-9770

Min: 100,000 Max: 2,000,000 Opt: 500,000
Sizes: 1245
Bindings: HCO-CB0-GBO-LBO-
    PBI-SSI-SDI-SPO-WBO
Items: ABCDEFGHIKNPQRSWXYZ
Services: 4C-CS-DA-TY-TD-WA
Equipment: 5SO(to 58")-5WO(to 36")
Annual sales: $30,000,000
Number of employees: 125
Turnaround times: B3C3M3
Customers: BU50-CU10-MP30-NP5-SC5
Union shop: N
Year established: 1975
Terms: Net 30

Tapco MG
Fort Dix-Pemberton Road
Pemberton, NJ 08068
609-894-2282

Min: 10,000 Max: 1,000,000 Opt:
Sizes: 25X
Bindings: SSI
Items: CDIKNPX
Services: 4C-TY
Equipment: SO-WO

Comments: Their specialties are tabloids, mini-tabs, and digest-sized books.

Taylor Publishing Company BK
1550 W Mockingbird Lane
Dallas, TX 75235
214-637-2800

Min: 1,000 Max: 50,000 Opt: 5,000
Sizes: 2345X
Bindings: HCI-CBX-PBX-SBX
Items: BFO
Services: 4C-CS-TY
Equipment: many SO
Annual sales: $97,389,000
Number of employees: 1,850

PRINTED ITEMS							
A	Annual Reports	G	Galley Copies	N	Workbooks	U	Greeting Cards
B	Books	H	Journals	O	Yearbooks	V	Labels / Stickers
C	Booklets	I	Magazines	P	Brochures	W	Maps
D	Catalogs	J	Mass-Market Books	Q	Calendars	X	Newspapers
E	Cookbooks	K	Newsletters	R	Comic Books	Y	Postcards
F	Directories	L	Software Manuals	S	Direct Mail Letters	Z	Posters
		M	Textbooks	T	Envelopes	1	Stationery

Comments: A division of Insilco Corporation, Taylor is a publisher as well as printer. Their specialty is school and college yearbooks.

GC
Technical Communication Service
David Teeters
110 West 12th Avenue
North Kansas City, MO 64116
816-842-9770; Fax: 816-842-0628

Min: 100 **Max:** 10,000 **Opt:** 5,000
Sizes: 2345
Bindings: HCO-CBI-LBI-PBI-
   SSI-SDI-SBI-WBI
Items: BDEFHKLMNQT
Services: FF-AF-TY-WA
Equipment: SO
Annual sales: $15,000,000
Number of employees: 50
Turnaround times: B3M3
Customers: BP55-NP25-OR20
Union shop: N
Year established: 1970
Terms: Net 30

Statement: We offer quality and service for our clients plus a competitive price.

MG
Telegraph Press
Cameron & Kelker Streets
P O Box 1831
Harrisburg, PA 17105
717-234-5091

Min: 5,000 **Max:** 2,000,000 **Opt:**
Sizes: 2356X
Bindings: GBI-PBI-SSI
Items: CDFIKNPX
Services: 4C-CS-DA-FF-WA
Equipment: SO-WO
Annual sales: $12,000,000
Number of employees: 240
Year established: 1831

Comments: A subsidiary of Commonwealth Communications Services, Telegraph prints magazines, tabloids, catalogs, and paperback books.

CA
Texas Color Printers
4100 Spring Valley Road #704
P O Box 809067
Dallas, TX 75234
214-233-3400; Toll-free: 800-678-6299

Min: 250,000 **Max:** 2,000,000 **Opt:**
Sizes: 235X
Bindings: PBI-SSI
Items: DX
Services: 4C-CS-FF
Equipment: 8WO-13OT(gravure)

Comments: Texas Color Printers is a division of Quebecor Printing.

Thomson - Shore

BK
Thomson-Shore
Ned Thomson, President
7300 W Joy Road
P O Box 305
Dexter, MI 48130-0305
313-426-3939; Fax: 313-426-6219

Min: 25 **Max:** 6,000 **Opt:** 1,500
Sizes: 2345
Bindings: HCI-CBI-PBI-
   SSI-SDI-SBO-WBO
Items: BCDEFHLMN
Services: RA-AF-RP
Equipment: 9SO(25x35-42x55)
Annual sales: $17,000,000
Number of employees: 240
Turnaround times: B4M4
Customers: BP50-CU40-NP10
Union shop: N
Year established: 1972
Terms: Net 30

Statement: Quality is our strength. We operate without salespeople, nor do we advertise. We rely on customer recommendations and on keeping customers happy with our prices and performance. Write for a free copy of our *Printer's Ink* newsletter.

SERVICES				
4C	4-Color Printing	RA	Rachwal System	
CS	Color Separations	AF	Acid-Free Paper	
DA	Design / Artwork	RP	Recycled Paper	
FF	Fulfillment/Mailing	TY	Typesetting	
LM	List Maintenance	TD	Typeset w/ Disk	
OC	OptiCopy System	WA	Warehousing	

BINDINGS				
HC	Hardcover	SD	Side Stitching	
CB	Comb Binding	SB	Spiral Binding	
GB	Glue Binding	WB	Wire-O Binding	
LB	Loose-Leaf Binding	I	In-House	
PB	Perfect Binding	O	Out of House	
SS	Saddle Stitching	X	Unknown	

Times Litho
MS

2014 A Street, P O Box 7
Forest Grove, OR 97116
503-648-7165

Min: 5,000 **Max:** 200,000 **Opt:** 40,000
Sizes: 25
Bindings: LBI-SSI
Items: DEFIRS
Services: TY-WA
Equipment: 2SO(25"-40")-3WO(38"-39")
Annual sales: $12,000,000
Number of employees: 100
Turnaround times: B3C3M3
Customers: BP5-BU50-MP45
Union shop: N
Year established: 1950
Terms: Net 30

Times Printing
MS

453 Fifth Street, P O Box 325
Random Lake, WI 53075
414-994-4396

Min: 500 **Max:** 1,000,000 **Opt:** 100,000
Sizes: 123456X
Bindings: HCO-CBI-GBO-LBI-
   PBI-SSI-SDI-SBO-WBO
Items: ABCDEFGHIKLNPQRSTWXYZ1
Services: 4C-DA-FF-AF-TY-TD-WA
Equipment: 6SO(10x15-28x41)-
   2WO(to 22x37)
Annual sales: $5,000,000
Number of employees: 125
Turnaround times: B3C2M2
Customers: BU40-CU1-MP50-
   NP1-OR1-SC1-SP6
Union shop: N
Year established: 1954
Terms: Net 30

Todd Web Press
GC

Sharon Haney, Sales Manager
205 E Third, P O Box 269
Smithville, TX 78957
512-237-3546; Fax: 512-237-5358

Min: 2,500 **Max:** 2,000,000 **Opt:** 100,000
Sizes: 3456
Bindings: HCO-PBO-SSO

Items: BCDFIJKLMNPXZ
Services: 4C-CS-FF-OC-WA
Equipment: 3SO(23x25-43x60)-
   2WO(23x36)
Annual sales: $2,500,000
Number of employees: 25
Turnaround times: B3C2M2
Customers: CU25-MP50-NP5-State20
Union shop: N
Year established: 1975
Terms: C.O.D.

Statement: We strive to provide quality products for our customers within a reasonable time frame. Our emphasis is on our service and educating publishers to the printing industries.

Tompson & Rutter
BR

Frances T Rutter, President
Dunbar Hill Road
P O Box 297
Grantham, NH 03753
603-863-4392

S C Toof and Company
BK

670 S Cooper Street, P O Box 14607
Memphis, TN 38114
901-278-2200

Bindings: CBI
Items: E
Year established: 1864

Comments: Toof prints and distributes many community, organizational, and other fundraising cookbooks.

Town House Press
BR

Alvin Schultzberg, President
552 Fearrington Post
Pittsboro, NC 27312
919-542-6242; Fax: 919-542-3922

Min: 100 **Max:** 5,000 **Opt:** 2,000
Sizes: 123456X
Bindings: HCO-CBO
Items: BCEFHMN
Services: 4C-CS-DA-AF-TY-TD
Equipment: none

PRINTED ITEMS							
A	Annual Reports	G	Galley Copies	N	Workbooks	U	Greeting Cards
B	Books	H	Journals	O	Yearbooks	V	Labels / Stickers
C	Booklets	I	Magazines	P	Brochures	W	Maps
D	Catalogs	J	Mass-Market Books	Q	Calendars	X	Newspapers
E	Cookbooks	K	Newsletters	R	Comic Books	Y	Postcards
F	Directories	L	Software Manuals	S	Direct Mail Letters	Z	Posters
		M	Textbooks	T	Envelopes	1	Stationery

Annual sales: $1,000,000
Number of employees: 2
Turnaround times: B4
Customers: BP40-NP35-OR10-SP15
Union shop: N
Year established: 1970
Terms: Net 30 (qualified clients)

Statement: We broker book printing services for small publishing houses, non-profit publishers, and self-publishing ventures.

Tracor Publications   GC
6500 Tracor Lane
Austin, TX 78725
512-929-2222

Min: 50 Max: 50,000 Opt: 10,000
Sizes: 123456X
Bindings: CBI-PBI-SSI
Items: ABCDEFHIKNO
Services: 4C-DA-TY
Equipment: SO

Comments: Tracor is a commercial printer specializing in magazine production and fulfillment as well as the printing of annual reports, sales literature, and technical manuals.

Tri-Graphic Printing   BK
Doug Doane, Sales Manager
465 Industrial Avenue
Ottawa, Ontario K1G 0Z1 Canada
613-731-7441; Fax: 613-731-3741

Min: 2,000 Max: 1,000,000 Opt: 50,000
Sizes: 123456
Bindings: HCI-LBI-PBI-
    SSI-SDI-SBO-WBO
Items: BDEFHILMNPQ
Services: 4C-OC-AF-RP-TY-TD
Equipment: 7SO(11x15-28x40)-
    1WO(40x46)
Annual sales: $15,000,000
Number of employees: 115
Turnaround times: B3C3M3
Customers: BP30-BU30-
    CU20-MP10-OT10
Union shop: N
Year established: 1968
Terms: Net 30

Statement: We service publishers of trade books, college course calendars, and wholesale catalogs. We also have facilities for inserting, labelling, and mailing.

Tri-State Press   GC
K C MacNeill, President
P O Box 1866
Clayton, GA 30525
404-782-2134

Sizes: 123456X
Bindings: CBI-LBI-PBI-SSI-SBI-WBO
Items: ABCDEFHIKLMNOPQSTVWZ1
Services: 4C-DA-FF-LM-TY-TD-WA
Equipment: 8SO-1WO
Annual sales: $500,000
Number of employees: 25
Turnaround times: B5C4M3
Customers: BU10-CU5-NP5-SP80
Union shop: N
Year established: 1963
Terms: 1/3 down, 1/3 blues, 1/3 done

Statement: Our motto: Quality printing at a reasonable cost.

Triangle Printing Company   GC
61 Visco Court, P O Box 100854
Nashville, TN 37210
615-254-1879; Toll-free: 800-843-9529

Min: 300 Max: 10,000 Opt: 2,000
Sizes: 123456
Bindings: CBI-LBI-PBI-SSI-SDI
Items: ABCDEFKLNOPSTY1
Services: TY
Equipment: SO-WO
Turnaround times: B3C3
Customers: BP10-BU25-NP10-SC5-SP5
Union shop: N
Year established: 1976
Terms: 50% down, balance before ship

Statement: We produce short-run books and pamphlets in 5 to 12 working days.

TSO General Corporation   GC
44-02 11th Street
Long Island City, NY 11101
718-937-0680

SERVICES				BINDINGS			
4C	4-Color Printing	RA	Rachwal System	HC	Hardcover	SD	Side Stitching
CS	Color Separations	AF	Acid-Free Paper	CB	Comb Binding	SB	Spiral Binding
DA	Design / Artwork	RP	Recycled Paper	GB	Glue Binding	WB	Wire-O Binding
FF	Fulfillment/Mailing	TY	Typesetting	LB	Loose-Leaf Binding	I	In-House
LM	List Maintenance	TD	Typeset w/ Disk	PB	Perfect Binding	O	Out of House
OC	OptiCopy System	WA	Warehousing	SS	Saddle Stitching	X	Unknown

Min: 500 Max: 50,000 Opt: 25,000
Sizes: 235
Bindings: CBI-GBI-LBI-PBI-SSI-SBI-WBI
Items: ACDFIKLNPSY
Equipment: 3SO(28x40)
Annual sales: $5,000,000
Number of employees: 30
Turnaround times: B4C4
Customers: BP20-BU20-CU20-MP20-NP20
Union shop: N
Year established: 1969
Terms: Net 30

Statement: TSO is a cost-competitive
medium to high quality sheetfed printer
with major emphasis on quick turnaround
service.

Twin City Printery   GC
P O Box 890
Westminster Street
Lewiston, ME 04240
207-784-9181

Min: Max: 1,000,000 Opt: 50,000
Sizes: 23456
Bindings: CBI-GBI-PBI-SSI-SDI
Items: ABCDEFHIKMNPQTUVWXZ1
Services: 4C-CS-DA-TY-TD
Equipment: SO-WO
Annual sales: $4,000,000
Number of employees: 125
Turnaround times: B4C3M3
Customers: BP10-BU50-CU5-
    MP10-NP2-SP15-OT7
Union shop: N
Year established: 1946
Terms: 2% 10, Net 20

U

United Color   MS
351 Garver Road
Monroe, OH 45050
513-359-9991

Min: 20,000 Max: 2,000,000 Opt: 80,000
Sizes: 5X
Bindings: PBI-SSI
Items: DHIX

Services: 4C-FF
Equipment: 2SO(22x29-25x38)-
    4WO(to 22x38)
Annual sales: $26,000,000
Number of employees: 330
Turnaround times: C2M2
Customers: MP80
Union shop: Y
Year established: 1970
Terms: Net 30

Comments: United specializes in printing
trade magazines, catalogs, and directories.

United Litho   MG
P O Box 191
Falls Church, VA 22046
703-560-5700; Toll-free: 800-368-6100

Sizes: 5
Bindings: SSI
Items: I
Services: 4C-TY-TD
Annual sales: $17,000,000
Number of employees: 150

United Lithograph   GC
48 Third Avenue
Somerville, MA 02143
617-776-6400

Min: 1,000 Max: 10,000 Opt: 5,000
Items: BCK

Universal Printers   BK
Fred G Granger, Sales Manager
P O Box 804
Winnipeg, Manitoba R3C 2N8
Canada
204-775-8486; Fax: 204-783-0090

Min: 5,000 Max: 1,000,000 Opt: 250,000
Sizes: 1
Bindings: PBI
Items: J
Equipment: 2LP(36x59)
Annual sales: $7,500,000
Number of employees: 50
Turnaround times: B3
Customers: BP100

PRINTED ITEMS			
A Annual Reports	G Galley Copies	N Workbooks	U Greeting Cards
B Books	H Journals	O Yearbooks	V Labels / Stickers
C Booklets	I Magazines	P Brochures	W Maps
D Catalogs	J Mass-Market Books	Q Calendars	X Newspapers
E Cookbooks	K Newsletters	R Comic Books	Y Postcards
F Directories	L Software Manuals	S Direct Mail Letters	Z Posters
	M Textbooks	T Envelopes	1 Stationery

Union shop: Y
Year established: 1951
Terms: Net 30 days

Statement: Our company specializes in producing mass-market paperback books. That is our only product.

MS

Universal Printing Company
3100 NW 74th Avenue
Miami, FL 33122
305-888-2695

Min: 20,000 **Max:** 200,000 **Opt:** 100,000
Sizes: 1245
Bindings: SSI
Items: DIKPX
Services: 4C-CS-TY
Equipment: 2WO(21x35-22x37)
Annual sales: $5,000,000
Number of employees: 125
Turnaround times: C3M3
Customers: BU42-MP35-SC8-OT15
Union shop: N
Year established: 1964
Terms: Net 30

GC

Universal Printing Company
1701 Macklind Avenue
Saint Louis, MO 63110
314-771-6900

Bindings: PBI-SSI
Items: ABCDFHIKNPS
Services: 4C-CS
Equipment: LP-SO-WO
Annual sales: $49,000,000
Number of employees: 400

BK

University Press
21 East Street
Winchester, MA 01890
617-729-8000

Bindings: HCI
Items: B
Equipment: LP

Comments: A division of Publishers Book Bindery, they specialize in printing leather bound books on India paper.

V

BK

Vail Ballou Printing
187 Clinton Street
Binghamton, NY 13902
607-723-7981

Min: 500 **Max:** 250,000 **Opt:**
Sizes: 235
Bindings: HCI-CBI-PBI-SBI
Items: BCDE
Services: FF-TY-TD
Equipment: SO-WO
Annual sales: $65,000,000
Number of employees: 1,200
Year established: 1903
Terms: To be established

Statement: A printing division of Maple Vail.

MS

Valco Graphics
3104 Western Avenue
Seattle, WA 98121
206-284-1755

Min: 5,000 **Max:** 500,000 **Opt:** 50,000
Sizes: 23456
Bindings: HCO-CBO-GBI-LBO-
PBI-SSO-SDO-SBO-WBO
Items: DEFFHIKLMNOPRSWX
Services: 4C-TY-TD-WA
Equipment: 2SO(to 25x38)-2WO(22x36)
Annual sales: $5,000,000
Number of employees: 30
Turnaround times: B4C2M2
Customers: CU10-MP50-SC5-SP10
Union shop: Y
Year established: 1927
Terms: Net 30

Statement: Valco specializes in quick turnaround, medium-length runs, pleasing quality publications and tabloid.

BK

Van Volumes
Russell L Tate, President
400 High Street, P O Box 567
Thorndike, MA 01079
413-283-8556; Fax: 413-283-7884

SERVICES				BINDINGS			
4C	4-Color Printing	RA	Rachwal System	HC	Hardcover	SD	Side Stitching
CS	Color Separations	AF	Acid-Free Paper	CB	Comb Binding	SB	Spiral Binding
DA	Design / Artwork	RP	Recycled Paper	GB	Glue Binding	WB	Wire-O Binding
FF	Fulfillment/Mailing	TY	Typesetting	LB	Loose-Leaf Binding	I	In-House
LM	List Maintenance	TD	Typeset w/ Disk	PB	Perfect Binding	O	Out of House
OC	OptiCopy System	WA	Warehousing	SS	Saddle Stitching	X	Unknown

Min: 100 Max: 3,000 Opt: 1,000
Sizes: 12345
Bindings: CBO-PBI-SSI-SDI-SBO
Items: ABCEFGHLNZ1
Equipment: 3SO(14x20)
Annual sales: $350,000
Number of employees: 9
Turnaround times: B3
Customers: BP80-CU1-SP19
Union shop: N
Year established: 1984
Terms: 50% deposit, balance net 30

Statement: We print and bind books at reasonable rates for a good product. We also provide film lamination and 2-cover colors.

BK

Versa Press
Steve Kennell, VP Sales
RR #1, Spring Bay Road
P O Box 2460
East Peoria, IL 61611-2460
309-822-8272; Fax: 309-822-8141
Toll-free: 800-447-7829

Min: 1,000 Max: 20,000 Opt: 8,000
Sizes: 2345X
Bindings: LBI-PBI-SSI-SBI-WBI
Items: BCJLMN
Equipment: 3SO(14x20-28x40)
Annual sales: $7,000,000
Number of employees: 67
Turnaround times: B4
Customers: BP45-BU35-CU5-NP10-SP5
Union shop: N
Year established: 1936
Terms: Net 30 with approved credit

Statement: Our goal is to provide the publishing trade with quality paperback bound books at a competitive price within a time frame that is fair and acceptable to us and our customers.

BK

Vicks Lithograph & Printing
Commercial Drive
P O Box 270
Yorkville, NY 13495
315-736-9345

Min: 1,000 Max: 35,000 Opt: 10,000
Sizes: 456
Bindings: CBI-GBI-PBI-SSI-SDI-SBI
Items: BHLMN
Services: 4C-AF
Equipment: 9SO(to 64")-
    2WO(22x36-24x38)
Annual sales: $6,000,000
Number of employees: 75
Turnaround times: B4
Customers: BP40-BU40-CU10-NP10
Union shop: Y
Year established: 1957
Terms: Net 30

BK

Victor Graphics
200 N Bentalou
P O Box 4446
Baltimore, MD 21223
301-233-8300

Min: 500 Max: 30,000 Opt: 10,000
Sizes: 23456
Bindings: HCO-CBO-PBI-SSI-SBI
Items: ABCDEFHKNP
Services: 4C-TY
Equipment: SO-WO

BK

Viking Press
Tom McCoy, Vice President Sales
7000 Washington Avenue S
Eden Prairie, MN 55344
612-941-8780; Fax: 612-941-2154
Toll-free: 800-765-7327

Min: 5,000 Max: 200,000 Opt: 12,500
Sizes: 1356X
Bindings: LBI-PBI-SSI-WBI
Items: BDFLN
Services: OC-RA-AF-RP
Equipment: 7SO(25"-40")-4WO(19"-45")
Annual sales: $36,000,000
Number of employees: 245
Turnaround times: B4
Union shop: N
Year established: 1970
Terms: Net 30 with approved credit

Comments: Viking Press, a division of Banta Corporation, specializes in printing computer manuals.

PRINTED ITEMS					
A	Annual Reports	G	Galley Copies	N	Workbooks	U	Greeting Cards
B	Books	H	Journals	O	Yearbooks	V	Labels / Stickers
C	Booklets	I	Magazines	P	Brochures	W	Maps
D	Catalogs	J	Mass-Market Books	Q	Calendars	X	Newspapers
E	Cookbooks	K	Newsletters	R	Comic Books	Y	Postcards
F	Directories	L	Software Manuals	S	Direct Mail Letters	Z	Posters
		M	Textbooks	T	Envelopes	1	Stationery

BK

Vimach Associates
3039 Indianola Avenue
Columbus, OH 43202
614-262-0471

Year established: 1984

Statement: We are a subsidy publisher and book printer. We are small and do all of the work in-house, involving the author as much as he or she is willing to be involved.

GC

Vogue Printers
2421 Green Bay Road
North Chicago, IL 60064
312-689-4044

Min: 10 **Max:** 100,000 **Opt:**
Sizes: 2345X
Bindings: CBI-PBI-SSI-SBX
Items: ABCDEFKNPSTYZ1
Services: 4C-DA-TY-TD
Equipment: SO
Terms: Net 30

CA

Volkmuth Printers
P O Box 1007
Saint Cloud, MN 56301
612-690-7210; Toll-free: 800-678-6299

Min: 10,000 **Max:** 2,000,000 **Opt:**
Sizes: 5
Bindings: PBI-SSI
Items: FHI
Services: 4C-CS-DA-FF-TY
Equipment: SO-16WO

Comments: A division of Quebecor.

W

CA

Waldman Graphics
9100 Pennsauken Highway
Pennsauken, NJ 08110
609-662-9111; Fax: 609-665-1789
Toll-free: 800-543-0955

Bindings: SSI
Items: DH
Services: 4C-CS-TY

GC

Waldon Press
216 West 18th Street
New York, NY 10011
212-691-9220

Min: 3,000 **Max:** 25,000 **Opt:**
Sizes: 23456X
Bindings: PBI
Items: BCDFHIP
Services: 4C-TY
Equipment: SO-WO

BK

Wallace Press
Tom Franke, Sales Manager
4600 W Roosevelt Road
Hillside, IL 60162
708-449-8611; Fax: 708-449-5999

Min: 5,000 **Max:** 2,000,000 **Opt:** 500,000
Sizes: 25X
Bindings: PBI-SSI
Items: ABCDFKLNPQ
Services: 4C-CS-DA-FF-LM-OC-RP-TY-TD
Equipment: 2SO(28x41)-4WO(22-24-38)
Annual sales: $30,000,000
Number of employees: 270
Turnaround times: B3C3
Customers: BP10-BU70-NP10-SP10
Union shop: Y
Year established: 1908
Terms: Net 30

Statement: A division of Wallace Computer Services, we offer not just products, but solutions.

Walsworth Publishing Company

BK

Walsworth Publishing
Dave Schattgen, Sales Manager
306 N Kansas Avenue
Marceline, MO 64658
816-376-3543; Fax: 816-258-7798

SERVICES				BINDINGS			
4C	4-Color Printing	RA	Rachwal System	HC	Hardcover	SD	Side Stitching
CS	Color Separations	AF	Acid-Free Paper	CB	Comb Binding	SB	Spiral Binding
DA	Design / Artwork	RP	Recycled Paper	GB	Glue Binding	WB	Wire-O Binding
FF	Fulfillment/Mailing	TY	Typesetting	LB	Loose-Leaf Binding	I	In-House
LM	List Maintenance	TD	Typeset w/ Disk	PB	Perfect Binding	O	Out of House
OC	OptiCopy System	WA	Warehousing	SS	Saddle Stitching	X	Unknown

Min: 300 Max: 10,000 Opt: 5,000
Sizes: 123456X
Bindings: HCI-CBI-LBI-
    PBI-SSI-SDI-SBO-WBI
Items: BCDEFHMNO
Services: 4C-CS-OC-AF-TY-TD
Equipment: 16SO(23x36-29x41)
Annual sales: $35,000,000
Number of employees: 1,100
Turnaround times: B4C4
Customers: BP75-SP20-OT5
Union shop: N
Year established: 1937
Terms: 1/3 down, 1/3 blues, 1/3 Net 30

Statement: Our goal is to be a producer of high quality products and a provider of excellent services to all of our customers resulting in a fair profit necessary for continued growth, while providing a motivating, creative, and safe environment with growth opportunities for our employees.

Walter's Publishing
BK

215 Fifth Avenue SE
Waseca, MN 56093
507-835-3691; Toll-free: 800-447-3274

Min: 200 Max: 3,000 Opt: 500
Sizes: X
Bindings: CBI
Items: E
Services: TY
Customers: NP-OR-SC-(fundraisers)
Year established: 195?
Terms: Net 90

Comments: Walters produces personalized standard-format cookbooks for fundraising organizations. Send for their free cookbook fundraising kit.

Watkins Printing Company
CA

1401 East 17th Avenue
Columbus, OH 43211
614-297-8270; Fax: 614-291-1961

Min: 20,000 Max: 2,000,000 Opt:
Sizes: 2345
Bindings: CBI-SSI-SDI
Items: ACDI
Services: 4C-FF-TY
Equipment: SO-WO

Waverly Press
MS

1314 Guilford Avenue
Baltimore, MD 21202-3995
301-528-4000; Fax: 301-528-8556
Toll-free: 800-638-5198

Min: 1,000 Max: 125,000 Opt:
Sizes: 345
Bindings: HCO-CBO-GBO-LBO-
    PBI-SSI-SDO-SBO-WBO
Items: HI
Services: 4C-DA-FF-LM-AF-TY-TD-WA
Equipment: SO-WO
Annual sales: $44,710,000
Number of employees: 610
Union shop: N
Year established: 1889
Terms: Net 30 days

Statement: Waverly is a full service periodical printer which continually trives to live up to our corporate goal: without blemish.

Web Specialties
CA

401 S Milwaukee Avenue
Wheeling, IL 60090
312-459-0800

Min: 100,000 Max: 2,000,000
    Opt: 1,500,000
Sizes: X
Bindings: GBI-SSI
Items: CDEPSTVY
Services: 4C-CS-DA
Equipment: 22WO(all sizes)
Annual sales: $18,000,000
Number of employees: 45
Turnaround times: C2
Union shop: N
Year established: 1983
Terms: Net 30

Statement: We are manufacturer's reps for specialty printers of mini-catalogs and other unique direct response formats.

The Webb Company
CA

1999 Shepard Road
Saint Paul, MN 55116
800-832-6403; Toll-free: 800-322-9322

PRINTED ITEMS							
A	Annual Reports	**G**	Galley Copies	**N**	Workbooks	**U**	Greeting Cards
B	Books	**H**	Journals	**O**	Yearbooks	**V**	Labels / Stickers
C	Booklets	**I**	Magazines	**P**	Brochures	**W**	Maps
D	Catalogs	**J**	Mass-Market Books	**Q**	Calendars	**X**	Newspapers
E	Cookbooks	**K**	Newsletters	**R**	Comic Books	**Y**	Postcards
F	Directories	**L**	Software Manuals	**S**	Direct Mail Letters	**Z**	Posters
		M	Textbooks	**T**	Envelopes	**1**	Stationery

Min: 30,000 Max: 5,000,000 Opt:
Sizes: 5
Bindings: PBI-SSI
Items: CDHIP
Services: 4C-CS-DA-FF-TY
Equipment: SO-16WO
Customers: BU-CU-MP-NP-OR
Year established: 1884
Statement: Webb, now owned by
Quebecor Printing, prints both magazines
and catalogs.

Webcom Ltd   BK
Chris Wilkins
3480 Pharmacy Avenue
Scarborough, Ontario M1W 3G3 Canada
416-496-1000; Fax: 416-496-1537

Min: 1,000 Max: 250,000 Opt: 5,000
Sizes: 123456
Bindings: HCO-LBO-PBI-
    SBI-SSO-SBO-WBO
Items: BDEFHJLMN
Services: 4C-FF-OC-AF-RP-TY-TD-WA
Equipment: 2SO(29")-3WO(35" and 38")
Annual sales: $18,000,000
Number of employees: 175
Turnaround times: B4
Customers: BP50-BU35-CU10-SP5
Union shop: N
Year established: 1961
Terms: Net 25

Comments: One of the few North
American printers capable of Otabinding a
book, this company manufactures books,
catalogs, and directories.

Webcraft Technologies   GC
P O Box 185
Route 1 & Adams Station
New Brunswick, NJ 08902
201-297-5100; Toll-free: 800-628-2533

Min: 25,000 Max: 2,000,000 Opt:
Sizes: 23456X
Bindings: GBI
Items: DPST
Services: 4C-CS
Equipment: 25WO
Annual sales: $220,000,000
Number of employees: 1,900
Year established: 1969

Statement: Webcraft is the world's largest
printer of direct mail formats.

Webcrafters   BK
P O Box 7608, 2211 Fordem Avenue
Madison, WI 53707
608-356-8200; Fax: 608-244-5120
Toll-free: 800-356-8200

Min: 10,000 Max: 2,000,000 Opt:
Sizes: 2345X
Bindings: HCI-PBI-SSI
Items: BCDFILMN
Services: 4C
Equipment: SO-WO
Annual sales: $60,000,000
Number of employees: 620
Turnaround times: B4
Year established: 1893

F A Weber & Sons   GC
175 S Fifth Avenue, P O Box 449
Park Falls, WI 54552
715-762-3707

Min: 500 Max: 100,000 Opt: 60,000
Sizes: 123456
Bindings: CBX-GBX-LBX-PBX-SSX
Items: ABCDEFIKOPQSTUVWYZ1
Services: 4C-CS-DA-AF-TY-WA
Equipment: 4SO(10x14-18x23-25x38)
Annual sales: $500,000
Number of employees: 30
Turnaround times: B5C5M4
Customers: BU50-MP20-NP20-SP10
Union shop: N
Year established: 1965
Terms: Net 30

Comments: A general commercial printer
who prints book jackets and covers.

A D Weiss Lithograph   MG
2025 McKinley Street
Hollywood, FL 33020-3199
305-920-7300

Min: 40,000 Max: 800,000 Opt: 150,000
Sizes: 45
Bindings: PBI-SSI
Items: DIX

PRINTED ITEMS						
A	Annual Reports	G	Galley Copies	N	Workbooks	U	Greeting Cards
B	Books	H	Journals	O	Yearbooks	V	Labels / Stickers
C	Booklets	I	Magazines	P	Brochures	W	Maps
D	Catalogs	J	Mass-Market Books	Q	Calendars	X	Newspapers
E	Cookbooks	K	Newsletters	R	Comic Books	Y	Postcards
F	Directories	L	Software Manuals	S	Direct Mail Letters	Z	Posters
		M	Textbooks	T	Envelopes	1	Stationery

Services: 4C-FF
Equipment: 10WO(22x36)
Annual sales: $32,000,000
Number of employees: 375
Turnaround times: M2
Customers: MP65-OT35
Union shop: N
Year established: 1967
Terms: Net 30

CA

Wellesley Press
190 Fountain Street
Framingham, MA 01701
617-879-6510

Min: 5,000 Max: 1,000,000 Opt: 30,000
Sizes: 25
Bindings: HCO-CBO-GBI-LBO-
PBI-SSI-SDO-SBO-WBO
Items: ABCDEFHIKLPQXYZ
Services: 4C-FF-LM-TY
Equipment: 3SO(to 25x38)-2WO(17x26)
Annual sales: $7,000,000
Number of employees: 125
Turnaround times: B3C3M2
Customers: BP5-BU15-MP55-
NP5-SC10-SP10
Union shop: N
Year established: 1881
Terms: 2% 10, Net 30

GC

West Side Graphics
340 West 57th Street
New York, NY 10025
212-222-9304

Min: 1,000 Max: 20,000 Opt: 10,000
Sizes: 123456X
Bindings: HCX-PBX-SSX
Items: ABCHIKPYZ1
Services: DA-TY
Equipment: LP-SO
Terms: Net 60

BR

Western Publishers' Consortium
Bob Johnson, Vice President
P O Box 35819
Albuquerque, NM 87176-5819
505-243-5333; Fax: 505-243-4327
Toll-free: 800-873-2363

Min: 1,000 Max: 50,000 Opt: 5,000
Sizes: 123456
Bindings: HCO-CBI-LBI-
PBI-SSI-SDI-SBI-WBO
Items: ABCDEFHIKLMNPQATWYZ1
Services: 4C-CS-DA-LM-
RA-AF-RP-TY-WA
Equipment: 11SO(19x25-26x40)
Annual sales: $3,000,000
Number of employees: 25
Turnaround times: B4C3
Customers: SP100
Union shop: N
Year established: 1987
Terms: Net 30

BK

Western Publishing
Book Printing Division
1220 Mound Avenue
Racine, WI 53404
414-631-5264; Fax: 414-631-1436
Toll-free: 800-453-1222

Min: 10,000 Max: 2,000,000 Opt:
Sizes: 2345X
Bindings: HCI-PBI-SSI
Items: BCDLNRZ
Services: 4C-CS-DA-FF-TY-TD-WA
Equipment: CB-LP-SO(to 55x78)-
7WO(to 35x50)
Annual sales: $550,000,000
Number of employees: 2,500
Turnaround times: B4
Year established: 1907

Comments: This publisher also prints
books for other publishers.

GC

Western Web Printing
4005 S Western Avenue
P O Box 1184
Sioux Falls, SD 57101
605-339-2383; Fax: 605-335-6873
Toll-free: 800-843-6805

Min: 1,000 Max: 5,000,000 Opt: 50,000
Sizes: 123456X
Bindings: GBI-PBX-SSI-SDI-SBX-WBX
Items: ABCDEFGHIJKLMNPQSTXYZ1
Services: 4C-CS-DA-FF-LM-TY-TD-WA
Equipment: 1LP-8SO(to 29")-
10WO(22x35)

Annual sales: $5,000,000
Number of employees: 100
Turnaround times: B2C2M2
Customers: BP10-BU40-
CU10-MP10-NP20-OT10
Union shop: N
Year established: 1976
Terms: Net 30 to established accounts

Statement: We specialize in tabloids, broadsides, flexies, and coupon books.

Westview Press   BK
Sara Wetzig
5500 Central Avenue
Boulder, CO 80301
303-444-3541; Fax: 303-449-3356

Min: 100 **Max:** 3,000 **Opt:** 800
Sizes: 12356
Bindings: HCO-CBO-GBO-LBO-
PBI-SSI-SDO-SBO-WBO
Items: BEFGHKLMN
Services: AF-RP
Equipment: 4SO(13x18 maximum)
Annual sales: $2,500,000
Number of employees: 13
Turnaround times: B3M3
Customers: BP22-(in-house)78
Union shop: N
Year established: 1982
Terms: Net 30

Comments: Besides printing their own books and journals, they also print books/journals for other publishers.

White Arts   GC
Garry Hiott, Sales
1203 E Saint Clair Street
P O Box 623
Indianapolis, IN 46206
317-638-3564; Fax: 317-638-6793
Toll-free: 800-748-0323

Min: 5,000 **Max:** 100,000 **Opt:** 20,000
Sizes: 23456
Bindings: HCO-CBI-LBO-
PBO-SSI-SDI-SBO-WBO
Items: ACDKLNPSYZ
Services: 4C-AF-RP
Equipment: 6SO(20x26-41x54)

Annual sales: $15,000,000
Number of employees: 100
Turnaround times: B3C2
Customers: BP30-BU50-
CU5-MP5-NP5-OR5
Union shop: N
Year established: 1950
Terms: Net 30 with credit approval

Statement: We strive to provide quality printing service at a reasonable cost.

Whitehall Printing   BK
Mike Hirsch, President
1200 S Willis Avenue
Wheeling, IL 60090
708-541-9290; Fax: 708-541-5890
Toll-free: 800-321-9290

Min: 500 **Max:** 5,000 **Opt:**
Sizes: 235
Bindings: LBI-PBI-SSX
Items: BCDEFKLN
Equipment: SO
Year established: 1959

Comments: One of the lowest priced book printers in the country, but not suitable for books with lots of halftones or any that require high quality.

Wickersham Printing Company   BK
Steve Cooper, VP Sales
2959 Old Tree Drive
Lancaster, PA 17603-4080
717-299-5731; Fax: 717-393-7469
Toll-free: 800-437-7171

Min: 100 **Max:** 150,000 **Opt:** 5,000
Sizes: 123456X
Bindings: HCO-CBO-GBI-LBI-
PBI-SSI-SDI-SBO-WBO
Items: ABCDEFIKLMNPS
Services: FF-AF-TY-TD-WA
Equipment: 4SO(23x29-43x60)-1WO
Annual sales: $7,000,000
Number of employees: 115
Turnaround times: B4C4
Customers: BP75-BU5-
CU5-OR2-SC10-SP3
Union shop: Y
Year established: 1863
Terms: Net 30

PRINTED ITEMS						
A	Annual Reports	**G**	Galley Copies	**N**	Workbooks	**U**	Greeting Cards
B	Books	**H**	Journals	**O**	Yearbooks	**V**	Labels / Stickers
C	Booklets	**I**	Magazines	**P**	Brochures	**W**	Maps
D	Catalogs	**J**	Mass-Market Books	**Q**	Calendars	**X**	Newspapers
E	Cookbooks	**K**	Newsletters	**R**	Comic Books	**Y**	Postcards
F	Directories	**L**	Software Manuals	**S**	Direct Mail Letters	**Z**	Posters
		M	Textbooks	**T**	Envelopes	**1**	Stationery

Statement: Wickersham specializes in looseleaf and softcover books, directories, and manuals. We deliver on schedule with high quality at competitive prices.

BK
Williams Catello Printing
George Catello, Manager
19495 SW Teton Avenue
Tualatin, OR 97062
503-692-9200; Fax: 503-692-9005

Min: 3,000 **Max:** 100,000 **Opt:** 25,000
Sizes: 23456
Bindings: HCO-CBO-LBO-PBO-SSO-SDO-SBO-WBO
Items: BDEFLN
Services: FF-WA
Equipment: 3SO(25"-40")-1WO
Annual sales: $10,000,000
Number of employees: 50
Turnaround times: B4C3
Customers: BU90-OR9-SP1
Union shop: N
Year established: 1983
Terms: Net 30

Statement: We provide a turnkey operation for software publishers.

BK
Wimmer Brothers
P O Box 18408
4210 BF Goodrich Boulevard
Memphis, TN 38118
901-362-8900

Min: 3,000 **Max:** 50,000 **Opt:**
Sizes: 23
Bindings: HCO-CBI-GBO-LBO-PBO-SSO-SDO-SBO-WB0
Items: BCEIPW
Services: 4C-FF-WA
Equipment: 2WO(25x38)
Annual sales: $5,000,000
Number of employees: 100
Turnaround times: B6
Customers: BU20-NP40-OR20-SP10-OT10
Union shop: N
Year established: 1950

Statement: We serve cookbook fundraisers (design, consultation, manufacturing, fulfillment, storage, and distribution).

BR
Windsor Associates
4655 Cass Street #314
P O Box 90282
San Diego, CA 92109
619-270-1000

Min: 500 **Max:** 20,000 **Opt:**
Sizes: 12356
Bindings: HCX-CBX-GBX-PBX
Items: BCDEFLMO
Services: 4C-CS-DA-TY
Equipment: SO-WO
Turnaround times: B5C4
Customers: BU10-CU10-SC10-SP50-OT20
Union shop: N
Year established: 1978
Terms: Open

Comments: They offer complete self-publishing services: editing, typesetting, art/design, printing, binding, distribution, and copyright.

MG
Wisconsin Color Press
5400 W Good Hope Road
P O Box 552
Milwaukee, WI 53201
414-353-5400

Min: 25,000 **Max:** 3,000,000 **Opt:**
Sizes: 2345X
Bindings: PBI-SSI-SDI
Items: CDEFHINPQXZ
Services: 4C-CS-FF
Equipment: 1SO(25x38)-8WO(to 45x63)
Annual sales: $35,000,000
Number of employees: 325
Customers: BU20-MP80
Union shop: Y
Year established: 193?
Terms: 2% 10, Net 30

Statement: We specialize in medium to long-run production, newsstand distribution, and mailing services. We never miss a shipping date!

GC
Wolfer Printing
6670 Flotilla Street
City of Commerce, CA 90040-1816
213-721-5411

SERVICES				BINDINGS			
4C	4-Color Printing	RA	Rachwal System	HC	Hardcover	SD	Side Stitching
CS	Color Separations	AF	Acid-Free Paper	CB	Comb Binding	SB	Spiral Binding
DA	Design / Artwork	RP	Recycled Paper	GB	Glue Binding	WB	Wire-O Binding
FF	Fulfillment/Mailing	TY	Typesetting	LB	Loose-Leaf Binding	I	In-House
LM	List Maintenance	TD	Typeset w/ Disk	PB	Perfect Binding	O	Out of House
OC	OptiCopy System	WA	Warehousing	SS	Saddle Stitching	X	Unknown

Min: 30,000 Max: 10,000,000 Opt: 250,000
Sizes: 25
Bindings: HCO-CBO-GBO-LBO-
    PBO-SSO-SD0-SBO-WBO
Items: ADFIPQSZ
Services: 4C-CS-FF-WA
Equipment: 2WO(22x38)
Annual sales: $30,000,000
Number of employees: 100
Turnaround times: C2M2
Customers: BU60-MP10-OR30
Union shop: Y
Year established: 1913
Terms: Net 30

Wood & Jones   GC
Hanna Wood, Marketing Director
139 W Colorado Boulevard
Pasadena, CA 91105-1983
818-449-1144; Fax: 213-681-4048

Min: 500 Max: 50,000 Opt: 30,000
Sizes: 12345
Bindings: HCO-CBI-LBO-
    PBO-SSI-SDI-SBO-WBO
Items: ABCDLMT1
Services: 4C-RP-TY-TD
Equipment: 1LP-SO
Annual sales: $2,500,000
Number of employees: 25
Turnaround times: B2
Customers: BU75-OR15-SC5-OT5
Union shop: N
Year established: 1907
Terms: Net 30 with approved credit

Comments: Wood & Jones is a general
commercial printer who typesets and prints
many technical manuals.

The Wood Press   GC
515 East 41st Street
Paterson, NJ 07509
201-684-4472

Min: 5,000 Max: 2,000,000 Opt:
Sizes: 2345X
Items: PSVZ
Services: 4C-CS
Equipment: SO-WO

Comments: They specialize in printing
multicolor direct mail pieces, roll labels,
and pharmaceutical packaging.

World Color Press   CA
National Sales Office
485 Lexington Avenue
New York, NY 10017
212-986-2440

Min: 50,000 Max: 5,000,000 Opt:
Sizes: 5X
Bindings: SSI
Items: ADFIP
Services: 4C
Equipment: WO-OT(gravure)
Annual sales: $682,000,000
Number of employees: 6,000

Comments: This subsidiary of Kohlberg,
Kravis, Roberts & Company prints long-
run magazines and catalogs.

Worzalla Publishing Company   BK
John Butkus
3535 Jefferson Street
P O Box 307
Stevens Point, WI 54481
715-344-9600; Fax: 715-344-2578

Min: 2,000 Max: 200,000 Opt: 25,000
Sizes: 123456X
Bindings: HCI-CBI-GBI-LBO-
    PBI-SSI-SDI-SBO-WBO
Items: BDEFMN
Services: 4C-FF-OC-AF-RP-WA
Equipment: 7SO(19x25-41x55)-
    1WO(23x36)
Annual sales: $30,000,000
Number of employees: 300
Turnaround times: B5C3
Customers: BP100
Union shop: N
Year established: 1892
Terms: Net 30

Comments: Worzalla can print almost any
size book, including many odd sizes. Their
specialty is full-color illustrated children's
books. They offer competitive prices.

PRINTED ITEMS	G	Galley Copies	N	Workbooks	U	Greeting Cards
A Annual Reports	H	Journals	O	Yearbooks	V	Labels / Stickers
B Books	I	Magazines	P	Brochures	W	Maps
C Booklets	J	Mass-Market Books	Q	Calendars	X	Newspapers
D Catalogs	K	Newsletters	R	Comic Books	Y	Postcards
E Cookbooks	L	Software Manuals	S	Direct Mail Letters	Z	Posters
F Directories	M	Textbooks	T	Envelopes	1	Stationery

Henry Wurst Inc   **GC**
1331 Saline Street
North Kansas City, MO 64116
816-842-3113

Min: 25,000 **Max:** 2,000,000 **Opt:** 500,000
Sizes: 25
Bindings: SSI
Items: ADFIPQS
Services: 4C-CS-FF
Equipment: 7WO(23x38)
Annual sales: $52,000,000
Number of employees: 400
Turnaround times: C2M2
Customers: BP1-BU89-MP10
Union shop: N
Year established: 1952
Terms: Net 20

Y

Yates Publishing Company   **BK**
William A Yates, Owner
P O Box 237
Ozark, MO 65721
417-485-3426

Min: 25 **Max:** 500 **Opt:** 500
Sizes: 5
Bindings: SDI
Items: BCFK
Customers: OT(genealogists)
Year established: 1970
Terms: 50% deposit, balance B4 shipmen

Statement: We specialize in printing genealogies and other family histories.

Ye Olde Genealogie Shoppe   **GC**
Ray Gooldy, Owner
3851 S Post Road
P O Box 39128
Indianapolis, IN 46239
317-862-3330

Min: 25 **Max:** 1,000 **Opt:** 300
Sizes: 35X
Bindings: HCX-CBX-LBX-SDX-SBX
Items: BCDIKNPSTW

Services: SO
Customers: OT(genealogists)
Year established: 1980
Terms: Quotation by job

Statement: We specialize in printing family genealogies.

Last Minute Entries

These two printers came to our attention just days before this directory went to press. Hence, their listings are incomplete. Also, neither printer is included in any of the indexes.

Great Northern/Design Printing   **GC**
Tony Albert, President
5401 Fargo Avenue
Skokie, IL 60077
708-674-4740

Items: ADPQZ
Services: 4C-CS

Nies/Artcraft Printing Companies   **GC**
Ed Nies, Marketing Director
5900 Berthold Avenue
Saint Louis, MO 63110
314-647-3400

Items: AI
Services: 4C
Equipment: SO-WO
Customers: BU100
Year established: 1902

Statement: They specialize in corporate publications, from annual reports to company magazines.

SERVICES				BINDINGS			
4C	4-Color Printing	**RA**	Rachwal System	**HC**	Hardcover	**SD**	Side Stitching
CS	Color Separations	**AF**	Acid-Free Paper	**CB**	Comb Binding	**SB**	Spiral Binding
DA	Design / Artwork	**RP**	Recycled Paper	**GB**	Glue Binding	**WB**	Wire-O Binding
FF	Fulfillment/Mailing	**TY**	Typesetting	**LB**	Loose-Leaf Binding	**I**	In-House
LM	List Maintenance	**TD**	Typeset w/ Disk	**PB**	Perfect Binding	**O**	Out of House
OC	OptiCopy System	**WA**	Warehousing	**SS**	Saddle Stitching	**X**	Unknown

Chapter 6

Low-Cost Short-Run Color Printers

The following printers specialize in printing low-cost short runs of full-color catalog sheets, posters, postcards, and other such items. Many of these printers do gang-runs (that is, they print a number of 4-color jobs at the same time). Nonetheless, most do a good job for a low cost.

Ad Color
149 Westchester Avenue
Port Chester, NY 10573
914-937-0005

Min: 2,000 **Max:** 50,000 **Opt:** 10,000
Items: ACDPSTUY1
Services: 4C-CS-DA-TY
Equipment: 2SO(11X17-12X18)
Annual sales: $200,000
Number of employees: 5
Turnaround times: C3M3
Customers: BU60-NP30-OT10
Union shop: N
Year established: 1985
Terms: 50% COD, 50% upon delivery

American Color Printing
1731 NW 97th Avenue
Plantation, FL 33322
305-473-4392; Fax: 305-473-8621

Min: 2,500
Items: DPYZ
Services: 4C-CS

Apollo Graphics
Roy Innella
1085 Industrial Boulevard
Southampton, PA 18966
215-953-0500; Fax: 215-953-1144
Toll-free: 800-522-9006

Min: 1,000 **Max:** 500,000 **Opt:** 50,000
Sizes: 123456
Bindings: HCO-CBI-LBO-
   PBO-SSI-SDI-SBO-WBO
Items: ACDEFKPQSZ
Services: 4C-CS-DA-OC-TY-TD-WA
Equipment: 2SO(28x40)
Annual sales: $2,000,000
Number of employees: 40
Turnaround times: B3
Customers: BU60-Ad Agencies40
Union shop: N
Year established: 1985
Terms: Net 30

Statement: We offer ultimate service in high quality color prepress, separations, electronic retouching as well as printing and binding.

PRINTED ITEMS							
A Annual Reports	**G**	Galley Copies	**N**	Workbooks	**U**	Greeting Cards
B Books	**H**	Journals	**O**	Yearbooks	**V**	Labels / Stickers
C Booklets	**I**	Magazines	**P**	Brochures	**W**	Maps
D Catalogs	**J**	Mass-Market Books	**Q**	Calendars	**X**	Newspapers
E Cookbooks	**K**	Newsletters	**R**	Comic Books	**Y**	Postcards
F Directories	**L**	Software Manuals	**S**	Direct Mail Letters	**Z**	Posters
	M	Textbooks	**T**	Envelopes	**1**	Stationery

Catalog King
1 Entin Road
Clifton, NJ 07014
212-695-0711; Toll-free: 800-223-5751

Min: 5,000 **Max:** 1,000,000 **Opt:** 50,000
Sizes: 5
Bindings: SSI
Items: DPS
Services: 4C-CS-DA-TY

Catalogue Service of Westchester
159 Main Street, P O Box 1652
New Rochelle, NY 10802
212-823-1581

Min: 1,000 **Max:** 50,000 **Opt:** 10,000
Sizes: 2356
Items: ACDQSUZ
Services: 4C-CS-TY
Equipment: 4SO(26x36-23x29-18x25)
Turnaround times: C1
Customers: BU93-CU2-NP5
Union shop: N
Year established: 1950
Terms: Net 30

CatalogueACE
Trade Litho Inc
5301 NW 37th Avenue
Miami, FL 33142
305-633-9779; Fax: 305-633-2848
Toll-free: 800-367-5871

Min: 2,500 **Max:** 200,000 **Opt:** 10,000
Items: DP
Services: 4C-CS

Color Catalog Creations
11-20 46th Road
Long Island City, NY 11101
Fax: 718-937-0227
Toll-free: 800-621-6680

Min: 5,000 **Max:** **Opt:** 10,000
Items: DP
Services: 4C-CS

Color Express
2 Jenner Street
Irvine, CA 92718
714-727-9257; Toll-free: 800-872-0720

Min: 250 **Max:** 10,000 **Opt:**
Items: DPZ
Services: 4C-CS

Color Express
Butler Square #119, 100 N Sixth Street
Minneapolis, MN 55403
612-333-3932; Toll-free: 800-872-0720

Min: 250 **Max:** 10,000 **Opt:**
Services: 4C-CS

Color Express
1 Baltimore Place
Atlanta, GA 30308
404-872-6618; Toll-free: 800-872-0720

Min: 250 **Max:** 10,000 **Opt:**
Services: 4C-CS

Color Express
5885 Rickenbacker Road
Los Angeles, CA 90040
213-724-1588; Toll-free: 800-872-0720

Min: 250 **Max:** 10,000 **Opt:**
Services: 4C-CS

Chicago Color Express
512 N Franklin Street
Chicago, IL 60610
312-222-0662; Toll-free: 800-872-0720

Min: 250 **Max:** 10,000 **Opt:**
Services: 4C-CS

Chicago Color Express
1111 Pasquinelli Drive
Westmont, IL 60559
708-323-2232
Toll-free: 800-872-0720

Min: 250 **Max:** 10,000 **Opt:**
Services: 4C-CS

Color US Inc
4420A Commerce Circle
Atlanta, GA 30336
404-691-3201; Toll-free: 800-443-7377

Min: **Max:** **Opt:** 5,000
Items: DP
Services: 4C-CS

SERVICES		BINDINGS	
4C 4-Color Printing	**RA** Rachwal System	**HC** Hardcover	**SD** Side Stitching
CS Color Separations	**AF** Acid-Free Paper	**CB** Comb Binding	**SB** Spiral Binding
DA Design / Artwork	**RP** Recycled Paper	**GB** Glue Binding	**WB** Wire-O Binding
FF Fulfillment/Mailing	**TY** Typesetting	**LB** Loose-Leaf Binding	**I** In-House
LM List Maintenance	**TD** Typeset w/ Disk	**PB** Perfect Binding	**O** Out of House
OC OptiCopy System	**WA** Warehousing	**SS** Saddle Stitching	**X** Unknown

Colorlith Corporation
777 Hartford Avenue
Johnston, RI 02919
401-521-6000
Toll-free: 800-556-7171

Min: 2,500 **Max:** 50,000 **Opt:** 5,000
Items: DP
Services: 4C-CS

Communicolor
Standard Register Company
P O Box 400
Newark, OH 43055
614-928-6110
Toll-free: 800-848-7040

Items: PSTV
Services: 4C-FF-LM-TY

Comments: Besides color brochures, Communicolor prints many different direct mail formats including punch outs, scratch offs, labels, coupons, stamps, and brochures (with as many as 10 colors). They also offer ink-jet personalization, list maintenance, and mailing services. Communicolor is a division of the Standard Register printing company (which has sales of $450,000,000 and employs over 4000 people.

Dayal Graphics
111 Stephen Street
Lemont, IL 60439
708-257-2511; Fax: 708-257-2946

Items: DP
Services: 4C-CS

Direct Press/Modern Litho
386 Oakwood Road
P O Box 8104
Huntington Station, NY 11746
516-271-7000; Toll-free: 800-347-3285

Min: 2,000 **Max:** 500,000 **Opt:** 50,000
Sizes: 25
Bindings: CBO-GBO-LBO-
    PBO-SSI-SDI-SBO-WBO
Items: CDPYZ
Services: 4C-CS-DA-TY
Equipment: 5SO(12x17-28x40)-
    1WO(20x26)
Turnaround times: C4
Customers: BU100

Union shop: Y
Terms: 1/2 deposit, balance COD

Flower City Printing
P O Box 12744
Rochester, NY 14612
716-663-9000

Items: DPZ
Services: 4C-CS

Full Color Graphics
Sheldon Morgan, Sales Manager
P O Box 581
Plainview, NY 11083
516-937-0920; Fax: 516-937-1547
Toll-free: 800-323-5452

Min: 5,000 **Max:** 100,000 **Opt:** 10,000
Sizes: 123456
Bindings: HCO-CBO-LBO-
    PBO-SSO-SDO-SBO-WBO
Items: ABCDFHKLMNPQYZ
Services: 4C-CS-DA-TY
Annual sales: $250,000
Number of employees: 4
Turnaround times: B4C3
Customers: BP10-BU80-OT10
Union shop: N
Year established: 1970
Terms: Net 30

Statement: A printing broker of full-color products.

Hi-Tech Color House
Albert Stevens, President
5901 N Cicero Avenue
Chicago, IL 60646
312-588-8200
Toll-free: 800-621-4004

Min: 1,000 **Max:** 2,000,000 **Opt:** 7,500
Sizes: 25
Bindings: SSI
Items: DPZ
Services: 4C-CS
Equipment: 2SO

Instant Web
7951 Powers Boulevard
Chanhassen, MN 55317
612-474-0961

PRINTED ITEMS						
A	Annual Reports	G	Galley Copies	N	Workbooks	U Greeting Cards
B	Books	H	Journals	O	Yearbooks	V Labels / Stickers
C	Booklets	I	Magazines	P	Brochures	W Maps
D	Catalogs	J	Mass-Market Books	Q	Calendars	X Newspapers
E	Cookbooks	K	Newsletters	R	Comic Books	Y Postcards
F	Directories	L	Software Manuals	S	Direct Mail Letters	Z Posters
		M	Textbooks	T	Envelopes	1 Stationery

Min: 50,000 **Max:** 2,000,000 **Opt:**
Sizes: 5X
Bindings: GBI
Items: PST
Services: 4C-FF
Equipment: 20WO
Annual sales: $38,000,000
Number of employees: 200

McGrew Color Graphics
P O Box 19716
1615 Grand Avenue
Kansas City, MO 64141
816-221-6560

Min: 2,000 **Max:** 100,000 **Opt:**
Sizes: 25X
Bindings: SSI-SBI
Items: ACDPQSTUYZ1
Services: 4C-CS
Equipment: SO(to 28x40)

Mitchell Graphics
2230 E Mitchell
Petoskey, MI 49770
616-347-5650; Fax: 616-347-9255
Toll-free: 800-841-6793

Min: 1,500 **Max:** 50,000 **Opt:** 5,000
Sizes: 5
Bindings: SSI
Items: DPZ
Services: 4C-TY
Equipment: 3SO
Annual sales: $2,500,000
Number of employees: 50
Union shop: N
Terms: variety of options

Statement: We specialize in producing
quality full-color direct mail products at an
affordable price.

Modern Graphic Arts
3131 13th Avenue N
Saint Petersburg, FL 33713
813-323-3131; Toll-free: 800-237-8474

Min: 5,000 **Max:** 2,000,000 **Opt:**
Sizes: 5X
Bindings: SSI
Items: DPSTX
Services: 4C-CS-DA-FF-TY
Equipment: 1SO(28x40)-
    2WO(17x26-22x38)

Annual sales: $10,000,000
Number of employees: 125

Comments: A subsidiary of Times Publishing, MGA specializes in printing special
format catalogs.

MultiPrint Company
Bob Sanders, Vice President
555 W Howard Street
Skokie IL 60077
708-677-7770; Fax: 708-677-7544
Toll-free: 800-858-9999

Min: 250 **Max:** 500,000 **Opt:** 25,000
Sizes: 123456
Bindings: PBO-SSO-SDO-SBO-WBO
Items: CDKPYZ
Services: 4C-CS-DA-FF-TY-WA
Turnaround times: B4C3
Customers: BU95-SC2-OT3
Union shop: N
Year established: 1967
Terms: 1% 10, Net 30; 50% deposit

Comments: Write for their price list for
full color printing of sales sheets, posters,
ad reprints, postcards, brochures, and catalogs in quantities from 500 to 25,000.

MWM Dexter
Customer Service Department
107 Washington, P O Box 261
Aurora, MO 65605
417-678-2135; Fax: 417-678-3626
Toll-free: 800-641-3398

Min: 1,000 **Max:** 200,000 **Opt:** 10,000
Sizes: 123456
Bindings: SSI-SBI-WBO
Items: CDPQUYZ
Services: 4C-CS-TY
Equipment: SO
Annual sales: $15,000,000
Number of employees: 150
Turnaround times: C4
Customers: BU80-CU4-OT16
Union shop: N
Year established: 1920
Terms: C.O.D.

Statement: Our specialty is short-run fast-
turnaround 4-color advertising products:
postcards, brochures, greeting cards, catalog sheets, business cards, and posters. All
are produced within 5 to 25 days.

SERVICES				BINDINGS			
4C	4-Color Printing	RA	Rachwal System	HC	Hardcover	SD	Side Stitching
CS	Color Separations	AF	Acid-Free Paper	CB	Comb Binding	SB	Spiral Binding
DA	Design / Artwork	RP	Recycled Paper	GB	Glue Binding	WB	Wire-O Binding
FF	Fulfillment/Mailing	TY	Typesetting	LB	Loose-Leaf Binding	I	In-House
LM	List Maintenance	TD	Typeset w/ Disk	PB	Perfect Binding	O	Out of House
OC	OptiCopy System	WA	Warehousing	SS	Saddle Stitching	X	Unknown

Ohio Valley Litho Color
Econocolor Catalog, 7405 Industrial Road
Florence, KY 41042
606-525-7405; Fax: 606-525-7654
Toll-free: 800-877-7405

Min: 5,000 Max: 250,000 Opt: 20,000
Items: DPZ
Services: 4C-CS

Penn Colour Graphics
99 Buck Road
Huntington Valley, PA 19006
215-364-4000

Items: D
Services: 4C-CS-DA

Pinecliffe Printers
1815 N Harrison
Shawnee, OK 74801
405-275-7351

Sizes: 5
Services: 4C-CS

The Press
18780 West 78th Street
Chanhassen, MN 55317
612-937-9764; Toll-free: 800-336-2680

Min: 2,000 Max: 2,000,000 Opt:
Sizes: 25
Bindings: SSI
Items: ACDNPSUWYZ
Services: 4C-CS-FF
Equipment: 3SO(19x26)-7WO(20x23-38")

Rapidocolor Corporation
A Daniel Gabaldon, Sales Manager
101 Brandywine Parkway, P O Box 2540
West Chester, PA 19380
215-344-0500; Fax: 215-344-0506
Toll-free: 800-872-7436

Min: 50 Max: Opt: 5,000
Items: DPZ
Services: 4C

Saltzman Printers
Combo Color
50 Madison Street
Maywood, IL 60153-2399
312-344-4500; Toll-free: 800-952-2800

Items: DPSZ
Services: 4C-CS
Turnaround times: C2

Service Web Offset
2568 S Dearborn Street
Chicago, IL 60616
312-567-7000; Toll-free: 800-621-1567

Min: 25,000 Max: 1,000,000 Opt: 75,000
Sizes: 25X
Bindings: SSI
Items: CDP
Services: 4C
Equipment: WO
Annual sales: $20,000,000
Number of employees: 150

Ultra-Color Corporation
1814 Washington Avenue
Saint Louis, MO 63103
314-241-0300

Min: 1,000 Max: 50,000 Opt: 10,000
Sizes: 25
Bindings: SSI
Items: DP
Services: 4C-CS-DA-TY

US Press
Michael R Jetter, VP Marketing
1628A James P Rodgers Drive
P O Box 640
Valdosta, GA 31603-0640
912-244-5634; Fax: 912-247-4405
Toll-free: 800-227-7377

Min: 1,000 Max: 100,000 Opt: 10,000
Sizes: 25X
Bindings: SSI
Items: ACDKPY
Services: 4C-CS-DA-TY-TD
Equipment: 3SO(19x25)
Annual sales: $3,000,000
Number of employees: 27
Turnaround times: C3
Union shop: N
Terms: 50% with order, balance C.O.D.

Statement: We specialize in producing short-run color literature with a focus on quality, quick turnaround, and competitive pricing. From postcards to catalog sheets, brochures, catalogs, and more, US Press is your best printing value.

PRINTED ITEMS					
A	Annual Reports	G	Galley Copies	N	Workbooks
B	Books	H	Journals	O	Yearbooks
C	Booklets	I	Magazines	P	Brochures
D	Catalogs	J	Mass-Market Books	Q	Calendars
E	Cookbooks	K	Newsletters	R	Comic Books
F	Directories	L	Software Manuals	S	Direct Mail Letters
		M	Textbooks	T	Envelopes

U	Greeting Cards	
V	Labels / Stickers	
W	Maps	
X	Newspapers	
Y	Postcards	
Z	Posters	
1	Stationery	

Chapter 7

Overseas Printers and Printing Brokers

How to Work with Overseas Printers

We generally do not recommend having overseas printers do the printing for your books or other publications unless you have had years of experience in specifying your print requirements and in dealing with printers. Nevertheless, for those of you who are considering working with such printers, we will list some of the advantages and disadvantages of having your printing done overseas, and then give some guidelines on how to work most effectively with such printers.

Advantages of Overseas Printers

- **Less Expensive** – Overseas printers are usually cheaper, especially for full-color work and highly illustrated books.
- **Quality** – Some of the overseas printers offer good quality, often superb full-color reproduction. Dai Nippon and Toppan, for example, have both won numerous awards for their printing excellence.
- **Typesetting** – Hong Kong or Singapore printers can often give good prices for intricate typesetting,
- **Service** – Asian printers like long-term relationships and do whatever they can to develop satisfied customers.

Disadvantages of Overseas Printers

- **Language Differences** – Differences in language and other cultural factors can cause misunderstandings regarding your requirements and specifications.
- **Communication costs** – Communication can be more difficult due to time zone gaps and the higher cost of phone calls or telexes.

- **Turnaround times** – Shipping time adds to the usual time for production. This can cause delays of four weeks or more, especially when shipping proofs back and forth for approval.

- **Piracy** – Piracy of copyrighted material can be a problem in Taiwan, Korea, the Philippines, and Indonesia because they have weaker copyright standards. This situation, however, is changing as the international publishing community puts more and more pressure on these countries to improve their enforcement of copyright laws.

- **Paper Standards** – The high humidity of Southeast Asia and the lack of warehousing space (in Hong Kong) limits the amount of paper they can keep in storage; hence, most printers tend to buy paper by the job (which can delay your job, especially if you require special paper).

  Also, paper stocks are not the same. Hence, you must be sure that the paper they plan to use for your job matches the standards you require. Be sure to see samples before going ahead with the job.

- **Quality Control** – To ensure that you get quality printing and reliable, on-time delivery, you must stay on top of the situation at all times. Printing overseas requires more supervision and monitoring.

- **Proofing Jobs** – If you have a full-color job that requires precise registration, you might have to fly to the plant to check the press proofs and the printed job as it comes off the press. The travel and lodging expenses, of course, add to the final cost of the job (and may wipe out any savings you gained by printing overseas). Don't forget to figure in cost of your own time in calculating the final costs of any print job.

- **Reprints** – Because of the greater time required to print overseas, you can't expect the overseas printer to provide you with quick turnaround on your reprint needs. Hence, you must forecast your needs accurately and well enough ahead of time to allow for the delivery delays.

- **Payments** – In most cases you will have to get a letter of credit from your bank to send to the overseas printer. In most cases, this Letter of Credit must be bought prior to the printing job. Hence, not only do you have a payment outside your normal bookkeeping channels, but you also incur additional financing costs.

- **Getting Bumped** – Many Asian printers favor long-term relationships with their customers; if you're new or only doing a one-time job with them, your job may be bumped for one of their steady customers.

- **Proofreading** – Proofreading of typesetting done by foreign printers can delay your book by many weeks since it is not safe to leave it to the typesetters (where English is often a second language at best).

- **Customs** – Your shipment will have to clear customs. In most cases, you will find it easier and more cost-effective to work with a shipping broker rather than try to clear the shipment yourself. Nonetheless, this is just another stumbling block you don't have to deal with when working with printers here.

The primary benefit of printing overseas is that the job can cost half as much as the same job printed in the United States. Yet, when making a decision to print overseas, you should not overlook the hidden costs involved. Generally speaking, printing overseas pays off only if you have the experience to work closely with the printers or their local representatives *and* intend to develop a long-term relationship them. The savings for a one-shot deal rarely justifies the added expenditure of your time and efforts in organizing and monitoring the job.

Guidelines for Working with Foreign Printers

For those of you who do plan to use overseas printers, the following guidelines gives you some pointers on how best to work with them.

- Clearly define all your specifications in writing. Make sure the printer understands exactly what you expect. When sending requests for quotation, be sure to include samples of the paper, binding, and print quality you expect.
- Examine bids carefully for any differences from your specifications.
- Check to see that the standard operating assumptions of the printing trade in that country match your own assumptions. Write to the local printers association for their standard terms and conditions.
- Get references. And check them out thoroughly.
- Have them send you samples of their work. Indeed, ask them to make a dummy of your proposed job so you can see exactly how they see your job. Inspect those samples very carefully.
- Monitor all stages of the manufacturing process. Be sure to get updated regularly on the progress of your job.
- Note that each country has its busy season when printers are less likely to offer you the best prices and delivery. The busy season for Japanese book printers is August through December (because their school year starts in April), while the busy season for most other Asian printers is March through September (when they are printing books for the school and holiday seasons).
- You'll probably want to install a fax machine or telex machine to facilitate quick and inexpensive communication between you and the printer.
- Set a production schedule that allows plenty of leeway for delays. Allow at least four extra weeks in your marketing plan.
- Make sure the shipment of books is insured.
- Arrange to have a shipping broker clear the books or other printed items through customs. Note that while books and magazines are duty-free, postcards and greeting cards are charged a duty. Check with customs to see if any duty applies to whatever you are having printed.

- When possible, work with their sales representatives in this country. Let them deal with the language barrier and time differences.

- Whenever possible, work toward establishing a lasting relationship with the overseas printer. As one Japanese printer noted in *Publishers Weekly*, "If U.S. publishers were willing to think in the long term, and to guarantee work for the low season as well as the peak time, we would certainly look forward to having that sort of customer." Asians especially appreciate such customer loyalty and reciprocate with better service.

Overseas Printers: The Listings

On the following eight pages, we list more than 120 foreign printers of books, catalogs, magazines, and other bound publications. Most of the information in this section is taken from material we gathered from foreign trade offices and printers who exhibited at the American Bookseller Convention during the past few years. Because this information is compiled from less up-to-date sources (rather than surveys), some of the addresses may no longer be correct.

Since we did not survey any of these printers, we list only their names, addresses, and phone numbers—and any special details that made the printers stand out in our minds. Note, however, that the PrintBase data files do contain more details about each of these overseas printers. For more information about the PrintBase data files, write to **Ad-Lib Publications, 51 N. Fifth Street, P. O. Box 1102, Fairfield, IA 52556-1102**, or call toll-free **(800) 669-0773**.

Overseas Printers: A Listing

China

Wenwu Jardine Printing Company
No 21 Bei Street
Xihuangchenggen, HichengDistrict
Beijing, China
66-2595

Columbia

Carvajal S.A.
Calle 29 North, No. 6A-40
P O Box 46
Cali, Columbia
675-011; Fax: 661-581

Statement: Specialty: pop-up books. They have done pop-ups for Hallmark Cards and Intervisual Communications.

Ediciones Laser Saenz Hurtado
Raul E Urquijo Puerto, Manager
Calle 11 No. 22-01, P O Box 34905
Bogota, Columbia
247-2640; Fax: 201-6780

Ediciones Lerner
Jack Grimberg, Manager
Calle 8-B, No. 68A-41
P O Box 8304
Bogota, Columbia
571-262-8200; Fax: 571-262-4459

Statement: Specialty: pop-up books and other hand-intensive books.

Educar
Calle 44 No. 15-28
P O Box 45616
Bogota, Columbia
287-1055; Fax: 288-3369

Impresora Feriva Ltda
Calle 18 No. 3-33
P O Box 4342
Cali, Columbia
283-1595; Fax: 283-5788

Intergraficas Ltda
Carrera 34A No. 10-47
Bogota, Columbia
247-0445

Op Graficas Ltda
Calle 11 No. 22-51
Bogota, Columbia
201-0211

Rei Nades Ltda
Avenida 40A No. 13-09
P O Box 21834
Bogota, Columbia
287-5334

Roto/Offset - Cano Isaza Y Cia
Avenida Carrera 68, No. 23-71
P O Box 3341
Bogota, Columbia
571-290-5555; Fax: 571-262-2323

Statement: The commercial division of El Espectador, Columbia's second largest newspaper. Specialties: magazines and children's books.

Saenz Y Cia Ltda
Calle 55 No. 13-19
P O Box 024000
Bogota, Columbia
217-9788; Fax: 249-8911

Susaeta Ediciones
Calle 50 No. 46A-6
P O Box 1742
Medellin, Columbia
288-4422

Tecimpre S.A.
Calle 15A No. 69-84
P O Box 82514
Bogota, Columbia
292-4900; Fax: 292-5558

Tempora Impresores S.A.
Avenida El Dorado No. 79-34
P O Box 98916
Bogota, Columbia
295-0511; Fax: 295-4713

Costa Rica

Trejos International
Alvaro Trejos, President
P O Box 10096
San Jose 1000, Costa Rica
506-24-2411

Hong Kong

Amko Color Graphics
445 Fifth Avenue #27H
New York, NY 10016
212-213-1277

Amko Color Graphics
156-8 Chodong, Chung Ku
Seoul, Korea
272-7975; Fax: 273-1284.

Bookbuilders
Ian Green, Managing Director
Tonic Industrial Centre 10F B13
19 Lam Hing Street
Kowloon Bay, Hong Kong
3-7968123; Fax: 3-7968267

C & C Joint Printing Company
Daniel Tam, Sales Manager
75 Pau Chung Street
Tokwawan, Kowloon, Hong Kong
3-7135175

Colorcraft Ltd
Daniel K C Chung, Director
502-3 Citicorp Centre
18 Whitfield Road
Causeway Bay, Hong Kong
5-786301; Fax: 5-8072005

Creative Printing
William Shue, Managing Director
5/F, Wah Ha Factory Building #B
8 Shipyard Lane
Quarry Bay, Hong Kong
5-632187

Dah Hua Printing Press
Bernard Chan, Sales Director
9/F Chai Wan Industrial Building
26 Lee Chung Street
Chaiwan, Hong Kong
5-560221

Dai Nippon Printing Company
2-5/F, Tsuen Wan Industrial Ctr
220-248, Texaco Road
Tsuen Wan, NT Hong Kong
0-499-1031; Fax: 0-499-5710

Dow Jones Printing (Asia)
GPO Box 9825
2/F AIA Building, 1 Stubbs Road
Hong Kong
5-8910794

Earl & Associates Ltd
13/F Jubilee Commercial Building
42-46 Gloucester Road
Hong Kong
5-286275

Everbest Printing Company
Kofai Industrial Building 10/F
7 Ko Fai Road
Yau Tong, Kowloon, Hong Kong
3-727-4433; Fax: 3-772-7687

Golden Cup Printing Company
5 Seapower Industrial Centre
177 Hoi Bun Road
Kwun Tong, Kowloon, Hong Kong
852-3-434255; Fax: 852-3-415426

Great Wall Graphics
Philip Rosenberg, Director
27 Stanley Street, 11/F
Central, Hong Kong
852-5-257021; Fax: 852-5-81057

Hip Shing Offset Printing
95 How Ming Street 1/F
Kwun Tong, Kowloon, Hong Kong
3-434254

Hung Hing Printing Ltd
Matthew Yum, Director
4/F Blue Box Factory Building
15 Hing Wo Street, Tin Wan
Aberdeen, Hong Kong
5-534191

J P Printing Press
3/F East Sun Industrial Building
16 Shing Yip Street
Kwun Tong, Kowloon, Hong Kong
3-440255

Jardine Printing
Alex Wong, Marketing Manager
10/F, Mappin House, 98 Texaco Road
Tsuen Wan, Hong Kong
0-411-3371; Fax: 0-413-5181
Toll-free: 800-637-7101

Liang Yu Printing Factory
Eric Hui, General Manager
Hip Shing Industrial Building
9-11 Sai Wan Ho Street
Shaukiwan, Hong Kong
5-677563; Fax: 5-8858099

Libra Press
56 Wong Chuk Hang Road #5D
Hong Kong
5-528147

Mandarin Offset
David Pryor, Sales Director
One Madison Avenue, 25th Floor
New York, NY 10010
212-481-7170; Fax: 212-683-0882

Mandarin Offset
6/F Toppan Building
22A Westlands Road
Quarry Bay, Hong Kong
852-5-636251; Fax: 852-5-657417

Pacific Offset Printing
Timmy Ng, General Manager
Block A, 6/F Wah Ha Factory Building
8 Shipyard Lane
Quarry Bay, Hong Kong
5-616146

Paper Communication Intl.
4A Dragon Industrial Building
93 King Lam St, Cheung Sha Wan
Kowloon, Hong Kong
852-786-4191; Fax: 852-786-4498

US office: 230 Miller Avenue
South San Francisco CA 94080
415-875-3804; Fax: 415-483-0537

Pointex Company Ltd
10/F, Wyndham Street
Hong Kong
5-215392

Professional Printers Ltd
65 Wyndham Street, 1st-3rd Floor
Hong Kong, Hong Kong
852-5-210195; Fax: 852-58453681

Sheck Way Tong Pringing Press
653 King's Road 1/F
North Point, Hong Kong
5-614959

Sing Cheong Printing Company
651 King's Road 1/F
North Point, Hong Kong
5-626317; Fax: 5-659467

South China Printing Company
James Binnie, Director
Aik San Factory Bldg, 14th Floor
14 Westlands Rd, Quarry Bay
North Point, Hong Kong
5-628261; Fax: 5-811-0221

South Sea International Press
Jeeves Norombaba, General Mgr
20/F Eastern Centre Building #3
1065 King's Road
Quarry Bay, Hong Kong

Times-Ringier Ltd
Room B, 9th Floor, Cindic Tower
128 Gloucester Road
Wanchai, Hong Kong
5-834-1033; Fax: 5-834-0790

Toppan Printing Company
Walter Lee, General Manager
Toppan Building
22 Westlands Road
Quarry Bay, Hong Kong
5-510101

NY Office: 680 Fifth Avenue
New York NY 10019
212-489-7740; Fax: 212-969-9349

Travel Publishing Asia Ltd
Roy Howard, Managing Director
1801 World Trade Centre
Causeway Bay, Hong Kong
5-8903067

Wing King Tong Company
Alex Yan, General Manager
200, Texaco Road 3/F
Leader Industrial Centre
Tsuen Wan, New Territories, Hong Kong
0-411-2287; Fax: 0-411-0330

Winson Printing Company
2/F Aiksan Factory Building
14 Westlands Road
Quarry Bay, Hong Kong
5-635257

Wishing Printing Company
8 Shipyard Lane, Block C, 1/F
Quarry Bay, Hong Kong
5-614131

Yee Tin Tong Printing Press
Jim Viney, General Manager
South China Morning Post Building 4/F
Tong Chong Street
Quarry Bay, Hong Kong
852-5-652222; Fax: 852-5-659833

Hungary

Kultura Budapest
Agnes Tompa, Export Sales Manager
Printing Department
1389 Budapest 62, P O Box 149
Budapest, Hungary
361-180-3194; Fax: 361-180-3306

Statement: Hungarian Foreign Trading
Company represents printers of all sorts of
materials.

Indonesia

P T Victory Offset Prima
Jalan Raya Pegangsaan Dua #17
Jakarta Utara 14250
Indonesia
489-6084; Fax: 489-6032

Italy

American Pizzi Offset Corp
141 East 44th Street
New York, NY 10017
212-986-1658; Fax: 212-286-1887

Statement: Subsidiary of Arti Grafiche
Amilcare Pizzi of Milan, Italy.

Mondadori-AME Publishing
740 Broadway
New York, NY 10003
212-505-7900

New Interlitho USA
Elaine Freedman, President
50 West 34th Street #8A7
New York, NY 10001
212-947-0653; Fax: 212-947-1203

New Interlitho SPA
Via Curiel 19
20090 Trezzano sul Naviglio
Milano, Italy
02-445-6741; Fax: 02-445-0653.

Japan

Dai Nippon Printing Company
1-1, Ichigaya Kagacho 1-chrome
Shinjuku-ku
Tokyo, Japan
03-266-2111

New York office: DNP America
2 Park Avenue #1405
New York NY 10016
212-686-1919; Fax: 212-686-3250.

Nissha Printing
149 Madison Avenue
New York, NY 10016
212-889-6970

Japan: 3 Hanicho Myby Nakakyoky
Kyoto, Japan
075-811-8111; Fax: 075-801-8250.

Korea

Overseas Printing Corporation
Hal Belmont
2806 Van Ness Avenue
San Francisco, CA 94109-1426
415-441-7725; Fax: 415-441-7618

Sung In Printing
60-4 Garibong-Dong, Guro-Gu
P O Box 38
Seoul, Korea
02-864-6121; Fax: 02-866-6156.

Malaysia

Web Printers Sdn Bhd
Ashraf Ali, Marketing Manager
P O Box 40, 46700 Petaling Jaya
Selangor, Malaysia
03-756-3577

Mexico

Litoart
Rafael Sevilla, Manager
Ferrocarril de Cuernavaca 683
D.F. 11520, Mexico
525-250-3482

Singapore

C.O.S. Printers
5 Kian Teck Way
Singapore 2262
265-9022; Fax: 265-9074

Chin Chang Press
Poh But Chay, Manager
113 Eunos Avenue 3
#04-08 Gordon Industrial Building
Singapore 1440
746-6025; Fax: 748-9108

Chong Moh Offset Printing
Koo Chan Kwan, Managing Director
19 Joo Koon Road
Singapore 2262
862-2701; Fax: 862-4335

Colourwork Press
Cho Jock Min, Managing Director
21 Mandai Estate
Singapore 0512
368-4048; Fax: 368-9107

Continental Press
Danny Ng, Proprietor
1160 Depot Road #03-01/07
Telok Blangah JTC Industrial Est
Singapore 0410
65-271-0602; Fax: 65-278-3850

Craft Print
Dora Chan, Managing Director
18 Pasir Panjang Road #06-13/17
Singapore 0511
65-278-5816; Fax: 65-272-2398

Creative Graphics International
Yoh Jinno, Vice President
10 East 23rd Street
New York, NY 10010
212-420-0610; Fax: 212-420-0746
Statement: Agent for Eurasia Press.

Des Meyer Press
2021 Bukit Batok ST23
Industrial Park A #04-210
Singapore
65-5660629; Fax: 65-5661952

Dominie Press
T H Oh, Managing Director
Blk 1200 Depot Close #01-21/27
Telok Blangah Industrial Estate
Singapore 0410
65-273-0755; Fax: 65-273-0060
Statement: Specialties: jigsaw puzzles, pop-up cards, and items involving handwork.

Eurasia Press
Allan Fong, Marketing Director
10/14 Kampong Ampat
Singapore 1336
280-5522; Fax: 280-0593

FEP International
Richard Toh, General Manager
348 Jalan Boon Lay Jurong
Singapore 2261
265-0311; Fax: 265-5103

Fong & Sons Printers
Tony Fong, Marketing Director
1090 Lower Delta Road #0110-0116
Tiong Bahru JTC Flatted Factory
Singapore 0316
272-0154; Fax: 273-3855

General Printing Services
Lee Joachim, Managing Director
2 Soon Wing Road #03-09
Soon Wing Industrial Building
Singapore 1334
747-2657; Fax: 746-4681

Hiap Seng Press
Eddie Yam, Managing Director
77 Lorong 19 Geylang #01-00
Singapore 1438
747-5391; Fax: 743-3251

Ho Printing Company
Tan Bak Choon, Sales Manager
11-15 Harper Road
Singapore 1336
65-280-9322; Fax: 65-289-6065

Hofer Press
Chan Ying Lock, Director
3 Gul Crescent
Singapore 2262
65-861-2755; Fax: 65-861-6438
Statement: Specialty: guide books and maps.

Hoong Fatt Press
George S W Wong, Manager
9 Harper Road
Singapore 1336
65-288-2243; Fax: 65-280-5943

Huntsmen Offset Printing
Heung Yam Yuen, General Manager
12 Fan Yoong Road
Jurong Town
Singapore 2262
265-0600; Fax: 265-8575
Statement: Specialties: Bibles, diaries, directories.

Hup Khoon Press
Ng Eng Kiat, Managing Director
Block 173 Stirling Road #01-1045
Singapore 0314
65-479-8350; Fax: 65-473-1118

International Press Company
Low Song Take, Managing Director
32 Kallang Place
Singapore 1233
65-298-3800; Fax: 65-297-1668

Jin Jin Printing Industry
See Cheng Tee, Managing Director
Block 1013
Eunos Avenue 5 #01-02
Singapore 1440
65-745-5166; Fax: 65-747-1232

Khai Wah Litho
Lau Sum Wing, Managing Director
16 Kallang Place #07-02
Singapore 1233
65-296-8644; Fax: 65-297-1540

Kim Hup Lee Printing
Lim Geok Khoon, Director
22 Lim Teck Boo Road
Kim Hup Lee Building
Singapore 1953
65-283-3306; Fax: 65-288-9222

Kin Keong Printing
H L Wong, Executive Director
Block 3015A Ubi Road 1 #05-04/07
Singapore 1440
65-744-0915; Fax: 65-743-0692

Kok Wah Press
3 Gul Crescent
Singapore 2262
861-7966

Kyodo-Shing Loong Printing
Yoshiki Ishii, General Manager
112 Neythal Road
Singapore 2262
265-2955; Fax: 264-4939

Lenco Printing
Poon Yeow Wah, Managing Director
37 Kallang Pudding Road #04-14
Tong Lee Building, Block B
Singapore 1334
747-5573; Fax: 743-3928
Statement: Also boxes and packaging.

Lolitho Pte
Peter Loh, General Manager
5055 Ang Mo Kio Industrial
    Park 2 #01-1141
Singapore 2056
457-8390; Fax: 456-9297

MCD Pte
Philip Chew, Director
18 Pasir Panjang Road #04-01
PSA Multi Storey Complex
Singapore 0511
273-6888; Fax: 273-8328

Monocrafts Pte
Alan Sim, Managing Director
34 Kallang Place
Singapore 1233
298-1088; Fax: 298-2624
Statement: Specialty: Diaries.

Nissin Printcraft
Wong Yat Bor, Managing Director
No 3 Kallang Way 3
Singapore 1334
747-2992
Statement: Specialties: diaries and calendars.

PacPress Industries
Sai Yong Mong, Managing Director
25/27 Tannery Lane
Singapore 1334
746-3939; Fax: 748-9242

Saik Wah Press
Anthony Tham, Marketing Director
Block 5021 Kallang Bahru #01-21
Singapore 1233
65-292-8759; Fax: 65-296-0638
Statement: Specialty: Pop-up books

Sin Sin Lithographers
Michael Tsu, Director
Block 115-A Commonwealth Drive #02-30
Singapore 0314
474-5692; Fax: 473-3817
Statement: Specialties: cassette and CD casecards.

Sing Chew Press
Tan Kay Tiak, Managing Director
38 Genting Lane #02-01/04
Metal House Building
Singapore 1334
746-6611; Fax: 746-5209

Singapore National Printers
Henry Pang, Marketing Manager
303 Upper Serangoon Road
Singapore 1334
282-0611; Fax: 288-7246
Toll-free: 800-446-4767

NY office: Palace Press
268 West 23rd Street, 4th Floor
New York NY 10011
212-627-0092; Fax: 212-691-5331

San Diego office: Palace Press
Lori Comtois, Sales Manager
7723 Fay Street #8
La Jolla CA 92037
619-459-2733; Fax: 619-459-8214

Stamford Press
Joseph Edison, Marketing Manager
48 Lorong 21 Geylang #04-03
Singapore 1438
65-748-5111; Fax: 65-746-7310

Sydney Press Indusprint
Ng Ghin, Managing Director
Block 3011
Bedok North Avenue 4 #04-2012
Bedok Industrial Park E
Singapore 1648
445-6006; Fax: 449-7634

Tien Mah Litho Printing
David Chew, Marketing Director
2 Jalan Jentera
Jurong Town
Singapore 2261
261-0988; Fax: 265-0549
Statement: Specialty: children's books.

Tien Wah Press
574 Broome Street
New York, NY 10013
212-206-8090; Fax: 212-645-1429

Tien Wah Press
Roger Phua, Sales Manager
977 Bukit Timah Road
Singapore 2158
466-6222; Fax: 469-3894
Statement: A division of Dai Nippon. Specialties: thin casebound books, pop-ups, special handwork.

Times Offset
Ricky Ang, General Manager
Koon Wah Printing
18 Tuas Avenue 5
Singapore 2263
862-3333; Fax: 862-1313
Statement: Formerly Koon Wah Printing

Times Printers
Ricky Ang, General Manager
Commercial Printing Group
2 Jurong Port Road
Singapore 2261
65-265-8855; Fax: 65-268-5979
Statement: Specialties: time-critical publications and periodicals.

Toppan Printing Company
Ee Swee Kiat, General Manager
38 Liu Fang Road
Jurong Town, Singapore 2262
265-1811; Fax: 265-8298

Viva Lithographers
Michael Oh, Managing Director
22 Pasir Panjang Road #06-22/23
PSA Multi-Storey Complex
Singapore 0511
272-1880; Fax: 273-5425

Welpac Printing & Packaging
Joe Yip, Sales Manager
36 Lok Yang Way
Singapore 2262
261-5555; Fax: 265-7961

Spain

Novograph S.A.
19 West 44th Street #510
New York, NY 10036
212-921-0357; Fax: 212-921-0395

Novograph S.A.
Ctra. de Irun, km. 12,450
Madrid, Spain
341-734-7100; Fax: 341-734-0375.

Taiwan

Morion Company
Simon Huang, General Manager
P O Box 43-396
Taipei 10657, Taiwan
02-704-1715; Fax: 02-704-8197

Taipei Yung Chang Printing
49-15 Chuanyuan Road
Peitou (112)
Taipei, Taiwan

Thailand

Thai Watana Panich Press
Thira T Suwan, Managing Director
891 Rama 1 Road
Bangkok 10500, Thailand
662-215-0060; Fax: 662-215-2360

United Kingdom

Anthony Rowe Ltd
Bumper's Way, Bristol Road
Chippenham SN14 6LH England
0249-659706

BAS Printers Ltd
Paul Gumn, Sales Director
Over Wallop, Stockbridge
Hants SO2O 8JD, England
264-781711; Fax: 264-781116

Bourne Offset Ltd
Tim Staples, Managing Director
2 The Ridgeway, Iver
Buckinghamshire SL0 9HR, England
753-652004

Cradley Print
Chris Jordan, Managing Director
P O Box 34
Chester Road Cradley Heath Warly
West Midlands B64 6AB, England

Pensord Press
David Seabrook, Director
The Old Tram Road
Southend-on-Sea
Essex SS2 6UN, England
495-223721

The Phoenix Press
John Oliver, Managing Director
Unit 6 Birch Road
Eastbourne
E Sussex BN23 6PE, England
323-411090; Fax: 323-411060

Thamesmouth Printing Group
Ian Cuthbert, Managing Director
17-21 Hovefields Avenue
Burnt Mills Ind Est, Basildon
Essex SS13 1EB, England

Yugoslavia

Gorenjski Tisk Printing Company
Boris Kozely, Export Manager
Mdse Pijadeja 1
64000 Kranj, Yugoslavia
064-23-341; Fax: 064-24-475

Printing Brokers

Chanticleer Company
424 Madison Avenue
New York, NY 10017
212-486-3900

Codra Enterprises
20695 S Western Avenue #116
Torrance, CA 90501
213-212-7155

Faron Melrose Inc
Penny Melrose
1333 Lawrence Expressway #150
Santa Clara, CA 95051
408-737-9494

Four Colour Imports
George Dick, President
2235 Millvale Road
Louisville, KY 40205
502-456-6033; Fax: 502-473-1437
Statement: US representative of Cayfosa
Industria Grafica, D W Friesen, Everbest
Printing, and Coloursplendor Graphics.

Imago Sales (USA)
Joseph Braff, President
310 Madison Avenue #2103
New York, NY 10017
212-370-4411

Interprint
Ken Coburn, President
2447 Petaluma Boulevard N
Petaluma, CA 94952
707-765-6116; Fax: 707-765-6018

Chapter 8

Other Publishing Services

This chapter features a few other publishing suppliers and services that you might want to use in designing, producing, and marketing your books. In compiling this short list, we sent surveys to over 300 companies. To limit the size of this section, however, we asked companies to pay a small listing fee if they wanted to be featured here. Obviously, the companies which chose to be listed here are eager for your business. For a more complete list of such services, see the *Book Publishing Resource Guide*. To order, call Ad-Lib Publications toll-free: **800-669-0773**.

Book Binders

Pease Bindery
G Steven Bock, President
2348 N Street
Lincoln, NE 68510
402-476-1303; Fax: 402-476-2978

Statement: Pease Bindery offers short-run book manufacturing (Smyth sewn case binding) to printers and publishers. In recent years, Pease has experienced an exciting growth period by providing timely, high quality, cost efficient book manufacturing for our U.S. customers.

Bar Codes

Infinity Symbology
Fred Bauries or Scott Bauries
2277 Science Parkway
Okemos, MI 48864
517-349-4635; Fax: 517-349-7608

Statement: UPC and Bookland EAN bar code masters. Same day turnaround. Knowledgeable telephone assistance.

Design Services

Comp-Type Inc
Cynthia Frank
155 Cypress Street
Fort Bragg, CA 95437
707-964-9520; Fax: 707-964-7531

Statement: Complete editorial and book production services. Call or write for a free brochure describing the full range of services we provide small press and self-publishers, including: 1) Manuscript evaluation, editing, proofreading, high-quality phototypesetting or economical laser printing, design, illustration, and page make-up. 2) Print brokering for paperback and hardcover books. 3) Promotion, direct mail, and fulfillment services.

Desktop Studio
Janet Andrews
290 Larkspur Plaza Drive
Larkspur, CA 94939
415-924-8036

Statement: Book design, typography, and full production services. We specialize in quality design and production for the small to medium size publisher. Our services include planning and specifying physical and visual attributes of a book. We then execute the design, coordinating all suppliers and the printer. We use Ventura Publisher and Adobe fonts for our typography.

Distribution Services

Quality Books
Amy Mascillino
918 Sherwood Drive
Lake Bluff, IL 60044-2204
708-295-2010; Fax: 708-295-1556

Statement: Quality Books is the leading national library distributor of small press books and independently produced special interest videos. We sell books and videos to libraries through direct sales representation and provide a full complement of marketing and distribution services.

Fulfillment Services

Publishers Storage & Shipping
E B Quick
46 Development Road
Fitchburg, MA 01420
508-345-2121; Fax: 508-348-1233

Statement: We provide book storage and order fulfillment. We presently serve about 200 small publishers from warehouses in Massachusetts and Michigan.

Upper Access Fulfillment Service
Gay Muller
P O Box 457
Hinesburg, VT 05461
Toll-free: 800-356-9315

Statement: Retail book fulfillment. 800 number for credit card sales. We charge no "front" money or warehousing fee and require no minimum sales. We pay monthly (50% discount to us). We periodically make available to you the list of customers. Once an agreement is signed and books are in stock, you may use our 800 number throughout your promotions.

Loose-Leaf Binders

American Thermoplastic Co.
Attn: Customer Service
622 Second Avenue
Pittsburgh, PA 15219-2086
412-261-6657; Fax: 412-642-7464
Toll-free: 800-456-6602

Statement: We manufacture all types of binders and related loose-leaf products, custom-made and imprinted to your specifications. We offer a wide variety of products, sizes, and vinyl colors to choose from. QuickShop 10 Service is available on many items.

Marketing Services

Northwest Publishers Consortium
Heather Kibbey
15800 SW Boones Ferry Road #A-14
Lake Oswego, OR 97035
503-697-7964

Statement: Promotion a la carte for independent publishers, including exhibits, mailings, and the unique Promote-A-Great-Book program of in-store promotion. We offer a free newsletter for book publishers which gives information on upcoming promotional events.

Planned Television Arts
Rick Frishman
25 West 43rd Street
New York, NY 10036
212-921-5111

Planned Television Arts
Rick Frishman
25 West 43rd Street
New York, NY 10036
212-921-5111

Statement: We provide book and author publicity, especially radio and TV interview tours. We may be the right PR firm for you. We'll book you (or your author) on at least four quality interviews in each city you visit...or you don't pay! Our clients include some of the country's largest book publishers—yet our prices are still affordable for the little guy.

Radio-TV Interview Report
Bill Harrison
Bradley Communications
101 W Baltimore Avenue
P O Box JK-1206
Lansdowne, PA 19050-1206
215-259-1070

Statement: Want more radio/TV exposure with less cost and effort? Then advertise in the *Radio-TV Interview Report*, the magazine producers read to find guests. For as little as $215, you can pitch your authors to over 4,700 producers and editors across the country. Most advertisers get five or more interviews the first time. Many do far better.

Sensible Solutions
Judith Appelbaum
275 Madison Avenue #1518
New York, NY 10016-1101
212-687-1761; Fax: 212-986-3218

Statement: Judith Appelbaum, author of *How to Get Happily Published*, and Florence Janovic are book marketing consultants who can help you sell your book once it's printed. We provide targeted marketing plans for cost-effective ways to reach your readers.

Paper / Cover Suppliers

Holliston Mills - Pajco
Jeffrey A Hopkins
P O Box 478
Kingsport, TN 37662
615-357-6141; Fax: 615-357-8840

Statement: Holliston Mills and Pajco Products manufacture a complete line of woven and nonwoven book covering materials. We also manufacture and distribute all forms of bindery supply items.

Papyrus Newton Falls Inc
Thomas M Hanley
P O Box 253
Newton Falls, NY 13666
315-848-3321; Fax: 315-848-2081
Toll-free: 800-448-8900

Statement: We manufacture coated papers in gloss and matte finishes, distributed throughout the U.S. and Canada. All products are alkaline based, and papers containing recycled fibers are available.

Penntech Papers
William E Curtis, VP Sales
3 Barker Avenue
White Plains, NY 10601
914-997-1600; Fax: 914-997-1238

Statement: We manufacture book publishing papers for the trade, text, reference, juvenile, and specialty publishing markets.

Software for Book Publishers

The Edge
Connie Lowery
911 Lyttleton Street
P O Box 1195
Camden, SC 29020
803-432-7674; Fax: 803-425-5064

Statement: We produce the Selection of the Month Club system, a PC-based system for handling continuity and negative option invoicing and order fulfillment. Use it to add an additional sales channel for direct marketing your books, tapes, or other products.

Metagroup Consultants
Marek Karon
12103 S Brookhurst Street #E-410
Garden Grove, CA 92642-3065
714-638-8663

Statement: Mail Business Manager is a comprehensive PC computer program providing support for all aspects of publishing, mail order, and related businesses. It provides fast customer file searching and retrieval, customer tracking, order taking and processing, shipping, personalized invoices, payment processing, response tracking, inventory, back orders, returns, accounts receivable, mailing lists with file export, management reporting, and marketing analysis.

PIIGS Software
Lisa Carlson
Upper Access Inc.
P O Box 457
Hinesburg, VT 05461
Toll-free: 800-356-9315

Statement: This computer program for book publishers is designed by a small publisher. It provides order entry, invoices, statements, fulfillment, inventory control, back orders, royalties, consignments, and much more. The program is so easy to use you'll hardly need the manual. PIIGS is the friendly program for only $500.

Typesetting

Heritage Publishing Company
Derek Wood
2402 Wildwood Avenue
Sherwood, AR 72116
501-835-5000, Extension 1409
Fax: 501-835-5834; Toll-free: 800-643-8822

Statement: Typesetting and composition services. Over 30 years experience. Producing quality digital/paginated camera-ready pages. We will type copy or import text from your disk. Call us for our introductory rate. Sample pages on request.

Counter-Top Book Displays

Ad-Lib Publications is now stocking two counter-top white corrugated cardboard displays designed for books that are either 6" x 9" (5 1/2" x 8 1/2") or 8 1/2" x 11".

These displays are designed to be put together by the publisher, then filled with books, and finally shipped inside a carton that fits the display. It has been our experience that displays are much more likely to be used if the retailer doesn't have to do anything but take the display out of the shipping carton and put it on the shelf.

Since we stock these displays, you can order as few as 10 or as many as 200 or more without having to buy cutting dies or overstock. Here are the prices for orders of 10 or more displays (the minimum order is 10 displays, though it is more convenient for us to ship in units of 25 displays):

60¢   6" wide x 9" tall x 6" deep counter-top display

35¢   shipping box to fit the 6" x 9" x 6" display

70¢   8 1/2" wide x 11" tall x 6" deep counter-top display

40¢   shipping box to fit the 8 1/2" x 11" x 6" display

Shipping costs are $6.00 per 25 or fewer displays and $6.00 per 25 or fewer shipping boxes. Hence, if you were to order 25 6" x 9" displays and 25 boxes, your total cost would be $15.00 (25 x 60¢) for the displays, plus $8.75 (25 x 35¢) for the shipping boxes, plus $12.00 ($6.00 plus $6.00) for shipping and handling = $35.75.

If you'd like to see a sample display before ordering larger quantities, send $5.00 for a sample display and shipping carton. Please note which size display you'd like to have.

To order, call toll-free 800-669-0773, or write to:

Ad-Lib Publications, 51 N. Fifth Street, Fairfield IA 52556

Glossary

The definitions for this glossary have been adapted for the most part from Braun-Brumfield's *Book Manufacturing Glossary*. Write to them for a copy of the complete booklet as well as their paper samples book and paper bulk chart.

A

Across the Grain — The direction 90 degrees, or at a right angle, to the paper grain.

Acid-Free Paper — Paper which is free from acid or other ingredients likely to have a destructive effect. Libraries prefer books with acid free paper, because such books last longer.

Actual Value Shipment — A truck shipment insured for the actual value of the commodity, rather than the amount specified by ICC regulations. In the case of books, the standard insurance is $1.65 each, rather than the actual value, which may be more or less. An actual value shipment is at a higher freight rate.

Advance Copies — Finished books sent to a customer, usually by air mail, prior to bulk shipment of the balance of the order.

Aluminum Plate — A thin sheet of aluminum used in lithography for some press plates; used for both surface-type and deep-etch offset plates.

Alterations — In composition, changes made in the copy after it has been set in type.

Antique — A natural or cream-white color of paper.

Antique Finish — A term describing the surface, usually on book and cover papers, that has a natural rough finish.

Appendix — An addition to the back matter of a book listing material related to the subject but not necessarily essential to its completeness.

Art Work — A general term used to describe photographs, drawings, paintings, hand lettering, and the like, prepared to illustrate printed matter.

Author's Alterations (A.A.'s) — Changes from original copy, or author's corrections.

B

BMI (Book Manufacturing Institute) — A graphic arts industry organization consisting of book manufacturers and related companies.

Back Lining — (1) A paper or fabric strip used to reinforce the spine of a casebound book after rounding and backing. It provides the means for a firm connection between book and case. (2) The paper stiffening used in the backbone of a case, between the binder's boards.

Back Matter — Material printed at the end of a book; usually includes appendix, addenda, glossary, index, and bibliography.

Back Up — To print the reverse side of a sheet already printed on one side. Printing is said to back up when the printing areas on both sides are exactly opposite one another.

Backbone — The back of a bound book connecting the two covers; also called the Spine.

Back Cover — Back outside surface of a casebound or softcover book.

Back Margin — The distance between live matter of a left hand page and live matter of a right hand page — always measured in even PICAS, for example: 8, 10, or 12 picas. This measurement is critical in producing a good design and continuity to your printed product. It is also used as a guide in stripping and becomes the bible for finishing and bindery.

Band — (1) A strip of paper, printed or unprinted, which wraps around loose sheets (in lieu of binding with a cover) or assembled pieces. (2) The operation of putting a paper band around loose sheets or assembled pieces. (3) Metal straps wrapped around skids of cartons to secure the contents to the skid for shipment.

Basis Weight — A term used to distinguish the various weights of paper. For example, a basis weight of 60 pounds means a ream (500 sheets) of such paper in size 25" x 38" weighs 60 pounds. The 25" x 38" size is standard for book papers. Other kinds of paper (bond, bristol, cover, newsprint, etc.) determine their basis weight on different base sizes, and thus weights are not comparable with book paper weights.

Benday — A method of laying a screen (dots, line, and other textures) on artwork or plates to obtain various tones and shadings.

Bill of Lading (B/L) — The document that originates a shipment; it contains all the necessary information for the carrier to handle the shipment in transit, such as special instructions for protection from the elements as well as delivery information. A Bill of Lading is: a) The contract of carriage, b) Documentary evidence of title, and c) Receipt for the goods.

Bind — To join pages of a book together with thread, wire, adhesive or other means; to enclose them in a cover when so specified.

Bind Margin — The gutter or inner margin, from the binding to the beginning of the printed area.

Binder's Boards — A stiff, high-grade composition board used in book binding, inside the cloth of the case; more dense than chipboard.

Binding Edge — Edge of sheet or page that is nearest the saddle of the book. Right-hand pages are bound at the left side, left-hand pages at the right side. Ample space between the line matter and the binding edge should be allowed.

Black and White — Originals and reproductions displayed in monochrome (single color) as distinguished from polychrome or multicolor.

Blank — An unprinted page.

Bleed — Any part of the printed area (usually a photograph or some non-illustrative artwork; never headlines or copy) that extends beyond the trim edge of the page.

Blind Embossing — A design which is stamped without gold leaf or ink, giving a bas-relief effect.

Blind Stamp — A design which is impressed (stamped) without foil or ink, giving a bas-relief effect.

Blowup — An enlargement of the original size.

Blues or **Blueprint** — See: Silverprint.

Book Cloth — Cotton gray goods, woven as for any other fabric and finished in one of three ways; starch-filled, pyroxlin impregnated, or plastic coated. Cloth comes in different weights and weaves. The quality of the cloth is determined by the number of threads per inch and the tensile strength of the threads.

Booklet — Any pamphlet sewn, wired, or bound with adhesive, containing a few pages and generally not produced for permanence.

Book Paper — A class or group of papers having common physical characteristics that, in general, are most suitable for book manufacture. Book paper is made to close tolerances on caliper (pages per inch).

Broadside — A broadside may be printed on both sides or on portions of a single fold. Product size is usually 22" x 16 ½" folded to 8 ¼" x 11" — heads not trimmed.

Buckram — A book cloth which can be identified by heavy, coarse threads; available in a number of grades.

Bulk — (1) The stacked thickness of paper, usually expressed as pages per inch (ppi). (2) The thickness of a book, exclusive of cover.

Bulking Dummy — Unprinted sheets folded in the signature size and signature number of a given job, to determine the actual bulk; used to establish dimensions for cover art preparation or by the binder to determine case size for a casebound book.

C

C1S (Coated One Side) — Cover or text paper which has been coated on one side only; usually used for covers and dust jackets.

C2S (Coated Two Sides) — Cover or text paper which has been coated on both sides.

Calendered Paper — Paper which has been glazed during manufacture by passing it through a stack of polished metal rollers called calenders.

Caliper — The thickness of a single sheet of paper; usually expressed in thousandths of an inch.

Camera Ready Copy — Customer furnished material suitable for photographing and reproduction. See: Copy.

Case Bound — A term denoting a book bound with a stiff or hard cover.

Casebinding — A method of binding in which the cover is made separately and consists of rigid or flexible boards covered with cloth, paper or other material, in such a manner that the covering material surrounds the outside and edges of the board. Covers always project beyond the edges of the text pages.

Check Copy — (1) A folded and gathered but unbound copy of a book sent to a customer for approval before binding. (2) The gathered, trimmed copy which is inspected and approved prior to any binding operations; used as a guide in bindery for assembling in the proper sequence, including inserts, furnished items, etc.

Chipboard — A less expensive and less durable single ply substitute for binder's boards; also used as a backing for padded forms. It is more likely to absorb moisture or to warp than binder's boards.

Close Register — Used to describe low trap allowance, requiring more press printing position accuracy; also known as Tight Register.

Clothbound — See: Casebound.

Coated Paper — Paper having a surface coating which produces a smooth gloss finish. When producing four color process printing, high quality halftones or heavy ink coverages, coated papers will produce the best results. Magazines, books, booklets, trade journals, and catalogs use these papers for high-quality printing.

Cold Type — Text composition prepared for photomechanical reproduction with a typewriter, by hand-lettering, or by photocomposition. Hot type is set using melted lead to form the type. All typesetting not using melted lead is known as Cold Type.

Collate — In binding, collating is the gathering (assembling) of sections (signatures in proper sequence) for binding.

Color Key — Color proofing material from 3-M (available as positive or negative) of a light-sensitive polyester-base film, supplied in any one of a number of colors.

Color Process Work—A reproduction of color made by means of photographic separations. The printing is done using cyan, magenta, yellow, and black inks, each requiring its own negative. This is the means of full color reproduction in printing; also called Four Color.

Color Separation—(1) In photography, the division of colors of a continuous-tone full color original, each of which will be reproduced by a separate printing plate carrying a color. (2) In lithographic platemaking, manual separation of colors by handwork performed directly on the printing surface. (3) For some kinds of color reproduction, a paste-up artist can prepare separate overlays for each color.

Comb—See: Plastic Comb Binding.

Composition—The assembling of characters into words, lines, and paragraphs of texts or body matter for reproduction by printing.

Confirming Proof—A proof confirming to the customer that the page, as shown by the proof, is the way the page will print. No approval will be required or expected.

Contact Print—A photographic print made from either a negative or a positive, exposed in contact with sensitized paper or film, instead of by projection.

Continuous Tone—A photographic image without a halftone dot screen containing gradient tones from black to white.

Copy—The photograph, paste-up, art, or other material furnished for reproduction. A better term is Original, since it is from this material that reproduction originates. Most commonly, the term Photocopy is used. See also Camera Ready Copy.

Corner Marks—Open parts of squares placed on original copy as a positioning guide.

Covers—**Cover 1**: Outside front cover. **Cover 2**: Inside front cover. **Cover 3**: Inside back cover. **Cover 4**: Outside back cover.

Crop Marks—Marks along the margins of an illustration indicating the part of the illustration to be reproduced.

Cropping—The process of defining the reproduction image area of line and continuous-tone art by drawing crop marks or of continuous-tone art by producing windows in negatives by means of dropout masks.

Cross Grain—A fold at right angles to the binding edge of a book, or at right angles to the direction of the grain in the paper or board; also called Against the Grain.

Customer Furnished (CF)—Any material supplied by the customer, for example, paper, printed covers, or separations.

Cutoff—The paper dimension fixed by the size of the press cylinder, which limits the cutoff at right angles to the travel of the web.

D

Data Conversion—Taking the data produced on one system (e.g., a word processor) and transferring it to another system (e.g., a phototypesetter) by changing the codes and the format via an interface, but leaving the text alone, thereby saving proofreading and keyboarding time. Data may be delivered for conversion over telephone lines or by sending the media (disks) through the mail.

Density—(1) The specific gravity of paper, or weight per unit volume. (2) A measure of the degree of blackness. (3) The blackness and weight of type set in phototypesetting.

Die Cutting—The use of sharp steel rules to cut special shapes, like labels, boxes and containers, from printed or unprinted material. Die-cutting can be done on flat-bed or rotary presses.

Digest—A size of publication that is usually 5¼ x 8¼ inches.

Dividers—Tabbed sheets of index or other heavy stock, used to identify and separate specific sections of a book; used in looseleaf and bound books (tipped in on bound books).

Dot Gain—The slight enlargement of a halftone dot during exposure, development, or on the printing press.

Dot Spread—In printing, a defect in which dots print larger than they should, causing darker tones or colors.

Drill(ing)—Punching of holes in folded sections, trimmed or untrimmed, or in finished books, which will permit their insertion over rings or posts in a binder.

Drop-Out—A halftone negative exposed to eliminate the extreme highlight dots so the white background of the artwork will not produce a printing dot on the negative. This technique can also be used to eliminate printing of shadow dots.

Dull Coated Paper—Coated paper that has a dull finish. Such paper may have a dull finish on one side for text and a glossy finish on the other side for fine color work or halftones. The dull finish eliminates glare for reading solid copy.

Dummy—(1) A preliminary drawing or layout showing the positioning of illustrations and text as they are to appear in the final reproduction. (2) A set of blank pages made up in advance to show the size, shape, form, and general style of a piece of printing.

Duotone—A term for a two-color halftone reproduction from a one-color original, requiring two halftone negatives for opposite ends of the gray scale, one emphasizing highlights and the other emphasizing shadows. One plate usually is printed in dark ink, the other in a lighter one.

Dust Jacket—The printed or unprinted wrapper, usually paper, placed around a case bound book.

Dylux (Silverprint) — A pre-press proof of negatives made by photographic techniques. A DuPont product.

E

Edition Binding — See: Casebinding.

Embossed Finish — Paper with a raised or depressed surface resembling wood, cloth, leather, or other pattern.

Embossing — (1) Impressing an image in relief to achieve a raised or depressed surface, either over printing or on blank paper for decorative purposes. (2) The swelling of the image on an offset blanket, due to its absorbing solvents from the ink. (3) A finish on paper or cloth.

Emulsion Side — The side of a photographic film to which the emulsion is applied, and on which the image is developed; the side on which scratching or scribing can be done.

Endsheets — Four pages each at the beginning and end of a casebound book, one leaf of each being solidly pasted against the inside board of the case. Stock is stronger and heavier than text stock; may be white or colored stock, printed or unprinted. Other common terms frequently used are Endpapers, Endleaves or Lining Paper.

Estimate — A price provided to a customer, based on the specifications outlined on the estimate form; it is normally sent prior to entry of an order and prices may change if the order specifications are not the same as the estimate specifications.

Exposure — A step in photographic processes during which light produces an image on the light-sensitive coating on film or plates; in photography, called Shot; in platemaking, called Burn.

F

F & G — A term used to refer to a folded and gathered, but unbound, copy of a book; sometimes called a Check Copy.

F.O.B. (Free on Board) — The f.o.b. point is usually the inland point of departure, or the port of shipment. The buyer pays all shipping charges beyond the f.o.b. point.

Filling In — A condition in offset lithography where ink fills the area between the halftone dots or plugs up the type; also known as Plugging or Filling Up.

Film Lamination — See: Laminate.

Finish — The general surface properties of paper, determined by various manufacturing techniques.

Finishing — Any post-press operations, such as folding, binding, etc.

Flat – A stripped flat, in photographic platemaking for offset lithography, is an assembled (stripped) composite of negatives or positives from which a printing plate is made.

Foil – Tissue-thin material, faced with metal or pigment, used in book stamping with a Stamping Die.

Foldout – An insert which is wider than the page width of a publication. In some cases, one or more vertical folds are required so that it will occupy the same area as the page. Foldouts are used to accommodate large illustrations, charts, and the like.

Folio – (1) A page number. (2) Sometimes used to refer to a sheet that has been folded once.

Foreword – A statement forming part of the front matter of a book, often written by an expert, other than the author, to give the book greater promotability and authority.

Four Color Process Printing – The overprinting of specially made plates of four separate colors of transparent ink (magenta, cyan, yellow, and black). The result is a finished printed page which matches the color proof by combining to reproduce all colors.

Four-Sided Trim (Trim 4) – After the job is printed and folded, a trim will be taken off of all four sides to remove any reference or registration marks and give a clean edge to the pile of sheets.

Front Flap – The inside fold on the front of a dust jacket.

Front Matter – The pages preceding the text of a book.

Frontispiece – An illustration facing the title page of a book; also called Frontis.

Fulfillment – A system of storage and mailing upon customer request of title and quantity specified.

Full Color Printing – See: Four Color Process Printing.

G

Galley – Typeset material before it has been arranged into page form.

Galley Copies – Bound galleys (generally printed before proofing and final typeset corrections) which are used in prepublication review mailings.

Galley Proof – Proof of typeset material in galley form prior to page makeup.

Gatefold – A four page insert having foldouts on either side of the center spread.

Gathering – Collecting, by hand or machine, the signatures of a book in the sequence in which they are to be bound; also called Collating.

Grain—(1) In paper, the machine direction in papermaking along which the majority of fibers are aligned. This governs some paper properties such as increased size change with relative humidity across the grain, and better folding qualities along the grain.

Gray Scale—A strip of standard gray tones, ranging from white to black, placed at the side of original copy during photography, or beside the negative or positive during plate exposure, to measure the tonal range obtained.

Gripper Margin—The margin on the forward or leading edge of paper held by grippers of the printing press which feeds and controls paper as it is printed. Because this area cannot be used for a printed image, allowance must be made for gripper edges.

Gutter—(1) In multi-column composition, the space between columns on a page. (2) Short for Gutter Margin.

Gutter Bleed—Occurs when a page bleeds or prints to the binding edge.

Gutter Margin—In binding, the blank space where two pages meet; the inside margin at the binding edge; also called Back Margin or Bind Margin.

H

Hairline Register—The joining or butting of two or more colors, with no color overlapping. Also called Close Register or Tight Register.

Halftone—The reproduction of a continuous tone original, such as a photograph, in which detail and tone values are represented by a series of evenly spaced dots of varying size and shape. The dot areas vary in direct proportion to the intensity of the tones they represent. A halftone screen is placed in front of the negative during photography.

Halftone Screen—A screen placed in front of the negative material in a process camera to break up a continuous tone image into dot formation.

Hand Tip—To attach a leaf, foldout, etc. to a signature or bound book by hand operations of gluing and placement of the item.

Handwork—Any operation which can only be accomplished by hand. This includes hand operations in Composition or Plate Prep, as well as those performed in Bindery.

Hard Copy—Any output from a machine, or as a result of machine processing, which is readable copy on paper or film. Examples are computer printouts and phototypesetting output on film or paper.

Hardbound—Another term for Casebound.

Headband—A small band of silk or cotton glued at the top or bottom (or both) of a casebound book to fill the gap normally formed between the spine of the book and the cover. The only purpose is decorative.

Hickey — An imperfection in offset press work due to a number of causes, such as dirt on the press, hardened specks of ink, or any dry hard particle working into the ink or onto the plate or offset blanket. It is characterized by a solid center area surrounded by a white ring.

High Bulk Paper — A paper specifically manufactured to retain a thickness not found in other papers of the same basis weight.

House Sheet — Paper stocked by the printer.

I

Illustrations — The drawings, photographs, etc., used to supplement the text of printed matter.

Imposition — The laying out of pages in press form so that they will be in the correct sequence after the printed sheet is folded.

Index — A list at the end of a book showing individual terms from the text contents in alphabetical order and listing the pages on which each entry appears.

Insert — (1) In stripping, a section of film carrying printing detail that is spliced into a larger piece of film. (2) In printing, a page, etc., that is printed separately and then placed into or bound with the main publication. (3) In typesetting, copy to be added.

Inside Delivery — Delivery made inside a door or garage on the ground level. It will not necessarily include breaking of skid bands and unloading cartons. There is an additional charge for Inside Delivery.

J

Jacket — See: Dust Jacket.

Jacketing — The application of dust jackets on finished casebound books.

Joint — The flexible hinge where the cover of a casebound book meets the spine, permitting the cover to open without breaking the spine of the book or breaking apart signatures; also called Hinge.

K

Keyline — In artwork, an outline drawing of finished art to indicate the exact shape, position, and size for such elements as halftones and type.

Knock Out — See: Reverse

Kraft — Paper or board made from unbleached woodpulp by the sulfate process; it is brown in color. Kraft paper is often used to wrap books and journals for mailings of individual copies.

L

Laid Paper — Paper which, when held up to the light, shows fine parallel lines (wire-marks) and crosslines (chain-marks).

Laminate — Bonding plastic film by adhesives or heat and pressure to a sheet of paper; especially used to protect the covers of paperback books and improve their appearance.

Layout — (1) The drawing or sketch of a proposed printed piece; the working diagram for a printer to follow. (2) Brief for Layout Sheet. (3) Another term for Plate Prep.

Layout Sheet — The imposition form; indicates the sequence and positioning of negatives on the flat, which corresponds to printed pages on the press sheet. Pages are not sequential on the Layout Sheet — it is a folding imposition. Once the sheet is folded, pages will be in consecutive order.

Leaf — (1) Each separate piece of paper in a book, with a page on each side. (2) A pigmented stamping material used to decorate cases.

Library Binding — A book bound in accordance with the standards of the American Library Association, having strong endpapers, muslin reinforced end signatures, sewing with four-cord thread, canton flannel backlining, and covers of Library or Caxton Buckram cloth with round corners.

Lightweight Paper — Paper in the 17 to 35 lb. weight range.

Line Copy — Any copy suitable for reproduction without using a halftone screen; copy composed of lines or dots as distinguished from copy composed of continuous tones. Lines or dots may be small and close together so as to simulate tones, but are still regarded as line copy if they can be faithfully reproduced without a halftone screen.

Line Drawing — A drawing containing no grays or middle tones. In general, any drawing that can be reproduced without the use of halftone techniques.

Linen Finish — Book Cloth which has a two-tone effect due to the white threads which show through the color.

Lint — Small fuzzy particles in paper.

Lithography — A generic term for any printing process in which the image area and nonimage area exist on the same plane (plate) and are separated by chemical repulsion.

Long Grain — Paper made with the machine direction of fibers in the longest dimension of the sheet.

Long Run — A print run in excess of 20,000 copies.

Loose Register — Color or other copy that fits loosely, where positioning (register) is not critical.

Low Bulk Paper — A paper with a smooth surface; a thin sheet.

M

M – The abbreviation for a quantity of 1000.

Machine Finish (m.f.) – A term applied to paper which has been made smooth and somewhat glossy by passing through several rolls of the calendering machine.

Magenta – Process red, a purplish red, one of the four process colors.

Makeready – (1) On an offset press, all work done before running a job, such as adjusting the feeder and side guide, putting a plate on press and ink in the fountain, etc. (2) Any machine adjustments made for size, bulk, etc., prior to performing the required operation.

Manuscript (mss) – A written or typewritten work, which the typesetter follows as a guide in setting copy.

Matte Finish – Dull paper finish without gloss or luster.

Mechanical – Camera-ready copy (usually for a cover or dust jacket) showing exact placement of every element and carrying actual or simulated type and artwork.

Mechanical Binding – Individual leaves fastened by means of an independent binding device such as Plastic Comb, Wire-O, or Spiral.

Moire – The undesirable wave-like or checkered effect that results when a halftone is photographed through a screen. The second screen must be angled at 15 degrees away from that of the halftone to avoid this effect.

N

Natural – A paper color such as cream, white, or ivory.

Natural Finish – A book cloth characterized by a soft, slightly fuzzy appearance due to to the finishing process.

Negative – Photographic image on film, in which black values in the original subject are transparent, and white values are opaque; light grays are dark, and dark grays are light.

Neutral pH Paper – See: Acid-free Paper.

Newsprint – Paper made mostly from ground wood pulp and small amounts of chemical pulp; used for newspaper printing.

Nick – A small tear on the head of a saddlestitched book that occurs during the trim operation.

Notch Bind – An adhesive binding similar to Perfect Binding. Pieces of text stock (notches) are removed on the binding edge during folding to allow greater adhesive penetration without trimming the spine; primarily used for adhesive binding of coated paper.

O

Odd Sizes—Any nonstandard paper or book size.

Offset—In printing, the term refers to the transfer of the image from the plate to a rubber blanket to stock as in photo-offset lithography.

Offset Lithography—Lithography produced on an offset lithographic press. A right-reading plate is used and an intermediate rubber-covered offset cylinder transfers the image from the plate cylinder to the paper, cloth, metal or other material being printed.

Offset Paper—Paper which is strong enough to resist the tacky inks and considerable moisture encountered in offset printing.

Opacity—That property of paper which minimizes the show-through of printing from the back side or the sheet under it.

Opaque—(1) An area or material which completely blocks out unwanted light; a filter may be opaque to only certain colors. (2) A red or black liquid used to block out or cover unwanted clear or grey areas on a negative. (3) White opaque used to cover unwanted black images in an original copy (on white paper). (4) To paint out areas on a negative which are not to print. (5) In paper, the property which makes it less transparent.

Opti-Copy—A computerized camera that uses a Slo-Syn numerical control to position images on film in proper position for printing on a flat-size piece of film; the exposed film contains the matter to be printed on one side of the press sheet.

Original—The artwork, mechanical, or other material furnished for printing reproduction; usually refers to photographs or drawings for halftone reproduction. More commonly called Photocopy.

Out of Register—(1) Descriptive of pages on both sides of the sheet which do not back up accurately. (2) Two or more colors are not in the proper position when printed; register does not match.

Overlay—In artwork, a clear acetate sheet or tissue with color separated as it is to be photographed.

Overrun—Additional copies above the number ordered to be printed.

P

PMS (Pantone Matching System)—An ink color system widely used in the graphic arts. There are approximately 500 basic colors, for both coated and uncoated paper. The color number and formula for each color are shown beneath the color swath in the ink book.

PMT (Photomechanical Transfer Prints)—Camera-generated positive prints used for pasteup and for making paper contacts without the need for a negative.

Page Makeup—The hand or electronic assembly of the elements that comprise a page.

Page Proof—Proof of type, in page form.

Pagination—The numbering of pages of a book.

Paperbound—A paper covered book; also called Paperback or Soft Cover.

Pasteup—The assembling of type elements, illustrations, etc., into final page form ready for photographing. See also: Mechanical and Page Makeup.

Perfect Binding—A binding method, usually for paper-covered books, with adhesive (glue) the only binding medium; also known as Adhesive Binding.

Perfecting Press—A printing press that prints both sides of the paper in one pass through the press.

Perforate—To make slits in the paper during folding, at the fold, to prevent wrinkles and allow air to escape. Books with perfect bind are perforated on the spine fold to aid in binding.

Phototypesetting—The process of setting type via a photographic process directly onto film or paper film.

Pica—Printer's unit of measurement used in printing, principally for measuring lines. One pica is equal to 12 points, and is approximately 1/6 of an inch. The pica is used to measure the width and length of pages, columns, slugs, and so on.

Pin Register—The use of accurately positioned holes and special pins on copy, film, plates, and presses to insure proper register or fit of colors.

Pinhole—A small, unwanted transparent area in the developed emulsion of a negative or black area on a positive; usually due to dust or other defects on the copy, copyboard glass, or the film.

Plastic Comb Binding—A type of mechanical binding using a piece of rigid vinyl plastic sheeting diecut in the shape of a comb or rake and rolled to make a cylinder of any thickness. The book is punched with slots along the binding edge through which this comb is inserted.

Plastic Shrink Wrap—A method of packaging in plastic film. The material to be wrapped is inserted into a folded roll of polyethylene film, which is heat-sealed around it. The package then goes through a heat tunnel where the film shrinks tightly around the package.

Plate—Brief for printing plate; a thin sheet of metal that carries the printing image, whose surface is treated so that only that image is ink receptive.

Plate Prep—Those operations after camera and before plate making; includes opaquing of negatives, strip-ins of halftones, stripping of negative flats, and any other operations needed to make negative flats ready for platemaking.

Point—A unit of measurement, based on the pica used to measure type sizes. A point measures .013 of an inch. There are approximately 72 points to an inch.

Positive—Photographic image usually made from a negative, in which the dark and light values are the same as the original. A positive on paper is called a print; one on a transparent base such as film is called a positive transparency.

Prep—In the prep department, work is assembled and made ready for the printing process. Litho camera, stripping, proofing, and platemaking are done in the prep department of a printing company.

Prepress—All manufacturing operations prior to press.

Press Proof—Actual press sheets to show image, tone value, and color. A few sheets are run and approval received from the customer prior to printing the job.

Printer's Error (PE)—Usually refers to a typesetting or other compositor error as distinguished from an author's alteration. Correction costs are not chargeable to the customer.

Process Color Separation Negative—A color picture is actually printed with the four process colors. To obtain the negatives for each of these colors requires a complicated darkroom process. Basically, filters are used to block out all but the desired color for each color negative, and for each a different angle screen is employed. Usually special color correction masks must be used to improve colors for each negative.

Process Color—(1) Yellow (2) Cyan Blue (3) Magenta Red (4) Black. When these colors are used in various strengths and combinations, they make it possible to produce thousands of colors with a minimum of photography, platemaking, and presswork.

Progressive Proofs—Proofs of plates for color printing, showing each color separately and also the combined colors in the order they are to print (second color on first; third on second and first; fourth on third, second, and first): used to indicate color quality and as a guide for printing; also called Progs.

Proportional Wheel—A circular scale used to determine proportional reductions and enlargements of copy. Linear scales may be used for the same purpose.

R

Recto—A right-hand page of a book, usually odd-numbered.

Recycled Paper—Paper made from old paper pulp; used paper is cooked in chemicals and reduced back to pulp after it is deinked. Recycled Paper might also include pulp made from mill waste.

Register — (1) Exact correspondence in the position of pages or other printed matter on both sides of a sheet or in relation to other matter already ruled or printed on the same side of the sheet. (2) In photoreproduction and color printing, the correct relative position of two or more colors, so that no color is out of its proper position.

Register Marks — (1) Small crosses, guides, or patterns placed on originals before reproduction; used for positioning the negatives for stripping or for color register. (2) Similar marks added to a negative flat to print along the margins of a press sheet; used as a guide for correct alignment, backing, and color register in printing.

Reprints — Articles for which negatives are relaid so the articles are produced in booklet form.

Reproduction Proof (Repro) — Carefully printed proofs from type forms; used as camera-ready copy for reproduction.

Reverse — Type appearing in white on a black or color background or in a dark area of a photograph.

Ring Binder — A looseleaf mechanism comprised of a metal housing to which heavy wire rings are attached. These rings open in the center. Such binders are used in looseleaf binding.

Rounding and Backing — In binding, the process of rounding gives books a convex spine and a concave fore-edge. The process of backing makes the spine wider than the rest by the thickness of the covers, thus providing a shoulder against which the boards of the front and back covers fit (i.e., the crease or joint).

Rub-Off — (1) Ink on printed sheets, after sufficient drying, which smears or comes off on the fingers when handled. (2) Ink which comes off the cover during shipment and transfers to other covers or to the shipping carton or mailer; also called Scuffing.

Run — The total number of copies ordered.

Running Head — A headline or title repeated at the top of each page for the quick reference of the reader.

S

Saddlestitch — A binding method which inserts sections into sections, then fastens them with wires (stitches) through the middle fold of the sheets. The limiting factor in this type of binding is bulk (thickness) Also called: Saddlewire.

Screened Print — Halftone illustration made on photographic paper. It can be mounted with line copy on a page layout so that the entire page can be photographed at the same time as line copy for reproduction.

Screened Print — A print made from continuous tone copy which was screened during exposure.

Screentone—A halftone film having a uniform dot size over its area and rated by its approximate printing dot size value, such as 20%; also called Screen Tint.

Self-Cover—A cover of the same paper as the inside text pages.

Sheet-Fed Press—A printing press which takes paper previously cut into sheets, as opposed to paper in a continuous roll (web press).

Short Grain Paper—Paper made with the direction of the majority of fibers in the shortest sheet dimension.

Show Through—The ability to see the printing from the back of a sheet because the ink is too oily, too opaque, or the paper too transparent.

Shrink Wrap—See: Plastic Shrink Wrap.

Sidestitching—Method of mechanical binding in which a booklet or a signature is stitched at the sides. "At the sides" means that the booklet or signature is stitched in the closed position. The pages therefore cannot be opened to their full width.

Sidesewing—An entire book is sewn together along the binding edge without any sewing of individual sections, as is done with Smyth Sewing. A sidesewn book will not lie open flat.

Signature—A sheet of paper printed on both sides and folded to make up part of a publication. For example, a sheet of paper with 2 printed pages on each side is folded once to form a 4-page signature. One with 4 pages on each side is folded twice to form an 8-page signature, and so on up to a 64-page signature with 32 pages on each side of the sheet.

Silkscreen Printing—A piece of silk is stretched on a frame and blocked out in the nonprinting areas. A rubber squeegee pushes ink or paint through the porous areas of the design onto the material to be printed.

Silverprint—A paper print made from a single negative or a flat, used primarily as a proof, to check content and/or positioning; also called Brownline, Brownprint, Bluelines, Blues, or Van Dykes.

Single-Color Press—A printing press capable of printing only one color at a time.

Sizing—The treatment of paper which gives it resistance to the penetration of liquids (water) or vapors.

Skid—(1) A platform support, made of wood, on which sheets of paper are delivered, and on which printed sheets or folded sections are stacked. Also used to ship materials, usually in cartons which have been strapped (banded) to the skid.

Slip Case—A decorated slide box in which the finished book or books are inserted so that the spine(s) remains visible.

Smearing—A press condition in which the impression is slurred and unclear because too much ink was used or sheets were handled or rubbed before the ink was dry.

Smyth Sewing—A method of fastening side-by-side signatures so that each is linked with thread to its neighbor as well as saddle sewn through its own center fold. Smyth-sewn books open flat. The stitching is on the back of the fold.

Softcover—Another term for paperback or paperbound books.

Spec (Specification) Sheet—A form which is the primary source document for estimate and order specifications. Pricing is based on these written specifications and orders are entered based on the data on this form. Also known as a Request for Quotation or RFQ.

Special Handling—Intended for preferential handling in dispatch and transportation of third and fourth-class mail. A special fee is assessed for each piece, in addition to the regular postage.

Spine—The back of a book connecting the two covers.

Spiral Binding—A type of mechanical binding which uses a continuous wire of corkscrew or spring coil form run through round holes punched in the binding edge; the wire can be exposed, semi-concealed or concealed.

Split Bind—Refers to an order with two or more bind types, such as perfect and case.

Spot Varnish—Press varnish applied to a portion of the sheet as opposed to an overall application of the varnish.

Stamping—Pressing a design onto a book cover using metal foil colored foil or ink, applied with metal dies.

Stapling—Binding a book or loose sheets with one or more wire staples.

Stripping—(1) The act of positioning or inserting copy elements in negative or positive film to make a complete negative; the positioning of photographic negatives or positives on a lithographic flat or form imposition.

T

Tare Weight—The weight of packing material (cartons, skids, pallets, etc.).

Text—The body matter of a page or book as distinguished from the headings.

Text Paper—A general term applied to high quality antique or laid papers, made in white and colors; used for books, booklets, etc.

Three-M(3M)—See: Color Key.

Tip-Ins—Any separate page (or pages) pasted in a book, such as foldouts, frontispiece, etc.; it may be pasted by hand or machine.

Tip-Ons—Endsheets or other material attached to the outside of folded sections by machine application of a thin strip of adhesive.

Tissue Overlay — A thin translucent paper placed over artwork for protection and correction. Register marks are used on the overlay to ensure proper register for corrections. Any light, inexpensive onionskin that does not have oily characteristics may serve as an overlay.

Tolerance — The acceptable amount of variance from stated specifications.

Transparency — (1) A monochrome or full-color photographic positive or picture on a transparent support, the image intended for viewing and reproduction by transmitted light. (2) The quality that allows images to be seen through a sheet.

Trim — To cut away the folded or uneven edges to form a smooth even edge and permit all pages to open.

Trim Margin — The margin of the open side away from the bind. Also called the Outside Margin.

Trim Size — The finished size of a book after binding and trimming.

Turnaround — Time from the acceptance or beginning of a job until the completed job is delivered.

Typo — Short for typographical error.

U

Underinked — Not enough ink used, resulting in light printing.

Underrun — A shortage in the number of copies completed; a quanity less than the amount ordered.

Undertrimmed — Trimmed to a size smaller than the specified trim size.

Upright — In bookbinding, a book bound on its long dimension, as opposed to oblong binding which is on the short dimension.

V

Vandyke — See: Silverprint.

Varnish — A thin, protective coating applied to a printed sheet for protection or appearance; generally cheaper than lamination, but with less gloss and providing less protection.

Vellum Finish — (1) In paper, a toothy finish which is relatively absorbent for fast ink penetration. (2) A smooth finish, solid color book cloth.

Velox — Print of a photograph or other continuous-tone copy which has been prescreened before paste-up.

Verso — A left-hand page of a book, usually even numbered.

Vignette — An illustration in which the background fades gradually away until it blends into the unprinted paper.

W

Washup – The process of cleaning the rollers, form or plate, and sometimes the fountain of a printing press.

Web Offset Printing – Lithographic printing from rolled stock. The paper manufacturer refers to the roll as a web. The printer uses the term "web" not only for the roll but for the paper itself as it feeds through the press.

Widow – A short single line at the top of a page or column, usually the last line of a paragraph. Widows are to be avoided in good typesetting. Also a single word or syllable standing alone as the last line of a paragraph. An orphan, on the other hand, is a single line at the bottom of a page or column from a paragraph that runs to the next page or column.

Wire-O-Binding – A type of mechanical binding which uses a series of double wire loops formed from single continuous wire, run through longitudinal slots along the bind edge, which must be crimped closed after insertion of trimmed text sheets.

With the Grain – A term applied to folding paper parallel to the grain of the paper.

Wrap – (1) To place jackets on finished books. (2) A folded section, such as four pages, into which another folded section is hand inserted; the outside section wraps around the inside section; (3) To package in kraft paper or plastic film (shrink wrapping).

Wrap-Around Mailer – A single piece corrugated pad which is wrapped or rolled around a book, then stapled closed at both ends; also called: Book-Wrap Mailer.

Wrinkles – Creases in paper occurring during printing or folding.

Indexes

An Introduction to the Indexes

Because of the amount of details contained in each complete listing, we have provided indexes to highlight those printers who are capable of providing the type of service or support that any user might require. The following 79 pages of indexes are divided into six sections, as follows:

- **Index of Book Printers, Etc.** — Indicates which printers can print books, magazines, catalogs, in long or short runs.

- **Index of Other Printed Items** — Indicates which printers can print annual reports, calendars, comics, computer documentation, cookbooks, directories, galley copies, journals, maps, mass-market paperbacks, postcards, posters, textbooks, workbooks, and yearbooks.

- **Index of Binding Capabilities** — Indicates which printers can do case binding, comb binding, loose-leaf binding, perfect binding, spiral binding, and wire-o binding.

- **Index of Printing Equipment** — Indicates which printers use Cameron belt, letterpress, gravure, sheetfed offset, and web offset presses.

- **Index of Printing Services** — Indicates which printers can print full-color publications, do color separations, design and lay out material, provide fulfillment, maintain lists, typeset copy, or warehouse books. Also indicates which printers stock acid-free and/or recycled papers. And, finally, also indicates which printers use union labor, have toll-free phone numbers, and/or have fax numbers.

- **Index of Printers by State** — Lists printers by their location so you can find printers who are located near you who might be able to provide the services you need.

Index: Book Printers, Etc.

This set of indexes lists those printers who can print books, catalogs, and magazines. The set of indexes that follows lists printers of other items and bound publications.

Book Printers

Those printers marked with a bold **B** specialize in printing books.

Academy Books (Rutland, VT) **B**
Accurate Web (Central Islip, NY) **B**
Ad Infinitum (Mount Vernon, NY) **B**
The Adams Group (New York, NY)
Adams Press (Chicago, IL) **B**
Advanced Duplicating (Edina, MN) **B**
Adviser Graphics (Red Deer, AB) **B**
Alger Press Ltd (Oshawa, ON) **B**
Allied Printing (Akron, OH)
Alonzo Printing (S San Francisco, CA)
Alpine Press (Stoughton, MA) **B**
American Offset (Los Angeles, CA) **B**
American Printers (Chicago, IL)
Americomp (Brattleboro, VT) **B**
Anderson, Barton, Dalby (Atlanta, GA) **B**
Andover Press (New York, NY) **B**
Anundsen Publishing (Decorah, IA)
Arcata Graphics (Fairfield, PA) **B**
Arcata Graphics (West Hanover, MA) **B**
Arcata Graphics (Kingsport, TN) **B**
Arcata Graphics (Martinsburg, WV) **B**
Artex Publishing (Stevens Point, WI) **B**
Atelier (New York, NY)
Automated Graphic (White Plains, MD) **B**
Baker Johnson (Dexter, MI) **B**
Balan Printing (Brooklyn, NY)
Bang Printing (Brainerd, MN) **B**
Banta Corporation (Menasha, WI) **B**
Banta-Harrisonburg (Harrisonburg, VA) **B**
Bawden Printing (Eldridge, IA) **B**
Bay Port Press (National City, CA) **B**
Beacon Press (Richmond, VA)
Beacon Wholesale Printing (Seattle, WA)
Bell Publications (Iowa City, IA)
Harold Berliner (Nevada City, CA) **B**
Berryville Graphics (Berryville, VA) **B**
Bertelsmann Printing (New York, NY) **B**
Beslow Associates (Chicago, IL)
T H Best Printing (Don Mills, ON) **B**
Blake Printery (San Luis Obispo, CA) **B**
Blue Dolphin Press (Grass Valley, CA) **B**
Bolger Publications (Minneapolis, MN)

Book Makers Inc (Kenosha, WI) **B**
The Book Press (Brattleboro, VT) **B**
The Book Printer (Laurens, IA) **B**
Book-Mart Press (North Bergen, NJ) **B**
BookCrafters (Chelsea, MI) **B**
BookCrafters (Fredericksburg, VA) **B**
Booklet Publishing (Elk Grove Village, IL)
BookMasters (Ashland, OH) **B**
William Boyd Printing (Albany, NY) **B**
Braceland Brothers (Philadelphia, PA)
Braun-Brumfield (Ann Arbor, MI) **B**
William Brown Printing (Dubuque, IA) **B**
Brunswick Publish (Lawrenceville, VA) **B**
R L Bryan Company (Columbia, SC)
BSC Litho (Harrisburg, PA)
C & M Press (Thornton, CO) **B**
Cal Central Press (Sacramento, CA)
Caldwell Printers (Arcadia, CA) **B**
Camelot Book (Ormond Beach, FL) **B**
Camelot Fine Printing (Albuquerque, NM)
Canterbury Press (Rome, NY)
Capital City Press (Montpelier, VT) **B**
Capital Printing (Austin, TX)
Carter Rice (Boston, MA) **B**
Centax of Canada (Regina, SK) **B**
Central Publishing (Indianapolis, IN)
Clarkwood Corporation (Totowa, NJ) **B**
Coach House Press (Toronto, ON) **B**
Cody Publications (Kissimmee, FL)
A Colish Inc (Mount Vernon, NY) **B**
The College Press (Collegedale, TN)
Colonial Graphics (Paterson, NJ)
Color House (Grand Rapids, MI) **B**
Color World Printers (Bozeman, MT)
Colortone Press (Washington, DC) **B**
Columbus Book (Columbus, GA) **B**
Commercial Printing (Medford, OR) **B**
Community Press (Provo, UT) **B**
Comput-A-Print (Reno, NV)
Coneco Laser Graphics (Glen Falls, NY) **B**
Consolidated Printers (Berkeley, CA)
Copen Press (Brooklyn, NY)
Copple House (Lakemont, GA) **B**
Corley Printing (Earth City, MO)
Cornay Web (New Orleans, LA) **B**
Country Press (Mohawk, NY)
Crane Duplicating (W Barnstable, MA) **B**
Crest Litho (Watervliet, NY) **B**

Book Printers

Crusader Printing (East Saint Louis, IL)
Cushing-Malloy (Ann Arbor, MI) **B**
D D Associates (Santa Clara, CA)
Daamen Printing (West Rutland, VT) **B**
Danner Press (Canton, OH) **B**
Dataco (Albuquerque, NM)
Dellas Graphics (Syracuse, NY)
Delmar Printing (Charlotte, NC) **B**
Delta Lithograph (Valencia, CA) **B**
Desaulniers Printing (Milan, IL)
John Deyell Company (Lindsay, ON) **B**
Dharma Press (Oakland, CA)
Diamond Graphics (Milwaukee, WI)
Dickinson Press (Grand Rapids, MI) **B**
Dinner & Klein (Seattle, WA)
Diversified Printing (Brea, CA)
Dollco Printing (Ottawa, ON)
Donihe Graphics (Kingsport, TN)
R R Donnelley (Crawfordsville, IN) **B**
R R Donnelley (Chicago, IL) **B**
R R Donnelley (Harrisonburg, VA) **B**
R R Donnelley (Willard, OH) **B**
Dragon Press (Delta Junction, AK) **B**
East Village Enterprises (New York, NY)
Eastern Press (New Haven, CT) **B**
Eastwood Printing (Denver, CO)
Edison Litho (North Bergen, NJ) **B**
Edison Press (Glen Rock, NJ)
Edwards & Broughton (Raleigh, NC)
Edwards Brothers (Ann Arbor, MI) **B**
Edwards Brothers (Lillington, NC) **B**
Eerdmans Printing (Grand Rapids, MI) **B**
Einson Freeman Graphics (Fairlawn, NJ)
Eureka Printing Company (Eureka, CA)
Eusey Press (Leominster, MA) **B**
Evangel Press (Nappanee, IN) **B**
Everton Publishers (Logan, UT) **B**
Faculty Press (Brooklyn, NY) **B**
Fast Print (Fort Wayne, IN)
Federated Litho (Providence, RI) **B**
Fort Orange Press (Albany, NY) **B**
Four Corners Press (Grand Rapids, MI) **B**
Friesen Printers (Altona R0G 0B0, MB) **B**
Full Color Graphics (Plainview, NY)
Futura Printing (Boynton Beach, FL)
Gagne Printing (Louiseville, PQ) **B**
Ganis & Harris (New York, NY) **B**
Gateway Press (Louisville, KY)
Gaylord Ltd (West Hollywood, CA) **B**
Geiger Brothers (Lewiston, ME) **B**
General Offset (Jersey City, NJ)
George Lithograph (San Francisco, CA)
Germac Printing (Tigard, OR)
Geryon Press (Tunnel, NY)
Giant Horse (Daly City, CA) **B**
Gilliland Printing (Arkansas City, KS) **B**
Gladstone Press (Ottawa, ON)
Golden Horn Press (Berkeley, CA) **B**
Goodway Graphics (Springfield, VA) **B**
Gorham Printing (Rochester, WA)

Graphic Design (Center Line, MI) **B**
Graphic Litho Corp (Lawrence, MA) **B**
Graphic Printing (New Carlisle, OH) **B**
The Gregath Company (Cullman, AL)
Griffin Printing (Glendale, CA) **B**
Griffin Printing (Sacramento, CA) **B**
GRT Book Printing (Oakland, CA) **B**
GTE Directories (Des Plaines, IL) **B**
Gulf Printing (Houston, TX)
Guynes Printing (Albuquerque, NM)
Haddon Craftsmen (Scranton, PA) **B**
Hamilton Printing (Rensselaer, NY) **B**
Harlo Press (Detroit, MI) **B**
Hart Graphics (Austin, TX)
Hawkes Publishing (Salt Lake City, UT) **B**
Heart of the Lakes (Interlaken, NY) **B**
Heffernan Press (Worcester, MA) **B**
Henington Publishing (Wolfe City, TX) **B**
Heritage Printers (Charlotte, NC) **B**
D B Hess Company (Woodstock, IL) **B**
Hignell Printing (Winnepeg, MB) **B**
A B Hirschfeld Press (Denver, CO)
Hoechstetter Printing (Pittsburgh, PA)
Holladay-Tyler (Glenn Dale, MD)
Holyoke Lithography (Springfield, MA) **B**
Hooven-Dayton Corp (Dayton, OH) **B**
Horowitz/Rae (Fairfield, NJ) **B**
Hunter Publishing (Winston-Salem, NC)
Independent (Long Island City, NY) **B**
Independent Publishing (Sarasota, FL) **B**
Infopress (Saratoga Springs, NY) **B**
Inland Lithograph (Elk Grove Village, IL)
Interstate Printers (Danville, IL) **B**
Interstate Printing (Omaha, NE)
Jersey Printing (Bayonne, NJ)
The Job Shop (Woods Hole, MA)
Johnson & Hardin (Cincinnati, OH)
Johnson Publishing (Boulder, CO)
Jostens (Clarksville, TN) **B**
Jostens (State College, PA) **B**
Jostens (Topeka, KS) **B**
Jostens (Visalia, CA) **B**
Julin Printing (Monticello, IA)
K/P Graphics (Escondido, CA)
Kern International (Duxbury, MA)
Kimberly Press (Santa Barbara, CA) **B**
KNI Book Mfg (Anaheim, CA) **B**
C J Krehbiel Company (Cincinnati, OH) **B**
Lancaster Press (Lancaster, PA)
The Lane Press (Burlington, VT)
Legacy Books (Minneapolis, MN) **B**
Les Editions Marquis (Montmagny, PQ) **B**
Liberty York Graphic (Hempstead, NY)
Litho Prestige (Drummondville, PQ) **B**
Litho Specialties (Saint Paul, MN)
Lithocolor Press (Westchester, IL) **B**
LithoCraft (Carlstadt, NJ)
Little River Press (Miami, FL) **B**
John D Lucas Printing (Baltimore, MD) **B**
Mackintosh Typo. (Santa Barbara, CA) **B**
The Mad Printers (Mattituck, NY) **B**
Malloy Lithographing (Ann Arbor, MI) **B**

Book Printers

Maple-Vail (York, PA) **B**
Mariposa Press (Benicia, CA)
Mark IV Press (Hauppauge, NY) **B**
Marrakech Express (Tarpon Springs FL) **B**
Maverick Publications (Bend, OR) **B**
The Mazer Corporation (Dayton, OH)
McClain Printing (Parson, WV)
McDowell Publications (Utica, KY) **B**
McGregor & Werner (Washington, DC) **B**
McNaughton & Gunn (Saline, MI) **B**
Meaker the Printer (Phoenix, AZ)
Mercury Printing (Memphis, TN)
Messenger Graphics (Phoenix, AZ) **B**
Mitchell Press (Vancouver, BC)
Mitchell-Shear (Ann Arbor, MI) **B**
MMI Press (Harrisville, NH) **B**
Monument Printers (Verplanck, NY) **B**
Moran Colorgraphic (Baton Rouge, LA)
Morgan Press (Dobbs Ferry, NY)
Morgan Printing (Austin, TX) **B**
Morningrise Printing (Costa Mesa, CA)
Multiprint Inc (Chatham, NY) **B**
Murphy's Printing (Campbell, CA)
Murray Printing (Kendallville, IN) **B**
Murray Printing (Westford, MA) **B**
National Graphics Corp (Columbus, OH)
National Publishing (Philadelphia, PA) **B**
National Reproductions (Livonia, MI) **B**
Naturegraph (Happy Camp, CA) **B**
Neibauer Press (Warminster, PA)
Newsfoto Publishing (San Angelo, TX) **B**
Neyenesch Printers (San Diego, CA)
Nimrod Press (Boston, MA)
Noble Book Press (New York, NY) **B**
North Plains Press (Aberdeen, SD)
Northeast Web (Farmingdale, NY)
Northlight Studio Press (Barre, VT)
Nystrom Publishing (Maple Grove, MN)
O'Neil Data Systems (Los Angeles, CA) **B**
Oaks Printing Company (Bethlehem, PA)
Odyssey Press (Dover, NH) **B**
Offset Paperback (Dallas, PA) **B**
Omnipress (Madison, WI) **B**
Optic Graphics (Glen Burnie, MD) **B**
Original Copy Centers (Cleveland, OH)
Ortlieb Press (Baton Rouge, LA)
Ovid Bell Press (Fulton, MO)
Oxford Group (Norway, ME) **B**
Oxford Group (Berlin, NH) **B**
Oxmoor Press (Birmingham, AL) **B**
Pantagraph Printing (Bloomington, IL) **B**
Paraclete Press (Orleans, MA) **B**
Patterson Printing (Benton Harbor, MI) **B**
Paust Inc (Richmond, IN)
Pearl Pressman (Philadelphia, PA) **B**
Pentagram (Minneapolis, MN) **B**
PFP Printing Corp (Gaithersburg, MD) **B**
Phillips Brothers (Springfield, IL) **B**
Pioneer Press (Wilmette, IL)
Plus Communications (Saint Louis, MO) **B**

Port City Press (Pikesville, MD) **B**
Practical Graphics (New York, NY)
Preferred Graphics (Winona, MN) **B**
The Press of Ohio (Brimfield, OH) **B**
Princeton University (Lawrenceville, NJ) **B**
Prinit Press (Dublin, IN) **B**
Printing Corp (Pompano Beach, FL)
Printing Dimensions (Beltsville, MD)
Progress Printing (Lynchburg, VA)
Progressive Typo. (Emigsville, PA) **B**
ProLitho (Provo, UT)
Publishers Press (Salt Lake City, UT) **B**
Publishers Printing (Shepherdsville, KY)
Quebecor America (New York, NY) **B**
Quinn-Woodbine (Woodbine, NJ) **B**
Quintessence Press (Amador City, CA) **B**
Quixott Press (Doylestown, PA) **B**
RBW Graphics (Owen Sound, ON)
Realtron Multi-Lith (Denver, CO) **B**
Recorder Sunset (San Francisco, CA)
Regensteiner Press (West Chicago, IL)
Repro-Tech (West Patterson, NJ)
Reproductions Inc (Rockville, MD)
Rich Printing (Nashville, TN) **B**
Rich Publishing (Houston, TX) **B**
Ringier America (Itasca, IL)
Ringier America (Brookfield, WI)
Ringier America (New Berlin, WI) **B**
Ringier America (Olathe, KS) **B**
Ringier America (Senatobia, MS)
John Roberts (Minneapolis, MN)
Rollins Press (Orlando, FL) **B**
Ronalds Printing (Montreal, PQ)
Ronalds Printing (Vancouver, BC)
Rose Printing (Tallahassee, FL) **B**
Roxbury Publishing (Los Angeles, CA) **B**
Sabre Printers (Rogersville, TN) **B**
Saint Mary's Press (Hollywood, MD) **B**
Sanders Printing (Garretson, SD) **B**
Saybrook Press (Old Saybrook, CT) **B**
Schiff Printers (Pittsburgh, PA)
Science Press (Ephrata, PA) **B**
Semline Inc (Braintree, MA) **B**
Service Printing (San Leandro, CA) **B**
Sexton Printing (West Saint Paul, MN)
Skillful Means Press (Oakland, CA)
Snohomish Publishing (Snohomish, WA) **B**
Southam Printing (Weston M9N 3R3, ON)
Southeastern Printing (Stuart, FL)
Southern Tennessee (Waynesboro, TN) **B**
Sowers Printing (Lebanon, PA)
Staked Plains Press (Canyon, TX)
Standard Printing (Chicago, IL) **B**
Stephenson Inc (Alexandria, VA)
Stewart Publishing (Marble Hill, MO) **B**
Stinehour Press (Lunenburg, VT) **B**
The Studley Press (Dalton, MA) **B**
John S Swift Company (Saint Louis, MO)
John S Swift (Chicago, IL)
John S Swift (Cincinnati, OH)
John S Swift (Teterboro, NJ)
T A S Graphics (Detroit, MI)

Book Printers

Taylor Publishing (Dallas, TX) **B**
Technical Commu. (N Kansas City, MO)
Thomson-Shore (Dexter, MI) **B**
Times Printing (Random Lake, WI)
Todd Web Press (Smithville, TX)
Town House Press (Pittsboro, NC) **B**
Tracor Publications (Austin, TX)
Tri-Graphic Printing (Ottawa, ON) **B**
Tri-State Press (Clayton, GA)
Triangle Printing (Nashville, TN)
Twin City Printery (Lewiston, ME)
United Lithograph (Somerville, MA)
Universal Printing (Saint Louis, MO)
University Press (Winchester, MA) **B**
Vail Ballou Printing (Binghamton, NY) **B**
Van Volumes (Thorndike, MA) **B**
Versa Press (East Peoria, IL) **B**
Vicks Lithograph (Yorkville, NY) **B**
Victor Graphics (Baltimore, MD) **B**
Viking Press (Eden Prairie, MN) **B**
Vogue Printers (North Chicago, IL)
Waldon Press (New York, NY)
Wallace Press (Hillside, IL) **B**
Walsworth Publishing (Marceline, MO) **B**
Webcom Ltd (Scarborough, ON) **B**
Webcrafters (Madison, WI) **B**
F A Weber & Sons (Park Falls, WI)
Wellesley Press (Framingham, MA)
West Side Graphics (New York, NY)
Western Publishers (Albuquerque, NM) **B**
Western Publishing (Racine, WI) **B**
Western Web Printing (Sioux Falls, SD)
Westview Press (Boulder, CO) **B**
Whitehall Printing (Wheeling, IL) **B**
Wickersham Printing (Lancaster, PA) **B**
Williams Catello Printing (Tualatin, OR) **B**
Wimmer Brothers (Memphis, TN) **B**
Windsor Associates (San Diego, CA) **B**
Wood & Jones (Pasadena, CA)
Worzalla Publishing (Stevens Point, WI) **B**
Yates Publishing (Ozark, MO) **B**
Ye Olde Genealogie (Indianapolis, IN)

Catalog Printers

The following printers all can print catalogs. Those marked with a bold **C** specialize as catalog printers, while those marked with a bold **G** are general commercial printers. Those that are unmarked specialize in printing books or magazines.

Academy Books (Rutland, VT)
Accurate Web (Central Islip, NY)
Ad Color (Port Chester, NY) **C**
The Adams Group (New York, NY) **G**
Adams Press (Chicago, IL)
Adviser Graphics (Red Deer, AB)

Alden Press (Elk Grove Village, IL) **C**
Algen Press (College Point, NY) **G**
Allied Graphics Arts (New York, NY) **C**
Allied Printing (Akron, OH) **G**
Alonzo Printing (S San Francisco, CA) **G**
American Color (Plantation, FL) **C**
American Offset (Los Angeles, CA)
American Press Inc (Oakton, VA)
American Printers (Chicago, IL) **G**
American Signature (Dallas, TX) **C**
American Signature (Costa Mesa, CA) **C**
American Signature (New York, NY) **C**
American Signature (Memphis, TN) **C**
Amidon Graphics (Saint Paul, MN) **G**
Apollo Graphics (Southampton, PA) **C**
Arandell-Schmidt (Menomonee, WI) **C**
Arcata Graphics (Nashville, TN)
Arcata Graphics (Depew, NY)
Arcata Graphics (Fairfield, PA)
Arcata Graphics (Kingsport, TN)
Arcata Graphics (Martinsburg, WV)
Arcata Graphics (San Jose, CA)
Argus Press (Niles, IL) **C**
Arizona Litho (Tucson, AZ) **G**
Artcraft Press (Waterloo, WI) **G**
Associated Printers (Grafton, ND) **G**
Automated Graphics (White Plains, MD)
B & R Printing (Post Falls, ID) **G**
Baker Johnson (Dexter, MI)
Balan Printing (Brooklyn, NY) **C**
Banta Catalog Group (Saint Paul, MN) **C**
Banta Corporation (Menasha, WI)
Banta-Harrisonburg (Harrisonburg, VA)
Bawden Printing (Eldridge, IA)
Bay Port Press (National City, CA)
Beacon Press (Richmond, VA) **G**
Beacon Wholesale (Seattle, WA) **G**
Bell Publications (Iowa City, IA) **G**
Beslow Associates (Chicago, IL)
Blake Printery (San Luis Obispo, CA)
Blazing Graphics (Cranston, RI) **C**
Blue Dolphin Press (Grass Valley, CA)
Bolger Publications (Minneapolis, MN)
Book Makers Inc (Kenosha, WI)
The Book Press (Brattleboro, VT)
Book-Mart Press (North Bergen, NJ)
BookCrafters (Chelsea, MI)
BookCrafters (Fredericksburg, VA)
Booklet Pub. (Elk Grove Village, IL) **G**
BookMasters (Ashland, OH)
Braceland Brothers (Philadelphia, PA)
Bradley Printing (Des Plaines, IL) **C**
Braun-Brumfield (Ann Arbor, MI)
Brookshore (Elk Grove Village, IL) **G**
Brown Printing (Waseca, MN)
Brown Printing (East Greenville, PA) **C**
Brown Printing (Franklin, KY)
Brunswick Publishing (Lawrenceville, VA)
R L Bryan Company (Columbia, SC) **G**
BSC Litho (Harrisburg, PA) **G**
C & M Press (Thornton, CO)
Caldwell Printers (Arcadia, CA)

Catalog Printers

California Offset (Glendale, CA)
Camelot Book (Ormond Beach, FL)
Camelot Fine (Albuquerque, NM) G
Canterbury Press (Rome, NY)
Capital Printing (Austin, TX) G
Carlson Color Graphics (Ocala, FL)
Cascio-Wolf (Springfield, VA) C
Case-Hoyt Corp (Rochester, NY) C
Catalog King (Clifton, NJ) C
Catalogue Pub. (Martinsburg, WV) C
Catalogue Service (New Rochelle, NY) C
CatalogueACE (Miami, FL) C
Central Publishing (Indianapolis, IN) G
Champion Printing (Cincinnati, OH) G
Charles Communications (New York, NY) C
City Printing (North Haven, CT) G
Clark Printing (Kansas City, MO)
Cody Publications (Kissimmee, FL)
The College Press (Collegedale, TN) G
Colonial Graphics (Paterson, NJ) G
Color Catalog (Long Island City, NY) C
Color Express (Irvine, CA) C
Color Express (Minneapolis, MN) C
Color Express (Atlanta, GA) C
Color Express (Los Angeles, CA) C
Chicago Color Express (Chicago, IL) C
Chicago Color Express (Westmont, IL) C
Color House (Grand Rapids, MI)
Color US Inc (Atlanta, GA) C
Color World Printers (Bozeman, MT) G
ColorGraphics (Tulsa, OK) G
Colorlith Corporation (Johnston, RI) C
Colortone Press (Washington, DC)
Columbus Book Printers (Columbus, GA)
Combined Comm. (Columbia, MO)
Combined Communication (Mendota, IL)
Community Press (Provo, UT)
Comput-A-Print (Reno, NV) G
Concord Litho (Concord, NH) G
Connecticut Printers (Bloomfield, CT)
Consolidated Printers (Berkeley, CA) G
Continental Web (Itasca, IL) G
Copen Press (Brooklyn, NY) C
Corley Printing (Earth City, MO) G
Cornay Web Graphics (New Orleans, LA)
Country Press (Mohawk, NY) G
Craftsman Press (Seattle, WA) C
Crane Duplicating (West Barnstable, MA)
Crest Litho (Watervliet, NY)
Crusader Printing (E Saint Louis, IL) G
Cushing-Malloy (Ann Arbor, MI)
D D Associates (Santa Clara, CA) G
Danbury Printing (Danbury, CT) C
Danner Press (Canton, OH)
Dartmouth Printing (Hanover, NH)
Dataco (Albuquerque, NM) G
Dayal Graphics (Lemont, IL) C
Dellas Graphics (Syracuse, NY) G
Delmar Printing (Charlotte, NC)
Delta Lithograph (Valencia, CA)

Democrat Printing (Little Rock, AR)
Des Plaines Publishing (Des Plaines, IL) G
Desaulniers Printing (Milan, IL) G
Dharma Press (Oakland, CA) G
Diamond Graphics (Milwaukee, WI) G
Dickinson Press (Grand Rapids, MI)
The Dingley Press (Lisbon, ME) C
Dinner & Klein (Seattle, WA) C
Direct Press (Huntington Station, NY) C
Diversified Printing (Brea, CA) C
Dollco Printing (Ottawa, ON) G
Donihe Graphics (Kingsport, TN) C
R R Donnelley (Crawfordsville, IN)
R R Donnelley (Chicago, IL)
Dragon Press (Delta Junction, AK)
Dynagraphics (Carlsbad, CA)
E & D Web (Cicero, IL) C
Eagle Web Press (Salem, OR) G
East Village (New York, NY) G
Eastwood Printing (Denver, CO) G
Economy Printing (Berne, IN)
Edison Litho (North Bergen, NJ)
Edison Press (Glen Rock, NJ) G
Editors Press (Hyattsville, MD)
Edwards & Broughton (Raleigh, NC) G
Edwards Brothers (Ann Arbor, MI)
Edwards Brothers (Lillington, NC)
Eerdmans Printing (Grand Rapids, MI)
Einson Freeman (Fairlawn, NJ) G
Eureka Printing (Eureka, CA) G
Faculty Press (Brooklyn, NY)
Fast Print (Fort Wayne, IN) G
William Feathers (Oberlin, OH) G
Federated Litho (Providence, RI)
Fetter Printing (Louisville, KY) G
Fisher Web Printers (Cedar Rapids, IA)
Fleetwood Litho (New York, NY) G
Flower City (Rochester, NY) C
Foote & Davies (Atlanta, GA) C
Foote & Davies (Lincoln, NE)
Fort Orange Press (Albany, NY)
Full Color Graphics (Plainview, NY) C
Futura Printing (Boynton Beach, FL) G
Gagne Printing (Louiseville, PQ)
Gateway Press (Louisville, KY) G
Gaylord Ltd (West Hollywood, CA)
Gaylord Printing (Detroit, MI) G
General Offset (Jersey City, NJ) G
George Lithograph (San Francisco, CA) G
Germac Printing (Tigard, OR) G
Geryon Press (Tunnel, NY) G
Giant Horse (Daly City, CA)
Gibbs-Inman (Louisville, KY) C
Gilliland Printing (Arkansas City, KS)
Gladstone Press (Ottawa, ON) G
Globe-Comm (San Antonio, TX) G
Glundal Color (E Syracuse, NY) C
Goodway Graphics (Springfield, VA)
Gorham Printing (Rochester, WA) G
Gowe Printing (Medina, OH) G
Graftek Press (Woodstock, IL)
Graphic Arts Center (Portland, OR) C

Catalog Printers

Graphic Arts Publishing (Boise, ID) C
Graphic Design (Center Line, MI)
Graphic Litho Corp (Lawrence, MA)
Graphic Printing (New Carlisle, OH)
Gray Printing (Fostoria, OH)
Greater Buffalo Press (Buffalo, NY)
Gregath Company (Cullman, AL) G
Griffin Printing (Glendale, CA)
Griffin Printing (Sacramento, CA)
Grit Commercial (Williamsport, PA) G
Gulf Printing (Houston, TX) G
Guynes Printing (Albuquerque, NM) G
Hamilton Printing (Rensselaer, NY)
Harlin Litho (Ossining, NY)
Harlo Press (Detroit, MI)
Hart Graphics (Austin, TX) G
Hart Press (Long Prairie, MN)
Heartland Press (Spencer, IA)
Herbick & Held (Pittsburgh, PA) G
D B Hess Company (Woodstock, IL)
Hi-Tech Color (Chicago, IL) C
Hignell Printing (Winnepeg, MB)
Hinz Lithographing (Mt Prospect, IL) G
A B Hirschfeld Press (Denver, CO) G
Hoechstetter Printing (Pittsburgh, PA) G
Holladay-Tyler (Glenn Dale, MD)
Holyoke Lithography (Springfield, MA)
Hooven-Dayton Corp (Dayton, OH)
Horowitz/Rae (Fairfield, NJ)
Humboldt National (N Abington, MA) G
Hunter Publishing (Winston-Salem, NC) G
Independent Publishing (Sarasota, FL)
Infopress/Saratoga (Saratoga Springs, NY)
Inland Litho (Elk Grove Village, IL) G
Intelligencer Printing (Lancaster, PA) C
Interstate Printers (Danville, IL)
Interstate Printing (Omaha, NE) C
Japs-Olson (Minneapolis, MN) G
Jersey Printing (Bayonne, NJ)
The Job Shop (Woods Hole, MA) G
JohnsBryne Microdot (Niles, IL)
Johnson & Hardin (Cincinnati, OH)
Johnson Graphics (East Dubuque, IL) G
Johnson Publishing (Boulder, CO) G
Jostens / Clarksville (Clarksville, TN)
Jostens / State College (State College, PA)
Jostens / Topeka (Topeka, KS)
Jostens / Visalia (Visalia, CA)
Julin Printing (Monticello, IA) G
K & S Graphics (Nashville, TN) G
K-B Offset Printing (State College, PA) C
K/P Graphics (Escondido, CA) G
Kable Printing (Mount Morris, IL) C
Kaufman Press (Syracuse, NY) G
Kern International (Duxbury, MA) G
KNI Book Manufacturing (Anaheim, CA)
The Kordet Group (Oceanside, NY) C
C J Krehbiel Company (Cincinnati, OH)
Lancaster Press (Lancaster, PA)
The Lane Press (Burlington, VT)

Lasky Company (Milburn, NJ) C
Latham Process Corp (New York, NY) G
Lawson Graphics (Toronto, ON) G
Lehigh Press / Cadillac (Broadview, IL) G
Lehigh Press / Dallas (Dallas, TX)
Lehigh Press (Pennsauken, NJ) G
Les Éditions Marquis (Montmagny, PQ)
Liberty York Graphic (Hempstead, NY) G
Litho Prestige (Drummondville, PQ)
Litho Specialties (St Paul, MN) G
Lithocolor Press (Westchester, IL)
LithoCraft (Carlstadt, NJ) G
Little River Press (Miami, FL)
Long Island Web (Jericho, NY) C
John D Lucas Printing (Baltimore, MD)
Mack Printing (Easton, PA)
Mackintosh Typo. (Santa Barbara, CA)
Maclean Hunter (Willowdale, ON)
Mail-O-Graph (Kewanne, IL) C
Malloy Lithographing (Ann Arbor, MI)
Maple Leaf Press (Brattleboro, VT) C
Maple-Vail (York, PA)
Maquoketa Web (Maquoketa, IA) G
Mariposa Press (Benicia, CA) G
Mark IV Press (Hauppauge, NY)
Marrakech Express (Tarpon Springs, FL)
Mazer Corporation (Dayton, OH) G
McClain Printing (Parson, WV) G
McFarland Company (Harrisburg, PA)
McGregor & Werner (Washington, DC)
McGrew Color (Kansas City, MO) C
McKay Printing Services (Dolton, IL) G
McNaughton & Gunn (Saline, MI)
Meaker the Printer (Phoenix, AZ) G
Media Printing (Miami, FL) C
Meehan-Tooker (E Rutherford, NJ) G
Mercury Printing (Memphis, TN) G
Meredith/Burda (Des Moines, IA)
Messenger Graphics (Phoenix, AZ)
Metromail Corp (Lincoln, NE) G
Metroweb (Erlanger, KY)
Mideastern Printing (Brookfield, CT) G
Mitchell Graphics (Petoskey, MI) C
Mitchell Press (Vancouver, BC) G
Mitchell-Shear (Ann Arbor, MI)
MMI Press (Harrisville, NH)
Modern Graphic (St Petersburg, FL) C
Moebius Printing (Milwaukee, WI) C
Monument Printers (Verplanck, NY)
Moore Response (Libertyville, IL) G
Moran Colorgraphic (Baton Rouge, LA) G
Morgan Press (Dobbs Ferry, NY) G
Morgan Printing (Austin, TX)
Morningrise Printing (Costa Mesa, CA) G
Motheral Printing (Fort Worth, TX) C
Muller Printing (Santa Clara, CA) G
MultiPrint Company (Skokie, IL) C
Murphy's Printing (Campbell, CA) G
MWM Dexter (Aurora, MO) C
National Bickford (Providence, RI) C
National Graphics (Columbus, OH) G
National Publishing (Philadelphia, PA)

Catalog Printers

National Reproductions (Livonia, MI)
Nationwide Printing (Burlington, KY) G
Naturegraph (Happy Camp, CA)
Neibauer Press (Warminster, PA) G
Nevada Web Graphics (Sparks, NV) C
Neyenesch Printers (San Diego, CA)
Nielsen Litho (Cincinnati, OH) G
Nimrod Press (Boston, MA) G
Noble Book Press (New York, NY)
Noll Printing (Huntington, IN) C
North Plains Press (Aberdeen, SD)
Northeast Web (Farmingdale, NY) G
Northlight Studio (Barre, VT) G
Northprint (Grand Rapids, MN)
Northwest Web (Eugene, OR) C
Nystrom Publishing (Maple Grove, MN) G
O'Neil Data Systems (Los Angeles, CA)
Oaks Printing (Bethlehem, PA) G
Ohio Valley Litho (Florence, KY) C
Oklahoma Graphics (Oklahoma City, OK)
Olympic Litho (Brooklyn, NY) G
Omaha Printing (Omaha, NE) G
Original Copy Centers (Cleveland, OH) G
Ortlieb Press (Baton Rouge, LA) G
Outstanding Graphics (Kenosha, WI) G
Oxmoor Press (Birmingham, AL)
Pacific Litho (San Francisco, CA) G
PAK Discount Printing (Zion, IL) G
Paraclete Press (Orleans, MA)
Park Press (South Holland, IL) G
Parker Graphics (Fuquay-Varina, NC) G
Paust Inc (Richmond, IN) G
Pendell Printing (Midland, MI)
Penn Colour (Huntington Valley, PA) C
PennWell Printing (Tulsa, OK)
Penton Press (Berea, OH)
Perlmuter Printing (Independence, OH) C
Perry Printing (Waterloo, WI) C
Perry/Baraboo (Baraboo, WI) G
Petty Printing (Effingham, IL) G
PFP Printing Corp (Gaithersburg, MD)
Phillips Brothers (Springfield, IL)
Pine Hill Press (Freeman, SD) G
Pioneer Press (Wilmette, IL) G
Plain Talk Publishing (Des Moines, IA) G
Plus Communications (St Louis, MO)
Port City Press (Pikesville, MD)
Port Publications (Port Washington, WI)
Practical Graphics (New York, NY) G
Precision Offset (Upper Darby, PA) G
Preferred Graphics (Winona, MN)
Press America (Chicago, IL) G
The Press of Ohio (Brimfield, OH)
The Press (Chanhassen, MN) C
Princeton University (Lawrenceville, NJ)
Prinit Press (Dublin, IN)
Print Northwest (Tacoma, WA) G
The Printer Inc (Maple Grove, MN) C
Printing Corp (Pompano Beach, FL) G
Printing Dimensions (Beltsville, MD) G

Progress Printing (Lynchburg, VA) G
Progressive Typographers (Emigsville, PA)
ProLitho (Provo, UT) G
Promotional Printing (Houston, TX) C
Providence Gravure (Providence, RI) C
Publishers Press (Salt Lake City, UT)
Publishers Printing (Shepherdsville, KY)
Quad/Graphics (Lomira, WI)
Quad/Graphics (Pewaukee, WI)
Quad/Graphics (Saratoga Springs, NY)
Quad/Graphics (Sussex, WI) C
Quebecor America (New York, NY)
Rapid Printing (Omaha, NE) G
Rapidocolor Corp (West Chester, PA) C
RBW Graphics (Owen Sound, ON) C
Realtron Multi-Lith (Denver, CO)
Recorder Sunset (San Francisco, CA)
Regensteiner Press (West Chicago, IL)
Repro-Tech (W Patterson, NJ) G
Reproductions Inc (Rockville, MD) G
Rich Printing (Nashville, TN)
Ringier America (Itasca, IL) G
Ringier America (Brookfield, WI)
Ringier America (Corinth, MS)
Ringier America (Jonesboro, AR) C
Ringier America (New Berlin, WI)
Ringier America (Olathe, KS)
Ringier America (Phoenix, AZ) C
Ringier America (Pontiac, IL) C
Ringier America (Senatobia, MS)
Riverside Press (Dallas, TX) G
John Roberts Co (Minneapolis, MN) C
Ronalds Printing (Montreal, PQ) C
Ronalds Printing (Vancouver, BC) G
S Rosenthal & Company (Cincinnati, OH)
Royle Printing (Sun Prairie, WI) G
RPP Enterprises (Libertyville, IL) G
Saint Croix Press (New Richmond, WI)
Saint Joseph Printing (Toronto, ON) G
Saint Mary's Press (Hollywood, MD)
Saltzman Printers (Maywood, IL) C
Schiff Printers (Pittsburgh, PA) G
Science Press (Ephrata, PA)
Semline Inc (Braintree, MA)
Service Printing (San Leandro, CA)
Service Web (Chicago, IL) C
Sexton Printing (W Saint Paul, MN)
Shepard Poorman (Indianapolis, IN)
Sheridan Press (Hanover, PA)
Sheridan Printing (Alpha, NJ)
Skillful Means Press (Oakland, CA) G
R E Smith Printing (Fall River, MA) G
Smith-Edwards (Phildelphia, PA) G
Snohomish Publishing (Snohomish, WA)
Southam Printing (Weston, ON)
Southeastern Printing (Stuart, FL) G
Sowers Printing (Lebanon, PA)
Speaker-Hines & Thomas (Lansing, MI) G
Spencer Press (Hingham, MA) C
Spencer Press (Wells, ME) C
Standard Publishing (Cincinnati, OH) C
Stephenson Inc (Alexandria, VA) C

Catalog Printers

Stewart Publishing (Marble Hill, MO)
Straus Printing (Madison, WI) **G**
Suburban Publishers (Exeter, PA) **C**
Sun Graphics (Parsons, KS) **C**
Sweet Printing (Round Rock, TX) **C**
John S Swift (Saint Louis, MO) **G**
John S Swift (Chicago, IL) **G**
John S Swift (Cincinnati, OH) **G**
John S Swift (Teterboro, NJ) **G**
T A S Graphics (Detroit, MI) **G**
Tapco (Pemberton, NJ)
Technical Comm. (N Kansas City, MO) **G**
Telegraph Press (Harrisburg, PA)
Texas Color Printers (Dallas, TX) **C**
Thomson-Shore (Dexter, MI)
Times Litho (Forest Grove, OR)
Times Printing (Random Lake, WI)
Todd Web Press (Smithville, TX) **G**
Tracor Publications (Austin, TX) **G**
Tri-Graphic Printing (Ottawa, ON)
Tri-State Press (Clayton, GA) **G**
Triangle Printing (Nashville, TN) **G**
TSO General (Long Island City, NY) **G**
Twin City Printery (Lewiston, ME) **G**
Ultra-Color Corp (Saint Louis, MO) **C**
United Color (Monroe, OH)
Universal Printing (Miami, FL)
Universal Printing (St Louis, MO) **G**
US Press (Valdosta, GA) **C**
Vail Ballou Printing (Binghamton, NY)
Valco Graphics (Seattle, WA)
Victor Graphics (Baltimore, MD)
Viking Press (Eden Prairie, MN)
Vogue Printers (North Chicago, IL) **G**
Waldman Graphics (Pennsauken, NJ) **C**
Waldon Press (New York, NY) **G**
Wallace Press (Hillside, IL)
Walsworth Publishing (Marceline, MO)
Watkins Printing (Columbus, OH) **C**
Web Specialties (Wheeling, IL) **C**
Webb Company (Saint Paul, MN) **C**
Webcom Ltd (Scarborough, ON)
Webcraft (New Brunswick, NJ) **G**
Webcrafters (Madison, WI)
F A Weber & Sons (Park Falls, WI) **G**
A D Weiss Lithograph (Hollywood, FL)
Wellesley Press (Framingham, MA) **C**
Western Publishers (Albuquerque, NM)
Western Publishing (Racine, WI)
Western Web (Sioux Falls, SD) **G**
White Arts (Indianapolis, IN) **G**
Wickersham Printing (Lancaster, PA)
Williams Catello (Tualatin, OR)
Windsor Associates (San Diego, CA)
Wisconsin Color Press (Milwaukee, WI)
Wolfer Printing (Commerce, CA) **G**
Wood & Jones (Pasadena, CA) **G**
World Color Press (New York, NY) **C**
Worzalla Publishing (Stevens Point, WI)
Henry Wurst (North Kansas City, MO) **G**

Magazine Printers

The following printers all can print magazines. Those marked with a bold **M** specialize as magazine printers.

Academy Books (Rutland, VT)
The Adams Group (New York, NY)
Adams Press (Chicago, IL)
Allied Printing (Akron, OH)
Alonzo Printing (S San Francisco, CA)
American Press Inc (Oakton, VA) **M**
American Signature (Dallas, TX)
American Signature (Costa Mesa, CA)
American Signature (New York, NY)
American Signature (Memphis, TN)
American Web (Denver, CO) **M**
Americomp (Brattleboro, VT)
Amos Press (Sidney, OH) **M**
Arcata Graphics (Nashville, TN) **M**
Arcata Graphics (Depew, NY) **M**
Arcata Graphics (San Jose, CA) **M**
Arizona Lithographers (Tucson, AZ)
Artcraft Press (Waterloo, WI)
Artex Publishing (Stevens Point, WI)
Associated Printers (Grafton, ND)
Autumn House (Hagerstown, MD) **M**
Balan Printing (Brooklyn, NY)
Banta Catalog Group (St Paul, MN)
Banta-Harrisonburg (Harrisonburg, VA)
Beacon Press (Richmond, VA)
Beslow Associates (Chicago, IL) **M**
Blake Printery (San Luis Obispo, CA)
Bolger Publications (Minneapolis, MN) **M**
William Boyd Printing (Albany, NY)
Braceland Brothers (Philadelphia, PA) **M**
Brown Printing (Waseca, MN) **M**
Brown Printing (East Greenville, PA)
Brown Printing (Franklin, KY) **M**
R L Bryan Company (Columbia, SC)
BSC Litho (Harrisburg, PA)
William Byrd Press (Richmond, VA) **M**
Cal Central Press (Sacramento, CA)
California Offset (Glendale, CA) **M**
Camelot Fine Printing (Albuquerque, NM)
Canterbury Press (Rome, NY) **M**
Capital City Press (Montpelier, VT)
Capital Printing (Austin, TX)
Carlson Color Graphics (Ocala, FL) **M**
Central Publishing (Indianapolis, IN)
Charles Comm. (New York, NY) **M**
Citizen Prep (Beaver Dam, WI) **M**
City Printing (North Haven, CT)
Clark Printing (Kansas City, MO) **M**
Cody Publications (Kissimmee, FL) **M**
The College Press (Collegedale, TN)
Color World Printers (Bozeman, MT)
Colortone Press (Washington, DC)
Columbus Book Printers (Columbus, GA)

Magazine Printers

Combined Comm. (Columbia, MO) **M**
Combined Comm. (Mendota, IL) **M**
Community Press (Provo, UT)
Coneco Laser Graphics (Glen Falls, NY)
Connecticut Printers (Bloomfield, CT) **M**
Continental Web (Itasca, IL)
Cornay Web Graphics (New Orleans, LA)
Country Press (Mohawk, NY)
Craftsman Press (Seattle, WA)
Creative Web Systems (Inglewood, CA)
Crest Litho (Watervliet, NY)
Crusader Printing (E Saint Louis, IL)
Cummings Printing (Manchester, NH) **M**
D D Associates (Santa Clara, CA)
Danner Press (Canton, OH)
Dartmouth Printing (Hanover, NH) **M**
Dataco (Albuquerque, NM)
Democrat Printing (Little Rock, AR) **M**
Des Plaines Publishing (Des Plaines, IL)
Desaulniers Printing (Milan, IL)
Dharma Press (Oakland, CA)
Diamond Graphics (Milwaukee, WI)
Dickinson Press (Grand Rapids, MI)
The Dingley Press (Lisbon, ME)
Dollco Printing (Ottawa, ON)
Donihe Graphics (Kingsport, TN)
R R Donnelley (Crawfordsville, IN)
R R Donnelley (Chicago, IL)
Dynagraphics (Carlsbad, CA) **M**
Eastwood Printing (Denver, CO)
Economy Printing (Berne, IN) **M**
Edison Litho (North Bergen, NJ)
Editors Press (Hyattsville, MD) **M**
Edwards & Broughton (Raleigh, NC)
Einson Freeman Graphics (Fairlawn, NJ)
Evangel Press (Nappanee, IN)
Faculty Press (Brooklyn, NY)
Fetter Printing (Louisville, KY)
Fisher Web Printers (Cedar Rapids, IA) **M**
Foote & Davies (Atlanta, GA)
Foote & Davies (Lincoln, NE) **M**
Futura Printing (Boynton Beach, FL)
Gagne Printing (Louiseville, PQ)
Gateway Press (Louisville, KY)
Gaylord Ltd (West Hollywood, CA)
George Lithograph (San Francisco, CA)
Gladstone Press (Ottawa, ON)
Glundal Color Service (E Syracuse, NY)
Gowe Printing Company (Medina, OH)
Graftek Press (Woodstock, IL) **M**
Gray Printing (Fostoria, OH) **M**
Greater Buffalo Press (Buffalo, NY) **M**
Greenfield Printing (Greenfield, OH) **M**
Gregath Company (Cullman, AL)
Griffin Printing (Glendale, CA)
Grit Commercial Print (Williamsport, PA)
Gulf Printing (Houston, TX)
Guynes Printing (Albuquerque, NM)
Hamilton Printing (Rensselaer, NY)
Harlin Litho (Ossining, NY)

Hart Graphics (Sampsonville, SC) **M**
Hart Press (Long Prairie, MN) **M**
Heartland Press (Spencer, IA) **M**
Hinz Lithographing (Mt Prospect, IL)
A B Hirschfeld Press (Denver, CO)
Hoechstetter Printing (Pittsburgh, PA)
Holladay-Tyler (Glenn Dale, MD) **M**
Hooven-Dayton Corp (Dayton, OH)
Humboldt National (N Abington, MA)
Hunter Publishing (Winston-Salem, NC)
Independent Publishing (Sarasota, FL)
Infopress/Saratoga (Saratoga Springs, NY)
Insert Color Press (Ronkonkoma, NY) **M**
Intelligencer Printing (Lancaster, PA)
Interstate Printers (Danville, IL)
Jersey Printing (Bayonne, NJ) **M**
JohnsBryne Microdot (Niles, IL) **M**
Johnson & Hardin (Cincinnati, OH) **M**
Johnson Graphics (East Dubuque, IL)
Jostens / Clarksville (Clarksville, TN)
Jostens / State College (State College, PA)
Jostens / Topeka (Topeka, KS)
Jostens / Visalia (Visalia, CA)
Judd Inc. (Washington, DC) **M**
Julin Printing (Monticello, IA)
K-B Offset Printing (State College, PA)
K/P Graphics (Escondido, CA)
Kaufman Press (Syracuse, NY)
Kimberly Press (Santa Barbara, CA)
Lancaster Press (Lancaster, PA) **M**
The Lane Press (Burlington, VT) **M**
Lasky Company (Milburn, NJ)
Latham Process Corp (New York, NY)
Lawson Graphics (Toronto, ON)
Lehigh Press (Broadview, IL)
Lehigh Press (Dallas, TX) **M**
The Lehigh Press (Pennsauken, NJ)
Lithocolor Press (Westchester, IL)
LithoCraft (Carlstadt, NJ)
Little River Press (Miami, FL)
John D Lucas Printing (Baltimore, MD)
Mack Printing (Easton, PA) **M**
Mackintosh Typo. (Santa Barbara, CA)
Maclean Hunter (Willowdale, ON) **M**
Mariposa Press (Benicia, CA)
Marrakech Express (Tarpon Springs, FL)
Mars Graphic Services (Westville, NJ)
McClain Printing (Parson, WV)
McFarland Company (Harrisburg, PA) **M**
McKay Printing (Dolton, IL)
Meaker the Printer (Phoenix, AZ)
Mercury Printing (Memphis, TN)
Meredith/Burda (Des Moines, IA) **M**
Messenger Graphics (Phoenix, AZ)
Metroweb (Erlanger, KY) **M**
Mideastern Printing (Brookfield, CT)
Mitchell Press (Vancouver, BC)
Moebius Printing (Milwaukee, WI)
Moran Colorgraphic (Baton Rouge, LA)
Morgan Printing (Austin, TX)
Motheral Printing (Fort Worth, TX)
Muller Printing (Santa Clara, CA)

Magazine Printers

National Bickford (Providence, RI)
National Graphics (Columbus, OH)
Neibauer Press (Warminster, PA)
Neyenesch Printers (San Diego, CA) M
Nielsen Litho (Cincinnati, OH)
Nimrod Press (Boston, MA)
Noll Printing (Huntington, IN)
North Plains Press (Aberdeen, SD) M
Northprint (Grand Rapids, MN) M
Northwest Web (Eugene, OR)
Nystrom Publishing (Maple Grove, MN)
Oaks Printing (Bethlehem, PA)
Oklahoma (Oklahoma City, OK) M
Omaha Printing (Omaha, NE)
Ortlieb Press (Baton Rouge, LA)
Ovid Bell Press (Fulton, MO) M
Oxford Group (Norway, ME)
Oxford Group (Berlin, NH)
Paraclete Press (Orleans, MA)
Patterson Printing (Benton Harbor, MI)
Paust Inc (Richmond, IN)
Pendell Printing (Midland, MI) M
PennWell Printing (Tulsa, OK) M
Penton Press (Berea, OH) M
Perlmuter Printing (Independence, OH)
Perry Printing (Waterloo, WI)
Perry/Baraboo (Baraboo, WI)
PFP Printing Corp (Gaithersburg, MD)
Pioneer Press (Wilmette, IL)
Plain Talk Publishing (Des Moines, IA)
Port City Press (Pikesville, MD)
Port Pubns (Port Washington, WI) M
Practical Graphics (New York, NY)
Preferred Graphics (Winona, MN)
The Press of Ohio (Brimfield, OH)
Print Northwest (Tacoma, WA)
The Printer Inc (Maple Grove, MN)
Printing Dimensions (Beltsville, MD)
Progress Printing (Lynchburg, VA)
Progressive Typographers (Emigsville, PA)
Promotional Printing (Houston, TX)
Publishers Printing (Shepherdsville KY) M
Quad Graphics (Thomaston, GA) M
Quad/Graphics (Lomira, WI) M
Quad/Graphics (Pewaukee, WI) M
Quad/Graphics (Saratoga Springs, NY) M
Quad/Graphics (Sussex, WI)
RBW Graphics (Owen Sound, ON)
Recorder Sunset (San Francisco, CA) M
Regensteiner Press (West Chicago, IL) M
Reproductions Inc (Rockville, MD)
George Rice & Sons (Los Angeles, CA)
Rich Printing (Nashville, TN)
Ringier America (Itasca, IL)
Ringier America (Brookfield, WI) M
Ringier America (Corinth, MS) M
Ringier America (Jonesboro, AR)
Ringier America (Phoenix, AZ)
Ringier America (Pontiac, IL)
Ringier America (Senatobia, MS) M

Ronalds Printing (Montreal, PQ)
Ronalds Printing (Vancouver, BC)
Rose Printing Company (Tallahassee, FL)
S Rosenthal (Cincinnati, OH) M
Royle Printing (Sun Prairie, WI)
Saint Croix Press (New Richmond, WI) M
Saint Joseph Printing (Toronto, ON)
Schumann Printers (Fall River, WI) M
Sexton Printing (W Saint Paul, MN) M
Shepard Poorman (Indianapolis, IN) M
Sheridan Press (Hanover, PA) M
Sheridan Printing (Alpha, NJ) M
SLC Graphics (Pittston, PA) M
R E Smith Printing (Fall River, MA)
Smith-Edwards-Dunlap (Phildelphia, PA)
Snohomish Publishing (Snohomish, WA)
Southam Printing (Weston, ON) M
Southeastern Printing (Stuart, FL)
Southern California (Culver City, CA) M
Sowers Printing (Lebanon, PA) M
Speaker-Hines & Thomas (Lansing, MI)
Stephenson Inc (Alexandria, VA)
Straus Printing (Madison, WI)
The Studley Press (Dalton, MA)
Suburban Publishers (Exeter, PA)
Sundance Press (Tucson, AZ) M
Sweet Printing (Round Rock, TX)
T A S Graphics (Detroit, MI)
Tapco (Pemberton, NJ) M
Telegraph Press (Harrisburg, PA) M
Times Litho (Forest Grove, OR) M
Times Printing (Random Lake, WI) M
Todd Web Press (Smithville, TX)
Tracor Publications (Austin, TX)
Tri-Graphic Printing (Ottawa, ON)
Tri-State Press (Clayton, GA)
TSO General (Long Island City, NY)
Twin City Printery (Lewiston, ME)
United Color (Monroe, OH) M
United Litho (Falls Church, VA) M
Universal Printing (Miami, FL) M
Universal Printing (Saint Louis, MO)
Valco Graphics (Seattle, WA) M
Volkmuth Printers (Saint Cloud, MN)
Waldon Press (New York, NY)
Watkins Printing (Columbus, OH)
Waverly Press (Baltimore, MD) M
The Webb Company (Saint Paul, MN)
Webcrafters (Madison, WI)
F A Weber & Sons (Park Falls, WI)
A D Weiss Litho (Hollywood, FL) M
Wellesley Press (Framingham, MA)
West Side Graphics (New York, NY)
Western Publishers (Albuquerque, NM)
Western Web (Sioux Falls, SD)
Wickersham Printing (Lancaster, PA)
Wimmer Brothers (Memphis, TN)
Wisconsin Color Press (Milwaukee, WI) M
Wolfer Printing (City of Commerce, CA)
World Color Press (New York, NY)
Henry Wurst Inc (N Kansas City, MO)
Ye Olde Genealogie (Indianapolis, IN)

Magazine Short-Run Printers

The following magazine printers specialize in printing magazines in runs from 10,000 on up to 100,000 copies.

Allen Press (Lawrence, KS)
American Press Inc (Oakton, VA)
American Web Offset (Denver, CO)
Amos Press (Sidney, OH)
Bolger Publications (Minneapolis, MN)
Braceland Brothers (Philadelphia, PA)
Brown Printing (Waseca, MN)
William Byrd Press (Richmond, VA)
California Offset (Glendale, CA)
Canterbury Press (Rome, NY)
Carlson Color Graphics (Ocala, FL)
Citizen Prep & Printing (Beaver Dam, WI)
Clark Printing (Kansas City, MO)
Cody Publications (Kissimmee, FL)
Combined Comm. (Columbia, MO)
Combined Communication (Mendota, IL)
Cummings Printing (Manchester, NH)
Dartmouth Printing (Hanover, NH)
Democrat Printing (Little Rock, AR)
Dynagraphics (Carlsbad, CA)
Ebsco Media (Birmingham, AL)
Editors Press (Hyattsville, MD)
Graftek Press (Woodstock, IL)
Gray Printing (Fostoria, OH)
Greenfield Printing (Greenfield, OH)
Hart Press (Long Prairie, MN)
Heartland Press (Spencer, IA)
Holladay-Tyler Printing (Glenn Dale, MD)
Jersey Printing Company (Bayonne, NJ)
JohnsBryne Microdot (Niles, IL)
Johnson & Hardin (Cincinnati, OH)
Judd's Incorporated (Washington, DC)
Lancaster Press (Lancaster, PA)
Lane Press (Burlington, VT)
Mack Printing (Easton, PA)
McFarland Company (Harrisburg, PA)
Metroweb (Erlanger, KY)
Neyenesch Printers (San Diego, CA)
Northprint (Grand Rapids, MN)
Ovid Bell Press (Fulton, MO)
Pendell Printing (Midland, MI)
PennWell Printing (Tulsa, OK)
Port Publications (Port Washington, WI)
Publishers Printing (Shepherdsville, KY)
Ringier America (Senatobia, MS)
S Rosenthal & Company (Cincinnati, OH)
Saint Croix Press (New Richmond, WI)
Schumann Printers (Fall River, WI)
Sexton Printing (West Saint Paul, MN)
Sheridan Press (Hanover, PA)
Sheridan Printing (Alpha, NJ)
Southern California (Culver City, CA)
Sundance Press (Tucson, AZ)
Times Litho (Forest Grove, OR)
Times Printing (Random Lake, WI)
United Color (Monroe, OH)
Universal Printing (Miami, FL)
Valco Graphics (Seattle, WA)
Waverly Press (Baltimore, MD)

Ultra-Short-Run Book Printers

The following printers specialize in printing books in runs of less than 1,000 copies.

Advanced Duplicating (Edina, MN)
Americomp (Brattleboro, VT)
Anundsen Publishing (Decorah, IA)
Harold Berliner Printer (Nevada City, CA)
Book Makers Inc (Kenosha, WI)
BookMasters (Ashland, OH)
C & M Press (Thornton, CO)
Camelot Book (Ormond Beach, FL)
Canterbury Press (Rome, NY)
Coach House Press (Toronto, ON)
Country Press (Middleborough, MA)
Crane Duplicating (West Barnstable, MA)
Edison Press (Glen Rock, NJ)
Everton Publishers (Logan, UT)
Fast Print (Fort Wayne, IN)
Geryon Press (Tunnel, NY)
GRT Book Printing (Oakland, CA)
Henington Publishing (Wolfe City, TX)
Independent Print (Long Island City, NY)
Independent Publishing (Sarasota, FL)
The Job Shop (Woods Hole, MA)
Kern International (Duxbury, MA)
McDowell Publications (Utica, KY)
Morgan Printing (Austin, TX)
Cookbooks by Morris Press (Kearney, NE)
Multiprint Inc (Chatham, NY)
National Reproductions (Livonia, MI)
Odyssey Press (Dover, NH)
Omnipress (Madison, WI)
Original Copy Centers (Cleveland, OH)
Paust Inc (Richmond, IN)
Pentagram (Minneapolis, MN)
PFP Printing Corp (Gaithersburg, MD)
Pine Hill Press (Freeman, SD)
Quinn-Woodbine (Woodbine, NJ)
Quintessence Press (Amador City, CA)
Quixott Press (Doylestown, PA)
Realtron Multi-Lith (Denver, CO)
Southern Tennessee (Waynesboro, TN)
Van Volumes (Thorndike, MA)
Walter's Publishing (Waseca, MN)
Westview Press (Boulder, CO)
Yates Publishing (Ozark, MO)
Ye Olde Genealogie (Indianapolis, IN)

Short-Run Book Printers

The following book printers report an optimum print run somewhere between 1,001 copies and 10,000 copies.

Academy Books (Rutland, VT)
Ad Color (Port Chester, NY)
Adams Press (Chicago, IL)
Adviser Graphics (Red Deer, AB)
Allen Press (Lawrence, KS)
Andover Press (New York, NY)
Arcata Graphics (W Hanover, MA)
B & R Printing (Post Falls, ID)
Baker Johnson (Dexter, MI)
Bay Port Press (National City, CA)
Beacon Wholesale Printing (Seattle, WA)
T H Best Printing (Don Mills, ON)
Blake Printery (San Luis Obispo, CA)
Blue Dolphin Press (Grass Valley, CA)
Book-Mart Press (North Bergen, NJ)
BookCrafters (Chelsea, MI)
BookCrafters (Fredericksburg, VA)
Booklet Publishing (Elk Grove Village, IL)
Braun-Brumfield (Ann Arbor, MI)
Brennan Printing (Deep River, IA)
Brunswick Publishing (Lawrenceville, VA)
Caldwell Printers (Arcadia, CA)
Capital City Press (Montpelier, VT)
Capital Printing Company (Austin, TX)
Cody Publications (Kissimmee, FL)
Color House (Grand Rapids, MI)
Community Press (Provo, UT)
Comput-A-Print (Reno, NV)
Coneco Laser Graphics (Glen Falls, NY)
Cookbook Publishers (Olathe, KS)
Corley Printing (Earth City, MO)
Cushing-Malloy (Ann Arbor, MI)
D D Associates (Santa Clara, CA)
Daamen Printing (West Rutland, VT)
Dataco (Albuquerque, NM)
Delmar Printing (Charlotte, NC)
Delta Lithograph (Valencia, CA)
Diamond Graphics (Milwaukee, WI)
Dickinson Press (Grand Rapids, MI)
Dragon Press (Delta Junction, AK)
Eastwood Printing (Denver, CO)
Edwards Brothers (Ann Arbor, MI)
Edwards Brothers (Lillington, NC)
Evangel Press (Nappanee, IN)
William Exline Inc (Cleveland, OH)
Faculty Press (Brooklyn, NY)
Four Corners Press (Grand Rapids, MI)
Friesen Printers (Altona R0G 0B0, MB)
Fundcraft (Collierville, TN)
Gagne Printing (Louiseville, PQ)
Ganis & Harris (New York, NY)
Gaylord Ltd (West Hollywood, CA)
George Lithograph (San Francisco, CA)

Germac Printing (Tigard, OR)
Giant Horse (Daly City, CA)
Gilliland Printing (Arkansas City, KS)
Graphic Printing (New Carlisle, OH)
Griffin Printing (Glendale, CA)
Griffin Printing (Sacramento, CA)
Guynes Printing (Albuquerque, NM)
Haddon Craftsmen (Scranton, PA)
Harlo Press (Detroit, MI)
Heart of the Lakes (Interlaken, NY)
Heffernan Press (Worcester, MA)
Heritage Printers (Charlotte, NC)
Hignell Printing (Winnepeg, MB)
Infopress/Saratoga (Saratoga Springs, NY)
Jersey Printing (Bayonne, NJ)
Johnson Publishing (Boulder, CO)
Jostens / Clarksville (Clarksville, TN)
Jostens / State College (State College, PA)
Jostens / Topeka (Topeka, KS)
Jostens / Visalia (Visalia, CA)
Julin Printing (Monticello, IA)
K/P Graphics (Escondido, CA)
Kimberly Press (Santa Barbara, CA)
KNI Book Manufacturing (Anaheim, CA)
Les Editions Marquis (Montmagny, PQ)
Litho Specialties (Saint Paul, MN)
Mackintosh Typo. (Santa Barbara, CA)
Malloy Lithographing (Ann Arbor, MI)
Marrakech Express (Tarpon Springs, FL)
Maverick Publications (Bend, OR)
The Mazer Corporation (Dayton, OH)
McClain Printing (Parson, WV)
McFarland Company (Harrisburg, PA)
McGregor & Werner (Washington, DC)
McNaughton & Gunn (Saline, MI)
Meaker the Printer (Phoenix, AZ)
Messenger Graphics (Phoenix, AZ)
Metromail Corporation (Lincoln, NE)
Mitchell Graphics (Petoskey, MI)
Mitchell-Shear (Ann Arbor, MI)
Monument Printers (Verplanck, NY)
Morningrise Printing (Costa Mesa, CA)
Murphy's Printing (Campbell, CA)
Naturegraph (Happy Camp, CA)
Neibauer Press (Warminster, PA)
Nimrod Press (Boston, MA)
Northlight Studio Press (Barre, VT)
Nystrom Publishing (Maple Grove, MN)
Oaks Printing Company (Bethlehem, PA)
Optic Graphics (Glen Burnie, MD)
Outstanding Graphics (Kenosha, WI)
PAK Discount Printing (Zion, IL)
Paraclete Press (Orleans, MA)
Parker Graphics (Fuquay-Varina, NC)
Patterson Printing (Benton Harbor, MI)
Preferred Graphics (Winona, MN)
Princeton University (Lawrenceville, NJ)
Prinit Press (Dublin, IN)
Publishers Press (Salt Lake City, UT)
Repro-Tech (West Patterson, NJ)
Ringier America (Olathe, KS)
Rose Printing (Tallahassee, FL)

Short-Run Book Printers

Sabre Printers (Rogersville, TN)
Saint Mary's Press (Hollywood, MD)
Science Press (Ephrata, PA)
Service Printing (San Leandro, CA)
Sexton Printing (W Saint Paul, MN)
The Sheridan Press (Hanover, PA)
Snohomish Publishing (Snohomish, WA)
Stewart Publishing (Marble Hill, MO)
The Studley Press (Dalton, MA)
Sundance Press (Tucson, AZ)
Taylor Publishing (Dallas, TX)
Technical Comm. (N Kansas City, MO)
Thomson-Shore (Dexter, MI)
Town House Press (Pittsboro, NC)
Tracor Publications (Austin, TX)
Triangle Printing (Nashville, TN)
United Lithograph (Somerville, MA)
Versa Press (East Peoria, IL)
Vicks Lithograph (Yorkville, NY)
Victor Graphics (Baltimore, MD)
Walsworth Publishing (Marceline, MO)
Webcom Ltd (Scarborough, ON)
West Side Graphics (New York, NY)
Western Publishers (Albuquerque, NM)
Wickersham Printing (Lancaster, PA)

Index: Other Printed Items

The following indexes list some of the printers who are capable of printing various items, from annual reports to software manuals, from calendars to posters. These indexes, like all the other indexes, are derived from the surveys returned by printers (plus other sources describing the capabilities of those printers who did not respond to the survey).

Annual Reports

Academy Books (Rutland, VT)
Ad Color (Port Chester, NY)
The Adams Group (New York, NY)
Adams Press (Chicago, IL)
Adviser Graphics (Red Deer, AB)
Allied Printing (Akron, OH)
American Printers (Chicago, IL)
American Signature (Dallas, TX)
American Signature (Costa Mesa, CA)
American Signature (New York, NY)
American Signature (Memphis, TN)
Apollo Graphics (Southampton, PA)
Arcata Graphics (Kingsport, TN)
Argus Press (Niles, IL)
Arizona Lithographers (Tucson, AZ)
Artcraft Press (Waterloo, WI)
B & R Printing (Post Falls, ID)
Banta Catalog Group (Saint Paul, MN)
Beacon Wholesale Printing (Seattle, WA)
Bell Publications (Iowa City, IA)
T H Best Printing (Don Mills, ON)
Blue Dolphin Press (Grass Valley, CA)
Bolger Publications (Minneapolis, MN)
Book-Mart Press (North Bergen, NJ)
Bradley Printing (Des Plaines, IL)
Brown Printing (Waseca, MN)
Brunswick Publishing (Lawrenceville, VA)
R L Bryan Company (Columbia, SC)
BSC Litho (Harrisburg, PA)
C & M Press (Thornton, CO)
Cal Central Press (Sacramento, CA)
Camelot Fine (Albuquerque, NM)
Canterbury Press (Rome, NY)
Capital Printing Company (Austin, TX)
Cascio-Wolf (Springfield, VA)
Catalogue Publishing (Martinsburg, WV)
Catalogue Service (New Rochelle, NY)
Central Publishing (Indianapolis, IN)
City Printing Company (North Haven, CT)
Cody Publications (Kissimmee, FL)
The College Press (Collegedale, TN)
Colonial Graphics (Paterson, NJ)
Color House (Grand Rapids, MI)

Color World Printers (Bozeman, MT)
ColorGraphics (Tulsa, OK)
Colortone Press (Washington, DC)
Commercial Printing (Medford, OR)
Community Press (Provo, UT)
Comput-A-Print (Reno, NV)
Coneco Laser Graphics (Glen Falls, NY)
Consolidated Printers (Berkeley, CA)
Continental Web (Itasca, IL)
Copen Press (Brooklyn, NY)
Cornay Web Graphics (New Orleans, LA)
Country Press (Mohawk, NY)
Crane Duplicating (West Barnstable, MA)
Crest Litho (Watervliet, NY)
Crusader Printing (East Saint Louis, IL)
D D Associates (Santa Clara, CA)
Daamen Printing (West Rutland, VT)
Danbury Printing (Danbury, CT)
Dataco (Albuquerque, NM)
Dellas Graphics (Syracuse, NY)
Delmar Printing (Charlotte, NC)
Delta Lithograph (Valencia, CA)
Desaulniers Printing (Milan, IL)
Dharma Press (Oakland, CA)
Diamond Graphics (Milwaukee, WI)
Dinner & Klein (Seattle, WA)
Diversified Printing (Brea, CA)
Dollco Printing (Ottawa, ON)
Donihe Graphics (Kingsport, TN)
R R Donnelley (Crawfordsville, IN)
R R Donnelley (Chicago, IL)
East Village Enterprises (New York, NY)
Eastwood Printing (Denver, CO)
Editors Press (Hyattsville, MD)
Edwards & Broughton (Raleigh, NC)
Eerdmans Printing (Grand Rapids, MI)
Einson Freeman Graphics (Fairlawn, NJ)
Faculty Press (Brooklyn, NY)
Fast Print (Fort Wayne, IN)
Foote & Davies (Atlanta, GA)
Fort Orange Press (Albany, NY)
Foster Printing (Michigan City, IN)
Full Color Graphics (Plainview, NY)
Futura Printing (Boynton Beach, FL)
Gateway Press (Louisville, KY)
Gaylord Printing (Detroit, MI)

Annual Reports

General Offset (Jersey City, NJ)
George Lithograph (San Francisco, CA)
Germac Printing (Tigard, OR)
Giant Horse (Daly City, CA)
Gladstone Press (Ottawa, ON)
Globe-Comm (San Antonio, TX)
Glundal Color (East Syracuse, NY)
Graphic Arts Center (Portland, OR)
Graphic Design (Center Line, MI)
Graphic Litho Corp (Lawrence, MA)
Gray Printing (Fostoria, OH)
The Gregath Company (Cullman, AL)
Griffin Printing (Glendale, CA)
Grit Commercial Print (Williamsport, PA)
Gulf Printing (Houston, TX)
Guynes Printing (Albuquerque, NM)
Harlin Litho (Ossining, NY)
Harlo Press (Detroit, MI)
Hennegan Company (Cincinnati, OH)
Herbick & Held Printing (Pittsburgh, PA)
Hinz Lithographing (Mt Prospect, IL)
A B Hirschfeld Press (Denver, CO)
Hooven-Dayton Corp (Dayton, OH)
Hunter Publishing (Winston-Salem, NC)
Infopress/Saratoga (Saratoga Springs, NY)
Inland Lithograph (Elk Grove Village, IL)
Intelligencer Printing (Lancaster, PA)
Interstate Printers (Danville, IL)
Interstate Printing (Omaha, NE)
Jersey Printing (Bayonne, NJ)
Johnson & Hardin (Cincinnati, OH)
Johnson Graphics (East Dubuque, IL)
Julin Printing (Monticello, IA)
K & S Graphics (Nashville, TN)
K-B Offset Printing (State College, PA)
K/P Graphics (Escondido, CA)
Kaufman Press Printing (Syracuse, NY)
Kern International (Duxbury, MA)
Lasky Company (Milburn, NJ)
Lawson Graphics (Toronto, ON)
Lehigh Press (Broadview, IL)
Lehigh Press (Dallas, TX)
The Lehigh Press (Pennsauken, NJ)
Les Editions Marquis (Montmagny, PQ)
Liberty York Graphic (Hempstead, NY)
Litho Specialties (Saint Paul, MN)
LithoCraft (Carlstadt, NJ)
Little River Press (Miami, FL)
John D Lucas Printing (Baltimore, MD)
Marrakech Express (Tarpon Springs, FL)
McClain Printing (Parson, WV)
McFarland Company (Harrisburg, PA)
McGrew Color (Kansas City, MO)
Meaker the Printer (Phoenix, AZ)
Meehan-Tooker (E Rutherford, NJ)
Mercury Printing (Memphis, TN)
Messenger Graphics (Phoenix, AZ)
Mideastern Printing (Brookfield, CT)
Mitchell Press (Vancouver, BC)
Mitchell-Shear (Ann Arbor, MI)

Moebius Printing (Milwaukee, WI)
Moran Colorgraphic (Baton Rouge, LA)
Morgan Press (Dobbs Ferry, NY)
Motheral Printing (Fort Worth, TX)
Muller Printing (Santa Clara, CA)
Murphy's Printing (Campbell, CA)
National Bickford (Providence, RI)
National Graphics (Columbus, OH)
Nationwide Printing (Burlington, KY)
Naturegraph (Happy Camp, CA)
Neibauer Press (Warminster, PA)
Neyenesch Printers (San Diego, CA)
Nielsen Lithographing (Cincinnati, OH)
Nimrod Press (Boston, MA)
Northlight Studio Press (Barre, VT)
Nystrom Publishing (Maple Grove, MN)
Oaks Printing Company (Bethlehem, PA)
Omaha Printing (Omaha, NE)
Optic Graphics (Glen Burnie, MD)
Ortlieb Press (Baton Rouge, LA)
Pacific Lithograph (San Francisco, CA)
Paraclete Press (Orleans, MA)
Paust Inc (Richmond, IN)
Pendell Printing (Midland, MI)
Perlmuter Printing (Independence, OH)
Perry Printing (Waterloo, WI)
Perry/Baraboo (Baraboo, WI)
Plain Talk Publishing (Des Moines, IA)
Port City Press (Pikesville, MD)
Port Publications (Port Washington, WI)
Practical Graphics (New York, NY)
Precision Offset (Upper Darby, PA)
Preferred Graphics (Winona, MN)
The Press (Chanhassen, MN)
Print Northwest (Tacoma, WA)
The Printer Inc (Maple Grove, MN)
Printing Corp. (Pompano Beach, FL)
Progress Printing (Lynchburg, VA)
ProLitho (Provo, UT)
Quad/Graphics (Lomira, WI)
Quad/Graphics (Pewaukee, WI)
Quad/Graphics (Saratoga Springs, NY)
Quad/Graphics (Sussex, WI)
Regensteiner Press (West Chicago, IL)
Repro-Tech (West Patterson, NJ)
Reproductions Inc (Rockville, MD)
George Rice & Sons (Los Angeles, CA)
Ringier America (Brookfield, WI)
Ringier America (Jonesboro, AR)
Ringier America (New Berlin, WI)
Ringier America (Phoenix, AZ)
Ringier America (Pontiac, IL)
Ringier America (Senatobia, MS)
The Riverside Press (Dallas, TX)
John Roberts Co (Minneapolis, MN)
Ronalds Printing (Montreal, PQ)
S Rosenthal & Company (Cincinnati, OH)
Royle Printing (Sun Prairie, WI)
RPP Enterprises (Libertyville, IL)
Schiff Printers (Pittsburgh, PA)
Science Press (Ephrata, PA)
Sexton Printing (West Saint Paul, MN)

Annual Reports

Shepard Poorman (Indianapolis, IN)
R E Smith Printing (Fall River, MA)
Smith-Edwards-Dunlap (Phildelphia, PA)
Snohomish Publishing (Snohomish, WA)
Southam Printing (Weston, ON)
Southeastern Printing (Stuart, FL)
Southern California (Culver City, CA)
Spencer Press (Hingham, MA)
Spencer Press (Wells, ME)
Stephenson Inc (Alexandria, VA)
Stewart Publishing (Marble Hill, MO)
Stinehour Press (Lunenburg, VT)
Straus Printing Company (Madison, WI)
The Studley Press (Dalton, MA)
Suburban Publishers (Exeter, PA)
Sweet Printing (Round Rock, TX)
John S Swift Company (Saint Louis, MO)
John S Swift (Chicago, IL)
John S Swift (Cincinnati, OH)
John S Swift (Teterboro, NJ)
T A S Graphics (Detroit, MI)
Times Printing (Random Lake, WI)
Tracor Publications (Austin, TX)
Tri-State Press (Clayton, GA)
Triangle Printing (Nashville, TN)
TSO General Corp (Long Island City, NY)
Twin City Printery (Lewiston, ME)
Universal Printing (Saint Louis, MO)
US Press (Valdosta, GA)
Van Volumes (Thorndike, MA)
Victor Graphics (Baltimore, MD)
Vogue Printers (North Chicago, IL)
Wallace Press (Hillside, IL)
Watkins Printing (Columbus, OH)
F A Weber & Sons (Park Falls, WI)
Wellesley Press (Framingham, MA)
West Side Graphics (New York, NY)
Western Publishers (Albuquerque, NM)
Western Web Printing (Sioux Falls, SD)
White Arts (Indianapolis, IN)
Wickersham Printing (Lancaster, PA)
Wolfer Printing (City of Commerce, CA)
Wood & Jones (Pasadena, CA)
World Color Press (New York, NY)
Henry Wurst Inc (N Kansas City, MO

Calendars

Adviser Graphics (Red Deer, AB)
Allied Printing (Akron, OH)
Apollo Graphics (Southampton, PA)
Arcata Graphics (Martinsburg, WV)
Argus Press (Niles, IL)
Bertelsmann Printing (New York, NY)
Blake Printery (San Luis Obispo, CA)
Bolger Publications (Minneapolis, MN)
Bradley Printing (Des Plaines, IL)
R L Bryan Company (Columbia, SC)

BSC Litho (Harrisburg, PA)
Camelot Fine (Albuquerque, NM)
Catalogue Service (New Rochelle, NY)
City Printing (North Haven, CT)
Colonial Graphics (Paterson, NJ)
Color World Printers (Bozeman, MT)
Colortone Press (Washington, DC)
Community Press (Provo, UT)
Comput-A-Print (Reno, NV)
Coneco Laser Graphics (Glen Falls, NY)
Copen Press (Brooklyn, NY)
Cornay Web Graphics (New Orleans, LA)
Country Press (Mohawk, NY)
Crusader Printing (East Saint Louis, IL)
Dataco (Albuquerque, NM)
Delmar Printing (Charlotte, NC)
Desaulniers Printing (Milan, IL)
Dharma Press (Oakland, CA)
Diamond Graphics (Milwaukee, WI)
Donihe Graphics (Kingsport, TN)
R R Donnelley (Crawfordsville, IN)
R R Donnelley (Chicago, IL)
Dynagraphics (Carlsbad, CA)
Edwards & Broughton (Raleigh, NC)
Eerdmans Printing (Grand Rapids, MI)
Faculty Press (Brooklyn, NY)
Fast Print (Fort Wayne, IN)
Federated Lithographers (Providence, RI)
Friesen Printers (Altona, MB)
Full Color Graphics (Plainview, NY)
Gateway Press (Louisville, KY)
General Offset (Jersey City, NJ)
Globe-Comm (San Antonio, TX)
Glundal Color Service (East Syracuse, NY)
Graphic Design (Center Line, MI)
Graphic Litho Corp (Lawrence, MA)
Grit Commercial Print (Williamsport, PA)
Guynes Printing (Albuquerque, NM)
Harlo Press (Detroit, MI)
Herbick & Held Printing (Pittsburgh, PA)
Hinz Lithographing (Mt Prospect, IL)
A B Hirschfeld Press (Denver, CO)
Holyoke Lithography (Springfield, MA)
Hunter Publishing (Winston-Salem, NC)
Infopress/Saratoga (Saratoga Springs, NY)
Inland Lithograph (Elk Grove Village, IL)
Intelligencer Printing (Lancaster, PA)
Interstate Printing (Omaha, NE)
Jersey Printing (Bayonne, NJ)
JohnsBryne Microdot (Niles, IL)
Jostens / Clarksville (Clarksville, TN)
Jostens / State College (State College, PA)
Jostens / Topeka (Topeka, KS)
Jostens / Visalia (Visalia, CA)
Julin Printing (Monticello, IA)
K/P Graphics (Escondido, CA)
Kaufman Press Printing (Syracuse, NY)
Kern International (Duxbury, MA)
Lawson Graphics (Toronto, ON)
Litho Specialties (Saint Paul, MN)
LithoCraft (Carlstadt, NJ)
John D Lucas Printing (Baltimore, MD)

Calendars

McClain Printing (Parson, WV)
McFarland Company (Harrisburg, PA)
McGrew Color (Kansas City, MO)
Mercury Printing (Memphis, TN)
Messenger Graphics (Phoenix, AZ)
Mideastern Printing (Brookfield, CT)
Mitchell-Shear (Ann Arbor, MI)
Moebius Printing (Milwaukee, WI)
Moran Colorgraphic (Baton Rouge, LA)
Morgan Press (Dobbs Ferry, NY)
Muller Printing (Santa Clara, CA)
MWM Dexter (Aurora, MO)
Nationwide Printing (Burlington, KY)
Neibauer Press (Warminster, PA)
Nielsen Lithographing (Cincinnati, OH)
Olympic Litho (Brooklyn, NY)
Omaha Printing (Omaha, NE)
Ortlieb Press (Baton Rouge, LA)
Paraclete Press (Orleans, MA)
Paust Inc (Richmond, IN)
Perlmuter Printing (Independence, OH)
Plain Talk Publishing (Des Moines, IA)
Plus Communications (Saint Louis, MO)
Preferred Graphics (Winona, MN)
Prinit Press (Dublin, IN)
Print Northwest (Tacoma, WA)
Printing Corp (Pompano Beach, FL)
Printing Dimensions (Beltsville, MD)
Progress Printing (Lynchburg, VA)
Quebecor America (New York, NY)
RBW Graphics (Owen Sound, ON)
Reproductions Inc (Rockville, MD)
Ringier America (Brookfield, WI)
Ringier America (Jonesboro, AR)
Ringier America (New Berlin, WI)
Ringier America (Phoenix, AZ)
Ringier America (Pontiac, IL)
Ringier America (Senatobia, MS)
Ronalds Printing (Vancouver, BC)
S Rosenthal & Company (Cincinnati, OH)
RPP Enterprises (Libertyville, IL)
Saint Joseph Printing (Toronto, ON)
R E Smith Printing (Fall River, MA)
Snohomish Publishing (Snohomish, WA)
Southeastern Printing (Stuart, FL)
Stinehour Press (Lunenburg, VT)
Straus Printing (Madison, WI)
John S Swift Company (Saint Louis, MO)
John S Swift (Chicago, IL)
John S Swift (Cincinnati, OH)
John S Swift (Teterboro, NJ)
T A S Graphics (Detroit, MI)
Technical Comm. (N Kansas City, MO)
Times Printing (Random Lake, WI)
Tri-Graphic Printing (Ottawa, ON)
Tri-State Press (Clayton, GA)
Twin City Printery (Lewiston, ME)
Wallace Press (Hillside, IL)
F A Weber & Sons (Park Falls, WI)
Wellesley Press (Framingham, MA)

Western Publishers (Albuquerque, NM)
Western Web Printing (Sioux Falls, SD)
Wisconsin Color Press (Milwaukee, WI)
Wolfer Printing (City of Commerce, CA)
Henry Wurst Inc (N Kansas City, MO)

Computer Documentation

While all the printers listed below print computer documentation (software and hardware manuals), the printers marked with an asterick (*) specialize in this area.

Advanced Duplicating (Edina, MN)
Alger Press Ltd (Oshawa, ON)
American Offset (Los Angeles, CA)
Americomp (Brattleboro, VT)
Arcata Graphics (Fairfield, PA)
Arcata Graphics (Kingsport, TN)
Arcata Graphics (Martinsburg, WV)
B & R Printing (Post Falls, ID)
Baker Johnson (Dexter, MI)
Banta Corporation (Menasha, WI)
Banta-Harrisonburg (Harrisonburg, VA)
Bawden Printing (Eldridge, IA)
Bay Port Press (National City, CA)
Beacon Wholesale Printing (Seattle, WA)
Bertelsmann Printing (New York, NY)
T H Best Printing (Don Mills, ON)
Bolger Publications (Minneapolis, MN)
Book Makers (Kenosha, WI)
The Book Press (Brattleboro, VT)
Book-Mart Press (North Bergen, NJ)
BookCrafters (Chelsea, MI)
BookCrafters (Fredericksburg, VA)
Booklet Publishing (Elk Grove Village, IL)
William Boyd Printing (Albany, NY)
Bradley Printing (Des Plaines, IL)
Brunswick Publishing (Lawrenceville, VA)
C & M Press (Thornton, CO) *
California Offset Printers (Glendale, CA)
Camelot Book (Ormond Beach, FL)
Camelot Fine Printing (Albuquerque, NM)
Capital Printing (Austin, TX)
Central Publishing (Indianapolis, IN)
Clarkwood Corporation (Totowa, NJ)
The College Press (Collegedale, TN)
Colonial Graphics (Paterson, NJ)
Color World Printers (Bozeman, MT)
Columbus Book Printers (Columbus, GA)
Commercial Printing (Medford, OR) *
Comput-A-Print (Reno, NV)
Coneco Laser Graphics (Glen Falls, NY)
Consolidated Printers (Berkeley, CA)
Corley Printing (Earth City, MO)
Country Press (Mohawk, NY)
Crusader Printing (East St Louis, IL)

Computer Documentation

Cushing-Malloy (Ann Arbor, MI)
D D Associates (Santa Clara, CA) *
Dataco (Albuquerque, NM)
Dellas Graphics (Syracuse, NY)
Delta Lithograph (Valencia, CA)
Dharma Press (Oakland, CA)
Diamond Graphics (Milwaukee, WI)
Diversified Printing (Brea, CA) *
Donihe Graphics (Kingsport, TN)
R R Donnelley (Crawfordsville, IN)
R R Donnelley (Chicago, IL)
R R Donnelley (Harrisonburg, VA)
R R Donnelley (Willard, OH)
East Village Enterprises (New York, NY)
Eastwood Printing (Denver, CO)
Economy Printing (Berne, IN)
Edison Press (Glen Rock, NJ)
Edwards Brothers (Ann Arbor, MI)
Edwards Brothers (Lillington, NC)
Eerdmans Printing (Grand Rapids, MI)
Eusey Press (Leominster, MA)
Faculty Press (Brooklyn, NY)
Federated Lithographers (Providence, RI)
Full Color Graphics (Plainview, NY)
Futura Printing (Boynton Beach, FL)
Gaylord Ltd (West Hollywood, CA)
General Offset Company (Jersey City, NJ)
George Lithograph (San Francisco, CA) *
Giant Horse (Daly City, CA)
Gilliland Printing (Arkansas City, KS)
Goodway Graphics (Springfield, VA)
Gorham Printing (Rochester, WA)
Graphic Printing (New Carlisle, OH)
Gray Printing (Fostoria, OH)
Griffin Printing (Glendale, CA)
Griffin Printing (Sacramento, CA)
GRT Book Printing (Oakland, CA)
Guynes Printing (Albuquerque, NM)
Haddon Craftsmen (Scranton, PA)
Harlo Press (Detroit, MI)
Heffernan Press (Worcester, MA)
A B Hirschfeld Press (Denver, CO)
Holyoke Lithography (Springfield, MA)
Hooven-Dayton Corp (Dayton, OH)
Hunter Publishing (Winston-Salem, NC)
Infopress/Saratoga (Saratoga Springs, NY)
Inland Lithograph (Elk Grove Village, IL)
Interstate Printers (Danville, IL)
The Job Shop (Woods Hole, MA)
Johnson & Hardin (Cincinnati, OH)
Johnson Publishing (Boulder, CO)
Jostens (Visalia, CA)
K/P Graphics (Escondido, CA)
Kaufman Press Printing (Syracuse, NY)
Kern International (Duxbury, MA)
KNI Book Manufacturing (Anaheim, CA)
Latham Process Corp (New York, NY)
Les Editions Marquis (Montmagny, PQ)
Lithocolor Press (Westchester, IL)
Mack Printing (Easton, PA)

Malloy Lithographing (Ann Arbor, MI)
Mark IV Press (Hauppauge, NY)
Marrakech Express (Tarpon Springs, FL)
Maverick Publications (Bend, OR)
The Mazer Corporation (Dayton, OH)
McClain Printing Company (Parson, WV)
McFarland Company (Harrisburg, PA)
McGregor & Werner (Washington, DC)
McNaughton & Gunn (Saline, MI)
Mercury Printing (Memphis, TN)
Messenger Graphics (Phoenix, AZ)
Mideastern Printing (Brookfield, CT)
Mitchell-Shear (Ann Arbor, MI)
Moran Colorgraphic (Baton Rouge, LA)
Morningrise Printing (Costa Mesa, CA)
Muller Printing (Santa Clara, CA)
Multiprint Inc (Chatham, NY)
Murray Printing (Kendallville, IN)
Murray Printing (Westford, MA)
National Reproductions (Livonia, MI)
Nationwide Printing (Burlington, KY)
Neibauer Press (Warminster, PA)
Nimrod Press (Boston, MA)
Noble Book Press (New York, NY)
Odyssey Press (Dover, NH)
Omnipress (Madison, WI) *
Optic Graphics (Glen Burnie, MD) *
Original Copy Centers (Cleveland, OH)
Ortlieb Press (Baton Rouge, LA)
Paust Inc (Richmond, IN)
PFP Printing (Gaithersburg, MD)
Phillips Brothers (Springfield, IL)
Plain Talk Publishing (Des Moines, IA)
Plus Communications (Saint Louis, MO)
Print Northwest (Tacoma, WA)
Printing Dimensions (Beltsville, MD)
Progress Printing (Lynchburg, VA)
ProLitho (Provo, UT) *
Publishers Press (Salt Lake City, UT)
Quebecor America (New York, NY)
Realtron Multi-Lith (Denver, CO) *
Recorder Sunset (San Francisco, CA)
Repro-Tech (West Patterson, NJ)
Reproductions Inc (Rockville, MD)
Ronalds Printing (Montreal, PQ)
Ronalds Printing (Vancouver, BC)
Rose Printing Company (Tallahassee, FL)
Saint Mary's Press (Hollywood, MD)
Schiff Printers (Pittsburgh, PA)
Science Press (Ephrata, PA)
Semline Inc (Braintree, MA)
Service Printing (San Leandro, CA) *
R E Smith Printing (Fall River, MA)
Snohomish Publishing (Snohomish, WA)
Southeastern Printing (Stuart, FL)
Staked Plains Press (Canyon, TX)
Technical Comm (Kansas City, MO) *
Thomson-Shore (Dexter, MI)
Times Printing (Random Lake, WI)
Todd Web Press (Smithville, TX)
Tri-Graphic Printing (Ottawa, ON)
Tri-State Press (Clayton, GA)

Computer Documentation

Triangle Printing (Nashville, TN)
TSO General Corp (Long Island City, NY)
Valco Graphics (Seattle, WA)
Van Volumes (Thorndike, MA)
Versa Press (East Peoria, IL)
Vicks Lithograph (Yorkville, NY)
Viking Press (Eden Prairie, MN) *
Wallace Press (Hillside, IL)
Webcom Ltd (Scarborough, ON)
Webcrafters (Madison, WI)
Wellesley Press (Framingham, MA)
Western Publishers (Albuquerque, NM)
Western Publishing (Racine, WI)
Western Web Printing (Sioux Falls, SD)
Westview Press (Boulder, CO)
White Arts (Indianapolis, IN)
Whitehall Printing (Wheeling, IL)
Wickersham Printing (Lancaster, PA) *
Williams Catello (Tualatin, OR)
Windsor Associates (San Diego, CA)
Wood & Jones (Pasadena, CA) *

Cookbooks

The companies noted with an asterick (*)
specialize in printing cookbooks for
fundraising organizations.

Academy Books (Rutland, VT)
Adams Press (Chicago, IL)
Adviser Graphics (Red Deer, AB)
Alger Press Ltd (Oshawa, ON)
American Printers (Chicago, IL)
Andover Press (New York, NY)
Apollo Graphics (Southampton, PA)
Arcata Graphics (Fairfield, PA)
Arcata Graphics (Kingsport, TN)
Arcata Graphics (Martinsburg, WV)
Atelier (New York, NY)
Automated Graphic (White Plains, MD)
B & R Printing (Post Falls, ID)
Baker Johnson (Dexter, MI)
Balan Printing (Brooklyn, NY)
Banta Corporation (Menasha, WI)
Bay Port Press (National City, CA)
Beacon Wholesale Printing (Seattle, WA)
Berryville Graphics (Berryville, VA)
Bertelsmann Printing (New York, NY)
T H Best Printing (Don Mills, ON)
Blake Printery (San Luis Obispo, CA)
Blue Dolphin Press (Grass Valley, CA)
Bolger Publications (Minneapolis, MN)
Book Makers Inc (Kenosha, WI)
The Book Press (Brattleboro, VT)
Book-Mart Press (North Bergen, NJ)
BookCrafters (Chelsea, MI)
BookCrafters (Fredericksburg, VA)
BookMasters (Ashland, OH)

William Boyd Printing (Albany, NY)
Braun-Brumfield (Ann Arbor, MI)
Brennan Printing (Deep River, IA) *
Brunswick (Lawrenceville, VA)
R L Bryan (Columbia, SC)
BSC Litho (Harrisburg, PA)
C & M Press (Thornton, CO)
Camelot Book (Ormond Beach, FL)
Camelot Fine (Albuquerque, NM)
Capital Printing (Austin, TX)
Centax of Canada (Regina, SK)
Central Publishing (Indianapolis, IN)
Cody Publications (Kissimmee, FL)
The College Press (Collegedale, TN)
Colonial Graphics (Paterson, NJ)
Color House Graphics (Grand Rapids MI)
Color World Printers (Bozeman, MT)
Colortone Press (Washington, DC)
Community Press (Provo, UT)
Comput-A-Print (Reno, NV)
Consolidated Printers (Berkeley, CA)
Cookbook Publishers (Olathe, KS) *
Cookbooks by Morris (Kearney, NE) *
Copen Press (Brooklyn, NY)
Copple House (Lakemont, GA)
Cornay Web Graphics (New Orleans, LA)
Country Press (Mohawk, NY)
Crane Duplicating (Barnstable, MA)
Crest Litho (Watervliet, NY)
Crusader Printing (East St Louis, IL)
Cushing-Malloy (Ann Arbor, MI)
D D Associates (Santa Clara, CA)
Daamen Printing (West Rutland, VT)
Delmar Printing Company (Charlotte, NC)
Delta Lithograph (Valencia, CA)
John Deyell Company (Lindsay, ON)
Diamond Graphics (Milwaukee, WI)
Donihe Graphics (Kingsport, TN)
R R Donnelley (Crawfordsville, IN)
R R Donnelley (Chicago, IL)
R R Donnelley (Harrisonburg, VA)
R R Donnelley, Willard (Willard, OH)
Economy Printing Concern (Berne, IN)
Edwards & Broughton (Raleigh, NC)
Edwards Brothers (Lillington, NC)
Eerdmans Printing (Grand Rapids, MI)
Evangel Press (Nappanee, IN)
Faculty Press (Brooklyn, NY)
Fast Print (Fort Wayne, IN)
Federated Lithographers (Providence, RI)
Fort Orange Press (Albany, NY)
Friesen Printers (Altona, MB)
Fundcraft (Collierville, TN) *
Futura Printing (Boynton Beach, FL)
Gagne Printing (Louiseville, PQ)
Gateway Press (Louisville, KY)
Gaylord Ltd (West Hollywood, CA)
General Offset (Jersey City, NJ)
Geryon Press (Tunnel, NY)
Giant Horse (Daly City, CA)
Gilliland Printing (Arkansas City, KS)
Goodway Graphics (Springfield, VA)

Cookbooks

Graphic Litho (Lawrence, MA)
The Gregath Company (Cullman, AL)
Griffin Printing (Glendale, CA)
Griffin Printing (Sacramento, CA)
Grit Commercial Print (Williamsport, PA)
GRT Book Printing (Oakland, CA)
Guynes Printing (Albuquerque, NM)
Haddon Craftsmen (Scranton, PA)
Harlin Litho (Ossining, NY)
Harlo Press (Detroit, MI)
Heritage Printers (Charlotte, NC)
A B Hirschfeld Press (Denver, CO)
Holyoke Lithography (Springfield, MA)
Hooven-Dayton Corp (Dayton, OH)
Horowitz/Rae (Fairfield, NJ)
Hunter Publishing (Winston-Salem, NC)
Independent Publishing (Sarasota, FL)
Infopress/Saratoga (Saratoga Springs, NY)
Inland Lithograph (Elk Grove Village, IL)
Interstate Printers (Danville, IL)
Johnson & Hardin (Cincinnati, OH)
Johnson Publishing (Boulder, CO)
Jostens (Clarksville, TN)
Jostens (State College, PA)
Jostens (Topeka, KS)
Jostens (Visalia, CA)
Julin Printing (Monticello, IA)
K/P Graphics (Escondido, CA)
Kern International (Duxbury, MA)
KNI Book Mfg (Anaheim, CA)
Les Editions Marquis (Montmagny, PQ)
Litho Specialties (St Paul, MN)
LithoCraft (Carlstadt, NJ)
Malloy Lithographing (Ann Arbor, MI)
Maple-Vail (York, PA)
Mark IV Press (Hauppauge, NY)
Marrakech Express (Tarpon Springs, FL)
Maverick Publications (Bend, OR)
The Mazer Corp (Dayton, OH)
McClain Printing (Parson, WV)
McNaughton & Gunn (Saline, MI)
Meaker the Printer (Phoenix, AZ)
Mercury Printing (Memphis, TN)
Messenger Graphics (Phoenix, AZ)
Mideastern Printing (Brookfield, CT)
Mitchell-Shear (Ann Arbor, MI)
Moran Colorgraphic (Baton Rouge, LA)
Murray Printing (Kendallville, IN)
Murray Printing (Westford, MA)
National Reproductions (Livonia, MI)
Naturegraph (Happy Camp, CA)
Neibauer Press (Warminster, PA)
Nimrod Press (Boston, MA)
Northlight Studio (Barre, VT)
Oaks Printing Company (Bethlehem, PA)
Omaha Printing (Omaha, NE)
Ortlieb Press (Baton Rouge, LA)
Paraclete Press (Orleans, MA)
Parker Graphics (Fuquay-Varina, NC)
PFP Printing Corp (Gaithersburg, MD)

Phillips Brothers (Springfield, IL)
Plain Talk Publishing (Des Moines, IA)
Preferred Graphics (Winona, MN)
Prinit Press (Dublin, IN)
Print Northwest (Tacoma, WA)
Progress Printing (Lynchburg, VA)
Publishers Press (Salt Lake City, UT)
Quebecor America (New York, NY)
Quintessence Press (Amador City, CA)
Quixott Press (Doylestown, PA)
Repro-Tech (West Patterson, NJ)
Reproductions Inc (Rockville, MD)
Ringier America (Itasca, IL)
Ronalds Printing (Montreal, PQ)
Rose Printing (Tallahassee, FL)
Roxbury Publishing (Los Angeles, CA)
Sabre Printers (Rogersville, TN)
Saint Croix Press (New Richmond, WI)
Science Press (Ephrata, PA)
Semline Inc (Braintree, MA)
The Sheridan Press (Hanover, PA)
Snohomish Publishing (Snohomish, WA)
Southeastern Printing (Stuart, FL)
Staked Plains Press (Canyon, TX)
Stewart Publishing (Marble Hill, MO)
Straus Printing (Madison, WI)
T A S Graphic (Detroit, MI)
Technical Comm. (Kansas City MO)
Thomson-Shore (Dexter, MI)
Times Litho (Forest Grove, OR)
Times Printing (Random Lake, WI)
S C Toof (Memphis, TN) *
Town House Press (Pittsboro, NC)
Tracor Publications (Austin, TX)
Tri-Graphic Printing (Ottawa, ON)
Tri-State Press (Clayton, GA)
Triangle Printing (Nashville, TN)
Twin City Printery (Lewiston, ME)
Vail Ballou (Binghamton, NY)
Valco Graphics (Seattle, WA)
Van Volumes (Thorndike, MA)
Victor Graphics (Baltimore, MD)
Vogue Printers (North Chicago, IL)
Walsworth Publishing (Marceline, MO)
Walter's Publishing (Waseca, MN) *
Web Specialties (Wheeling, IL)
Webcom Ltd (Scarborough, ON)
F A Weber (Park Falls, WI)
Wellesley Press (Framingham, MA)
Western Publishers (Albuquerque, NM)
Western Web Printing (Sioux Falls, SD)
Westview Press (Boulder, CO)
Whitehall Printing (Wheeling, IL)
Wickersham Printing (Lancaster, PA)
Williams Catello (Tualatin, OR)
Wimmer Brothers (Memphis, TN) *
Windsor Associates (San Diego, CA)
Wisconsin Color Press (Milwaukee, WI)
Worzalla Publishing (Stevens Point, WI)

Directories

Accurate Web (Central Islip, NY)
Ad Infinitum Press (Mount Vernon, NY)
The Adams Group (New York, NY)
Advanced Duplicating (Edina, MN)
Adviser Graphics (Red Deer, AB)
Alger Press Ltd (Oshawa, ON)
Alpine Press (Stoughton, MA)
American Offset (Los Angeles, CA)
Apollo Graphics (Southampton, PA)
Arcata Graphics (Fairfield, PA)
Arcata Graphics (Kingsport, TN)
Arcata Graphics (Martinsburg, WV)
Artcraft Press (Waterloo, WI)
Automated Graphics (White Plains, MD)
B & R Printing (Post Falls, ID)
Baker Johnson (Dexter, MI)
Balan Printing (Brooklyn, NY)
Banta Catalog Group (Saint Paul, MN)
Banta Corporation (Menasha, WI)
Banta-Harrisonburg (Harrisonburg, VA)
Bawden Printing (Eldridge, IA)
Bay Port Press (National City, CA)
Bertelsmann Printing (New York, NY)
Beslow Associates (Chicago, IL)
T H Best Printing (Don Mills, ON)
Blue Dolphin Press (Grass Valley, CA)
Bolger Publications (Minneapolis, MN)
Book Makers Inc (Kenosha, WI)
The Book Press (Brattleboro, VT)
Book-Mart Press (North Bergen, NJ)
BookCrafters (Chelsea, MI)
BookCrafters (Fredericksburg, VA)
Booklet Publishing (Elk Grove Village, IL)
BookMasters (Ashland, OH)
William Boyd Printing (Albany, NY)
Braceland Brothers (Philadelphia, PA)
Bradley Printing (Des Plaines, IL)
Braun-Brumfield (Ann Arbor, MI)
Brown Printing (Waseca, MN)
Brunswick Publishing (Lawrenceville, VA)
R L Bryan Company (Columbia, SC)
BSC Litho (Harrisburg, PA)
C & M Press (Thornton, CO)
Cal Central Press (Sacramento, CA)
California Offset (Glendale, CA)
Camelot Book (Ormond Beach, FL)
Camelot Fine (Albuquerque, NM)
Canterbury Press (Rome, NY)
Capital City Press (Montpelier, VT)
Capital Printing (Austin, TX)
Catalogue Publishing (Martinsburg, WV)
Central Publishing (Indianapolis, IN)
Cody Publications (Kissimmee, FL)
The College Press (Collegedale, TN)
Colonial Graphics (Paterson, NJ)
Color House (Grand Rapids, MI)
Color World Printers (Bozeman, MT)
Columbus Book Printers (Columbus, GA)
Community Press (Provo, UT)

Comput-A-Print (Reno, NV)
Coneco Laser Graphics (Glen Falls, NY)
Consolidated Printers (Berkeley, CA)
Martin Cook Associates (New York, NY)
Copen Press (Brooklyn, NY)
Copple House (Lakemont, GA)
Corley Printing (Earth City, MO)
Cornay Web Graphics (New Orleans, LA)
Country Press (Mohawk, NY)
Courier Corporation (Lowell, MA)
Crane Duplicating (West Barnstable, MA)
Crest Litho (Watervliet, NY)
Crusader Printing (East Saint Louis, IL)
Cushing-Malloy (Ann Arbor, MI)
D D Associates (Santa Clara, CA)
Dataco (Albuquerque, NM)
Delmar Printing (Charlotte, NC)
Delta Lithograph (Valencia, CA)
Des Plaines Publishing (Des Plaines, IL)
Desaulniers Printing (Milan, IL)
John Deyell Company (Lindsay, ON)
Dharma Press (Oakland, CA)
Diamond Graphics (Milwaukee, WI)
Dickinson Press (Grand Rapids, MI)
Dinner & Klein (Seattle, WA)
Diversified Printing (Brea, CA)
Dollco Printing (Ottawa, ON)
Donihe Graphics (Kingsport, TN)
R R Donnelley (Crawfordsville, IN)
R R Donnelley (Chicago, IL)
R R Donnelley (Harrisonburg, VA)
R R Donnelley (Willard, OH)
Dragon Press (Delta Junction, AK)
Dynagraphics (Carlsbad, CA)
East Village Enterprises (New York, NY)
Eastwood Printing (Denver, CO)
Economy Printing Concern (Berne, IN)
Edison Press (Glen Rock, NJ)
Edwards & Broughton (Raleigh, NC)
Edwards Brothers (Ann Arbor, MI)
Edwards Brothers (Lillington, NC)
Eerdmans Printing (Grand Rapids, MI)
Everton Publishers (Logan, UT)
Faculty Press (Brooklyn, NY)
Fast Print (Fort Wayne, IN)
Federated Lithographers (Providence, RI)
Fisher Web Printers (Cedar Rapids, IA)
Foote & Davies (Lincoln, NE)
Fort Orange Press (Albany, NY)
Four Corners Press (Grand Rapids, MI)
Full Color Graphics (Plainview, NY)
Futura Printing (Boynton Beach, FL)
Gagne Printing (Louiseville, PQ)
Ganis & Harris (New York, NY)
Gateway Press (Louisville, KY)
Gaylord Ltd (West Hollywood, CA)
George Lithograph (San Francisco, CA)
Germac Printing (Tigard, OR)
Giant Horse (Daly City, CA)
Gilliland Printing (Arkansas City, KS)
Gladstone Press (Ottawa, ON)
Globe-Comm (San Antonio, TX)

Directories

Glundal Color Service (East Syracuse, NY)
Goodway Graphics (Springfield, VA)
Gorham Printing (Rochester, WA)
Gowe Printing Company (Medina, OH)
Graftek Press (Woodstock, IL)
Graphic Design (Center Line, MI)
Graphic Litho Corp (Lawrence, MA)
Graphic Printing (New Carlisle, OH)
Gray Printing (Fostoria, OH)
The Gregath Company (Cullman, AL)
Griffin Printing (Glendale, CA)
Griffin Printing (Sacramento, CA)
Grit Commercial Print (Williamsport, PA)
GRT Book Printing (Oakland, CA)
GTE Directories (Des Plaines, IL)
Gulf Printing (Houston, TX)
Guynes Printing (Albuquerque, NM)
Haddon Craftsmen (Scranton, PA)
Hamilton Printing (Rensselaer, NY)
Harlin Litho (Ossining, NY)
Harlo Press (Detroit, MI)
Heart of the Lakes (Interlaken, NY)
Heartland Press (Spencer, IA)
Heffernan Press (Worcester, MA)
D B Hess Company (Woodstock, IL)
Hignell Printing (Winnepeg, MB)
Holladay-Tyler Printing (Glenn Dale, MD)
Holyoke Lithography (Springfield, MA)
Hooven-Dayton Corp (Dayton, OH)
Hunter Publishing (Winston-Salem, NC)
Independent Publishing (Sarasota, FL)
Infopress/Saratoga (Saratoga Springs, NY)
Inland Lithograph (Elk Grove Village, IL)
Interstate Printers (Danville, IL)
Jersey Printing (Bayonne, NJ)
The Job Shop (Woods Hole, MA)
Johnson & Hardin (Cincinnati, OH)
Johnson Graphics (East Dubuque, IL)
Johnson Publishing (Boulder, CO)
Jostens / Visalia (Visalia, CA)
Julin Printing (Monticello, IA)
K/P Graphics (Escondido, CA)
Kern International (Duxbury, MA)
KNI Book Manufacturing (Anaheim, CA)
Latham Process Corp (New York, NY)
Les Editions Marquis (Montmagny, PQ)
Liberty York Graphic (Hempstead, NY)
Litho Prestige (Drummondville, PQ)
Lithocolor Press (Westchester, IL)
Little River Press (Miami, FL)
Long Island Web (Jericho, NY)
John D Lucas Printing (Baltimore, MD)
Mack Printing (Easton, PA)
Mail-O-Graph (Kewanne, IL)
Malloy Lithographing (Ann Arbor, MI)
Mark IV Press (Hauppauge, NY)
Marrakech Express (Tarpon Springs, FL)
Maverick Publications (Bend, OR)
The Mazer Corporation (Dayton, OH)
McClain Printing (Parson, WV)

McDowell Publications (Utica, KY)
McFarland Company (Harrisburg, PA)
McGregor & Werner (Washington, DC)
McNaughton & Gunn (Saline, MI)
Meaker the Printer (Phoenix, AZ)
Mercury Printing (Memphis, TN)
Messenger Graphics (Phoenix, AZ)
Metromail Corporation (Lincoln, NE)
Mitchell Press (Vancouver, BC)
Mitchell-Shear (Ann Arbor, MI)
MMI Press (Harrisville, NH)
Monument Printers (Verplanck, NY)
Moran Colorgraphic (Baton Rouge, LA)
Morgan Printing (Austin, TX)
Multiprint Inc (Chatham, NY)
Murray Printing (Kendallville, IN)
Murray Printing (Westford, MA)
National Graphics (Columbus, OH)
National Publishing (Philadelphia, PA)
National Reproductions (Livonia, MI)
Neibauer Press (Warminster, PA)
Newsfoto Publishing (San Angelo, TX)
Neyenesch Printers (San Diego, CA)
Nimrod Press (Boston, MA)
Noll Printing Company (Huntington, IN)
North Plains Press (Aberdeen, SD)
Northlight Studio Press (Barre, VT)
Nystrom Publishing (Maple Grove, MN)
O'Neil Data Systems (Los Angeles, CA)
Oaks Printing Company (Bethlehem, PA)
Odyssey Press (Dover, NH)
Omnipress (Madison, WI)
Optic Graphics (Glen Burnie, MD)
Original Copy Centers (Cleveland, OH)
Ortlieb Press (Baton Rouge, LA)
Oxmoor Press (Birmingham, AL)
Pantagraph Printing (Bloomington, IL)
Paraclete Press (Orleans, MA)
Parker Graphics (Fuquay-Varina, NC)
Patterson Printing (Benton Harbor, MI)
Paust Inc (Richmond, IN)
Perry Printing (Waterloo, WI)
Perry/Baraboo (Baraboo, WI)
PFP Printing Corp (Gaithersburg, MD)
Phillips Brothers (Springfield, IL)
Pioneer Press (Wilmette, IL)
Plain Talk Publishing (Des Moines, IA)
Plus Communications (Saint Louis, MO)
Practical Graphics (New York, NY)
Preferred Graphics (Winona, MN)
Prinit Press (Dublin, IN)
Print Northwest (Tacoma, WA)
Printing Corp (Pompano Beach, FL)
Printing Dimensions (Beltsville, MD)
Progress Printing (Lynchburg, VA)
ProLitho (Provo, UT)
Publishers Press (Salt Lake City, UT)
Quebecor America (New York, NY)
Quinn-Woodbine (Woodbine, NJ)
Rapid Printing (Omaha, NE)
RBW Graphics (Owen Sound, ON)
Realtron Multi-Lith (Denver, CO)

Directories

Recorder Sunset (San Francisco, CA)
Repro-Tech (West Patterson, NJ)
Reproductions Inc (Rockville, MD)
Rich Printing Company (Nashville, TN)
Ringier America (Itasca, IL)
Rollins Press (Orlando, FL)
Ronalds Printing (Montreal, PQ)
Ronalds Printing (Vancouver, BC)
Rose Printing Company (Tallahassee, FL)
S Rosenthal & Company (Cincinnati, OH)
Roxbury Publishing (Los Angeles, CA)
Royle Printing (Sun Prairie, WI)
RPP Enterprises (Libertyville, IL)
Sabre Printers (Rogersville, TN)
Saint Croix Press (New Richmond, WI)
Saint Mary's Press (Hollywood, MD)
The Saybrook Press (Old Saybrook, CT)
Schiff Printers (Pittsburgh, PA)
Science Press (Ephrata, PA)
Semline Inc (Braintree, MA)
Service Printing (San Leandro, CA)
Sexton Printing (West Saint Paul, MN)
Shepard Poorman (Indianapolis, IN)
The Sheridan Press (Hanover, PA)
Skillful Means Press (Oakland, CA)
R E Smith Printing (Fall River, MA)
Snohomish Publishing (Snohomish, WA)
Southam Printing (Weston, ON)
Sowers Printing Company (Lebanon, PA)
Standard Printing (Chicago, IL)
Standard Publishing (Cincinnati, OH)
Stephenson Inc (Alexandria, VA)
Stewart Publishing (Marble Hill, MO)
Straus Printing (Madison, WI)
Suburban Publishers (Exeter, PA)
T A S Graphics (Detroit, MI)
Taylor Publishing (Dallas, TX)
Technical Comm. (N Kansas City, MO)
Telegraph Press (Harrisburg, PA)
Thomson-Shore (Dexter, MI)
Times Litho (Forest Grove, OR)
Times Printing (Random Lake, WI)
Todd Web Press (Smithville, TX)
Town House Press (Pittsboro, NC)
Tracor Publications (Austin, TX)
Tri-Graphic Printing (Ottawa, ON)
Tri-State Press (Clayton, GA)
Triangle Printing (Nashville, TN)
TSO General Corp (Long Island City, NY)
Twin City Printery (Lewiston, ME)
Universal Printing (Saint Louis, MO)
Valco Graphics (Seattle, WA)
Van Volumes (Thorndike, MA)
Victor Graphics (Baltimore, MD)
Viking Press (Eden Prairie, MN)
Vogue Printers (North Chicago, IL)
Volkmuth Printers (Saint Cloud, MN)
Waldon Press (New York, NY)
Wallace Press (Hillside, IL)
Walsworth Publishing (Marceline, MO)

Webcom Ltd (Scarborough, ON)
Webcrafters (Madison, WI)
F A Weber & Sons (Park Falls, WI)
Wellesley Press (Framingham, MA)
Western Publishers (Albuquerque, NM)
Western Web Printing (Sioux Falls, SD)
Westview Press (Boulder, CO)
Whitehall Printing (Wheeling, IL)
Wickersham Printing (Lancaster, PA)
Williams Catello Printing (Tualatin, OR)
Windsor Associates (San Diego, CA)
Wisconsin Color Press (Milwaukee, WI)
Wolfer Printing (City of Commerce, CA)
World Color Press (New York, NY)
Worzalla Publishing (Stevens Point, WI)
Henry Wurst Inc (N Kansas City, MO)
Yates Publishing (Ozark, MO)

Galley Copies

Those companies marked with an asterick (*) specialize in producing galley copies.

Ad Infinitum Press (Mount Vernon, NY) *
Americomp (Brattleboro, VT)
Arcata Graphics (Kingsport, TN)
Balan Printing (Brooklyn, NY)
Bertelsmann Printing (New York, NY)
Book Makers Inc (Kenosha, WI)
Camelot Book (Ormond Beach, FL)
Central Publishing (Indianapolis, IN)
Comput-A-Print (Reno, NV)
Country Press (Middleborough, MA) *
Country Press (Mohawk, NY)
Crane Duplicating (W Barnstable, MA) *
R R Donnelley (Crawfordsville, IN)
R R Donnelley (Chicago, IL)
East Village Enterprises (New York, NY)
Fort Orange Press (Albany, NY)
Foster Printing (Michigan City, IN)
Graphic Printing (New Carlisle, OH)
The Gregath Company (Cullman, AL)
Hunter Publishing (Winston-Salem, NC)
Independent Print. (Long Island City, NY)
Kern International (Duxbury, MA)
Kimberly Press (Santa Barbara, CA)
Mark IV Press (Hauppauge, NY)
The Mazer Corporation (Dayton, OH)
McGregor & Werner (Washington, DC)
Monument Printers (Verplanck, NY)
Moran Colorgraphic (Baton Rouge, LA)
Multiprint Inc (Chatham, NY)
National Reproductions (Livonia, MI)
Neibauer Press (Warminster, PA)
Northlight Studio Press (Barre, VT)
Oaks Printing Company (Bethlehem, PA)
Odyssey Press (Dover, NH)
Omnipress (Madison, WI)
PFP Printing Corp (Gaithersburg, MD)
Progress Printing (Lynchburg, VA)

Galley Copies

Repro-Tech (West Patterson, NJ)
Saint Mary's Press (Hollywood, MD)
T A S Graphics (Detroit, MI)
Times Printing (Random Lake, WI)
Van Volumes (Thorndike, MA)
Western Web Printing (Sioux Falls, SD)
Westview Press (Boulder, CO)

Genealogies

The following small companies specialize in printing genealogies and family histories for individuals. Of course, many of the other printers who manufacture books can also print genealogies.

Anundsen Publishing Co. (Decorah, IA)
Everton Publishers (Logan, UT)
Gateway Press (Baltimore, MD)
The Gregath Company (Cullman, AL)
Hawkes Publishing (Salt Lake City, UT)
Heart of the Lakes (Interlaken, NY)
Henington Publishing (Wolfe City, TX)
McDowell Publications (Utica, KY)
Yates Publishing Company (Ozark, MO)
Ye Olde Genealogie (Indianapolis, IN)

Journals

Academy Books (Rutland, VT)
Ad Infinitum Press (Mount Vernon, NY)
Adams Press (Chicago, IL)
Adviser Graphics (Red Deer, AB)
Allen Press (Lawrence, KS)
American Offset (Los Angeles, CA)
American Web Offset (Denver, CO)
Americomp (Brattleboro, VT)
Arcata Graphics (Kingsport, TN)
Arcata Graphics (Martinsburg, WV)
Artex Publishing (Stevens Point, WI)
Automated Graphics (White Plains, MD)
Baker Johnson (Dexter, MI)
Balan Printing (Brooklyn, NY)
Beacon Press (Richmond, VA)
Beslow Associates (Chicago, IL)
Blake Printery (San Luis Obispo, CA)
Bolger Publications (Minneapolis, MN)
Book-Mart Press (North Bergen, NJ)
BookCrafters (Chelsea, MI)
BookCrafters (Fredericksburg, VA)
BookMasters (Ashland, OH)
William Boyd Printing (Albany, NY)
Braceland Brothers (Philadelphia, PA)
Braun-Brumfield (Ann Arbor, MI)
Brown Printing (Waseca, MN)
Brown Printing (East Greenville, PA)

R L Bryan Company (Columbia, SC)
William Byrd Press (Richmond, VA)
Camelot Fine Printing (Albuquerque, NM)
Canterbury Press (Rome, NY)
Capital City Press (Montpelier, VT)
Capital Printing (Austin, TX)
Central Publishing (Indianapolis, IN)
Coach House Press (Toronto, ON)
Cody Publications (Kissimmee, FL)
Colonial Graphics (Paterson, NJ)
Color World Printers (Bozeman, MT)
Columbus Book Printers (Columbus, GA)
Combined Comm. (Columbia, MO)
Combined Communication (Mendota, IL)
Community Press (Provo, UT)
Coneco Laser Graphics (Glen Falls, NY)
Copple House (Lakemont, GA)
Cornay Web Graphics (New Orleans, LA)
Country Press (Mohawk, NY)
Crane Duplicating (West Barnstable, MA)
Crest Litho (Watervliet, NY)
Crusader Printing (East Saint Louis, IL)
Cummings Printing (Manchester, NH)
Cushing-Malloy (Ann Arbor, MI)
D D Associates (Santa Clara, CA)
Daamen Printing (West Rutland, VT)
Dataco (Albuquerque, NM)
Delta Lithograph (Valencia, CA)
Desaulniers Printing (Milan, IL)
John Deyell Company (Lindsay, ON)
Dharma Press (Oakland, CA)
Dollco Printing (Ottawa, ON)
R R Donnelley (Crawfordsville, IN)
R R Donnelley (Chicago, IL)
Dragon Press (Delta Junction, AK)
East Village Enterprises (New York, NY)
Ebsco Media (Birmingham, AL)
Edwards & Broughton (Raleigh, NC)
Edwards Brothers (Ann Arbor, MI)
Edwards Brothers (Lillington, NC)
Evangel Press (Nappanee, IN)
Faculty Press (Brooklyn, NY)
Fisher Web Printers (Cedar Rapids, IA)
Fort Orange Press (Albany, NY)
Four Corners Press (Grand Rapids, MI)
Friesen Printers (Altona, MB)
Full Color Graphics (Plainview, NY)
Ganis & Harris (New York, NY)
Gaylord Ltd (West Hollywood, CA)
George Lithograph (San Francisco, CA)
Giant Horse (Daly City, CA)
Gilliland Printing (Arkansas City, KS)
Gladstone Press (Ottawa, ON)
Goodway Graphics (Springfield, VA)
Graftek Press (Woodstock, IL)
Graphic Printing (New Carlisle, OH)
Gray Printing (Fostoria, OH)
The Gregath Company (Cullman, AL)
Griffin Printing (Glendale, CA)
GRT Book Printing (Oakland, CA)
Hamilton Printing (Rensselaer, NY)
Heart of the Lakes (Interlaken, NY)

Journals

Heartland Press (Spencer, IA)
Heffernan Press (Worcester, MA)
Heritage Printers (Charlotte, NC)
Hignell Printing (Winnepeg, MB)
A B Hirschfeld Press (Denver, CO)
Holladay-Tyler Printing (Glenn Dale, MD)
Hooven-Dayton Corp (Dayton, OH)
Hunter Publishing (Winston-Salem, NC)
Independent Print. (Long Island City, NY)
Infopress/Saratoga (Saratoga Springs, NY)
Jersey Printing (Bayonne, NJ)
Johnson & Hardin (Cincinnati, OH)
Johnson Publishing (Boulder, CO)
Jostens / Visalia (Visalia, CA)
Kaufman Press Printing (Syracuse, NY)
Kimberly Press (Santa Barbara, CA)
KNI Book Manufacturing (Anaheim, CA)
Lancaster Press (Lancaster, PA)
The Lane Press (Burlington, VT)
Latham Process Corp (New York, NY)
Liberty York Graphic (Hempstead, NY)
Little River Press (Miami, FL)
John D Lucas Printing (Baltimore, MD)
Mack Printing (Easton, PA)
Mackintosh Typo. (Santa Barbara, CA)
Maclean Hunter (Willowdale, ON)
The Mad Printers (Mattituck, NY)
Mail-O-Graph (Kewanne, IL)
Malloy Lithographing (Ann Arbor, MI)
Mariposa Press (Benicia, CA)
Marrakech Express (Tarpon Springs, FL)
The Mazer Corporation (Dayton, OH)
McClain Printing Company (Parson, WV)
McFarland Company (Harrisburg, PA)
McGregor & Werner (Washington, DC)
McNaughton & Gunn (Saline, MI)
Meaker the Printer (Phoenix, AZ)
Messenger Graphics (Phoenix, AZ)
Metroweb (Erlanger, KY)
Mitchell Press (Vancouver, BC)
Mitchell-Shear (Ann Arbor, MI)
Moran Colorgraphic (Baton Rouge, LA)
Morgan Press (Dobbs Ferry, NY)
Motheral Printing (Fort Worth, TX)
Muller Printing (Santa Clara, CA)
Multiprint Inc (Chatham, NY)
National Reproductions (Livonia, MI)
Nationwide Printing (Burlington, KY)
Neibauer Press (Warminster, PA)
Neyenesch Printers (San Diego, CA)
Nimrod Press (Boston, MA)
Noll Printing Company (Huntington, IN)
North Plains Press (Aberdeen, SD)
Nystrom Publishing (Maple Grove, MN)
Oaks Printing Company (Bethlehem, PA)
Odyssey Press (Dover, NH)
Omnipress (Madison, WI)
Ortlieb Press (Baton Rouge, LA)
Ovid Bell Press (Fulton, MO)
Oxford Group (Norway, ME)

Oxford Group (Berlin, NH)
Pantagraph Printing (Bloomington, IL)
Patterson Printing (Benton Harbor, MI)
PennWell Printing (Tulsa, OK)
Perry Printing (Waterloo, WI)
Perry/Baraboo (Baraboo, WI)
PFP Printing Corp (Gaithersburg, MD)
Plain Talk Publishing (Des Moines, IA)
Plus Communications (Saint Louis, MO)
Port City Press (Pikesville, MD)
Port Publications (Port Washington, WI)
Practical Graphics (New York, NY)
Preferred Graphics (Winona, MN)
Printing Corp (Pompano Beach, FL)
Printing Dimensions (Beltsville, MD)
Progress Printing (Lynchburg, VA)
Progressive Typographers (Emigsville, PA)
Publishers Press (Salt Lake City, UT)
Publishers Printing (Shepherdsville, KY)
Quinn-Woodbine (Woodbine, NJ)
Realtron Multi-Lith (Denver, CO)
Regensteiner Press (West Chicago, IL)
Reproductions Inc (Rockville, MD)
Rich Printing Company (Nashville, TN)
Ringier America (Itasca, IL)
Rollins Press (Orlando, FL)
Ronalds Printing (Montreal, PQ)
Ronalds Printing (Vancouver, BC)
S Rosenthal & Company (Cincinnati, OH)
Sabre Printers (Rogersville, TN)
Saint Croix Press (New Richmond, WI)
Saint Mary's Press (Hollywood, MD)
The Saybrook Press (Old Saybrook, CT)
Schumann Printers (Fall River, WI)
Science Press (Ephrata, PA)
Sexton Printing (West Saint Paul, MN)
Shepard Poorman (Indianapolis, IN)
The Sheridan Press (Hanover, PA)
Skillful Means Press (Oakland, CA)
Smith-Edwards-Dunlap (Phildelphia, PA)
Southam Printing (Weston, ON)
Southern Tennessee (Waynesboro, TN)
Sowers Printing (Lebanon, PA)
Speaker-Hines & Thomas (Lansing, MI)
Standard Publishing (Cincinnati, OH)
Stephenson Inc (Alexandria, VA)
Stewart Publishing (Marble Hill, MO)
Stinehour Press (Lunenburg, VT)
The Studley Press (Dalton, MA)
Sweet Printing (Round Rock, TX)
T A S Graphics (Detroit, MI)
Technical Comm. (N Kansas City, MO)
Thomson-Shore (Dexter, MI)
Times Printing (Random Lake, WI)
Town House Press (Pittsboro, NC)
Tracor Publications (Austin, TX)
Tri-Graphic Printing (Ottawa, ON)
Tri-State Press (Clayton, GA)
Twin City Printery (Lewiston, ME)
United Color (Monroe, OH)
Universal Printing (Saint Louis, MO)
Valco Graphics (Seattle, WA)

Journals

Van Volumes (Thorndike, MA)
Vicks Lithograph (Yorkville, NY)
Victor Graphics (Baltimore, MD)
Volkmuth Printers (Saint Cloud, MN)
Waldman Graphics (Pennsauken, NJ)
Waldon Press (New York, NY)
Walsworth Publishing (Marceline, MO)
Waverly Press (Baltimore, MD)
The Webb Company (Saint Paul, MN)
Webcom Ltd (Scarborough, ON)
Wellesley Press (Framingham, MA)
West Side Graphics (New York, NY)
Western Publishers (Albuquerque, NM)
Western Web Printing (Sioux Falls, SD)
Westview Press (Boulder, CO)
Wisconsin Color Press (Milwaukee, WI)

Maps

American Printers (Chicago, IL)
Arcata Graphics (Martinsburg, WV)
Banta Catalog Group (Saint Paul, MN)
Harold Berliner Printer (Nevada City, CA)
Bradley Printing (Des Plaines, IL)
Brown Printing (Waseca, MN)
R L Bryan Company (Columbia, SC)
Camelot Fine Printing (Albuquerque, NM)
Colonial Graphics (Paterson, NJ)
Connecticut Printers (Bloomfield, CT)
Continental Web (Itasca, IL)
Cornay Web Graphics (New Orleans, LA)
Delta Lithograph (Valencia, CA)
Dharma Press (Oakland, CA)
Dollco Printing (Ottawa, ON)
Donihe Graphics (Kingsport, TN)
R R Donnelley (Crawfordsville, IN)
R R Donnelley (Chicago, IL)
Eastwood Printing (Denver, CO)
Einson Freeman Graphics (Fairlawn, NJ)
Faculty Press (Brooklyn, NY)
Federated Lithographers (Providence, RI)
Fisher Web Printers (Cedar Rapids, IA)
Gateway Press (Louisville, KY)
Gaylord Printing (Detroit, MI)
General Offset (Jersey City, NJ)
Gladstone Press (Ottawa, ON)
Graphic Litho Corp (Lawrence, MA)
The Gregath Company (Cullman, AL)
Grit Commercial Print (Williamsport, PA)
Harlin Litho (Ossining, NY)
Hinz Lithographing (Mt Prospect, IL)
A B Hirschfeld Press (Denver, CO)
Infopress/Saratoga (Saratoga Springs, NY)
Inland Lithograph (Elk Grove Village, IL)
Interstate Printing (Omaha, NE)
Julin Printing (Monticello, IA)
Kaufman Press Printing (Syracuse, NY)
Kern International (Duxbury, MA)

Lehigh Press (Broadview, IL)
The Lehigh Press (Pennsauken, NJ)
Les Editions Marquis (Montmagny, PQ)
McFarland Company (Harrisburg, PA)
Meehan-Tooker (E Rutherford, NJ)
Mercury Printing (Memphis, TN)
Messenger Graphics (Phoenix, AZ)
Mideastern Printing (Brookfield, CT)
National Graphics Corp (Columbus, OH)
Neyenesch Printers (San Diego, CA)
Nystrom Publishing (Maple Grove, MN)
Oaks Printing Company (Bethlehem, PA)
Paraclete Press (Orleans, MA)
Paust Inc (Richmond, IN)
Preferred Graphics (Winona, MN)
The Press (Chanhassen, MN)
Print Northwest (Tacoma, WA)
Progress Printing (Lynchburg, VA)
Quad/Graphics (Lomira, WI)
Quad/Graphics (Pewaukee, WI)
Quad/Graphics (Saratoga Springs, NY)
Quad/Graphics (Sussex, WI)
Quebecor America (New York, NY)
Ringier America (Corinth, MS)
Ronalds Printing (Vancouver, BC)
Southeastern Printing (Stuart, FL)
Stephenson Inc (Alexandria, VA)
Straus Printing (Madison, WI)
Sweet Printing (Round Rock, TX)
John S Swift Company (Saint Louis, MO)
John S Swift (Chicago, IL)
John S Swift (Cincinnati, OH)
John S Swift (Teterboro, NJ)
T A S Graphics (Detroit, MI)
Times Printing (Random Lake, WI)
Tri-State Press (Clayton, GA)
Twin City Printery (Lewiston, ME)
Valco Graphics (Seattle, WA)
F A Weber & Sons (Park Falls, WI)
Western Publishers (Albuquerque, NM)
Western Web Printing (Sioux Falls, SD)
Wimmer Brothers (Memphis, TN)
Ye Olde Genealogie (Indianapolis, IN)

Mass-Market Paperbacks

American Offset (Los Angeles, CA)
Arcata Graphics (Depew, NY) *
Arcata Graphics (Martinsburg, WV) *
Balan Printing (Brooklyn, NY)
Banta Corporation (Menasha, WI) *
Bertelsmann Printing (New York, NY) *
BookMasters (Ashland, OH)
C & M Press (Thornton, CO)
Country Press (Mohawk, NY)
Crusader Printing (East Saint Louis, IL)
Dickinson Press (Grand Rapids, MI)

Mass Market Paperbacks

R R Donnelley (Crawfordsville, IN)
R R Donnelley (Chicago, IL)
Eerdmans Printing (Grand Rapids, MI) *
Fort Orange Press (Albany, NY)
Gagne Printing (Louiseville, PQ)
Gilliland Printing (Arkansas City, KS)
Golden Horn Press (Berkeley, CA)
The Gregath Company (Cullman, AL)
Griffin Printing (Glendale, CA)
Guynes Printing (Albuquerque, NM)
Interstate Printers (Danville, IL)
Litho Prestige (Drummondville, PQ)
Lithocolor Press (Westchester, IL)
Little River Press (Miami, FL)
Mark IV Press (Hauppauge, NY)
Messenger Graphics (Phoenix, AZ)
MMI Press (Harrisville, NH)
Moebius Printing (Milwaukee, WI)
Noll Printing Company (Huntington, IN)
Offset Paperback (Dallas, PA) *
Paraclete Press (Orleans, MA)
Princeton Univ. Press (Lawrenceville, NJ)
Publishers Press (Salt Lake City, UT)
Quad Graphics (Thomaston, GA) *
Ringier America (Itasca, IL)
Ringier America (Dresden, TN) *
Ronalds Printing (Montreal, PQ)
Ronalds Printing (Toronto, ON)
Roxbury Publishing (Los Angeles, CA)
Stewart Publishing (Marble Hill, MO)
Todd Web Press (Smithville, TX)
Universal Printers (Winnipeg, MB)
Versa Press (East Peoria, IL)
Webcom (Scarborough, ON)
Western Web Printing (Sioux Falls, SD)

Postcards

Ad Color (Port Chester, NY)
Adviser Graphics (Red Deer, AB)
Algen Press Corp (College Point, NY)
American Color Printing (Plantation, FL)
Amidon Graphics (Saint Paul, MN)
Argus Press (Niles, IL)
Arizona Lithographers (Tucson, AZ)
Artcraft Press (Waterloo, WI)
B & R Printing (Post Falls, ID)
Bay Port Press (National City, CA)
Beacon Wholesale Printing (Seattle, WA)
Blake Printery (San Luis Obispo, CA)
Blue Dolphin Press (Grass Valley, CA)
Bolger Publications (Minneapolis, MN)
Bradley Printing (Des Plaines, IL)
Brookshore Litho (Elk Grove Village, IL)
BSC Litho (Harrisburg, PA)
Camelot Fine Printing (Albuquerque, NM)
Capital Printing (Austin, TX)
Catalogue Publishing (Martinsburg, WV)

Coach House Press (Toronto, ON)
Color World Printers (Bozeman, MT)
Comput-A-Print (Reno, NV)
Continental Web (Itasca, IL)
Copple House (Lakemont, GA)
Cornay Web Graphics (New Orleans, LA)
Country Press (Mohawk, NY)
Dataco (Albuquerque, NM)
Dellas Graphics (Syracuse, NY)
Dharma Press (Oakland, CA)
Diamond Graphics (Milwaukee, WI)
Direct Press (Huntington Station, NY)
Dollco Printing (Ottawa, ON)
Donihe Graphics (Kingsport, TN)
E & D Web (Cicero, IL)
Eagle Web Press (Salem, OR)
East Village Enterprises (New York, NY)
Edwards & Broughton (Raleigh, NC)
Fast Print (Fort Wayne, IN)
Full Color Graphics (Plainview, NY)
Geryon Press (Tunnel, NY)
Gladstone Press (Ottawa, ON)
Globe-Comm (San Antonio, TX)
Graphic Litho Corp (Lawrence, MA)
The Gregath Company (Cullman, AL)
Guynes Printing (Albuquerque, NM)
Harlin Litho (Ossining, NY)
Harlo Press (Detroit, MI)
A B Hirschfeld Press (Denver, CO)
Hunter Publishing (Winston-Salem, NC)
Infopress/Saratoga (Saratoga Springs, NY)
Interstate Printing (Omaha, NE)
Jersey Printing (Bayonne, NJ)
The Job Shop (Woods Hole, MA)
Jostens / Visalia (Visalia, CA)
Julin Printing (Monticello, IA)
K/P Graphics (Escondido, CA)
Kaufman Press Printing (Syracuse, NY)
Lehigh Press (Broadview, IL)
Lehigh Press (Dallas, TX)
The Lehigh Press (Pennsauken, NJ)
Longacrea Press (New Rochelle, NY)
John D Lucas Printing (Baltimore, MD)
Mackintosh Typo. (Santa Barbara, CA)
McGrew Color (Kansas City, MO)
Meaker the Printer (Phoenix, AZ)
Mercury Printing (Memphis, TN)
Messenger Graphics (Phoenix, AZ)
Mitchell-Shear (Ann Arbor, MI)
Moebius Printing (Milwaukee, WI)
Morgan Press (Dobbs Ferry, NY)
MultiPrint Company (Skokie, IL)
Murphy's Printing (Campbell, CA)
MWM Dexter (Aurora, MO)
Nationwide Printing (Burlington, KY)
Nielsen Lithographing (Cincinnati, OH)
Oaks Printing (Bethlehem, PA)
Olympic Litho (Brooklyn, NY)
Omaha Printing (Omaha, NE)
Ortlieb Press (Baton Rouge, LA)
Outstanding Graphics (Kenosha, WI)
PAK Discount Printing (Zion, IL)

Postcards

Paust Inc (Richmond, IN)
Perlmuter Printing (Independence, OH)
PFP Printing Corp (Gaithersburg, MD)
Plain Talk Publishing (Des Moines, IA)
Practical Graphics (New York, NY)
Preferred Graphics (Winona, MN)
The Press (Chanhassen, MN)
Prinit Press (Dublin, IN)
Print Northwest (Tacoma, WA)
Printing Corp (Pompano Beach, FL)
Printing Dimensions (Beltsville, MD)
Progress Printing (Lynchburg, VA)
ProLitho (Provo, UT)
Quintessence Press (Amador City, CA)
Quixott Press (Doylestown, PA)
Reproductions Inc (Rockville, MD)
Royle Printing (Sun Prairie, WI)
Skillful Means Press (Oakland, CA)
R E Smith Printing (Fall River, MA)
Southeastern Printing (Stuart, FL)
Stewart Publishing (Marble Hill, MO)
Stinehour Press (Lunenburg, VT)
Straus Printing Company (Madison, WI)
John S Swift Company (Saint Louis, MO)
John S Swift (Chicago, IL)
John S Swift (Cincinnati, OH)
T A S Graphics (Detroit, MI)
Times Printing (Random Lake, WI)
Triangle Printing (Nashville, TN)
TSO General Corp (Long Island City, NY)
Twin City Printery (Lewiston, ME)
US Press (Valdosta, GA)
Vogue Printers (North Chicago, IL)
Web Specialties (Wheeling, IL)
F A Weber & Sons (Park Falls, WI)
Wellesley Press (Framingham, MA)
West Side Graphics (New York, NY)
Western Publishers (Albuquerque, NM)
Western Web Printing (Sioux Falls, SD)
White Arts (Indianapolis, IN)

Posters

The Adams Group (New York, NY)
Adviser Graphics (Red Deer, AB)
Algen Press Corp (College Point, NY)
American Color Printing (Plantation, FL)
American Printers (Chicago, IL)
American Signature (Dallas, TX)
American Signature (Costa Mesa, CA)
American Signature (New York, NY)
American Signature (Memphis, TN)
Apollo Graphics (Southampton, PA)
Argus Press (Niles, IL)
Artcraft Press (Waterloo, WI)
Balan Printing (Brooklyn, NY)
Banta Catalog Group (Saint Paul, MN)
Bell Publications (Iowa City, IA)

Harold Berliner Printer (Nevada City, CA)
Bertelsmann Printing (New York, NY)
Blake Printery (San Luis Obispo, CA)
Blue Dolphin Press (Grass Valley, CA)
Bolger Publications (Minneapolis, MN)
Bradley Printing (Des Plaines, IL)
Brookshore Litho (Elk Grove Village, IL)
Brown Printing (Waseca, MN)
R L Bryan Company (Columbia, SC)
Cal Central Press (Sacramento, CA)
Camelot Book (Ormond Beach, FL)
Camelot Fine Printing (Albuquerque, NM)
Capital Printing (Austin, TX)
Catalogue Service (New Rochelle, NY)
Coach House Press (Toronto, ON)
Colonial Graphics (Paterson, NJ)
Color Express (Irvine, CA)
Color Express (Minneapolis, MN)
Color Express (Atlanta, GA)
Color Express (Los Angeles, CA)
Chicago Color Express (Chicago, IL)
Chicago Color Express (Westmont, IL)
Color World Printers (Bozeman, MT)
ColorGraphics (Tulsa, OK)
Colortone Press (Washington, DC)
Community Press (Provo, UT)
Comput-A-Print (Reno, NV)
Coneco Laser Graphics (Glen Falls, NY)
Continental Web (Itasca, IL)
Martin Cook Associates (New York, NY)
Copple House (Lakemont, GA)
Country Press (Mohawk, NY)
Creative Web Systems (Inglewood, CA)
Crusader Printing (East Saint Louis, IL)
Dataco (Albuquerque, NM)
Dellas Graphics (Syracuse, NY)
Delta Lithograph (Valencia, CA)
Desaulniers Printing (Milan, IL)
Dharma Press (Oakland, CA)
Diamond Graphics (Milwaukee, WI)
Direct Press (Huntington Station, NY)
Dollco Printing (Ottawa, ON)
Donihe Graphics (Kingsport, TN)
E & D Web (Cicero, IL)
Eagle Web Press (Salem, OR)
East Village Enterprises (New York, NY)
Eastwood Printing (Denver, CO)
Edison Lithographing (North Bergen, NJ)
Edwards & Broughton (Raleigh, NC)
Einson Freeman Graphics (Fairlawn, NJ)
Faculty Press (Brooklyn, NY)
Fast Print (Fort Wayne, IN)
Federated Lithographers (Providence, RI)
Fisher Web Printers (Cedar Rapids, IA)
Fleetwood Litho (New York, NY)
Flower City Printing (Rochester, NY)
Fort Orange Press (Albany, NY)
Foster Printing (Michigan City, IN)
Full Color Graphics (Plainview, NY)
Gateway Press (Louisville, KY)
Gaylord Printing (Detroit, MI)
General Offset (Jersey City, NJ)

Posters

Geryon Press (Tunnel, NY)
Giant Horse (Daly City, CA)
Gladstone Press (Ottawa, ON)
Globe-Comm (San Antonio, TX)
Glundal Color Service (East Syracuse, NY)
Graphic Litho Corp (Lawrence, MA)
Gray Printing (Fostoria, OH)
The Gregath Company (Cullman, AL)
Gulf Printing (Houston, TX)
Guynes Printing (Albuquerque, NM)
Harlin Litho (Ossining, NY)
Harlo Press (Detroit, MI)
Hennegan Company (Cincinnati, OH)
Herbick & Held Printing (Pittsburgh, PA)
Hi-Tech Color House (Chicago, IL)
Hinz Lithographing (Mt Prospect, IL)
A B Hirschfeld Press (Denver, CO)
Hunter Publishing (Winston-Salem, NC)
Infopress/Saratoga (Saratoga Springs, NY)
Inland Lithograph (Elk Grove Village, IL)
Intelligencer Printing (Lancaster, PA)
Interstate Printing (Omaha, NE)
Jersey Printing (Bayonne, NJ)
JohnsBryne Microdot (Niles, IL)
Jostens / Clarksville (Clarksville, TN)
Jostens / State College (State College, PA)
Jostens / Topeka (Topeka, KS)
Jostens / Visalia (Visalia, CA)
Julin Printing (Monticello, IA)
K & S Graphics (Nashville, TN)
K/P Graphics (Escondido, CA)
Kaufman Press (Syracuse, NY)
Lasky Company (Milburn, NJ)
Lehigh Press (Broadview, IL)
Lehigh Press (Dallas, TX)
The Lehigh Press (Pennsauken, NJ)
Les Editions Marquis (Montmagny, PQ)
Litho Specialties (Saint Paul, MN)
LithoCraft (Carlstadt, NJ)
Longacrea Press (New Rochelle, NY)
John D Lucas Printing (Baltimore, MD)
Mackintosh Typo. (Santa Barbara, CA)
The Mazer Corporation (Dayton, OH)
McClain Printing (Parson, WV)
McFarland Company (Harrisburg, PA)
McGrew Color (Kansas City, MO)
Meaker the Printer (Phoenix, AZ)
Meehan-Tooker (E Rutherford, NJ)
Mercury Printing (Memphis, TN)
Messenger Graphics (Phoenix, AZ)
Mideastern Printing (Brookfield, CT)
Mitchell Graphics (Petoskey, MI)
Mitchell-Shear (Ann Arbor, MI)
Moebius Printing (Milwaukee, WI)
Moran Colorgraphic (Baton Rouge, LA)
Morgan Press (Dobbs Ferry, NY)
Morgan Printing (Austin, TX)
Motheral Printing (Fort Worth, TX)
Muller Printing (Santa Clara, CA)
MultiPrint Company (Skokie, IL)

Murphy's Printing (Campbell, CA)
MWM Dexter (Aurora, MO)
National Bickford (Providence, RI)
National Graphics (Columbus, OH)
Nationwide Printing (Burlington, KY)
Neibauer Press (Warminster, PA)
Neyenesch Printers (San Diego, CA)
Nielsen Lithographing (Cincinnati, OH)
Noll Printing (Huntington, IN)
Oaks Printing (Bethlehem, PA)
Ohio Valley Litho (Florence, KY)
Olympic Litho (Brooklyn, NY)
Omaha Printing (Omaha, NE)
Ortlieb Press (Baton Rouge, LA)
Outstanding Graphics (Kenosha, WI)
Pacific Lithograph (San Francisco, CA)
PAK Discount Printing (Zion, IL)
Paraclete Press (Orleans, MA)
Paust Inc (Richmond, IN)
Pendell Printing (Midland, MI)
Perlmuter Printing (Independence, OH)
Perry Printing (Waterloo, WI)
Perry/Baraboo (Baraboo, WI)
Plain Talk Publishing (Des Moines, IA)
Port Publications (Port Washington, WI)
Practical Graphics (New York, NY)
Precision Offset (Upper Darby, PA)
Preferred Graphics (Winona, MN)
The Press (Chanhassen, MN)
Prinit Press (Dublin, IN)
Print Northwest (Tacoma, WA)
Printing Corp (Pompano Beach, FL)
Printing Dimensions (Beltsville, MD)
Progress Printing (Lynchburg, VA)
ProLitho (Provo, UT)
Quebecor America (New York, NY)
Quintessence Press (Amador City, CA)
Quixott Press (Doylestown, PA)
Rapidocolor Corp (West Chester, PA)
Reproductions Inc (Rockville, MD)
Ringier America - Corinth (Corinth, MS)
The Riverside Press (Dallas, TX)
John Roberts Co (Minneapolis, MN)
Ronalds Printing (Montreal, PQ)
Ronalds Printing (Vancouver, BC)
S Rosenthal & Company (Cincinnati, OH)
Royle Printing (Sun Prairie, WI)
Saint Croix Press (New Richmond, WI)
Saltzman Printers (Maywood, IL)
Skillful Means Press (Oakland, CA)
R E Smith Printing (Fall River, MA)
Smith-Edwards-Dunlap (Phildelphia, PA)
Southeastern Printing (Stuart, FL)
Standard Publishing (Cincinnati, OH)
Stephenson Inc (Alexandria, VA)
Stewart Publishing (Marble Hill, MO)
Stinehour Press (Lunenburg, VT)
Straus Printing (Madison, WI)
Sweet Printing (Round Rock, TX)
John S Swift Company (Saint Louis, MO)
John S Swift (Chicago, IL)
John S Swift (Cincinnati, OH)

Posters

John S Swift (Teterboro, NJ)
T A S Graphics (Detroit, MI)
Times Printing (Random Lake, WI)
Todd Web Press (Smithville, TX)
Tri-State Press (Clayton, GA)
Twin City Printery (Lewiston, ME)
Van Volumes (Thorndike, MA)
Vogue Printers (North Chicago, IL)
F A Weber & Sons (Park Falls, WI)
Wellesley Press (Framingham, MA)
West Side Graphics (New York, NY)
Western Publishers (Albuquerque, NM)
Western Publishing (Racine, WI)
Western Web Printing (Sioux Falls, SD)
White Arts (Indianapolis, IN)
Wisconsin Color Press (Milwaukee, WI)
Wolfer Printing (City of Commerce, CA)
The Wood Press (Paterson, NJ)

Textbooks

Ad Infinitum Press (Mount Vernon, NY)
Adams Press (Chicago, IL)
Advanced Duplicating (Edina, MN)
Alger Press Ltd (Oshawa, ON)
Alpine Press (Stoughton, MA)
American Offset (Los Angeles, CA)
Arcata Graphics (Fairfield, PA)
Arcata Graphics (West Hanover, MA)
Arcata Graphics (Kingsport, TN)
Arcata Graphics (Martinsburg, WV)
B & R Printing (Post Falls, ID)
Baker Johnson (Dexter, MI)
Balan Printing (Brooklyn, NY)
Banta Corporation (Menasha, WI)
Bay Port Press (National City, CA)
Bertelsmann Printing (New York, NY)
T H Best Printing (Don Mills, ON)
Bolger Publications (Minneapolis, MN)
The Book Press (Brattleboro, VT)
Book-Mart Press (North Bergen, NJ)
BookCrafters (Chelsea, MI)
BookCrafters (Fredericksburg, VA)
BookMasters (Ashland, OH)
Braceland Brothers (Philadelphia, PA)
Braun-Brumfield (Ann Arbor, MI)
C & M Press (Thornton, CO)
Camelot Book (Ormond Beach, FL)
Camelot Fine Printing (Albuquerque, NM)
Centax of Canada (Regina, SK)
The College Press (Collegedale, TN)
Color House (Grand Rapids, MI)
Color World Printers (Bozeman, MT)
Columbus Book Binders (Columbus, GA)
Community Press (Provo, UT)
Comput-A-Print (Reno, NV)
Country Press (Mohawk, NY)
Crane Duplicating (West Barnstable, MA)

Crest Litho (Watervliet, NY)
Crusader Printing (East Saint Louis, IL)
Cushing-Malloy (Ann Arbor, MI)
D D Associates (Santa Clara, CA)
Daamen Printing (West Rutland, VT)
Danner Press (Canton, OH)
Delmar Printing (Charlotte, NC)
Delta Lithograph (Valencia, CA)
John Deyell Company (Lindsay, ON)
Diamond Graphics (Milwaukee, WI)
Dickinson Press (Grand Rapids, MI)
Diversified Printing (Brea, CA)
Dollco Printing (Ottawa, ON)
R R Donnelley (Crawfordsville, IN)
R R Donnelley (Chicago, IL)
R R Donnelley (Harrisonburg, VA)
R R Donnelley (Willard, OH)
Dragon Press (Delta Junction, AK)
Eastwood Printing (Denver, CO)
Edwards Brothers (Ann Arbor, MI)
Edwards Brothers (Lillington, NC)
Eerdmans Printing (Grand Rapids, MI)
Federated Lithographers (Providence, RI)
Fort Orange Press (Albany, NY)
Four Corners Press (Grand Rapids, MI)
Friesen Printers (Altona, MB)
Full Color Graphics (Plainview, NY)
Gagne Printing (Louiseville, PQ)
Ganis & Harris (New York, NY)
Gateway Press (Louisville, KY)
Gaylord Ltd (West Hollywood, CA)
Gladstone Press (Ottawa, ON)
Graphic Litho Corp (Lawrence, MA)
Graphic Printing (New Carlisle, OH)
The Gregath Company (Cullman, AL)
Griffin Printing (Glendale, CA)
Griffin Printing (Sacramento, CA)
GRT Book Printing (Oakland, CA)
Haddon Craftsmen (Scranton, PA)
Hamilton Printing (Rensselaer, NY)
Harlo Press (Detroit, MI)
Heffernan Press (Worcester, MA)
D B Hess Company (Woodstock, IL)
Hignell Printing (Winnepeg, MB)
Holyoke Lithography (Springfield, MA)
Hooven-Dayton Corp (Dayton, OH)
Horowitz/Rae (Fairfield, NJ)
Hunter Publishing (Winston-Salem, NC)
Infopress/Saratoga (Saratoga Springs, NY)
Inland Lithograph (Elk Grove Village, IL)
Interstate Printers (Danville, IL)
Johnson & Hardin (Cincinnati, OH)
K/P Graphics (Escondido, CA)
Kern International (Duxbury, MA)
KNI Book Manufacturing (Anaheim, CA)
Latham Process Corp (New York, NY)
Les Editions Marquis (Montmagny, PQ)
Litho Prestige (Drummondville, PQ)
John D Lucas Printing (Baltimore, MD)
Malloy Lithographing (Ann Arbor, MI)
Marrakech Express (Tarpon Springs, FL)
Maverick Publications (Bend, OR)

Textbooks

The Mazer Corporation (Dayton, OH)
McClain Printing (Parson, WV)
McFarland Company (Harrisburg, PA)
McGregor & Werner (Washington, DC)
McNaughton & Gunn (Saline, MI)
Mercury Printing (Memphis, TN)
Messenger Graphics (Phoenix, AZ)
Mitchell-Shear (Ann Arbor, MI)
MMI Press (Harrisville, NH)
Multiprint Inc (Chatham, NY)
Murray Printing (Kendallville, IN)
Murray Printing (Westford, MA)
National Publishing (Philadelphia, PA)
National Reproductions (Livonia, MI)
Nationwide Printing (Burlington, KY)
Neibauer Press (Warminster, PA)
Nimrod Press (Boston, MA)
Oaks Printing Company (Bethlehem, PA)
Omnipress (Madison, WI)
Pantagraph Printing (Bloomington, IL)
Patterson Printing (Benton Harbor, MI)
Pearl Pressman Liberty (Philadelphia, PA)
PFP Printing Corp (Gaithersburg, MD)
Phillips Brothers (Springfield, IL)
Plus Communications (Saint Louis, MO)
The Press of Ohio (Brimfield, OH)
Princeton University (Lawrenceville, NJ)
Publishers Press (Salt Lake City, UT)
Quebecor America (New York, NY)
Rapid Printing (Omaha, NE)
Reproductions Inc (Rockville, MD)
Ringier America (Itasca, IL)
Ringier America (Brookfield, WI)
Ringier America (Jonesboro, AR)
Ringier America (New Berlin, WI)
Ringier America (Phoenix, AZ)
Ringier America (Pontiac, IL)
Ringier America (Senatobia, MS)
Ronalds Printing (Vancouver, BC)
Rose Printing Company (Tallahassee, FL)
Roxbury Publishing (Los Angeles, CA)
Saint Mary's Press (Hollywood, MD)
Science Press (Ephrata, PA)
Semline Inc (Braintree, MA)
Southeastern Printing (Stuart, FL)
Standard Printing (Chicago, IL)
Technical Comm. (N Kansas City, MO)
Thomson-Shore (Dexter, MI)
Todd Web Press (Smithville, TX)
Town House Press (Pittsboro, NC)
Tri-Graphic Printing (Ottawa, ON)
Tri-State Press (Clayton, GA)
Twin City Printery (Lewiston, ME)
Valco Graphics (Seattle, WA)
Versa Press (East Peoria, IL)
Vicks Lithograph (Yorkville, NY)
Walsworth Publishing (Marceline, MO)
Webcom Ltd (Scarborough, ON)
Webcrafters (Madison, WI)
Western Publishers (Albuquerque, NM)

Western Web Printing (Sioux Falls, SD)
Westview Press (Boulder, CO)
Wickersham Printing (Lancaster, PA)
Windsor Associates (San Diego, CA)
Wood & Jones (Pasadena, CA)
Worzalla Publishing (Stevens Point, WI)

Workbooks

Academy Books (Rutland, VT)
Ad Infinitum Press (Mount Vernon, NY)
The Adams Group (New York, NY)
Adams Press (Chicago, IL)
Advanced Duplicating (Edina, MN)
Alger Press Ltd (Oshawa, ON)
Allied Printing (Akron, OH)
Alonzo Printing (S San Francisco, CA)
American Offset (Los Angeles, CA)
Americomp (Brattleboro, VT)
Amidon Graphics (Saint Paul, MN)
Arcata Graphics (Kingsport, TN)
Arcata Graphics (Martinsburg, WV)
Arizona Lithographers (Tucson, AZ)
Artcraft Press (Waterloo, WI)
B & R Printing (Post Falls, ID)
Baker Johnson (Dexter, MI)
Balan Printing (Brooklyn, NY)
Banta Catalog (Saint Paul, MN)
Banta Corporation (Menasha, WI)
Banta-Harrisonburg (Harrisonburg, VA)
Bawden Printing (Eldridge, IA)
Bay Port Press (National City, CA)
Beacon Wholesale Printing (Seattle, WA)
Bell Publications (Iowa City, IA)
Bertelsmann Printing (New York, NY)
T H Best Printing (Don Mills, ON)
Bolger Publications (Minneapolis, MN)
Book Makers Inc (Kenosha, WI)
The Book Press (Brattleboro, VT)
Book-Mart Press (North Bergen, NJ)
BookCrafters (Chelsea, MI)
BookCrafters (Fredericksburg, VA)
Booklet Publishing (Elk Grove Village, IL)
BookMasters (Ashland, OH)
Braceland Brothers (Philadelphia, PA)
Braun-Brumfield (Ann Arbor, MI)
Brunswick Publishing (Lawrenceville, VA)
C & M Press (Thornton, CO)
Cal Central Press (Sacramento, CA)
California Offset (Glendale, CA)
Camelot Book (Ormond Beach, FL)
Camelot Fine Printing (Albuquerque, NM)
Canterbury Press (Rome, NY)
Capital Printing (Austin, TX)
Champion Printing (Cincinnati, OH)
Cody Publications (Kissimmee, FL)
The College Press (Collegedale, TN)
Color House (Grand Rapids, MI)
Color World Printers (Bozeman, MT)
Colortone Press (Washington, DC)

Workbooks

Columbus Book Printers (Columbus, GA)
Community Press (Provo, UT)
Comput-A-Print (Reno, NV)
Connecticut Printers (Bloomfield, CT)
Consolidated Printers (Berkeley, CA)
Copple House (Lakemont, GA)
Corley Printing (Earth City, MO)
Country Press (Mohawk, NY)
Crane Duplicating (West Barnstable, MA)
Crest Litho (Watervliet, NY)
Crusader Printing (East Saint Louis, IL)
D D Associates (Santa Clara, CA)
Daamen Printing (West Rutland, VT)
Danner Press (Canton, OH)
Delmar Printing (Charlotte, NC)
Delta Lithograph (Valencia, CA)
Desaulniers Printing (Milan, IL)
John Deyell Company (Lindsay, ON)
Dharma Press (Oakland, CA)
Diamond Graphics (Milwaukee, WI)
Dickinson Press (Grand Rapids, MI)
Dinner & Klein (Seattle, WA)
Diversified Printing (Brea, CA)
Donihe Graphics (Kingsport, TN)
R R Donnelley (Crawfordsville, IN)
R R Donnelley (Chicago, IL)
R R Donnelley (Harrisonburg, VA)
R R Donnelley (Willard, OH)
Dragon Press (Delta Junction, AK)
Eastwood Printing (Denver, CO)
Economy Printing Concern (Berne, IN)
Edwards & Broughton (Raleigh, NC)
Edwards Brothers (Ann Arbor, MI)
Edwards Brothers (Lillington, NC)
Eerdmans Printing (Grand Rapids, MI)
Einson Freeman Graphics (Fairlawn, NJ)
Eusey Press (Leominster, MA)
Faculty Press (Brooklyn, NY)
Fast Print (Fort Wayne, IN)
Federated Litho (Providence, RI)
Fisher Web Printers (Cedar Rapids, IA)
Foote & Davies (Lincoln, NE)
Fort Orange Press (Albany, NY)
Four Corners Press (Grand Rapids, MI)
Friesen Printers (Altona, MB)
Full Color Graphics (Plainview, NY)
Gagne Printing (Louiseville, PQ)
Ganis & Harris (New York, NY)
Gateway Press (Louisville, KY)
Gaylord Ltd (West Hollywood, CA)
Gaylord Printing (Detroit, MI)
General Offset (Jersey City, NJ)
George Lithograph (San Francisco, CA)
Germac Printing (Tigard, OR)
Giant Horse (Daly City, CA)
Goodway Graphics (Springfield, VA)
Gorham Printing (Rochester, WA)
Gowe Printing Company (Medina, OH)
Graphic Litho Corp (Lawrence, MA)
Graphic Printing (New Carlisle, OH)

Gray Printing (Fostoria, OH)
The Gregath Company (Cullman, AL)
Griffin Printing (Glendale, CA)
Griffin Printing (Sacramento, CA)
GRT Book Printing (Oakland, CA)
Hamilton Printing (Rensselaer, NY)
Harlo Press (Detroit, MI)
Heffernan Press (Worcester, MA)
D B Hess Company (Woodstock, IL)
Hignell Printing (Winnepeg, MB)
Hoechstetter Printing (Pittsburgh, PA)
Holladay-Tyler Printing (Glenn Dale, MD)
Holyoke Lithography (Springfield, MA)
Hooven-Dayton Corp (Dayton, OH)
Hunter Publishing (Winston-Salem, NC)
Infopress/Saratoga (Saratoga Springs, NY)
Inland Lithograph (Elk Grove Village, IL)
Interstate Printers (Danville, IL)
Interstate Printing (Omaha, NE)
The Job Shop (Woods Hole, MA)
Johnson & Hardin (Cincinnati, OH)
Johnson Graphics (East Dubuque, IL)
Jostens / Clarksville (Clarksville, TN)
Jostens / State College (State College, PA)
Jostens / Topeka (Topeka, KS)
Jostens / Visalia (Visalia, CA)
K/P Graphics (Escondido, CA)
Kern International (Duxbury, MA)
KNI Book Manufacturing (Anaheim, CA)
C J Krehbiel Company (Cincinnati, OH)
Latham Process Corp (New York, NY)
Les Editions Marquis (Montmagny, PQ)
Liberty York Graphic (Hempstead, NY)
Litho Prestige (Drummondville, PQ)
Lithocolor Press (Westchester, IL)
Little River Press (Miami, FL)
John D Lucas Printing (Baltimore, MD)
Malloy Lithographing (Ann Arbor, MI)
Maverick Publications (Bend, OR)
The Mazer Corporation (Dayton, OH)
McClain Printing (Parson, WV)
McGregor & Werner (Washington, DC)
McKay Printing Services (Dolton, IL)
McNaughton & Gunn (Saline, MI)
Meaker the Printer (Phoenix, AZ)
Mercury Printing (Memphis, TN)
Messenger Graphics (Phoenix, AZ)
Metromail Corporation (Lincoln, NE)
Mideastern Printing (Brookfield, CT)
Mitchell Press (Vancouver, BC)
MMI Press (Harrisville, NH)
Morgan Printing (Austin, TX)
Multiprint Inc (Chatham, NY)
Murray Printing (Kendallville, IN)
Murray Printing (Westford, MA)
National Graphics (Columbus, OH)
National Reproductions (Livonia, MI)
Nationwide Printing (Burlington, KY)
Neibauer Press (Warminster, PA)
Neyenesch Printers (San Diego, CA)
Nimrod Press (Boston, MA)
O'Neil Data Systems (Los Angeles, CA)

Workbooks

Oaks Printing Company (Bethlehem, PA)
Odyssey Press (Dover, NH)
Omnipress (Madison, WI)
Optic Graphics (Glen Burnie, MD)
Original Copy Centers (Cleveland, OH)
Ortlieb Press (Baton Rouge, LA)
Oxmoor Press (Birmingham, AL)
PAK Discount Printing (Zion, IL)
Pantagraph Printing (Bloomington, IL)
Paraclete Press (Orleans, MA)
Parker Graphics (Fuquay-Varina, NC)
Patterson Printing (Benton Harbor, MI)
Paust Inc (Richmond, IN)
Perlmuter Printing (Independence, OH)
Perry Printing (Waterloo, WI)
Perry/Baraboo (Baraboo, WI)
PFP Printing Corp (Gaithersburg, MD)
Pine Hill Press (Freeman, SD)
Plus Communications (Saint Louis, MO)
Press America (Chicago, IL)
The Press of Ohio (Brimfield, OH)
The Press (Chanhassen, MN)
Printing Corp (Pompano Beach, FL)
Progress Printing (Lynchburg, VA)
ProLitho (Provo, UT)
Publishers Press (Salt Lake City, UT)
Quebecor America (New York, NY)
Rapid Printing (Omaha, NE)
RBW Graphics (Owen Sound, ON)
Realtron Multi-Lith (Denver, CO)
Recorder Sunset (San Francisco, CA)
Repro-Tech (West Patterson, NJ)
Reproductions Inc (Rockville, MD)
Rich Printing Company (Nashville, TN)
The Riverside Press (Dallas, TX)
John Roberts Co (Minneapolis, MN)
Rollins Press (Orlando, FL)
Ronalds Printing (Vancouver, BC)
Rose Printing Company (Tallahassee, FL)
Roxbury Publishing (Los Angeles, CA)
Royle Printing (Sun Prairie, WI)
Saint Mary's Press (Hollywood, MD)
Schiff Printers (Pittsburgh, PA)
Science Press (Ephrata, PA)
Semline Inc (Braintree, MA)
Service Printing (San Leandro, CA)
Sexton Printing (W Saint Paul, MN)
Skillful Means Press (Oakland, CA)
R E Smith Printing (Fall River, MA)
Smith-Edwards-Dunlap (Phildelphia, PA)
Snohomish Publishing (Snohomish, WA)
Southam Printing (Weston M9N 3R3, ON)
Sowers Printing (Lebanon, PA)
Speaker-Hines & Thomas (Lansing, MI)
Standard Publishing (Cincinnati, OH)
Stephenson Inc (Alexandria, VA)
Stewart Publishing (Marble Hill, MO)
Sweet Printing (Round Rock, TX)
T A S Graphics (Detroit, MI)
Tapco (Pemberton, NJ)

Technical Comm. (N Kansas City, MO)
Telegraph Press (Harrisburg, PA)
Thomson-Shore (Dexter, MI)
Times Printing (Random Lake, WI)
Todd Web Press (Smithville, TX)
Town House Press (Pittsboro, NC)
Tracor Publications (Austin, TX)
Tri-Graphic Printing (Ottawa, ON)
Tri-State Press (Clayton, GA)
Triangle Printing (Nashville, TN)
TSO General Corp (Long Island City, NY)
Twin City Printery (Lewiston, ME)
Universal Printing (Saint Louis, MO)
Valco Graphics (Seattle, WA)
Van Volumes (Thorndike, MA)
Versa Press (East Peoria, IL)
Vicks Lithograph (Yorkville, NY)
Victor Graphics (Baltimore, MD)
Viking Press (Eden Prairie, MN)
Vogue Printers (North Chicago, IL)
Wallace Press (Hillside, IL)
Walsworth Publishing (Marceline, MO)
Webcom Ltd (Scarborough, ON)
Webcrafters (Madison, WI)
Western Publishers (Albuquerque, NM)
Western Publishing (Racine, WI)
Western Web Printing (Sioux Falls, SD)
Westview Press (Boulder, CO)
White Arts (Indianapolis, IN)
Whitehall Printing (Wheeling, IL)
Wickersham Printing (Lancaster, PA)
Williams Catello Printing (Tualatin, OR)
Wisconsin Color Press (Milwaukee, WI)
Worzalla Publishing (Stevens Point, WI)
Ye Olde Genealogie (Indianapolis, IN)

Yearbooks

The companies which are marked with asterisks (*) have divisions which are devoted solely to printing yearbooks.

Arcata Graphics (Kingsport, TN)
Arcata Graphics (Martinsburg, WV)
B & R Printing (Post Falls, ID)
Balan Printing (Brooklyn, NY)
T H Best Printing (Don Mills, ON) *
Book Makers (Kenosha, WI)
William Boyd Printing (Albany, NY)
Brunswick Publishing (Lawrenceville, VA)
Camelot Fine Printing (Albuquerque, NM)
Cascio-Wolf (Springfield, VA)
Color House (Grand Rapids, MI)
Community Press (Provo, UT) *
Comput-A-Print (Reno, NV)
Crusader Printing (East Saint Louis, IL)
Daamen Printing (West Rutland, VT)
Delmar Printing (Charlotte, NC) *
Diamond Graphics (Milwaukee, WI)
Dollco Printing (Ottawa, ON)

Yearbooks

Faculty Press (Brooklyn, NY)
Friesen Printers (Altona, MB) *
Gagne Printing (Louiseville, PQ)
Gaylord Ltd (West Hollywood, CA)
General Offset (Jersey City, NJ)
Giant Horse (Daly City, CA)
Gladstone Press (Ottawa, ON)
The Gregath Company (Cullman, AL)
Harlo Press (Detroit, MI)
Henington Publishing (Wolfe City, TX)
Hunter Publishing (Winston-Salem, NC) *
Jostens (Clarksville, TN) *
Jostens (State College, PA) *
Jostens (Topeka, KS) *
Jostens (Visalia, CA) *
Les Editions Marquis (Montmagny, PQ)
Marrakech Express (Tarpon Springs, FL)
McClain Printing (Parson, WV)
Mercury Printing (Memphis, TN)
Neibauer Press (Warminster, PA)
Newsfoto Publishing (San Angelo, TX)
Noble Book Press (New York, NY)
Ortlieb Press (Baton Rouge, LA)
Outstanding Graphics (Kenosha, WI)
PFP Printing (Gaithersburg, MD)
Progress Printing (Lynchburg, VA) *
Science Press (Ephrata, PA)
Stewart Publishing (Marble Hill, MO)
Taylor Publishing (Dallas, TX) *
Tracor Publications (Austin, TX)
Tri-State Press (Clayton, GA)
Triangle Printing (Nashville, TN)
Twin City Printery (Lewiston, ME)
Valco Graphics (Seattle, WA)
Walsworth Publishing (Marceline, MO) *
F A Weber (Park Falls, WI)
Western Web Printing (Sioux Falls, SD)
Windsor Associates (San Diego, CA)

Pop-ups

The following foreign printers specialize in producing pop-ups and other novelty books that require lots of intricate handwork.

Carvajal S.A. (Columbia)
Dominie Press (Singapore)
Ediciones Lerner (Columbia)
Saik Wah Press (Singapore)
Tien Wah Press (Singapore)

Comic Books

Amidon Graphics (Saint Paul, MN)
Arizona Lithographers (Tucson, AZ)
Balan Printing (Brooklyn, NY)
T H Best Printing (Don Mills, ON)
Delta Lithograph (Valencia, CA)
Diversified Printing (Brea, CA)
Gilliland Printing (Arkansas City, KS)
Interstate Printing (Omaha, NE)
KNI Book Manufacturing (Anaheim, CA)
Mercury Printing (Memphis, TN)
Ortlieb Press (Baton Rouge, LA)
Oxmoor Press (Birmingham, AL)
Port Publications (Port Washington, WI)
Reproductions Inc (Rockville, MD)
Ronalds Printing (Montreal, PQ)
T A S Graphics (Detroit, MI)
Times Litho (Forest Grove, OR)
Times Printing (Random Lake, WI)
Valco Graphics (Seattle, WA)
Western Publishing (Racine, WI)
Western Web Printing (Sioux Falls, SD)

Index: Binding Capabilities

These indexes list those printers who report that they have in-house binding capabilities for the following types of books.

Casebound Books

Academy Books (Rutland, VT)
Alpine Press (Stoughton, MA)
Arcata Graphics (Fairfield, PA)
Arcata Graphics (West Hanover, MA)
Arcata Graphics (Kingsport, TN)
Arcata Graphics (Martinsburg, WV)
Banta Corporation (Menasha, WI)
Berryville Graphics (Berryville, VA)
Bertelsmann Printing (New York, NY)
T H Best Printing (Don Mills, ON)
The Book Press (Brattleboro, VT)
Book-Mart Press (North Bergen, NJ)
BookCrafters (Chelsea, MI)
Braun-Brumfield (Ann Arbor, MI)
C & M Press (Thornton, CO)
Community Press (Provo, UT)
Delmar Printing Company (Charlotte, NC)
John Deyell Company (Lindsay, ON)
R R Donnelley (Crawfordsville, IN)
R R Donnelley (Chicago, IL)
R R Donnelley (Harrisonburg, VA)
R R Donnelley (Willard, OH)
Edwards Brothers (Ann Arbor, MI)
Eerdmans Printing (Grand Rapids, MI)
Fort Orange Press (Albany, NY)
Friesen Printers (Altona, MB)
Ganis & Harris (New York, NY)
Germac Printing (Tigard, OR)
Graphic Arts Center (Portland, OR)
Haddon Craftsmen (Scranton, PA)
Hamilton Printing (Rensselaer, NY)
Henington Publishing (Wolfe City, TX)
Hignell Printing (Winnepeg, MB)
A B Hirschfeld Press (Denver, CO)
Horowitz/Rae (Fairfield, NJ)
Hunter Publishing (Winston-Salem, NC)
Interstate Printers (Danville, IL)
Jostens / Clarksville (Clarksville, TN)
Jostens / State College (State College, PA)
Jostens / Topeka (Topeka, KS)
Jostens / Visalia (Visalia, CA)
Kimberly Press (Santa Barbara, CA)
C J Krehbiel Company (Cincinnati, OH)
John D Lucas Printing (Baltimore, MD)

Maple-Vail (York, PA)
MMI Press (Harrisville, NH)
Murray Printing Company (Westford, MA)
National Publishing (Philadelphia, PA)
Newsfoto Publishing (San Angelo, TX)
Optic Graphics (Glen Burnie, MD)
Preferred Graphics (Winona, MN)
Publishers Press (Salt Lake City, UT)
Quebecor America (New York, NY)
Quinn-Woodbine (Woodbine, NJ)
Quintessence Press (Amador City, CA)
RBW Graphics (Owen Sound, ON)
Recorder Sunset (San Francisco, CA)
Ringier America (Itasca, IL)
Ringier America (New Berlin, WI)
Ringier America (Olathe, KS)
Rose Printing Company (Tallahassee, FL)
The Saybrook Press (Old Saybrook, CT)
Standard Printing Service (Chicago, IL)
Stinehour Press (Lunenburg, VT)
The Studley Press (Dalton, MA)
Taylor Publishing Company (Dallas, TX)
Thomson-Shore (Dexter, MI)
Tri-Graphic Printing (Ottawa, ON)
University Press (Winchester, MA)
Vail Ballou Printing (Binghamton, NY)
Walsworth Publishing (Marceline, MO)
Webcrafters (Madison, WI)
Western Publishing (Racine, WI)
Worzalla Publishing (Stevens Point, WI)

Comb-Bound Books

Advanced Duplicating (Edina, MN)
Alger Press Ltd (Oshawa, ON)
Alpine Press (Stoughton, MA)
Apollo Graphics (Southampton, PA)
Arcata Graphics (West Hanover, MA)
Arcata Graphics (Kingsport, TN)
Arcata Graphics (Martinsburg, WV)
Automated Graphic (White Plains, MD)
B & R Printing (Post Falls, ID)
Banta Corporation (Menasha, WI)
Bawden Printing (Eldridge, IA)
Beacon Wholesale Printing (Seattle, WA)

Comb-Bound Books

Blake Printery (San Luis Obispo, CA)
Blue Dolphin Press (Grass Valley, CA)
Book Makers Inc (Kenosha, WI)
Book-Mart Press (North Bergen, NJ)
BookCrafters (Chelsea, MI)
Braceland Brothers (Philadelphia, PA)
Brennan Printing (Deep River, IA)
Brunswick Publishing (Lawrenceville, VA)
C & M Press (Thornton, CO)
Camelot Book (Ormond Beach, FL)
Camelot Fine Printing (Albuquerque, NM)
Canterbury Press (Rome, NY)
Case-Hoyt Corporation (Rochester, NY)
Centax of Canada (Regina, SK)
The College Press (Collegedale, TN)
Color House (Grand Rapids, MI)
Color World Printers (Bozeman, MT)
Columbus Book Printers (Columbus, GA)
Community Press (Provo, UT)
Comput-A-Print (Reno, NV)
Coneco Laser Graphics (Glen Falls, NY)
Cookbook Publishers (Olathe, KS)
Country Press (Mohawk, NY)
Crane Duplicating (West Barnstable, MA)
Crest Litho (Watervliet, NY)
Crusader Printing (East Saint Louis, IL)
Dataco (Albuquerque, NM)
Dellas Graphics (Syracuse, NY)
Delmar Printing (Charlotte, NC)
Desaulniers Printing (Milan, IL)
Diamond Graphics (Milwaukee, WI)
Diversified Printing (Brea, CA)
R R Donnelley (Crawfordsville, IN)
R R Donnelley (Chicago, IL)
East Village Enterprises (New York, NY)
Edison Press (Glen Rock, NJ)
Edwards & Broughton (Raleigh, NC)
Edwards Brothers (Ann Arbor, MI)
Fort Orange Press (Albany, NY)
Friesen Printers (Altona, MB)
Fundcraft (Collierville, TN)
Ganis & Harris (New York, NY)
Gateway Press (Louisville, KY)
George Lithograph (San Francisco, CA)
Giant Horse (Daly City, CA)
Goodway Graphics (Springfield, VA)
Graphic Design (Center Line, MI)
Graphic Litho Corp (Lawrence, MA)
Graphic Printing (New Carlisle, OH)
Gray Printing (Fostoria, OH)
GRT Book Printing (Oakland, CA)
Guynes Printing (Albuquerque, NM)
Hamilton Printing (Rensselaer, NY)
Harlo Press (Detroit, MI)
Heffernan Press (Worcester, MA)
Henington Publishing (Wolfe City, TX)
A B Hirschfeld Press (Denver, CO)
Hooven-Dayton Corp (Dayton, OH)
Independent Print. (Long Island City, NY)
Infopress/Saratoga (Saratoga Springs, NY)

Interstate Printers (Danville, IL)
The Job Shop (Woods Hole, MA)
Johnson Publishing (Boulder, CO)
Jostens / Clarksville (Clarksville, TN)
Jostens / State College (State College, PA)
Jostens / Topeka (Topeka, KS)
Julin Printing (Monticello, IA)
Kern International (Duxbury, MA)
C J Krehbiel Company (Cincinnati, OH)
Liberty York Graphic (Hempstead, NY)
Malloy Lithographing (Ann Arbor, MI)
Maple-Vail (York, PA)
Mark IV Press (Hauppauge, NY)
The Mazer Corporation (Dayton, OH)
McClain Printing Company (Parson, WV)
McGregor & Werner (Washington, DC)
McNaughton & Gunn (Saline, MI)
Meaker the Printer (Phoenix, AZ)
Mercury Printing (Memphis, TN)
Mideastern Printing (Brookfield, CT)
Mitchell-Shear (Ann Arbor, MI)
Morgan Printing (Austin, TX)
Cookbooks by Morris Press (Kearney, NE)
Multiprint Inc (Chatham, NY)
National Reproductions (Livonia, MI)
Naturegraph (Happy Camp, CA)
Nimrod Press (Boston, MA)
Northlight Studio Press (Barre, VT)
O'Neil Data Systems (Los Angeles, CA)
Omnipress (Madison, WI)
Optic Graphics (Glen Burnie, MD)
Ortlieb Press (Baton Rouge, LA)
Parker Graphics (Fuquay-Varina, NC)
Patterson Printing (Benton Harbor, MI)
PFP Printing Corp (Gaithersburg, MD)
Phillips Brothers (Springfield, IL)
Plus Communications (Saint Louis, MO)
Practical Graphics (New York, NY)
Print Northwest (Tacoma, WA)
Printing Dimensions (Beltsville, MD)
Progress Printing (Lynchburg, VA)
Quebecor America (New York, NY)
Quintessence Press (Amador City, CA)
Recorder Sunset (San Francisco, CA)
Reproductions Inc (Rockville, MD)
Ringier America (Itasca, IL)
Ringier America (Olathe, KS)
Roxbury Publishing (Los Angeles, CA)
Saint Mary's Press (Hollywood, MD)
Semline Inc (Braintree, MA)
Southeastern Printing (Stuart, FL)
Staked Plains Press (Canyon, TX)
John S Swift Company (Saint Louis, MO)
John S Swift (Chicago, IL)
John S Swift (Cincinnati, OH)
John S Swift (Teterboro, NJ)
Technical Comm. (N Kansas City, MO)
Thomson-Shore (Dexter, MI)
Times Printing (Random Lake, WI)
S C Toof and Company (Memphis, TN)
Tracor Publications (Austin, TX)
Tri-State Press (Clayton, GA)

Comb-Bound Books

Triangle Printing (Nashville, TN)
TSO General Corp (Long Island City, NY)
Twin City Printery (Lewiston, ME)
Vail Ballou Printing (Binghamton, NY)
Vicks Lithograph (Yorkville, NY)
Vogue Printers (North Chicago, IL)
Walsworth Publishing (Marceline, MO)
Walter's Publishing (Waseca, MN)
Watkins Printing (Columbus, OH)
Western Publishers (Albuquerque, NM)
White Arts (Indianapolis, IN)
Wimmer Brothers (Memphis, TN)
Wood & Jones (Pasadena, CA)
Worzalla Publishing (Stevens Point, WI)

Loose-Leaf Binding

Advanced Duplicating (Edina, MN)
Arcata Graphics (Kingsport, TN)
Arcata Graphics (Martinsburg, WV)
Argus Press (Niles, IL)
B & R Printing (Post Falls, ID)
Baker Johnson (Dexter, MI)
Bay Port Press (National City, CA)
Beacon Wholesale Printing (Seattle, WA)
Bell Publications (Iowa City, IA)
Bolger Publications (Minneapolis, MN)
Book-Mart Press (North Bergen, NJ)
BookCrafters (Chelsea, MI)
William Boyd Printing (Albany, NY)
Brennan Printing (Deep River, IA)
Brunswick Publishing (Lawrenceville, VA)
C & M Press (Thornton, CO)
Camelot Fine Printing (Albuquerque, NM)
Central Publishing (Indianapolis, IN)
Clarkwood Corporation (Totowa, NJ)
Color World Printers (Bozeman, MT)
Comput-A-Print (Reno, NV)
Coneco Laser Graphics (Glen Falls, NY)
Country Press (Mohawk, NY)
Daamen Printing (West Rutland, VT)
Dataco (Albuquerque, NM)
Diamond Graphics (Milwaukee, WI)
Eastwood Printing (Denver, CO)
Fort Orange Press (Albany, NY)
Gagne Printing Ltd (Louiseville, PQ)
Gateway Press (Louisville, KY)
Geiger Brothers (Lewiston, ME)
Giant Horse (Daly City, CA)
Globe-Comm (San Antonio, TX)
Graphic Printing (New Carlisle, OH)
The Gregath Company (Cullman, AL)
Griffin Printing (Glendale, CA)
GRT Book Printing (Oakland, CA)
Guynes Printing (Albuquerque, NM)

Hamilton Printing (Rensselaer, NY)
Heffernan Press (Worcester, MA)
A B Hirschfeld Press (Denver, CO)
Independent Print. (Long Island City, NY)
The Job Shop (Woods Hole, MA)
Johnson Publishing (Boulder, CO)
Julin Printing (Monticello, IA)
K/P Graphics (Escondido, CA)
Kaufman Press (Syracuse, NY)
Kern International (Duxbury, MA)
Latham Process Corp (New York, NY)
Malloy Lithographing (Ann Arbor, MI)
Mark IV Press (Hauppauge, NY)
Marrakech Express (Tarpon Springs, FL)
The Mazer Corporation (Dayton, OH)
McClain Printing (Parson, WV)
McGregor & Werner (Washington, DC)
Mideastern Printing (Brookfield, CT)
Cookbooks by Morris Press (Kearney, NE)
Muller Printing (Santa Clara, CA)
Multiprint Inc (Chatham, NY)
Neibauer Press (Warminster, PA)
Oaks Printing Company (Bethlehem, PA)
Omnipress (Madison, WI)
Optic Graphics (Glen Burnie, MD)
Parker Graphics (Fuquay-Varina, NC)
Patterson Printing (Benton Harbor, MI)
Paust Inc (Richmond, IN)
PFP Printing Corp (Gaithersburg, MD)
Plus Communications (Saint Louis, MO)
Printing Dimensions (Beltsville, MD)
Progress Printing (Lynchburg, VA)
Quebecor America (New York, NY)
Reproductions Inc (Rockville, MD)
Saint Mary's Press (Hollywood, MD)
Semline Inc (Braintree, MA)
Technical Comm. (N Kansas City, MO)
Times Litho (Forest Grove, OR)
Times Printing (Random Lake, WI)
Tri-Graphic Printing (Ottawa, ON)
Tri-State Press (Clayton, GA)
Triangle Printing (Nashville, TN)
TSO General Corp (Long Island City, NY)
Versa Press (East Peoria, IL)
Viking Press (Eden Prairie, MN)
Walsworth Publishing (Marceline, MO)
Western Publishers (Albuquerque, NM)
Whitehall Printing (Wheeling, IL)
Wickersham Printing (Lancaster, PA)

Perfectbound Books

Academy Books (Rutland, VT)
Accurate Web (Central Islip, NY)
Ad Infinitum Press (Mount Vernon, NY)
The Adams Group (New York, NY)
Adams Press (Chicago, IL)

Perfectbound Books

Advanced Duplicating (Edina, MN)
Alger Press Ltd (Oshawa, ON)
Allen Press (Lawrence, KS)
Allied Printing (Akron, OH)
Alpine Press (Stoughton, MA)
American Signature (Dallas, TX)
American Signature (Costa Mesa, CA)
American Signature (New York, NY)
American Signature (Memphis, TN)
American Web Offset (Denver, CO)
Americomp (Brattleboro, VT)
Anundsen Publishing (Decorah, IA)
Arcata Graphics (Nashville, TN)
Arcata Graphics (Depew, NY)
Arcata Graphics (Fairfield, PA)
Arcata Graphics (West Hanover, MA)
Arcata Graphics (Kingsport, TN)
Arcata Graphics (Martinsburg, WV)
Arcata Graphics (San Jose, CA)
Argus Press (Niles, IL)
Arizona Lithographers (Tucson, AZ)
Artcraft Press (Waterloo, WI)
Artex Publishing (Stevens Point, WI)
Automated Graphic (White Plains, MD)
B & R Printing (Post Falls, ID)
Baker Johnson (Dexter, MI)
Balan Printing (Brooklyn, NY)
Banta Corporation (Menasha, WI)
Banta-Harrisonburg (Harrisonburg, VA)
Bawden Printing (Eldridge, IA)
Bay Port Press (National City, CA)
Beacon Press (Richmond, VA)
Bell Publications (Iowa City, IA)
Berryville Graphics (Berryville, VA)
Bertelsmann Printing (New York, NY)
Beslow Associates (Chicago, IL)
T H Best Printing (Don Mills, ON)
Blazing Graphics (Cranston, RI)
Blue Dolphin Press (Grass Valley, CA)
Bolger Publications (Minneapolis, MN)
The Book Press (Brattleboro, VT)
Book-Mart Press (North Bergen, NJ)
BookCrafters (Chelsea, MI)
Booklet Publishing (Elk Grove Village, IL)
William Boyd Printing (Albany, NY)
Braceland Brothers (Philadelphia, PA)
Bradley Printing (Des Plaines, IL)
Braun-Brumfield (Ann Arbor, MI)
Brennan Printing (Deep River, IA)
Brown Printing (Waseca, MN)
Brown Printing (East Greenville, PA)
Brown Printing (Franklin, KY)
William C Brown Printing (Dubuque, IA)
Brunswick Publishing (Lawrenceville, VA)
R L Bryan Company (Columbia, SC)
C & M Press (Thornton, CO)
Camelot Book (Ormond Beach, FL)
Canterbury Press (Rome, NY)
Capital City Press (Montpelier, VT)
Capital Printing (Austin, TX)

Case-Hoyt Corporation (Rochester, NY)
Clark Printing (Kansas City, MO)
The College Press (Collegedale, TN)
Color House (Grand Rapids, MI)
Color World Printers (Bozeman, MT)
ColorGraphics (Tulsa, OK)
Columbus Book Printers (Columbus, GA)
Combined Comm. (Columbia, MO)
Combined Communication (Mendota, IL)
Commercial Printing (Medford, OR)
Comput-A-Print (Reno, NV)
Coneco Laser Graphics (Glen Falls, NY)
Connecticut Printers (Bloomfield, CT)
Consolidated Printers (Berkeley, CA)
Copen Press (Brooklyn, NY)
Corley Printing (Earth City, MO)
Country Press (Middleborough, MA)
Country Press (Mohawk, NY)
Courier Corporation (Lowell, MA)
Craftsman Press (Seattle, WA)
Crane Duplicating (West Barnstable, MA)
Crest Litho (Watervliet, NY)
Cummings Printing (Manchester, NH)
Cushing-Malloy (Ann Arbor, MI)
Daamen Printing (West Rutland, VT)
Danner Press (Canton, OH)
Dartmouth Printing (Hanover, NH)
Delta Lithograph (Valencia, CA)
Desaulniers Printing (Milan, IL)
Deven Lithographers (Brooklyn, NY)
John Deyell Company (Lindsay, ON)
Diamond Graphics (Milwaukee, WI)
Dickinson Press (Grand Rapids, MI)
Dinner & Klein (Seattle, WA)
Dittler Brothers (Atlanta, GA)
Diversified Printing (Brea, CA)
Dollco Printing (Ottawa, ON)
R R Donnelley (Crawfordsville, IN)
R R Donnelley (Chicago, IL)
R R Donnelley (Harrisonburg, VA)
R R Donnelley (Willard, OH)
Dragon Press (Delta Junction, AK)
Dynagraphics (Carlsbad, CA)
Eastern Press (New Haven, CT)
Eastwood Printing (Denver, CO)
Economy Printing Concern (Berne, IN)
Editors Press (Hyattsville, MD)
Edwards & Broughton (Raleigh, NC)
Edwards Brothers (Ann Arbor, MI)
Eerdmans Printing (Grand Rapids, MI)
Einson Freeman Graphics (Fairlawn, NJ)
Evangel Press (Nappanee, IN)
Faculty Press (Brooklyn, NY)
Foote & Davies (Atlanta, GA)
Foote & Davies (Lincoln, NE)
Fort Orange Press (Albany, NY)
Foster Printing (Michigan City, IN)
Friesen Printers (Altona, MB)
Gagne Printing (Louiseville, PQ)
Ganis & Harris (New York, NY)
Gateway Press (Louisville, KY)
George Lithograph (San Francisco, CA)

Perfectbound Books

Germac Printing (Tigard, OR)
Geryon Press (Tunnel, NY)
Giant Horse (Daly City, CA)
Gilliland Printing (Arkansas City, KS)
Gladstone Press (Ottawa, ON)
Goodway Graphics (Springfield, VA)
Graftek Press (Woodstock, IL)
Graphic Arts Center (Portland, OR)
Graphic Design (Center Line, MI)
Graphic Litho Corp (Lawrence, MA)
Graphic Printing (New Carlisle, OH)
Gray Printing (Fostoria, OH)
Greenfield Printing (Greenfield, OH)
The Gregath Company (Cullman, AL)
Griffin Printing (Glendale, CA)
Griffin Printing (Sacramento, CA)
GTE Directories (Des Plaines, IL)
Gulf Printing (Houston, TX)
Guynes Printing (Albuquerque, NM)
Haddon Craftsmen (Scranton, PA)
Hamilton Printing (Rensselaer, NY)
Harlo Press (Detroit, MI)
Hart Graphics (Austin, TX)
Hart Graphics (Sampsonville, SC)
Hart Press (Long Prairie, MN)
Heart of the Lakes (Interlaken, NY)
Heffernan Press (Worcester, MA)
Henington Publishing (Wolfe City, TX)
Hennegan Company (Cincinnati, OH)
D B Hess Company (Woodstock, IL)
Hignell Printing (Winnepeg, MB)
A B Hirschfeld Press (Denver, CO)
Hoechstetter Printing (Pittsburgh, PA)
Hooven-Dayton Corp (Dayton, OH)
Horowitz/Rae (Fairfield, NJ)
Hunter Publishing (Winston-Salem, NC)
Independent Print. (Long Island City, NY)
Independent Publishing (Sarasota, FL)
Intelligencer Printing (Lancaster, PA)
Interstate Printers (Danville, IL)
Jersey Printing (Bayonne, NJ)
The Job Shop (Woods Hole, MA)
Johnson Publishing (Boulder, CO)
Jostens / Clarksville (Clarksville, TN)
Jostens / State College (State College, PA)
Jostens / Topeka (Topeka, KS)
Jostens / Visalia (Visalia, CA)
Judd's Incorporated (Washington, DC)
Julin Printing (Monticello, IA)
Kable Printing (Mount Morris, IL)
Kern International (Duxbury, MA)
Kimberly Press (Santa Barbara, CA)
C J Krehbiel Company (Cincinnati, OH)
Lancaster Press (Lancaster, PA)
The Lane Press (Burlington, VT)
Latham Process Corp (New York, NY)
Les Editions Marquis (Montmagny, PQ)
Liberty York Graphic (Hempstead, NY)
Litho Prestige (Drummondville, PQ)
Lithocolor Press (Westchester, IL)

Little River Press (Miami, FL)
John D Lucas Printing (Baltimore, MD)
Mack Printing (Easton, PA)
Mackintosh Typo. (Santa Barbara, CA)
Maclean Hunter (Willowdale, ON)
The Mad Printers (Mattituck, NY)
Malloy Lithographing (Ann Arbor, MI)
Maple-Vail (York, PA)
Mariposa Press (Benicia, CA)
Mark IV Press (Hauppauge, NY)
Marrakech Express (Tarpon Springs, FL)
The Mazer Corporation (Dayton, OH)
McClain Printing Company (Parson, WV)
McFarland Company (Harrisburg, PA)
McGregor & Werner (Washington, DC)
McNaughton & Gunn (Saline, MI)
Mercury Printing (Memphis, TN)
Meredith/Burda (Des Moines, IA)
Messenger Graphics (Phoenix, AZ)
Metromail Corporation (Lincoln, NE)
Metroweb (Erlanger, KY)
Mitchell Press (Vancouver, BC)
Mitchell-Shear (Ann Arbor, MI)
MMI Press (Harrisville, NH)
Moran Colorgraphic (Baton Rouge, LA)
Morgan Printing (Austin, TX)
Multiprint Inc (Chatham, NY)
Murray Printing (Kendallville, IN)
Murray Printing (Westford, MA)
National Bickford (Providence, RI)
National Graphics Corp (Columbus, OH)
National Publishing (Philadelphia, PA)
National Reproductions (Livonia, MI)
Naturegraph (Happy Camp, CA)
Neyenesch Printers (San Diego, CA)
Nielsen Litho (Cincinnati, OH)
Nimrod Press (Boston, MA)
Noll Printing (Huntington, IN)
Northlight Studio (Barre, VT)
O'Neil Data Systems (Los Angeles, CA)
Odyssey Press (Dover, NH)
Offset Paperback (Dallas, PA)
Omnipress (Madison, WI)
Optic Graphics (Glen Burnie, MD)
Ortlieb Press (Baton Rouge, LA)
Ovid Bell Press (Fulton, MO)
Paraclete Press (Orleans, MA)
Parker Graphics (Fuquay-Varina, NC)
Patterson Printing (Benton Harbor, MI)
Pendell Printing (Midland, MI)
PennWell Printing (Tulsa, OK)
Pentagram (Minneapolis, MN)
Penton Press (Berea, OH)
Perry Printing (Waterloo, WI)
Perry/Baraboo (Baraboo, WI)
PFP Printing Corp (Gaithersburg, MD)
Phillips Brothers (Springfield, IL)
Plus Communications (Saint Louis, MO)
Port City Press (Pikesville, MD)
Practical Graphics (New York, NY)
Preferred Graphics (Winona, MN)
The Press of Ohio (Brimfield, OH)

Perfectbound Books

Prinit Press (Dublin, IN)
Print Northwest (Tacoma, WA)
The Printer Inc (Maple Grove, MN)
Printing Corp (Pompano Beach, FL)
Printing Dimensions (Beltsville, MD)
Progress Printing (Lynchburg, VA)
Providence Gravure (Providence, RI)
Publishers Press (Salt Lake City, UT)
Publishers Printing (Shepherdsville, KY)
Quad Graphics (Thomaston, GA)
Quad/Graphics (Lomira, WI)
Quad/Graphics (Pewaukee, WI)
Quad/Graphics (Saratoga Springs, NY)
Quad/Graphics (Sussex, WI)
Quebecor America (New York, NY)
Quinn-Woodbine (Woodbine, NJ)
Quixott Press (Doylestown, PA)
RBW Graphics (Owen Sound, ON)
Realtron Multi-Lith (Denver, CO)
Recorder Sunset (San Francisco, CA)
Regensteiner Press (West Chicago, IL)
Rich Printing (Nashville, TN)
Ringier America (Itasca, IL)
Ringier America (Brookfield, WI)
Ringier America (Dresden, TN)
Ringier America (New Berlin, WI)
Ringier America (Olathe, KS)
Ringier America (Senatobia, MS)
Rollins Press (Orlando, FL)
Ronalds Printing (Montreal, PQ)
Ronalds Printing (Vancouver, BC)
Rose Printing (Tallahassee, FL)
S Rosenthal & Company (Cincinnati, OH)
Roxbury Publishing (Los Angeles, CA)
Royle Printing (Sun Prairie, WI)
Sabre Printers (Rogersville, TN)
Saint Croix Press (New Richmond, WI)
Saint Mary's Press (Hollywood, MD)
The Saybrook Press (Old Saybrook, CT)
Schiff Printers (Pittsburgh, PA)
Schumann Printers (Fall River, WI)
Science Press (Ephrata, PA)
Semline Inc (Braintree, MA)
The Sheridan Press (Hanover, PA)
Sheridan Printing (Alpha, NJ)
SLC Graphics (Pittston, PA)
Snohomish Publishing (Snohomish, WA)
Southeastern Printing (Stuart, FL)
Sowers Printing (Lebanon, PA)
Speaker-Hines & Thomas (Lansing, MI)
Standard Publishing (Cincinnati, OH)
Stephenson Inc (Alexandria, VA)
Stewart Publishing (Marble Hill, MO)
Stinehour Press (Lunenburg, VT)
Straus Printing (Madison, WI)
The Studley Press (Dalton, MA)
Suburban Publishers (Exeter, PA)
Sweet Printing (Round Rock, TX)
John S Swift Company (Saint Louis, MO)
John S Swift (Chicago, IL)

John S Swift (Cincinnati, OH)
John S Swift (Teterboro, NJ)
T A S Graphics (Detroit, MI)
Technical Comm. (N Kansas City, MO)
Telegraph Press (Harrisburg, PA)
Texas Color Printers (Dallas, TX)
Thomson-Shore (Dexter, MI)
Times Printing (Random Lake, WI)
Tracor Publications (Austin, TX)
Tri-Graphic Printing (Ottawa, ON)
Tri-State Press (Clayton, GA)
Triangle Printing (Nashville, TN)
TSO General Corp (Long Island City, NY)
Twin City Printery (Lewiston, ME)
United Color (Monroe, OH)
Universal Printers (Winnipeg, MB)
Universal Printing (Saint Louis, MO)
Vail Ballou Printing (Binghamton, NY)
Valco Graphics (Seattle, WA)
Van Volumes (Thorndike, MA)
Versa Press (East Peoria, IL)
Vicks Lithograph (Yorkville, NY)
Victor Graphics (Baltimore, MD)
Viking Press (Eden Prairie, MN)
Vogue Printers (North Chicago, IL)
Volkmuth Printers (Saint Cloud, MN)
Waldon Press (New York, NY)
Wallace Press (Hillside, IL)
Walsworth Publishing (Marceline, MO)
Waverly Press (Baltimore, MD)
The Webb Company (Saint Paul, MN)
Webcom Ltd (Scarborough, ON)
Webcrafters (Madison, WI)
A D Weiss Lithograph (Hollywood, FL)
Wellesley Press (Framingham, MA)
Western Publishers (Albuquerque, NM)
Western Publishing (Racine, WI)
Westview Press (Boulder, CO)
Whitehall Printing (Wheeling, IL)
Wickersham Printing (Lancaster, PA)
Wisconsin Color Press (Milwaukee, WI)
Worzalla Publishing (Stevens Point, WI)

Spiral Bound Books

Adams Press (Chicago, IL)
Advanced Duplicating (Edina, MN)
Adviser Graphics (Red Deer, AB)
Alger Press Ltd (Oshawa, ON)
Alpine Press (Stoughton, MA)
Arcata Graphics (West Hanover, MA)
Arcata Graphics (Kingsport, TN)
Arcata Graphics (Martinsburg, WV)
Argus Press (Niles, IL)
Atelier (New York, NY)
Automated Graphic (White Plains, MD)
Balan Printing (Brooklyn, NY)

Spiral Bound Books

Banta Corporation (Menasha, WI)
Bawden Printing (Eldridge, IA)
Beacon Wholesale Printing (Seattle, WA)
Blue Dolphin Press (Grass Valley, CA)
BookCrafters (Chelsea, MI)
C & M Press (Thornton, CO)
Camelot Fine Printing (Albuquerque, NM)
Case-Hoyt Corporation (Rochester, NY)
Centax of Canada (Regina, SK)
Color House (Grand Rapids, MI)
Commercial Printing (Medford, OR)
Community Press (Provo, UT)
Comput-A-Print (Reno, NV)
Consolidated Printers (Berkeley, CA)
Country Press (Mohawk, NY)
Crane Duplicating (West Barnstable, MA)
Crest Litho (Watervliet, NY)
Diversified Printing (Brea, CA)
R R Donnelley (Crawfordsville, IN)
R R Donnelley (Chicago, IL)
Edwards & Broughton (Raleigh, NC)
Edwards Brothers (Ann Arbor, MI)
Fast Print (Fort Wayne, IN)
Federated Litho (Providence, RI)
Fort Orange Press (Albany, NY)
Friesen Printers (Altona, MB)
Gagne Printing (Louiseville, PQ)
Ganis & Harris (New York, NY)
Gateway Press (Louisville, KY)
Geiger Brothers (Lewiston, ME)
George Lithograph (San Francisco, CA)
Gilliland Printing (Arkansas City, KS)
Graphic Arts Center (Portland, OR)
Graphic Printing (New Carlisle, OH)
Guynes Printing (Albuquerque, NM)
Hamilton Printing (Rensselaer, NY)
Harlo Press (Detroit, MI)
D B Hess Company (Woodstock, IL)
A B Hirschfeld Press (Denver, CO)
Interstate Printers (Danville, IL)
Johnson Publishing (Boulder, CO)
Jostens / Clarksville (Clarksville, TN)
Jostens / State College (State College, PA)
Jostens / Topeka (Topeka, KS)
Julin Printing (Monticello, IA)
Kern International (Duxbury, MA)
C J Krehbiel Company (Cincinnati, OH)
Liberty York Graphic (Hempstead, NY)
Maple-Vail (York, PA)
Mark IV Press (Hauppauge, NY)
The Mazer Corporation (Dayton, OH)
McGregor & Werner (Washington, DC)
McGrew Color (Kansas City, MO)
Cookbooks by Morris Press (Kearney, NE)
MWM Dexter (Aurora, MO)
Nimrod Press (Boston, MA)
Omnipress (Madison, WI)
Paust Inc (Richmond, IN)
Progress Printing (Lynchburg, VA)
Quebecor America (New York, NY)

Recorder Sunset (San Francisco, CA)
Ringier America (Olathe, KS)
Saint Mary's Press (Hollywood, MD)
Semline Inc (Braintree, MA)
Staked Plains Press (Canyon, TX)
Stewart Publishing (Marble Hill, MO)
John S Swift Company (Saint Louis, MO)
John S Swift (Chicago, IL)
John S Swift (Cincinnati, OH)
John S Swift (Teterboro, NJ)
Technical Comm. (N Kansas City, MO)
Tri-State Press (Clayton, GA)
TSO General Corp (Long Island City, NY)
Vail Ballou Printing (Binghamton, NY)
Versa Press (East Peoria, IL)
Vicks Lithograph (Yorkville, NY)
Victor Graphics (Baltimore, MD)
Webcom Ltd (Scarborough, ON)
Western Publishers (Albuquerque, NM)

Wire-O Bound Books

Adams Press (Chicago, IL)
Advanced Duplicating (Edina, MN)
Alger Press Ltd (Oshawa, ON)
Alpine Press (Stoughton, MA)
Arcata Graphics (Kingsport, TN)
Arcata Graphics (Martinsburg, WV)
Banta Corporation (Menasha, WI)
Bawden Printing (Eldridge, IA)
T H Best Printing (Don Mills, ON)
BookCrafters (Chelsea, MI)
C & M Press (Thornton, CO)
Color House (Grand Rapids, MI)
Commercial Printing (Medford, OR)
Delmar Printing (Charlotte, NC)
Delta Lithograph (Valencia, CA)
Diversified Printing (Brea, CA)
R R Donnelley (Crawfordsville, IN)
R R Donnelley (Chicago, IL)
Eastwood Printing (Denver, CO)
Edwards Brothers (Ann Arbor, MI)
Federated Lithographers (Providence, RI)
Friesen Printers (Altona, MB)
Graphic Arts Center (Portland, OR)
Graphic Design (Center Line, MI)
Graphic Printing (New Carlisle, OH)
Gray Printing (Fostoria, OH)
The Gregath Company (Cullman, AL)
Guynes Printing (Albuquerque, NM)
Hamilton Printing (Rensselaer, NY)
Harlo Press (Detroit, MI)
Heffernan Press (Worcester, MA)
Henington Publishing (Wolfe City, TX)
A B Hirschfeld Press (Denver, CO)
Independent Print. (Long Island City, NY)
Johnson Publishing (Boulder, CO)

Wire-O Bound Books

Julin Printing (Monticello, IA)
Kern International (Duxbury, MA)
The Mazer Corporation (Dayton, OH)
McGregor & Werner (Washington, DC)
Print Northwest (Tacoma, WA)
Quebecor America (New York, NY)
Saint Mary's Press (Hollywood, MD)
Semline Inc (Braintree, MA)
Southeastern Printing (Stuart, FL)
Technical Comm. (N Kansas City, MO)
TSO General Corp (Long Island City, NY)
Versa Press (East Peoria, IL)
Viking Press (Eden Prairie, MN)
Walsworth Publishing (Marceline, MO)

Index: Printing Equipment

This index lists those printers which have the following printing equipment in-house. Since not all printers responded to our survey forms, this index lists only those printers which could be verified as having the printing equipment indexed here.

Cameron Belt Press Printers

For more information about the Cameron belt press, write to **Cameron Graphic Arts, Somerset Technologies, P. O. Box 791, New Brunswick NJ 08903; (201) 356-6000.**. They will send you a booklet describing how a Cameron belt press works and why it is cost-effective for certain publications.

Arcata Graphics (Fairfield, PA)
Arcata Graphics (Kingsport, TN)
Arcata Graphics (Martinsburg, WV)
Banta-Harrisonburg (Harrisonburg, VA)
The Book Press (Brattleboro, VT)
BookCrafters (Fredericksburg, VA)
R R Donnelley (Harrisonburg, VA)
Eusey Press (Leominster, MA)
Interstate Printing Company (Omaha, NE)
Litho Prestige (Drummondville, PQ)
MMI Press (Harrisville, NH)
Practical Graphics (New York, NY)
Quebecor America Group (New York NY)
Western Publishing (Racine, WI)

Gravure Printers

Arcata Graphics (Depew, NY)
Brown Printing (Franklin, KY)
Dittler Brothers (Atlanta, GA)
R R Donnelley & Sons (Chicago, IL)
Kable Printing Co. (Mount Morris, IL)
Kaumagraph Corp (Wilmington, DE)
Meredith/Burda (Des Moines, IA)
Providence Gravure (Providence, RI)
Quad/Graphics, Lomira (Lomira, WI)
Ringier America (Itasca, IL)
Ringier America (Corinth, MS)
Southam Printing (Weston, ON)
Texas Color Printers (Dallas, TX)
World Color Press (New York, NY)

Letterpress Printers

Ad Infinitum Press (Mount Vernon, NY)
Adviser Graphics (Red Deer, AB)
American Printers & Litho (Chicago, IL)
Anderson Lithograph (Los Angeles, CA)
Anundsen Publishing Co. (Decorah, IA)
Argus Press (Niles, IL)
Banta (Saint Paul, MN)
Bawden Printing (Eldridge, IA)
Beacon Wholesale Printing (Seattle, WA)
Harold Berliner Printer (Nevada City, CA)
Berryville Graphics (Berryville, VA)
Blue Dolphin Press (Grass Valley, CA)
Book Makers Inc (Kenosha, WI)
Bradley Printing (Des Plaines, IL)
R L Bryan Company (Columbia, SC)
BSC Litho (Harrisburg, PA)
Cal Central Press (Sacramento, CA)
City Printing Company (North Haven, CT)
Coach House Press (Toronto, ON)
A Colish Inc (Mount Vernon, NY)
Commercial Printing (Medford, OR)
Crusader Printing (East Saint Louis, IL)
Dollco Printing (Ottawa, ON)
Einson Freeman Graphics (Fairlawn, NJ)
Fast Print (Fort Wayne, IN)
Fort Orange Press (Albany, NY)
Foster Printing (Michigan City, IN)
Geiger Brothers (Lewiston, ME)
Geryon Press (Tunnel, NY)
Gladstone Press (Ottawa, ON)
Globe-Comm (San Antonio, TX)
Graphic Design (Center Line, MI)
Greater Buffalo Press (Buffalo, NY)
Gregath Company (Cullman, AL)
Hart Graphics (Austin, TX)
Hennegan Company (Cincinnati, OH)
Heritage Printers (Charlotte, NC)
Interstate Printing Company (Omaha, NE)
Jersey Printing Company (Bayonne, NJ)
Johnson & Hardin Co. (Cincinnati, OH)
Kaufman Press Printing (Syracuse, NY)

Letterpress Printers

Mackintosh Typo. (Santa Barbara, CA)
The Mazer Corporation (Dayton, OH)
Mercury Printing Co. (Memphis, TN)
Messenger Graphics (Phoenix, AZ)
Moran Colorgraphic (Baton Rouge, LA)
Morgan Press (Dobbs Ferry, NY)
Neyenesch Printers (San Diego, CA)
Omaha Printing (Omaha, NE)
Ortlieb Press (Baton Rouge, LA)
Oxmoor Press (Birmingham, AL)
Pentagram (Minneapolis, MN)
Plain Talk Publishing (Des Moines, IA)
Preferred Graphics (Winona, MN)
Print Northwest (Tacoma, WA)
Progress Printing (Lynchburg, VA)
Quintessence Press (Amador City, CA)
Quixott Press (Doylestown, PA)
RBW Graphics (Owen Sound, ON)
John Roberts Co. (Minneapolis, MN)
Rollins Press (Orlando, FL)
Ronalds Printing (Vancouver, BC)
RPP Enterprises (Libertyville, IL)
Sexton Printing (West Saint Paul, MN)
R E Smith Printing (Fall River, MA)
Smith-Edwards-Dunlap (Phildelphia, PA)
Southam Printing (Weston, ON)
Speaker-Hines & Thomas (Lansing, MI)
Stinehour Press (Lunenburg, VT)
Universal Printers (Winnipeg, MB)
Universal Printing (Saint Louis, MO)
University Press (Winchester, MA)
West Side Graphics (New York, NY)
Western Publishing (Racine, WI)
Western Web Printing (Sioux Falls, SD)
Wood & Jones (Pasadena, CA)

Sheetfed Offset Printers

Academy Books (Rutland, VT)
Ad Color (Port Chester, NY)
Ad Infinitum Press (Mount Vernon, NY)
The Adams Group (New York, NY)
Adams Press (Chicago, IL)
Advanced Duplicating (Edina, MN)
Adviser Graphics (Red Deer, AB)
Alger Press Ltd (Oshawa, ON)
Allen Press (Lawrence, KS)
Allied Printing (Akron, OH)
Alpine Press (Stoughton, MA)
American Offset (Los Angeles, CA)
American Printers & Litho (Chicago, IL)
American Signature Graphics (Dallas, TX)
American Signature (Costa Mesa, CA)
American Signature (Memphis, TN)
Americomp (Brattleboro, VT)

Amherst Printing Corp (New York, NY)
Anderson Lithograph (Los Angeles, CA)
Anundsen Publishing (Decorah, IA)
Apollo Graphics (Southampton, PA)
Arandell-Schmidt (Menomonee Falls, WI)
Arcata Graphics (Fairfield, PA)
Arcata Graphics (Kingsport, TN)
Arcata Graphics (Martinsburg, WV)
Arcata Graphics (West Hanover, MA)
Argus Press (Niles, IL)
Arizona Lithographers (Tucson, AZ)
Artcraft Press (Waterloo, WI)
Autumn House (Hagerstown, MD)
B & R Printing (Post Falls, ID)
Baker Johnson (Dexter, MI)
Balan Printing (Brooklyn, NY)
Banta (Saint Paul, MN)
Banta Corporation (Menasha, WI)
Banta-Harrisonburg (Harrisonburg, VA)
Bawden Printing (Eldridge, IA)
Bay Port Press (National City, CA)
Beacon Press (Richmond, VA)
Beacon Wholesale Printing (Seattle, WA)
Bell Publications (Iowa City, IA)
Harold Berliner Printer (Nevada City, CA)
Berryville Graphics (Berryville, VA)
Bertelsmann Printing (New York, NY)
Beslow Associates (Chicago, IL)
T H Best Printing Co. (Don Mills, ON)
Blazing Graphics (Cranston, RI)
Blue Dolphin Press (Grass Valley, CA)
Bolger Publications (Minneapolis, MN)
Book Makers Inc (Kenosha, WI)
The Book Press (Brattleboro, VT)
Book-Mart Press (North Bergen, NJ)
BookCrafters (Chelsea, MI)
BookCrafters (Fredericksburg, VA)
Booklet Publishing (Elk Grove Village, IL)
William Boyd Printing (Albany, NY)
Braceland Brothers (Philadelphia, PA)
Bradley Printing (Des Plaines, IL)
Braun-Brumfield (Ann Arbor, MI)
Brennan Printing (Deep River, IA)
Brunswick Publishing (Lawrenceville, VA)
R L Bryan Company (Columbia, SC)
BSC Litho (Harrisburg, PA)
William Byrd Press (Richmond, VA)
C & M Press (Thornton, CO)
Cal Central Press (Sacramento, CA)
Camelot Fine Printing (Albuquerque, NM)
Canterbury Press (Rome, NY)
Capital City Press (Montpelier, VT)
Capital Printing Company (Austin, TX)
Cascio-Wolf (Springfield, VA)
Case-Hoyt Corporation (Rochester, NY)
Catalogue Publishing (Martinsburg, WV)
Catalogue Service (New Rochelle, NY)
Centax of Canada (Regina, SK)
Central Publishing (Indianapolis, IN)
Charles Communications (New York, NY)
City Printing Company (North Haven, CT)
Clarkwood Corporation (Totowa, NJ)

Sheetfed Offset Printers

Cody Publications (Kissimmee, FL)
A Colish Inc (Mount Vernon, NY)
The College Press (Collegedale, TN)
Colonial Graphics (Paterson, NJ)
Color Express (Irvine, CA)
Color Express (Minneapolis, MN)
Color Express (Atlanta, GA)
Color Express (Los Angeles, CA)
Chicago Color Express (Chicago, IL)
Chicago Color Express (Westmont, IL)
Color Graphics (Delran, NJ)
Color House (Grand Rapids, MI)
Color US Inc (Atlanta, GA)
Color World Printers (Bozeman, MT)
ColorGraphics (Tulsa, OK)
Combined Comm. (Columbia, MO)
Combined Communication (Mendota, IL)
Commercial Printing (Medford, OR)
Community Press (Provo, UT)
Comput-A-Print (Reno, NV)
Concord Litho Company (Concord, NH)
Coneco Laser Graphics (Glen Falls, NY)
Connecticut Printers (Bloomfield, CT)
Consolidated Printers (Berkeley, CA)
Copen Press (Brooklyn, NY)
Copple House (Lakemont, GA)
Corley Printing Co. (Earth City, MO)
Country Press (Middleborough, MA)
Country Press (Mohawk, NY)
Courier Graphics (Louisville, KY)
Craftsman Press (Seattle, WA)
Crane Duplicating (West Barnstable, MA)
Crest Litho (Watervliet, NY)
Crusader Printing (East Saint Louis, IL)
Cummings Printing (Manchester, NH)
Cushing-Malloy (Ann Arbor, MI)
D D Associates (Santa Clara, CA)
Daamen Printing (West Rutland, VT)
Danbury Printing (Danbury, CT)
Danner Press (Canton, OH)
Dartmouth Printing (Hanover, NH)
Dataco (Albuquerque, NM)
Dellas Graphics (Syracuse, NY)
Delmar Printing Company (Charlotte, NC)
Delta Lithograph (Valencia, CA)
Desaulniers Printing (Milan, IL)
John Deyell Company (Lindsa, ON)
Dharma Press (Oakland, CA)
Diamond Graphics (Milwaukee, WI)
Dickinson Press (Grand Rapids, MI)
Dinner & Klein (Seattle, WA)
Direct Press (Huntington Station, NY)
Dittler Brothers (Atlanta, GA)
Diversified Printing (Brea, CA)
Dollco Printing (Ottawa K1G 3M5, ON)
Donihe Graphics (Kingsport, TN)
R R Donnelley (Crawfordsville, IN)
R R Donnelley (Chicago, IL)
R R Donnelley (Harrisonburg, VA)
R R Donnelley (Willard, OH)

East Village Enterprises (New York, NY)
Eastwood Printing (Denver, CO)
Ebsco Media (Birmingham, AL)
Economy Printing Concern (Berne, IN)
Edison Lithographing (North Bergen, NJ)
Editors Press (Hyattsville, MD)
Edwards & Broughton (Raleigh, NC)
Edwards Brothers (Ann Arbor, MI)
Eerdmans Printing (Grand Rapids, MI)
Einson Freeman Graphics (Fairlawn, NJ)
Eva-Tone (Clearwater, FL)
Evangel Press (Nappanee, IN)
Faculty Press (Brooklyn, NY)
Fast Print (Fort Wayne, IN)
Federated Lithographers (Providence, RI)
Fetter Printing (Louisville, KY)
Fisher Printing (Galion, OH)
Foote & Davies (Atlanta, GA)
Fort Orange Press (Albany, NY)
Foster Printing (Michigan City, IN)
Friesen Printers (Altona, MB)
Futura Printing (Boynton Beach, FL)
Gagne Printing (Louiseville, PQ)
Gateway Press (Louisville, KY)
Gaylord Ltd (West Hollywood, CA)
Gaylord Printing (Detroit, MI)
Geiger Brothers (Lewiston, ME)
General Offset Company (Jersey City, NJ)
George Lithograph (San Francisco, CA)
Germac Printing (Tigard, OR)
Giant Horse (Daly City, CA)
Gilliland Printing Co. (Arkansas City, KS)
Gladstone Press (Ottawa K2P 0Z1, ON)
Globe-Comm (San Antonio, TX)
Glundal Color Service (East Syracuse, NY)
Goodway Graphics (Springfield, VA)
Gowe Printing Company (Medina, OH)
Graftek Press (Woodstock, IL)
Graphic Arts Center (Portland, OR)
Graphic Arts Publishing (Boise, ID)
Graphic Design (Center Line, MI)
Graphic Litho Corp (Lawrence, MA)
Graphic Printing (New Carlisle, OH)
Gray Printing (Fostoria, OH)
Greenfield Printing (Greenfield, OH)
The Gregath Company (Cullman, AL)
Griffin Printing (Glendale, CA)
Griffin Printing (Sacramento, CA)
Grit Commercial Print (Williamsport, PA)
GRT Book Printing (Oakland, CA)
Gulf Printing (Houston, TX)
Guynes Printing (Albuquerque, NM)
Hamilton Printing (Rensselaer, NY)
Harlo Press (Detroit, MI)
Hart Graphics (Austin, TX)
Heffernan Press (Worcester, MA)
Henington Publishing (Wolfe City, TX)
Hennegan Company (Cincinnati, OH)
D B Hess Company (Woodstock, IL)
Hi-Tech Color House (Chicago, IL)
Hignell Printing (Winnepeg, MB)
Hinz Lithographing (Mt Prospect, IL)

Sheetfed Offset Printers

A B Hirschfeld Press (Denver, CO)
Hoechstetter Printing (Pittsburgh, PA)
Holyoke Lithography (Springfield, MA)
Horowitz/Rae (Fairfield, NJ)
Humboldt National (North Abington MA)
Hunter Publishing (Winston-Salem, NC)
Independent Print. (Long Island City, NY)
Independent Publishing (Sarasota, FL)
Infopress/Saratoga (Saratoga Springs, NY)
Inland Lithograph (Elk Grove Village, IL)
Intelligencer Printing (Lancaster, PA)
Interstate Printers (Danville, IL)
Interstate Printing Company (Omaha, NE)
Japs-Olson Company (Minneapolis, MN)
Jersey Printing Company (Bayonne, NJ)
The Job Shop (Woods Hole, MA)
JohnsBryne Microdot (Niles, IL)
Johnson & Hardin Co. (Cincinnati, OH)
Johnson Graphics (East Dubuque, IL)
Johnson Publishing (Boulder, CO)
Jostens / Clarksville (Clarksville, TN)
Jostens / State College (State College, PA)
Jostens / Topeka (Topeka, KS)
Jostens / Visalia (Visalia, CA)
Julin Printing (Monticello, IA)
K/P Graphics San Diego (Escondido, CA)
Kaufman Press Printing (Syracuse, NY)
Kern International (Duxbury, MA)
KNI Book Manufacturing (Anaheim, CA)
The Kordet Group (Oceanside, NY)
C J Krehbiel Company (Cincinnati, OH)
Lancaster Press (Lancaster, PA)
The Lane Press (Burlington, VT)
Lasky Company (Milburn, NJ)
Latham Process Corp (New York, NY)
Les Editions Marquis (Montmagny, PQ)
Liberty York Graphic (Hempstead, NY)
Litho Specialties (Saint Paul, MN)
Lithocolor Press (Westchester, IL)
LithoCraft (Carlstadt, NJ)
Longacrea Press (New Rochelle, NY)
John D Lucas Printing (Baltimore, MD)
Mack Printing (Easton, PA)
Mackintosh Typo. (Santa Barbara, CA)
Maclean Hunter (Willowdale, ON)
The Mad Printers (Mattituck, NY)
Malloy Lithographing (Ann Arbor, MI)
Maple-Vail (York, PA)
Mark IV Press (Hauppauge, NY)
Marrakech Express (Tarpon Springs, FL)
Maverick Publications (Bend, OR)
The Mazer Corporation (Dayton, OH)
McClain Printing Company (Parson, WV)
McFarland Company (Harrisburg, PA)
McGregor & Werner (Washington, DC)
McGrew Color (Kansas City, MO)
McNaughton & Gunn (Saline, MI)
Meehan-Tooker (East Rutherford, NJ)
Mercury Printing (Memphis, TN)
Messenger Graphics (Phoenix, AZ)

Metromail Corporation (Lincoln, NE)
Mideastern Printing (Brookfield, CT)
Mitchell Graphics (Petoskey, MI)
Mitchell Press (Vancouver, BC)
Mitchell-Shear (Ann Arbor, MI)
Modern Graphic Arts (St Petersburg, FL)
Moebius Printing (Milwaukee, WI)
Monument Printers (Verplanck, NY)
Moran Colorgraphic (Baton Rouge, LA)
Morgan Press (Dobbs Ferry, NY)
Morgan Printing (Austin, TX)
Morningrise Printing (Costa Mesa, CA)
Cookbooks by Morris Press (Kearney, NE)
Motheral Printing (Fort Worth, TX)
Muller Printing (Santa Clara, CA)
Multiprint Inc (Chatham, NY)
Murray Printing (Kendallville, IN)
Murray Printing (Westford, MA)
MWM Dexter (Aurora, MO)
National Bickford (Providence, RI)
National Graphics Corp (Columbus, OH)
National Reproductions (Livonia, MI)
Nationwide Printing (Burlington, KY)
Naturegraph (Happy Camp, CA)
Neibauer Press (Warminster, PA)
Newsfoto Publishing (San Angelo, TX)
Neyenesch Printers (San Diego, CA)
Nielsen Lithographing (Cincinnati, OH)
North Plains Press (Aberdeen, SD)
Northlight Studio Press (Barre, VT)
Nystrom Publishing (Maple Grove, MN)
O'Neil Data Systems (Los Angeles, CA)
Oaks Printing Company (Bethlehem, PA)
Odyssey Press (Dover, NH)
Offset Paperback (Dallas, PA)
Olympic Litho (Brooklyn, NY)
Omaha Printing (Omaha, NE)
Optic Graphics (Glen Burnie, MD)
Ortlieb Press (Baton Rouge, LA)
Outstanding Graphics (Kenosha, WI)
Ovid Bell Press (Fulton, MO)
Oxford Group (Norway, ME)
Oxford Group (Berlin, NH)
Oxmoor Press (Birmingham, AL)
Pacific Lithograph (San Francisco, CA)
PAK Discount Printing (Zion, IL)
Pantagraph Printing (Bloomington, IL)
Paraclete Press (Orleans, MA)
Parker Graphics (Fuquay-Varina, NC)
Patterson Printing (Benton Harbor, MI)
Paust Inc (Richmond, IN)
Pearl Pressman Liberty (Philadelphia, PA)
Pendell Printing (Midland, MI)
Penn Colour (Huntington Valley, PA)
PennWell Printing (Tulsa, OK)
Penton Press (Berea, OH)
Perlmuter Printing (Independence, OH)
Petty Printing Company (Effingham, IL)
PFP Printing Corp (Gaithersburg, MD)
Phillips Brothers Printing (Springfield, IL)
Pinecliffe Printers (Shawnee, OK)
Pioneer Press (Wilmette, IL)

Sheetfed Offset Printers

Plain Talk Publishing (Des Moines, IA)
Plus Communications (Saint Louis, MO)
Port City Press (Pikesville, MD)
Port Publications (Port Washington, WI)
Practical Graphics (New York, NY)
Precision Offset (Upper Darby, PA)
Preferred Graphics (Winona, MN)
Press America (Chicago, IL)
The Press of Ohio (Brimfield, OH)
The Press (Chanhassen, MN)
Prinit Press (Dublin, IN)
Print Northwest (Tacoma, WA)
Printing Dimensions (Beltsville, MD)
Progress Printing (Lynchburg, VA)
Progressive Typographers (Emigsville, PA)
ProLitho (Provo, UT)
Publishers Press (Salt Lake City, UT)
Publishers Printing (Shepherdsville, KY)
Quebecor America (New York, NY)
Quinn-Woodbine (Woodbine, NJ)
Rapid Printing & Mailing (Omaha, NE)
RBW Graphics (Owen Sound, ON)
Realtron Multi-Lith (Denver, CO)
Repro-Tech (West Patterson, NJ)
Reproductions Inc (Rockville, MD)
Rich Printing Company (Nashville, TN)
Ringier America (Itasca, IL)
The Riverside Press (Dallas, TX)
John Roberts (Minneapolis, MN)
Rollins Press (Orlando, FL)
Ronalds Printing (Montreal, PQ)
Ronalds Printing (Vancouver, BC)
Rose Printing Company (Tallahassee, FL)
S Rosenthal & Company (Cincinnati, OH)
Roxbury Publishing (Los Angeles, CA)
Royle Printing (Sun Prairie, WI)
RPP Enterprises (Libertyville, IL)
Sabre Printers (Rogersville, TN)
Saint Croix Press (New Richmond, WI)
Saint Mary's Press (Hollywood, MD)
The Saybrook Press (Old Saybrook, CT)
Schiff Printers (Pittsburgh, PA)
Science Press (Ephrata, PA)
Semline Inc (Braintree, MA)
Service Printing (San Leandro, CA)
Sexton Printing (West Saint Paul, MN)
The Sheridan Press (Hanover, PA)
Skillful Means Press (Oakland, CA)
R E Smith Printing (Fall River, MA)
Smith-Edwards-Dunlap (Phildelphia, PA)
Snohomish Publishing (Snohomish, WA)
Southeastern Printing (Stuart, FL)
Southern Tennessee (Waynesboro, TN)
Sowers Printing Company (Lebanon, PA)
Speaker-Hines & Thomas (Lansing, MI)
Staked Plains Press (Canyon, TX)
Standard Printing Service (Chicago, IL)
Standard Publishing (Cincinnati, OH)
Stephenson Inc (Alexandria, VA)
Stewart Printing (Marble Hill, MO)

Stinehour Press (Lunenburg, VT)
Straus Printing Company (Madison, WI)
The Studley Press (Dalton, MA)
Sundance Press (Tucson, AZ)
Sweet Printing (Round Rock, TX)
John S Swift Company (Saint Louis, MO)
John S Swift (Chicago, IL)
John S Swift (Cincinnati, OH)
John S Swift (Teterboro, NJ)
T A S Graphics (Detroit, MI)
Tapco (Pemberton, NJ)
Taylor Publishing Company (Dallas, TX)
Technical Comm. (N Kansas City, MO)
Telegraph Press (Harrisburg, PA)
Thomson-Shore (Dexter, MI)
Times Litho (Forest Grove, OR)
Times Printing (Random Lake, WI)
Todd Web Press (Smithville, TX)
Tracor Publications (Austin, TX)
Tri-Graphic Printing (Ottawa, ON)
Tri-State Press (Clayton, GA)
Triangle Printing (Nashville, TN)
TSO General Corp (Long Island City, NY)
Twin City Printery (Lewiston, ME)
United Color (Monroe, OH)
Universal Printing (Saint Louis, MO)
US Press (Valdosta, GA)
Vail Ballou Printing (Binghamton, NY)
Valco Graphics (Seattle, WA)
Van Volumes (Thorndike, MA)
Versa Press (East Peoria, IL)
Vicks Lithograph (Yorkville, NY)
Victor Graphics (Baltimore, MD)
Viking Press (Eden Prairie, MN)
Vogue Printers (North Chicago, IL)
Volkmuth Printers (Saint Cloud, MN)
Waldon Press (New York, NY)
Wallace Press (Hillside, IL)
Walsworth Publishing (Marceline, MO)
Watkins Printing (Columbus, OH)
Waverly Press (Baltimore, MD)
The Webb Company (Saint Paul, MN)
Webcom Ltd (Scarborough, ON)
Webcrafters (Madison, WI)
F A Weber & Sons (Park Falls, WI)
Wellesley Press (Framingham, MA)
West Side Graphics (New York, NY)
Western Publishers (Albuquerque, NM)
Western Publishing (Racine, WI)
Western Web Printing (Sioux Falls, SD)
Westview Press (Boulder, CO)
White Arts (Indianapolis, IN)
Whitehall Printing (Wheeling, IL)
Wickersham Printing (Lancaster, PA)
Williams Catello Printing (Tualatin, OR)
Windsor Associates (San Diego, CA)
Wisconsin Color Press (Milwaukee, WI)
Wood & Jones (Pasadena, CA)
The Wood Press (Paterson, NJ)
Worzalla Publishing (Stevens Point, WI)

Web Offset Printers

Accurate Web (Central Islip, NY)
The Adams Group (New York, NY)
Advanced Duplicating (Edina, MN)
Adviser Graphics (Red Deer, AB)
Alden Press (Elk Grove Village, IL)
Alger Press Ltd (Oshawa, ON)
Allied Printing (Akron, OH)
Alonzo Printing (S San Francisco, CA)
Alpine Press (Stoughton, MA)
American Offset (Los Angeles, CA)
American Press Inc (Oakton, VA)
American Signature (Dallas, TX)
American Signature (Costa Mesa, CA)
American Signature (New York, NY)
American Signature (Memphis, TN)
American Web Offset (Denver, CO)
Amidon Graphics (Saint Paul, MN)
Arandell-Schmidt (Menomonee Falls, WI)
Arcata Graphics (Nashville, TN)
Arcata Graphics (Depew, NY)
Arcata Graphics (Kingsport, TN)
Arcata Graphics (Martinsburg, WV)
Arcata Graphics (San Jose, CA)
Artcraft Press (Waterloo, WI)
Autumn House (Hagerstown, MD)
Balan Printing (Brooklyn, NY)
Banta (Saint Paul, MN)
Banta Corporation (Menasha, WI)
Banta-Harrisonburg (Harrisonburg, VA)
Bawden Printing (Eldridge, IA)
Bay Port Press (National City, CA)
Beacon Press (Richmond, VA)
Beacon Wholesale Printing (Seattle, WA)
Bell Publications (Iowa City, IA)
Berryville Graphics (Berryville, VA)
Bertelsmann Printing (New York, NY)
Beslow Associates (Chicago, IL)
The Book Press (Brattleboro, VT)
William Boyd Printing (Albany, NY)
Braceland Brothers (Philadelphia, PA)
Bradley Printing (Des Plaines, IL)
Brookshore Litho (Elk Grove Village, IL)
Brown Printing (Waseca, MN)
Brown Printing (East Greenville, PA)
BSC Litho (Harrisburg, PA)
William Byrd Press (Richmond, VA)
Cal Central Press (Sacramento, CA)
California Offset Printers (Glendale, CA)
Carlson Color Graphics (Ocala, FL)
Cascio-Wolf (Springfield, VA)
Case-Hoyt Corporation (Rochester, NY)
Catalogue Publishing (Martinsburg, WV)
Centax of Canada (Regina, SK)
Charles Communications (New York, NY)
Citizen Prep & Printing (Beaver Dam, WI)
City Printing Company (North Haven, CT)
Clark Printing (Kansas City, MO)

Clarkwood Corporation (Totowa, NJ)
Colonial Graphics (Paterson, NJ)
Color Graphics (Delran, NJ)
ColorGraphics (Tulsa, OK)
Combined Comm. (Columbia, MO)
Combined Communication (Mendota, IL)
Commercial Printing (Medford, OR)
Concord Litho Company (Concord, NH)
Connecticut Printers (Bloomfield, CT)
Consolidated Printers (Berkeley, CA)
Continental Web (Itasca, IL)
Copen Press (Brooklyn, NY)
Corley Printing (Earth City, MO)
Craftsman Press (Seattle, WA)
Creative Web Systems (Inglewood, CA)
Crest Litho (Watervliet, NY)
Crusader Printing (East Saint Louis, IL)
Danbury Printing & Litho (Danbury, CT)
Danner Press (Canton, OH)
Dartmouth Printing (Hanover, NH)
Dataco (Albuquerque, NM)
Delta Lithograph (Valencia, CA)
Des Plaines Publishing (Des Plaines, IL)
Desaulniers Printing Company (Milan, IL)
Deven Lithographers (Brooklyn, NY)
Dickinson Press (Grand Rapids, MI)
The Dingley Press (Lisbon, ME)
Dinner & Klein (Seattle, WA)
Direct Press (Huntington Station, NY)
Dittler Brothers (Atlanta, GA)
Diversified Printing (Brea, CA)
Dollco Printing (Ottawa, ON)
Donihe Graphics (Kingsport, TN)
R R Donnelley (Crawfordsville, IN)
R R Donnelley (Chicago, IL)
R R Donnelley (Harrisonburg, VA)
R R Donnelley (Willard, OH)
Dynagraphics (Carlsbad, CA)
E & D Web (Cicero, IL)
Eagle Web Press (Salem, OR)
East Village Enterprises (New York, NY)
Eastwood Printing (Denver, CO)
Economy Printing Concern (Berne, IN)
Editors Press (Hyattsville, MD)
Edwards & Broughton (Raleigh, NC)
Edwards Brothers (Ann Arbor, MI)
Eerdmans Printing (Grand Rapids, MI)
Einson Freeman Graphics (Fairlawn, NJ)
William Feathers Printer (Oberlin, OH)
Fetter Printing (Louisville, KY)
Fisher Printing (Galion, OH)
Fisher Web Printers (Cedar Rapids, IA)
Foote & Davies (Atlanta, GA)
Foote & Davies (Lincoln, NE)
Gagne Printing (Louiseville, PQ)
Gateway Press (Louisville, KY)
Gaylord Printing (Detroit, MI)
Gibbs-Inman Company (Louisville, KY)
Gladstone Press (Ottawa, ON)
Globe-Comm (San Antonio, TX)
Glundal Color Service (East Syracuse, NY)
Goodway Graphics (Springfield, VA)

Web Offset Printers

Gowe Printing Company (Medina, OH)
Graftek Press (Woodstock, IL)
Graphic Arts Center (Portland, OR)
Graphic Arts Publishing (Boise, ID)
Graphic Design (Center Line, MI)
Gray Printing (Fostoria, OH)
Greater Buffalo Press (Buffalo, NY)
Greenfield Printing (Greenfield, OH)
Griffin Printing (Glendale, CA)
Griffin Printing (Sacramento, CA)
Grit Commercial Print (Williamsport, PA)
GTE Directories (Des Plaines, IL)
Gulf Printing (Houston, TX)
Haddon Craftsmen (Scranton, PA)
Harlo Press (Detroit, MI)
Hart Graphics (Austin, TX)
Hart Graphics (Sampsonville, SC)
Hart Press (Long Prairie, MN)
Heartland Press (Spencer, IA)
Hennegan Company (Cincinnati, OH)
Herbick & Held Printing (Pittsburgh, PA)
D B Hess Company (Woodstock, IL)
Hinz Lithographing (Mt Prospect, IL)
A B Hirschfeld Press (Denver, CO)
Holladay-Tyler Printing (Glenn Dale, MD)
Horowitz/Rae (Fairfield, NJ)
Humboldt National (North Abington MA)
Independent Print. (Long Island City, NY)
Inland Lithograph (Elk Grove Village, IL)
Instant Web (Chanhassen, MN)
Intelligencer Printing (Lancaster, PA)
Interstate Printers (Danville, IL)
Interstate Printing Company (Omaha, NE)
Japs-Olson Company (Minneapolis, MN)
Johnson & Hardin (Cincinnati, OH)
Johnson Publishing (Boulder, CO)
Kable Printing (Mount Morris, IL)
Kaufman Press Printing (Syracuse, NY)
Kaumagraph Corp (Wilmington, DE)
KNI Book Manufacturing (Anaheim, CA)
C J Krehbiel Company (Cincinnati, OH)
Lancaster Press (Lancaster, PA)
The Lane Press (Burlington, VT)
Lasky Company (Milburn, NJ)
Latham Process Corp (New York, NY)
Lawson Graphics (Toronto, ON)
Lehigh Press / Cadillac (Broadview, IL)
Lehigh Press / Dallas (Dallas, TX)
The Lehigh Press (Pennsauken, NJ)
Litho Prestige (Drummondville, PQ)
Litho Specialties (Saint Paul, MN)
Lithocolor Press (Westchester, IL)
LithoCraft (Carlstadt, NJ)
Long Island Web Printing (Jericho, NY)
John D Lucas Printing (Baltimore, MD)
Mack Printing (Easton, PA)
Maclean Hunter (Willowdale, ON)
Mail-O-Graph (Kewanne, IL)
Malloy Lithographing (Ann Arbor, MI)
Maple-Vail (York, PA)

Maquoketa Web Printing (Maquoketa, IA)
Mariposa Press (Benicia, CA)
Mars Graphic Services (Westville, NJ)
The Mazer Corporation (Dayton, OH)
McNaughton & Gunn (Saline, MI)
Media Printing (Miami, FL)
Meehan-Tooker (East Rutherford, NJ)
Meredith/Burda (Des Moines, IA)
Messenger Graphics (Phoenix, AZ)
Metromail Corporation (Lincoln, NE)
Metroweb (Erlanger, KY)
Mitchell Press (Vancouver, BC)
Modern Graphic Arts (St Petersburg, FL)
Moebius Printing (Milwaukee, WI)
Moore Response (Libertyville, IL)
Motheral Printing (Fort Worth, TX)
Muller Printing (Santa Clara, CA)
Murray Printing (Kendallville, IN)
Murray Printing (Westford, MA)
National Bickford (Providence, RI)
National Graphics Corp (Columbus, OH)
National Publishing (Philadelphia, PA)
Nevada Web Graphics (Sparks, NV)
Neyenesch Printers (San Diego, CA)
Nielsen Lithographing (Cincinnati, OH)
Noll Printing Company (Huntington, IN)
North Plains Press (Aberdeen, SD)
Northeast Web (Farmingdale, NY)
Northprint (Grand Rapids, MN)
Northwest Web (Eugene, OR)
O'Neil Data Systems (Los Angeles, CA)
Offset Paperback (Dallas, PA)
Oklahoma Graphics (Oklahoma City, OK)
Omaha Printing (Omaha, NE)
Ortlieb Press (Baton Rouge, LA)
Oxford Group (Norway, ME)
Oxford Group (Berlin, NH)
Pacific Lithograph (San Francisco, CA)
Pantagraph Printing (Bloomington, IL)
Park Press (South Holland, IL)
Parker Graphics (Fuquay-Varina, NC)
Patterson Printing (Benton Harbor, MI)
Pendell Printing (Midland, MI)
PennWell Printing (Tulsa, OK)
Penton Press (Berea, OH)
Perlmuter Printing (Independence, OH)
Perry Printing (Waterloo, WI)
Perry/Baraboo (Baraboo, WI)
Petty Printing Company (Effingham, IL)
Phillips Brothers Printing (Springfield, IL)
Pioneer Press (Wilmette, IL)
Plus Communications (Saint Louis, MO)
Port City Press (Pikesville, MD)
Port Publications (Port Washington, WI)
Practical Graphics (New York, NY)
The Press of Ohio (Brimfield, OH)
The Press (Chanhassen, MN)
Print Northwest (Tacoma, WA)
The Printer Inc (Maple Grove, MN)
Progress Printing (Lynchburg, VA)
ProLitho (Provo, UT)
Promotional Printing Corp (Houston, TX)

Web Offset Printers

Providence Gravure (Providence, RI)
Publishers Press (Salt Lake City, UT)
Publishers Printing (Shepherdsville, KY)
Quad Graphics (Thomaston, GA)
Quad/Graphics (Lomira, WI)
Quad/Graphics (Pewaukee, WI)
Quad/Graphics (Saratoga Springs, NY)
Quad/Graphics (Sussex, WI)
Quebecor America Book (New York, NY)
Rapid Printing & Mailing (Omaha, NE)
RBW Graphics (Owen Sound, ON)
Recorder Sunset (San Francisco, CA)
Regensteiner Press (West Chicago, IL)
Reproductions Inc (Rockville, MD)
Rich Printing Company (Nashville, TN)
Ringier America (Itasca, IL)
Ringier America (Brookfield, WI)
Ringier America (Corinth, MS)
Ringier America (Jonesboro, AR)
Ringier America (New Berlin, WI)
Ringier America (Phoenix, AZ)
Ringier America (Pontiac, IL)
Ringier America (Senatobia, MS)
The Riverside Press (Dallas, TX)
John Roberts (Minneapolis, MN)
Ronalds Printing (Montreal, PQ)
Ronalds Printing (Vancouver, BC)
Rose Printing Company (Tallahassee, FL)
S Rosenthal & Company (Cincinnati, OH)
Roxbury Publishing (Los Angeles, CA)
Royle Printing (Sun Prairie, WI)
RPP Enterprises (Libertyville, IL)
Saint Croix Press (New Richmond, WI)
Schumann Printers (Fall River, WI)
Science Press (Ephrata, PA)
Semline Inc (Braintree, MA)
Service Web Offset (Chicago, IL)
SLC Graphics (Pittston, PA)
R E Smith Printing (Fall River, MA)
Smith-Edwards-Dunlap (Phildelphia, PA)
Snohomish Publishing (Snohomish, WA)
Southam Printing (Weston, ON)
Sowers Printing Company (Lebanon, PA)
Speaker-Hines & Thomas (Lansing, MI)
Spencer Press (Hingham, MA)
Spencer Press (Wells, ME)
Standard Printing Service (Chicago, IL)
Standard Publishing (Cincinnati, OH)
Stephenson Inc (Alexandria, VA)

Straus Printing Company (Madison, WI)
Suburban Publishers (Exeter, PA)
Sweet Printing (Round Rock, TX)
John S Swift Company (Saint Louis, MO)
John S Swift (Chicago, IL)
John S Swift (Cincinnati, OH)
John S Swift (Teterboro, NJ)
T A S Graphics (Detroit, MI)
Tapco (Pemberton, NJ)
Telegraph Press (Harrisburg, PA)
Texas Color Printers (Dallas, TX)
Times Litho (Forest Grove, OR)
Times Printing (Random Lake, WI)
Todd Web Press (Smithville, TX)
Tri-Graphic Printing (Ottawa, ON)
Tri-State Press (Clayton, GA)
Triangle Printing (Nashville, TN)
Twin City Printery (Lewiston, ME)
United Color (Monroe, OH)
Universal Printing (Miami, FL)
Universal Printing (Saint Louis, MO)
Vail Ballou Printing (Binghamton, NY)
Valco Graphics (Seattle, WA)
Vicks Lithograph (Yorkville, NY)
Victor Graphics (Baltimore, MD)
Viking Press (Eden Prairie, MN)
Volkmuth Printers (Saint Cloud, MN)
Waldon Press (New York, NY)
Wallace Press (Hillside, IL)
Watkins Printing (Columbus, OH)
Waverly Press (Baltimore, MD)
Web Specialties (Wheeling, IL)
The Webb Company (Saint Paul, MN)
Webcom Ltd (Scarborough, ON)
Webcraft (New Brunswick, NJ)
Webcrafters (Madison, WI)
A D Weiss Lithograph (Hollywood, FL)
Wellesley Press (Framingham, MA)
Western Publishing (Racine, WI)
Western Web Printing (Sioux Falls, SD)
Wickersham Printing (Lancaster, PA)
Williams Catello Printing (Tualatin, OR)
Wimmer Brothers (Memphis, TN)
Windsor Associates (San Diego, CA)
Wisconsin Color Press (Milwaukee, WI)
Wolfer Printing (City of Commerce, CA)
The Wood Press (Paterson, NJ)
World Color Press (New York, NY)
Worzalla Publishing (Stevens Point, WI)
Henry Wurst Inc (N Kansas City, MO)

Index: Printing Services

These indexes lists those printers who provide additional services such as color separations, typesetting, warehousing, etc. Separate indexes note those printers who stock acid free and/or recycled paper.

4-Color Printers

Ad Color (Port Chester, NY)
Ad Infinitum Press (Mount Vernon, NY)
The Adams Group (New York, NY)
Adams Press (Chicago, IL)
Adviser Graphics (Red Deer, AB)
Alden Press (Elk Grove Village, IL)
Algen Press (College Point, NY)
Alger Press (Oshawa, ON)
Allen Press (Lawrence, KS)
Allied Graphics Arts (New York, NY)
Allied Printing (Akron, OH)
Alonzo Printing (S San Francisco, CA)
American Color Printing (Plantation, FL)
American Offset (Los Angeles, CA)
American Press Inc (Oakton, VA)
American Printers (Chicago, IL)
American Signature (Dallas, TX)
American Signature (Costa Mesa, CA)
American Signature (New York, NY)
American Signature (Memphis, TN)
American Web Offset (Denver, CO)
Amidon Graphics (Saint Paul, MN)
Anundsen Publishing (Decorah, IA)
Apollo Graphics (Southampton, PA)
Arandell-Schmidt (Menomonee Falls, WI)
Arcata Graphics (Nashville, TN)
Arcata Graphics (Depew, NY)
Arcata Graphics (Kingsport, TN)
Arcata Graphics (Martinsburg, WV)
Arcata Graphics (San Jose, CA)
Argus Press (Niles, IL)
Arizona Lithographers (Tucson, AZ)
Artcraft Press (Waterloo, WI)
Associated Printers (Grafton, ND)
Autumn House (Hagerstown, MD)
Baker Johnson (Dexter, MI)
Balan Printing (Brooklyn, NY)
Banta Catalog Group (Saint Paul, MN)
Banta Corporation (Menasha, WI)
Banta-Harrisonburg (Harrisonburg, VA)
Beacon Press (Richmond, VA)
Beacon Wholesale Printing (Seattle, WA)
Berryville Graphics (Berryville, VA)
Bertelsmann Printing (New York, NY)
Beslow Associates (Chicago, IL)

Blake Printery (San Luis Obispo, CA)
Blazing Graphics (Cranston, RI)
Blue Dolphin Press (Grass Valley, CA)
Bolger Publications (Minneapolis, MN)
BookCrafters (Chelsea, MI)
BookCrafters (Fredericksburg, VA)
William Boyd Printing (Albany, NY)
Bradley Printing (Des Plaines, IL)
Brookshore Litho (Elk Grove Village, IL)
Brown Printing (Waseca, MN)
Brown Printing (East Greenville, PA)
Brown Printing (Franklin, KY)
R L Bryan Company (Columbia, SC)
BSC Litho (Harrisburg, PA)
Cal Central Press (Sacramento, CA)
California Offset (Glendale, CA)
Camelot Fine Printing (Albuquerque, NM)
Canterbury Press (Rome, NY)
Capital Printing Company (Austin, TX)
Carlson Color Graphics (Ocala, FL)
Cascio-Wolf (Springfield, VA)
Case-Hoyt Corporation (Rochester, NY)
Catalog King (Clifton, NJ)
Catalogue Publishing (Martinsburg, WV)
Catalogue Service (New Rochelle, NY)
CatalogueACE (Miami, FL)
Centax of Canada (Regina, SK)
Central Publishing (Indianapolis, IN)
Charles Communications (New York, NY)
Citizen Prep & Printing (Beaver Dam, WI)
City Printing Company (North Haven, CT)
Clark Printing (Kansas City, MO)
Coach House Press (Toronto, ON)
Cody Publications (Kissimmee, FL)
The College Press (Collegedale, TN)
Color Catalog (Long Island City, NY)
Color Express (Irvine, CA)
Color Express (Minneapolis, MN)
Color Express (Atlanta, GA)
Color Express (Los Angeles, CA)
Chicago Color Express (Chicago, IL)
Chicago Color Express (Westmont, IL)
Color Graphics (Delran, NJ)
Color House (Grand Rapids, MI)
Color US Inc (Atlanta, GA)
Color World Printers (Bozeman, MT)
ColorGraphics (Tulsa, OK)
Colorlith Corporation (Johnston, RI)

4-Color Printers

Colortone Press (Washington, DC)
Combined Comm. (Columbia, MO)
Combined Communication (Mendota, IL)
Commercial Printing (Medford, OR)
Communicolor (Newark, OH)
Community Press (Provo, UT)
Concord Litho (Concord, NH)
Connecticut Printers (Bloomfield, CT)
Continental Web (Itasca, IL)
Cookbook Publishers (Olathe, KS)
Copple House (Lakemont, GA)
Coral Graphic Services (Plainview, NY)
Corley Printing (Earth City, MO)
Cornay Web Graphics (New Orleans, LA)
Country Press (Mohawk, NY)
Craftsman Press (Seattle, WA)
Crane Duplicating (West Barnstable, MA)
Creative Web Systems (Inglewood, CA)
Crest Litho (Watervliet, NY)
Crusader Printing (East Saint Louis, IL)
D D Associates (Santa Clara, CA)
Danbury Printing (Danbury, CT)
Danner Press (Canton, OH)
Dartmouth Printing (Hanover, NH)
Dataco (Albuquerque, NM)
Dayal Graphics (Lemont, IL)
Dellas Graphics (Syracuse, NY)
Delmar Printing (Charlotte, NC)
Delta Lithograph (Valencia, CA)
Des Plaines Publishing (Des Plaines, IL)
Desaulniers Printing (Milan, IL)
Deven Lithographers (Brooklyn, NY)
Dharma Press (Oakland, CA)
Diamond Graphics (Milwaukee, WI)
Dickinson Press (Grand Rapids, MI)
The Dingley Press (Lisbon, ME)
Direct Press (Huntington Station, NY)
Dollco Printing (Ottawa, ON)
Donihe Graphics (Kingsport, TN)
R R Donnelley (Crawfordsville, IN)
R R Donnelley (Chicago, IL)
R R Donnelley (Harrisonburg, VA)
R R Donnelley (Willard, OH)
Dynagraphics (Carlsbad, CA)
E & D Web (Cicero, IL)
East Village Enterprises (New York, NY)
Eastern Press (New Haven, CT)
Eastwood Printing (Denver, CO)
Ebsco Media (Birmingham, AL)
Economy Printing Concern (Berne, IN)
Editors Press (Hyattsville, MD)
Edwards & Broughton (Raleigh, NC)
Edwards Brothers (Ann Arbor, MI)
Edwards Brothers (Lillington, NC)
Eerdmans Printing (Grand Rapids, MI)
Einson Freeman Graphics (Fairlawn, NJ)
Eusey Press (Leominster, MA)
Eva-Tone (Clearwater, FL)
Faculty Press (Brooklyn, NY)
William Feathers (Oberlin, OH)

Federated Lithographers (Providence, RI)
Fetter Printing (Louisville, KY)
Fisher Printing (Galion, OH)
Fisher Web Printers (Cedar Rapids, IA)
Fleetwood Litho (New York, NY)
Flower City Printing (Rochester, NY)
Foote & Davies (Atlanta, GA)
Foote & Davies (Lincoln, NE)
Fort Orange Press (Albany, NY)
Foster Printing (Michigan City, IN)
Friesen Printers (Altona, MB)
Full Color Graphics (Plainview, NY)
Fundcraft (Collierville, TN)
Futura Printing (Boynton Beach, FL)
Gagne Printing (Louiseville, PQ)
Ganis & Harris (New York, NY)
Gateway Press (Louisville, KY)
Gaylord Ltd (West Hollywood, CA)
Gaylord Printing (Detroit, MI)
General Offset (Jersey City, NJ)
Gilliland Printing (Arkansas City, KS)
Gladstone Press (Ottawa, ON)
Globe-Comm (San Antonio, TX)
Glundal Color (East Syracuse, NY)
Gowe Printing Company (Medina, OH)
Graftek Press (Woodstock, IL)
Graphic Arts Center (Portland, OR)
Graphic Litho Corp (Lawrence, MA)
Graphic Printing (New Carlisle, OH)
Gray Printing (Fostoria, OH)
Greater Buffalo Press (Buffalo, NY)
Greenfield Printing (Greenfield, OH)
Gregath Company (Cullman, AL)
Griffin Printing (Glendale, CA)
Grit Commercial Print (Williamsport, PA)
Gulf Printing (Houston, TX)
Guynes Printing (Albuquerque, NM)
Haddon Craftsmen (Scranton, PA)
Hamilton Printing (Rensselaer, NY)
Harlin Litho (Ossining, NY)
Harlo Press (Detroit, MI)
Hart Graphics (Austin, TX)
Hart Graphics (Sampsonville, SC)
Hart Press (Long Prairie, MN)
Henington Publishing (Wolfe City, TX)
Hennegan Company (Cincinnati, OH)
Herbick & Held (Pittsburgh, PA)
D B Hess Company (Woodstock, IL)
Hi-Tech Color House (Chicago, IL)
Hignell Printing (Winnepeg, MB)
Hinz Lithographing (Mt Prospect, IL)
A B Hirschfeld Press (Denver, CO)
Hoechstetter Printing (Pittsburgh, PA)
Holladay-Tyler Printing (Glenn Dale, MD)
Holyoke Lithography (Springfield, MA)
Horowitz/Rae (Fairfield, NJ)
Humboldt National (N Abington, MA)
Hunter Publishing (Winston-Salem, NC)
Infopress/Saratoga (Saratoga Springs, NY)
Inland Lithograph (Elk Grove Village, IL)
Instant Web (Chanhassen, MN)
Intelligencer Printing (Lancaster, PA)

4-Color Printers

Interstate Printers (Danville, IL)
Interstate Printing (Omaha, NE)
Japs-Olson Company (Minneapolis, MN)
Jersey Printing Company (Bayonne, NJ)
JohnsBryne Microdot (Niles, IL)
Johnson & Hardin Co (Cincinnati, OH)
Johnson Publishing (Boulder, CO)
Jostens / Clarksville (Clarksville, TN)
Jostens / State College (State College, PA)
Jostens / Topeka (Topeka, KS)
Jostens / Visalia (Visalia, CA)
Julin Printing (Monticello, IA)
K & S Graphics (Nashville, TN)
K-B Offset (State College, PA)
K/P Graphics (Escondido, CA)
Kable Printing (Mount Morris, IL)
Kaufman Press Printing (Syracuse, NY)
Kimberly Press (Santa Barbara, CA)
The Kordet Group (Oceanside, NY)
C J Krehbiel Company (Cincinnati, OH)
Lancaster Press (Lancaster, PA)
The Lane Press (Burlington, VT)
Lasky Company (Milburn, NJ)
Latham Process Corp (New York, NY)
Lawson Graphics (Toronto, ON)
Lehigh Press (Broadview, IL)
Lehigh Press (Dallas, TX)
The Lehigh Press (Pennsauken, NJ)
Les Editions Marquis (Montmagny, PQ)
Litho Prestige (Drummondville, PQ)
Litho Specialties (Saint Paul, MN)
Lithocolor Press (Westchester, IL)
LithoCraft (Carlstadt, NJ)
Little River Press (Miami, FL)
Long Island Web (Jericho, NY)
Longacrea Press (New Rochelle, NY)
John D Lucas Printing (Baltimore, MD)
Mack Printing (Easton, PA)
Mackintosh Typo. (Santa Barbara, CA)
Maclean Hunter (Willowdale, ON)
Mail-O-Graph (Kewanne, IL)
Maquoketa Web Printing (Maquoketa, IA)
Mariposa Press (Benicia, CA)
Mark IV Press (Hauppauge, NY)
Marrakech Express (Tarpon Springs, FL)
Mars Graphic Services (Westville, NJ)
Maverick Publications (Bend, OR)
The Mazer Corporation (Dayton, OH)
McClain Printing (Parson, WV)
McFarland Company (Harrisburg, PA)
McGregor & Werner (Washington, DC)
McGrew Color (Kansas City, MO)
McNaughton & Gunn (Saline, MI)
Meaker the Printer (Phoenix, AZ)
Media Printing (Miami, FL)
Meehan-Tooker (East Rutherford, NJ)
Mercury Printing (Memphis, TN)
Meredith/Burda (Des Moines, IA)
Messenger Graphics (Phoenix, AZ)
Metroweb (Erlanger, KY)

Mideastern Printing (Brookfield, CT)
Mitchell Graphics (Petoskey, MI)
Mitchell Press (Vancouver, BC)
Mitchell-Shear (Ann Arbor, MI)
MMI Press (Harrisville, NH)
Modern Graphic Arts (St Petersburg, FL)
Moebius Printing (Milwaukee, WI)
Moran Colorgraphic (Baton Rouge, LA)
Morgan Press (Dobbs Ferry, NY)
Morgan Printing (Austin, TX)
Cookbooks by Morris Press (Kearney, NE)
Motheral Printing (Fort Worth, TX)
Muller Printing (Santa Clara, CA)
MultiPrint Company (Skokie, IL)
Murphy's Printing (Campbell, CA)
MWM Dexter (Aurora, MO)
National Bickford (Providence, RI)
National Graphics Corp (Columbus, OH)
National Reproductions (Livonia, MI)
Nationwide Printing (Burlington, KY)
Naturegraph (Happy Camp, CA)
Neibauer Press (Warminster, PA)
Nevada Web Graphics (Sparks, NV)
Newsfoto Publishing (San Angelo, TX)
Neyenesch Printers (San Diego, CA)
Nielsen Lithographing (Cincinnati, OH)
Nimrod Press (Boston, MA)
Noble Book Press (New York, NY)
Noll Printing (Huntington, IN)
North Plains Press (Aberdeen, SD)
Northlight Studio Press (Barre, VT)
Northwest Web (Eugene, OR)
Nystrom Publishing (Maple Grove, MN)
Oaks Printing Company (Bethlehem, PA)
Offset Paperback (Dallas, PA)
Ohio Valley Litho (Florence, KY)
Oklahoma Graphics (Oklahoma City, OK)
Olympic Litho (Brooklyn, NY)
Omaha Printing (Omaha, NE)
Ortlieb Press (Baton Rouge, LA)
Outstanding Graphics (Kenosha, WI)
Ovid Bell Press (Fulton, MO)
Pacific Lithograph (San Francisco, CA)
Paraclete Press (Orleans, MA)
Parker Graphics (Fuquay-Varina, NC)
Patterson Printing (Benton Harbor, MI)
Paust Inc (Richmond, IN)
Pearl Pressman Liberty (Philadelphia, PA)
Pendell Printing (Midland, MI)
Penn Colour (Huntington Valley, PA)
PennWell Printing (Tulsa, OK)
Penton Press (Berea, OH)
Perlmuter Printing (Independence, OH)
Perry Printing (Waterloo, WI)
Perry Printing (Baraboo, WI)
Pinecliffe Printers (Shawnee, OK)
Pioneer Press (Wilmette, IL)
Plain Talk Publishing (Des Moines, IA)
Plus Communications (Saint Louis, MO)
Port City Press (Pikesville, MD)
Port Publications (Port Washington, WI)
Practical Graphics (New York, NY)

4-Color Printers

Precision Offset (Upper Darby, PA)
Preferred Graphics (Winona, MN)
The Press of Ohio (Brimfield, OH)
The Press (Chanhassen, MN)
Prinit Press (Dublin, IN)
Print Northwest (Tacoma, WA)
The Printer Inc (Maple Grove, MN)
Printing Corp (Pompano Beach, FL)
Progress Printing (Lynchburg, VA)
ProLitho (Provo, UT)
Promotional Printing (Houston, TX)
Providence Gravure (Providence, RI)
Publishers Press (Salt Lake City, UT)
Publishers Printing (Shepherdsville, KY)
Quad Graphics (Thomaston, GA)
Quad/Graphics (Lomira, WI)
Quad/Graphics (Pewaukee, WI)
Quad/Graphics (Saratoga Springs, NY)
Quad/Graphics (Sussex, WI)
Quebecor America (New York, NY)
Rapid Printing (Omaha, NE)
Rapidocolor Corp (West Chester, PA)
RBW Graphics (Owen Sound, ON)
Recorder Sunset (San Francisco, CA)
Regensteiner Press (West Chicago, IL)
Reproductions Inc (Rockville, MD)
Rich Printing Company (Nashville, TN)
Ringier America (Itasca, IL)
Ringier America (Brookfield, WI)
Ringier America (Corinth, MS)
Ringier America (Jonesboro, AR)
Ringier America (New Berlin, WI)
Ringier America (Olathe, KS)
Ringier America (Phoenix, AZ)
Ringier America (Pontiac, IL)
Ringier America (Senatobia, MS)
The Riverside Press (Dallas, TX)
John Roberts Co (Minneapolis, MN)
Ronalds Printing (Montreal, PQ)
Ronalds Printing (Vancouver, BC)
S Rosenthal & Company (Cincinnati, OH)
Roxbury Publishing (Los Angeles, CA)
Royle Printing (Sun Prairie, WI)
RPP Enterprises (Libertyville, IL)
Saint Croix Press (New Richmond, WI)
Saint Mary's Press (Hollywood, MD)
Saltzman Printers (Maywood, IL)
The Saybrook Press (Old Saybrook, CT)
Schiff Printers (Pittsburgh, PA)
Schumann Printers (Fall River, WI)
Science Press (Ephrata, PA)
Semline Inc (Braintree, MA)
Service Web Offset (Chicago, IL)
Sexton Printing (West Saint Paul, MN)
The Sheridan Press (Hanover, PA)
Sheridan Printing (Alpha, NJ)
Skillful Means Press (Oakland, CA)
SLC Graphics (Pittston, PA)
R E Smith Printing (Fall River, MA)
Smith-Edwards-Dunlap (Phildelphia, PA)

Snohomish Publishing (Snohomish, WA)
Southam Printing (Weston, ON)
Southeastern Printing (Stuart, FL)
Southern Tennessee (Waynesboro, TN)
Sowers Printing (Lebanon, PA)
Speaker-Hines & Thomas (Lansing, MI)
Spencer Press (Hingham, MA)
Spencer Press (Wells, ME)
Staked Plains Press (Canyon, TX)
Standard Publishing (Cincinnati, OH)
Stephenson Inc (Alexandria, VA)
Stewart Publishing (Marble Hill, MO)
Stinehour Press (Lunenburg, VT)
Straus Printing (Madison, WI)
The Studley Press (Dalton, MA)
Suburban Publishers (Exeter, PA)
Sun Graphics (Parsons, KS)
Sweet Printing (Round Rock, TX)
John S Swift Company (Saint Louis, MO)
John S Swift (Chicago, IL)
John S Swift (Cincinnati, OH)
John S Swift (Teterboro, NJ)
T A S Graphics (Detroit, MI)
Tapco (Pemberton, NJ)
Taylor Publishing (Dallas, TX)
Telegraph Press (Harrisburg, PA)
Texas Color Printers (Dallas, TX)
Times Printing (Random Lake, WI)
Todd Web Press (Smithville, TX)
Town House Press (Pittsboro, NC)
Tracor Publications (Austin, TX)
Tri-Graphic Printing (Ottawa, ON)
Tri-State Press (Clayton, GA)
Twin City Printery (Lewiston, ME)
Ultra-Color Corp (Saint Louis, MO)
United Color (Monroe, OH)
United Litho (Falls Church, VA)
Universal Printing (Miami, FL)
Universal Printing (Saint Louis, MO)
US Press (Valdosta, GA)
Valco Graphics (Seattle, WA)
Vicks Lithograph (Yorkville, NY)
Victor Graphics (Baltimore, MD)
Vogue Printers (North Chicago, IL)
Volkmuth Printers (Saint Cloud, MN)
Waldman Graphics (Pennsauken, NJ)
Waldon Press (New York, NY)
Wallace Press (Hillside, IL)
Walsworth Publishing (Marceline, MO)
Watkins Printing (Columbus, OH)
Waverly Press (Baltimore, MD)
Web Specialties (Wheeling, IL)
The Webb Company (Saint Paul, MN)
Webcom Ltd (Scarborough, ON)
Webcraft (New Brunswick, NJ)
Webcrafters (Madison, WI)
F A Weber & Sons (Park Falls, WI)
A D Weiss Lithograph (Hollywood, FL)
Wellesley Press (Framingham, MA)
Western Publishers (Albuquerque, NM)
Western Publishing (Racine, WI)
Western Web Printing (Sioux Falls, SD)

4-Color Printers

White Arts (Indianapolis, IN)
Wimmer Brothers (Memphis, TN)
Windsor Associates (San Diego, CA)
Wisconsin Color Press (Milwaukee, WI)
Wolfer Printing (City of Commerce, CA)
Wood & Jones (Pasadena, CA)
The Wood Press (Paterson, NJ)
World Color Press (New York, NY)
Worzalla Publishing (Stevens Point, WI)
Henry Wurst Inc (North Kansas City, MO)

Color
Separations

Ad Color (Port Chester, NY)
Ad Infinitum Press (Mount Vernon, NY)
The Adams Group (New York, NY)
Algen Press Corp (College Point, NY)
Allied Graphics Arts (New York, NY)
American Color (Plantation, FL)
American Offset (Los Angeles, CA)
American Press Inc (Oakton, VA)
American Signature (Dallas, TX)
American Signature (Costa Mesa, CA)
American Signature (New York, NY)
American Signature (Memphis, TN)
American Web Offset (Denver, CO)
Amidon Graphics (Saint Paul, MN)
Apollo Graphics (Southampton, PA)
Arcata Graphics (Depew, NY)
Arcata Graphics (Kingsport, TN)
Arcata Graphics (Martinsburg, WV)
Argus Press (Niles, IL)
Autumn House (Hagerstown, MD)
Baker Johnson (Dexter, MI)
Banta Catalog Group (Saint Paul, MN)
Banta Corporation (Menasha, WI)
Banta-Harrisonburg (Harrisonburg, VA)
Bertelsmann Printing (New York, NY)
Beslow Associates (Chicago, IL)
Blazing Graphics (Cranston, RI)
Bolger Publications (Minneapolis, MN)
Bradley Printing (Des Plaines, IL)
Brown Printing (Waseca, MN)
Brown Printing (East Greenville, PA)
Brown Printing (Franklin, KY)
R L Bryan Company (Columbia, SC)
Cal Central Press (Sacramento, CA)
Camelot Fine Printing (Albuquerque, NM)
Cascio-Wolf (Springfield, VA)
Catalog King (Clifton, NJ)
Catalogue Service (New Rochelle, NY)
CatalogueACE (Miami, FL)
Central Publishing (Indianapolis, IN)
Clark Printing (Kansas City, MO)
Cody Publications (Kissimmee, FL)

The College Press (Collegedale, TN)
Color Catalog (Long Island City, NY)
Color Express (Irvine, CA)
Color Express (Minneapolis, MN)
Color Express (Atlanta, GA)
Color Express (Los Angeles, CA)
Chicago Color Express (Chicago, IL)
Chicago Color Express (Westmont, IL)
Color US Inc (Atlanta, GA)
Colorlith Corporation (Johnston, RI)
Combined Comm (Columbia, MO)
Combined Communication (Mendota, IL)
Commercial Printing (Medford, OR)
Concord Litho Company (Concord, NH)
Continental Web (Itasca, IL)
Martin Cook Associates (New York, NY)
Copple House (Lakemont, GA)
Coral Graphic Services (Plainview, NY)
Cornay Web Graphics (New Orleans, LA)
Craftsman Press (Seattle, WA)
Crane Duplicating (West Barnstable, MA)
D D Associates (Santa Clara, CA)
Danbury Printing (Danbury, CT)
Danner Press (Canton, OH)
Dartmouth Printing (Hanover, NH)
Dayal Graphics (Lemont, IL)
Delmar Printing (Charlotte, NC)
Desaulniers Printing (Milan, IL)
The Dingley Press (Lisbon, ME)
Direct Press (Huntington Station, NY)
Dollco Printing (Ottawa, ON)
Donihe Graphics (Kingsport, TN)
R R Donnelley (Harrisonburg, VA)
R R Donnelley (Willard, OH)
Dynagraphics (Carlsbad, CA)
Eastern Press (New Haven, CT)
Eastwood Printing (Denver, CO)
Economy Printing Concern (Berne, IN)
Edwards Brothers (Ann Arbor, MI)
Faculty Press (Brooklyn, NY)
Fetter Printing (Louisville, KY)
Fisher Web Printers (Cedar Rapids, IA)
Fleetwood Litho (New York, NY)
Flower City Printing (Rochester, NY)
Foote & Davies (Atlanta, GA)
Friesen Printers (Altona, MB)
Full Color Graphics (Plainview, NY)
Gaylord Ltd (West Hollywood, CA)
Gaylord Printing (Detroit, MI)
General Offset (Jersey City, NJ)
Gladstone Press (Ottawa K2P 0Z1, ON)
Globe-Comm (San Antonio, TX)
Glundal Color (East Syracuse, NY)
Graftek Press (Woodstock, IL)
Graphic Arts Center (Portland, OR)
Greater Buffalo Press (Buffalo, NY)
Greenfield Printing (Greenfield, OH)
The Gregath Company (Cullman, AL)
Griffin Printing (Glendale, CA)
Gulf Printing (Houston, TX)
Guynes Printing (Albuquerque, NM)
Harlin Litho (Ossining, NY)

Color Separations

Hart Graphics (Austin, TX)
Hart Press (Long Prairie, MN)
Hennegan Company (Cincinnati, OH)
Hi-Tech Color House (Chicago, IL)
Hinz Lithographing (Mt Prospect, IL)
A B Hirschfeld Press (Denver, CO)
Horowitz/Rae (Fairfield, NJ)
Hunter Publishing (Winston-Salem, NC)
Intelligencer Printing (Lancaster, PA)
Jersey Printing Company (Bayonne, NJ)
JohnsBryne Microdot (Niles, IL)
Jostens / Clarksville (Clarksville, TN)
Jostens / State College (State College, PA)
Jostens / Topeka (Topeka, KS)
Jostens / Visalia (Visalia, CA)
Julin Printing (Monticello, IA)
K/P Graphics (Escondido, CA)
Kable Printing (Mount Morris, IL)
Kaufman Press (Syracuse, NY)
The Kordet Group (Oceanside, NY)
Lancaster Press (Lancaster, PA)
Lasky Company (Milburn, NJ)
Lehigh Press (Broadview, IL)
Lehigh Press (Dallas, TX)
The Lehigh Press (Pennsauken, NJ)
Les Editions Marquis (Montmagny, PQ)
Litho Specialties (Saint Paul, MN)
LithoCraft (Carlstadt, NJ)
Longacrea Press (New Rochelle, NY)
John D Lucas Printing (Baltimore, MD)
Mackintosh Typo. (Santa Barbara, CA)
Maclean Hunter (Willowdale, ON)
Mark IV Press (Hauppauge, NY)
Marrakech Express (Tarpon Springs, FL)
Maverick Publications (Bend, OR)
McClain Printing Company (Parson, WV)
McGrew Color (Kansas City, MO)
McNaughton & Gunn (Saline, MI)
Meehan-Tooker (East Rutherford, NJ)
Meredith/Burda (Des Moines, IA)
Mideastern Printing (Brookfield, CT)
Mitchell Press (Vancouver, BC)
Mitchell-Shear (Ann Arbor, MI)
Modern Graphic Arts (St Petersburg, FL)
Moebius Printing (Milwaukee, WI)
Muller Printing (Santa Clara, CA)
MultiPrint Company (Skokie, IL)
MWM Dexter (Aurora, MO)
National Bickford (Providence, RI)
National Reproductions (Livonia, MI)
Neibauer Press (Warminster, PA)
Newsfoto Publishing (San Angelo, TX)
Neyenesch Printers (San Diego, CA)
Nielsen Lithographing (Cincinnati, OH)
Noble Book Press (New York, NY)
Noll Printing (Huntington, IN)
Offset Paperback (Dallas, PA)
Ohio Valley Litho (Florence, KY)
Olympic Litho (Brooklyn, NY)
Omaha Printing (Omaha, NE)

Ortlieb Press (Baton Rouge, LA)
Outstanding Graphics (Kenosha, WI)
Pacific Lithograph (San Francisco, CA)
Paust Inc (Richmond, IN)
Pendell Printing (Midland, MI)
Penn Colour (Huntington Valley, PA)
Perlmuter Printing (Independence, OH)
Pinecliffe Printers (Shawnee, OK)
The Press of Ohio (Brimfield, OH)
The Press (Chanhassen, MN)
Printing Corp (Pompano Beach, FL)
Progress Printing (Lynchburg, VA)
Promotional Printing (Houston, TX)
Providence Gravure (Providence, RI)
Quad/Graphics (Lomira, WI)
Quad/Graphics (Pewaukee, WI)
Quad/Graphics (Saratoga Springs, NY)
Quad/Graphics (Sussex, WI)
Regensteiner Press (West Chicago, IL)
Ringier America (Itasca, IL)
Ringier America (Brookfield, WI)
Ringier America (Jonesboro, AR)
Ringier America (New Berlin, WI)
Ringier America (Phoenix, AZ)
Ringier America (Pontiac, IL)
Ringier America (Senatobia, MS)
The Riverside Press (Dallas, TX)
John Roberts Co (Minneapolis, MN)
S Rosenthal & Company (Cincinnati, OH)
Roxbury Publishing (Los Angeles, CA)
Saltzman Printers (Maywood, IL)
Schiff Printers (Pittsburgh, PA)
Schumann Printers (Fall River, WI)
SLC Graphics (Pittston, PA)
Southam Printing (Weston, ON)
Speaker-Hines & Thomas (Lansing, MI)
Spencer Press (Hingham, MA)
Spencer Press (Wells, ME)
Staked Plains Press (Canyon, TX)
Stephenson Inc (Alexandria, VA)
Stinehour Press (Lunenburg, VT)
Straus Printing (Madison, WI)
Suburban Publishers (Exeter, PA)
Sun Graphics (Parsons, KS)
Sweet Printing (Round Rock, TX)
T A S Graphics (Detroit, MI)
Taylor Publishing (Dallas, TX)
Telegraph Press (Harrisburg, PA)
Texas Color Printers (Dallas, TX)
Todd Web Press (Smithville, TX)
Town House Press (Pittsboro, NC)
Twin City Printery (Lewiston, ME)
Ultra-Color Corp (Saint Louis, MO)
Universal Printing (Miami, FL)
Universal Printing (Saint Louis, MO)
US Press (Valdosta, GA)
Volkmuth Printers (Saint Cloud, MN)
Waldman Graphics (Pennsauken, NJ)
Wallace Press (Hillside, IL)
Walsworth Publishing (Marceline, MO)
Web Specialties (Wheeling, IL)
The Webb Company (Saint Paul, MN)

Color Separations

Webcraft (New Brunswick, NJ)
F A Weber & Sons (Park Falls, WI)
Western Publishers (Albuquerque, NM)
Western Publishing (Racine, WI)
Western Web Printing (Sioux Falls, SD)
Windsor Associates (San Diego, CA)
Wisconsin Color Press (Milwaukee, WI)
Wolfer Printing (City of Commerce, CA)
The Wood Press (Paterson, NJ)
Henry Wurst Inc (N Kansas City, MO)

Design and Artwork

Ad Color (Port Chester, NY)
Ad Infinitum Press (Mount Vernon, NY)
Adams & Abbott (Boston, MA)
The Adams Group (New York, NY)
Allied Graphics Arts (New York, NY)
American Press Inc (Oakton, VA)
Amos Press (Sidney, OH)
Anderson, Barton & Dalby (Atlanta, GA)
Andover Press (New York, NY)
Apollo Graphics (Southampton, PA)
Automated Graphics (White Plains, MD)
Autumn House (Hagerstown, MD)
B & R Printing (Post Falls, ID)
Banta Catalog Group (Saint Paul, MN)
Bay Port Press (National City, CA)
Blake Printery (San Luis Obispo, CA)
Blazing Graphics (Cranston, RI)
Blue Dolphin Press (Grass Valley, CA)
Bolger Publications (Minneapolis, MN)
Book Makers Inc (Kenosha, WI)
BookMasters (Ashland, OH)
William Boyd Printing (Albany, NY)
Braceland Brothers (Philadelphia, PA)
Bradley Printing (Des Plaines, IL)
R L Bryan Company (Columbia, SC)
BSC Litho (Harrisburg, PA)
Caldwell Printers (Arcadia, CA)
Camelot Book (Ormond Beach, FL)
Camelot Fine Printing (Albuquerque, NM)
Capital Printing Company (Austin, TX)
Carlson Color Graphics (Ocala, FL)
Catalog King (Clifton, NJ)
Catalogue Publishing (Martinsburg, WV)
Citizen Prep (Beaver Dam, WI)
Cody Publications (Kissimmee, FL)
A Colish Inc (Mount Vernon, NY)
The College Press (Collegedale, TN)
Color World Printers (Bozeman, MT)
ColorGraphics (Tulsa, OK)
Colortone Press (Washington, DC)
Community Press (Provo, UT)
Martin Cook Associates (New York, NY)

Copple House (Lakemont, GA)
Cornay Web Graphics (New Orleans, LA)
Country Press (Mohawk, NY)
Crane Duplicating (West Barnstable, MA)
Crusader Printing (East Saint Louis, IL)
Danbury Printing (Danbury, CT)
Dataco (Albuquerque, NM)
Dellas Graphics (Syracuse, NY)
Delmar Printing (Charlotte, NC)
Delta Lithograph (Valencia, CA)
Diamond Graphics (Milwaukee, WI)
Direct Press (Huntington Station, NY)
Donihe Graphics (Kingsport, TN)
R R Donnelley (Harrisonburg, VA)
R R Donnelley (Willard, OH)
East Village Enterprises (New York, NY)
Economy Printing Concern (Berne, IN)
Edwards & Broughton (Raleigh, NC)
Faculty Press (Brooklyn, NY)
Fast Print (Fort Wayne, IN)
Fetter Printing (Louisville, KY)
Fort Orange Press (Albany, NY)
Four Corners Press (Grand Rapids, MI)
Full Color Graphics (Plainview, NY)
Fundcraft (Collierville, TN)
Ganis & Harris (New York, NY)
George Lithograph (San Francisco, CA)
Germac Printing (Tigard, OR)
Geryon Press (Tunnel, NY)
Gilliland Printing (Arkansas City, KS)
Globe-Comm (San Antonio, TX)
Glundal Color (East Syracuse, NY)
Gorham Printing (Rochester, WA)
Graphic Design (Center Line, MI)
Gray Printing (Fostoria, OH)
Greater Buffalo (Buffalo, NY)
The Gregath Company (Cullman, AL)
Griffin Printing (Glendale, CA)
Grit Commercial Print (Williamsport, PA)
Harlo Press (Detroit, MI)
Heart of the Lakes (Interlaken, NY)
Herbick & Held Printing (Pittsburgh, PA)
A B Hirschfeld Press (Denver, CO)
Hunter Publishing (Winston-Salem, NC)
Independent Publishing (Sarasota, FL)
Interstate Printers (Danville, IL)
Jersey Printing (Bayonne, NJ)
The Job Shop (Woods Hole, MA)
Johnson Publishing (Boulder, CO)
Jostens / Clarksville (Clarksville, TN)
Jostens / State College (State College, PA)
Jostens / Topeka (Topeka, KS)
Jostens / Visalia (Visalia, CA)
Julin Printing (Monticello, IA)
K & S Graphics (Nashville, TN)
K/P Graphics (Escondido, CA)
Kaufman Press (Syracuse, NY)
Kern International (Duxbury, MA)
The Kordet Group (Oceanside, NY)
Long Island Web (Jericho, NY)
Mack Printing (Easton, PA)
Mackintosh Typo. (Santa Barbara, CA)

Design and Artwork

Mark IV Press (Hauppauge, NY)
Maverick Publications (Bend, OR)
The Mazer Corporation (Dayton, OH)
Meaker the Printer (Phoenix, AZ)
Mercury Printing (Memphis, TN)
Mideastern Printing (Brookfield, CT)
Mitchell Press (Vancouver, BC)
Modern Graphic Arts (St Petersburg, FL)
Moran Colorgraphic (Baton Rouge, LA)
Morgan Press (Dobbs Ferry, NY)
Morningrise Printing (Costa Mesa, CA)
Cookbooks by Morris Press (Kearney, NE)
MultiPrint Company (Skokie, IL)
Neibauer Press (Warminster, PA)
Noble Book Press (New York, NY)
North Plains Press (Aberdeen, SD)
Northeast Web (Farmingdale, NY)
Olympic Litho (Brooklyn, NY)
Ortlieb Press (Baton Rouge, LA)
Outstanding Graphics (Kenosha, WI)
Paraclete Press (Orleans, MA)
Paust Inc (Richmond, IN)
Pendell Printing (Midland, MI)
Penn Colour (Huntington Valley, PA)
Pentagram (Minneapolis, MN)
Perlmuter Printing (Independence, OH)
Plus Communications (Saint Louis, MO)
Port City Press (Pikesville, MD)
Practical Graphics (New York, NY)
Preferred Graphics (Winona, MN)
Prinit Press (Dublin, IN)
Printing Corp (Pompano Beach, FL)
Printing Dimensions (Beltsville, MD)
Progress Printing (Lynchburg, VA)
Quintessence Press (Amador City, CA)
Quixott Press (Doylestown, PA)
Rapid Printing & Mailing (Omaha, NE)
Repro-Tech (West Patterson, NJ)
Reproductions Inc (Rockville, MD)
Rich Publishing (Houston, TX)
S Rosenthal & Company (Cincinnati, OH)
Roxbury Publishing (Los Angeles, CA)
RPP Enterprises (Libertyville, IL)
Sexton Printing (West Saint Paul, MN)
The Sheridan Press (Hanover, PA)
Southern Tennessee (Waynesboro, TN)
Stewart Publishing (Marble Hill, MO)
Stinehour Press (Lunenburg, VT)
The Studley Press (Dalton, MA)
Suburban Publishers (Exeter, PA)
Sweet Printing (Round Rock, TX)
T A S Graphics (Detroit, MI)
Telegraph Press (Harrisburg, PA)
Times Printing (Random Lake, WI)
Town House Press (Pittsboro, NC)
Tracor Publications (Austin, TX)
Tri-State Press (Clayton, GA)
Twin City Printery (Lewiston, ME)
Ultra-Color Corp (Saint Louis, MO)
US Press (Valdosta, GA)

Vogue Printers (North Chicago, IL)
Volkmuth Printers (Saint Cloud, MN)
Wallace Press (Hillside, IL)
Waverly Press (Baltimore, MD)
Web Specialties (Wheeling, IL)
The Webb Company (Saint Paul, MN)
F A Weber & Sons (Park Falls, WI)
West Side Graphics (New York, NY)
Western Publishers (Albuquerque, NM)
Western Publishing (Racine, WI)
Western Web Printing (Sioux Falls, SD)
Windsor Associates (San Diego, CA)

Fulfillment and Mailing Services

Alden Press (Elk Grove Village, IL)
Alger Press (Oshawa, ON)
Allen Press (Lawrence, KS)
Allied Printing (Akron, OH)
Alonzo Printing (S San Francisco, CA)
American Offset (Los Angeles, CA)
American Press Inc (Oakton, VA)
American Signature (Dallas, TX)
American Signature (Costa Mesa, CA)
American Signature (New York, NY)
American Signature (Memphis, TN)
Amos Press (Sidney, OH)
Arcata Graphics (Nashville, TN)
Arcata Graphics (Depew, NY)
Arcata Graphics (Kingsport, TN)
Arcata Graphics (Martinsburg, WV)
Arcata Graphics (San Jose, CA)
Argus Press (Niles, IL)
Artcraft Press (Waterloo, WI)
Associated Printers (Grafton, ND)
Automated Graphic (White Plains, MD)
Autumn House (Hagerstown, MD)
Balan Printing (Brooklyn, NY)
Banta Catalog Group (Saint Paul, MN)
Banta Corporation (Menasha, WI)
Banta-Harrisonburg (Harrisonburg, VA)
Bawden Printing (Eldridge, IA)
Beacon Wholesale Printing (Seattle, WA)
Bertelsmann Printing (New York, NY)
Beslow Associates (Chicago, IL)
Book-Mart Press (North Bergen, NJ)
BookCrafters (Chelsea, MI)
BookCrafters (Fredericksburg, VA)
BookMasters (Ashland, OH)
William Boyd Printing (Albany, NY)
Braceland Brothers (Philadelphia, PA)
Bradley Printing (Des Plaines, IL)
Braun-Brumfield (Ann Arbor, MI)
Brown Printing (Waseca, MN)
Brown Printing (East Greenville, PA)
Brown Printing (Franklin, KY)
R L Bryan Company (Columbia, SC)

Fulfillment and Mailing Services

California Offset (Glendale, CA)
Capital City Press (Montpelier, VT)
Capital Printing (Austin, TX)
Carlson Color Graphics (Ocala, FL)
Cascio-Wolf (Springfield, VA)
Case-Hoyt Corporation (Rochester, NY)
Catalogue Publishing (Martinsburg, WV)
Champion Printing (Cincinnati, OH)
Clark Printing (Kansas City, MO)
Clarkwood Corporation (Totowa, NJ)
Cody Publications (Kissimmee, FL)
Colonial Graphics (Paterson, NJ)
Color World Printers (Bozeman, MT)
ColorGraphics (Tulsa, OK)
Combined Comm. (Columbia, MO)
Combined Communication (Mendota, IL)
Commercial Printing (Medford, OR)
Communicolor (Newark, OH)
Connecticut Printers (Bloomfield, CT)
Cornay Web Graphics (New Orleans, LA)
Craftsman Press (Seattle, WA)
Crusader Printing (East Saint Louis, IL)
Cummings Printing (Manchester, NH)
D D Associates (Santa Clara, CA)
Danner Press (Canton, OH)
Dartmouth Printing (Hanover, NH)
Dataco (Albuquerque, NM)
Dellas Graphics (Syracuse, NY)
Delmar Printing (Charlotte, NC)
Delta Lithograph (Valencia, CA)
Des Plaines Publishing (Des Plaines, IL)
Desaulniers Printing (Milan, IL)
Dharma Press (Oakland, CA)
Diamond Graphics (Milwaukee, WI)
The Dingley Press (Lisbon, ME)
Diversified Printing (Brea, CA)
Donihe Graphics (Kingsport, TN)
R R Donnelley (Crawfordsville, IN)
R R Donnelley (Chicago, IL)
R R Donnelley (Harrisonburg, VA)
R R Donnelley (Willard, OH)
Ebsco Media (Birmingham, AL)
Editors Press (Hyattsville, MD)
Edwards Brothers (Ann Arbor, MI)
Edwards Brothers (Lillington, NC)
Eva-Tone (Clearwater, FL)
Fetter Printing (Louisville, KY)
Fisher Web Printers (Cedar Rapids, IA)
Fleetwood Litho (New York, NY)
Foote & Davies (Atlanta, GA)
Foote & Davies (Lincoln, NE)
Friesen Printers (Altona, MB)
Gateway Press (Louisville, KY)
Gaylord Ltd (West Hollywood, CA)
Globe-Comm (San Antonio, TX)
Graphic Arts Center (Portland, OR)
Greater Buffalo Press (Buffalo, NY)
Greenfield Printing (Greenfield, OH)
Griffin Printing (Glendale, CA)
Grit Commercial Print (Williamsport, PA)

Gulf Printing (Houston, TX)
Guynes Printing (Albuquerque, NM)
Haddon Craftsmen (Scranton, PA)
Hamilton Printing (Rensselaer, NY)
Harlo Press (Detroit, MI)
Hart Graphics (Austin, TX)
Hart Graphics (Sampsonville, SC)
Hart Press (Long Prairie, MN)
Heffernan Press (Worcester, MA)
Hennegan Company (Cincinnati, OH)
D B Hess Company (Woodstock, IL)
A B Hirschfeld Press (Denver, CO)
Horowitz/Rae (Fairfield, NJ)
Humboldt National (N Abington, MA)
Instant Web (Chanhassen, MN)
Interstate Printers (Danville, IL)
Interstate Printing (Omaha, NE)
Japs-Olson Company (Minneapolis, MN)
Jersey Printing (Bayonne, NJ)
Johnson Graphics (East Dubuque, IL)
Johnson Publishing (Boulder, CO)
K/P Graphics (Escondido, CA)
Kable Printing (Mount Morris, IL)
Kaufman Press (Syracuse, NY)
Kern International (Duxbury, MA)
Kimberly Press (Santa Barbara, CA)
Lancaster Press (Lancaster, PA)
The Lane Press (Burlington, VT)
LithoCraft (Carlstadt, NJ)
Mack Printing (Easton, PA)
Maple-Vail (York, PA)
Mariposa Press (Benicia, CA)
Mark IV Press (Hauppauge, NY)
Marrakech Express (Tarpon Springs, FL)
The Mazer Corporation (Dayton, OH)
McClain Printing (Parson, WV)
McKay Printing (Dolton, IL)
McNaughton & Gunn (Saline, MI)
Media Printing (Miami, FL)
Mercury Printing (Memphis, TN)
Meredith/Burda (Des Moines, IA)
Messenger Graphics (Phoenix, AZ)
Metroweb (Erlanger, KY)
Mideastern Printing (Brookfield, CT)
Modern Graphic Arts (St Petersburg, FL)
Moebius Printing (Milwaukee, WI)
MultiPrint Company (Skokie, IL)
National Bickford (Providence, RI)
National Graphics (Columbus, OH)
National Publishing (Philadelphia, PA)
Neibauer Press (Warminster, PA)
Noll Printing Company (Huntington, IN)
North Plains Press (Aberdeen, SD)
Nystrom Publishing (Maple Grove, MN)
O'Neil Data Systems (Los Angeles, CA)
Odyssey Press (Dover, NH)
Offset Paperback (Dallas, PA)
Oklahoma Graphics (Oklahoma City, OK)
Omnipress (Madison, WI)
Ortlieb Press (Baton Rouge, LA)
Patterson Printing (Benton Harbor, MI)
Pearl Pressman Liberty (Philadelphia, PA)

Fulfillment and Mailing Services

PennWell Printing (Tulsa, OK)
Perlmuter Printing (Independence, OH)
Perry Printing (Waterloo, WI)
Perry/Baraboo (Baraboo, WI)
Petty Printing Company (Effingham, IL)
PFP Printing Corp (Gaithersburg, MD)
Plus Communications (Saint Louis, MO)
Port City Press (Pikesville, MD)
The Press (Chanhassen, MN)
The Printer Inc (Maple Grove, MN)
Progress Printing (Lynchburg, VA)
Providence Gravure (Providence, RI)
Publishers Press (Salt Lake City, UT)
Publishers Printing (Shepherdsville, KY)
Quad Graphics (Thomaston, GA)
Quad/Graphics (Lomira, WI)
Quad/Graphics (Pewaukee, WI)
Quad/Graphics (Saratoga Springs, NY)
Quad/Graphics (Sussex, WI)
Rapid Printing (Omaha, NE)
RBW Graphics (Owen Sound, ON)
Regensteiner Press (West Chicago, IL)
Ringier America (Itasca, IL)
Ringier America (Corinth, MS)
Ronalds Printing (Montreal, PQ)
Ronalds Printing (Vancouver, BC)
S Rosenthal & Company (Cincinnati, OH)
Roxbury Publishing (Los Angeles, CA)
Royle Printing (Sun Prairie, WI)
Saint Croix Press (New Richmond, WI)
Schumann Printers (Fall River, WI)
Science Press (Ephrata, PA)
Sexton Printing (West Saint Paul, MN)
The Sheridan Press (Hanover, PA)
Sheridan Printing (Alpha, NJ)
SLC Graphics (Pittston, PA)
Smith-Edwards-Dunlap (Phildelphia, PA)
Southeastern Printing (Stuart, FL)
Sowers Printing (Lebanon, PA)
Speaker-Hines & Thomas (Lansing, MI)
Spencer Press (Hingham, MA)
Spencer Press / Wells (Wells, ME)
Standard Publishing (Cincinnati, OH)
Stephenson Inc (Alexandria, VA)
Stinehour Press (Lunenburg, VT)
Sweet Printing (Round Rock, TX)
Technical Comm. (N Kansas City, MO)
Telegraph Press (Harrisburg, PA)
Texas Color Printers (Dallas, TX)
Times Printing (Random Lake, WI)
Todd Web Press (Smithville, TX)
Tri-State Press (Clayton, GA)
United Color (Monroe, OH)
Vail Ballou Printing (Binghamton, NY)
Volkmuth Printers (Saint Cloud, MN)
Wallace Press (Hillside, IL)
Watkins Printing (Columbus, OH)
Waverly Press (Baltimore, MD)
The Webb Company (Saint Paul, MN)
Webcom Ltd (Scarborough, ON)

A D Weiss Lithograph (Hollywood, FL)
Wellesley Press (Framingham, MA)
Western Publishing (Racine, WI)
Western Web Printing (Sioux Falls, SD)
Wickersham Printing (Lancaster, PA)
Williams Catello Printing (Tualatin, OR)
Wimmer Brothers (Memphis, TN)
Wisconsin Color Press (Milwaukee, WI)
Wolfer Printing (City of Commerce, CA)
Worzalla Publishing (Stevens Point, WI)
Henry Wurst Inc (North Kansas City, MO)

List Maintenance

Adviser Graphics (Red Deer, AB)
Allen Press (Lawrence, KS)
Balan Printing (Brooklyn, NY)
Beacon Wholesale Printing (Seattle, WA)
William Boyd Printing (Albany, NY)
Catalogue Publishing (Martinsburg, WV)
Clark Printing (Kansas City, MO)
Clarkwood Corporation (Totowa, NJ)
Cody Publications (Kissimmee, FL)
Communicolor (Newark, OH)
Crusader Printing (East Saint Louis, IL)
D D Associates (Santa Clara, CA)
Dataco (Albuquerque, NM)
Dellas Graphics (Syracuse, NY)
Delta Lithograph (Valencia, CA)
Desaulniers Printing (Milan, IL)
Diamond Graphics (Milwaukee, WI)
R R Donnelley (Harrisonburg, VA)
R R Donnelley (Willard, OH)
East Village Enterprises (New York, NY)
Editors Press (Hyattsville, MD)
Globe-Comm (San Antonio, TX)
The Gregath Company (Cullman, AL)
Griffin Printing (Glendale, CA)
Hart Press (Long Prairie, MN)
Kern International (Duxbury, MA)
Lehigh Press (Broadview, IL)
Lehigh Press (Dallas, TX)
The Lehigh Press (Pennsauken, NJ)
Mack Printing (Easton, PA)
Meredith/Burda (Des Moines, IA)
Noll Printing Company (Huntington, IN)
North Plains Press (Aberdeen, SD)
Ortlieb Press (Baton Rouge, LA)
Paust Inc (Richmond, IN)
PennWell Printing (Tulsa, OK)
Practical Graphics (New York, NY)
Rapid Printing (Omaha, NE)
Repro-Tech (West Patterson, NJ)
Sexton Printing (West Saint Paul, MN)
The Sheridan Press (Hanover, PA)
Sowers Printing (Lebanon, PA)
Suburban Publishers (Exeter, PA)
Tri-State Press (Clayton, GA)
Wallace Press (Hillside, IL)

List Maintenance

Waverly Press (Baltimore, MD)
Wellesley Press (Framingham, MA)
Western Publishers (Albuquerque, NM)
Western Web Printing (Sioux Falls, SD)

Opti-Copy Systems

Apollo Graphics (Southampton, PA)
Arcata Graphics (Depew, NY)
Arcata Graphics (Kingsport, TN)
Banta Corporation (Menasha, WI)
Banta-Harrisonburg (Harrisonburg, VA)
Bawden Printing (Eldridge, IA)
Berryville Graphics (Berryville, VA)
Bertelsmann Printing (New York, NY)
T H Best Printing (Don Mills, ON)
Bolger Publications (Minneapolis, MN)
The Book Press (Brattleboro, VT)
Braun-Brumfield (Ann Arbor, MI)
Capital Printing (Austin, TX)
Colonial Graphics (Paterson, NJ)
Country Press (Mohawk, NY)
Danner Press (Canton, OH)
Delta Lithograph (Valencia, CA)
R R Donnelley (Crawfordsville, IN)
R R Donnelley (Chicago, IL)
Edwards Brothers (Ann Arbor, MI)
Griffin Printing (Sacramento, CA)
Malloy Lithographing (Ann Arbor, MI)
Messenger Graphics (Phoenix, AZ)
Metroweb (Erlanger, KY)
Murray Printing (Westford, MA)
The Press of Ohio (Brimfield, OH)
Publishers Press (Salt Lake City, UT)
Quebecor America (New York, NY)
Rose Printing Company (Tallahassee, FL)
Science Press (Ephrata, PA)
Semline Inc (Braintree, MA)
Sexton Printing (West Saint Paul, MN)
Shepard Poorman (Indianapolis, IN)
Todd Web Press (Smithville, TX)
Tri-Graphic Printing (Ottawa, ON)
Viking Press (Eden Prairie, MN)
Wallace Press (Hillside, IL)
Walsworth Publishing (Marceline, MO)
Webcom Ltd (Scarborough, ON)
Worzalla Publishing (Stevens Point, WI)

Rachwal System

Alpine Press (Stoughton, MA)
Arcata Graphics (Kingsport, TN)

Berryville Graphics (Berryville, VA)
Bertelsmann Printing (New York, NY)
Braun-Brumfield (Ann Arbor, MI)
Dickinson Press (Grand Rapids, MI)
Malloy Lithographing (Ann Arbor, MI)
The Mazer Corporation (Dayton, OH)
McNaughton & Gunn (Saline, MI)
Patterson Printing (Benton Harbor, MI)
Science Press (Ephrata, PA)
Thomson-Shore (Dexter, MI)
Viking Press (Eden Prairie, MN)
Western Publishers (Albuquerque, NM)

Stock Acid-Free Paper

Academy Books (Rutland, VT)
Adams Press (Chicago, IL)
Adviser Graphics (Red Deer, AB)
Allen Press (Lawrence, KS)
American Offset (Los Angeles, CA)
Anundsen Publishing (Decorah, IA)
Arcata Graphics (Fairfield, PA)
Arcata Graphics (Kingsport, TN)
Arcata Graphics (Martinsburg, WV)
B & R Printing (Post Falls, ID)
Baker Johnson (Dexter, MI)
Banta Corporation (Menasha, WI)
Banta-Harrisonburg (Harrisonburg, VA)
Bawden Printing (Eldridge, IA)
Bay Port Press (National City, CA)
Beacon Wholesale Printing (Seattle, WA)
Berryville Graphics (Berryville, VA)
Bertelsmann Printing (New York, NY)
Blue Dolphin Press (Grass Valley, CA)
Book-Mart Press (North Bergen, NJ)
BookCrafters (Chelsea, MI)
Braun-Brumfield (Ann Arbor, MI)
Brunswick Publishing (Lawrenceville, VA)
Canterbury Press (Rome, NY)
Capital Printing (Austin, TX)
Cody Publications (Kissimmee, FL)
Color World Printers (Bozeman, MT)
Coneco Laser Graphics (Glen Falls, NY)
Continental Web (Itasca, IL)
Crane Duplicating (West Barnstable, MA)
Cushing-Malloy (Ann Arbor, MI)
Delmar Printing (Charlotte, NC)
Delta Lithograph (Valencia, CA)
Dharma Press (Oakland, CA)
Dickinson Press (Grand Rapids, MI)
Dollco Printing (Ottawa, ON)
R R Donnelley (Crawfordsville, IN)
R R Donnelley (Chicago, IL)
Edwards Brothers (Lillington, NC)
Eerdmans Printing (Grand Rapids, MI)
Faculty Press (Brooklyn, NY)

Stock Acid-Free Paper

Friesen Printers (Altona, MB)
Gagne Printing (Louiseville, PQ)
Gaylord Ltd (West Hollywood, CA)
General Offset (Jersey City, NJ)
Gladstone Press (Ottawa, ON)
The Gregath Company (Cullman, AL)
Griffin Printing (Glendale, CA)
Grit Commercial Print (Williamsport, PA)
Guynes Printing (Albuquerque, NM)
Harlo Press (Detroit, MI)
Heffernan Press (Worcester, MA)
Heritage Printers (Charlotte, NC)
Hignell Printing (Winnepeg, MB)
Horowitz/Rae (Fairfield, NJ)
Infopress/Saratoga (Saratoga Springs, NY)
Johnson Publishing (Boulder, CO)
Julin Printing (Monticello, IA)
Les Editions Marquis (Montmagny, PQ)
Litho Specialties (Saint Paul, MN)
Lithocolor Press (Westchester, IL)
Malloy Lithographing (Ann Arbor, MI)
Marrakech Express (Tarpon Springs, FL)
The Mazer Corporation (Dayton, OH)
McClain Printing Company (Parson, WV)
McNaughton & Gunn (Saline, MI)
Mercury Printing (Memphis, TN)
Metroweb (Erlanger, KY)
Mitchell-Shear (Ann Arbor, MI)
Moran Colorgraphic (Baton Rouge, LA)
Morgan Printing (Austin, TX)
Murray Printing (Kendallville, IN)
Murray Printing (Westford, MA)
Noble Book Press (New York, NY)
Noll Printing (Huntington, IN)
Odyssey Press (Dover, NH)
Outstanding Graphics (Kenosha, WI)
Ovid Bell Press (Fulton, MO)
Paraclete Press (Orleans, MA)
Paust Inc (Richmond, IN)
Pentagram (Minneapolis, MN)
PFP Printing Corp (Gaithersburg, MD)
Preferred Graphics (Winona, MN)
Publishers Press (Salt Lake City, UT)
Quintessence Press (Amador City, CA)
Roxbury Publishing (Los Angeles, CA)
Schiff Printers (Pittsburgh, PA)
Science Press (Ephrata, PA)
Technical Comm. (N Kansas City, MO)
Thomson-Shore (Dexter, MI)
Times Printing (Random Lake, WI)
Town House Press (Pittsboro, NC)
Tri-Graphic Printing (Ottawa, ON)
Vicks Lithograph (Yorkville, NY)
Viking Press (Eden Prairie, MN)
Walsworth Publishing (Marceline, MO)
Waverly Press (Baltimore, MD)
Webcom Ltd (Scarborough, ON)
F A Weber & Sons (Park Falls, WI)
Western Publishers (Albuquerque, NM)
Westview Press (Boulder, CO)

White Arts (Indianapolis, IN)
Wickersham Printing (Lancaster, PA)
Worzalla Publishing (Stevens Point, WI)

Stock Recycled Paper

Arcata Graphics (Fairfield, PA)
Banta Corporation (Menasha, WI)
Banta-Harrisonburg (Harrisonburg, VA)
Bawden Printing (Eldridge, IA)
Beacon Wholesale Printing (Seattle, WA)
Bertelsmann Printing (New York, NY)
T H Best Printing (Don Mills, ON)
Bolger Publications (Minneapolis, MN)
BookCrafters (Chelsea, MI)
Braun-Brumfield (Ann Arbor, MI)
Canterbury Press (Rome, NY)
Capital Printing (Austin, TX)
Country Press (Mohawk, NY)
Crane Duplicating (West Barnstable, MA)
Crusader Printing (East Saint Louis, IL)
Delta Lithograph (Valencia, CA)
Dharma Press (Oakland, CA)
Dollco Printing (Ottawa, ON)
R R Donnelley (Crawfordsville, IN)
R R Donnelley (Chicago, IL)
Edwards Brothers (Ann Arbor, MI)
Faculty Press (Brooklyn, NY)
Friesen Printers (Altona, MB)
Gladstone Press (Ottawa, ON)
Grit Commercial Print (Williamsport, PA)
Guynes Printing (Albuquerque, NM)
Heffernan Press (Worcester, MA)
Hignell Printing (Winnepeg, MB)
A B Hirschfeld Press (Denver, CO)
Infopress/Saratoga (Saratoga Springs, NY)
Johnson Publishing (Boulder, CO)
Litho Specialties (Saint Paul, MN)
Malloy Lithographing (Ann Arbor, MI)
Marrakech Express (Tarpon Springs, FL)
The Mazer Corporation (Dayton, OH)
McNaughton & Gunn (Saline, MI)
Metroweb (Erlanger, KY)
Morgan Printing (Austin, TX)
Multiprint Inc (Chatham, NY)
Northlight Studio Press (Barre, VT)
Nystrom Publishing (Maple Grove, MN)
Omnipress (Madison, WI)
PFP Printing Corp (Gaithersburg, MD)
Practical Graphics (New York, NY)
Preferred Graphics (Winona, MN)
Quintessence Press (Amador City, CA)
Rose Printing Company (Tallahassee, FL)
Schiff Printers (Pittsburgh, PA)
Science Press (Ephrata, PA)
Thomson-Shore (Dexter, MI)

Stock Recycled Paper

Tri-Graphic Printing (Ottawa, ON)
Viking Press (Eden Prairie, MN)
Wallace Press (Hillside, IL)
Webcom Ltd (Scarborough, ON)
Western Publishers (Albuquerque, NM)
Westview Press (Boulder, CO)
White Arts (Indianapolis, IN)
Wood & Jones (Pasadena, CA)
Worzalla Publishing (Stevens Point, WI)

Typesetting

Ad Color (Port Chester, NY)
Ad Infinitum Press (Mount Vernon, NY)
Adams & Abbott (Boston, MA)
The Adams Group (New York, NY)
Adams Press (Chicago, IL)
Adviser Graphics (Red Deer, AB)
Allen Press (Lawrence, KS)
Americomp (Brattleboro, VT)
Amos Press (Sidney, OH)
Andover Press (New York, NY)
Anundsen Publishing (Decorah, IA)
Apollo Graphics (Southampton, PA)
Arcata Graphics (Kingsport, TN)
Arcata Graphics (Martinsburg, WV)
Argus Press (Niles, IL)
Artex Publishing (Stevens Point, WI)
Associated Printers (Grafton, ND)
Automated Graphics (White Plains, MD)
Autumn House (Hagerstown, MD)
B & R Printing (Post Falls, ID)
Balan Printing (Brooklyn, NY)
Banta Catalog Group (Saint Paul, MN)
Bawden Printing (Eldridge, IA)
Bay Port Press (National City, CA)
Beacon Wholesale Printing (Seattle, WA)
Bell Publications (Iowa City, IA)
Berryville Graphics (Berryville, VA)
Beslow Associates (Chicago, IL)
Blake Printery (San Luis Obispo, CA)
Blazing Graphics (Cranston, RI)
Blue Dolphin Press (Grass Valley, CA)
Bolger Publications (Minneapolis, MN)
Book Makers Inc (Kenosha, WI)
The Book Printer (Laurens, IA)
BookCrafters (Chelsea, MI)
BookMasters (Ashland, OH)
William Boyd Printing (Albany, NY)
Braceland Brothers (Philadelphia, PA)
Braun-Brumfield (Ann Arbor, MI)
Brennan Printing (Deep River, IA)
Brown Printing (Waseca, MN)
Brown Printing (East Greenville, PA)
Brunswick Publishing (Lawrenceville, VA)
R L Bryan Company (Columbia, SC)
BSC Litho (Harrisburg, PA)

William Byrd Press (Richmond, VA)
Cal Central Press (Sacramento, CA)
Caldwell Printers (Arcadia, CA)
Camelot Book (Ormond Beach, FL)
Camelot Fine Printing (Albuquerque, NM)
Canterbury Press (Rome, NY)
Capital City Press (Montpelier, VT)
Carlson Color Graphics (Ocala, FL)
Case-Hoyt Corporation (Rochester, NY)
Catalog King (Clifton, NJ)
Catalogue Publishing (Martinsburg, WV)
Catalogue Service (New Rochelle, NY)
Central Publishing (Indianapolis, IN)
Citizen Prep (Beaver Dam, WI)
Coach House Press (Toronto, ON)
Cody Publications (Kissimmee, FL)
A Colish Inc (Mount Vernon, NY)
The College Press (Collegedale, TN)
Colonial Graphics (Paterson, NJ)
Color World Printers (Bozeman, MT)
ColorGraphics (Tulsa, OK)
Colortone Press (Washington, DC)
Columbus Book Binders (Columbus, GA)
Combined Comm. (Columbia, MO)
Combined Communication (Mendota, IL)
Commercial Printing (Medford, OR)
Communicolor (Newark, OH)
Community Press (Provo, UT)
Comput-A-Print (Reno, NV)
Coneco Laser Graphics (Glen Falls, NY)
Connecticut Printers (Bloomfield, CT)
Copple House (Lakemont, GA)
Cornay Web Graphics (New Orleans, LA)
Country Press (Mohawk, NY)
Craftsman Press (Seattle, WA)
Crane Duplicating (West Barnstable, MA)
Crusader Printing (East Saint Louis, IL)
Cummings Printing (Manchester, NH)
D D Associates (Santa Clara, CA)
Daamen Printing (West Rutland, VT)
Danbury Printing (Danbury, CT)
Dartmouth Printing (Hanover, NH)
Dataco (Albuquerque, NM)
Dellas Graphics (Syracuse, NY)
Delmar Printing (Charlotte, NC)
Delta Lithograph (Valencia, CA)
Des Plaines Publishing (Des Plaines, IL)
Desaulniers Printing (Milan, IL)
John Deyell Company (Lindsay, ON)
Dharma Press (Oakland, CA)
Diamond Graphics (Milwaukee, WI)
Direct Press (Huntington Station, NY)
Dollco Printing (Ottawa, ON)
Donihe Graphics (Kingsport, TN)
East Village Enterprises (New York, NY)
Eastern Press (New Haven, CT)
Eastwood Printing (Denver, CO)
Economy Printing Concern (Berne, IN)
Edison Lithographing (North Bergen, NJ)
Edwards & Broughton (Raleigh, NC)
Edwards Brothers (Ann Arbor, MI)
Edwards Brothers (Lillington, NC)

Typesetting

Evangel Press (Nappanee, IN)
Fast Print (Fort Wayne, IN)
Fetter Printing (Louisville, KY)
Fleetwood Litho (New York, NY)
Foote & Davies (Atlanta, GA)
Fort Orange Press (Albany, NY)
Foster Printing (Michigan City, IN)
Four Corners Press (Grand Rapids, MI)
Full Color Graphics (Plainview, NY)
Fundcraft (Collierville, TN)
Futura Printing (Boynton Beach, FL)
Gagne Printing (Louiseville, PQ)
Ganis & Harris (New York, NY)
Gateway Press (Louisville, KY)
Gaylord Ltd (West Hollywood, CA)
George Lithograph (San Francisco, CA)
Germac Printing (Tigard, OR)
Geryon Press (Tunnel, NY)
Gilliland Printing (Arkansas City, KS)
Gladstone Press (Ottawa, ON)
Globe-Comm (San Antonio, TX)
Gorham Printing (Rochester, WA)
Graphic Arts Center (Portland, OR)
Graphic Design (Center Line, MI)
Gray Printing (Fostoria, OH)
Greater Buffalo Press (Buffalo, NY)
The Gregath Company (Cullman, AL)
Griffin Printing (Glendale, CA)
Grit Commercial Print (Williamsport, PA)
Guynes Printing (Albuquerque, NM)
Haddon Craftsmen (Scranton, PA)
Harlin Litho (Ossining, NY)
Harlo Press (Detroit, MI)
Hart Graphics (Austin, TX)
Hawkes Publishing (Salt Lake City, UT)
Heart of the Lakes (Interlaken, NY)
Herbick & Held Printing (Pittsburgh, PA)
Heritage Printers (Charlotte, NC)
Hignell Printing (Winnepeg, MB)
Hinz Lithographing (Mt Prospect, IL)
A B Hirschfeld Press (Denver, CO)
Hooven-Dayton Corp (Dayton, OH)
Humboldt National (N Abington, MA)
Hunter Publishing (Winston-Salem, NC)
Independent Publishing (Sarasota, FL)
Infopress/Saratoga (Saratoga Springs, NY)
Interstate Printers (Danville, IL)
Interstate Printing (Omaha, NE)
Japs-Olson Company (Minneapolis, MN)
Jersey Printing Company (Bayonne, NJ)
The Job Shop (Woods Hole, MA)
Johnson & Hardin Co (Cincinnati, OH)
Johnson Publishing (Boulder, CO)
Jostens / Clarksville (Clarksville, TN)
Jostens / State College (State College, PA)
Jostens / Topeka (Topeka, KS)
Jostens / Visalia (Visalia, CA)
K & S Graphics (Nashville, TN)
K/P Graphics (Escondido, CA)
Kaufman Press (Syracuse, NY)

Kern International (Duxbury, MA)
The Kordet Group (Oceanside, NY)
Lancaster Press (Lancaster, PA)
The Lane Press (Burlington, VT)
Lasky Company (Milburn, NJ)
Latham Process Corp (New York, NY)
Les Editions Marquis (Montmagny, PQ)
Liberty York Graphic (Hempstead, NY)
Long Island Web (Jericho, NY)
John D Lucas Printing (Baltimore, MD)
Mack Printing (Easton, PA)
Mackintosh Typo. (Santa Barbara, CA)
Maclean Hunter (Willowdale, ON)
The Mad Printers (Mattituck, NY)
Mail-O-Graph (Kewanne, IL)
Maple Leaf Press (Brattleboro, VT)
Maple-Vail (York, PA)
Mark IV Press (Hauppauge, NY)
Marrakech Express (Tarpon Springs, FL)
Maverick Publications (Bend, OR)
The Mazer Corporation (Dayton, OH)
McClain Printing (Parson, WV)
Meaker the Printer (Phoenix, AZ)
Mercury Printing (Memphis, TN)
Messenger Graphics (Phoenix, AZ)
Metromail Corporation (Lincoln, NE)
Mideastern Printing (Brookfield, CT)
Mitchell Graphics (Petoskey, MI)
Mitchell Press (Vancouver, BC)
Modern Graphic Arts (St Petersburg, FL)
Monument Printers (Verplanck, NY)
Moran Colorgraphic (Baton Rouge, LA)
Morgan Press (Dobbs Ferry, NY)
Morgan Printing (Austin, TX)
Morningrise Printing (Costa Mesa, CA)
Cookbooks by Morris Press (Kearney, NE)
MultiPrint Company (Skokie, IL)
MWM Dexter (Aurora, MO)
National Graphics Corp (Columbus, OH)
Neibauer Press (Warminster, PA)
Newsfoto Publishing (San Angelo, TX)
Neyenesch Printers (San Diego, CA)
Nimrod Press (Boston, MA)
Noll Printing (Huntington, IN)
North Plains Press (Aberdeen, SD)
Northlight Studio Press (Barre, VT)
Northwest Web (Eugene, OR)
Nystrom Publishing (Maple Grove, MN)
O'Neil Data Systems (Los Angeles, CA)
Oaks Printing Company (Bethlehem, PA)
Odyssey Press (Dover, NH)
Omaha Printing (Omaha, NE)
Ortlieb Press (Baton Rouge, LA)
Ovid Bell Press (Fulton, MO)
Oxford Group (Norway, ME)
Oxford Group (Berlin, NH)
PAK Discount Printing (Zion, IL)
Pantagraph Printing (Bloomington, IL)
Paraclete Press (Orleans, MA)
Parker Graphics (Fuquay-Varina, NC)
Paust Inc (Richmond, IN)
Pearl Pressman Liberty (Philadelphia, PA)

Typesetting

Pendell Printing (Midland, MI)
PennWell Printing (Tulsa, OK)
Pentagram (Minneapolis, MN)
Perlmuter Printing (Independence, OH)
Petty Printing Company (Effingham, IL)
PFP Printing Corp (Gaithersburg, MD)
Pioneer Press (Wilmette, IL)
Plus Communications (Saint Louis, MO)
Port City Press (Pikesville, MD)
Practical Graphics (New York, NY)
Preferred Graphics (Winona, MN)
Princeton Univ. Press (Lawrenceville, NJ)
Prinit Press (Dublin, IN)
The Printer Inc (Maple Grove, MN)
Printing Corp (Pompano Beach, FL)
Printing Dimensions (Beltsville, MD)
Progress Printing (Lynchburg, VA)
Progressive Typographers (Emigsville, PA)
Promotional Printing (Houston, TX)
Quad Graphics (Thomaston, GA)
Quad/Graphics (Lomira, WI)
Quad/Graphics (Pewaukee, WI)
Quad/Graphics (Saratoga Springs, NY)
Quad/Graphics (Sussex, WI)
Quintessence Press (Amador City, CA)
Quixott Press (Doylestown, PA)
Rapid Printing (Omaha, NE)
RBW Graphics (Owen Sound, ON)
Realtron Multi-Lith (Denver, CO)
Recorder Sunset (San Francisco, CA)
Repro-Tech (West Patterson, NJ)
Reproductions Inc (Rockville, MD)
Rich Printing Company (Nashville, TN)
Ringier America (Brookfield, WI)
Ringier America (Jonesboro, AR)
Ringier America (New Berlin, WI)
Ringier America (Olathe, KS)
Ringier America (Phoenix, AZ)
Ringier America (Pontiac, IL)
Ringier America (Senatobia, MS)
Rollins Press (Orlando, FL)
Ronalds Printing (Vancouver, BC)
S Rosenthal & Company (Cincinnati, OH)
Roxbury Publishing (Los Angeles, CA)
Saint Croix Press (New Richmond, WI)
Sanders Printing (Garretson, SD)
The Saybrook Press (Old Saybrook, CT)
Schiff Printers (Pittsburgh, PA)
Science Press (Ephrata, PA)
Sexton Printing (West Saint Paul, MN)
Shepard Poorman (Indianapolis, IN)
The Sheridan Press (Hanover, PA)
Sheridan Printing (Alpha, NJ)
Skillful Means Press (Oakland, CA)
R E Smith Printing (Fall River, MA)
Smith-Edwards-Dunlap (Phildelphia, PA)
Snohomish Publishing (Snohomish, WA)
Southam Printing (Weston, ON)
Southern Tennessee (Waynesboro, TN)
Spencer Press (Hingham, MA)

Spencer Press (Wells, ME)
Staked Plains Press (Canyon, TX)
Standard Printing (Chicago, IL)
Standard Publishing (Cincinnati, OH)
Stewart Publishing (Marble Hill, MO)
Stinehour Press (Lunenburg, VT)
The Studley Press (Dalton, MA)
Suburban Publishers (Exeter, PA)
Sun Graphics (Parsons, KS)
Sweet Printing (Round Rock, TX)
John S Swift Company (Saint Louis, MO)
John S Swift (Chicago, IL)
John S Swift (Cincinnati, OH)
John S Swift (Teterboro, NJ)
T A S Graphics (Detroit, MI)
Tapco (Pemberton, NJ)
Taylor Publishing (Dallas, TX)
Technical Comm. (N Kansas City, MO)
Times Litho (Forest Grove, OR)
Times Printing (Random Lake, WI)
Town House Press (Pittsboro, NC)
Tracor Publications (Austin, TX)
Tri-Graphic Printing (Ottawa, ON)
Tri-State Press (Clayton, GA)
Triangle Printing (Nashville, TN)
Twin City Printery (Lewiston, ME)
Ultra-Color Corp (Saint Louis, MO)
United Litho (Falls Church, VA)
Universal Printing (Miami, FL)
US Press (Valdosta, GA)
Vail Ballou Printing (Binghamton, NY)
Valco Graphics (Seattle, WA)
Victor Graphics (Baltimore, MD)
Vogue Printers (North Chicago, IL)
Volkmuth Printers (Saint Cloud, MN)
Waldman Graphics (Pennsauken, NJ)
Waldon Press (New York, NY)
Wallace Press (Hillside, IL)
Walsworth Publishing (Marceline, MO)
Walter's Publishing (Waseca, MN)
Watkins Printing (Columbus, OH)
Waverly Press (Baltimore, MD)
The Webb Company (Saint Paul, MN)
Webcom Ltd (Scarborough, ON)
F A Weber & Sons (Park Falls, WI)
Wellesley Press (Framingham, MA)
West Side Graphics (New York, NY)
Western Publishers (Albuquerque, NM)
Western Publishing (Racine, WI)
Western Web Printing (Sioux Falls, SD)
Wickersham Printing (Lancaster, PA)
Windsor Associates (San Diego, CA)
Wood & Jones (Pasadena, CA)

Typesetting Via Modem or Disk

Adams Press (Chicago, IL)
Adviser Graphics (Red Deer, AB)
Allen Press (Lawrence, KS)
Americomp (Brattleboro, VT)
Apollo Graphics (Southampton, PA)
Arcata Graphics (Kingsport, TN)
Arcata Graphics (Martinsburg, WV)
Automated Graphics (White Plains, MD)
B & R Printing (Post Falls, ID)
Balan Printing (Brooklyn, NY)
Bay Port Press (National City, CA)
Berryville Graphics (Berryville, VA)
Bertelsmann Printing (New York, NY)
Beslow Associates (Chicago, IL)
Blazing Graphics (Cranston, RI)
Blue Dolphin Press (Grass Valley, CA)
Bolger Publications (Minneapolis, MN)
Book Makers Inc (Kenosha, WI)
BookMasters (Ashland, OH)
Braceland Brothers (Philadelphia, PA)
Braun-Brumfield (Ann Arbor, MI)
Brunswick Publishing (Lawrenceville, VA)
R L Bryan Company (Columbia, SC)
William Byrd Press (Richmond, VA)
Camelot Fine Printing (Albuquerque, NM)
Canterbury Press (Rome, NY)
Capital City Press (Montpelier, VT)
Central Publishing (Indianapolis, IN)
Clark Printing (Kansas City, MO)
Coach House Press (Toronto, ON)
Cody Publications (Kissimmee, FL)
The College Press (Collegedale, TN)
Color World Printers (Bozeman, MT)
Colortone Press (Washington, DC)
Columbus Book Printers (Columbus, GA)
Commercial Printing (Medford, OR)
Coneco Laser Graphics (Glen Falls, NY)
Connecticut Printers (Bloomfield, CT)
Country Press (Mohawk, NY)
Crane Duplicating (West Barnstable, MA)
Crusader Printing (East Saint Louis, IL)
D D Associates (Santa Clara, CA)
Dartmouth Printing (Hanover, NH)
Dellas Graphics (Syracuse, NY)
Delmar Printing (Charlotte, NC)
Des Plaines Publishing (Des Plaines, IL)
Dharma Press (Oakland, CA)
Diamond Graphics (Milwaukee, WI)
Dollco Printing (Ottawa, ON)
East Village Enterprises (New York, NY)
Eastwood Printing (Denver, CO)
Edwards & Broughton (Raleigh, NC)
Edwards Brothers (Ann Arbor, MI)
Edwards Brothers (Lillington, NC)
Fast Print (Fort Wayne, IN)
Fort Orange Press (Albany, NY)

Gagne Printing (Louiseville, PQ)
George Lithograph (San Francisco, CA)
Gilliland Printing (Arkansas City, KS)
Gladstone Press (Ottawa K2P 0Z1, ON)
Graphic Design (Center Line, MI)
Gray Printing (Fostoria, OH)
Griffin Printing (Glendale, CA)
Grit Commercial Print (Williamsport, PA)
Guynes Printing (Albuquerque, NM)
Harlo Press (Detroit, MI)
Hart Press (Long Prairie, MN)
Herbick & Held Printing (Pittsburgh, PA)
Hignell Printing (Winnepeg, MB)
A B Hirschfeld Press (Denver, CO)
Hunter Publishing (Winston-Salem, NC)
Independent Publishing (Sarasota, FL)
Infopress/Saratoga (Saratoga Springs, NY)
Interstate Printing (Omaha, NE)
Jersey Printing (Bayonne, NJ)
The Job Shop (Woods Hole, MA)
Johnson Publishing (Boulder, CO)
Jostens / Clarksville (Clarksville, TN)
Jostens / State College (State College, PA)
Jostens / Topeka (Topeka, KS)
K/P Graphics San Diego (Escondido, CA)
Kern International (Duxbury, MA)
Lancaster Press (Lancaster, PA)
The Lane Press (Burlington, VT)
Latham Process Corp (New York, NY)
Les Editions Marquis (Montmagny, PQ)
Mack Printing (Easton, PA)
Mackintosh Typo. (Santa Barbara, CA)
The Mad Printers (Mattituck, NY)
Maple-Vail (York, PA)
Mark IV Press (Hauppauge, NY)
Marrakech Express (Tarpon Springs, FL)
Maverick Publications (Bend, OR)
The Mazer Corporation (Dayton, OH)
McClain Printing (Parson, WV)
Meaker the Printer (Phoenix, AZ)
Mercury Printing (Memphis, TN)
Messenger Graphics (Phoenix, AZ)
Metroweb (Erlanger, KY)
Mideastern Printing (Brookfield, CT)
Monument Printers (Verplanck, NY)
Moran Colorgraphic (Baton Rouge, LA)
Morgan Printing (Austin, TX)
Neibauer Press (Warminster, PA)
Nimrod Press (Boston, MA)
Noll Printing (Huntington, IN)
Northlight Studio Press (Barre, VT)
Nystrom Publishing (Maple Grove, MN)
O'Neil Data Systems (Los Angeles, CA)
Oaks Printing Company (Bethlehem, PA)
Odyssey Press (Dover, NH)
Omaha Printing (Omaha, NE)
Ovid Bell Press (Fulton, MO)
Oxford Group (Norway, ME)
Oxford Group (Berlin, NH)
PennWell Printing (Tulsa, OK)
Perry Printing (Waterloo, WI)
Perry/Baraboo (Baraboo, WI)

Typesetting Via Modem or Disk

PFP Printing Corp (Gaithersburg, MD)
Plus Communications (Saint Louis, MO)
Practical Graphics (New York, NY)
Preferred Graphics (Winona, MN)
Princeton Univ. Press (Lawrenceville, NJ)
Printing Dimensions (Beltsville, MD)
Progress Printing (Lynchburg, VA)
Progressive Typographers (Emigsville, PA)
RBW Graphics (Owen Sound, ON)
Realtron Multi-Lith (Denver, CO)
Recorder Sunset (San Francisco, CA)
Repro-Tech (West Patterson, NJ)
Ronalds Printing (Vancouver, BC)
Rose Printing Company (Tallahassee, FL)
S Rosenthal & Company (Cincinnati, OH)
Roxbury Publishing (Los Angeles, CA)
Sanders Printing (Garretson, SD)
Schiff Printers (Pittsburgh, PA)
Science Press (Ephrata, PA)
Sexton Printing (W Saint Paul, MN)
The Sheridan Press (Hanover, PA)
Snohomish Publishing (Snohomish, WA)
Stewart Publishing (Marble Hill, MO)
Stinehour Press (Lunenburg, VT)
The Studley Press (Dalton, MA)
T A S Graphics (Detroit, MI)
Times Printing (Random Lake, WI)
Town House Press (Pittsboro, NC)
Tri-Graphic Printing (Ottawa, ON)
Tri-State Press (Clayton, GA)
Twin City Printery (Lewiston, ME)
United Litho (Falls Church, VA)
US Press (Valdosta, GA)
Vail Ballou Printing (Binghamton, NY)
Valco Graphics (Seattle, WA)
Vogue Printers (North Chicago, IL)
Wallace Press (Hillside, IL)
Walsworth Publishing (Marceline, MO)
Waverly Press (Baltimore, MD)
Webcom Ltd (Scarborough, ON)
Western Publishing (Racine, WI)
Western Web Printing (Sioux Falls, SD)
Wickersham Printing (Lancaster, PA)
Wood & Jones (Pasadena, CA)

Printers Who Warehouse

Ad Infinitum Press (Mount Vernon, NY)
Alger Press Ltd (Oshawa, ON)
Allen Press (Lawrence, KS)
American Offset (Los Angeles, CA)
Apollo Graphics (Southampton, PA)
Arcata Graphics (Depew, NY)
Arcata Graphics (Kingsport, TN)

Arcata Graphics (Martinsburg, WV)
Argus Press (Niles, IL)
Automated Graphics (White Plains, MD)
Baker Johnson (Dexter, MI)
Balan Printing (Brooklyn, NY)
Banta Corporation (Menasha, WI)
Banta-Harrisonburg (Harrisonburg, VA)
Bawden Printing (Eldridge, IA)
Beacon Wholesale Printing (Seattle, WA)
Berryville Graphics (Berryville, VA)
Bertelsmann Printing (New York, NY)
T H Best Printing (Don Mills, ON)
Book Makers Inc (Kenosha, WI)
Book-Mart Press (North Bergen, NJ)
BookCrafters (Chelsea, MI)
BookMasters (Ashland, OH)
William Boyd Printing (Albany, NY)
Braun-Brumfield (Ann Arbor, MI)
R L Bryan Company (Columbia, SC)
BSC Litho (Harrisburg, PA)
Canterbury Press (Rome, NY)
Catalogue Publishing (Martinsburg, WV)
Colonial Graphics (Paterson, NJ)
Commercial Printing (Medford, OR)
Community Press (Provo, UT)
Comput-A-Print (Reno, NV)
Connecticut Printers (Bloomfield, CT)
Continental Web (Itasca, IL)
Crest Litho (Watervliet, NY)
D D Associates (Santa Clara, CA)
Dellas Graphics (Syracuse, NY)
Delta Lithograph (Valencia, CA)
Desaulniers Printing (Milan, IL)
Diamond Graphics (Milwaukee, WI)
Dollco Printing (Ottawa, ON)
Donihe Graphics (Kingsport, TN)
Economy Printing Concern (Berne, IN)
Editors Press (Hyattsville, MD)
Edwards Brothers (Ann Arbor, MI)
Edwards Brothers (Lillington, NC)
Fetter Printing (Louisville, KY)
Fort Orange Press (Albany, NY)
Friesen Printers (Altona, MB)
Gagne Printing (Louiseville, PQ)
George Lithograph (San Francisco, CA)
Gladstone Press (Ottawa, ON)
Globe-Comm (San Antonio, TX)
Griffin Printing (Glendale, CA)
Grit Commercial Print (Williamsport, PA)
Haddon Craftsmen (Scranton, PA)
Harlo Press (Detroit, MI)
Heffernan Press (Worcester, MA)
A B Hirschfeld Press (Denver, CO)
Hooven-Dayton Corp (Dayton, OH)
Horowitz/Rae (Fairfield, NJ)
Hunter Publishing (Winston-Salem, NC)
Interstate Printers (Danville, IL)
Interstate Printing (Omaha, NE)
Jersey Printing (Bayonne, NJ)
Johnson Publishing (Boulder, CO)
K/P Graphics (Escondido, CA)
Kaufman Press (Syracuse, NY)

Printers Who Warehouse Books

Kern International (Duxbury, MA)
Mack Printing (Easton, PA)
Mail-O-Graph (Kewanne, IL)
Marrakech Express (Tarpon Springs, FL)
The Mazer Corporation (Dayton, OH)
McClain Printing (Parson, WV)
Mercury Printing (Memphis, TN)
Metroweb (Erlanger, KY)
Mitchell-Shear (Ann Arbor, MI)
Moran Colorgraphic (Baton Rouge, LA)
Morgan Press (Dobbs Ferry, NY)
MultiPrint Company (Skokie, IL)
Neibauer Press (Warminster, PA)
Nystrom Publishing (Maple Grove, MN)
Odyssey Press (Dover, NH)
Offset Paperback (Dallas, PA)
Omaha Printing (Omaha, NE)
Ortlieb Press (Baton Rouge, LA)
Pendell Printing (Midland, MI)
PennWell Printing (Tulsa, OK)
Perry Printing (Waterloo, WI)
Perry/Baraboo (Baraboo, WI)
Plus Communications (Saint Louis, MO)
Port City Press (Pikesville, MD)
Printing Dimensions (Beltsville, MD)
Progress Printing (Lynchburg, VA)
Rapid Printing (Omaha, NE)
Repro-Tech (West Patterson, NJ)
Ringier America (Brookfield, WI)
Ringier America (Jonesboro, AR)
Ringier America (New Berlin, WI)
Ringier America (Olathe, KS)
Ringier America (Phoenix, AZ)
Ringier America (Pontiac, IL)
Ringier America (Senatobia, MS)
Ronalds Printing (Montreal, PQ)
S Rosenthal & Company (Cincinnati, OH)
Roxbury Publishing (Los Angeles, CA)
RPP Enterprises (Libertyville, IL)
Science Press (Ephrata, PA)
SLC Graphics (Pittston, PA)
Southeastern Printing (Stuart, FL)
Stinehour Press (Lunenburg, VT)
Suburban Publishers (Exeter, PA)
T A S Graphics (Detroit, MI)
Technical Comm. (N Kansas City, MO)
Telegraph Press (Harrisburg, PA)
Times Litho (Forest Grove, OR)
Times Printing (Random Lake, WI)
Todd Web Press (Smithville, TX)
Tri-State Press (Clayton, GA)
Valco Graphics (Seattle, WA)
Waverly Press (Baltimore, MD)
Webcom Ltd (Scarborough, ON)
F A Weber & Sons (Park Falls, WI)
Western Publishers (Albuquerque, NM)
Western Publishing (Racine, WI)
Western Web Printing (Sioux Falls, SD)
Wickersham Printing (Lancaster, PA)
Williams Catello Printing (Tualatin, OR)

Wimmer Brothers (Memphis, TN)
Wolfer Printing (City of Commerce, CA)
Worzalla Publishing (Stevens Point, WI)

Union Printers

The following printers all employ union workers.

Allied Printing (Akron, OH)
American Offset (Los Angeles, CA)
American Printers (Chicago, IL)
Arcata Graphics (Depew, NY)
Arcata Graphics (Kingsport, TN)
Balan Printing (Brooklyn, NY)
Banta Corporation (Menasha, WI)
Banta-Harrisonburg (Harrisonburg, VA)
Bawden Printing (Eldridge, IA)
Bertelsmann Printing (New York, NY)
The Book Press (Brattleboro, VT)
Bradley Printing (Des Plaines, IL)
California Offset Printers (Glendale, CA)
Canterbury Press (Rome, NY)
Central Publishing (Indianapolis, IN)
Clark Printing (Kansas City, MO)
Copen Press (Brooklyn, NY)
Danner Press (Canton, OH)
Dickinson Press (Grand Rapids, MI)
Direct Press (Huntington Station, NY)
Eastwood Printing (Denver, CO)
Editors Press (Hyattsville, MD)
Faculty Press (Brooklyn, NY)
Federated Lithographers (Providence, RI)
Foster Printing Service (Michigan City, IN)
Gagne Printing (Louiseville, PQ)
General Offset Company (Jersey City, NJ)
Gray Printing (Fostoria, OH)
Grit Commercial Print (Williamsport, PA)
Hart Press (Long Prairie, MN)
Herbick & Held Printing (Pittsburgh, PA)
A B Hirschfeld Press (Denver, CO)
Holyoke Lithography (Springfield, MA)
Inland Lithograph (Elk Grove Village, IL)
Interstate Printing Company (Omaha, NE)
Jersey Printing Company (Bayonne, NJ)
Kaufman Press Printing (Syracuse, NY)
Latham Process Corp (New York, NY)
Lawson Graphics (Toronto, ON)
Les Editions Marquis (Montmagny, PQ)
LithoCraft (Carlstadt, NJ)
Mail-O-Graph (Kewanne, IL)
McFarland Company (Harrisburg, PA)
Messenger Graphics (Phoenix, AZ)
Moran Colorgraphic (Baton Rouge, LA)
National Publishing (Philadelphia, PA)
Noll Printing Company (Huntington, IN)
Oaks Printing Company (Bethlehem, PA)
Offset Paperback (Dallas, PA)
PennWell Printing (Tulsa, OK)

Union Printers

Perry Printing (Waterloo, WI)
Perry/Baraboo (Baraboo, WI)
Phillips Brothers Printing (Springfield, IL)
Plain Talk Publishing (Des Moines, IA)
Port Publications (Port Washington, WI)
Print Northwest (Tacoma, WA)
Quebecor America (New York, NY)
Ronalds Printing (Montreal H1E 2S7, PQ)
Ronalds Printing (Vancouver, BC)
S Rosenthal & Company (Cincinnati, OH)
Roxbury Publishing (Los Angeles, CA)
Saint Croix Press (New Richmond, WI)
Semline Inc (Braintree, MA)
SLC Graphics (Pittston, PA)
United Color (Monroe, OH)
Universal Printers (Winnipeg, MB)
Valco Graphics (Seattle, WA)
Vicks Lithograph (Yorkville, NY)
Wallace Press (Hillside, IL)
Wickersham Printing (Lancaster, PA)
Wisconsin Color Press (Milwaukee, WI)
Wolfer Printing (City of Commerce, CA)

Printers with Toll-Free Phone Numbers

Allied Printing (800-824-8719)
Alpine Press (800-343-5901)
American Press (800-283-4666)
Americomp (800-451-4328)
Amidon Graphics (800-328-6502)
Amos Press (800-848-4406)
Apollo Graphics (800-522-9006)
Arandell-Schmidt (800-558-8724)
Arcata Graphics (800-356-0603)
Automated Graphics (800-678-8760)
Autumn House Graphics (800-444-7532)
Banta Corporation (800-722-3324)
Beacon Wholesale Printing (800-426-0244)
Blake Printery (800-792-6946)
Bolger Publications (800-999-6311)
The Book Press (800-732-7310)
BookMasters (800-537-6727)
Braceland Brothers (800-338-1280)
Brookshore Lithographers (800-323-6112)
Carter Rice (800-225-6673)
Catalog King (800-223-5751)
CatalogueACE (800-367-5871)
Champion Printing (800-543-1957)
Cody Publications (800-432-9192)
The College Press (800-277-7377)
Color Catalog Creations (800-621-6680)

Color Express (800-872-0720)
Chicago Color Express (800-872-0720)
Color Graphics (800-257-9569)
Color US Inc (800-443-7377)
Color World Printers (800-332-3303)
Colorlith Corporation (800-556-7171)
Columbus Book Printers (800-553-7314)
Communicolor (800-848-7040)
Concord Litho Company (800-258-3662)
Cookbook Publishers (800-821-5745)
Cornay Web Graphics (800-888-9426)
Danbury Printing (800-231-8712)
Delmar Printing (800-438-1504)
Delta Lithograph (800-323-3582)
Des Plaines Publishing (800-283-1776)
Direct Press/Modern Litho (800-347-3285)
Dittler Brothers (800-927-0777)
Donihe Graphics (800-251-0337)
R R Donnelley (800-428-0832)
E & D Web (800-323-5733)
Ebsco Media (800-624-9454)
Eusey Press (800-678-6299)
Eva-Tone (800-382-8663)
Evangel Press (800-822-5919)
William Exline Inc (800-321-3062)
Fort Orange Press (800-448-4468)
Foster Printing Service (800-382-0808)
Full Color Graphics (800-323-5452)
Fundcraft (800-351-7822)
Gagne Printing Ltd (800-567-2154)
Gibbs-Inman Company (800-626-2365)
Gilliland Printing (800-332-8200)
Graphic Arts Publishing (800-523-9675)
Graphic Design & Printing (800-343-5840)
Greenfield Printing (800-543-3881)
Griffin Printing (800-826-4049)
Griffin Printing (800-448-3511)
Grit Commercial Print (800-223-8455)
Gulf Printing (800-423-9537)
Haddon Craftsmen (800-225-6538)
Hart Graphics (800-531-5471)
Heartland Press (800-932-9675)
Heffernan Press (800-343-6016)
Hi-Tech Color House (800-621-4004)
Holladay-Tyler Printing (800-444-8953)
Humboldt National (800-344-1033)
Insert Color Press (800-356-3943)
Intelligencer Printing (800-233-0107)
Kable Printing Company (800-678-6299)
Legacy Books (800-367-BOOK)
LithoCraft (800-223-0574)
John D Lucas Printing (800-638-2850)
Malloy Lithographing (800-722-3231)
Marrakech Express (800-940-6566)
Maverick Publications (800-627-7932)
McKay Printing Services (800-227-1432)
Media Printing (800-544-WEBS)
Messenger Graphics (800-847-2844)
Mitchell Graphics (800-841-6793)
MMI Press (800-367-1888)
Modern Graphic Arts (800-237-8474)
Monument Printers (800-227-2081)

Printers with Toll-Free Numbers

Moore Response Graphics (800-722-9001)
Cookbooks by Morris Press (800-445-6621)
MultiPrint Company (800-858-9999)
MWM Dexter (800-641-3398)
Noll Printing Company (800-348-2886)
Northprint (800-346-5767)
Ohio Valley Litho (800-877-7405)
Omnipress (800-828-0305)
Optic Graphics (800-638-7107)
Ovid Bell Press (800-835-8919)
Paraclete Press (800-451-5006)
Pendell Printing (800-448-4200)
Perlmuter Printing (800-321-6228)
Preferred Graphics (800-247-7841)
The Press (800-336-2680)
Progress Printing (800-572-7804)
Providence Gravure (800-678-6299)
Publishers Press (800-456-6600)
Publishers Printing (800-626-5801)
Rapidocolor Corporation (800-872-7436)
Ringier America - Olathe (800-678-0003)
Rose Printing Company (800-227-3725)
S Rosenthal & Company (800-325-7200)
Saint Croix Press (800-826-6622)
Saltzman Printers (800-952-2800)
Sanders Printing Company (800-648-3738)
Service Web Offset (800-621-1567)
The Sheridan Press (800-352-2210)
Southeastern Printing (800-228-1583)
Sowers Printing (800-233-7028)
Speaker-Hines & Thomas (800-292-2630)
Spencer Press (800-343-5690)
Standard Publishing (800-543-1301)
Stephenson Inc (800-336-4637)
Sun Graphics (800-835-0588)
Sundance Press (800-528-4827)
Texas Color Printers (800-678-6299)
Tri-Graphic Printing (800-267-9750)
Triangle Printing (800-843-9529)
United Litho (800-368-6100)
US Press (800-227-7377)
Versa Press (800-447-7829)
Viking Press (800-765-7327)
Volkmuth Printers (800-678-6299)
Waldman Graphics (800-543-0955)
Walter's Publishing (800-447-3274)
Waverly Press (800-638-5198)
The Webb Company (800-322-9322)
Webcraft Technologies (800-628-2533)
Webcrafters (800-356-8200)
Western Publishers (800-873-2363)
Western Publishing (800-453-1222)
Western Web Printing (800-843-6805)
White Arts (800-748-0323)
Whitehall Printing (800-321-9290)
Wickersham Printing (800-437-7171)

Printers with Fax Numbers

Advanced Duplicating (612-944-9683)
Algen Press Corporation (718-359-0384)
Allied Printing (216-753-0870)
Alpine Press (617-341-3973)
American Color Printing (305-473-8621)
American Press Inc (703-255-9857)
American Printers (312-267-6553)
Americomp (802-254-5240)
Anderson, Barton & Dalby (404-231-9427)
Anundsen Publishing (319-382-5150)
Apollo Graphics (215-953-1144)
Arcata / Baird Ward (615-297-8539)
Arcata Graphics / Buffalo (716-684-5191)
Arcata Graphics / Fairfield (717-642-8485)
Arcata Graphics / Halliday (617-826-6653)
Arcata / Kingsport (615-378-1109)
Arcata / Martinsburg (304-267-0989)
Arcata Graphics / San Jose (408-435-2383)
Automated Graphics (301-843-6339)
Baker Johnson (313-426-0301)
Banta Corporation (414-722-8541)
Bawden Printing (319-285-4828)
Bay Port Press (619-420-2217)
Beacon Wholesale Printing (206-726-8394)
Berryville Graphics (703-955-4268)
Bertelsmann Printing (212-984-7600)
T H Best Printing (416-447-7444)
Bolger Publications (612-645-1750)
The Book Press (802-257-9439)
Book-Mart Press (201-864-7559)
BookCrafters (313-475-7337)
BookCrafters (703-475-8591)
Booklet Publishing (312-364-0284)
William Boyd Printing (518-436-7433)
Braceland Brothers (215-492-8538)
Braun-Brumfield (313-662-1667)
Brunswick Publishing (804-848-0607)
Canterbury Press (315-337-4070)
Capital Printing (512-441-1448)
Carlson Color Graphics (904-351-5199)
Case-Hoyt Corporation (716-889-3418)
CatalogueACE (305-633-2848)
Champion Printing (513-541-9398)
The College Press (615-238-3546)
Colonial Graphics (201-345-0083)
Color Catalog Creations (718-937-0227)
Color House Graphics (616-245-5494)
Columbus Book Printers (800-553-2987)
Commercial Printing (503-773-1832)
Continental Web (312-773-1909)
Coral Graphic Services (516-935-5902)
Corley Printing (314-739-1436)
Courier Corporation (508-453-0344)
Crane Duplicating (508-362-5445)
Crusader Printing (618-271-2045)
Cushing-Malloy (313-663-5731)
Daamen Printing (802-438-5477)

Index: Printers by State

This index lists printers alphabetically by the state in which they are located. Canadian printers are listed at the end of this index.

A B Hirschfeld Press (Denver, CO)
Johnson Publishing (Boulder, CO)
Realtron Multi-Lith (Denver, CO)
Westview Press (Boulder, CO)

Connecticut

City Printing (North Haven, CT)
Connecticut Printers (Bloomfield, CT)
Danbury Printing (Danbury, CT)
Eastern Press (New Haven, CT)
Mideastern Printing (Brookfield, CT)
The Saybrook Press (Old Saybrook, CT)

DC

Colortone Press (Washington, DC)
Judd's Incorporated (Washington, DC)
McGregor & Werner (Washington, DC)

Delaware

Kaumagraph Corp (Wilmington, DE)

Florida

American Color Printing (Plantation, FL)
Camelot Book (Ormond Beach, FL)
Carlson Color Graphics (Ocala, FL)
CatalogueACE (Miami, FL)
Cody Publications (Kissimmee, FL)
Eva-Tone (Clearwater, FL)
Futura Printing (Boynton Beach, FL)
Independent Publishing (Sarasota, FL)
Little River Press (Miami, FL)
Marrakech Express (Tarpon Springs, FL)
Media Printing (Miami, FL)
Modern Graphic Arts (St Petersburg, FL)
Printing Corporation (Pompano Bch, FL)
Rollins Press (Orlando, FL)
Rose Printing Company (Tallahassee, FL)
Southeastern Printing (Stuart, FL)
Universal Printing (Miami, FL)
A D Weiss Lithograph (Hollywood, FL)

Georgia

Anderson, Barton & Dalby (Atlanta, GA)
Color Express (Atlanta, GA)
Color US Inc (Atlanta, GA)
Columbus Book Printers (Columbus, GA)
Copple House (Lakemont, GA)
Dittler Brothers (Atlanta, GA)
Foote & Davies (Atlanta, GA)
Quad Graphics (Thomaston, GA)
Tri-State Press (Clayton, GA)
US Press (Valdosta, GA)

Idaho

B & R Printing (Post Falls, ID)
Graphic Arts Publishing (Boise, ID)

Illinois

Adams Press (Chicago, IL)
Alden Press (Elk Grove Village, IL)
American Printers (Chicago, IL)
Argus Press (Niles, IL)
Beslow Associates (Chicago, IL)
Booklet Publishing (Elk Grove Village, IL)
Bradley Printing (Des Plaines, IL)
Brookshore Litho (Elk Grove Village, IL)
Chicago Color Express (Westmont, IL)
Chicago Color Express (Chicago, IL)
Combined Comm. (Mendota, IL)
Continental Web (Itasca, IL)
Crusader Printing (East Saint Louis, IL)
Dayal Graphics (Lemont, IL)
Des Plaines Publishing (Des Plaines, IL)
Desaulniers Printing (Milan, IL)
R R Donnelley & Sons (Chicago, IL)
E & D Web (Cicero, IL)
Graftek Press (Woodstock, IL)
GTE Directories (Des Plaines, IL)
D B Hess Company (Woodstock, IL)
Hi-Tech Color House (Chicago, IL)
Hinz Lithographing (Mt Prospect, IL)
Inland Lithograph (Elk Grove Village, IL)
Interstate Printers (Danville, IL)
JohnsBryne Microdot (Niles, IL)
Johnson Graphics (East Dubuque, IL)
Kable Printing (Mount Morris, IL)
Lehigh Press (Broadview, IL)
Lithocolor Press (Westchester, IL)
Mail-O-Graph (Kewanne, IL)
McKay Printing (Dolton, IL)
Moore Response (Libertyville, IL)
MultiPrint Company (Skokie, IL)
PAK Discount Printing (Zion, IL)
Pantagraph Printing (Bloomington, IL)
Park Press (South Holland, IL)
Petty Printing (Effingham, IL)
Phillips Brothers (Springfield, IL)
Pioneer Press (Wilmette, IL)
Press America (Chicago, IL)

Regensteiner Press (West Chicago, IL)
Ringier America (Itasca, IL)
Ringier America (Pontiac, IL)
RPP Enterprises (Libertyville, IL)
Saltzman Printers (Maywood, IL)
Service Web Offset (Chicago, IL)
Standard Printing (Chicago, IL)
John S Swift, Chicago (Chicago, IL)
Versa Press (East Peoria, IL)
Vogue Printers (North Chicago, IL)
Wallace Press (Hillside, IL)
Web Specialties (Wheeling, IL)
Whitehall Printing (Wheeling, IL)

Indiana

Central Publishing (Indianapolis, IN)
R R Donnelley (Crawfordsville, IN)
Economy Printing (Berne, IN)
Evangel Press (Nappanee, IN)
Fast Print (Fort Wayne, IN)
Foster Printing (Michigan City, IN)
Murray Printing (Kendallville, IN)
Noll Printing (Huntington, IN)
Paust Inc (Richmond, IN)
Prinit Press (Dublin, IN)
Shepard Poorman (Indianapolis, IN)
White Arts (Indianapolis, IN)
Ye Olde Genealogie (Indianapolis, IN)

Iowa

Anundsen Publishing (Decorah, IA)
Bawden Printing (Eldridge, IA)
Bell Publications (Iowa City, IA)
The Book Printer (Laurens, IA)
Brennan Printing (Deep River, IA)
William C Brown Printing (Dubuque, IA)
Fisher Web Printers (Cedar Rapids, IA)
Heartland Press (Spencer, IA)
Julin Printing (Monticello, IA)
Maquoketa Web Printing (Maquoketa, IA)
Meredith/Burda (Des Moines, IA)
Plain Talk Publishing (Des Moines, IA)

Kansas

Allen Press (Lawrence, KS)
Cookbook Publishers (Olathe, KS)
Gilliland Printing (Arkansas City, KS)
Jostens (Topeka, KS)
Ringier America (Olathe, KS)
Sun Graphics (Parsons, KS)

Kentucky

Brown Printing (Franklin, KY)
Courier Graphics (Louisville, KY)
Fetter Printing (Louisville, KY)
Gateway Press (Louisville, KY)
Gibbs-Inman Company (Louisville, KY)
McDowell Publications (Utica, KY)
Metroweb (Erlanger, KY)
Nationwide Printing (Burlington, KY)
Ohio Valley Litho (Florence, KY)
Publishers Printing (Shepherdsville, KY)
Rand McNally (Versailles, KY)

Louisiana

Cornay Web Graphics (New Orleans, LA)
Moran Colorgraphic (Baton Rouge, LA)
Ortlieb Press (Baton Rouge, LA)

Maine

The Dingley Press (Lisbon, ME)
Geiger Brothers (Lewiston, ME)
Oxford Group (Norway, ME)
Spencer Press (Wells, ME)
Twin City Printery (Lewiston, ME)

Maryland

Automated Graphic (White Plains, MD)
Autumn House (Hagerstown, MD)
Editors Press (Hyattsville, MD)
Gateway Press (Baltimore, MD)
Holladay-Tyler Printing (Glenn Dale, MD)
John D Lucas Printing (Baltimore, MD)
Optic Graphics (Glen Burnie, MD)
PFP Printing Corp (Gaithersburg, MD)
Port City Press (Pikesville, MD)
Printing Dimensions (Beltsville, MD)
Reproductions Inc (Rockville, MD)
Saint Mary's Press (Hollywood, MD)
Victor Graphics (Baltimore, MD)
Waverly Press (Baltimore, MD)

Massachusetts

Adams & Abbott (Boston, MA)
Alpine Press (Stoughton, MA)
Arcata Graphics (West Hanover, MA)

Carter Rice (Boston, MA)
Country Press (Middleborough, MA)
Courier Corporation (Lowell, MA)
Crane Duplicating (West Barnstable, MA)
Eusey Press (Leominster, MA)
Graphic Litho Corp (Lawrence, MA)
Heffernan Press (Worcester, MA)
Holyoke Lithography (Springfield, MA)
Humboldt National (N Abington, MA)
The Job Shop (Woods Hole, MA)
Kern International (Duxbury, MA)
Murray Printing (Westford, MA)
Nimrod Press (Boston, MA)
Paraclete Press (Orleans, MA)
Semline Inc (Braintree, MA)
R E Smith Printing (Fall River, MA)
Spencer Press (Hingham, MA)
The Studley Press (Dalton, MA)
United Lithograph (Somerville, MA)
University Press (Winchester, MA)
Van Volumes (Thorndike, MA)
Wellesley Press (Framingham, MA)

Michigan

Baker Johnson (Dexter, MI)
BookCrafters (Chelsea, MI)
Braun-Brumfield (Ann Arbor, MI)
Color House Graphics (Grand Rapids MI)
Cushing-Malloy (Ann Arbor, MI)
Dickinson Press (Grand Rapids, MI)
Edwards Brothers (Ann Arbor, MI)
Eerdmans Printing (Grand Rapids, MI)
Four Corners Press (Grand Rapids, MI)
Gaylord Printing (Detroit, MI)
Graphic Design (Center Line, MI)
Harlo Press (Detroit, MI)
Malloy Lithographing (Ann Arbor, MI)
McNaughton & Gunn (Saline, MI)
Mitchell Graphics (Petoskey, MI)
Mitchell-Shear (Ann Arbor, MI)
National Reproductions (Livonia, MI)
Patterson Printing (Benton Harbor, MI)
Pendell Printing (Midland, MI)
Speaker-Hines & Thomas (Lansing, MI)
T A S Graphics (Detroit, MI)
Thomson-Shore (Dexter, MI)

Minnesota

Advanced Duplicating (Edina, MN)
Amidon Graphics (Saint Paul, MN)
Bang Printing (Brainerd, MN)
Banta Catalog Group (Saint Paul, MN)
Bolger Publications (Minneapolis, MN)
Brown Printing (Waseca, MN)
Color Express (Minneapolis, MN)

Hart Press (Long Prairie, MN)
Instant Web (Chanhassen, MN)
Japs-Olson (Minneapolis, MN)
Legacy Books (Minneapolis, MN)
Litho Specialties (Saint Paul, MN)
Northprint (Grand Rapids, MN)
Nystrom Publishing (Maple Grove, MN)
Pentagram (Minneapolis, MN)
Preferred Graphics (Winona, MN)
The Press (Chanhassen, MN)
The Printer Inc (Maple Grove, MN)
John Roberts Co. (Minneapolis, MN)
Sexton Printing (West Saint Paul, MN)
Viking Press (Eden Prairie, MN)
Volkmuth Printers (Saint Cloud, MN)
Walter's Publishing (Waseca, MN)
The Webb Company (Saint Paul, MN)

Mississippi

Ringier America (Corinth, MS)
Ringier America (Senatobia, MS)

Missouri

Clark Printing (Kansas City, MO)
Combined Comm. (Columbia, MO)
Corley Printing (Earth City, MO)
McGrew Color (Kansas City, MO)
MWM Dexter (Aurora, MO)
Ovid Bell Press (Fulton, MO)
Plus Communications (Saint Louis, MO)
Stewart Publishing (Marble Hill, MO)
John S Swift Company (Saint Louis, MO)
Technical Comm, (N Kansas City, MO)
Ultra-Color Corp (Saint Louis, MO)
Universal Printing (Saint Louis, MO)
Walsworth Publishing (Marceline, MO)
Henry Wurst Inc (North Kansas City, MO)
Yates Publishing (Ozark, MO)

Montana

Color World Printers (Bozeman, MT)

Nebraska

Foote & Davies (Lincoln, NE)
Interstate Printing (Omaha, NE)
Metromail Corporation (Lincoln, NE)
Cookbooks by Morris Press (Kearney, NE)
Omaha Printing (Omaha, NE)
Rapid Printing (Omaha, NE)

Nevada

Comput-A-Print (Reno, NV)
Nevada Web Graphics (Sparks, NV)

New Hampshire

Concord Litho (Concord, NH)
Cummings Printing (Manchester, NH)
Dartmouth Printing (Hanover, NH)
MMI Press (Harrisville, NH)
Odyssey Press (Dover, NH)
Oxford Group (Berlin, NH)
Tompson & Rutter (Grantham, NH)

New Jersey

Book-Mart Press (North Bergen, NJ)
Catalog King (Clifton, NJ)
Clarkwood Corporation (Totowa, NJ)
Colonial Graphics (Paterson, NJ)
Color Graphics (Delran, NJ)
Edison Litho (North Bergen, NJ)
Edison Press (Glen Rock, NJ)
Einson Freeman (Fairlawn, NJ)
General Offset (Jersey City, NJ)
Horowitz/Rae (Fairfield, NJ)
Jersey Printing (Bayonne, NJ)
Lasky Company (Milburn, NJ)
The Lehigh Press (Pennsauken, NJ)
LithoCraft (Carlstadt, NJ)
Mars Graphic Services (Westville, NJ)
Meehan-Tooker & Co (E Rutherford, NJ)
Princeton University (Lawrenceville, NJ)
Quinn-Woodbine (Woodbine, NJ)
Repro-Tech (West Patterson, NJ)
Sheridan Printing (Alpha, NJ)
John S Swift (Teterboro, NJ)
Tapco (Pemberton, NJ)
Waldman Graphics (Pennsauken, NJ)
Webcraft Tech (New Brunswick, NJ)
The Wood Press (Paterson, NJ)

New Mexico

Camelot Fine Printing (Albuquerque, NM)
Dataco (Albuquerque, NM)
Guynes Printing (Albuquerque, NM)
Western Publishers (Albuquerque, NM)

New York

Accurate Web (Central Islip, NY)
Ad Color (Port Chester, NY)
Ad Infinitum Press (Mount Vernon, NY)
The Adams Group (New York, NY)
Algen Press Corp (College Point, NY)
Allied Graphics Arts (New York, NY)
American Signature (New York, NY)
Amherst Printing (New York, NY)
Andover Press (New York, NY)
Arcata Graphics (Depew, NY)
Atelier (New York, NY)
Balan Printing (Brooklyn, NY)
Bertelsmann Printing (New York, NY)
William Boyd Printing (Albany, NY)
Canterbury Press (Rome, NY)
Case-Hoyt Corporation (Rochester, NY)
Catalogue Service (New Rochelle, NY)
Charles Communications (New York, NY)
A Colish Inc (Mount Vernon, NY)
Color Catalog (Long Island City, NY)
Coneco Laser Graphics (Glen Falls, NY)
Martin Cook Associates (New York, NY)
Copen Press (Brooklyn, NY)
Coral Graphics (Plainview, NY)
Country Press (Mohawk, NY)
Crest Litho (Watervliet, NY)
Dellas Graphics (Syracuse, NY)
Deven Lithographers (Brooklyn, NY)
Direct Press (Huntington Station, NY)
East Village Enterprises (New York, NY)
Faculty Press (Brooklyn, NY)
Fleetwood Litho (New York, NY)
Flower City Printing (Rochester, NY)
Fort Orange Press (Albany, NY)
Full Color Graphics (Plainview, NY)
Ganis & Harris (New York, NY)
Geryon Press (Tunnel, NY)
Glundal Color Service (E Syracuse, NY)
Greater Buffalo Press (Buffalo, NY)
Hamilton Printing (Rensselaer, NY)
Hamilton Repro (Poughkeepsie, NY)
Harlin Litho (Ossining, NY)
Heart of the Lakes (Interlaken, NY)
Independent Print. (Long Island City, NY)
Infopress/Saratoga (Saratoga Springs, NY)
Insert Color Press (Ronkonkoma, NY)
Kaufman Press Printing (Syracuse, NY)
The Kordet Group (Oceanside, NY)
Latham Process Corp (New York, NY)
Liberty York Graphic (Hempstead, NY)
Long Island Web (Jericho, NY)
Longacrea Press (New Rochelle, NY)
The Mad Printers (Mattituck, NY)
Mark IV Press (Hauppauge, NY)
Monument Printers (Verplanck, NY)
Morgan Press (Dobbs Ferry, NY)
Multiprint Inc (Chatham, NY)
Noble Book Press (New York, NY)
Northeast Web (Farmingdale, NY)

Olympic Litho (Brooklyn, NY)
Practical Graphics (New York, NY)
Quad/Graphics (Saratoga Springs, NY)
Quebecor America (New York, NY)
Slater Lithographers (New York, NY)
TSO General Corp (Long Island City, NY)
Vail Ballou Printing (Binghamton, NY)
Vicks Lithograph (Yorkville, NY)
Waldon Press (New York, NY)
West Side Graphics (New York, NY)
World Color Press (New York, NY)

North Carolina

Celo Press (Burnsville, NC)
Delmar Printing (Charlotte, NC)
Edwards & Broughton (Raleigh, NC)
Edwards Brothers (Lillington, NC)
Heritage Printers (Charlotte, NC)
Hunter Publishing (Winston-Salem, NC)
Parker Graphics (Fuquay-Varina, NC)
Town House Press (Pittsboro, NC)

North Dakota

Associated Printers (Grafton, ND)

Ohio

Allied Printing (Akron, OH)
Amos Press (Sidney, OH)
BookMasters (Ashland, OH)
Champion Printing (Cincinnati, OH)
Communicolor (Newark, OH)
Danner Press (Canton, OH)
R R Donnelley (Willard, OH)
William Exline (Cleveland, OH)
William Feathers Printer (Oberlin, OH)
Fisher Printing (Galion, OH)
Gowe Printing (Medina, OH)
Graphic Printing (New Carlisle, OH)
Gray Printing (Fostoria, OH)
Greenfield Printing (Greenfield, OH)
Hennegan Company (Cincinnati, OH)
Hooven-Dayton Corp (Dayton, OH)
Johnson & Hardin (Cincinnati, OH)
C J Krehbiel Company (Cincinnati, OH)
Mazer Corporation (Dayton, OH)
National Graphics (Columbus, OH)
Nielsen Lithographing (Cincinnati, OH)
Original Copy Centers (Cleveland, OH)
Penton Press (Berea, OH)
Perlmuter Printing (Independence, OH)

The Press of Ohio (Brimfield, OH)
S Rosenthal & Company (Cincinnati, OH)
Schlasbach Printers (Sugarcreek, OH)
Standard Publishing (Cincinnati, OH)
John S Swift (Cincinnati, OH)
United Color (Monroe, OH)
Vimach Associates (Columbus, OH)
Watkins Printing (Columbus, OH)

Oklahoma

ColorGraphics (Tulsa, OK)
Oklahoma Graphics (Oklahoma City, OK)
PennWell Printing (Tulsa, OK)
Pinecliffe Printers (Shawnee, OK)

Oregon

Commercial Printing (Medford, OR)
Eagle Web Press (Salem, OR)
Germac Printing (Tigard, OR)
Graphic Arts Center (Portland, OR)
Maverick Publications (Bend, OR)
Northwest Web (Eugene, OR)
Times Litho (Forest Grove, OR)
Williams Catello Printing (Tualatin, OR)

Pennsylvania

Apollo Graphics (Southampton, PA)
Arcata Graphics (Fairfield, PA)
Braceland Brothers (Philadelphia, PA)
Brown Printing (East Greenville, PA)
BSC Litho (Harrisburg, PA)
Grit Commercial Print (Williamsport, PA)
Haddon Craftsmen (Scranton, PA)
Herbick & Held Printing (Pittsburgh, PA)
Hoechstetter Printing (Pittsburgh, PA)
Intelligencer Printing (Lancaster, PA)
Jostens (State College, PA)
K-B Offset Printing (State College, PA)
Lancaster Press (Lancaster, PA)
Mack Printing (Easton, PA)
Maple-Vail (York, PA)
McFarland Company (Harrisburg, PA)
National Publishing (Philadelphia, PA)
Neibauer Press (Warminster, PA)
Oaks Printing (Bethlehem, PA)
Offset Paperback (Dallas, PA)
Pearl Pressman Liberty (Philadelphia, PA)
Penn Colour (Huntington Valley, PA)
Precision Offset (Upper Darby, PA)
Progressive Typographers (Emigsville, PA)

Quixott Press (Doylestown, PA)
Rapidocolor Corp (West Chester, PA)
Schiff Printers (Pittsburgh, PA)
Science Press (Ephrata, PA)
The Sheridan Press (Hanover, PA)
SLC Graphics (Pittston, PA)
Smith-Edwards-Dunlap (Phildelphia, PA)
Sowers Printing (Lebanon, PA)
Suburban Publishers (Exeter, PA)
Telegraph Press (Harrisburg, PA)
Wickersham Printing (Lancaster, PA)

Rhode Island

Blazing Graphics (Cranston, RI)
Colorlith Corporation (Johnston, RI)
Federated Litho (Providence, RI)
National Bickford (Providence, RI)
Providence Gravure (Providence, RI)

South Carolina

R L Bryan Company (Columbia, SC)
Hart Graphics (Sampsonville, SC)

South Dakota

North Plains Press (Aberdeen, SD)
Pine Hill Press (Freeman, SD)
Sanders Printing (Garretson, SD)
Western Web Printing (Sioux Falls, SD)

Tennessee

American Signature (Memphis, TN)
Arcata Graphics (Nashville, TN)
Arcata Graphics (Kingsport, TN)
The College Press (Collegedale, TN)
Donihe Graphics (Kingsport, TN)
Fundcraft (Collierville, TN)
Jostens (Clarksville, TN)
K & S Graphics (Nashville, TN)
Mercury Printing (Memphis, TN)
Rich Printing (Nashville, TN)
Ringier America (Dresden, TN)
Sabre Printers (Rogersville, TN)
Southern Tennessee (Waynesboro, TN)
S C Toof and Company (Memphis, TN)
Triangle Printing (Nashville, TN)
Wimmer Brothers (Memphis, TN)

Texas

American Signature (Dallas, TX)
Capital Printing (Austin, TX)
Globe-Comm (San Antonio, TX)
Gulf Printing (Houston, TX)
Hart Graphics (Austin, TX)
Henington Publishing (Wolfe City, TX)
Lehigh Press (Dallas, TX)
Morgan Printing (Austin, TX)
Motheral Printing (Fort Worth, TX)
Newsfoto Publishing (San Angelo, TX)
Promotional Printing (Houston, TX)
Rich Publishing (Houston, TX)
The Riverside Press (Dallas, TX)
Staked Plains Press (Canyon, TX)
Sweet Printing (Round Rock, TX)
Taylor Publishing (Dallas, TX)
Texas Color Printers (Dallas, TX)
Todd Web Press (Smithville, TX)
Tracor Publications (Austin, TX)

Utah

Community Press (Provo, UT)
Everton Publishers (Logan, UT)
Hawkes Publishing (Salt Lake City, UT)
ProLitho (Provo, UT)
Publishers Press (Salt Lake City, UT)

Virginia

American Press (Oakton, VA)
Banta (Harrisonburg, VA)
Beacon Press (Richmond, VA)
Berryville Graphics (Berryville, VA)
BookCrafters (Fredericksburg, VA)
Brunswick Publishing (Lawrenceville, VA)
William Byrd Press (Richmond, VA)
Cascio-Wolf (Springfield, VA)
R R Donnelley (Harrisonburg, VA)
Goodway Graphics (Springfield, VA)
Progress Printing (Lynchburg, VA)
Stephenson Inc (Alexandria, VA)
United Litho (Falls Church, VA)

Vermont

Academy Books (Rutland, VT)
Americomp (Brattleboro, VT)
The Book Press (Brattleboro, VT)
Capital City Press (Montpelier, VT)
Daamen Printing (West Rutland, VT)

The Lane Press (Burlington, VT)
Maple Leaf Press (Brattleboro, VT)
Northlight Studio Press (Barre, VT)
Stinehour Press (Lunenburg, VT)

Washington

Beacon Wholesale Printing (Seattle, WA)
Craftsman Press (Seattle, WA)
Dinner & Klein (Seattle, WA)
Gorham Printing (Rochester, WA)
Print Northwest (Tacoma, WA)
Snohomish Publishing (Snohomish, WA)
Valco Graphics (Seattle, WA)

West Virginia

Arcata Graphics (Martinsburg, WV)
Catalogue Publishing (Martinsburg, WV)
McClain Printing (Parson, WV)

Wisconsin

Arandell-Schmidt (Menomonee Falls, WI)
Artcraft Press (Waterloo, WI)
Artex Publishing (Stevens Point, WI)
Banta Corporation (Menasha, WI)
Book Makers Inc (Kenosha, WI)
Citizen Prep (Beaver Dam, WI)
Diamond Graphics (Milwaukee, WI)
Moebius Printing (Milwaukee, WI)
Omnipress (Madison, WI)
Outstanding Graphics (Kenosha, WI)
Perry Printing (Waterloo, WI)
Perry Printing (Baraboo, WI)
Port Publications (Port Washington, WI)
Quad/Graphics (Lomira, WI)
Quad/Graphics (Pewaukee, WI)
Quad/Graphics (Sussex, WI)
Ringier America (Brookfield, WI)
Ringier America (New Berlin, WI)
Royle Printing (Sun Prairie, WI)
Saint Croix Press (New Richmond, WI)
Schumann Printers (Fall River, WI)
Straus Printing (Madison, WI)
Times Printing (Random Lake, WI)
Webcrafters (Madison, WI)
F A Weber & Sons (Park Falls, WI)
Western Publishing (Racine, WI)
Wisconsin Color Press (Milwaukee, WI)
Worzalla Publishing (Stevens Point, WI)

Canadian Printers

Alberta

Adviser Graphics (Red Deer, AB)

British Columbia

Mitchell Press (Vancouver, BC)
Ronalds Printing (Vancouver, BC)

Manitoba

Friesen Printers (Altona, MB)
Hignell Printing (Winnepeg, MB)
Universal Printers (Winnipeg, MB)

Ontario

Alger Press Ltd (Oshawa, ON)
T H Best Printing (Don Mills, ON)
Coach House Press (Toronto, ON)
John Deyell Company (Willowdale, ON)
Dollco Printing (Ottawa, ON)
Gladstone Press (Ottawa, ON)
Lawson Graphics (Toronto, ON)
Maclean Hunter (Willowdale, ON)
RBW Graphics (Owen Sound, ON)
Ronalds Printing (L4C 3C6, ON)
Saint Joseph Printing Ltd (Toronto, ON)
Southam Printing (Weston, ON)
Tri-Graphic Printing (Ottawa, ON)
Webcom Ltd (Scarborough, ON)

Quebec

Gagne Printing (Louiseville, PQ)
Les Editions Marquis (Montmagny, PQ)
Litho Prestige (Drummondville, PQ)
Ronalds Printing (Montreal, PQ)

Saskatchewan

Centax of Canada (Regina, SK)

Bibliography

Books on Editing, Design, and Printing

These books will help you do a better job editing, designing, and producing your books. If the titles highlighted in **bold** are not available at your local bookstore, you can order them from Ad-Lib Publications, P. O. Box 1102, Fairfield, IA 52556-1102; Fax: (515) 472-3186; Toll-free: (800) 669-0773. We accept VISA, MasterCard, and American Express credit cards. Add $2.50 postage and handling for the first book ordered and 50¢ for each additional book. When ordering 3 or more books, deduct 10%.

- Barker, Malcolm E., **Book Design & Production**, (San Francisco, CA: Londonborn Publications, 1990), 233 pages, softcover, $24.95.

  This new book is a superb step-by-step guide to designing and producing your books. Learn how and why to use a grid, how to choose the perfect typeface to match your book's content, how to design the front and back matter to make them more accessible to readers, and much more. Very good and very thorough. A wonderful book!

- Beach, Mark; Steve Shepro, and Ken Russon, **Getting It Printed: How to Work with Printers and Graphic Arts Services to Assure Quality, Stay on Schedule, and Control Costs**, (Portland, OR: Coast to Coast Books, 1985), 236 pages, hardcover, $42.50; softcover, $29.50.

  Of all the books on printing and graphics that I have read, this book is a standout. It is detailed, well-designed, and easy to use. It covers everything from planning the printing job, writing specifications, requesting quotations, working with typesetters, preparing camera-ready copy, proofing, and working with your printer to get the best job. Plus it provides specific criteria for checking every step of the process. **If every printer and book publisher had this book, 90% of all printing problems would disappear.**

- Beach, Mark, and Ken Russon, *Papers for Printing: How to Choose the Right Paper at the Right Price for Any Printing Job*, (Portland, OR: Coast to Coast, 1989), 40 sample sheets, 64 pages, softcover, $34.50.

  This booklet shows how to buy and specify paper for your various printing jobs. It includes 40 printed sample sheets, a chart that compares the costs of all 40 samples, a list of 678 paper brands, a list of 591 paper merchants, and a glossary of 214 paper terms.

- Bodian, Nat G., **How to Choose a Winning Title**, (Phoenix: Oryx Press, 1989), 176 pages, softcover, $23.50.

  If you've ever agonized over the title of a book, this new guide will provide you with all the tips, insights, and real-life examples you'll need to come up with selling titles. These same tips might also help you come up with selling headlines and product names.

- Burke, Clifford, **Printing It: A Guide to Graphic Techiniques for the Impecunious**, (Berkeley, CA: Wingbow Press, 1974), 127 pages, softcover, $4.95.

  A short guide that provides all the basics you need to know to prepare your own camera-ready copy for printers.

- *The Chicago Manual of Style*, (Chicago: University of Chicago Press, 1982), hardcover.

  The handbook of style for books. When you have questions about capitalization, punctuation, and usage, this book is the first place to look for answers. It will help you make the most acceptable choice when editing and copyediting your books.

- Graham, Walter B., **Complete Guide to Pasteup, Third Edition**, (Omaha, NE: Dot Pasteup Supply, 1987), 236 pages, softcover, $19.95.

  This is the classic book on how to prepare camera-ready copy for printing. If you are a newcomer to pasteup or have just hired a novice, this is the book to use. Very detailed and complete. Indeed, if this book has any faults, it would be the fact that it could very well overwhelm you with its details.

- International Paper Company, *Pocket Pal: A Graphics Arts Production Handbook*, (New York: International Paper Company, 1987), 216 pages, softcover, $6.95.

  A wonderful compendium of information on pre-press and printing processes. A basic reference book that still fits in your pocket!

- Judd, Karen, **Copyediting: A Practical Guide**, (Los Altos, CA: Crisp Publications, 1988), 287 pages, hardcover, $19.95.

When you have questions regarding the appropriate places to use numerals versus spelling out numbers, how to use the standard punctuation marks, how to mark changes in a manuscript (with standard proofreading symbols), how to typeset equations, or how to format bibliographies and footnotes, look to this book for the answers. A very complete and easy-to-use guide. Highly recommended for your editors and copyeditors.

- Lippi, Robert, *How to Buy Good Printing & Save Money*, (New York: Art Direction, 1987), 144 pages, hardcover, $15.75; softcover, $12.50.

  A good, basic, easy-to-understand guide to buying printing services. While this book is a good book, it is not nearly as attractive, comprehensive, or detailed as *Getting It Printed*.

- Middletown, Tony, **A Desktop Publisher's Guide to Pasteup,** (Colorado Springs: PLUSware, 1987), 228 pages, softcover, $15.95.

  Not just for desktop publishers. Indeed, this book is one of the most readable books on how to lay out and paste up books, advertisements, and other printed items. A practical guide for preparing camera-ready copy for the printer.

- Parker, Roger, **Looking Good in Print: A Guide to Basic Design for Desktop Publishing,** (Chapel Hill, NC: Ventana Press, 1988), 221 pages, softcover, $23.95.

  Shows how to use computers to design and produce more effective brochures, newsletters, manuals, and catalogs. Also describes the common design pitfalls and how to avoid them.

- Poynter, Dan, **Publishing Short-Run Books, Fourth Edition,** Santa Barbara: Para Publishing, 1987), 121 pages, softcover, $5.95.

  A how-to book on preparing and reproducing small books using your local copy shop. It teaches how to set type inexpensively, pasteup camera-ready copy, print using your local copy shop, and bind your books yourself. A superb guide to producing your books and reports in short runs of 200 or less in a matter of days.

- Rice, Stanley, *Book Design: Systematic Aspects*, (New York: R. R. Bowker, 1978), 274 pages, hardcover, $29.95.

  A systematic and clear delineation of all the steps involved in producing a book, from editorial design decisions to printing and binding. Includes schedules, transmittal forms, press layouts, and other charts and forms to ensure that everything proceeds smoothly and efficiently. This books covers everything a book production manager needs to know to produce well-designed books on time and on budget. Highly recommended.

• Rice, Stanley, *Book Design: Text Format Models*, (New York:
  R. R. Bowker, 1978), 215 pages, hardcover, $29.95.
  An extensive collection of samples for typesetting standard text, lists,
  tables, poems, plays, footnotes, glossaries, bibliographies, captions, indexes, and more. These samples are a handy way to visualize the look
  of your book, choose the style you want, and specify the type.

• Stoughton, Mary, **Substance & Style**, (Alexandria, VA: Editorial
  Experts, 1989), 351 pages, softcover, $28.00.
  Good book design also requires careful editing. If you want your
  books to pass all the tests (from reviewer to retailer to reader), make
  sure that they contain no errors in grammar, usage, or punctuation.
  This book, with all its practical exercises, is the perfect tool for teach-
  ing your editors and proofreaders all the little details that must be
  covered when copyediting any books.

• Vandermeulen, Carl, **Photography for Student Publications**,
  (Orange City, IA: Middleburg Press, 1979), 160 pages, hardcover,
  $16.95; softcover, $12.95.
  This book should really be titled *Photography for Small Publications*
  because it is a good basic text for beginners of all kinds. It provides
  excellent advice on how to produce natural poses and better photos
  overall. It covers everything from handling cameras to setting ex-
  posures, composing photos, developing them, making prints, shooting
  for layouts, and much more.

• White, Jan V., *Editing by Design: A Guide to Effective Word-and-
  Picture Communication for Editors and Designers, Second Edition*,
  (New York: R. R. Bowker, 1982), 264 pages, softcover, $24.95.
  A graphic design guide for magazine editors and designers that shows
  how words and images can enhance each other and make for a more
  effective presentation. With the increasingly graphic nature of books
  today, this guide could help you to strengthen the visual impact of
  your books.

• White, Jan V., *Graphic Design for the Electronic Age*, (New York:
  Watson-Guptill, 1988), 224 pages, hardcover, $30.00; softcover, $24.95.
  This book has more to offer the book designer than the above book. It
  describes how to select a typeface and size, how to select a column
  style, how to handle illustrations, and how to put together and in-
  tegrate a complete publication (front matter, text, and back matter).

Ad-Lib Bibliography

Books from Ad-Lib Publications

The following books, reports, newsletters, and data files are published by **Ad-Lib Publications, 51 N. Fifth Street, Fairfield, IA 52556; (515) 472-6617; Fax: (515) 472-3186; Toll-free: (800) 669-0773.**

- Kremer, John, **Book Marketing Made Easier,** $14.95

  This book provides forms and procedures to help any book publisher prepare and carry out an effective marketing plan. Over 70 forms help you through all the steps: preparing your marketing strategy ... planning your budget ... forecasting your sales ... getting listed in the book publishing records ... researching the media ... sending out publicity releases ... obtaining reviews ... organizing author tours ... getting distribution ... setting up sales representation ... working with bookstores ... exhibiting your books ... submitting your books to catalogs ... granting subsidiary rights ... and dealing with authors. These forms take all the fuss out of book publishing. 160 pages, softcover. A new edition will be published in late spring of 1991.

- Kremer, John, **Book Marketing No-Frills Database,** $149.95

  These data files are continuously updated. You get the latest version on the day you order. Includes more than 3100 specialty booksellers, 350 distributors, 488 wholesalers, 380 paperback jobbers, 160 sales representatives, 39 fulfillment services, 300 chain stores, 150 top independent booksellers, 180 book clubs, 450 mail order catalogs, 200 mailing list sources, 250 publicity and marketing services, 320 card packs, 83 book fairs and conventions, 100 publishing associations, and much, much more! No other book marketing database offers so much for so little cost—about 2¢ a contact. 7600+ records available in various data file formats for IBM-PCs, Macintoshes, or compatibles.

- Kremer, John, **Book Marketing Update** newsletter, $48.00 per year

  A bimonthly newsletter for anyone wanting to sell more books. Here are a few comments from our readers: "The management of our two companies have found your newsletter to be the finest newsletter about our business that we have ever seen." ... "As each issue comes, I think *There's no way you can top this* — and your next one does." ... "This is what we've been looking for since we started in publishing 3 years ago—at last someone is giving us what we need.!" 32 pages.

- Kremer, John, **Book Publishing Resource Guide**, $25.00

  This directory includes detailed listings for about 4000 book marketing contacts (wholesalers, distributors, sales reps, chain stores, book clubs, and more) plus 3500 newspaper and 750 magazine editors. All the key contacts and resources you need to publish and market books and other information products. 320 pages, softcover. Updated April, 1990.

- Kremer, John, **How to Make the News: A step-by-step guide to getting free publicity for your product, service, event, group, or idea**, $19.95

  This guide provides all the details anyone needs to get free national publicity for their products and services—how to write effective news releases, how to book national TV shows, how to research the media, how to conduct a radio phone interview tour from your home, how to track responses to your publicity, and much more. Includes worksheets and sample news releases to make it easy to carry out a national PR campaign. 192 pages, softcover. To be published in May, 1991.

- Kremer, John, **How to Sell to Mail Order Catalogs**, $30.00

  This report not only describes all the steps you need to follow to sell a book or other product to mail order catalog houses, but it also lists 550 catalogs that carry books, tapes, and other items. Current names, addresses, buyers, phone numbers, subject interests, and products carried are listed for each catalog. 34 pages, report. Updated regularly.

- Kremer, John, **Mail Order Selling Made Easier**, $19.95

  This book is an easy-to-use introduction to running a mail order operation. It includes worksheets, tables, sample letters, flow charts plus instructions to help anyone develop and carry out a successful direct response marketing program. It makes all the time-consuming details so much easier to handle. The book also features an extensive listing of resources and an annotated review of over 100 books. 288 pages, hardcover. Published in September, 1990.

  "If you have any questions about the nitty-gritty of mail order, you can find the answer here," says Jeannie Spears, publisher of *The Professional Quilter*. "The material is short, concise, information-packed and easy to find. An excellent resource!"

- Kremer, John, **Mail Order Worksheet Kit**, $15.00

  This kit includes full-size master copies of all the worksheets and sample letters outlined in *Mail Order Selling Made Easier*. Use these copies to organize your direct marketing programs. 60 master copies in a kit. Available for only $10.00 when ordered with the book.

- Kremer, John, **1001 Ways to Market Your Books — For Authors and Publishers**, hardcover, $19.95; softcover, $14.95

  The book features more than 1000 tips, techniques, and examples of how you can market your books more effectively. It covers traditional markets as well as special sales, subsidiary rights, direct mail, telemarketing, foreign sales, and much, much more. This book will help you to sell more books—and have fun doing it. This book includes two special chapters especially designed to help writers market their books and get the most out of the publication of their books. 448 pages. A new third edition was just published in September, 1990.

- Kremer, John, **PR FLASH No-Frills Data Files**, $149.95

  These data files provide key contact names, addresses, phone and fax numbers, subject interests, and other details for 11,450 media, including 3800 newspaper editors, 3400 magazine editors, 2530 radio shows, 975 TV shows, and 740 syndicated columns. The 11,450 records are available in a variety of file formats to use with your favorite database program on the IBM-PC, Macintosh, or compatibles. No other database or directory offers so much for so little cost. Updated regularly.

- Kremer, John, **Radio Phone Interview Shows: How to Do an Interview Tour from Your Home**, $30.00

  This report lists more than 950 radio shows that feature phone interviews with authors and other experts. This report includes 32 pages of addresses formatted to copy onto labels with any photocopy machine, plus 40 more pages of details about each show: radio station, show name, contact person, address, phone number, subject interests, hosts, times, and much more. Radio phone interviews are one of the most cost-effective ways to promote your products and services. 72 page report, updated every six months.

- Kremer, John, **The Top 200 National TV News / Talk / Magazine Shows**, $30.00

  This report features the top 200 national TV news, talk, and magazine shows. Not only does it describe how to book guests on such shows, but it also lists the addresses and phone numbers of each show, who to contact, what subjects the show is interested in, the hosts, and other pertinent details. This report is indispensable for anyone wanting to book a guest appearance on a national TV talk show or place a story on the national news. 200 page report updated every six months.

About the Author

John Kremer is the publisher of Ad-Lib Publications in Fairfield, Iowa. He is the author of a number of books on publishing and marketing, including *1001 Ways to Market Your Books — For Authors and Publishers*; *Book Marketing Made Easier*; *Mail Order Selling Made Easier*, *Specialty Booksellers Directory*; *Book Publishing Resource Guide*, and *How to Make the News: A Step-by-Step Guide to Getting Free Publicity for Your Product, Service, Event, Group, or Idea*.

He is also the author of four special reports, including *How to Sell to Mail Order Catalogs*; *Radio Phone Interview Shows: How to Do an Author Tour from Home*; *The Top 200 National TV News, Talk, and Magazine Shows*; and *How to Sell to Premium and Incentive Users*. In addition, he is the developer of the *Book Marketing No-Frills Data Files*, the *PR FLASH No-Frills Data Files*, the *Mail Order Worksheet Kit*, and the *Mail Order Spreadsheet Kit*.

John Kremer is the editor and publisher of the bimonthly *Book Marketing Update* newsletter and the weekly *Book Promotion Hotline* newsletter. He also writes the Books for the Trade book review column for *Small Press* magazine.

Finally, he is also the author of *Tinseltowns, U.S.A.*, a trivia quiz book about towns and cities in the United States which have been featured in movies and TV shows. He is currently working on a series of trivia tour guides and a marketing resource directory.

John is chairman of the board for the Mid-America Publishers Association. He is also a member of COSMEP, Publishers Marketing Association, Book Publicists of Southern California, Minnesota Independent Publishers Association, American Booksellers Association, and Marin Small Publishers Association.

John is single, 42 years old, never been married, but highly eligible. Besides being a superb slow-pitch softball pitcher, he also plays volleyball, walleyball, basketball, and radios. He rides a three-speed bicycle to work.